U. S. STORIES

Regional Stories from the Forty-eight States

U. S. STORIES

REGIONAL STORIES FROM THE FORTY-EIGHT STATES

Selected with a Foreword by

MARTHA FOLEY *and*
ABRAHAM ROTHBERG

Hendricks House–Farrar Straus · New York

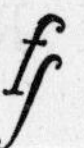

Manufactured in the U.S.A. by
The Colonial Press Inc., Clinton, Massachusetts
Designed by Stefan Salter

TO

DAVID BURNETT

AND

LOTTIE ROTHBERG

ACKNOWLEDGMENT

The editors of U. S. STORIES wish to express their gratitude to the following persons for their very kind assistance: Professor Augustus H. Able 3rd, University of Delaware, Newark, Delaware; Professor Albert Howard Carter, University of Arkansas, Fayetteville, Arkansas; Professor Joseph Warren Beach, University of Minnesota, Minneapolis, Minnesota; Professor John Cushman, University of Idaho, Moscow, Idaho; Professor Francis Wolle, University of Colorado, Boulder, Colorado; Professor Donald L. Clark, Columbia University, New York City; and Mr. Brewster Ghiselin, University of Utah, Salt Lake City, Utah; Mr. Ray B. West Jr., Editor, *The Western Review;* Mr. Nelson Antrim Crawford, Editor, *Household Magazine;* Mr. Paul Bixler, Editor, *Antioch Review;* Desmond Powell, Associate Editor, *Arizona Quarterly;* Elizabeth Stover, *Southwest Review;* Eleanor Stierham and Geraldine Rhodes, Fiction Editor and Editor in Chief, *Today's Woman;* Miss Marjorie Price; Misses Jean and Miriam Conwell; Helen McFarland, Librarian, Kansas State Historical Society; the Librarians at the New York Public Library, Fifth Avenue and Forty-second Street.

Grateful acknowledgment is also made to authors and publishers who have given their permission for the use of copyrighted material.

CONTENTS

THE STATES ACCORDING TO THE DATES
OF THEIR ENTRANCE INTO THE UNION

FOREWORD

As history goes, it is only a short time since an English editor, Sydney Smith, could ask, "In the four quarters of the globe, who reads an American book? Or goes to an American play? Or looks at an American picture or statue? What does the world yet owe to American physicians and surgeons? What new substances have their chemists discovered? Or what old ones have they analyzed? What new constellations have been discovered by the telescopes of Americans? What have they done in mathematics? Who drinks out of American glasses? Or eats from American plates? Or wears American coats or gowns? Or sleeps in American blankets?"

His questions, of course, were rhetorical. He expected no one to disagree with him, and no one did. When Sydney Smith asked those questions America still was provincial. A little more than a century later, it is a great world force. And today all his questions would seem laughable.

But when he asked them, American culture, particularly literature, was a second-hand affair. We looked to Europe for most of our books and we looked to Europe for approval of what few writers we had. Then something happened. To quote another famous editor, Edward J. O'Brien, "The American writer discovered the story on his own doorstep, learned to surprise the expression on the face of the man next door."

In other words, Americans, whether they were a Thoreau or a Mark Twain, a Whitman or a Hawthorne, wrote about *special* places in their America and of lives as they were lived in those special places. Life on the edge of the Mississippi or on the edge of Walden Pond. American writing came into its own.

When, a couple of years ago, a magazine, *Today's Woman,* asked one of the editors of this volume to edit a series of regional stories for it, two surprising things were learned. The first was that no such volume as this, offering to a reader the tremendous richness and variety of stories in America, state by state, had been done before. The other amazing thing was the enormous amount of enthusiastic letters, the largest number in its history, which the magazine received about the series. They showed the great interest the general reader has in seeing the regional aspect of writing emphasized, an interest which many literary scholars mistakenly have assumed was a limited one.

Only twelve stories could be used in the magazine series and many readers were disappointed because all of the forty-eight states had not been included. Therefore, the editors of this volume set to work searching out stories for every state in the union.

Each story has been chosen, not because it was written by an author who happened to be born in a certain state, or because it may have been the best ever written in that state from a purely literary standpoint, but because it gives the flavor, the feeling of life in the state as lived by its people. A second qualification is needed here. In choosing a story like "Bright and Morning Star," by Richard Wright, the editors do not mean to imply that life in Tennessee is limited to lynching any more than in selecting "Dawn of Remembered Spring" do they mean to suggest that all of life in Kentucky is represented by a boy out killing snakes. What we have tried to do is present a vivid facet of life in a state, rather than embrace the whole.

If, too, some of the stories tend to deal with less happy aspects of American life, this is easily understandable. It is part of the nation's growing up before Americans can understand the structure of their own culture and its worth. U. S. STORIES tries to show America from the heart, not as a travelogue or as a book on state politics or scenery but in fiction which lays bare the feelings of people in ways that are unique to various parts of the country.

American literature's most triumphant achievement is the short story. No other nation has produced in its history the harvest of short story writing and talent and achievement which the United States has reaped in the last fifty years. Just why the short story has been a form of expression so dear to Americans is hard to explain. Perhaps it is due to the fact that here in America we live a hurried life and this is reflected in the artist's use of the shorter length. Perhaps it is because the artist, as yet, has no real social or economic status in American culture and so can produce only briefly between spells at making a living and doing other things. Also, novel writing and play writing require long periods of gestation and this tranquillity needed to work is dearly, and rarely, bought in a country of split-second timing, one-arm counter lunches and general hustle-bustle.

Whatever the reason for it, the fact stands that the short story seems to be the form most indigenous to American expression. In other countries there are two or three fine short story writers: a Pirandello and a Grazia Deledda, a de Maupassant and a Daudet, a Mansfield and a Joyce, a Chekhov and a Pushkin, but what literature, save American, has produced a host like Sherwood Anderson, Hemingway, Faulkner, Saroyan, Irwin Shaw, Katherine Anne Porter, Nancy Hale, Steinbeck, Erskine Caldwell, Jesse Stuart, Oliver La Farge, to mention but a few.

The wide range of our geography is reflected in their writing. The sands of Arizona and the snows of northern Wisconsin, the far west of California and the austerity of Maine are shown in the different kinds of writing they produce and contribute to the great variety of our short stories. The reader, we hope, will find pleasure in studying the varied picture and the richness of the American literary scene. He will note that even the rhythms of the language pattern change according to locality. Compare, for instance, the dialogue in Nelson Algren's Chicago story with that of Marjorie Kinnan Rawlings' Florida story, or the contrast in feeling between the highly sophisticated urban story of an Irwin Shaw and the powerful, down-to-earth story of Oliver La Farge.

There are beauty, variety, vigor and courage in this writing from the forty-eight states. Of it Americans can be proud.

Martha Foley
Abraham Rothberg

U. S. STORIES

Regional Stories from the Forty-eight States

"O beautiful, for spacious skies, for amber waves of grain,
For purple mountain majesty above the fruited plain.
America, America, God shed His Grace on thee,
And crown thy good with brotherhood from sea to shining sea."

DELAWARE

The Offending Eye

ELLA MIDDLETON TYBOUT

Brother Noah Hyatt, one of the chief pillars of the church, a member of the Sessions, a leader of class-meeting, and especially gifted in exhortation, had a certain peculiarity which was a matter of comment in Poketown. This was his apparent ability to fix one eye sternly upon an objective point while the other rolled independently about, seeking for new worlds to conquer. The stationary orb was light blue, while its roving companion was brown.

Brother Jacob Sutton was pondering upon this eccentricity of nature as the two men walked home from class-meeting one Friday night, and at last summoned courage to give utterance to his thoughts.

"Hit jes' entah meh mine, Brothah Hyatt," he remarked casually, "tuh wondah huccum yo' haid tuh suppoht a blue eye on de lef' an' a brown eye on de right. Hit done make yo' 'peah pow'ful exting'ished, tuh be sho'. Does yo' know huccum de Lawd tuh favah yo' dat a-way?"

The brown eye of Brother Hyatt flashed angrily, in direct opposition to the pleasant smile of the blue member of the firm.

"Reckon He done hit fuh de same reason He tuck an' favah yo' wid one straight laig an' one bow laig," he returned indifferently, and Brother Sutton felt impelled to change the subject.

"De case o' James Pollahd am gwine tuh be laid befo' de chu'ch nex' class night," he remarked hastily; "yo' 'membahs dat he done tuck a paiah o' pants f'om de Jew sto' on Main Street, an' dey come an' 'rested him 'caze dey seen him gwine tuh chu'ch in 'em."

"Dem plaid pants done lay him low fo' sho'," said Brother Hyatt reflectively.

From *Poketown People* by Ella Middleton Tybout. Published by J. B. Lippincott. Used by permission.

"'Peahs like, bein' ez he done wuck out he time in jail, de sin am spashiated 'nuff," hinted Brother Sutton, who was inclined to be lenient.

"Ef plaid pants am de undoin' o' James Pollahd," said Brother Hyatt unctuously, "den he got tuh stick tuh plain goods. Sich am de konsekinses o' vanity."

"Po' James! 'Peahs like I kin see him now, standin' up in dem pants an' givin' in he sperience fuh de old yeah when day tuck an' 'rested him," said Brother Sutton, indulging in momentary retrospection.

"De chu'ch," said Brother Hyatt severely as he paused at his own gate, "am obligated tuh sterminate sich acks. Dem whut 'dulges in cuss wo'ds had ought tuh slit dey tongues; dem whut takes de goods o' othahs had ought tuh chop dey han's offen dey body."

"Sof'ly, Brothah, sof'ly," ejaculated Mr. Sutton.

"Dem am de wo'ds o' de Book," affirmed Brother Hyatt, focussing his wandering eye upon the hands of his companion, which involuntarily sought the privacy of his pockets. "Kin yo' ahgify 'g'inst dat, Brothah Sutton?"

Brother Sutton could not. He therefore took his leave, and Mr. Hyatt entered his house and closed the door. Within those four walls he was monarch of all he surveyed, and he intended to remain so.

"Dem ez has 'scaped de clutches of a female woman, by de grace o' Gawd," he was wont to assert, "had bettah keep deyse'fs *tuh* deyse'fs, 'caze dey ain' no knowin' whut gwine tuh happen ef yo' gits tuh passin' de time o' day too frequent."

Almost simultaneously with closing the door he removed his left eye and placed it carefully in his waistcoat pocket, over the edge of which it smiled bravely on, a small blue island on a sea of white. The existence of this glass eye was the skeleton in the closet of Brother Hyatt, and he guarded the secret jealously. When bargaining for its purchase it had been suggested to him that perhaps brown would be a better choice than blue, owing to the prevailing custom of having such appendages to match when possible, but he had repudiated the suggestion with scorn.

"Whut yo' reckon I wants tuh git a brown eye fo'?" he demanded argumentatively. "Ain' I jes' done wo' one clean out? I's gwine tuh get a blue eye, dat's whut I's gwine tuh do."

And blue it was.

Going to his back door, Brother Hyatt opened it and surveyed the landscape. The quiet of an August night reigned supreme, and overhead the moon shone with enticing brilliancy. Beyond two adjoining fields an irregular dark outline was plainly visible. It was the watermelon patch of a neighboring truck farm.

Brother Jacob Sutton, after leaving his companion, paused at his own residence to procure an empty grain-sack. When one hunts one naturally carries a game-bag. Brother Sutton was bent on a still-hunt, and wished to be properly equipped.

"De speckled pullet ovah tuh de fahm mus' be 'bout at de fryin' aige now," he reflected as he climbed the fence.

And the speckled pullet, with several companions, soon fluttered uneasily in the seclusion of the grain-bag.

"Mought ez well come home thu de watahmillion patch," he reflected, his errand accomplished to his satisfaction.

The dew lay thick upon the vines, glistening brightly in the light of the moon, and scattered closely about the field were the melons themselves, large and luscious, and most tempting to the palate.

"Ovah in de cohnah by de crick," ruminated Mr. Sutton, "de sun shine wahmes' an' de fruit tas'e sweetes'."

Accordingly he repaired to the corner by the creek, bent upon refreshment of the inner man, but someone was before him. Brother Sutton hesitated an instant, then approached boldly.

"James Pollahd," he exclaimed sternly, 'whut yo' doin' hyah?"

James Pollard, he of the plaid trousers, turned apprehensively around, then gave vent to a relieved chuckle.

"Clah tuh goodness," he remarked, "I done thunk hit wuh ole man Noahy Hyatt."

"James," said Brother Sutton solemnly, "yo' done lef' de jail yistidday; is yo' gwine tuh zume evil ackshuns 'mej'ate?"

The unhappy James entered into a rambling explanation of his reasons for the nocturnal expedition, but the attention of his companion wandered perceptibly as his eyes became fixed upon the partly consumed fruit at his feet.

"James," he interrupted suddenly, *"am she ripe?"*

Over the brow of the hill now appeared a third figure, walking slowly and stooping now and then to tap a melon inquiringly with thumb and finger.

"Pow'ful quare," he muttered; "I done make meh mahk on de top so's dey wouldn' be no trubble 'bout it. I done mahked it wid a cross an' 'lowed I'd come tuh-night an' git it."

Brother Hyatt paused in his search and listened intently. He heard a murmur of voices, which gradually grew more distinct. Hastily his hand sought his waistcoat pocket and fumbled there unavailingly: his eye was gone.

A famous general has said that the best mode of defence is by attack, and it is apparently true that great minds run in the same channels, for Brother Noah Hyatt promptly advanced to meet the enemy, with one hand held over the empty eyesocket and the other raised in stern denunciation.

"Brothah Sutton," he exclaimed, "whut yo' aftah, Brothah Sutton? Whuh yo' 'ligion, Brothah Sutton, whuh yo' 'ligion?"

Mr. Sutton pointed towards his companion, guiltily trembling at his side, clad in the identical plaid trousers which had occasioned his downfall, purchased and presented by a sympathizing friend upon his release from prison.

"I come hyah, Brothah Hyatt," he responded loftily, "tuh snatch de brand f'om de burnin'. I done come tuh wras'le wid dis Son o' Sin an' Wickedness, an' tuh keep he feet f'om strayin' whuh dey done strayed befo'."

"Hope tuh die," stammered the wretched James, visions of the county jail rising vividly before his mind's eye,—"hope tuh die, Brothah Hyatt, I ain' done nawthin'. He tuck an' eat ez much ez me."

"James," said Brother Sutton in tones of patient reproach, "I zorts yo' not tuh add lyin' tuh yo' crap o' sins. Yo's got 'nuff tuh spashiate an' tuh sterminate 'thout dat, James."

"Ax him whut he got in he baig," muttered James, his knees knocking together as he encountered the brown eye of Brother Hyatt fixed upon him,—"ax him whut he got in he baig."

Brother Sutton shifted the bag to the other shoulder, and its occupants stirred uneasily as he did so.

"I got mus'rats in meh baig," returned Mr. Sutton promptly. "I done been down tuh de crick aftah mus'rats."

Mr. Hyatt passed to the rear and squeezed the bag between his hands; a muffled squawk resulted from the pressure.

" 'Peahs like de lanwidge o' mus'rats done been changed sence yistidday," he remarked dryly as he replaced his hand before his eye and resumed his former location.

"Whut yo' doin' hyah yo'se'f, Brothah Hyatt?" inquired Mr. Sutton, rallying sufficiently to return the attack. "Kin yo' splain yo' own ackshuns?"

Brother Hyatt saw his way of escape and took immediate advantage of it.

"Brothah Sutton," he replied, "I done come hyah 'caze ole Satan he beckon me; dat's huccum me tuh be hyah. He done drug me ovah de fence an' tuck an' p'inted out de ripes' million in de patch. I sets meh eye on hit, Brothah Sutton, I sets meh eye on hit, an' I wants hit, y-a-a-s, I wants hit pow'ful bad. I couldn't git meh eye f'om offen hit nohow; de zire growed an' swelled in meh buzzom twell I feel fit tuh bus'. Whut yo' think I done, Brothah Sutton, whut yo' think I done?"

"Reckon yo' tuck an' cut de million," said Brother Sutton, speaking as from experience.

"No, sah," returned Brother Hyatt piously, "I didn't do dat nohow. I 'membahs de wo'ds o' de Book, 'if yo' eye offen' yo', pluck hit out an' cas' hit f'om yo',' an' dat's whut I done, Brothah Sutton, dat's whut I done."

He dramatically removed his hand at the concluding word, and the eyelid collapsed into the cavernous socket presented for inspection. The two men gasped with astonishment, and Brother Hyatt resumed:

"She come out po'ful hahd," he said pathetically; "dem roots wuh sho'ly in good an' tight, but I kep' a-pullin',—y-a-a-s, I kep' a-pullin', 'caze I ain' gwine tuh suppoht no onruly membahs tuh my body. No, sah! I's gwine tuh cas' 'em f'om me. An' aftah I done fling dat sinful blue eye intuh de crick de Lawd come down in a ch'iot o' fiah an' stanched de bleedin' an' tuck away de huht. He sez tuh me, sez He, 'Well done, Noahy Hyatt!' sez He."

"I nevah hyah no sperience de ekil o' dat," said Mr. Sutton in awestruck tones.

"Does yo' still hone fuh de million, Brothah Hyatt?" inquired James Pollard curiously.

"James," said Brother Hyatt severely, "I tells yo' mighty solemn dat ef yo' reaches out yo' han' tuh tech dem millions (whut don' b'long tuh yo'), yo's gwine tuh see a' Eye lookin' at yo'. Dat Eye am wotchin' yo' cyahful, an' yo' kaint hide f'om hit nohow. Has yo' disremembah 'bout de All-Pervadin' Eye, Brothah Sutton? Huccum you do dat? Huccum yo', Brothah Sutton? Hit done been spyin' aftah yo' dis night. De Session am gwine tuh hyah 'bout dem mus'rats, sho's yo' bawn. Dey's somebody sides James Pollahd fo' de chu'ch tuh deal wid, Brothah Sutton."

With which concluding remark Mr. Hyatt turned and walked majestically away, complete master of the situation.

"James," said Mr. Sutton reproachfully when they were alone, "yo' didn' have no call tuh 'trac' 'tention tuh de baig, nohow."

"Has yo' got mus'rats in dat baig, sho' 'nuff?" asked James, who was an inquiring youth.

"I leaves yo' hyah, James, tuh yo' own 'fleckshuns; aftah whut yo' done 'pinionated 'bout dis baig, I reckon I don' wan' yo' s'ciety home nohow."

So saying, Brother Sutton walked sorrowfully off. His heart was heavy within him, owing to the unfortunate contretemps, and his soul was awed with the Spartan resistance of Brother Hyatt to the prompting of the devil. Gradually, however, he succumbed to the witchery of his surroundings and forgot everything but the fact that it was pleasant to be alive and to wander at will in a watermelon patch alone in the moonlight.

"Reckon I mought ez well tote one home tuh 'Cindy," he reflected, and looked about him preparatory to a careful selection. The dew shone white and sparkling upon the dark-green rind of his choice; it was necessary to push aside some leaves to find the stem, and Brother Sutton did so. With a loud yell of terror he jumped up and started to run, but caught his foot in the tangle of melon vines and fell heavily forward.

"De Eye!" he gasped, "de Eye!"

And, indeed, beneath the sheltering leaves a stern blue eye lay upon the ground and gazed up at him in silent accusation.

The countenance of Mr. Sutton was covered with an ashen bloom of fright, and large drops of perspiration stood out upon his brow as he stared fixedly at it, quite motionless from its irresistible magnetism. He felt it incumbent upon him to follow the example of Brother Hyatt, yet shrank weakly from the pruning process.

"Lawd," he gasped, moistening his trembling lips, "I knows whut yo' spec's me tuh take an' do. Meh eyes done res' 'pon de million, but, O Lawd, 'tain't one eye no mo' den t'othah. How I gwine tuh git 'long ef dey's bofe cas' out? I done seen hit lookin' up at me; I done seen dat Wotchful Eye, Lawd, dat yo' keeps tuh sick on wicked pussons. Y-a-a-s, oh, y-a-a-s, I done seen it plain as day."

Here his breath failed for an instant, and the chickens in the bag upon his back stirred slightly.

"I's gwine tuh give dem chickins back, good Lawd," continued the uncertain voice; "I don' 'peah tuh cyah 'bout 'em nohow."

He sat cautiously upright and fumbled at the neck of the bag, finally shaking his prisoners out one by one.

"Git home," he cried, heading off first one and then another, as they rushed madly about after the manner of all chickens; "shoo! git outen meh sight. Shoo!"

The speckled pullet, spreading her wings until they touched the ground, started for home on the double-quick, followed by her companions, all squawking loudly. And Brother Sutton, with a hasty but apprehensive glance behind him, did likewise.

Now James Pollard, when left alone beside the creek, pondered thoughtfully upon the events of the evening without arriving at any definite conclusion; he was sadly puzzled.

"Ole man Noahy Hyatt nevah done pull out dat eye hisse'f nohow," he said aloud. "Yit, huccum dat hole in he haid?"

James scratched his own head thoughtfully as he finally started homeward. Heading wildly down the hill, and scuttling as though for their lives, came the speckled pullet and company.

"De mus'rats makin' fuh dey roos'," remarked James as he stood aside to let them pass, and then continued on his way, wondering greatly.

Observing what seemed to be an especially fine melon, he paused and bent over to examine it. What was that looking up at him from among the dark leaves? James's heart was in his mouth for a minute; then, gathering his courage together, he made the effort of his life, and putting forth a cautious finger touched the object, with fear and trembling at first, and then with curiosity and contempt.

James Pollard laughed long and loud as he disrespectfully thrust the accusing eye in the pocket of the plaid trousers, then quietly cut the stem of the melon, placed it upon his shoulder, and proceeded on his way rejoicing until he reached the neighborhood of Brother Noah Hyatt, who sat in the shadow of an oak-tree refreshing himself with the produce of the field after the exhausting events of the night. He deeply regretted the loss of his eye, but felt that its absence would give him added prestige in class-meetings, therefore he bore it with fortitude.

"I's gwine tuh make 'em dance Juba nex' class-night," he reflected as he cut a large piece directly out the heart of the melon; "jes' let me git aftah 'em befo' de Session."

"I done pick up whut yo' drap a ways back," said the voice of James Pollard from behind the tree as he produced the glass eye. The lower jaw of Mr. Hyatt dropped with astonishment and he was speechless; James was quite at his ease.

"I don' like dem stripy ones nohow," he remarked, turning over a bit of the rind with his foot, "dis yeah's de kine fuh me," and he deposited his burden upon the ground. Brother Hyatt pointed at the blue eye, which seemed to possess a far-away, unfamiliar look.

"Huccum," he gasped, "huccum——"

"Brothah Hyatt," said James, "I knows all 'bout yo', an' I's pow'ful glad I does. I ain' gwine to expose yo' humbuggery, 'caze I wants tuh git back intuh de bes' s'ciety of Poketown. Ef yo' he'ps me, I he'ps yo'."

James paused and looked searchingly at his companion.

"Ef de chu'ch take an' hol' out huh ahms tuh me, Brothah Hyatt, an' fuhgit de plaid pants an' de jail; ef de best s'ciety in Poketown am zorted tuh open de do' tuh me, I reckon de Lawd mought wuck a merrycle an' a' eye mought up an' spring out same ez Jonah's gourd tuck an' growed in a night. 'Peahs like tuh me," added James enticingly, "I kin see hit sproutin' now."

"James," said Brother Hyatt, rising, "come home wid me an 'go intuh meh back do'. De Lawd done favah yo' wid secon' sight, James."

There was a full attendance the next class-night, rumors of an unusual and interesting nature having excited the curiosity of Poketown to its highest point.

Brother Hyatt rose to address the meeting, and a stifled exclamation came from Brother Jacob Sutton, who half rose to his feet, then sat down again.

"Brothah Sutton," said Brother Hyatt impressively, "I calls on yo' fo' yo' sperience las' Friday night, jes' aftah I done pull out meh lef' eye an' cas' hit f'om me 'caze hit res' too long on de goods o' othahs,—las' Friday night, Brothah Sutton, when yo' done went aftah mus'rats. Tell de chu'ch I's speechifyin' de truf 'bout dat eye."

And Brother Sutton, in faltering accents, testified that he had met and conversed with Brother Hyatt when the eye was lacking. A thrill ran through the congregation as the story progressed with graphic details.

"James Pollahd," said Brother Hyatt, as Brother Sutton resumed his seat, "yo' done seen dat eye resto'ed tuh meh haid. Speak up now an' give in yo' sperience."

"Me an' Brothah Hyatt," said Mr. Pollard, "wuh settin' on he do'-step an' he wuh p'intin' out de way tuh heav'n tuh a po sinnah like me, when dey come a light, same ez de light when de meule stables on de towpath tuck fiah."

"Y-a-a-s! dey come a light. Praise Gawd!" interpolated Brother Hyatt.

"An' I done hyah a Voice outen de middle o' de light," resumed James; "hit say, 'Brothah Hyatt, de Lawd am pleased wid yo'. Hyah am yo' eye back ag'in, good ez new.' "

"An' den I done feel a ticklin' way back in de roots," said Brother Hyatt, taking up the thread of the discourse, "an' somethin' come a-bulgin' an' a-scrouchin' outen meh haid—glory! glory! hallelujah!—outen meh haid intuh de hole. Glory!"

"De light done fade," said James solemnly, "an' I up an' sez tuh Brothah Hyatt, I sez, 'Yo' got yo' same ole eye back ag'in,' I sez."

"But 'twa'n't de same ole eye," interrupted Brother Hyatt, " 'case I done see diff'unt wid hit. Dis hyah eye done been in glory, an' de way hit see now am de right way fo' sho'. Hit done tell me plain whut am de duty o' de chu'ch to'ds hits wanderin' lambs. I axes yo', meh brothahs an' meh sistahs, tuh welcome back James Pollahd tuh yo' midst; I zorts yo' tuh open yo' do's wide tuh him."

Brother Hyatt reached for the hand of James Pollard and led him forward before the pulpit.

"Brothah Sutton," he said, fixing that trembling gentleman with his brown eye, "I knows dat you's gwine tuh be 'mongst de fust tuh welcome Brothah Pollahd back tuh de ahms o' de chu'ch."

But Brother Sutton shook his head solemnly and rose, as though to protest.

"Brothah Sutton," admonished Brother Hyatt, " 'tain't no time tuh speechify 'bout mus'rats; I sho'ly would hate tuh be obligated tuh tell all I knows 'bout 'em dis night. Step up, Brothah Sutton, an' welcome de lamb back tuh de fole; step up lively now, an' set de zample tuh de res' o' de Session."

And Brother Sutton stepped.

PENNSYLVANIA

The Doctor's Son

JOHN O'HARA

My father came home at four o'clock one morning in the fall of 1918, and plumped down on a couch in the living room. He did not get awake until he heard the noise of us getting breakfast and getting ready to go to school, which had not yet closed down. When he got awake he went out front and shut off the engine of the car, which had been running while he slept, and then he went to bed and stayed, sleeping for nearly two days. Up to that morning he had been going for nearly three days with no more than two hours' sleep at a stretch.

There were two ways to get sleep. At first he would get it by going to his office, locking the rear office door, and stretching out on the floor or on the operating table. He would put a revolver on the floor beside him or in the tray that was bracketed to the operating table. He had to have the revolver, because here and there among the people who would come to his office, there would be a wild man or woman, threatening him, shouting that they would not leave until he left with them, and that if their baby died they would come back and kill him. The revolver, lying on the desk, kept the more violent patients from becoming too violent, but it really did no good so far as my father's sleep was concerned; not even a doctor who had kept going for days on coffee and quinine would use a revolver on an Italian who had just come from a bedroom where the last of five children was being strangled by influenza. So my father, with a great deal of profanity, would make it plain to the Italian that he was not being intimidated, but would go, and go without sleep.

There was one other way of getting sleep. We owned the building

---

in which he had his office, so my father made an arrangement with one of the tenants, a painter and paperhanger, so he could sleep in the room where the man stored rolls of wallpaper. This was a good arrangement, but by the time he had thought of it, my father's strength temporarily gave out and he had to come home and go to bed.

Meanwhile there was his practice, which normally was about forty patients a day, including office calls and operations, but which he had lost count of since the epidemic had become really bad. Ordinarily if he had been ill his practice would have been taken over by one of the young physicians; but now every young doctor was as busy as the older men. Italians who knew me would even ask me to prescribe for their children, simply because I was the son of Mister Doctor Malloy. Young general practitioners who would have had to depend upon friends of their families and fraternal orders and accidents and gonorrhea for their start, were seeing—hardly more than seeing—more patients in a day than in normal times they could have hoped to see in a month.

The mines closed down almost with the first whiff of influenza. Men who for years had been drilling rock and had chronic miner's asthma never had a chance against the mysterious new disease; and even younger men were keeling over, so the coal companies had to shut down the mines, leaving only maintenance men, such as pump men, in charge. Then the Commonwealth of Pennsylvania closed down the schools and churches, and forbade all congregating. If you wanted an ice cream soda you had to have it put in a cardboard container; you couldn't have it at the fountain in a glass. We were glad when school closed, because it meant a holiday, and the epidemic had touched very few of us. We lived in Gibbsville; it was in the tiny mining villages—"patches"—that the epidemic was felt immediately.

The State stepped in, and when a doctor got sick or exhausted so he literally couldn't hold his head up any longer, they would send a young man from the graduating class of one of the Philadelphia medical schools to take over the older man's practice. This was how Doctor Myers came to our town. I was looking at the pictures of the war in the Review of Reviews, my father's favorite magazine, when the doorbell rang and I answered it. The young man looked like the young men who came to our door during the summer selling magazines. He was wearing a short coat with a sheepskin collar, which I recognized as an S.A.T.C. issue coat.

"Is this Doctor Malloy's residence?" he said.

"Yes."

"Well, I'm Mr. Myers from the University."

"Oh," I said. "My father's expecting you." I told my father and he said: "Well, why didn't you bring him in?"

Doctor Myers went to my father's bedroom and they talked, and then the maid told me my father wanted to speak to me. When I went to the bedroom I could see my father and Doctor Myers were getting along nicely. That was natural; my father and Doctor Myers were University men, which meant the University of Pennsylvania; and University men shared a contempt for men who had studied at Hahnemann or Jefferson or Medico-Chi. Myers was not an M.D., but my father called him Doctor, and as I had been brought up to tip my hat to a doctor as I did to a priest, I called him Doctor too, although Doctor Myers made me feel like a lumberjack; I was so much bigger and obviously stronger than he. I was fifteen years old.

"Doctor Myers, this is my boy James," my father said, and without waiting for either of us to acknowledge the introduction, he went on: "Doctor Myers will be taking over my practice for the time being and you're to help him. Take him down to Handricks. Go over the names of our patients and help him arrange some kind of a schedule. Doctor Myers doesn't drive a car; you'll drive for him. Now your mother and I think the rest of the children ought to be on the farm, so you take them there in the big Buick and then bring it back and have it overhauled. Leave the little Buick where it is, and you use the Ford. You'll understand, Doctor, when you see our roads. If you want any money your mother'll give it to you. And no cigarettes, d'you understand?" Then he handed Doctor Myers a batch of prescription blanks, upon which were lists of patients to be seen, and said good-by and lay back on his pillow for more sleep.

Doctor Myers was almost tiny and that was the reason I could forgive him for not being in the Army. His hair was so light that you could hardly see his little mustache. In conversation between sentences his nostrils would twitch and like all doctors he had acquired a posed gesture which was becoming habitual. His was to stroke the skin in front of his right ear with his forefinger. He did that now downstairs in the hall. "Well, I'll just take a walk back to the hotel and wait till you get back from the farm. That suit you, James?" It did, and he left and I performed the chores my father had ordered, and then I went to the hotel in the Ford and picked up Doctor Myers.

He was catlike and dignified when he jumped in the car. "Well, here's a list of names. Where do you think we ought to go first? Here's a couple of prescription blanks with only four names apiece. Let's clean them up first."

"Well, I don't know about that, Doctor. Each one of those names means at least twenty patients. For instance, Kelly's. That's a saloon and there'll be a lot of people waiting. They all meet there and wait for my father. Maybe we'd better go to some single calls first."

"Okay, James. Here's a list." He handed it to me. "Oh, your father said something about going to Collieryville to see a family named Evans."

I laughed. "Which Evans? There's seventy-five thousands Evanses in Collieryville. Evan Evans. William W. Evans. Davis W. Evans. Davis W. Evans, Junior. David Evans?"

"David Evans sounds like it. The way your father spoke they were particular friends of his."

"David Evans," I said. "Well, he didn't say who's sick there, did he?"

"No. I don't think anybody. He just suggested we drop in to see if they're all well."

I was relieved, because I was in love with Edith Evans. She was nearly two years older than I, but I liked girls a little older. I looked at his list and said: "I think the best idea is to go there first and then go around and see some of the single cases in Collieryville." He was ready to do anything I suggested. He was affable and trying to make me feel that we were pals, but I could tell he was nervous, and I had sense enough to know that he had better look at some flu before tackling one of those groups at the saloons.

We drove to Collieryville to the David Evans home. Mr. Evans was district superintendent of one of the largest mining corporations, and therefore Collieryville's third citizen. He would not be there all the time, because he was a good man and due for promotion to a bigger district, but so long as he was there he was ranked with the leading doctor and the leading lawyer. After him came the Irish priest, the cashier of the larger bank (of which the doctor or the lawyer or the superintendent of the mines is president), the brewer and the leading merchant. David Evans had been born in Collieryville, the son of a superintendent, and was popular, a thirty-second-degree Mason, a graduate of Lehigh and a friend of my father's. They would see each other less than ten times a year, but they would go hunting rabbit and quail and pheasant together every autumn and always exchanged expensive Christmas gifts. When my mother had large parties she would invite Mrs. Evans but the two women were not close friends. Mrs. Evans was a Collieryville girl, half Polish, and my mother had gone to an expensive school and spoke French, and played bridge long before Mrs. Evans had learned to play "500." The Evanses had two children: Edith, my girl, and Rebecca, who was about five.

The Evans Cadillac, which was owned by the coal company, was standing in front of the Evans house, which also was owned by the coal company. I called to the driver, who was sitting behind the steering wheel, hunched up in a sheepskin coat and with a checkered cap pulled down over his eyes. "What's the matter, Pete?" I called. "Can't the company get rid of that old Caddy?"

"Go on wid you," said Pete. "What's the wrong wid the doctorin' business? I notice Mike Malloy ain't got nothin' better than Buicks."

"I'll have you fired, you round-headed son of a so and so," I said. "Where's the big lad?"

"Up Mike's. Where'd you t'ink he is?"

I parked the Ford and Doctor Myers and I went to the door and were let in by the pretty Polish maid. Mr. Evans came out of his den, wearing a raccoon coat and carrying his hat. I introduced Doctor Myers. "How do you do, sir?" he said. "Doctor Malloy just asked me to stop in and see if everything was all right with your family."

"Oh, fine," said Mr. Evans. "Tell the dad that was very thoughtful, James, and thank you too, Doctor. We're all okay here, thank the Lord, but while you're here I'd like to have you meet Mrs. Evans. Adele!"

Mrs. Evans called from upstairs that she would be right down. While we waited in the den Mr. Evans offered Doctor Myers a cigar, which was declined. Doctor Myers, I could see, preferred to sit, because Mr. Evans was so large that he had to look up to him. While Mr. Evans questioned him about his knowledge of the anthracite region, Doctor Myers spoke with a barely discernible hostility which was lost on Mr. Evans, the simplest of men. Mrs. Evans appeared in a house dress. She looked at me shyly, as she always did. She always embarrassed me, because when I went in a room where she was sitting she would rise to shake hands, and I would feel like telling her to sit down. She was in her middle thirties and still pretty, with rosy cheeks and pale blue eyes and nothing "foreign" looking about her except her high cheek bones and the lines of her eyebrows, which looked as though they had been drawn with crayon. She shook hands with Doctor Myers and then clasped her hands in front of her and looked at Mr. Evans when he spoke, and then at Doctor Myers and then at me, smiling and hanging on Mr. Evans' words. He was used to that. He gave her a half smile without looking at her and suggested we come back for dinner, which in Collieryville was at noon. Doctor Myers asked me if we would be in Collieryville at that time and I said we would, so we accepted his invitation. Mr. Evans said: "That's fine. Sorry I won't be here, but I have to go to Wilkes-Barre right away." He looked at his watch. "By George! By now I ought to be half way there." He grabbed his hat and kissed his wife and left.

When he had gone Mrs. Evans glanced at me and smiled and said: "Edith will be glad to see you, James."

"Oh, I'll bet she will," I said. "Where's she been keeping herself?"

"Oh, around the house. She's my eldest," she said to Doctor Myers. "Seventeen."

"Seventeen?" he repeated. "You have a daughter seventeen? I can hardly believe it, Mrs. Evans. Nobody would ever think you had a daughter seventeen." His voice was a polite protest, but there was nothing protesting in what he saw in Mrs. Evans. I looked at her myself now, thinking of her for the first time as someone besides Edith's mother. . . . No, I couldn't see her. We left to make some calls, promising to be back at twelve-thirty.

Our first call was on a family named Loughran, who lived in a neat two-story house near the Collieryville railroad station. Doctor Myers went in. He came out in less than two minutes, followed by Mr. Loughran. Loughran walked over to me. "You," he said. "Ain't we good enough for your dad no more? What for kind of a thing is this he does be sending us?"

"My father is sick in bed, just like everybody else, Mr. Loughran. This is the doctor that is taking all his calls till he gets better."

"It is, is it? So that's what we get, and doctorin' with Mike Malloy sincet he come from college, and always paid the day after payday. Well, young man, take this back to Mike Malloy. You tell him for me if my woman pulls through it'll be no thanks to him. And if she don't pull through and dies, I'll come right down to your old man's office and kill him wid a rock. Now you and this one get the hell outa here before I lose me patience."

We drove away. The other calls we made were less difficult, although

I noticed that when he was leaving one or two houses the people, who were accustomed to my father's quick, brusque calls, would stare at Doctor Myers' back. He stayed too long and probably was too sympathetic. We returned to the Evans home.

Mrs. Evans had changed her dress to one that I thought was a little too dressy for the occasion. She asked us if we wanted "a little wine," which we didn't, and Doctor Myers was walking around with his hands in his trousers pockets, telling Mrs. Evans what a comfortable place this was, when Edith appeared. I loved Edith but the only times I ever saw her were at dancing school, to which she would come every Saturday afternoon. She was quite small, but long since her legs had begun to take shape, and she had breasts. It was her father, I guess, who would not let her put her hair up; she often told me he was very strict and I knew that he was making her stay in Collieryville High School a year longer than was necessary because he thought her too young to go away. Edith called me Jimmy—one of the few who did. When we danced together at dancing school she scarcely spoke at all. I suspected her of regarding me as very young. All the little kids at dancing school called me James, and the oldest girls called me sarcastic. "James Malloy," they would say, "you think you're sarcastic. You think you're clever, but you're not. I consider the source of that remark." The remark might be that I had heard that Wallace Reid was waiting for that girl to grow up—and so was I. But I never said things like that to Edith. I would say: "How's everything out in the metropolis of Collieryville?" and she would say they were all right. It was no use trying to be romantic. One time I offered her the carnation that we had to wear at dancing school, and she refused it because the pin might tear her dress. It was useless to try to be dirty with her; there was no novelty in it for a girl who had gone to Collieryville High. I told her one story, and she said her grandmother fell out of the cradle laughing at that one.

When Edith came in she took a quick look at Doctor Myers which made me slightly jealous. He turned and smiled at her and his nostrils began to twitch. Mrs. Evans rubbed her hands together nervously and it was plain to see that she was not sure how to introduce Doctor Myers. Before she had a chance to make any mistakes I shook hands with Edith and she said, "Oh, hello, Jimmy," in a very offhand way, and I said: "Edith, this is Doctor Myers."

"How do you do?" said Edith.

"How are you?" said the doctor.

"Oh, very well, thank you," Edith said, and realized that it wasn't quite the thing to say.

"Well," said Mrs. Evans, "I don't know if you gentlemen want to wash up. Jimmy, you know where the bathroom is." It was the first time she had called me Jimmy. I glanced at her curiously and then the doctor and I went to wash our hands. Upstairs he said: "That your girl, James?"

"Oh, no," I said. "We're good friends. She isn't that kind."

"What kind? I didn't mean anything." He was amused.

"Well, I didn't know what you meant."

"Edith certainly looks like her mother," he said.

"Oh, I don't think so," I said, not really giving it a thought, but I was annoyed by the idea of talking about Edith in the bathroom. We came downstairs.

Dinner was a typical meal of that part of the country: sauerkraut and pork and some stuff called nep, which was nothing but dough, and mashed potatoes and lima beans, coffee, tea, and two kinds of pie, and you were expected to take both kinds. It was a meal I liked, and I ate a lot. Mrs. Evans got some courage from somewhere and was now talkative, now quiet, addressing most of her remarks to Doctor Myers and then turning to me. Edith kept looking at her and then turning to the doctor. She paid no attention to me except when I had something to say. Rebecca, whose table manners were being neglected, had nothing to contribute except to stick out her plate and say: "More mash potatoes with butter on."

"Say please," said Edith, but Rebecca only looked at her with the scornful blankness of five.

After dinner we went to the den and Doctor Myers and I smoked. I noticed he did not sit down; he was actually a little taller than Edith, and just about the same height as her mother. He walked around the room, standing in front of enlarged snapshots of long-deceased setter dogs, one of which my father had given Mr. Evans. Edith watched him and her mother and said nothing, but just before we were getting ready to leave Mrs. Evans caught Edith staring at her and they exchanged mysterious glances. Edith looked defiant and Mrs. Evans seemed puzzled and somehow alarmed. I could not figure it out.

In the afternoon Doctor Myers decided he would like to go to one of the patches where the practice of medicine was wholesale, so I suggested Kelly's. Kelly's was the only saloon in a patch of about one hundred families, mostly Irish, and all except one family were Catholics. In the spring they have procession in honor of the Blessed Virgin at Kelly's patch, and a priest carries the Blessed Sacrament the length of the patch, in the open air, to the public school grounds, where they hold Benediction. The houses are older and stauncher than in most patches, and they look like pictures of Ireland, except that there are no thatched roofs. Most patches were simply unbroken rows of company houses, made of slatty wood, but Kelly's had more ground between the houses and grass for the goats and cows to feed on, and the houses had plastered walls. Kelly's saloon was frequented by the whole patch because it was the post office substation, and it had a good reputation. For many years it had the only telephone in the patch.

Mr. Kelly was standing on the stoop in front of the saloon when I swung the Ford around. He took his pipe out of his mouth when he recognized the Ford and then frowned slightly when he saw that my father was not with me. He came to my side of the car.

"Where's the dad? Does he be down wid it now himself?"

"No," I said. "He's just all tired out and is getting some sleep. This is Doctor Myers that's taking his place till he gets better."

Mr. Kelly spat some tobacco juice on the ground and took a wad of tobacco out of his mouth. He was a white-haired, sickly man of middle age. "I'm glad to make your acquaintance," he said.

"How do you do, sir?" said Doctor Myers.

"I guess James here told you what to be expecting?"

"Well, more or less," said Doctor Myers. "Nice country out here. This is the nicest I've seen."

"Yes, all right I guess, but there does be a lot of sickness now. I guess you better wait a minute here till I have a few words with them inside there. I have to keep them orderly, y'understand."

He went in and we could hear his loud voice: ". . . young Malloy said his dad is seriously ill . . . great expense out of his own pocket secured a famous young specialist from Philadelphee so as to not have the people of the patch without a medical man. . . . And any lug of a lunkhead that don't stay in line will have me to answer to. . . ." Mr. Kelly then made the people line up and he came to the door and asked Doctor Myers to step in.

There were about thirty women in the saloon as Mr. Kelly guided Doctor Myers to an oilcloth-covered table. One Irishman took a contemptuous look at Doctor Myers and said: "Jesus, Mary and Joseph," and walked out, sneering at me before he closed the door. The others probably doubted that the doctor was a famous specialist, but they had not had a doctor in two or three days. Two others left quietly but the rest remained. "I guess we're ready, Mr. Kelly," said Doctor Myers.

Most of the people were Irish, but there was a few Hunkies in the patch, although not enough to warrant Mr. Kelly's learning any of their languages as the Irish had had to do in certain other patches. It was easy enough to deal with the Irish: a woman would come to the table and describe for Doctor Myers the symptoms of her sick man and kids in language that was painfully polite. My father had trained them to use terms like "bowel movement" instead of those that came more quickly to mind. After a few such encounters and wasting a lot of time, Doctor Myers more or less got the swing of prescribing for absent patients. I stood leaning against the bar, taking down the names of patients I didn't know by sight, and wishing I could have a cigarette, but that was out of the question because Mr. Kelly did not approve of cigarettes and might have told my father. I was standing there when the first of the Hunkie women had her turn. She was a worried-looking woman who even I could see was pregnant and had been many times before, judging by her body. She had on a white knitted cap and a black silk shirtwaist—nothing underneath—and a nondescript skirt. She was wearing a man's overcoat and a pair of Pacs, which are short rubber boots that men wear in the mines. When Doctor Myers spoke to her she became voluble in her own tongue. Mr. Kelly interrupted: "Wait a minute, wait a minute," he said. "You sick?"

"No, no. No me sick. Man sick." She lapsed again into her own language.

"She has a kid can speak English," said Mr. Kelly. "Hey, you. Leetle girl Mary, you daughter, her sick?" He made so-high with his hand. The woman caught on.

"Mary. Sick. Yah, Mary sick." She beamed.

Mr. Kelly looked at the line of patients and spoke to a woman. "Mame," he said. "You live near this lady. How many has she got sick?"

Mame said: "Well, there's the man for one. Dyin' from the way they was carryin' on yesterday and the day before. I ain't seen none of the kids. There's four little girls and they ain't been out of the house for a couple of days. And no wonder they're sick, runnin' around wild widout no—" "Never mind about that, now," said Mr. Kelly. "I guess,

Doctor, the only thing for you to do is go to this woman's house and take a look at them."

The woman Mame said: "To be sure, and ain't that nice? Dya hear that, everybody? Payin' a personal visit to the likes of that but the decent people take what they get. A fine how-do-ya-do."

"You'll take what you get in the shape of a puck in the nose," said Mr. Kelly. "A fine way you do be talking wid the poor dumb Hunkie not knowing how to talk good enough to say what's the matter wid her gang. So keep your two cents out of this, Mame Brannigan, and get back into line."

Mame made a noise with her mouth, but she got back into line. Doctor Myers got through the rest pretty well, except for another Hunkie who spoke some English but knew no euphemisms. Mr. Kelly finally told her to use monosyllables, which embarrassed Doctor Myers because there were some Irishwomen still in line. But "We can't be wasting no time on politeness," said Mr. Kelly. "This here's a doctor's office now." Finally all the patients except the Hunkie woman were seen to.

Mr. Kelly said: "Well, Doctor, bein's this is your first visit here you gotta take a little something on the house. Would you care for a brandy?"

"Why, yes, that'd be fine," said the doctor.

"James, what about you? A sass?"

"Yes, thank you," I said. A sass was a sarsaparilla.

Mr. Kelly opened a closet at the back of the bar and brought out a bottle. He set it on the bar and told the doctor to help himself. The doctor poured himself a drink and Mr. Kelly poured one and handed it to the Hunkie woman. "There y'are, Mary," he said. "Put hair on your chest." He winked at the doctor.

"Not joining us, Mr. Kelly?" said the doctor.

Mr. Kelly smiled. "Ask James there. No, I never drink a drop. Handle too much of it. Why, if I took a short beer every time I was asked to, I'd be drunk three quarters of the time. And another advantage is when this here Pro'bition goes into effect I won't miss it. Except financially. Well, I'll take a bottle of temperance just to be sociable." He opened a bottle of ginger ale and took half a glassful. The Hunkie woman raised her glass and said something that sounded more like a prayer than a toast, and put her whole mouth around the mouth of the glass and drank. She was happy and grateful. Doctor Myers wanted to buy another round, but Mr. Kelly said his money was no good there that day; if he wanted another drink he was to help himself. The doctor did not want another, but he said he would like to buy one for the Hunkie woman, and Mr. Kelly permitted him to pay for it, then we said good-by to Mr. Kelly and departed, the Hunkie woman getting in the car timidly, but once in the car her bottom was so large that the doctor had to stand on the running board until we reached her house.

The herd of goats in various stages of parturition gave us the razz when we stopped at the house. The ground around the house had a goaty odor because the wire which was supposed to keep them out was torn in several places. The yard was full of old wash boilers and rubber boots, tin cans and the framework of an abandoned baby carriage. The house was a one-and-a-half story building. We walked around to the back door, as the front door is reserved for the use of the priest when he comes on sick calls. The Hunkie woman seemed happier and encouraged, and prattled away as we followed her into the house, the doctor carefully picking his way through stuff in the yard.

The woman hung up her coat and hat on a couple of pegs on the kitchen wall, from which also hung a lunch can and a tin coffee bottle, the can suspended on a thick black strap, and the bottle on a braided black cord. A miner's cap with a safety lamp and a dozen buttons of the United Mine Workers of America was on another peg, and in a pile on the floor were dirty overalls and jumper and shirt. The woman sat down on a backless kitchen chair and hurriedly removed her boots, which left her barefoot. There was an awful stink of cabbage and dirty feet in the house, and I began to feel nauseated as I watched the woman flopping around, putting a kettle on the stove and starting the fire, which she indicated she wanted to do before going to look at the sick. Her bosom swung to and fro and her large hips jounced up and down, and the doctor smirked at these things, knowing that I was watching, but not knowing that I was trying to think of the skinniest girl I knew, and in the presence of so much woman I was sorry for all past thoughts or desires. Finally the woman led the way to the front of the house. In one of the two front rooms was an old-fashioned bed. The windows were curtained, but when our eyes became accustomed to the darkness we could see four children lying on the bed. The youngest and oldest were lying together. The oldest, a girl about five years old, was only half covered by the torn quilt that covered the others. The baby coughed as we came in. The other two were sound asleep. The half-covered little girl got awake, or opened her eyes and looked at the ceiling. She had a half-sneering look about her nose and mouth, and her eyes were expressionless. Doctor Myers leaned over her and so did her mother, speaking to the girl, but the girl apparently made no sense even in the Hunkie language. She sounded as though she were trying to clear her throat of phlegm. The doctor turned to me and said dramatically: "James, take this woman out and get her to boil more water, and go out to the car and get your father's instrument case." I grabbed the woman's arm and pulled her to the kitchen and made signs for her to boil the water, then I went out to the Ford and wrestled with the lid of the rear compartment, wondering what Myers wanted with the instrument case, wondering whether he himself knew what he wanted with it. At last I yanked the lid open and was walking back with the leather case in my hand when I heard a loud scream. It sounded more deliberate than wild, it started so low and suddenly went so high. I hurried back to the bedroom and saw Doctor Myers trying to pull the heavy woman away from her daughter. He was not strong enough for her, but he kept pulling and there were tears in his eyes: "Come away, damn it! Come away from her, you damn fool!" He turned to me for help and said: "James, this is awful. The little girl just died. Keep away from her. She had diphtheria!"

"I couldn't open the back of the car," I said.

"Oh, it wasn't your fault. Even a tracheotomy wouldn't have saved her, the poor little thing. But we've got to do something for these others. The baby has plenty of spots, and I haven't even looked at the other two." The other two had been awakened by their mother's screams and were sitting up and crying, not very loud. The woman had the dead girl in her arms. She did not need the English language to know that the child was dead. She was rocking her back and forth and kissing her and looking up at us with fat streams of tears running from her eyes. She would stop crying for a second, but would start again, crying with her mouth open and the tears, unheeded, sliding in over her upper lip.

Doctor Myers took some coins from his pocket and tried to make friends with the in-between kids, but they did not know what money was, so I left him to go in to see how the man was. I walked across the hall to the other bedroom and pulled up the curtains. The man was lying in his underwear; gaunt, bearded and dead.

I knew he was dead, but I said: "Hyuh, John, hyuh." The sound of my voice made me feel silly, then sacrilegious, and then I had to vomit. I had seen men brought in from railroad wrecks and mine explosions and other violent-accident cases, but I had been prepared for them if only by the sound of an ambulance bell. This was different. Doctor Myers heard me being sick and came in. I was crying. He took a few seconds to see that the man was dead and then he took me by the arm and said: "That's all right, kid. Come out in the air." He led me outside into the cold afternoon and I felt better and hungry.

He let go of my arm. "Listen," he said. "As soon as you feel well enough, take the car and go to the hospital. The first thing you do there is get them to give you twenty thousand units of antitoxin, and while you're doing that tell them to send an ambulance out here right away. Don't go near anybody if you can help it except a doctor." He paused. "You'd better find out about an undertaker."

"You'll need more than twenty thousand units of antitoxin," I said. I had had that much in my own back when I was eight years old.

"Oh, no. You didn't understand me. The antitoxin's for you. You tell whoever's in charge at the hospital how many are sick out here, and they'll know what to send."

"What about you?"

"Oh, I'll stay here and go back in the ambulance. Don't worry about me. I want to stay here and do what I can for these kids." I suddenly had a lot of respect for him. I got into the Ford and drove away. Doctors' cars carried cardboard signs which said By Order State Department of Health, which gave them the right to break speed laws, and I broke them on my way to the hospital. I pulled in at the porte-cochere and met Doctor Kleiber, a friend of my father's, and told him everything. He gave me antitoxin. He smiled when I mentioned getting an undertaker. "Lucky if they get a wooden rough box, even, James. These people aren't patients of Daddy's, are they, James?"

"No."

"Well then, I guess maybe we have to send an Army doctor. I'm full up so I haven't a minute except for Daddy's patients. Now go home and I'll take care of everything. You'll be stiff in the back and you want to rest. Good-by now." So I drove home and went to bed.

I was stiff the next morning from the antitoxin, but it had not been so bad as the other time I had taken it, and I was able to pick up Doctor Myers at the hotel. "I feel pretty damn useless, not being able to drive a car," he said. "But I never had much chance to learn. My mother never had enough money to get one. You know that joke: we can't afford a Ford."

"Oh, well," I said, "in Philadelphia you don't need one. They're a nuisance in the city."

"All the same I'd like to have one. I guess I'll have to when I start practicing. Well, where to first?" We outlined a schedule and for the next couple of days we were on the go almost continually. We hardly noticed how the character of the region was changed. There was little traffic in the streets, but the few cars tore madly. Most of them were Cadillacs; black, company-owned Cadillacs which were at the disposal of young men like Doctor Myers and the two drunken Gibbsville doctors who did not own cars; and gray Cadillacs from the USAAC base in Allentown, which took officers of the Army Medical Corps around to the emergency hospitals. At night the officers would use the cars for their fun, and there were a few scandals. One officer was rumored to be psychopathic and had to be sent elsewhere. Opinion among us boys was divided; some said he was taken away and shot, some said he was sent to Leavenworth, others said he was dishonorably discharged. The ambulances were being driven by members of the militia, who wore uniforms resembling those of the marine corps. The militia was made up of young men who were exempt from active service. They had to make one ambulance driver give up his job, because he would drive as fast as the ambulance would go even when he was only going to a drug store for a carton of soap. Another volunteer driver made so much noise with the ambulance bell that the sick persons inside would be worse off than if they had walked. The women of wealth who could drive their own cars drove them, fetching and carrying blankets and cots, towels and cotton, but their husbands made some of the women stop because of the dangers of influenza and Army medical officers. Mrs. Barlow, the leader of society, did not stop, and her husband knew better than to try to insist. She was charming and stylish and looked very English in her Red Cross canteen division uniform. She assumed charge of the emergency hospital in the armory and bossed the Catholic sisters and the graduate nurses around and made them like it. Her husband gave money and continued to ride a sorrel hunter about the countryside. The rector of the Second Presbyterian Church appeared before the Board of Health and demanded that the nuns be taken out of the hospitals on the ground that they were baptizing men and women who were about to die, without ascertaining whether they were Catholics or Protestants. The *Standard* had a story on the front page which accused unnamed undertakers of profiteering on "rough boxes," charging as much for pine board boxes as they had for mahogany caskets before the epidemic.

Doctor Myers at first wore a mask over his nose and mouth when making calls, and so did I, but the gauze stuck to my lips and I stopped wearing it and so did the doctor. It was too much of a nuisance to put them on and take them off every time we would go to a place like Kelly's, and also it was rather insulting to walk in on a group of people with a mask on your face when nobody in the group was wearing one. I was very healthy and was always glad to go in with the doctor because it gave me something to do. Of course I could have cleaned spark plugs or shot some air into the tires while waiting for the doctor, but I hated to monkey around the car almost as much as I liked to drive it.

In a few days Doctor Myers had begun to acquire some standing among the patients and he became more confident. One time after coming from my father's bedroom he got in the car with some prescriptions in his hand and we started out. To himself he said, looking up from a prescription: "Digitalis . . . now I wonder?" I turned suddenly, because it was the first time in my life I had heard anyone criticize a prescription of my father's. "Oh, I'm sorry, Jimmy," he said.

"You better not ever let him hear you say anything about his prescriptions."

"Yes, I know. He doesn't want anyone to argue with him. He doesn't think I'm seeing as many people as I should."

"What does he expect?" I said.

"Oh, he isn't unreasonable, but he doesn't want his patients to think he's neglecting them. By the way, he wants us to stop in at the Evanses in Collieryville. The David Evanses. Mrs. Evans phoned and said their maid is sick."

"That's okay with me," I said.

"I thought it would be," he said.

Collieryville seemed strange with the streets so deserted as on some new kind of holiday. The mines did not work on holydays of obligation, and the miners would get dressed and stand around in front of poolrooms and saloons, but now they were not standing around, and there was none of the activity of a working day, when coal wagons and trucks rumble through the town, and ten-horse teams, guided by the shouted "gee" and "haw" of the driver, would pull loads of timber through the streets on the way to the mines. Collieryville, a town of about four thousand persons, was quiet as though the people were afraid to come out in the cold November gray.

We were driving along the main street when I saw Edith. She was coming out of the P. O. S. of A. Hall, which was a poolroom on the first floor and had lodge rooms on the two upper stories. It was being used as an emergency hospital. I pulled up at the curb and called to Edith. "Come on, I'll give you a ride home," I said.

"Can't. I have to get some things at the drug store," she said.

"Well, we're going to your house anyway. I'll see you there," I said.

We drove to the Evans house and I told the doctor I would wait outside until Edith came. She appeared in about five minutes and I told her to sit in the car and talk to me. She said she would.

"Well, I'm a nurse, Jimmy," she said.

"Yes, you are," I said scornfully. "That's how your maid got sick."

"What!"

"Why, you hanging around at the P. O. S. of A. Hall is probably the way your maid got sick. You probably brought home the flu—"

"Oh, my Lord!" she said. She was nervous and pale. She suddenly jumped out of the car and I followed her. She swung open the front door and ran toward the kitchen, and I was glad she did; for although I followed her to the kitchen, I caught a glimpse of Mrs. Evans and Doctor Myers in Mr. Evans' den. Through the half-closed doors I could see they were kissing.

I didn't stop, I know, although I felt that I had slowed up. I followed Edith into the kitchen and saw that she was half crying, shaking her hands up and down. I couldn't tell whether she had seen what I had seen, but something was wrong that she knew about. I blurted out, "Don't go in your father's den," and was immediately sorry I had said it; but then I saw that she had guessed. She looked weak and took hold of my arms; not looking at me, not even speaking to me, she said: "Now it's him. Oh, why didn't I come home with you? Sarah isn't sick at all. That was just an excuse to get that Myers to come here." She bit her lip and squeezed my arms. "Jimmy, you mustn't ever let on. Promise me."

"I give you my word of honor," I said. "God can strike me dead if I ever say anything."

Edith kissed me, then she called out: "Hey, where is everybody?"

She whispered to me: "Pretend you're chasing me like as if I pulled your necktie."

"Let go!" I yelled, as loud as I could. Then we left the kitchen, and Edith would pull my necktie at every step.

Mrs. Evans came out of the den. "Here, what's going on here?"

"I'm after your daughter for pulling my tie," I said.

"Now Edith, be a good girl and don't fight with James. I don't understand what's the matter with you two. You usedn't to ever fight, and now you fight like cats and dogs. You oughtn't to. It's not nice."

"Oh—" Edith said, and then she burst into tears and went upstairs.

I was genuinely surprised, and said: "I'm sorry, Mrs. Evans, we were only fooling."

"Oh, it's not your fault, James. She feels nervous anyhow and I guess the running was too much for her." She looked at the doctor as if to imply that it was something he would understand.

"I guess I'll go out and sit in the car," I said.

"I'll be right out," said the doctor.

I sat in the car and smoked, now and then looking at the second floor window where I knew Edith's room was, but Edith did not come to the window and in about twenty minutes the doctor came out.

"The maid wasn't sick after all," he said. "It was Mrs. Evans. She has a slight cold but she didn't want to worry your father. I guess she thought if she said she was sick, your father'd come out himself."

"Uh-huh," I said. "Where to now?"

"Oh, that Polish saloon out near the big coal banks."

"You mean Wisniewski's," I said.

Doctor Myers must have known I suspected him, and he might even have suspected that I had *seen* him kissing Mrs. Evans. I was not very good at hiding my likes and dislikes, and I began to dislike him, but I tried not to show it. I didn't dare, for he might have told my father I was unsatisfactory, and my father would have given me hell. Or if I had told my father what I'd seen, he'd have given Doctor Myers a terrible beating. My father never drank or smoked, and he was a good savage amateur boxer, with no scruples against punching anyone smaller than himself. Less than a year before all this took place my father had been stopped by a traffic policeman while he was hurrying to an "OBS." The policeman knew my father's car, and could have guessed why he was in a hurry, but he stopped him. My father got out of the car, walked to the front of it, and in the middle of a fairly busy intersection he took a crack at the policeman and broke his jaw. Then he got back and drove around the unconscious policeman and on to the confinement case. It cost my father nearly a thousand dollars, and the policeman's friends and my father's enemies said: "Damn Mike Malloy, he ought to be put in jail." But my father was a staunch Republican and he got away with it.

I thought of this now and I thought of what my father would have done to Doctor Myers if he found out. Not only would he have beaten him up, but I am sure he would have used his influence at the University to keep Myers from getting his degree.

So I hid, as well as I could, my dislike for Doctor Myers, and the next day, when we stopped at my home, I was glad I did. My father had invented a signal system to save time. Whenever there was a white slip stuck in the window at home or at the office, that meant he was to stop and pick up a message. This day the message in the window read: "Mrs. David Evans, Collieryville."

Doctor Myers looked at it and showed it to me. "Well, on to Collieryville," he said.

"Okay, but would you mind waiting a second? I want to see my mother."

He was slightly suspicious. "You don't need any money, do you? I have some."

"No, I just wanted to see if she would get my father to let me have the car tonight." So I went in and telephoned to the Evanses. I got Edith on the phone and told her that her mother had sent for Doctor Myers.

"I know," she said. "I knew she would. She didn't get up this morning and she's faking sick."

"Well, when we get there you go upstairs with the doctor, and if he wants you to leave the bedroom, you'll have to leave, but tell your mother you'll be right outside, see?"

"Okay," said Edith.

I returned to the car. "How'd you make out?" said Doctor Myers.

"She thinks she can get him to let me have it," I said, meaning that my father would let me have the car.

When we arrived at the Evans house I had an inspiration. I didn't want him to suspect that we had any plan in regard to him, so I told him I was going in with him to apologize to Edith for our fight of the day before. There was the chance that Edith would fail to follow my advice and would come downstairs, but there was the equally good chance that she would stay upstairs.

The plan worked. In some respects Edith was dumb, but not in this. Doctor Myers stayed upstairs scarcely five minutes, but it was another five before Edith came down. Doctor Myers had gone out to wait in the Ford.

Edith appeared. "Oh, Jimmy, you're so nice to me, and I'm often mean to you. Why is that?"

"Because I love you." I kissed her and she kissed me.

"Listen, if my dad ever finds this out he'll kill her. It's funny, you and me. I mean if you ever told me a dirty story, like about *you* know—people—"

"I did once."

"Did you? I mustn't have been listening. Anyhow it's funny to think of you and me, and I'm older than you, but we know something that fellows and girls our age, they only guess at."

"Oh, I've known about it a long time, ever since I went to sisters' school."

"And I guess from your father's doctor books. But this isn't the same when it's your own mother, and I bet this isn't the first time. My dad must have suspicions, because why didn't he send me away to boarding school this year? I graduated from high last year. I bet he wanted me to be here to keep an eye on her."

"Who was the other man?"

"Oh, I can't tell you. Nobody you know. Anyhow, I'm not sure, so I wouldn't tell you. Listen, Jimmy, promise to telephone me every time before he comes here. If I'm not here I'll be at the Bordelmans' or at the Haltensteins', or if not there, the Callaways'. I'll stay home as much as I can, though. How long is he going to be around here, that doctor?"

"Lord knows," I said.

"Oh, I hope he goes. Now give me a good-by kiss, Jimmy, and then you have to go." I kissed her. "I'm worse than she is," she said.

"No, you're not," I said. "You're the most darling girl there is. Good-by, Ede," I said.

Doctor Myers was rubbing the skin in front of his ear when I came out. "Well, did you kiss and make up?"

"Oh, we don't go in for that mushy stuff," I said.

"Well, you will," he said. "Well . . . on to Wizziski's."

"It's a good thing you're not going to be around here long," I said.

"Why? Why do you say that?"

"Because you couldn't be in business or practice medicine without learning Hunkie names. If you stayed around here you'd have to be able to pronounce them and spell them." I started the car. I was glad to talk. "But I tell you where you'd have trouble. That's in the patches where they're all Irish with twenty or thirty cousins living in the same patch and all with the same name."

"Oh, come on."

"Well, it isn't as bad as it used to be," I said. "But my father told me about one time he went to Mass at Forganville, about fifteen miles from here, where they used to be all Irish. Now it's half Polack. Anyhow my father said the priest read the list of those that gave to the monthly collection, and the list was like this: John J. Coyle, $5; Jack Coyle, $2; Johnny Coyle, $2; J. J. Coyle, $5; Big John Coyle, $5; Mrs. John Coyle, saloonkeeper's window, $10; the Widow Coyle, $2. And then a lot of other Coyles."

He did not quite believe this, but he thought it was a good story, and we talked about college—my father had told me I could go to Oxford or Trinity College, Dublin, if I promised to study medicine—until we reached Wisniewski's.

This was a saloon in a newer patch than Kelly's. It was entirely surrounded by mine shafts and breakers and railroads and mule yards, a flat area broken only by culm banks until half a mile away there was a steep, partly wooded hill which was not safe to walk on because it was all undermined and cave-ins occurred so frequently that they did not bother to build fences around them. The houses were the same height as in Kelly's patch, but they were built in blocks of four and six houses each. Technically Wisniewski's saloon was not in the patch; that is, it was not on company ground, but at a crossroads at one end of the rows of houses. It was an old stone house which had been a tavern in the days of the King's Highway. Now it was a beery smelling place with a tall bar and no tables or chairs. It was crowded, but still it had a deserted appearance. The reason was that there was no one behind the bar, and no cigars or cartons of chewing tobacco on the back bar. The only decorations were a calendar from which the October leaf had not been torn, depicting a voluptuous woman stretched out on a divan, and an Old Overholt sign hanging askew on the toilet door.

The men and women recognized Doctor Myers and me, and made a lane for us to pass through. Wisniewski himself was sick in bed, and everybody understood that the doctor would see him first, before prescribing for the mob in the barroom.

Doctor Myers and I went to Wisniewski's room, which was on the first floor. Wisniewski was an affable man, between forty and fifty, with a Teutonic haircut that never needed brushing. His body under the covers made big lumps. He was shaking hands with another Polack whose name was Stiney. He said to us: "Oh, hyuh, Cheem, hyuh, Cheem. Hyuh, Doc."

"Hyuh, Steve," I said. "Yoksheemosh?"

"Oh, fine dandy. How's yaself? How's Poppa? You tell Poppa what he needs is lay off this here booze." He roared at this joke. "Ya, you tell him I said so, lay off this booze." He looked around at the others in the room, and they all laughed, because my father used to pretend that he was going to have Steve's saloon closed by the County. "You wanna drink, Cheem?" he asked, and reached under the bed and pulled the bottle away. "Na na na na na. Poppa closed up my place wit' the County, I give you a drink. Ya know, miners drink here, but no minors under eighteen, hey?" He passed the bottle around, and all the other men in the room took swigs.

Doctor Myers was horrified. "You oughtn't to do that. You'll give the others the flu."

"Too late now, Doc," he said. "T'ree bottle now already."

"You'll lose all your customers, Steve," I said.

"How ya figure dat out?" said Steve. "Dis flu make me die, dis bottle make dem die. Fwit! Me and my customers all togeder in hell, so I open a place in hell. Fwit!"

"Well, anyhow, how are you feeling?" said the doctor. He placed a thermometer under Steve's arm. The others and Steve were silent until the temperature had been taken. "Hm," said Doctor Myers. He frowned at the thermometer.

" 'M gonna die, Doc?" said Steve.

"Well, maybe not, but you—" he stopped talking. The door opened and there was a blast of sweaty air from the barroom, and Mr. Evans stood in the doorway, his hand on the knob. I felt weak.

"Doctor Myers, I'd like to see you a minute, please," said Mr. Evans.

"Hyuh, Meester Ivvins," called Steve. Evans is one name which is consistently pronounced the same by the Irish, Slavs, Germans, and even the Portuguese and Negroes in the anthracite.

"Hello, Steve, I see you're drunk," said Mr. Evans.

"Not yet, Meester Ivvins. Wanna drink?"

"No, thanks. Doctor, will you step outside with me?"

Doctor Myers stalled. "I haven't prescribed for this man, Mr. Evans, If you'll wait?"

"My God, man! I can't wait. It's about my wife."

"What about her?" asked the doctor.

"For God's sake," cried Evans. "She's sick, isn't she? Aren't you attending her, or don't you remember your patients?"

I sighed, and Doctor Myers sighed louder. "Oh," he said. "You certainly—frightened me, Mr. Evans. I was afraid something had happened. Why, you have no need to worry, sir. She has hardly any temperature. A very slight cold, and she did just the sensible thing by going to bed."

"Well, why didn't you say so?" Mr. Evans sat down. "Go ahead, then, finish with Steve. I'll wait till you get through. I'm sorry if I seemed rude, but I was worried. You see I just heard from my timber boss that he saw Doctor Malloy's car in front of my house, and I called up and found out that Mrs. Evans was sick in bed, and my daughter sounded so excited I thought it must be serious. I'll take a drink now, Steve."

"Better not drink out of that bottle, Mr. Evans," said the doctor, who was writing a prescription.

"Oh, hell, it won't hurt me. So anyhow, where was I? Oh, yes. Well, I went home and found Mrs. Evans in bed and she seemed very pale, so I wanted to be sure it wasn't flu. I found out you were headed this way so I came right out to ask if you wouldn't come back and take another look. That's good liquor, Steve. I'll buy a case of that."

"I give you a case, Meester Ivvins. Glad to give you a case any time," said Steve.

"All right, we'll call it a Christmas present," said Mr. Evans. "Thanks very much." He was sweating and he opened his raccoon coat. He took another drink, then he handed the bottle to Stiney. "Well, James, I hear you and Edith were at it again."

"Oh, it was just in fun. You know. Pulling my tie," I said.

"Well, don't let her get fresh with you," he said. "You have to keep these women in their place." He punched me playfully. "Doctor, I wonder if you could come to the house now and make sure everything's all right."

"I would gladly, Mr. Evans, but there's all that crowd in the barroom, and frankly, Mrs. Evans isn't what you'd call a sick woman, so my duty as a—physician is right here. I'll come if you'd like to wait."

The Hunkies, hearing the Super talked to in this manner, probably expected Meester Ivvins to get up and belt the doctor across the face, but he only said: "Well, if you're sure an hour couldn't make any difference."

"Couldn't possibly, Mr. Evans," said Doctor Myers.

He finished with Steve and told him to stop drinking and take his medicine, then he turned to leave. Steve reached under his pillow and drew out a bundle of money. He peeled off a fifty-dollar bill and handed it to the doctor.

"Oh, no, thanks," said Doctor Myers. "Doctor Malloy will send you a bill."

"Aw, don't worry about him, eh, Cheem? I always pay him firs' the mont', eh, Cheem? Naw, Doc, dis for you. Go have a good time. Get twenty-five woman, maybe get drunk wit' boilo." I could imagine Doctor Myers drinking boilo, which is hot moonshine. I nudged him and he took the money and we went to the barroom.

I carried the chair and table and set them in place, and the Hunkies lined up docilely. Mr. Evans waited in Steve's room, taking a swig out of the bottle now and then until Doctor Myers had finished with the crowd. It was the same as usual. It was impractical to get detailed descriptions from each patient, so the flu doctor would ask each person three or four questions and then pretend to prescribe for each case individually. Actually they gave the same prescription to almost all of the patients, not only to save time, but because drug supplies in the village and city pharmacies were inadequate and it was physically impossible for druggists to meet the demand. They would make up large batches of each doctor's standard prescription and dole out boxes and bottles as the patrons presented the prescriptions.

It took about two hours to dispose of the crowd at Steve's. Mr. Evans told Doctor Myers to come in the Cadillac because it was faster than the Ford—which I denied. I followed in the Ford and got to the Evans house about three minutes after the Cadillac. Edith met me at the door. "Oh, what a scare!" she said.

"If you think you were scared, what about me?" I said. I told her how I had felt when her father appeared at Steve's.

"Your father phoned and wants you to take that Myers home," she said.

"Did he say why?" I asked.

"No, he just said you weren't to make any more calls this afternoon."

"I wonder why."

"I hope it hasn't got anything to do with him and my mother," she said.

"How could it? Only four people know about it. He couldn't guess it and nobody would tell him. Maybe he's got up and wants me to drive for him."

"Maybe . . . I can't think. I'm afraid of them up there. Oh, I hope he goes away." I kissed her and she pushed me away. "You're a bad actor, James Malloy. You're bad enough now, but wait till you grow up."

"What do you mean grow up? I'm almost six feet."

"But you're only a kid. I'm seventeen and you're only fifteen."

"I'll be in my seventeenth year soon." We heard footsteps on the stairs, and Doctor Myers' voice: ". . . absolutely nothing to worry about. I'll come in again tomorrow. Good-by, Mr. Evans. Good-by, Edith. Ready, Jim?"

I gave him my father's message and we drove home fast. When we got there one of the Buicks was in front of the house, and we went in.

"Well, Doctor Myers," my father said. "Back in harness again. Fit as a fiddle and I want to thank you for the splendid attention you've given my practice. I don't know what my patients would have done without you."

"Oh, it's been a privilege, Doctor. I'd like to be able to tell you how much I've appreciated working for you. I wouldn't have missed it for the world. I think I'd like to serve my interneship in a place like this."

"Well, I'm glad to hear it. I'm chief of staff at our hospital, and I'm sorry I can't offer you anything here, but you ought to try some place like Scranton General. Get the benefit of these mining cases. Damn interesting fractures, by the way. I trephined a man, forty-eight years old—all right, James, I'll call you when I need you." I left the room and they talked for half an hour, and then my father called me. "Doctor Myers wants to say good-by."

"I couldn't leave without saying good-by to my partner," said the doctor. "And by the way, Doctor Malloy, I think I ought to give part of this check to James. He did half the work."

"If he did I'll see that he gets his share. James knows that. He wants one of these damn raccoon coats. When I was a boy the only people that wore them drove hearses. Well—" My father indicated that it was time for the doctor and me to shake hands.

"Quite a grip James has," said the doctor.

"Perfect hands for a surgeon. Wasted, though," my father said. "Probably send him to some damn agricultural school and make a farmer out of him. I want him to go to Dublin, then Vienna. That's where the surgeons are. Dublin and Vienna. Good luck, Doctor."

"Thank you, many thanks, Doctor Malloy."

"James will drive you to the hotel." I took him to the hotel and we shook hands. "If you ever want a place to stay in Philadelphia you're always welcome at my house." He gave me the address of a fraternity house. "Say good-by to the Evanses for me, will you, Jim?"

"Sure," I said and left.

My Father was standing on the porch, waiting impatiently. "We'll use the Buick," he said. "That Ford probably isn't worth the powder to blow it to hell after you've been using it. Do you really want one of those livery stable coats?"

"Sure I do."

"All right. Now, ah, drive to Kelly's." We drove to Kelly's, where there was an ovation, not too loud, because there were one or two in the crowd on whom my father was liable to turn and say: "You, ya dirty so and so, you haven't paid me a cent since last February. What are you cheering for?" We paid a few personal visits in the patch. At one of them my father slapped a pretty Irish girl's bottom; at another he gave a little boy a dollar and told him to stop picking his nose; at another he sent me for the priest, and when I came back he had gone on foot to two other houses, and was waiting for me at the second. "What the hell kept you? Go to Terry Loughran's, unless the skunk got another doctor."

"He probably did," I said jovially. "He probably got Lucas."

"*Doctor* Lucas. Doctor Lucashinsky. Ivan the Terrible. Well, if he got Lucas it serves him right. Go to Hartenstein's."

We drove until one o'clock the next morning, taking coffee now and then, and once we stopped for a fried-egg sandwich. Twice I very nearly fell asleep while driving. The second time I awoke to hear my father saying: ". . . And my God! To think that a son of mine would rather rot in a dirty stinking newspaper office than do this. Why, I do more good and make more money in twenty minutes in the operating room than you'll be able to make the first three years you're out of college. If you *go* to college. Don't drive so fast!"

It was like that for the next two days. I slept when he allowed me to. We were out late at night and out again early in the morning. We drove fast and a couple of times I bounded along corduroy roads with tanks of oxygen (my father was one of the first, if not the first, to use oxygen in pneumonia) ready to blow me to hell. I developed a fine cigarette cough, but my father kept quiet about it, because I was not taking quinine and he was. We got on each other's nerves and had one terrible scene. He became angered by my driving and punched me on the shoulder. I stopped the car and took a tire iron from the floor of the car.

"Now just try that again," I said.

He did not move from the back seat. "Get back in this car." And I got back. But that night we got home fairly early and the next morning, when he had to go out at four o'clock, he drove the car himself and let me sleep. I was beginning to miss Doctor Myers. It was about eight o'clock when I came down for breakfast, and I saw my father sitting in the living room, looking very tired, staring straight ahead, his arms lying on the arms of the chair. I said hello, but he did not answer.

My mother brought me my breakfast. "Did you speak to your father?"

"Oh, I said hello, but he's in a stupor or something. I'm getting sick of all this."

"Hold your tongue. Your father has good reason to be unhappy this morning. He just lost one of the dearest friends he had in the world. Mr. Evans."

"Mr. Evans!" I said. "When'd he die?"

"At about four o'clock this morning. They called your father but he died before he got there. Poor Mrs. Evans—"

"What he die of? The flu?"

"Yes." I thought of the bottle that he had shared with Steve and the other Hunkies, and Mrs. Evans' illness, and Doctor Myers. It was all mixed up in my mind. "Now you be careful how you behave with your father today," my mother said.

I called up Edith, but she would not come to the phone. I wrote her a note and drove to Collieryville with some flowers, but she would not see me.

Even after the epidemic died down and the schools were reopened she would not see me. Then she went away to school and did not come home for the Easter holidays, and in May or June I fell in love with another girl and was surprised, but only surprised, when Edith eloped. Now I never can remember her married name.

NEW JERSEY

★

Christ in Concrete

PIETRO DI DONATO

March whistled stinging snow against the brick walls and up the gaunt girders. Geremio, the foreman, swung his arms about, and gaffed the men on.

Old Nick, the 'Lean,' stood up from over a dust-flying brick pile, and tapped the side of his nose.

'Master Geremio, the devil himself could not break his tail any harder than we here.'

Burly Vincenzo of the walrus moustache, and known as the 'Snoutnose,' let fall the chute door of the concrete hopper and sang over in the Lean's direction: 'Mari-Annina's belly and the burning night will make of me once more a milk-mouthed strippling lad . . .'

The Lean loaded his wheelbarrow and spat furiously. 'Sons of two-legged dogs . . . despised of even the devil himself! Work! Sure! For America beautiful will eat you and spit your bones into the earth's hole! Work!' And with that his wiry frame pitched the barrow violently over the rough floor.

Snoutnose waved his head to and fro and with mock pathos wailed, 'Sing on, oh guitar of mine . . .'

Short, cherry-faced Joe Chiappa, the scaffoldman, paused with hatchet in hand and tenpenny spike sticking out from small dice-like teeth to tell the Lean as he went by, in a voice that all could hear, 'Ah, father of countless chicks, the old age is a carrion!'

Geremio chuckled and called to him: 'Hey, little Joe, who are you to talk? You and big-titted Cola can't even hatch an egg, whereas the

---

Lean has just to turn the doorknob of his bedroom and old Philomena becomes a balloon!'

Coarse throats tickled and mouths opened wide in laughter.

Mike, the 'Barrel-mouth,' pretended he was talking to himself and yelled out in his best English . . . he was always speaking English while the rest carried on in their native Italian: 'I don't know myself, but somebodys whose gotta bigga buncha keeds and he alla times talka from somebodys elsa!'

Geremio knew it was meant for him and he laughed. 'On the tomb of Saint Pimplelegs, this little boy my wife is giving me next week shall be the last! Eight hungry little Christians to feed is enough for any man.'

Joe Chiappa nodded to the rest. 'Sure, Master Geremio had a telephone call from the next bambino. Yes, it told him it had a little bell there instead of a rosebush . . . It even told him its name!'

'Laugh, laugh all of you,' returned Geremio, 'but I tell you that all my kids must be boys so that they some day will be big American builders. And then I'll help them to put the gold away in the basements for safe keeping!'

A great din of riveting shattered the talk among the fast-moving men. Geremio added a handful of 'Honest' tobacco to his corncob, puffed strongly, and cupped his hands around the bowl for a bit of warmth. The chill day caused him to shiver, and he thought to himself, 'Yes, the day is cold, cold . . . but who am I to complain when the good Christ himself was crucified?

'Pushing the job is all right (when has it been otherwise in my life?) but this job frightens me. I feel the building wants to tell me something; just as one Christian to another. I don't like this. Mr. Murdin tells me, "Push it up!" That's all he knows. I keep telling him that the underpinning should be doubled and the old material removed from the floors, but he keeps the inspector drunk and . . . "Hey, Ashes-ass! Get away from under that pilaster! Don't pull the old work. Push it away from you or you'll have a nice present for Easter if the wall falls on you!" . . . Well, with the help of God I'll see this job through. It's not my first, nor the . . . "Hey, Patsy number two! Put more cement in that concrete; we're putting up a building, not an Easter cake!"'

Patsy hurled his shovel to the floor and gesticulated madly. 'The padrone Murdin-sa tells me, "Too much, too much! Lil' bit is plenty!" And you tell me I'm stingy! The rotten building can fall after I leave!'

Six floors below, the contractor called: 'Hey Geremio! Is your gang of dagos dead?'

Geremio cautioned to the men: 'On your toes, boys. If he writes out slips, someone won't have big eels on the Easter table.'

The Lean cursed that 'the padrone could take the job and shove it . . . !'

Curly-headed Sandino, the roguish, pigeon-toed scaffoldman, spat a clod of tobacco-juice and hummed to his own music.

'Yes, certainly yes to your face, master padrone . . . and behind, this to you and all your kind!'

The day, like all days, came to an end. Calloused and bruised bodies sighed, and numb legs shuffled towards shabby railroad flats. . . .

'Ah, *bella casa mio*. Where my little freshets of blood, and my good woman await me. Home where my broken back will not ache so. Home where midst the monkey chatter of my piccolinos I will float off to blessed slumber with my feet on the chair and the head on the wife's soft full breast.'

These great child-hearted ones leave each other without words or ceremony, and as they ride and walk home, a great pride swells the breast. . . .

'Blessings to Thee, oh Jesus. I have fought winds and cold. Hand to hand I have locked dumb stones in place and the great building rises. I have earned a bit of bread for me and mine.'

The mad day's brutal conflict is forgiven, and strained limbs prostrate themselves so that swollen veins can send the yearning blood coursing and pulsating deliciously as though the body mountained leaping streams.

The job alone remained behind . . . and yet, they too, having left the bigger part of their lives with it. The cold ghastly beast, the Job, stood stark, the eerie March wind wrapping it in sharp shadows of falling dusk.

That night was a crowning point in the life of Geremio. He bought a house! Twenty years he had helped to mould the New World. And now he was to have a house of his own! What mattered that it was no more than a wooden shack? It was his own!

He had proudly signed his name and helped Annunziata to make her X on the wonderful contract that proved them owners. And she was happy to think that her next child, soon to come, would be born under their own rooftree. She heard the church chimes, and cried to the children: 'Children, to bed! It is near midnight. And remember, shut-mouth to the *paesanos!* Or they will send the evil eye to our new home even before we put foot.'

The children scampered off to the icy yellow bedroom where three slept in one bed and three in the other. Coltishly and friskily they kicked about under the covers; their black iron-cotton stockings not removed . . . what! and freeze the peanut-little toes?

Said Annunziata, 'The children are so happy, Geremio; let them be, for even I would a Tarantella dance.' And with that she turned blushing. He wanted to take her on her word. She patted his hands, kissed them, and whispered, 'Our children will dance for us . . . in the American style some day.'

Geremio cleared his throat and wanted to sing. 'Yes, with joy I could sing in a richer feeling than the great Caruso.' He babbled little old country couplets and circled the room until the tenant below tapped the ceiling.

Annunziata whispered: 'Geremio, to bed and rest. Tomorrow is a day for great things . . . and the day on which our Lord died for us.'

The children were now hard asleep. Heads under the cover, over . . . moist noses whistling, and little damp legs entwined.

In bed Geremio and Annunziata clung closely to each other. They mumbled figures and dates until fatigue stilled their thoughts. And with chubby Johnnie clutching fast his bottle and warmed between them . . . life breathed heavily, and dreams entertained in far, far worlds, the nation-builder's brood.

But Geremio and Annunziata remained for a while staring into darkness, silently.

'Geremio?'

'Yes?'

'This job you are now working. . . .'

'So?'

'You used always to tell about what happened on the jobs . . . who was jealous, and who praised. . . .'

'You should know by now that all work is the same. . . .'

'Geremio. The month you have been on this job, you have not spoken a word about the work . . . And I have felt that I am walking in a dream. Is the work dangerous? Why don't you answer . . .?'

Job loomed up damp, shivery grey. Its giant members waiting. Builders quietly donned their coarse robes, and waited.

Geremio's whistle rolled back into his pocket and the symphony of struggle began.

Trowel rang through brick and slashed mortar rivets were machine-gunned fast with angry grind Patsy number one check Patsy number two check the Lean three check Vincenzo four steel bellowed back at hammer donkey engines coughed purple Ashes-ass Pietro fifteen chisel point intoned stone thin steel whirred and wailed through wood liquid stone flowed with dull rasp through iron veins and hoist screamed through space Carmine the Fat twenty-four and Giacomo Sangini check . . . The multitudinous voices of a civilization rose from the surroundings and welded with the efforts of the Job.

To the intent ear, Nation was voicing her growing pains, but, hands that create are attached to warm hearts and not to calculating minds. The Lean as he fought his burden on looked forward to only one goal, the end. The barrow he pushed, he did not love. The stones that brutalized his palms, he did not love. The great God Job, he did not love. He felt a searing bitterness and a fathomless consternation at the queer consciousness that inflicted the ever mounting weight of structure that he HAD TO! HAD TO! raise above his shoulders! When, when and where would the last stone be? Never . . . did he bear his toil with the rhythm of song! Never . . . did his gasping heart knead the heavy mortar with lilting melody! A voice within him spoke a wordless language.

The language of worn oppression and the despair of realizing that his life had been left on brick piles. And always, there had been hunger and her bastard, the fear of hunger.

Murdin bore down upon Geremio from behind and shouted:

'Goddamnit, Geremio, if you're givin' the men two hours off today with pay, why the hell are they draggin' their tails? And why don't you turn that skinny old Nick loose, and put a young wop in his place?'

'Now, listen-a to me, Mister Murdin——'

'Don't give me that! And bear in mind that there are plenty of good barefoot men in the streets who'll jump for a day's pay!'

'Padrone—padrone, the underpinning gotta be make safe and——'

'Lissenyawopbastard! If you don't like it, you know what you can do!'

And with that he swung swaggering away.

The men had heard, and those who hadn't knew instinctively.

The new home, the coming baby, and his whole background, kept the fire from Geremio's mouth and bowed his head. 'Annunziata speaks of scouring the ashcans for the children's bread in case I didn't want to work on a job where . . . But am I not a man, to feed my own with these hands? Ah, but day will end and no boss in the world can then rob me of the joy of my home!'

Murdin paused for a moment before descending the ladder.

Geremio caught his meaning and jumped to, nervously directing the rush of work . . . No longer Geremio, but a machine-like entity.

The men were transformed into single, silent, beasts. Snoutnose steamed through ragged moustache whip-lashing sand into mixer Ashes-ass dragged under four by twelve beam Lean clawed wall knots jumping in jaws masonry crumbled dust billowed thundered choked. . . .

At noon, Geremio drank his wine from an old-fashioned magnesia bottle and munched a great pepper sandwich . . . no meat on Good Friday. Said one, 'Are some of us to be laid off? Easter is upon us and communion dresses are needed and . . .'

That, while Geremio was dreaming of the new house and the joys he could almost taste. Said he: 'Worry not. You should know Geremio.' It then all came out. He regaled them with his wonderful joy of the new house. He praised his wife and children one by one. They listened respectfully and returned him well wishes and blessings. He went on and on. . . . 'Paul made a radio—all by himself, mind you! One can hear Barney Google and many American songs! How proud he.'

The ascent to labour was made, and as they trod the ladder, heads turned and eyes communed with the mute flames of the brazier whose warmth they were leaving, not with willing heart, and in that fleeting moment, the breast wanted so, so much to speak of hungers that never reached the tongue.

About an hour later, Geremio called over to Pietro: 'Pietro, see if Mister Murdin is in the shanty and tell him I must see him! I will convince him that the work must not go on like this . . . just for the sake of a little more profit!'

Pietro came up soon. 'The padrone is not coming up. He was drinking from a large bottle of whisky and cursed in American words that if you did not carry out his orders——'

Geremio turned away disconcerted, stared dumbly at the structure and mechanically listed in his mind's eye the various violations of construction safety. An uneasy sensation hollowed him. The Lean brought down an old piece of wall and the structure palsied. Geremio's heart broke loose and out-thumped the floor's vibrations, a rapid wave of heat swept him and left a chill touch in its wake. He looked about to the men, a bit frightened. They seemed usual, life-size, and moved about with the methodical deftness that made the moment then appear no different than the task of toil had ever been.

Snoutnose's voice boomed into him. 'Master Geremio, the concrete is rea—dy!'

'Oh, yes, yes, Vincenz.' And he walked gingerly towards the chute, but, not without leaving behind some part of his strength, sending out his soul to wrestle with the limbs of Job, who threatened in stiff silence. He talked and joked with Snoutnose. Nothing said anything, nor seemed wrong. Yet a vague uneasiness was to him as certain as the foggy murk that floated about Job's stone and steel.

'Shall I let the concrete down now, Master Geremio?'

'Well, let me see—no, hold it a minute. Hey, Sandino! Tighten the chute cables!'

Snoutnose straightened, looked about, and instinctively rubbed the sore small of his spine. 'Ah,' sighed he, 'all the men feel as I—yes, I can tell. They are tired but happy that today is Good Friday and we quit at three o'clock . . .' And he swelled in human ecstasy at the anticipation of food, drink, and the hairy flesh-tingling warmth of wife, and then, extravagant rest. In truth, they all felt as Snoutnose, although perhaps with variations on the theme.

It was the Lean only who had lived, and felt otherwise. His soul, accompanied with time, had shredded itself in the physical war to keep the physical alive. Perhaps he no longer had a soul, and the corpse continued from momentum. May he not be the Slave, working on from the birth of Man—He of whom it was said, 'It was not for Him to reason?' And probably He who, never asking, taking, nor vaunting, created God and the creatable? Nevertheless, there existed in the Lean a sense of oppression suffered, so vast that the seas of time could never wash it away.

Geremio gazed about and was conscious of seeming to understand many things. He marvelled at the strange feeling which permitted him to sense the familiarity of life. And yet—all appeared unreal, a dream pungent and nostalgic. Life, dream, reality, unreality, spiralling ever about each other. 'Ha,' he chuckled, 'how and from where do these thoughts come?'

Snoutnose had his hand on the hopper latch and was awaiting the word from Geremio. 'Did you say something, Master Geremio?'

'Why, yes, Vincenz, I was thinking—funny! A—yes, what is the time —yes, that is what I was thinking.'

'My American can of tomatoes says ten minutes from two o'clock. It won't be long now, Master Geremio.'

Geremio smiled. 'No, about an hour . . . and then, home.'

'Oh, but first we stop at Mulberry Street, to buy their biggest eels, and the other finger-licking stuffs.'

Geremio was looking far off, and for a moment happiness came to his heart without words, a warm hand stealing over. Snoutnose's words sang to him pleasantly, and he nodded.

'And Master Geremio, we ought really to buy the seafruits with the shells—you know, for the much needed steam they put into the—'

He flushed despite himself and continued. 'It is true, I know it—especially the juicy clams . . . uhmm, my mouth waters like a pump.'

Geremio drew on his unlit pipe and smiled acquiescence. The men around him were moving to their tasks silently, feeling of their fatigue, but absorbed in contemplations the very same as Snoutnose's. The noise of labour seemed not to be noise, and as Geremio looked about, life settled over him a grey concert—grey forms, atmosphere, and grey notes . . . Yet his off-tone world felt so near, and familiar.

'Five minutes from two,' swished through Snoutnose's moustache.

Geremio automatically took out his watch, rewound, and set it. Sandino had done with the cables. The tone and movement of the scene seemed to Geremio strange, differently strange, and yet, a dream familiar from a timeless date. His hand went up in motion to Vincenzo. The molten stone gurgled low, and then with heightening rasp. His eyes followed the stone-cementy pudding, and to his ears there was no other sound than its flow. From over the roofs somewhere, the tinny voice of *Barney Google* whined its way, hooked into his consciousness and kept itself a revolving record beneath his skull-plate.

'Ah, yes, Barney Google, my son's wonderful radio machine . . . wonderful Paul.' His train of thought quickly took in his family, home and hopes. And with hope came fear. Something within asked, 'Is it not possible to breathe God's air without fear dominating with the pall of unemployment? And the terror of production for Boss, Boss and Job? To rebel is to lose all of the very little. To be obedient is to choke. Oh, dear Lord, guide my path.'

Just then, the floor lurched and swayed under his feet. The slipping of the underpinning below rumbled up through the undetermined floors.

Was he faint or dizzy? Was it part of the dreamy afternoon? He put his hands in front of him and stepped back, and looked up wildly. 'No! No!'

The men poised stricken. Their throats wanted to cry out and scream but didn't dare. For a moment they were a petrified and straining pageant. Then the bottom of their world gave way. The building shuddered violently, her supports burst with the crackling slap of wooden gunfire. The floor vomited upward. Geremio clutched at the air and shrieked agonizingly. 'Brothers, what have we done? Ahhhh-h, children of ours!' With the speed of light, balance went sickeningly awry and frozen men went flying explosively. Job tore down upon them madly. Walls, floors, beams became whirling, solid, splintering waves crashing with detonations that ground man and material in bonds of death.

The strongly shaped body that slept with Annunziata nights and was perfect in all the limitless physical quantities, thudded as a worthless sack amongst the giant debris that crushed fragile flesh and bone with centrifugal intensity.

Darkness blotted out his terror and the resistless form twisted, catapulted insanely in its directionless flight, and shot down neatly and deliberately between the empty wooden forms of a foundation wall pilaster in upright position, his blue swollen face pressed against the form and his arms outstretched, caught securely through the meat by the thin round bars of reinforcing steel.

The huge concrete hopper that was sustained by an independent structure of thick timber, wavered a breath or so, its heavy concrete rolling uneasily until a great sixteen-inch wall caught it squarely with all the terrific verdict of its dead weight and impelled it downward through joists, beams and masonry, until it stopped short, arrested by two girders, an arm's length above Geremio's head; the grey concrete gushing from the hopper mouth, and sealing up the mute figure.

Giacomo had been thrown clear of the building and dropped six floors to the street gutter, where he lay writhing.

The Lean had evinced no emotion. When the walls descended, he did not move. He lowered his head. One minute later he was hanging in mid-air, his chin on his chest, his eyes tearing loose from their sockets, a green foam bubbling from his mouth and his body spasming, suspended by the shreds left of his mashed arms pinned between a wall and a girder.

A two-by-four hooked little Joe Chiappa up under the back of his jumper and swung him around in a circle to meet a careening I-beam. In the flash that he lifted his frozen cherubic face, its shearing edge sliced through the top of his skull.

When Snoutnose cried beseechingly, 'Saint Michael!' blackness enveloped him. He came to in a world of horror. A steady stream, warm, thick, and sickening as hot wine bathed his face and clogged his nose, mouth, and eyes. The nauseous syrup that pumped over his face, clotted his moustache red and drained into his mouth. He gulped for air, and swallowed the rich liquid scarlet. As he breathed, the pain shocked him to oppressive semiconsciousness. The air was wormingly alive with cries, screams, moans and dust, and his crushed chest seared him with a thousand fires. He couldn't see, nor breathe enough to cry. His right hand moved to his face and wiped at the gelatinizing substance, but it kept coming on, and a heart-breaking moan wavered about him, not far. He wiped his eyes in subconscious despair. Where was he? What kind of dream was he having? Perhaps he wouldn't wake up in time for work, and then what? But how queer; his stomach beating him, his chest on fire, he sees nothing but dull red, only one hand moving about, and a moaning in his face!

The sound and clamour of the rescue squads called to him from far off.

Ah, yes, he's dreaming in bed, and far out in the streets, engines are going to a fire. Oh poor devils! Suppose his house were on fire? With the children scattered about in the rooms he could not remember! He must do his utmost to break out of this dream! He's swimming under water, not able to raise his head and get to the air. He must get back to consciousness to save his children!

He swam frantically with his one right hand, and then felt a face beneath its touch. A face! It's Angelina alongside of him! Thank God, he's awake! He tapped her face. It moved. It felt cold, bristly, and wet. 'It moves so. What is this?' His fingers slithered about grisly sharp bones and in a gluey, stringy, hollow mass, yielding as wet macaroni. Grey light brought sight, and hysteria punctured his heart. A girder lay across his chest his right hand clutched a grotesque human mask, and suspended almost on top of him was the twitching, faceless body of Joe Chiappa. Vincenzo fainted with an inarticulate sigh. His fingers loosed and the bodyless-headless face dropped and fitted to the side of his face while the drippings above came slower and slower.

The rescue men cleaved grimly with pick and axe.

Geremio came to with a start . . . far from their efforts. His brain told him instantly what had happened and where he was. He shouted wildly. 'Save me! Save me! I'm being buried alive!'

He paused exhausted. His genitals convulsed. The cold steel rod upon which they were impaled froze his spine. He shouted louder and louder. 'Save me! I am hurt badly! I can be saved, I can—save me before it's too late!' But the cries went no farther than his own ears. The icy wet concrete reached his chin. His heart was appalled. 'In a few seconds I shall be entombed. If I can only breathe, they will reach me. Surely they will!' His face was quickly covered, its flesh yielding to the solid, sharp-cut stones. 'Air! Air!' screamed his lungs as he was completely sealed. Savagely, he bit into the wooden form pressing upon his mouth. An eighth of an inch of its surface splintered off. Oh, if he could only hold out long enough to bite even the smallest hole through to air! He must! There can be no other way! He is responsible for his family! He cannot leave them like this! He didn't want to die! This could not be the answer to life! He had bitten half way through when his teeth snapped off to the gums in the uneven conflict. The pressure of the concrete was such, and its effectiveness so thorough, that the wooden splinters, stumps of teeth, and blood never left the choking mouth.

Why couldn't he go any farther?

Air! Quick! He dug his lower jaw into the little hollowed space and gnashed in choking agonized fury. 'Why doesn't it go through? Mother of Christ, why doesn't it give? Can there be a notch, or two-by-four stud behind it? Sweet Jesu! No! No! Make it give. . . . Air! Air!'

He pushed the bone-bare jaw maniacally; it splintered, cracked, and a jagged fleshless edge cut through the form, opening a small hole to air. With a desperate burst the lung-prisoned air blew an opening through the shredded mouth and whistled back greedily a gasp of fresh air. He tried to breathe, but it was impossible. The heavy concrete was settling immutably, and its rich cement-laden grout ran into his pierced face. His lungs would not expand, and were crushing in tighter and tighter under the settling concrete.

'Mother mine—mother of Jesu-Annunziata—children of mine—dear, dear, for mercy, Jesu-Guiseppe e 'Maria,' his blue-foamed tongue called. It then distorted in a shuddering coil and mad blood vomited forth. Chills and fire played through him and his tortured tongue stuttered, 'Mercy, blessed Father—salvation, most kind Father—Saviour—Saviour of His children help me—adored Saviour—I kiss your feet eternally—you are my Lord—there is but one God—you are my God of infinite mercy—Hail Mary divine Virgin—our Father who art in heaven hallowed be thy—name—our Father—my Father,' and the agony excruciated with never-ending mount, 'our Father—Jesu, Jesu, soon Jesu, hurry dear Jesu Jesu! Je-sssu . . .!' His mangled voice trebled hideously, and hung in jerky whimperings.

The unfeeling concrete was drying fast, and shrinking into monolithic density. The pressure temporarily de-sensitized sensation; leaving him petrified, numb, and substanceless. Only the brain remained miraculously alive.

'Can this be death? It is all too strangely clear. I see nothing nor feel nothing, my body and senses are no more, my mind speaks as it never did before. Am I or am I not Geremio? But I am Geremio! Can I be in the other world? I never was in any other world except the one I knew of; that of toil, hardship, prayer . . . of my wife who awaits with child for me, of my children and the first home I was to own. Where do I begin in this world? Where do I leave off? Why? I recall only a baffled life of cruelty from every direction. And hope was always as painful as fear, the fear of displeasing, displeasing the people and ideas whom I could never understand; laws, policemen, priests, bosses, and a rag with colours waving on a stick. I never did anything to these things. But what have I done with my life? Yes, my life! No one else's! Mine—mine—MINE—Geremio! It is clear. I was born hungry, and have always been hungry for freedom—life! I married and ran away to America so as not to kill and be killed in Tripoli for things they call "God and Country." I've never known the freedom I wanted in my heart. There was always an arm upraised to hit at me. What have I done to them? I did not want to make them toil for me. I did not raise my arm to them. In my life I could never breathe, and now without air, my mind breathes clearly for me. Wait! There has been a terrible mistake! A cruel crime! The world is not right! Murderers! Thieves! You have hurt me and my kind, and have taken my life from me! I have long felt it—yes, yes, yes, they have cheated me with flags, signs and fear . . . I say you can't take my life! I want to live! My life! To tell the cheated to rise and fight! Vincenz! Chiappa! Nick! Men! Do you hear me? We must follow the desires within us for the world has been taken from us; we, who made the world! Life!'

Feeling returned to the destroyed form.

'Ahhh-h, I am not dead yet. I knew it—you have not done with me. Torture away! I cannot believe you, God and Country, no longer!' His body was fast breaking under the concrete's closing wrack. Blood vessels burst like mashed flower stems. He screamed. 'Show yourself now, Jesu! Now is the time! Save me! Why don't you come! Are you there! I cannot stand it—ohhh, why do you let it happen—it is bestial—where are you! Hurry, hurry, hurry! You do not come! You make me suffer, and what have I done! Come, come—come now—now save me, save me now! Now, now, now! If you are God, save me!'

The stricken blood surged through a weltering maze of useless pipes and exploded forth from his squelched eyes and formless nose, ears and mouth, seeking life in the indifferent stone.

'Aie—aie, aie—devils and Saints—beasts! Where are you—quick, quick, it is death and I am cheated—cheat—ed! Do you hear, you whoring bastards who own the world? Ohhh-ohhhh aie-aie—hahahaha!' His bones cracked mutely and his sanity went sailing distorted in the limbo of the subconscious.

With the throbbing tones of an organ in the hollow background, the fighting brain disintegrated and the memories of a baffled lifetime sought outlet.

He moaned the simple songs of barefoot childhood, scenes flashed desperately on and off in disassociated reflex, and words and parts of words came pitifully high and low from his inaudible lips, the hysterical mind sang cringingly and breathlessly, 'Jesu my Lord my God my all Jesu my Lord my God my all Jesu my Lord my God my all Jesu my Lord my God my all,' and on as the whirling tempo screamed now far, now near, and came in soul-sickening waves as the concrete slowly contracted and squeezed his skull out of shape.

GEORGIA

★

The People vs. Abe Lathan, Colored

ERSKINE CALDWELL

Uncle Abe was shucking corn in the crib when Luther Bolick came down from the big white house on the hill and told him to pack up his household goods and move off the farm. Uncle Abe had grown a little deaf and he did not hear what Luther said the first time.

'These old ears of mine are bothering me again, Mr. Luther!' Uncle Abe said. 'I just can't seem to hear as good as I used to.'

Luther looked at the Negro and scowled. Uncle Abe had got up and was standing in the crib door where he could hear better.

'I said, I want you and your family to pack up your furniture and anything else that really belongs to you, and move off.'

Uncle Abe reached out and clutched at the crib door for support.

'Move off?' Uncle Abe said.

He looked into his landlord's face unbelievingly.

'Mr. Luther, you don't mean that, do you?' Uncle Abe asked, his voice shaking. 'You must be joking, ain't you, Mr. Luther?'

'You heard me right, even if you do pretend to be half deaf,' Luther said angrily, turning around and walking several steps. 'I want you off the place by the end of the week. I'll give you that much time if you don't try to make any trouble. And when you pack up your things, take care you don't pick up anything that belongs to me. Or, I'll have the law on you.'

Uncle Abe grew weak so quickly that he barely managed to keep from falling. He turned a little and slid down the side of the door and sat on the crib floor. Luther looked around to see what he was doing.

'I'm past sixty,' Uncle Abe said slowly, 'but me and my family works hard for you, Mr. Luther. We work as hard as anybody on your whole place. You know that's true, Mr. Luther. I've lived here, working for you, and your daddy before you, for all of forty years. I never mention to you about the shares, no matter how big the crop was that I raised for you. I've never asked much, just enough to eat and a few clothes, that's all. I raised up a houseful of children to help work, and none of them ever made any trouble for you, did they, Mr. Luther?'

Luther waved his arm impatiently indicating that he wanted the Negro to stop arguing. He shook his head, showing that he did not want to listen to anything Uncle Abe had to say.

'That's all true enough,' Luther said, 'but I've got to get rid of half the tenants on my place. I can't afford to keep eight or ten old people like you here any longer. All of you will have to move off and go somewhere else.'

'Ain't you going to farm this year, and raise cotton, Mr. Luther?' Uncle Abe asked. 'I can still work as good and hard as anybody else. It may take me a little longer sometimes, but I get the work done. Ain't I shucking this corn to feed the mules as good as anybody else could do?'

'I haven't got time to stand here and argue with you,' Luther said nervously. 'My mind is made up, and that's all there is to it. Now, you go on home as soon as you finish feeding the mules and start packing the things that belong to you like I told you.'

Luther turned away and started walking down the path toward the barn. When he got as far as the barnyard gate, he turned around and looked back. Uncle Abe had followed him.

'Where can me and my family move to, Mr. Luther?' Uncle Abe said. 'The boys are big enough to take care of themselves. But me and my wife have grown old. You know how hard it is for an old colored man like me to go out and find a house and land to work on shares. It don't cost you much to keep us, and me and my boys raise as much cotton as anybody else. The last time I mentioned to you about the shares has been a long way in the past, thirty years or more. I'm just content to work like I do and get some rations and a few clothes. You know that's true, Mr. Luther. I've lived in my little shanty over there for all of forty years, and it's the only home I've got. Mr. Luther, me and my wife is both old now, and I can't hire out to work by the day, because I don't have the strength any more. But I can still grow cotton as good as any other colored man in the country.'

Luther opened the barnyard gate and walked through it. He shook his head as though he was not even going to listen any longer. He turned his back on Uncle Abe and walked away.

Uncle Abe did not know what to say or do after that. When he saw Luther walk away, he became shaky all over. He clutched at the gate for something to hold on to.

'I just can't move away, Mr. Luther,' he said desperately. 'I just can't do that. This is the only place I've got to live in the world. I just can't move off, Mr. Luther.'

Luther walked out of sight around the corner of the barn. He did not hear Uncle Abe after that.

The next day, at a little after two o'clock in the afternoon, a truck drove up to the door of the three-room house where Uncle Abe, his wife, and their three grown sons lived. Uncle Abe and his wife were sitting by the fire trying to keep warm in the winter cold. They were the only ones at home then.

Uncle Abe heard the truck drive up and stop, but he sat where he was, thinking it was his oldest boy, Henry, who drove a truck sometimes for Luther Bolick.

After several minutes had passed, somebody knocked on the door, and his wife got up right away and went to see who it was.

There were two strange white men on the porch when she opened the door. They did not say anything at first, but looked inside the room to see who was there. Still not saying anything, they came inside and walked to the fireplace where Uncle Abe sat hunched over the hearth.

'Are you Abe Lathan?' one of the men, the oldest, asked.

'Yes, sir, I'm Abe Lathan,' he answered, wondering who they were, because he had never seen them before. 'Why do you want to know that?'

The man took a bright metal disk out of his pocket and held it in the palm of his hand before Uncle Abe's eyes.

'I'm serving a paper and a warrant on you,' he said. 'One is an eviction, and the other is for threatening to do bodily harm.'

He unfolded the eviction notice and handed it to Uncle Abe. The Negro shook his head bewilderedly, looking first at the paper and finally up at the two strange white men.

'I'm a deputy,' the older man said, 'and I've come for two things—to evict you from this house and to put you under arrest.'

'What does that mean—evict?' Uncle Abe asked.

The two men looked around the room for a moment. Uncle Abe's wife had come up behind his chair and put trembling hands on his shoulder.

'We are going to move your furniture out of this house and carry it off the property of Luther Bolick. Then, besides that, we're going to take you down to the county jail. Now, come on and hurry up, both of you.'

Uncle Abe got up, and he and his wife stood on the hearth not knowing what to do.

The two men began gathering up the furniture and carrying it out of the house. They took the beds, tables, chairs, and everything else in the three rooms except the cook-stove, which belonged to Luther Bolick. When they got all the things outside, they began piling them into the truck.

Uncle Abe went outside in front of the house as quickly as he could.

'White folks, please don't do that,' he begged. 'Just wait a minute while I go find Mr. Luther. He'll set things straight. Mr. Luther is my landlord, and he won't let you take all my furniture away like this. Please, sir, just wait while I go find him.'

The two men looked at each other.

'Luther Bolick is the one who signed these papers,' the deputy said, shaking his head. 'He was the one who got these court orders to carry off the furniture and put you in jail. It wouldn't do you a bit of good to try to find him now.'

'Put me in jail?' Uncle Abe said. 'What did he say to do that for?'

'For threatening bodily harm,' the deputy said. 'That's for threatening to kill him. Hitting him with a stick or shooting him with a pistol.'

The men threw the rest of the household goods into the truck and told Uncle Abe and his wife to climb into the back. When they made no effort to get in, the deputy pushed them to the rear and prodded them until they climbed into the truck.

While the younger man drove the truck, the deputy stood beside them in the body so they could not escape. They drove out the lane, past the other tenant houses, and then down the long road that went over the hill through Luther Bolick's land to the public highway. They passed the big white house where he lived, but he was not within sight.

'I never threatened to harm Mr. Luther,' Uncle Abe protested. 'I never did a thing like that in my whole life. I never said a mean thing about him, either. Mr. Luther is my boss, and I've worked for him ever since I was twenty years old. Yesterday he said he wanted me to move off his farm, and all I did was say that I thought he ought to let me stay. I won't have much longer to live, anyway. I told him I didn't want to move off. That's all I said to Mr. Luther, I ain't never said I was going to try to kill him. Mr. Luther knows that as well as I do. You ask Mr. Luther if that ain't so.'

They had left Luther Bolick's farm, and had turned down the highway toward the county seat, eleven miles away.

'For more than forty years I've lived here and worked for Mr. Luther,' Uncle Abe said, 'and I ain't never said a mean thing to his face or behind his back in all that time. He furnishes me with rations for me and my family, and a few clothes, and me and my family raise cotton for him, and I been doing that ever since I was twenty years old. I moved here and started working on shares for his daddy first, and then when he died, I kept right on like I have up to now. Mr. Luther knows I've worked hard and never answered him back, and only asked for rations and a few clothes all this time. You ask Mr. Luther.'

The deputy listened to all that Uncle Abe said, but he did not say anything himself. He felt sorry for the old Negro and his wife, but there was nothing he could do about it. Luther Bolick had driven to the courthouse early that morning and secured the papers for eviction and arrest. It was his job to serve the papers and execute the court orders. But even if it was his job, he could not keep from feeling sorry for the Negroes. He didn't think that Luther Bolick ought to throw them off his farm just because they had grown old.

When they got within sight of town, the deputy told the driver to stop. He drew the truck up beside the highway when they reached the first row of houses. There were fifteen or eighteen Negro houses on both sides of the road.

After they had stopped, the two white men began unloading the furniture and stacking it beside the road. When it was all out of the truck, the deputy told Uncle Abe's wife to get out. Uncle Abe started to get out, too, but the deputy told him to stay where he was. They drove off again, leaving Uncle Abe's wife standing in a dazed state of mind beside the furniture.

'What you going to do with me now?' Uncle Abe asked, looking back at his wife and furniture in the distance.

'Take you to the county jail and lock you up,' the deputy said.

'What's my wife going to do?' he asked.

'The people in one of those houses will probably take her in.'

'How long will you keep me in jail locked up?'

'Until your case comes up for trial.'

They drove through the dusty streets of the town, around the courthouse square, and stopped in front of a brick building with iron bars across the windows.

'Here's where we get out,' the deputy said.

Uncle Abe was almost too weak to walk by that time, but he managed to move along the path to the door. Another white man opened the door and told him to walk straight down the hall until he was told to stop.

Just before noon Saturday, Uncle Abe's oldest son, Henry, stood in Ramsey Clark's office, hat in hand. The lawyer looked at the Negro and frowned. He chewed his pencil for a while, then swung around in his chair and looked out the window into the courthouse square. Presently he turned around and looked at Uncle Abe's son.

'I don't want the case,' he said. 'I don't want to touch it.'

The boy stared at him helplessly. It was the third lawyer he had gone to see that morning, and all of them had refused to take his father's case.

'There's no money in it,' Ramsey Clark said, still frowning. 'I'd never get a dime out of you niggers if I took this case. And, besides, I don't want to represent any more niggers at court. Better lawyers than me have been ruined that way. I don't want to get the reputation of being a "nigger lawyer."'

Henry shifted the weight of his body from one foot to the other and bit his lips. He did not know what to say. He stood in the middle of the room trying to think of a way to get help for his father.

'My father never said he was going to kill Mr. Luther,' Henry protested. 'He's always been on friendly terms with Mr. Luther. None of us have ever given Mr. Luther any trouble. Anybody will tell you that. All the other tenants on Mr. Luther's place will tell you my father has always stood up for Mr. Luther. He never said he would try to hurt Mr. Luther in any way.'

The lawyer waved for him to stop. He had heard all he wanted to listen to.

'I told you I wouldn't touch the case,' he said angrily, snatching up papers and slamming them down on his desk. 'I don't want to go into court and waste my time arguing a case that won't make any difference one way or the other, anyway. It's a good thing for you niggers to get a turn on the 'gang every once in a while. It doesn't make any difference whether Abe Lathan threatened Mr. Bolick, or whether he didn't threaten him. Abe Lathan said he wasn't going to move off the farm after Mr. Bolick had told him to, didn't he? Well, that's enough to convict him in court. When the case comes up for trial, that's all the judge will want to hear. He'll be sent to the 'gang quicker than a flea can hop. No lawyer is going to spend a lot of time preparing a case when he knows how it's going to end. If there was money in it, it might be different. But you niggers don't have a thin dime to pay me with. No, I don't want the case. I wouldn't touch it with a ten-foot pole.'

Henry backed out of Ramsey Clark's office and went to the jail. He secured permission to see his father for five minutes.

Uncle Abe was sitting on his bunk in the cage looking through the bars when Henry entered. The jailer came and stood behind him at the cage door.

'Did you see a lawyer and tell him I never said anything like that to Mr. Luther?' Uncle Abe asked the first thing.

Henry looked at his father, but it was difficult for him to answer. He shook his head, dropping his gaze until he could see only the floor.

'You tried, didn't you, Henry?' Uncle Abe asked.

Henry nodded.

'But when you told the lawyers how I never said a mean thing about Mr. Luther, or his daddy before him, in all my whole life, didn't they say they would help me get out of jail?'

Henry shook his head.

'What did the lawyers say, Henry? When you told them how respectful I've always been to Mr. Luther, and how I've always worked hard for him all my life, and never mentioned to him about the shares, didn't they say they would help me then?'

Henry looked up at his father, moving his head sideways in order to see him between the bars of the cage. He had to swallow hard several times before he could speak at all.

'I've already been to see three lawyers,' he said finally. 'All of them said they couldn't do anything about it, and to just go ahead and let it come up for trial. They said there wasn't anything they could do, because the judge would give you a term on the 'gang, anyway.'

He stopped for a moment, looking down at his father's feet through the bars.

'If you want me to, I'll go see if I can try to find some other lawyers to take the case. But it won't do much good. They just won't do anything.'

Uncle Abe sat down on his bunk and looked at the floor. He could not understand why none of the lawyers would help him.

Presently he looked up through the bars at his son. His eyes were fast filling with tears that he could not control.

'Why did the lawyers say the judge would give me a term on the 'gang, anyway, Henry?' he asked.

Henry gripped the bars, thinking about all the years he had seen his father and mother working in the cotton fields for Luther Bolick and being paid in rations, a few clothes, and a house to live in, and nothing more.

'Why did they say that, Henry?" his father insisted.

'I reckon because we are colored folks,' Henry said at last. 'I don't know why else they would say things like that.'

The jailer moved up behind Henry, prodding him with his stick. 'Hurry along,' the jailer kept saying. 'Time's up! Time's up!' Henry walked down the hall between the rows of cages towards the door that led to the street. He did not look back.

CONNECTICUT

The Secret Life of Walter Mitty

JAMES THURBER

"We're going through!" The Commander's voice was like thin ice breaking. He wore his full-dress uniform, with the heavily braided white cap pulled down rakishly over one cold gray eye. "We can't make it, sir. It's spoiling for a hurricane, if you ask me." "I'm not asking you, Lieutenant Berg," said the Commander. "Throw on the power lights! Rev her up to 8,500! We're going through!" The pounding of the cylinders increased: ta-pocketa-pocketa-pocketa-*pocketa-pocketa*. The Commander stared at the ice forming on the pilot window. He walked over and twisted a row of complicated dials. "Switch on No. 8 auxiliary!" he shouted. "Switch on No. 8 auxiliary!" repeated Lieutenant Berg. "Full strength in No. 3 turret!" shouted the Commander. "Full strength in No. 3 turret!" The crew, bending to their various tasks in the huge, hurtling eight-engined Navy hydroplane, looked at each other and grinned. "The Old Man'll get us through," they said to one another. "The Old Man ain't afraid of Hell!" . . .

"Not so fast! You're driving too fast!" said Mrs. Mitty. "What are you driving so fast for?"

"Hmm?" said Walter Mitty. He looked at his wife, in the seat beside him, with shocked astonishment. She seemed grossly unfamiliar, like a strange woman who had yelled at him in a crowd. "You were up to fifty-five," she said. "You know I don't like to go more than forty. You were up to fifty-five." Walter Mitty drove on toward Waterbury in silence, the roaring of the SN202 through the worst storm in twenty years of Navy flying fading in the remote, intimate airways of his

---

mind. "You're tensed up again," said Mrs. Mitty. "It's one of your days. I wish you'd let Dr. Renshaw look you over."

Walter Mitty stopped the car in front of the building where his wife went to have her hair done. "Remember to get those overshoes while I'm having my hair done," she said. "I don't need overshoes," said Mitty. She put her mirror back into her bag. "We've been all through that," she said, getting out of the car. "You're not a young man any longer." He raced the engine a little. "Why don't you wear your gloves? Have you lost your gloves?" Walter Mitty reached in a pocket and brought out the gloves. He put them on, but after she had turned and gone into the building and he had driven on to a red light, he took them off again. "Pick it up, brother!" snapped a cop as the light changed, and Mitty hastily pulled on his gloves and lurched ahead. He drove around the streets aimlessly for a time, and then he drove past the hospital on his way to the parking lot.

. . . "It's the millionaire banker, Wellington McMillan," said the pretty nurse. "Yes?" said Walter Mitty, removing his gloves slowly. "Who has the case?" "Dr. Renshaw and Dr. Benbow, but there are two specialists here, Dr. Remington from New York and Dr. Pritchard-Mitford from London. He flew over." A door opened down a long, cool corridor and Dr. Renshaw came out. He looked distraught and haggard. "Hello, Mitty," he said. "We're having the devil's own time with McMillan, the millionaire banker and close personal friend of Roosevelt. Obstreosis of the ductal tract. Tertiary. Wish you'd take a look at him." "Glad to," said Mitty.

In the operating room there were whispered introductions: "Dr. Remington, Dr. Mitty, Dr. Pritchard-Mitford, Dr. Mitty." "I've read your book on streptothricosis," said Pritchard-Mitford, shaking hands. "A brilliant performance, sir." "Thank you," said Walter Mitty. "Didn't know you were in the States, Mitty," grumbled Remington. "Coals to Newcastle, bringing Mitford and me up here for a tertiary." "You are very kind," said Mitty. A huge, complicated machine, connected to the operating table, with many tubes and wires, began at this moment to go pocketa-pocketa-pocketa. "The new anesthetizer is giving way!" shouted an interne. "There is no one in the East who knows how to fix it!" "Quiet, man!" said Mitty, in a low, cool voice. He sprang to the machine, which was now going pocketa-pocketa-queep-pocketa-queep. He began fingering delicately a row of glistening dials. "Give me a fountain pen!" he snapped. Someone handed him a fountain pen. He pulled a faulty piston out of the machine and inserted the pen in its place. "That will hold for ten minutes," he said. "Get on with the operation." A nurse hurried over and whispered to Renshaw, and Mitty saw the man turn pale. "Coreopsis has set in," said Renshaw nervously. "If you would take over, Mitty?" Mitty looked at him and at the craven figure of Benbow, who drank, and at the grave, uncertain faces of the two great specialists. "If you wish," he said. They slipped a white gown on him; he adjusted a mask and drew on thin gloves; nurses handed him shining . . .

"Back it up, Mac! Look out for that Buick!" Walter Mitty jammed on the brakes. "Wrong lane, Mac," said the parking-lot attendant, looking at Mitty closely. "Gee. Yeh," muttered Mitty. He began cautiously to back out of the lane marked "Exit Only." "Leave her sit there," said the attendant. "I'll put her away." Mitty got out of the car. "Hey, better leave the key." "Oh," said Mitty, handing the man the ignition key. The attendant vaulted into the car, backed it up with insolent skill, and put it where it belonged.

They're so damn cocky, thought Walter Mitty, walking along Main Street; they think they know everything. Once he had tried to take his chains off, outside New Milford, and he had got them wound around the axles. A man had had to come out in a wrecking car and unwind them, a young, grinning garageman. Since then Mrs. Mitty always made him drive to a garage to have the chains taken off. The next time, he thought, I'll wear my right arm in a sling; they won't grin at me then. I'll have my right arm in a sling and they'll see I couldn't possibly take the chains off myself. He kicked at the slush on the sidewalk. "Overshoes," he said to himself, and he began looking for a shoe store.

When he came out into the street again, with the overshoes in a box under his arm, Walter Mitty began to wonder what the other thing was his wife had told him to get. She had told him twice before they set out from their house for Waterbury. In a way he hated these weekly trips to town—he was always getting something wrong. Kleenex, he thought, Squibb's, razor blades? No. Toothpaste, toothbrush, bicarbonate, corborundum, initiative and referendum? He gave it up. But she would remember it. "Where's the what's-its-name?" she would ask. "Don't tell me you forgot the what's-its-name." A newsboy went by shouting something about the Waterbury trial.

. . . "Perhaps this will refresh your memory." The District Attorney suddenly thrust a heavy automatic at the quiet figure on the witness stand. "Have you ever seen this before?" Walter Mitty took the gun and examined it expertly. "This is my Webley-Vickers 50.80," he said calmly. An excited buzz ran around the courtroom. The Judge rapped for order. "You are a crack shot with any sort of firearms, I believe?" said the District Attorney, insinuatingly. "Objection!" shouted Mitty's attorney. "We have shown that the defendant could not have fired the shot. We have shown that he wore his right arm in a sling on the night of the fourteenth of July." Walter Mitty raised his hand briefly and the bickering attorneys were stilled. "With any known make of gun," he said evenly, "I could have killed Gregory Fitzhurst at three hundred feet *with my left hand.*" Pandemonium broke loose in the courtroom. A woman's scream rose above the bedlam and suddenly a lovely, dark-haired girl was in Walter Mitty's arms. The District Attorney struck at her savagely. Without rising from his chair, Mitty let the man have it on the point of the chin. "You miserable cur!" . . .

"Puppy biscuit," said Walter Mitty. He stopped walking and the buildings of Waterbury rose up out of the misty courtroom and surrounded him again. A woman who was passing laughed. "He said 'Puppy biscuit,'" she said to her companion. "That man said 'Puppy biscuit' to himself." Walter Mitty hurried on. He went into an A. & P., not the first one he came to but a smaller one farther up the street. "I want some biscuit for small, young dogs," he said to the clerk. "Any special brand, sir?" The greatest pistol shot in the world thought a moment. "It says 'Puppies Bark for It' on the box," said Walter Mitty.

His wife would be through at the hair-dresser's in fifteen minutes, Mitty saw in looking at his watch, unless they had trouble drying it; sometimes they had trouble drying it. She didn't like to get to the hotel first; she would want him to be there waiting for her as usual. He found a big leather chair in the lobby, facing a window, and he put the overshoes and the puppy biscuit on the floor beside it. He picked up an old copy of *Liberty* and sank down into the chair. "Can Germany Conquer the World Through the Air?" Walter Mitty looked at the pictures of bombing planes and of ruined streets.

. . . "The cannonading has got the wind up in young Raleigh, sir," said the sergeant. Captain Mitty looked up at him through tousled hair. "Get him to bed," he said wearily, "with the others. I'll fly alone." "But you can't, sir," said the sergeant anxiously. "It takes two men to handle that bomber and the Archies are pounding hell out of the air. Von Richtman's circus is between here and Saulier." "Somebody's got to get that ammunition dump," said Mitty. "I'm going over. Spot of brandy?" He poured a drink for the sergeant and one for himself. War thundered and whined around the dugout and battered at the door. There was a rending of wood, and splinters flew through the room. "A bit of a near thing," said Captain Mitty carelessly. "The box barrage is closing in," said the sergeant. "We only live once, Sergeant," said Mitty, with his faint, fleeting smile. "Or do we?" He poured another brandy and tossed it off. "I never see a man could hold his brandy like you, sir," said the sergeant. "Begging your pardon, sir." Captain Mitty stood up and strapped on his huge Webley-Vickers automatic. "It's forty kilometers through hell, sir," said the sergeant. Mitty finished one last brandy. "After all," he said softly, "what isn't?" The pounding of the cannon increased; there was the rat-tat-tatting of machine guns, and from somewhere came the menacing pocketa-pocketa-pocketa of the new flame-throwers. Walter Mitty walked to the door of the dugout humming "Auprès de Ma Blonde." He turned and waved to the sergeant. "Cheerio!" he said. . . .

Something struck his shoulder. "I've been looking all over this hotel for you," said Mrs. Mitty. "Why do you have to hide in this old chair? How did you expect me to find you?" "Things close in," said Walter Mitty vaguely. "What?" Mrs. Mitty said. "Did you get the what's-its-name? The puppy biscuit? What's in that box?" "Overshoes," said Mitty. "Couldn't you have put them on in the store?" "I was thinking," said Walter Mitty. "Does it ever occur to you that I am sometimes thinking?" She looked at him. "I'm going to take your temperature when I get you home," she said.

They went out through the revolving doors that made a faintly derisive whistling sound when you pushed them. It was two blocks to the parking lot. At the drugstore on the corner she said, "Wait here for me. I forgot something. I won't be a minute." She was more than a minute. Walter Mitty lighted a cigarette. It began to rain, rain with sleet in it. He stood up against the wall of the drugstore, smoking. . . . He put his shoulders back and his heels together. "To hell with the handkerchief," said Walter Mitty scornfully. He took one last drag on his cigarette and snapped it away. Then, with that faint, fleeting smile playing about his lips, he faced the firing squad; erect and motionless, proud and disdainful, Walter Mitty the Undefeated, inscrutable to the last.

MASSACHUSETTS

The Revolt of Mother

MARY WILKINS FREEMAN

"Father!"

"What is it?"

"What are them men diggin' over in the field for?"

There was a sudden dropping and enlarging of the lower part of the old man's face, as if some heavy weight had settled therein; he shut his mouth tight, and went on harnessing the great bay mare. He hustled the collar on to her neck with a jerk.

"Father!"

The old man slapped the saddle on the mare's back.

"Look here, Father, I want to know what them men are diggin' over in the field for, an' I'm goin' to know."

"I wish you'd go into the house, Mother, an' tend to your own affairs," the old man said then. He ran his words together, and his speech was almost as inarticulate as a growl.

But the woman understood; it was her most native tongue. "I ain't goin' into the house till you tell me what them men are doin' over there in the field," said she.

Then she stood waiting. She was a small woman, short and straight-waisted like a child in her brown cotton gown. Her forehead was mild and benevolent between the smooth curves of gray hair; there were meek downward lines about her nose and mouth; but her eyes, fixed upon the old man, looked as if the meekness had been the result of her own will, never of the will of another.

They were in the barn, standing before the wide-open doors. The spring air, full of the smell of growing grass and unseen blossoms, came in their faces. The deep yard in front was littered with farm wag-

---

From *A New England Nun*. Published by Harper & Brothers. Used by permission.

ons and piles of wood; on the edges, close to the fence and the house, the grass was a vivid green, and there were some dandelions.

The old man glanced doggedly at his wife as he tightened the last buckles on the harness. She looked as immovable to him as one of the rocks in his pasture land, bound to the earth with generations of blackberry vines. He slapped the reins over the horse, and started forth from the barn.

"Father!" said she.

The old man pulled up. "What is it?"

"I want to know what them men are diggin' over there in that field for."

"They're diggin' a cellar, I s'pose, if you've got to know."

"A cellar for what?"

"A barn."

"A barn? You ain't goin' to build a barn over there where we was goin' to have a house, Father?"

The old man said not another word. He hurried the horse into the farm wagon and clattered out of the yard, jouncing as sturdily on his seat as a boy.

The woman stood a moment looking after him, then she went out of the barn across a corner of the yard to the house. The house, standing at right angles with the great barn and a long reach of sheds and outbuildings, was infinitesimal compared with them. It was scarcely as commodious for people as the little boxes under the barn eaves were for doves.

A pretty girl's face, pink and delicate as a flower, was looking out of one of the house windows. She was watching three men who were digging over in the field which bounded the yard near the road line. She turned quietly when the woman entered.

"What are they diggin' for, Mother?" said she. "Did he tell you?"

"They're diggin' for—a cellar for a new barn."

"Oh, Mother, he ain't going to build another barn?"

"That's what he says."

A boy stood before the kitchen glass combing his hair. He combed slowly and painstakingly, arranging his brown hair in a smooth hillock over his forehead. He did not seem to pay any attention to the conversation.

"Sammy, did you know Father was going to build a new barn?" asked the girl.

The boy combed assiduously.

"Sammy!"

He turned, and showed a face like his father's under his smooth crest of hair. "Yes, I s'pose I did," he said, reluctantly.

"How long have you known it?" asked his mother.

" 'Bout three months, I guess."

"Why didn't you tell of it?"

"Didn't think 'twould do no good."

"I don't see what Father wants another barn for," said the girl, in her sweet, slow voice. She turned again to the window and stared out at the digging men in the field. Her tender, sweet face was full of a gentle distress. Her forehead was as bald and innocent as a baby's, with the light hair strained from it in a row of curl papers. She was quite large, but her soft curves did not look as if they covered muscles.

Her mother looked sternly at the boy. "Is he goin' to buy more cows?" said she.

The boy did not reply; he was tying his shoes.

"Sammy, I want you to tell me if he's goin' to buy more cows."

"I s'pose he is."

"How many?"

"Four, I guess."

His mother said nothing more. She went into the pantry, and there was a clatter of dishes. The boy got his cap from a nail behind the door, took an old arithmetic from the shelf, and started for school. He was lightly built, but clumsy. He went out of the yard with a curious spring in his hips that made his loose homemade jacket tilt up in the rear.

The girl went to the sink and began to wash the dishes that were piled up there. Her mother came promptly out of the pantry and shoved her aside. "You wipe 'em," said she. "I'll wash. There's a good many this mornin'."

The mother plunged her hands vigorously into the water, the girl wiped the plates slowly and dreamily. "Mother," said she, "don't you think it's too bad Father's going to build that new barn, much as we need a decent house to live in?"

Her mother scrubbed a dish fiercely. "You ain't found out yet, we're womenfolks, Nanny Penn," said she. "You ain't seen enough of menfolks yet to. One of these days you'll find it out, and then you'll know that we know only what menfolks think we do, so far as any use of it goes, an' how we'd ought to reckon menfolks in with Providence, an' not complain of what they do any more than we do of the weather."

"I don't care; I don't believe George is anything like that, anyhow," said Nanny. Her delicate face flushed pink; her lips pouted softly, as if she were going to cry.

"You wait an' see. I guess George Eastman ain't no better than other men. You hadn't ought to judge Father, though. He can't help it, 'cause he don't look at things jest the way we do. An' we've been pretty comfortable here, after all. The roof don't leak—ain't never but once—that's one thing. Father's kept it shingled right up."

"I do wish we had a parlor."

"I guess it won't hurt George Eastman any to come to see you in a nice clean kitchen. I guess a good many girls don't have as good a place as this. Nobody's ever heard me complain."

"I ain't complained either, Mother."

"Well, I don't think you'd better, a good father an' a good home as you've got. S'pose your father made you go out an' work for your livin'? Lots of girls have to that ain't no better able to than you be."

Sarah Penn washed the frying pan with a conclusive air. She scrubbed the outside of it as faithfully as the inside. She was a masterly keeper of her box of a house. Her one living room never seemed to have in it any of the dust which the friction of life with inanimate matter produces. She swept, and there seemed to be no dirt to go before the broom; she cleaned, and one could see no difference. She was like an artist so perfect that he has apparently no art. Today she got out a mixing bowl and a board, and rolled some pies, and there was no more flour upon her than upon her daughter who was doing finer work. Nanny was to be married in the fall, and she was sewing on some white cambric and embroidery. She sewed industriously while her mother cooked; her soft milk-white hands and wrists showed whiter than her delicate work.

"We must have the stove moved out in the shed before long," said Mrs. Penn. "Talk about not havin' things, it's been a real blessin' to be able to put a stove up in that shed in hot weather. Father did one good thing when he fixed that stove pipe out there."

Sarah Penn's face as she rolled her pies had that expression of meek vigor which might have characterized one of the New Testament saints. She was making mince pies. Her husband, Adoniram Penn, liked them better than any other kind. She baked twice a week. Adoniram often liked a piece of pie between meals. She hurried this morning. It had been later than usual when she began, and she wanted to have a pie baked for dinner. However deep a resentment she might be forced to hold against her husband, she would never fail in sedulous attention to his wants.

Nobility of character manifests itself at loopholes when it is not provided with large doors. Sarah Penn's showed itself today in flaky dishes of pastry. She made the pies faithfully, while across the table she could see, when she glanced up from work, the sight that rankled in her patient and steadfast soul—the digging of the cellar of the new barn in the place where Adoniram forty years ago had promised her their new house should stand.

The pies were done for dinner. Adoniram and Sammy were home a few minutes after twelve o'clock. The dinner was eaten with serious haste. There was never much conversation at the table in the Penn family. Adoniram asked a blessing, and they ate promptly, then rose up and went about their work.

Sammy went back to school, taking soft sly lopes out of the yard like a rabbit. He wanted a game of marbles before school, and feared his father would give him chores to do. Adoniram hastened to the door and called after him, but he was out of sight.

"I don't see what you let him go for, Mother," said he. "I wanted him to help me unload that wood."

Adoniram went to work out in the yard unloading wood from the wagon. Sarah put away the dinner dishes, while Nanny took down her curl papers and changed her dress. She was going down to the store to buy some more embroidery and thread.

When Nanny was gone, Mrs. Penn went to the door. "Father!" she called.

"Well, what is it!"

"I want to see you jest a minute, Father."

"I can't leave this wood nohow. I've got to git it unloaded and go for a load of gravel afore two o'clock. Sammy had ought to help me. You hadn't ought to let him go to school so early."

"I want to see you jest a minute."

"I tell ye I can't, nohow, Mother."

"Father, you come here." Sarah Penn stood in the door like a queen; she held her head as if it bore a crown; there was that patience which makes authority royal in her voice. Adoniram went.

Mrs. Penn led the way into the kitchen, and pointed to a chair. "Sit down, Father," said she; "I've got somethin' I want to say to you."

He sat down heavily; his face was quite stolid, but he looked at her with restive eyes. "Well, what is it, Mother?"

"I want to know what you're buildin' that new barn for, Father?"

"I ain't got nothin' to say about it."

"It can't be you think you need another barn?"

"I tell ye I ain't got nothin' to say about it, Mother; an' I ain't goin' to say nothin'."

"Be you goin' to buy more cows?"

Adoniram did not reply; he shut his mouth tight.

"I know you be, as well as I want to. Now, Father, look here"—Sarah Penn had not sat down; she stood before her husband in the humble fashion of a Scripture woman—"I'm goin' to talk real plain to you; I never have sence I married you, but I'm goin' to now. I ain't never complained, an' I ain't goin' to complain now, but I'm goin' to talk plain. You see this room here, Father; you look at it well. You see there ain't no carpet on the floor, an' you see the paper is all dirty and droppin' off the walls. We ain't had no new paper on it for ten year, an' then I put it on myself, an' it didn't cost but nine cents a roll. You see this room, Father; it's all the one I've had to work in an' eat in an' sit in sence we was married. There ain't another woman in the whole town whose husband ain't got half the means you have but what's got better. It's all the room Nanny's got to have her company in; an' there ain't one of her mates but what's got better, an' their fathers not so able as hers is. It's all the room she'll have to be married in. What would you have thought, Father, if we had had our weddin' in a room no better than this? I was married in my mother's parlor, with a carpet on the floor, an' stuffed furniture, an' a mahogany card table. An' this is all the room my daughter will have to be married in. Look here, Father!"

Sarah Penn went across the room as though it were a tragic stage. She flung open a door and disclosed a tiny bedroom only large enough for a bed and bureau, with a path between. "There, Father," said she, "there's all the room I've had to sleep in in forty year. All my children were born there—the two that died an' the two that's livin'. I was sick with a fever, there."

She stepped to another door and opened it. It led into the small ill-lighted pantry. "Here," said she, "is all the buttery I've got—every place

I've got for my dishes, to set away my victuals in, an' to keep my milk pans in. Father, I've been takin' care of the milk of six cows in this place, an' now you're goin' to build a new barn, an' keep more cows, an' give me more to do in it."

She threw open another door. A narrow, crooked flight of stairs wound upward from it. "There, Father," said she, "I want you to look at the stairs that go up to them two unfinished chambers that are all the places our son and daughter have had to sleep in all their lives. There ain't a prettier girl in town nor a more ladylike one than Nanny, an' that's the place she has to sleep in. It ain't so good as your horse's stall; it ain't so warm an' tight."

Sarah Penn went back and stood before her husband. "Now, Father," said she, "I want to know if you think you're doin' right and accordin' to what you profess. Here, where we was married forty year ago, you promised me faithful that we should have a new house built in that lot over in the field before the year was out. You said you had money enough, an' you wouldn't ask me to live in no such place as this. It is forty year now, an' you've been makin' more money an' I've been savin' of it for you ever sence, an' you ain't built no house yet. You've built sheds an' cow houses an' one new barn, an' now you're goin' to build another. Father, I want to know if you think it's right. You're lodgin' your dumb beasts better than you are your own flesh and blood. I want to know if you think it's right."

"I ain't got nothin' to say."

"You can't say nothin' without ownin' it ain't right, Father. An' there's another thing—I ain't complained; I've got along forty year, an' I s'pose I should forty more, if it wa'n't for that—if we don't have another house, Nanny, she can't live with us after she's married. She'll have to go somewheres else to live away from us, an' it don't seem as if I could have it so, noways, Father. She wa'n't ever strong. She's got considerable color, but there wa'n't never any backbone to her. I've always took the heft of everything off her, an' she ain't fit to keep house an' do everything herself. Think of her doin' all the washin' and ironin' and bakin' with them soft white hands and arms, an' sweepin'! I can't have it so, noways, Father."

Mrs. Penn's face was burning; her mild eyes gleamed. She had pleaded her little cause like a Webster; she had ranged from severity to pathos; but her opponent employed that obstinate silence which makes eloquence futile with mocking echoes. Adoniram arose clumsily.

"Father, ain't you got nothin' to say?" said Mrs. Penn.

"I've got to go off after that load of gravel. I can't stan' talkin' all day."

"Father, won't you think it over an' have a house built there instead of a barn?"

"I ain't got nothin' to say."

Adoniram shuffled out. Mrs. Penn went into her bedroom. When she came out, her eyes were red. She had a roll of unbleached cotton. She spread it out on the kitchen table, and began cutting out some shirts for her husband. The men over in the field had a team to help them this afternoon; she could hear their halloos. She had a scanty pattern for the shirts; she had to plan and piece the sleeves.

Nanny came home with her embroidery and sat down with her needlework. She had taken down her curl papers, and there was a soft roll of fair hair like an aureole over her forehead; her face was as delicately fine and clear as porcelain. Suddenly she looked up and the tender red flamed over her face and neck. "Mother," said she.

"What say?"

"I've been thinking—I don't see how we're goin' to have any wedding in this room. I'd be ashamed to have his folks come if we didn't have anybody else."

"Mebbe we can have some new paper before then; I can put it on. I guess you won't have no call to be ashamed of your belongin's."

"We might have the wedding in the new barn," said Nanny, with gentle pettishness. "Why, Mother, what makes you look so?"

Mrs. Penn had started and was staring at her with a curious expression. She turned again to her work, and spread out a pattern carefully on the cloth. "Nothin'," said she.

Presently Adoniram clattered out of the yard in his two-wheeled dump cart, standing as proudly upright as a Roman charioteer. Mrs. Penn opened the door and stood there a minute looking out; the halloos of the men sounded louder.

It seemed to her all through the spring months that she heard nothing but the halloos and the noises of saws and hammers. The new barn grew fast. It was a fine edifice for this little village. Men came on pleasant Sundays, in their meeting suits and clean shirt bosoms, and stood around it admiringly. Mrs. Penn did not speak of it and Adoniram did not mention it to her, although sometimes upon a return from inspecting it, he bore himself with injured dignity.

"It's a strange thing how your mother feels about the new barn," he said, confidentially, to Sammy one day.

Sammy only grunted after an odd fashion for a boy; he had learned it from his father.

The barn was all completed ready for use by the third week in July. Adoniram had planned to move his stock in on Wednesday; on Tuesday he received a letter which changed his plans. He came in with it early in the morning. "Sammy's been to the post office," said he, "an' I've got a letter from Hiram." Hiram was Mrs. Penn's brother who lived in Vermont.

"Well," said Mrs. Penn, "what does he say about the folks?"

"I guess they're all right. He says he thinks if I come up country right off ther's a chance to buy jest the kind of a horse I want." He stared reflectively out of the window at the new barn.

Mrs. Penn was making pies. She went on clapping the rolling pin into the crust, although she was very pale, and her heart beat loudly.

"I dun' know but what I'd better go," said Adoniram. "I hate to go off jest now, right in the midst of hayin', but the ten-acre lot's cut, an' I guess Rufus an' the others can git along without me three or four days. I can't get a horse round here to suit me, nohow, an' I've got to have another for all that wood haulin' in the fall. I told Hiram to watch out an' if he got wind of a good horse to let me know. I guess I'd better go."

"I'll get out your clean shirt an' collar," said Mrs. Penn calmly.

She laid out Adoniram's Sunday suit and his clean clothes on the bed in the little bedroom. She got his shaving water and razor ready. At last she buttoned on his collar and fastened his black cravat.

Adoniram never wore his collar and cravat except on extra occasions. He held his head high, with a rasped dignity. When he was all ready, with coat and hat brushed, and a lunch of pie and cheese in a paper bag, he hesitated on the threshold of the door. He looked at his wife, and his manner was defiantly apologetic. "*If* them cows come today, Sammy can drive them into the new barn," said he, "an' when they bring the hay up they can pitch it in there."

"Well," replied Mrs. Penn.

Adoniram set his shaven face ahead and started. When he had cleared the doorstep, he turned and looked back with a kind of nervous solemnity. "I shall be back by Saturday if nothin' happens," said he.

"Do be careful, Father," returned his wife.

She stood in the door with Nanny at her elbow and watched him out of sight. Her eyes had a strange, doubtful expression in them; her peaceful forehead was contracted. Nanny sat sewing. Her wedding day was drawing nearer and she was getting pale and thin with her steady sewing. Her mother kept glancing at her.

"Have you got that pain in your side this mornin'?" she asked.

"A little."

Mrs. Penn's face as she worked, changed; her perplexed forehead smoothed; her eyes were steady, her lips firmly set. She formed a maxim for herself, although incoherently with her unlettered thoughts. "Unsolicited opportunities are the guideposts of the Lord to the new roads of Life," she repeated in effect, and she made up her mind to her course of action.

"S'posin' I *had* wrote to Hiram," she muttered once, when she was in the pantry. "S'posin' I had wrote and asked him if he knew of any horse? But I didn't, an' Father's goin' wa'n't any of my doin'. It looks like a providence." Her mother's voice rang out quite loud at the last.

"What you talkin' about, Mother?" called Nanny.

"Nothin'."

Mrs. Penn hurried her baking; at eleven o'clock it was all done. The load of hay from the west field came slowly down the cart track and drew up at the new barn. Mrs. Penn ran out. "Stop!" she screamed. "Stop!"

The men stopped and looked; Sammy upreared from the top of the load and stared at his mother.

"Stop!" she cried out again. "Don't you put the hay in that barn; put it in the old one."

"Why, he said to put it in here," returned one of the haymakers, wonderingly. He was a young man, a neighbor's son, whom Adoniram hired by the year to work on the farm.

"Don't you put the hay in the new barn; there's room enough in the old one, ain't there?" said Mrs. Penn.

"Room enough," returned the hired man, in his thick, rustic tones. "Didn't need the new barn, nohow, as far as room's concerned. Well, I s'pose he changed his mind." He took hold of the horses' bridles.

Mrs. Penn went back to the house. Soon the kitchen windows were darkened and a fragrance like warm honey came into the room.

Nanny laid down her work. "I thought Father wanted them to put the hay into the new barn?" she said, wonderingly.

"It's all right," replied her mother.

Sammy slid down from the load of hay and came in to see if dinner was ready.

"I ain't goin' to get a regular dinner today, as long as Father's gone," said his mother. "I've let the fire go out. You can have some bread an' milk an' pie. I thought we could get along. She set out some bowls of milk, some bread and a pie on the kitchen table. "You'd better eat your dinner now," said she. "You might jest as well get through with it. I want you to help me afterward."

Nanny and Sammy stared at each other. There was something strange in their mother's manner. Mrs. Penn did not eat anything herself. She went into the pantry and they heard her moving dishes while they ate. Presently she came out with a pile of plates. She got the clothes basket out of the shed and packed them in it. Nanny and Sammy watched. She brought out cups and saucers and put them in with the plates.

"What you goin' to do, Mother?" inquired Nanny, in a timid voice. A sense of something unusual made her tremble, as if it were a ghost. Sammy rolled his eyes over his pie.

"You'll see what I'm goin' to do," replied Mrs. Penn. "If you're through, Nanny, I want you to go upstairs and pack your things; an' I want you, Sammy, to help me take down the bed in the bedroom."

"Oh, Mother, what for?" gasped Nanny.

"You'll see."

During the next few hours a feat was performed by this simple, pious New England mother which was equal in its way to Wolfe's storming of the Heights of Abraham. It took no more genius and audacity of bravery for Wolfe to cheer his wondering soldiers up those steep precipices, under the sleeping eyes of the enemy, than for Sarah Penn, at the head of her children, to move all their little house-hold goods into the new barn while her husband was away.

Nanny and Sammy followed their mother's instructions without a murmur; indeed, they were overawed. There is a certain uncanny and super-human quality about all such purely original undertakings as their mother's was to them. Nanny went back and forth with her light loads and Sammy tugged with sober energy.

At five o'clock in the afternoon the little house in which the Penns had lived for forty years had emptied itself into the new barn.

Every builder builds somewhat for unknown purposes, and is in a measure a prophet. The architect of Adoniram Penn's barn, while he designed it for the comfort of four-footed animals, had planned better than he knew for the comfort of humans. Sarah Penn saw at a glance its possibilities. Those great box stalls, with quilts hung before them, would make better bedrooms than the one she had occupied for forty years, and there was a tight carriage room. The harness room, with its chimney and shelves, would make a kitchen of her dreams. The great middle space would make a parlor, by-and-by, fit for a palace. Upstairs there was as much room as down. With partitions and windows, what a house there would be! Sarah looked at the row of stanchions before the allotted space for cows, and reflected she would have a front entry there.

At six o'clock the stove was up in the harness room, the kettle was boiling, and the table set for tea. It looked almost as homelike as the abandoned house across the yard had ever done. The young hired man milked, and Sarah directed him calmly to bring the milk to the new barn. He came gasping, dropping little blots of foam from the brimming pails on the grass. Before the next morning he had spread the story of Adoniram Penn's wife moving into the new barn all over the little village. Men assembled in the store and talked it over; women with shawls over their heads scuttled into each other's houses before their work was done. Any deviation from the ordinary course of life in this quiet town was enough to stop all progress in it. Everybody paused to look at the staid, independent figure on the side track. There was a difference of opinion with regard to her. Some held her to be insane; some, of a lawless and rebellious spirit.

Friday the minister went to see her. It was in the forenoon, and she was at the barn door shelling peas for dinner. She looked up and returned his salutation with dignity; then she went on with her work. She did not invite him in. The saintly expression of her face remained fixed, but there was an angry flush over it.

The minister stood awkwardly before her, and talked. She handled the peas as if they were bullets. At last she looked up and her eyes showed a spirit that her meek front had covered for a lifetime.

"There ain't no use talkin', Mr. Hersey," said she. "I've thought it all over and over, an' I believe I'm doin' what's right. I've made it the subject of prayer, and it's betwixt me an' the Lord an' Adoniram. There ain't no call for nobody else to worry about it."

"Well, of course, if you have brought it to the Lord in prayer, and feel satisfied that you are doing right, Mrs. Penn," said the minister helplessly. His thin, gray-bearded face was pathetic. He was a sickly man; his youthful confidence had cooled; he had to scourge himself up to some of his pastoral duties, and then he was prostrated by the smart.

"I think it's right jest as much as I think it was right for our forefathers to come over from the old country 'cause they didn't have what belonged to 'em," said Mrs. Penn. She arose. The barn threshold might have been Plymouth Rock from her bearing. "I don't doubt you mean well, Mr. Hersey," said she, "but there are things people hadn't ought to interfere with. I've been a member of the church for over forty year. I've got my mind an' my own feet, an' I'm goin' to think my own thoughts an' go my own ways, an' nobody but the Lord is goin' to dictate to me unless I've a mind to have him. Won't you come in an' set down? How is Mis' Hersey?"

"She is well, I thank you," replied the minister. He added some more perplexed, apologetic remarks; then he retreated.

He could expound the intricacies of every character study in the Scriptures; he was competent to grasp the Pilgrim Fathers and all historical innovators; but Sarah Penn was beyond him. He could deal with primal cases, but parallel ones worsted him. But, after all, although it was aside from his province, he wondered more how Adoniram Penn would deal with his wife than how the Lord would. Everybody shared the wonder. When Adoniram's four new cows arrived, Sarah ordered three put in the old barn, the other in the house shed where the cooking stove had stood. That added to the excitement. It was whispered that all four cows were domiciled in the house.

Toward sunset on Saturday, when Adoniram was expected home, there was a knot of men in the road near the new barn. The hired man milked, but he still hung around the premises. There were brown bread and baked beans and a custard pie; it was the supper that Adoniram loved on a Saturday night. She had on a clean calico and she bore herself imperturbably. Nanny and Sammy kept close at her heels. Their eyes were large, and Nanny was full of nervous tremors. Still there was to them more pleasant excitement than anything else. An inborn confidence in their mother over their father asserted itself.

Sammy looked out of the harness-room window. "There he is," he announced, in an awed whisper. He and Nanny peeped around the casing. Mrs. Penn kept on about her work. The children watched Adoniram leave the new horse standing in the drive while he went to the house-door. It was fastened. Then he went around to the shed. That door was seldom locked, even when the family was away. The thought how her father would be confronted by the cow flashed upon Nanny. There was a hysterical sob in her throat. Adoniram emerged from the shed and stood looking about in a dazed fashion. His lips moved; he was saying something, but they could not hear what it was. The hired man was peeping around a corner of the old barn but nobody saw him.

Adoniram took the new horse by the bridle and led him across the yard to the new barn. Nanny and Sammy slunk close to their mother. The barn doors rolled back and there stood Adoniram, with the long mild face of the great Canadian farm horse looking over his shoulder.

Nanny kept behind her mother, but Sammy stepped suddenly forward and stood in front of her.

Adoniram stared at the group. "What on airth you all down here for?" said he. "What's the matter over to the house?"

"We've come here to live, Father," said Sammy. His shrill voice quavered out bravely.

"What—" Adoniram sniffed—"what is it smells like cookin'?" said he. He stepped forward and looked in at the open door of the harness room. Then he turned to his wife. His old bristling face was pale and frightened. "What on airth does this mean, Mother?"

"You come in here, Father," said Sarah. She led the way into the harness room and shut the door. "Now, Father," said she, "you needn't be scared. I ain't crazy. There ain't nothin' to be upset over. But we've come here to live an' we're goin' to live here. We've got jest as good a right here as new horses and cows. The house wa'n't fit for us to live in any longer, an' I made up my mind I wa'n't goin' to stay there. I've done my duty by you forty year an' I'm goin' to do it now, but I'm goin' to live here. You've got to put in some windows an' partitions, an' you'll have to buy some furniture."

"Why, Mother!" the old man gasped.

"You'd better take your coat off an' get washed—there's the wash basin—an' then we'll have supper."

"Why, Mother!"

Sammy went past the window, heading the new horse to the old barn. The old man saw him and shook his head speechlessly. He tried to take off his coat, but his arms seemed to lack the power. His wife helped him. She poured some water into the tin basin and put in a piece of soap. She got the comb and brush and smoothed his thin gray hair after he had washed. Then she put the beans, hot bread and tea on the table. Sammy came in and the family drew up. Adoniram sat looking dazedly at his plate and they waited.

"Ain't you goin' to ask a blessin', Father?" said Sarah.

And the old man bent his head and mumbled.

All through the meal he stopped eating at intervals and stared furtively at his wife, but he ate well. The home food tasted good to him and his old frame was too sturdily healthy to be affected by his mind. But after supper he went out and sat down on the step of the smaller door at the right of the barn, through which he had meant his Jerseys to pass in stately file, but which Sarah designed for her front housedoor, and he leaned his head on his hands.

After the supper dishes were cleared away and the milk pans washed, Sarah went out to him. The twilight was deepening. There was a clear green glow in the sky. Before them stretched the smooth level of field; in the distance was a cluster of haystacks like the huts of a village; the air was very calm and sweet. The landscape might have been an ideal one of peace.

Sarah bent over and touched her husband on one of his thin, sinewy shoulders. "Father!"

The old man's shoulders heaved; he was weeping.

"Why, don't do so, Father," said Sarah.

"I'll—put up the—partitions, an—everything you—want, Mother."

Sarah put her apron up to her face; she was overcome by her own triumph.

Adoniram was like a fortress whose walls had no active resistance, and went down the instant the right besieging tools were used. "Why, Mother," he said hoarsely, "I hadn't no idee you was so set on't it as all this comes to."

MARYLAND

The Manor

SARA HAARDT

Lucinda Vaughn stood in the door, and took a last look at her room. She knew that Ira and Nina were waiting downstairs, whispering nervously, but she took a deliberate pleasure in keeping them waiting this afternoon. She wanted to linger here, thinking all the sharp wounding thoughts she hadn't let herself think so long as she was a guest in their house. Her son's house! She didn't like the room, though she had been very comfortable in it: everything was too new, too expressive of her daughter-in-law's impeccable taste to suit her. Yet, she had to admit that she would have stayed on, if she hadn't felt she had worn her welcome out.

Oh, she could never explain it to any one but herself, but she could tell the difference! Nina had been just as sweet to her, even more insistent about all her little comforts, now that her heart had gone back on her, but she could feel Nina instinctively drawing away from her. Nina was young, her throat was a slim lovely column as smooth as marble, her eyes were as wide and as starry as freshly-opened flowers, and the sight of a crumbling old woman was naturally repulsive to her. But she didn't, really, care about Nina. It was Ira who filled her with a torturing guilt.

Ira's clearest picture of her was as a young woman, with silly ringlets and a devastating energy. She had been slender too, as slender as Nina, and prettier because of her rounded cheeks and arms. Nina was *too* thin! Later, of course, her hair had turned gray—a solid silver gray like the platinum blondness that was so fashionable now—but it had made her seem younger than ever. And she had never stopped going.

It was only in the last year that she had declined invitations of any moment.

Then, one day last Spring, she was suddenly aware that Ira was watching her climb the stairs. She was taking them slowly, her heart choking her with every breath, and she teetered about like a ship that had lost its ballast. After all, she *was* sixty-nine, and sixty-nine-year-old women didn't run up stairs like young girls, but she had winced at his horrified expression. He was seeing her for the first time as an old woman. He was fighting against the realization that she was failing, sinking slowly to her death, as he and Nina would one day fail and die.

After that she was conscious of his pained look every time he came near her, in spite of his efforts to be ordinary and cheerful. Oh, no, she wasn't deceiving herself—she had been through the same thing herself! It was natural for young people to shrink from old people. It was part of their gay ruthless make-believe not to want them around where they would be reminded of flesh that actually smelled musty and sagged in hideous purplish pouches. It seemed too terrible that *everybody* had to grow old!

She had thought the same thing herself, in the years that she had been young and gay, and she had made a secret vow that when her time came she would go off as the Eskimo women did and die all alone. A kind of primitive panic seized her as she stood there, her hands trembling with fatigue. She *had* to get away, out of reach of Nina's dutiful solicitude, of Ira's deploring glances. And yet, and yet—she hesitated in the door, scarcely breathing. She wasn't, in reality, like the Eskimo women who accepted their doom simply, implacably. She was a Virginian lady who regarded death as an indignity, an uninvited and presumptuous caller, and in spite of her promise, a Virginian lady she would remain to the end.

"Mother! If you are still set on going we had better be starting."

"I'm coming, my child."

They were waiting tensely, and she stood as rigidly in her pride.

"Do you really feel that you *have* to go this afternoon, Mother?" Nina asked in her smooth round voice. "It's a vile day to be out."

"I don't mind the rain," she said with a sprightliness she did not feel. She could take a melancholy pleasure in their sense of guilt at seeing her go in such weather. It was a gray November day, with a misty rain blowing. Pneumonia weather, for old ladies.

"We feel terribly about your deserting us for that old ladies' home,"

Nina protested prettily. "The only thing, it *is* near enough for us to visit back and forth."

Old ladies' home! In her coolly impudent way Nina had stated the exact incensing truth about the Manor. It had been the most elegant hotel in Baltimore when Lucinda first visited it with her parents in the late 'eighties, with the most commodious ballroom, and the most famous kitchen where the Virginians, who came up in droves after the war, could dine upon terrapin and chicken Maryland in the style to which they had been accustomed. But it had gradually deteriorated into a kind of genteel boarding-house where elderly mothers and grandmothers could be boarded reasonably, away from their families. It was really shocking how few old maids there were among them; they were all married women, like herself, widows who had reared large families—successful sons with pretty wives and adorable grandchildren, and charming daughters with prominent husbands and brilliant social careers.

There were Augusta Britt, and Rhoda Alexander, and Jennie Rountree, and Eliza France, and Mary Lightfoot—all potent, charming women in their day, and now huddling together in the musty rooms of the Manor for company, matching ills with one another, repeating endlessly their elaborate lies as to why they preferred the Manor for another Winter rather than visiting with the children. Well, they had all come along together; over her old life with them there was a sweetness of the past that had a depth beyond the present, but she wasn't the kind of plaguing old lady that they were. Oh, never!

"I shall enjoy being with my old friends," she reproved Nina gently. "I shall have very pleasant company at the Manor. Now, take care of yourself, my deah," Nina's smooth fragrant cheek lightly brushed her withered one. "Come in to see me when you can. I'll be in Sallie Holcombe's old room. Good-bye, my deah."

There was a wavering about her figure in the doorway. She had caught the slight irony of Nina's smile. Sallie Holcombe had died of heart failure in her room at the Manor last week. Her presence in Sallie's room signified, at the very least, that she was taking Sallie's place, weaving in faltering circles from the bureau to the window, from the window to her slipper-chair, from the slipper-chair back to the bureau, her mind weaving the while, as unfruitfully, as wearily.

Well, so she was taking Sallie's room, and so had she a bad heart like Sallie, but she'd never let on to them, though the roofs of fortune fell.

She squeezed her hands tightly together under the robe, clinging to her pain—her secret—as if, when the truth was known to them, it would be the one thing lost to her forever.

II

"Well, here we are," Ira was saying with a false note of cheer. "You'd better hurry on in, Mother. This is great weather for the flu."

Lucinda stood quite still, a solitary figure in the fog. The light from the crystal chandelier in the lobby lay in a wide golden swathe across the pavement reaching to her feet; voices floated out to her as the storm-door swung open. But a painted sickishness came over her. She was forsaking the true sound core of society to make her home among the sick and the aged. All her treasured youth was gone, never to be loosened again—all her brightness, laughter, bloom—gone. . . . She refused Ira's arm, and walked stiffly into the lobby.

Immediately there was a stir. Dexter, the head bellboy who ran the elevator at meal-times, came forward for her bags; Miss Fannie Eustace, a wizened little body with crimped hair and small blue-veined hands, spread her thin lips in a watery smile.

"It is such a pleasure to have Mrs. Vaughn," she drawled. "We are hoping that she will enjoy her Winter with us." Miss Fannie belonged to one of the proudest families among the Baltimore-Virginians; the Eustaces had come to Baltimore from Petersburg in the first migration after the war, and though they remained as poor as church mice, they banked as proudly as ever upon who they were.

"How d'ye do, Miss Fannie?"

Ira, who for one brief moment had looked irresolute and uncomfortable, youthfully squared his shoulders and wrote "Mrs. Ira Seaton Vaughn" with the mangy pen. He became businesslike as he instructed Miss Fannie in an undertone to send the weekly bill to his office. "I want her to have every comfort," he added. "If there are any little extras, you'll see that she gets them, won't you, Miss Fannie?"

Miss Fannie bobbed her head emphatically. Compared with Miss Fannie, Lucinda reflected, her life had been all velvet and roses. Miss Fannie obviously envied her the little extras so generously provided her by her tall handsome son; she should be reassured, uplifted to that triumphant spiritual plane known alone to the mothers of handsome sons, but she felt only the implied doom of her arrival here. The smile she might have bestowed upon poor starved Miss Fannie died on her lips.

Upstairs in her room, Ira laid the old-fashioned iron door-key on the marble-topped bureau. "Can't I help you get settled, Mother? Isn't there anything I can do?"

"No, thank you, my child. You hurry on now, or you'll keep dinner waiting." Swiftly she wanted him to go, before the tears loosed in a flood and blinded her. But he lingered; his dark eyes turned intently upon her, from the door.

"When are we going to see you again? You take it easy now, Mother. Your heart's all right but you'll have to go slowly for a while. Don't forget—we're expecting you back at the house at Christmas. You certainly must pay us a visit at Christmas."

She nodded glibly. Deeper down, though, in that dark of her mind where she had always stifled unpleasant thoughts, and where she stifled her pain now, she was yielding to the thought that Christmas was a long way off—as far off as Virginia, where the bells of all the plantations were stilled, and rows of black factories stretched along the rivers where, before, only gardens had grown.

When Jennie Rountree rapped on her door, an hour later, on her way down to dinner, Lucinda had changed to her plum-colored moiré, and was waiting for her. Jennie was over seventy, plump and pretty as a cameo, with a gushing manner that concealed her busy little mind continually agape for gossip. She made a little rush for her now, chirruping, "Lucinda, deah! Are you *alone?* I told Rhoda I'd peek in and see if Ira was still with you. The handsome scamp! *Is* he as handsome as ever? We were *so* in hopes he would dine with us this evening."

"No, I sent him off immediately." Lucinda set her lips, and proceeded spiritedly. "Ira opposed my coming away, of course, especially as I didn't tell him until I had made all the arrangements. But *you* can appreciate the situation, Jennie . . ."

Jennie Rountree nodded, and swallowed the saliva that always gathered in her mouth when she listened intently. Lucinda found herself lying instinctively, as Jennie had lied before her. "I wanted to be in town where I could get everywhere, and *see* things by myself. Nina and Ira were always *sweet* about bringing me in but I didn't stand the long drive so well of late. It isn't as if I were a girl any more."

"None of us are as young as we used to be," echoed Jennie, and Lucinda felt her focused gaze boring down to where her heart fluttered like a wounded bird; "but we still like to *go,* and to *do*. I'd pin my name and address inside my coat, if I were you Lucinda, in case anything *should* happen. Sallie and I always did, even when we went out together. Poor Sallie! She joined us in bridge every evening until the very last." She let her eyes rove about the room and continued in her sharp thread of a voice, "I see you've changed things from the way Sallie had them. She had her slipper-chair over there——"

"I brought a few little things with me," said Lucinda. She always spoke of her possessions deprecatingly; the habit had arisen among the Baltimore-Virginians after the war when their property was inseparable from their pride. As a matter of fact she had brought her famous Sheffield candlesticks, a priceless Stoddard flip glass for flowers, and two Peale miniatures.

"Those candlesticks always remind me of your Christmas dinners," mused Jennie with her fatuous smile. "None of us had much in those days, Lucinda, but I must say we made the most of it. I never tasted such oyster dressing as you used to serve with your turkey, before or since. And such syllabub! Where *are* the cooks in this generation?" She bounced up from her chair, and clenched uncertainly for the doorknob. "We'd better start down if we want any dinner."

Lucinda was suddenly conscious of a buzzing concerted movement throughout the building. Outside, in the corridor, Eliza France and Mary Lightfoot were hobbling along the Brussels carpet with their sticks.

"I'm afraid the doors are open," Eliza greeted her. "I was delayed at tea."

"This elevator is a death-trap, in my opinion," Mary cleared her throat with a cackle. "I like to get an early start when it isn't crowded. How d'ye do, Lucinda? I hope you left the children well."

"Very well, thank you," answered Lucinda, but her words, her very presence, were lost in the general scrimmage. The elevator doors banged; actually there was a rush for it, Eliza's stick clattered to the floor, and Jennie's breath blew in asthmatic gusts down her neck.

"Take it slowly, Dexter," commanded Mary. "We are in no hurry . . . no hurry."

She could barely wedge her way through the crowd gathered outside the dining-room downstairs. "Yonder are Augusta and Rhoda up near the front," shrilled Jennie. "Augusta's wearing her wisteria silk and cameos tonight in your honor."

Lucinda smiled, but over her masked sweetness there flooded the whole of her fear and her resentment. How loathsome old women were! No wonder their children didn't want them. Breeding, background—nothing saved them. These were Virginian ladies, yammering for their food; Eliza France was actually pounding the marble floor with her stick.

At last the doors swung back. Boston, the head waiter, sped before Augusta Britt, and pulled out her chair for her. There was a great to-do at the tables as the other waiters followed him.

"Whew!" breathed Augusta, and sinking into her chair, she fanned herself with the turkey-tail fan she carried Winter and Summer. "What was the matter, Boston? You're getting later every evening. Well, never mind, never mind. How d'ye do, Lucinda? Here, Boston, help Mrs. Vaughn to her place. I hope you left the children well, Lucinda." Augusta was still a very fine figure at eighty, with her high temper undiminished. She had been known to slap the little Negro girl who waited on her when she was out of humor.

Lucinda nodded. "Very well, thank you."

"We have been looking forward to your joining us," murmured Rhoda Alexander, and Lucinda nodded again. Rhoda, poor dear, never raised her voice except in acquiescence. She was small, with delicate features and a soft fluttery manner. She sat quietly, the hair brooch on her bosom rising and falling gently, but with a nervous eye eternally cocked at Augusta.

"Who d'ye suppose I met on the street today?" rattled Jennie, in her flighty voice. "I declare this clam broth is stone cold, Augusta. I've a good mind to send it back."

"Who?" demanded Augusta. "I'll speak to Boston at once. You, Boston! How dare you serve Mrs. Rountree cold broth!"

"Young Dr. Shackelford, of Christ Church! He told me he was speaking Sunday on the change in the prayerbook. They've left the word 'obey' out of the marriage ceremony. I say it's just as well, just as well!"

"I beg to differ with you," contradicted Augusta. She was a trifle deaf and spoke in a clarion voice. "They ought to leave prayerbooks and old things like that alone. The old things are best. They've stood the test of time, which is a lot more than you can say for these frisky young rectors. He'll never be the rector Dr. Braxton was, I'll warrant."

"He seemed a genteel young man to *me*," Jennie gushed in her high key, "and most at*ten*tive, *most* attentive."

"I see where they're burying Lucia Perry from Christ Church," interposed Rhoda, eternally at her gentle task of pacification. "My, my, it seems only yesterday she was being married there——"

"Here Boston, you Boston," Augusta interrupted her, "bring in some hot biscuit. How is your guinea, Lucinda? You haven't eaten a mouthful! Boston, I'd like a helping of sage dressing, while you're about it."

Lucinda protested faintly that her breast of guinea was delicious. The packing, and the trip into town, had tired her; her appetite would pick up tomorrow, after she was rested. She was preparing them for her escape to her room after dinner, when they gathered in Augusta's room for their rubber of bridge. She simply couldn't suffer another hour of their gluttony and bigotry and snobbery! She had dreaded parting with Ira and Nina but she hadn't realized until now how they had suckled her, or rather, how she had preyed upon their youth for her interests, her strength. She was hungry for them already, she longed to fly to them, away from these raucous old women, and her room upstairs smelling of Sallie Holcombe's stale heliotrope, and Sallie's dead face turned to the blank wall.

III

Lying drearily on her bed, Lucinda heard disquieting footsteps hurrying over the carpet outside her door, but she did not stir, except to put her hands over her eyes. She felt so utterly tired, once she was relaxed, that she had no curiosity about outside affairs. December was here, she said to herself incredulously, the end of the year—of many, many years—and the pain in her heart had deepened steadily. Often, now, she awoke in the night with it, and sat rocking on her bed in the dark, fearful of turning on the light lest some one see it shining through the transom, and rap on the door. Ah, the shame of it, crouching there in the shrouded blackness, to her who, in her proud narrow fashion, had thought of death as touching others but never herself.

There was a distinct bustle in the corridor but she lay still in that drained apathy she had come to know, after one of her bad nights. It was just as well. She would hear all about it from Jennie and Augusta and Rhoda when they came in to tea. She experienced a sense of relief at the thought that they would be too taken up with it to notice the blue circles under her eyes. She didn't feel like entertaining them this afternoon but it was her time to pour tea, and if she asked them not to come they would be reminded of the afternoon Sallie had disappointed them. Now she wouldn't have to exert herself, and they would have something to talk about besides her and Sallie.

Yes, she realized that she had taken Sallie's place, and there was nothing she could do about it. After all, there was a reassuring sense of custom in their company. She clung to any intimation of continuity, even if she had to swallow a certain amount of unpleasantness with it. What else could she do? Where else could she go?

She had one satisfaction: they did not know about her heart, or her visits to Dr. Deberniere's office. She had never yielded to the consolation of going over and over her symptoms with them, as they constantly did with each other, and as Sallie had done before her. Her terrible shame was intact. There was a pleasurable triumph in that—something that seemed an echo to her youth, her ability to take care of herself, to stand brilliantly alone.

She got up, and smoothed the counterpane where she had been lying down. They would be coming in a few minutes. She took her toilet articles off the top of the bureau and put them in the drawer; changed the water in a vase of laurel; hid her heart medicine in the back of the medicine closet.

A rap sounded on the door. "Oh, how d'ye do, Jennie."

"Mary's dead!"

It couldn't be. Why, not three hours ago, Mary had sat at the luncheon-table sipping her tea and secreting scraps of food in her napkin for her parrot. That terrible struggling unbelief came over her again. No, it simply couldn't be! But there were Augusta and Rhoda trailing in with solemn faces.

Jennie held the floor, screeching. "I tell you she was as spry as a cricket! I was talking to her not an hour before and she complained of her head but she was always subject to headaches. It wasn't any time before I heard a *clump* and she had dropped down dead! Just think of it! What will poor Eliza do without her?"

"Eliza'll have that bird on her hands, first thing she knows." Augusta had herself well in hand, though her lips were pinched. "I never did approve of Mary's keeping that bird with this parrot fever going round. Never did! But go on with your story, Jennie."

"It must have been a little after two," continued Jennie, quivering with excitement, "because I had just wound up my watch and I always wind it up early in the afternoon. I hurried out and called Eliza. She said Mary had probably gone out and the parrot had tipped his cage over, but we'd better see. We had to get Dexter to open the door. But by the time we got there she was . . . gone. Dr. Deberniere said it was cerebral hemorrhage. He said she was dead before she knew what hit her."

"What does Dr. Deberniere know about it?" shouted Augusta. "If he'd known so much he would have given her something."

"My, my," sighed Rhoda, "I thought Mary was looking better than she'd looked for years."

"I thought so, too," echoed Lucinda faintly, and flushed at the concealed reticence of her tone. She sat behind her repoussé service with a guilty, inturned expression. She was sorry about Mary, as sorry as she could be, but her own shame was the most that she could bear. "Can't I get you some sherry, Jennie, while Boston is bringing more hot water?" All the tea was gone, and the sandwiches and cakes—rich chicken-salad sandwiches, a meal in themselves, and devil's food cupcakes with creamy pecan icing. Mary's death, however saddening, hadn't affected their appetites.

"I take a sip of whiskey every morning," shrieked Jennie. "Elderly people really need it. Whiskey doesn't arouse me, it relaxes me. I put a little whiskey in a glass of Buffalo water, or French brandy if I can get it. It's the best tonic there is."

"It sounds like a vile dose to me," stated Augusta. "I don't believe in ruining good whiskey with fizz water. Never did!"

"Perhaps you'd rather have a toddy, Jennie?" asked Lucinda. "Can I mix you a little toddy?" She moved the tray, and brought two Waterford decanters out of her closet.

"The tea is delicious, Lucinda, but I believe I'll have a little toddy too." Augusta waved Jennie aside, and eyed the decanters greedily.

"Poor Mary!" sighed Rhoda. She declined her brandy glass and sniffed her bottle of lavender smelling-salts. "How she did enjoy good spirits!"

"Well, they never did her any harm," asserted Augusta, caressing the bowl of her glass.

"They're laying her out in the back parlor," Jennie said with her small hard clarity. "I saw Dexter wiping off the furniture."

IV

Lucinda had only glimpsed the back parlor since they had turned it into an undertaking parlor but the thought of Mary lying there with the light from the crystal chandelier shining in her dead eyes gave her the cold shivers. This couldn't be the festive little room where she had attended so many elegant gatherings, where she had sat in her rose silk, during an intermission at the Arlington Cotillion, shaking her silly ringlets at young Ira Seaton Vaughn!

Yes, it had the same stained glass windows, which had been so stylish in their day, but which now resembled the windows of a slightly rococo chapel. There was the old dark velvet carpet on the floor, the long centre table, on which the casket was placed, and the sofa and chairs upholstered in black horsehair round the walls. The mantelpiece of black marble with its brass candlesticks and borrowed crucifix made an appropriate altar. Only the crystal chandelier, and its cold sparkling prisms, resembling icicles rather than tears, seemed out of place.

"Well, when my time comes, I'll be ready to go," declaimed Augusta. The brandy had warmed her blood, but, as yet, it had not softened her tongue. "Mary was always complaining of her head, she said she couldn't see across the room, but I notice she could see the spots on the cards when she had a mind to."

"My, my, I can see her now," drooled Rhoda. Her eyes were streaming tears from smelling the lavender salts too closely. "She always knitted with white needles on dark wool or dark needles on light wool on account of her eyes. My, my, I suppose we all have to go some time."

"We'd *better* go, if we want any dinner," commanded Augusta. "It's been delightful, Lucinda. You're coming along, aren't you?"

Lucinda nodded. It was impossible to deny Augusta in her voracious gluttony, yet she herself was conscious of being always hungry, hungry, in the curious frantic way of the aged—fearful of losing one word, one morsel, before it was too late.

She found herself racing to the elevator now, clawing at Augusta's skirts ahead of her, the while Jennie and Rhoda clawed at hers from behind. In her haste she not only forgot Mary but also her own heart, contracted like a clenched fist, between her dry breasts.

"Hey, hey, you Dexter, you," called Augusta, thrashing her turkey-tail fan against the elevator shaft, "let us on—wait!—I tell you."

Dexter cracked the door tentatively. "Ah's got a full load now, Mis' Britt. Ah'll be back fur you 'fo Boston open up de dinin'-room."

"Open that door, I tell you," Augusta shouted, and swept past him. "Come on!"

Lucinda was close on her heels, crushed between Jennie and Rhoda so tightly she could turn neither to left nor to right. Behind her Dexter struggled with the safety door. The lock clicked faintly, there was a louder crack as a coiled black snake snapped over her head, and they pitched down . . . down . . .

Yet, in spite of the speed of the descent, every detail, the dangling of the broken cable, the smeary white faces with their bulging eyes, the loosened flakes of soot, were impressed upon her mind with a searing clarity. For one endless moment she seemed to be suspended in air; then they crashed.

There was an absolute and climactic hush of sound, and immediately after a salvo of voices. The elevator rested on the safety cushions in the basement, with the upper half of its body visible in the lobby. "Is anybody hurt?" screeched Miss Fannie, above the others. "Is anybody hurt? Come here, Boston, all of you—a terrible accident has happened!"

"Oh, Lawdy, Lawd," moaned Dexter, "whut we gwine do now, whut we gwine do now!"

"Shut up!" commanded Augusta, "shut up, the whole lot of you! Nobody's hurt. Get that tall stool from behind Miss Fannie's desk, Boston, and hand it down here. Now you climb up on it, Dexter, and help the rest of us out."

Rhoda obediently climbed up after him, clutching her lavender smelling-salts with her free hand. "My, my, it only goes to show we ought to be prepared for what's coming. I'll never budge a step without my smelling-salts after this. My, my, we were nearly ushered into eternity before we knew it!"

"I didn't have time to think where we were going," screamed Jennie, dabbing at the flecks of saliva in the corners of her mouth.

"We were going down in the cellar," snapped Augusta.

"Mary always said it was a death-trap," Eliza France whimpered. "She was wary of it to her dying day."

"Well, we came near to joining poor Mary tonight," jabbered Jennie. "I'm going to take an extra dose of my heart medicine to be on the safe side. But I can't walk up to the fourth floor to get it! How am I going to get up?"

"We'll have to walk up, no doubt about it," wailed Eliza. "I know I'm in for a siege with my sciatica after this."

"Who said so?" demanded Augusta. "We won't have to walk up any such. They'll fix that cable before we get up from the dinner table, or I'll know the reason why. I'll start a damage suit for endangering my life, if there's any argument about it!"

"The doors are open," interposed Rhoda faintly. "I think some hot broth will do us all good."

"Where's Lucinda?" yelled Augusta. "Well, I declare, Lucinda, what are you waiting on? Here, you no-account Dexter, get down there and help Mrs. Vaughn up!"

Lucinda hadn't moved. She stood in the elevator just where they had left her, a purplish flush creeping painfully under the wrinkled skin. For she knew something that was yet hidden from the others, she realized with a searing completeness that her secret shame had overtaken her at last. She was dying. It was useless to send Dexter down after her, or to send for Ira and Nina, or to hold Rhoda's lavender smelling-salts close to her nose so she could breathe. She was dying, sinking down, down, to death, another old ladies' home where her youth and her pride lay buried.

She could hear, faintly, a most unseemly commotion above. Her hands caught together, and her fingers interlaced; but when she looked up, the lobby, and all the gaping white faces, had receded into blackness.

SOUTH CAROLINA

The Half-Pint Flask

DUBOSE HEYWARD

I picked up the book and regarded it with interest. Even its format suggested the author: the practical linen-covered boards, the compact and exact paragraphing. I opened the volume at random. There he was again: 'There can be no doubt,' 'An undeniable fact,' 'I am prepared to assert.' A statement in the preface leaped from the context and arrested my gaze:

'The primitive American Negro is of a deeply religious nature, demonstrating in his constant attendance at church, his fervent prayers, his hymns, and his frequent mention of the Deity that he has cast aside the last vestiges of his pagan background, and has unreservedly espoused the doctrine of Christianity.'

I spun the pages through my fingers until a paragraph in the last chapter brought me up standing:

'I was hampered in my investigations by a sickness contracted on the island that was accompanied by a distressing insomnia, and, in its final stages, extreme delirium. But I already had sufficient evidence in hand to enable me to prove——'

Yes, there it was, fact upon fact. I was overwhelmed by the permanence, the unanswerable last word of the printed page. In the fact of it my own impressions became fantastic, discredited even in my own mind. In an effort at self-justification I commenced to rehearse my *impressions* of that preposterous month as opposed to Barksdale's *facts;* my feeling for effects and highly developed fiction writer's imagination on the one hand; and on the other, his cold record of a tight, three-dimensional world as reported by his five good senses.

Sitting like a crystal gazer, with the book in my hand, I sent my memory back to a late afternoon in August, when, watching from the shore near the landing on Ediwander Island, I saw the 'General Stonewall Jackson' slide past a frieze of palmetto trees, shut off her steam, and nose up to the tenuous little wharf against the ebb.

Two barefooted Negroes removed a section of the rail and prepared to run out the gang plank. Behind them gathered the passengers for Ediwander landing: ten or a dozen Negroes back from town with the proceeds of a month's labor transformed into flaming calico, amazing bonnets, and new, flimsy, yellow luggage; and trailing along behind them, the single white passenger.

I would have recognized my guest under more difficult circumstances and I experienced that inner satisfaction that comes from having a new acquaintance fit neatly into a preconceived pattern. The obstinacy of which I had been warned was evident in the thin immobile line of the mouth over the prognathous jaw. The eyes behind his thick glasses were a bright hard blue and moved methodically from object to object, allowing each its allotted time for classification, then passing unhurriedly on to the next. He was so like the tabloid portrait in the letter of the club member who had sent him down that I drew the paper from my pocket and refreshed my memory with a surreptitious glance.

'He's the museum, or collector type,' Spencer had written; 'spends his time collecting facts—some he sells—some he keeps to play with. Incidentally his hobby is American glass, and he has the finest private collection in the state.'

We stood eyeing each other over the heads of the noisy landing party without enthusiasm. Then when the last Negro had come ashore he picked up his bag with a meticulousness that vaguely exasperated me, and advanced up the gang plank.

Perfunctory introductions followed: 'Mr. Courtney?' from him, with an unnecessarily rising inflection; and a conventional 'Mr. Barksdale, I presume,' from me in reply.

The buckboard had been jogging along for several minutes before he spoke.

'Very good of Mr. Spencer to give me this opportunity,' he said in a close-clipped speech. 'I am doing a series of articles on Negroid Primates, and I fancy the chances for observation are excellent here.'

'Negroid Primates!' The phrase annoyed me. Uttered in that dissecting voice, it seemed to strip the human from the hundred or more

Negroes who were my only company except during the duck season when the club members dropped down for the shooting.

'There are lots of Negroes here,' I told him a little stiffly. 'Their ancestors were slaves when the island was the largest rice plantation in South Carolina, and isolation from modern life has kept them primitive enough, I guess.'

'Good!' he exclaimed. 'I will commence my studies at once. Simple souls, I fancy. I should have my data within a month.'

We had been traveling slowly through deep sand ruts that tugged the wheels like an undertow. On either side towered serried ranks of virgin long-leaf pine. Now we topped a gentle rise. Before us was the last outpost of the forest crowning a diminishing ridge. The straight columned trees were bars against a released splendor of sunset sky and sea.

Impulsively I called his attention to it:

'Rather splendid, don't you think?'

He raised his face, and I was immediately cognizant of the keen methodical scrutiny that passed from trees to sea, and from sea back to the last wooded ridge that fell away into the tumble of dunes.

Suddenly I felt his wire-tight grasp about my arm.

'What's that?' he asked, pointing with his free hand. Then with an air of authority, he snapped: 'Stop the cart. I've got to have a look at it.'

'That won't interest you. It's only a Negro burying ground. I'll take you to the quarters tomorrow, where you can study your "live primates."'

But he was over the wheel with surprising alacrity and striding up the slight ascent to the scattered mounds beneath the pines.

The sunset was going quickly, dragging its color from the sky and sea, rolling up leagues of delicately tinted gauze into tight little bales of primary color, then draping these with dark covers for the night. In sharp contrast against the light the burying ground presented its pitiful emblems of the departed. Under the pine needles, in common with all Negro graveyards of the region, the mounds were covered with a strange litter of half-emptied medicine bottles, tin spoons, and other futile weapons that had failed in the final engagement with the last dark enemy.

Barksdale was puttering excitedly about among the graves, peering at the strange assortment of crockery and glass. The sight reminded me of what Spencer had said of the man's hobby and a chill foreboding assailed me. I jumped from the buckboard.

'Here,' I called, 'I wouldn't disturb those things if I were you.'

But my words went unheeded. When I reached Barksdale's side, he was holding a small flat bottle, half filled with a sticky black fluid, and was rubbing the earth from it with his coat sleeve. The man was electric with excitement. He held the flask close to his glasses, then spun around upon me.

'Do you know what this is?' he demanded, then rushed on triumphantly with his answer: 'It's a first issue, half-pint flask of the old South Carolina state dispensary. It gives me the only complete set in existence. Not another one in America. I had hoped that I might get on the trail of one down here. But to fall upon it like this!'

The hand that held the flask was shaking so violently that the little palmetto tree and single X that marked it described small agitated circles. He drew out his handkerchief and wrapped it up tenderly, black contents and all.

'Come,' he announced, 'we'll go now.'

'Not so fast,' I cautioned him. 'You can't carry that away. It simply isn't done down here. We may have our moral lapses, but there are certain things that—well—can't be thought of. The graveyard is one. We let it alone.'

He placed the little linen-covered package tenderly in his inside pocket and buttoned his coat with an air of finality; then he faced me truculently.

'I have been searching for this flask for ten years,' he asserted. 'If you can find the proper person to whom payment should be made I will give a good price. In the meantime I intend to keep it. It certainly is of no use to anyone, and I shan't hesitate for a silly superstition.'

I could not thrash him for it and I saw that nothing short of physical violence would remove it from his person. For a second I was tempted to argue with him; tell him why he should not take the thing. Then I was frustrated by my own lack of a reason. I groped with my instinctive knowledge that it was not to be done, trying to embody the abstract into something sufficiently concrete to impress him. And all the while I felt his gaze upon me, hard, very blue, a little mocking, absolutely determined.

Behind the low crest of the ridge sounded a single burst of laughter, and the ring of a trace chain. A strange panic seized me. Taking him by the arm I rushed him across the short distance to the buckboard and into his seat; then leaped across him and took up the lines.

Night was upon us, crowding forward from the recesses of the forest, pushing out beyond us through the last scattered trees, flowing over the sea and lifting like level smoke into the void of sky. The horse started forward, wrenching the wheels from the clutching sand.

Before us, coming suddenly up in the dusk, a party of field Negroes filled the road. A second burst of laughter sounded, warm now, volatile and disarming. It made me ashamed of my panic. The party passed the vehicle, dividing and flowing by on both sides of the road. The last vestiges of day brought out high lights on their long earth-polished hoes. Teeth were a white accent here and there. Only eyes, and fallen sockets under the brows of the very old, seemed to defy the fading glimmer, bringing the night in them from the woods. Laughter and soft Gullah words were warm in the air about us.

'Howdy, Boss.'

'Ebenin', Boss.'

The women curtsied in their high tucked-up skirts; the men touched hat brims. Several mules followed, grotesque and incredible in the thickening dark, their trace chains dangling and chiming faintly.

The party topped the rise, then dropped behind it.

Silence, immediate and profound, as though a curtain had been run down upon the heels of the last.

'A simple folk,' clipped out my companion. 'I rather envy them starting out at zero, as it were, with everything to learn from our amazing civilization.'

'Zero, hell!' I flung out. 'They had created a Congo art before our ancestors drugged and robbed their first Indian.'

Barksdale consigned me to limbo with his mocking, intolerable smile.

The first few days at the club were spent by my guest in going through the preliminary routine of the systematic writer. Books were unpacked and arranged in the order of study, loose-leaf folders were laid out, and notes made for the background of his thesis. He was working at a table in his bedroom which adjoined my own, and as I also used my sleeping apartment as a study for the fabrication of the fiction which, with my salary as manager of the club, discharged my financial obligations, I could not help seeing something of him.

On the morning of the second day I glanced in as I passed his door, and surprised him gloating over his find. It was placed on the table before him, and he was gazing fixedly at it. Unfortunately, he looked up; our glances met and, with a self-consciousness that smote us simultaneously, remained locked. Each felt that the subject had better remain closed—yet there the flask stood evident and unavoidable.

After a strained space of time I managed to step into the room, pick up a book and say casually:

'I am rather interested in Negroes myself. Do you mind if I see what you have here?'

While I examined the volume he passed behind me and put the flask away, then came and looked at the book with me. 'African Religions and Superstitions,' he said, reading the title aloud; then supplemented:

'An interesting mythology for the American Negro, little more. The African Gullah Negro, from whom these are descended, believed in a God, you know, but he only created, then turned his people adrift to be preyed upon by malign spirits conjured up by their enemies. Really a religion, or rather a superstition, of senseless terror.'

'I am not so sure of the complete obsoleteness of the old rites and superstitions,' I told him, feeling as I proceeded that I was engaged in a useless mission. 'I know these Negroes pretty well. For them, Plat-eye, for instance, is a very actual presence. If you will notice the cook you will see that she seems to get along without a prayer book, but when she goes home after dark she sticks a sulphur match in her hair. Sulphur is a charm against Plat-eye.'

'Tell me,' he asked with a bantering light in his hard eyes, 'just what is Plat-eye?'

I felt that I was being laughed at and floundered ahead at the subject, anxious to be out of it as soon as possible.

'Plat-eye is a spirit which takes some form which will be particularly apt to lure its victims away. It is said to lead them into danger or lose them in the woods and, stealing their wits away, leave them to die alone.'

He emitted a short acid laugh.

'What amusing rot. And I almost fancy you believe it.'

'Of course I don't,' I retorted, but I experienced the feeling that my voice was over-emphatic and failed to convince.

'Well, well,' he said, 'I am not doing folk lore but religion. So that is out of my province. But it is amusing and I'll make a note of it. Plat-eye, did you say?'

The next day was Thursday. I remember that distinctly because, although nearly a week's wages were due, the last servant failed to arrive for work in the morning. The club employed three of them; two women and a man. Even in the off season this was a justifiable expense, for a servant could be hired on Ediwander for four dollars a week. When I went to order breakfast the kitchen was closed, and the stove cold.

After a makeshift meal I went out to find the yard boy. There were only a few Negroes in the village and these were women hoeing in the small garden patches before the cabins. There were the usual swarms of lean mongrel hounds, and a big sow lay nourishing her young in the warm dust of the road. The women looked up as I passed. Their soft voices, as they raised their heads one after another to say 'Mornin', Boss,' seemed like emanations from the very soil, so much a part of the earth did they appear.

But the curs were truculent that morning: strange, canny, candid little mongrels. If you want to know how you stand with a Negro, don't ask him—pat his dog.

I found Thomas, the hired boy, sitting before his cabin watching a buzzard carve half circles in the blue.

'When are you coming to work?' I demanded. 'The day's half done.'

'I gots de toot-ache, Boss. I can't git ober 'fore ter-morrer.' The boy knew that I did not believe him. He also knew that I would not take issue with him on the point. No Negro on the island will say 'no' to a white man. Call it 'good form' if you will, but what Thomas had said to me was merely the code for 'I'm through.' I did not expect him and I was not disappointed.

Noon of the following day I took the buckboard, crossed the ferry to the mainland, and returned at dark with a cheerful, wholesome Negress, loaned to me by a plantation owner, who answered for her faithfulness and promised that she would cook for us during the emergency. She got us a capital supper, retired to the room adjoining the kitchen that I had prepared for her, as I did not wish her to meet the Negroes in the village, and in the morning had vanished utterly. She must have left immediately after supper, for the bed was undisturbed.

I walked straight from her empty room to Barksdale's sanctum, entered, crossed to the closet where he had put the flask, and threw the door wide. The space was empty. I spun around and met his amused gaze.

'Thought I had better put it away carefully. It is too valuable to leave about.'

Our glances crossed like the slide of steel on steel. Then suddenly my own impotence to master the situation arose and overwhelmed me. I did not admit it even to myself, but that moment saw what amounted to my complete surrender.

We entered upon the haphazard existence inevitable with two preoccupied men unused to caring for their own comfort: impossible makeshift meals, got when we were hungry; beds made when we were ready to get into them; with me, hours put into work that had to be torn up and started over the next day; with Barksdale, regular tours of investigation about the island and two thousand words a day, no more, no less, written out in longhand, and methodically filed. We naturally saw less and less of each other—a fact which was evidently mutually agreeable.

It was therefore a surprise to me one night in the second week to leap from sleep into a condition of lucid consciousness and find myself staring at Barksdale who had opened the door between our rooms. There he stood like a bird of ill omen, tall and slightly stooping, with his ridiculous nightshirt and thin slightly bowed shanks.

'I'll leave this open if you don't mind,' he said with a new note of apology in his voice. 'Haven't been sleeping very well for a week or so, and thought the draft through the house might cool the air.'

Immediately I knew that there was something behind the apparently casual action of the man. He was the type who could lie through conviction; adopt some expedient point of view, convince himself that it was the truth, then assert it as a fact; but he was not an instinctive liar, and that new apologetic note gave him away. For a while after he went back to bed, I lay wondering what was behind his request.

Then for the first time I felt it; but hemmed in by the appalling limitations of human speech, how am I to make the experience plain to others!

Once I was standing behind the organ of a great cathedral when a bass chord was pressed upon the keys; suddenly the air about me was all sound and movement. The demonstration that night was like this a little, except that the place of the sound was taken by an almost audible silence, and the vibrations were so violent as to seem almost a friction against the nerve terminals. The wave of movement lasted for several minutes, then it abated slowly. But this was the strange thing about it: the agitation was not dissipated into the air; rather it seemed to settle slowly, heavily, about my body, and to move upon my skin like the multitudinous crawling of invisible and indescribably loathsome vermin.

I got up and struck a light. The familiar disorder of the room sprang into high relief, reassuring me, telling me coolly not to be a fool. I took the lamp into Barksdale's room. There he lay, his eyes wide and fixed, braced in his bed with every muscle tense. He gave me the impression of wrenching himself out of invisible bonds as he turned and sat up on the edge of his bed.

'Just about to get up and work,' he said in a voice that he could not manage to make casual. 'Been suffering from insomnia for a week, and it's beginning to get on my nerves.'

The strange sensation had passed from my body but the thought of sleep was intolerable. We went to our desks leaving the door ajar, and wrote away the four hours that remained until daylight.

And now a question arises of which due cognizance must be taken even though it may weaken my testimony. Is a man quite sane who has been without sleep for ten days and nights? Is he a competent witness? I do not know. And yet the phenomena that followed my first startled awakening entered into me and became part of my life experience. I live them over shudderingly when my resistance is low and memory has its way with me. I know that they transpired with that instinctive certainty which lies back of human knowledge and is immune from the skepticism of the cynic.

After that first night the house was filled with the vibrations. I closed the door to Barksdale's room, hoping a superstitious hope that I would be immune. After an hour I opened it again, glad for even his companionship. Only while I was wide awake and driving my brain to its capacity did the agitation cease. At the first drowsiness it would commence faintly, then swell up and up, fighting sleep back from the tortured brain, working under leaden eyelids upon the tired eyes.

Ten days and nights of it! Terrible for me: devastating for Barksdale. It wasted him like a jungle fever.

Once when I went near him and his head had dropped forward on his desk in the vain hope of relief, I made a discovery. He was the *center*. The moment I bent over him my nerve terminals seemed to become living antennae held out to a force that frayed and wasted them away. In my own room it was better. I went there and sat where I could still see him for what small solace there was in that.

I entreated him to go away, but with his insane obstinacy he would not hear of it. Then I thought of leaving him, confessing myself a coward—bolting for it. But again, something deeper than logic, some obscure tribal loyalty, held me bound. Two members of the same race; and out there the palmetto jungle, the village with its fires bronze against the midnight trees, the malign beleaguering presence. No, it could not be done.

But I did slip over to the mainland and arrange to send a wire to Spencer telling him to come and get Barksdale, that the man was ill.

During that interminable ten days and nights the fundamental difference between Barksdale and myself became increasingly evident. He would go to great pains to explain the natural causes of our malady. 'Simple enough,' he would say, while his bloodshot eyes, fixed on me, shouted the lie to his words. 'One of those damn swamp fevers. Livingstone complained of them, you will remember, and so did Stanley. Here in this subtropical belt we are evidently subject to the plague. Doubtless there is a serum. I should have inquired before coming down.'

To this I said nothing, but I confess now, at risk of being branded a coward, that I had become the victim of a superstitious terror. Frequently when Barksdale was out I searched for the flask without finding the least trace of it. Finally I capitulated utterly and took to carrying a piece of sulphur next to my skin. Nothing availed.

The strange commotion in the atmosphere became more and more persistent. It crowded over from the nights into the days. It came at noon; any time that drowsiness fell upon our exhausted bodies it was there waging a battle with it behind the closed lids. Only with the muscles tense and the eyes wide could one inhabit a static world. After the first ten days I lost count of time. There was a nightmare quality to its unbreakable continuity.

I remember only the night when I saw *her* in Barksdale's doorway, and I think that it must have been in the third week. There was a full moon, I remember, and there had been unusual excitement in the village. I have always had a passion for moonlight and I stood long on the piazza watching the great disc change from its horizon copper to gold, then cool to silver as it swung up into the immeasurable tranquillity of the southern night. At first I thought that the Negroes must be having a dance, for I could hear the syncopation of sticks on a cabin floor, and the palmettos and moss-draped live oaks that grew about the buildings could be seen the full quarter of a mile away, a ruddy bronze against the sky from a brush fire. But the longer I waited listening the less sure I became about the nature of the celebration. The rhythm became strange, complicated; and the chanting that rose and fell with the drumming rang with a new, compelling quality, and lacked entirely the abandon of dancers.

Finally I went into my room, stretched myself fully dressed on the bed, and almost achieved oblivion. Then suddenly I was up again, my fists clenched, my body taut. The agitation exceeded anything that I had before experienced. Before me, across Barksdale's room, were wide open double doors letting on the piazza. They molded the moonlight into a square shaft that plunged through the darkness of the room, cold, white, and strangely substantial among the half obliterated familiar objects. I had the feeling that it could be touched. That hands could be slid along its bright surface. It possessed itself of the place. It was the one reality in a swimming, nebulous cube. Then it commenced to tremble with the vibrations of the apartment.

And now the incredible thing happened. Incredible because belief arises in each of us out of the corroboration of our own life experience; and I have met no other white man who has beheld Plat-eye. I have no word, no symbol which can awaken recognition. But who has not seen heat shaking upward from hot asphalt, shaking upward until the things beyond it wavered and quaked? That is the nearest approach in the material world. Only the thing that I witnessed was colored a cold blue, and it was heavy with the perfume of crushed jasmine flowers.

I stood, muscle locked to muscle by terror.

The center of the shaft darkened; the air bore upon me as though some external force exerted a tremendous pressure in an effort to render an abstraction concrete: to mold moving unstable elements into something that could be seen—touched.

Suddenly it was done—accomplished. I looked—I saw *her*.

The shock released me, and I got a flare from several matches struck at once. Yellow light bloomed on familiar objects. I got the fire to a lamp wick, then looked again.

The shaft of moonlight was gone. The open doors showed only a deep blue vacant square. Beyond them something moved. The lamp light steadied, grew. It warmed the room like fire. It spread over the furniture, making it real again. It fell across Barksdale's bed, dragging my gaze with it. *The bed was empty.*

I got to the piazza just as he disappeared under a wide-armed live oak. The Spanish moss fell behind him like a curtain. The place was a hundred yards away. When I reached it, all trace of him had vanished.

I went back to the house, built a rousing fire, lit all the lamps, and stretched myself in a deep chair to wait until morning.

Then! an automobile horn on Ediwander Island. Imagine that! I could not place it at first. It crashed through my sleep like the trump of judgment. It called me up from the abysses into which I had fallen. It infuriated me. It reduced me to tears. Finally it tore me from unutterable bliss, and held me blinking in the high noon, with my silly lamps still burning palely about me.

'You're a hell of a fellow,' called Spencer. 'Think I've got nothing to do but come to this jungle in summer to nurse you and Barksdale.'

He got out of a big muddy machine and strode forward laughing. 'Oh, well,' he said, 'I won't row with you. It gave me a chance to try out the new bus. That's why I'm late. Thought I'd motor down. Had a hell of a time getting over the old ferry; but it was worth it to see the niggers when I started up on Ediwander. Some took to trees—one even jumped overboard.'

He ended on a hearty burst of laughter. Then he looked at me and broke off short. I remember how his face looked then, close to mine, white and frightened.

'My God, man!' he exclaimed, 'what's wrong? You aren't going to die on me, are you?'

'Not today,' I told him. 'We've got to find Barksdale first.'

We could not get a Negro to help us. They greeted Spencer, who had always been popular with them, warmly. They laughed their deep laughter—were just as they had always been with him. Mingo, his old Paddler, promised to meet us in half an hour with a gang. They never showed up; and later, when we went to the village to find them, there was not a human being on the premises. Only a pack of curs there that followed us as closely as they dared and hung just out of boot reach, snapping at our heels.

We had to go it alone: a stretch of jungle five miles square, a large part of it accessible only with bush hooks and machettes. We dared not take the time to go to the mainland and gather a party of whites.

Barksdale had been gone over twelve hours when we started and he would not last long in his emaciated condition.

The chances were desperately against us. Spencer, though physically a giant, was soft from office life. I was hanging on to consciousness only by a tremendous and deliberate effort. We took food with us, which we ate on our feet during breathing spells, and we fell in our tracks for rest when we could go no farther.

At night, when we were eating under the high, white moon, he told me more of the man for whom we were searching.

'I ought to have written you more fully at the start. You'd have been sorry for him then, not angry with him. He does not suggest Lothario now, but he was desperately in love once.

'She was the most fantastically imaginative creature, quick as light, and she played in circles around him. He was never dull in those days. Rather handsome, in the lean Gibson manner; but he was always—well—matter-of-fact. She had all there was of him the first day, and it was hers to do as she pleased with. Then one morning she saw quite plainly that he would bore her. She had to have someone who could *play*. Barksdale could have died for her, but he could not play. Like that,' and Spencer gave a snap of his fingers, 'she jugged him. It was at a house party. I was there and saw it. She was the sort of surgeon who believes in amputation and she gave it to Barksdale there without an anesthetic and with the crowd looking on.

'He changed after that. Wouldn't have anything he couldn't feel, see, smell. He had been wounded by something elusive, intangible. He was still scarred; and he hid behind the defenses of his five good senses. When I met him five years later he had gone in for facts and glass.'

He stopped speaking for a moment. The August dark crowded closer, pressing its low, insistent nocturne against our ears. Then he resumed in a musing voice: 'Strange the obsession that an imaginative woman can exercise over an unimaginative man. It is the sort of thing that can follow a chap to the grave. Celia's living in Europe now, married—children—but I believe that if she called him today he'd go. She was very beautiful, you know.'

'Yes,' I replied, 'I know. Very tall, blonde, with hair fluffed and shining about her head like a madonna's halo. Odd way of standing, too, with head turned to one side so that she might look at one over her shoulder. Jasmine perfume, heavy, almost druggy.'

Spencer was startled: 'You've seen her!'

'Yes, here. She came for Barksdale last night. I saw her as plainly as I see you.'

'But she's abroad, I tell you.'

I turned to Spencer with a sudden resolve: 'You've heard the Negroes here talk of Plat-eye?'

He nodded.

'Well, I've got to tell you something whether you believe it or not. Barksdale got in wrong down here. Stole a flask from the graveyard. There's been hell turned loose ever since: fires and singing every night in the village and a lot more. I am sure now what it all meant—conjuring, and Plat-eye, of course, to lead Barksdale away and do him in, at the same time emptying the house so that it could be searched for the flask.'

'But Celia; how could they know about her?'

'They didn't. But Barksdale knew. They had only to break him down and let his old obsession call her up. I probably saw her on the reflex from him, but I'll swear she was there.'

Spencer was leaning toward me, the moon shining full upon his face. I could see that he believed.

'Thank God you see it,' I breathed. 'Now you know why we've got to find him soon.'

In the hour just before dawn we emerged from the forest at the far side of the island. The moon was low and reached long fingers of pale light through the trees. The east was swinging nebula of half light and vapor. A flight of immense blue heron broke suddenly into the air before us, hurling the mist back into our faces from their beating wings. Spencer, who was ahead of me, gave a cry and darted forward, disappearing behind a palmetto thicket.

I grasped my machette and followed.

Our quest had ended. Barksdale lay face downward in the marsh with his head toward the east. His hands flung out before him were already awash in the rising tide.

We dragged him to high ground. He was breathing faintly in spasmodic gasps, and his pulse was a tiny thread of movement under our finger tips. Two saplings and our coats gave us a make-shift litter, and three hours of stumbling, agonizing labor brought us with our burden to the forest's edge.

I waited with him there, while Spencer went for his car and some wraps. When he returned his face was a study.

'Had a devil of a time finding blankets,' he told me, as we bundled Barksdale up for the race to town. 'House looks as though a tornado had passed through it; everything out on the piazza, and in the front yard.'

With what strength I had left I turned toward home. Behind me lay the forest, dark even in the summer noon; before me, the farthest hill, the sparse pines, and the tumble of mounds in the graveyard.

I entered the clearing and looked at the mound from which Barksdale had taken the flask. There it was again. While it had been gone the cavity had filled with water; now this had flooded out when the bottle had been replaced and still glistened gray on the sand, black on the pine needles.

I regained the road and headed for the club.

Up from the fields came the hands, dinner bound; fifteen or twenty of them; the women taking the direct sun indifferently upon their bare heads. Bright field hoes gleamed on shoulders. The hot noon stirred to deep laughter, soft Gullah accents:

'Mornin', Boss—howdy, Boss.'

They divided and flowed past me, women curtsying, men touching hat brims. On they went; topped the ridge; dropped from view.

Silence, immediate and profound.

NEW HAMPSHIRE

Death and Transfiguration

ALAN MARSHALL

The wind came in cold over the marshes, bending the crisp stubble of salt hay and printing ripples to be frozen upon the pools left at the ebb of tide; charged with the sea and the smell of distant snow, it knotted Grammer Weare's skirt across her knees, and it drove the mist of her breath back into her face and clustered it in hard beads on her blown hair, and snapped the fringes of her thick black shawl as if they had been small woolen whips. And, heavy and sickening with the scent of frost, the wind froze the damp in her nostrils and made them stick together so that she had to breathe through her mouth and let the wind pierce even the soft roots of her teeth, sending chill gimlets into her jaws and making her sick at her stomach with the pain of cold.

The whole of Folly Mill Road was hardened into troughs and crests of earth where the wagon wheels had been, and the hard earth crumbled under Grammer Weare's feet, now and again casting up yellow sparks from the flint. Grammer Weare clutched her green baize bag, spinning on its black cord and thumping against her shanks as she walked. Her tools and pans in the green bag clinked with a dull sound, like coins in a pocket. She hurried on, seeing the pines in Harper's Hollow, thinking of the warmth to be found behind their thick trunks where the wind was baffled and could not reach her and howled instead among the topmost branches. And an early light in a house seaward of the marsh gleamed like a yellow flower in all the desolation of flat, grey land; so Grammer Weare tucked her green bag under an armpit, keeping her eyes off the warm light, and hurried away from it.

From *Story in America: 1933-1934,* edited by Whit Burnett and Martha Foley,

The Vanguard Press, 1934. Used by permission of the author.

When she came to the mouth of the Hollow, dark under the thick boughs of pine that creaked with the frost in their joints, she ran a few steps into its shelter and seated herself upon a stone, laying her bag across her knees and working her fingers inside her mittens to scrape them warm against the rough wool. It was snug and not yet wholly dark, even in the wood; and only two miles were left. When she had been sitting there a moment or two she heard the sound of feet, and looked up, and saw that the man with the lantern was Poll's Matt walking in with a sack from the town.

'It's a foul night to be about, Grammer Weare,' said Poll's Matt.

'It's no worse than need be,' Grammer Weare said.

'There's snow toward,' Poll's Matt then said.

'Never this night,' Grammer Weare said.

Poll's Matt laid his lantern and sack on the ground. A spine of pebble tore a corner of the sack, letting the salt trickle out over the ground. Poll's Matt looked at Grammer's green bag and said:

'It'll be Ting's girl, won't it? Ting Seaver's girl Doll.'

Grammer Weare watched the white salt build a slow mound near the sack.

'Ting Seaver's no friend of yourn,' she said.

Poll's Matt laughed.

'She's been around big three months now,' Poll's Matt cried out. 'Too big to pole up autumn hay. Ting's got along now, too old to rake the marshes. Ting's old woman's too old to rake marshes. Ting's Hipper won't rake the marshes, he won't but trap lobster. It's up to Ting's girl Doll to rake the marshes now, but she was big this autumn haytime.'

'Ting's girl Doll is frail enough not to rake the marshes,' Grammer Weare said. 'She'll never be a strong woman, that one won't.'

Poll's Matt laughed again; Grammer watched his spilling salt spread in a white pool over the dark ground.

'It's Ting's girl Doll, big and needen you,' Poll's Matt said again, when he had laughed. 'I'll not be fubbed off, Grammer Weare.'

'The wine you drink is made of grapes, Poll's Matt,' she said. Then she laughed; and, warm again, she rose from the stone, dusting the seat of her skirt. She tucked her bag under her armpit and pointed at the sack near the man's feet. 'And the fish you eat is laid up in salt, too,' she said. 'May it not burn your tongue, Poll's Matt.'

Poll's Matt swore and knelt to scrape up the salt, sweeping with his cracked hands over the ground.

'You might have said!' he cried.

'I had naught to say,' Grammer Weare said. 'But now you can munch pebbles in your chowder.'

'Then you can tell Ting's Doll that I've spilled better salt nor this,' Poll's Matt said.

Grammer Weare laughed.

'I would have known that,' she said.

Poll's Matt rose, clutching a stone in his red fist. He stepped across the white stain of salt to Grammer Weare, cursing.

'What you've been told!' he cried. 'You don't know but that!'

Grammer stepped away from him.

'You'll not harm me, Poll's Matt,' she said.

Poll's Matt dropped his stone, and his hand, shaking in the fingers, began to pluck at his lower lip.

'You'll do well to keep an eye on yourself,' Grammer Weare said.

She began to walk away backwards, watching Poll's Matt until he turned and knelt again at his salt, and then she too turned and hurried away at a scuttling gait down the road and past the bend near Turkey Hill. The night had thickened, but was yet clear; for above the pines she could see a few stars blinking in the wind that ran high. But sometimes a gust of wind swept down over the earth and blew what it could find, blowing a pine-cone across the road. The pine-cones, though, were empty in the winter, and their fins were spread open so that they could lay their seeds.

Each man, woman and child of Seabrook village born in the last thirty years had been born into Grammer Weare's hands. Every one of them she had eased out of some woman; every one she had shucked out of some squirming pod of the bleeding flesh, and cut its cord and tied it, had washed the blood from its body and the gum from its eyes. Sometimes the child died, sometimes the mother; sometimes both. When the child died, it was simple; a thing so young—which, indeed, might never have had the breath in its lungs however much the Grammer swung it by its heels and breathed with her own lips into its nostrils—a thing so young and from the start of the woman's time wholly unliving, need only be put in a sack and buried like any thing too rank to keep. It was for Grammer to bury such infants; and if the mother died, to make her ready for burial, too. That also was simple: a matter of straightening the twisted legs, the racked arms, the clawing hands; and if death came later and there had been no one about to ease the dying one, so that there might be a cramp in the legs at death, it was a matter of hamstringing—of cutting the tendons at crotch or knee so that the legs might be brought decently together, side by side, calmly. Then it was a matter of washing the dead thing and changing sheets befouled in death; and, maybe, a matter of getting a pierced lip unclamped from the jaws that gripped it. And the face must be moulded gently, stroked by Grammer Weare's fingers out of anguish and terror, so that when the flesh hardened it would be a calm face, perhaps a face whose lips Grammer's moulding fingers had taught even to smile in peace and resignation.

Underground in the village graveyard there were many such faces, smiling gently; and each smile, until it seeped back into the earth or was chewed away by such things as crawl underground, was the work of Grammer Weare's fingers. Grammer Weare herself smiled, thinking of these things, as she walked out of Harper's Hollow and could see Ting Seaver's shack up the road. Ting Seaver's shack was near the factory which someone had built a year or two back; it was a factory for making shoes, and when the factory had started to make shoes most of the men and women and boys and girls of the village gave up their fishing, their trapping lobsters and digging clams. Before, they had fished through the bright summer, selling their lobsters and clams and salting away their cod and hake and flounders; and in the winter they made lobster-pots and new nets and lines, and ate salt fish. Now they worked in the factory, helping machines to cut and sew shoes, and they lived all year round on what they could buy from the village store. Only a few were left who fished, and husbanded salt hay off the marshes.

And the factory had brought some new blood to the village. There had been little new blood in the village for three hundred years. The Weares and the Seavers and the Morses and the Lowells and all the rest of the village three hundred years ago walked from the ship's landing at Portsmouth; and, finding a river which had fish in it and a harbour at its mouth for fishing-boats, there they had settled and called the place Seabrook, and built cabins and raised children. They had raised governors and lawmakers in the village at first, and sent them to build the state; and they had raised soldiers and sent them to fight the king;

and there had been sea-captains too, who had sailed across all the seas in the world; but then the blood of the village grew thin, and the names in the graveyard and in the village registers became fewer and fewer, although there were as many people in the village as ever there had been. For there were twenty or thirty Morses, and twenty or thirty Seavers, and so on; and then the village raised fishermen only—not men who sailed in ships, but who rowed out beyond the breakers in timid dories and who had large heads and drooping mouths and dull eyes.

Now there was the factory, where the men stood at machines all day long, helping the machines; for the machines could not have made shoes without the men, nor the men without the machines. These men of the village lived with their wives and families in small shacks scattered along the roadsides. The shacks were little wooden shells, chinked up with tar-paper and sometimes even with tufts of hay to keep out the winter cold; they rested among sparse trees or in the lee of spurs of New Hampshire granite which glaciers had dragged down from the mountainsides a million years before. Into this village of hovels few people ever came; motorists followed the Lafayette Highway, skirting the village and seeing only a few roadside farms, neat and well-kept. Young men and boys from over the line in Massachusetts used to hire buggies and drive into the village, hoping to entice girls to follow them into the darkly wooded roads; and the men of the village would set upon the invaders with stones and curses. But sometimes these foragers were successful; then the stock of the village was enriched.

Grammer Weare, walking toward Ting Seaver's shack to care for Ting's Doll, listened to the drone and clatter of the cutting and sewing machines, and to the high snarl of the automatic lathes which turned heels out of the beech forests of the village. Being in winter, it was early dark and the factory was all lighted, and Grammer Weare could see the men standing in rows at their machines, their heads bent over hands trained to work as fast as the machines demanded. Ting's shack was lighted, too, and Grammer Weare walked in without knocking.

Ting himself was seated at the table, trimming the wick of the oil lantern which he would carry when it was time for him to go to the factory and watch through the night when the men had stopped work. Ting's old woman, Gathy, stood at the fire stirring a broth of clams and milk which sent fragrant steam through the room, and almost buried the smell of clothes and bodies and kerosene smoke and tarred cord. Ting's Hipper sat weaving cord into the cone-shaped snare of a lobster-pot. And on a bed near the ladder going up to the loft, Ting's girl Doll lay, not looking up, but gazing at her fingers as they fiddled with a button at the waist of her blue gingham dress.

Grammer Weare shut the door behind her and walked to the table and laid her green baize bag upon its white, scarred surface. No one spoke. Grammer took off her thick shawl and folded it and laid it over the back of a chair and sat down. Hipper looked up at Grammer and then bent his head quickly to gnaw the end of a cord free for splicing. Ting lighted his lantern, and sheared a loose strand of wick so that the flame burned even and clear. And at last Ting's old woman, Gathy, dippered out a mouthful of the broth and tasted it, and put the cover back on the pot, and said to Grammer Weare:

'It's an evil night for you to come over with her, Grammer Weare.'

Grammer Weare stretched her thin legs in the warmth of the room, and looked to the window which was frozen thick at the bottom and spangled with water at the top.

'There's been colder,' she said.

'Will you not take off your bonnet?' Ting Seaver said.

Grammer took off her bonnet and knotted the strings again so that she could hang it over a chair. Then she looked at Ting's Doll, but Ting's Doll would not dare to look at anyone in the room, and lay looking at her own hands.

'She'll be needen you soon,' Ting's Gathy said, 'but we've not had a groan out of her yet.'

'The saucy tart!' Ting's Hipper cried, throwing down the lobster-pot, so that its wooden slats clattered on the floor. 'She'll want you soon, and may she sweat for it!'

'You shut your fat head,' Ting said.

Hipper walked over to the stove and seized up a ladle.

'Give me some broth,' he said.

Ting's Gathy faced him.

'That clam broth's for her,' Gathy said. 'There's none for you here. She'll want all her strength.'

Hipper ladled out a cup of the broth and sat with it in his hands, blowing the steam off the top, and drinking it so hot it burned him, and he swore.

'That's bad talk for now,' Ting said. 'Keep your tongue clean, do you hear?' Then Ting turned to Grammer. 'She'd go foinen at night,

night after night,' he said, 'and now she's got what, Grammer Weare.'

'There's been many a girl with child,' Grammer Weare said.

'Ay, Grammer Weare,' Ting's Gathy said. 'But the way she did it!'

Grammer Weare blew on her nails as if to warm her fingers and said:

'There's yet but one way for a girl to get with child, Ting's Gathy.'

'Every mother's son in this village!' Hipper shouted, with his mouth full of clams and potatoes.

'That's not true, you Hipper,' Ting's Doll said from the couch. Her voice was quiet, and there were tears on her cheeks. 'You might have picked your fill of me before.'

Hipper sprang to his feet again and walked to the bedside and stood looking down at the girl.

'You're a fine whoor to talk,' he said. 'I might whip you yet, you and your big belly.'

'And I might thank you for it,' Ting's Doll said.

'So you'll talk back, eh?' Ting's Hipper said. He plucked a hot clam out of his cup of broth and threw it at the girl. It struck her cheek, and stayed there.

'She would have done better to be whipped long since,' Ting said. 'What she's brought down on this roof!'

'We'll not hold up our heads more,' Ting's Hipper said, and walked back to his chair.

Grammer Weare walked over to the girl, who had not moved, and picked the clam off her cheek. Then she held the clam up to Hipper, and said:

'You'll want to eat this yet?'

Ting's Gathy laughed, but Ting said, 'Shut you up!' So Gathy turned to the fire and began rattling with the pots, putting more salt into the broth and saying, 'It's a caution the way we use salt in this house. When I was a girl we laid out sea water in pans and let the sun dry out the salt. Then it was hard to get and we spared it.'

But all this while Doll had been laughing softly, after she dried the clam broth from her cheek, and she turned to Hipper so that she could look at him, and said:

'Have you eat your clam yet?'

Hipper said nothing, but sat chewing in the corner, turning the tough clams over in his mouth. Ting looked at Doll and began to curse her.

'It ain't enough what you've yet done, but you must laugh,' he said.

'Well, you'll not laugh long, young one, when that babe leaps up in you. You'll sing to another tune then, you will.'

Grammer Weare stood up.

'The house will not be for men this night,' she said.

Ting had already closed his lantern and was pulling on his coat.

'It's time for me to go now,' he said. 'There's but a minute yet for the whistle.'

But Ting's Hipper had laid aside his cup of broth and picked up the lobster-pot and was weaving in the snare, having made the cone of mesh so that it would trap lobsters.

'She'll not drive a man from his work,' Hipper said. 'I can work here with such a blowze in labour.'

Doll laughed.

'Go out,' she cried. 'You'll not have sport of me.'

The whistle on the factory then blew, a siren that clamoured in the cold air and echoed on the hills inland. Then all the machines stopped with a falling note, like the sigh of a huge beast.

'Oh, I'll not?' Hipper said to Doll. 'I'll not, eh?'

Grammer Weare opened her bag and took out some sort of instrument, like a plier with ragged jaws.

'You pack your bones out of here,' Grammer Weare said.

Already the men from the factory were walking in the road past the house. Their voices were loud in the dry cold air, and their feet rang on the frozen earth like the shod hooves of animals. They could be heard laughing up the road, but when they came next to Ting's shack there was a hush fell upon them, and then they could be heard laughing down the road. Doll turned on the bed, groaning.

'What now?' Grammer Weare said, bending over Doll.

'It's not the hurt of my body grieves me, Grammer Weare,' Doll said.

'I know, girl,' said Grammer Weare.

Ting coughed. Then he turned to Hipper.

'You lead your damn feet out of here,' he shouted.

Hipper threw down his lobster-pot and rose and put on his coat. Ting said, 'I'll wait and see that you go, too, and if you show your nose in here before daylight I'll break the last bone under your skin.'

Hipper and Ting walked out, and a blast of chill air puffed through the open doorway. The flame in the lamp flickered, and Doll moaned. Grammer pushed the door shut against the wind and drew the bolt.

'We'll need water,' she said to Gathy.

'There's enough and more in the boiler,' Gathy said.

'And clean linens,' Grammer Weare said.

'I've a basket of clouts, fresh washed, Grammer,' Gathy said.

'Then we've naught to do but wait,' Grammer Weare said.

Doll drew up her legs, and, poising her body's weight upon her heels, moved her body, awkward with its size, across the bed a little. Then she swung over, so that she might rest on her side; but in a moment she rolled to her back again.

'There's suthin moves here, Grammer,' she said, drawing her hand across her belly's rise.

'Ay, but does it hurt you, girl?' Grammer Weare said.

Doll's knees collapsed and straightened, and the knees stiffened so that the toes shook. Her eyes closed and her head lay slowly back.

'Fit to mammock out the heart,' she said.

'Ay, girl,' Grammer Weare said.

Ting's Gathy stood at the stove cutting small cubes of salt pork into a pan. The fatty white flesh, striking the smooth iron, writhed and crackled in the heat, and turned crisp and brown and sent up threads of sharp smoke.

'It seems we might take a cup of broth now, Grammer,' Gathy said. She poured the melted fat and the browned meat into the stew of clams and potatoes, so that the fat lay in yellow pools floating upon the white milk. 'She'll want naught until daybreak.'

Doll cried out from the bed:

'Ah, Grammer, there's suthin toward here now!'

Grammer spooned up some of her broth and started to blow it cool. 'No,' she said. 'This will be a long night, girl.'

'You'll want to let Grammer Weare get the good of this hot,' Ting's Gathy said to Doll; and then she turned to Grammer, saying: 'A night this cold'll take the very heart out of a body.'

The two old women sat at the table, one opposite the other, eating their broth and savouring it slowly on their lips. Gathy ate cautiously, slicing each clam in two with the edge of her spoon upon the bottom of the dish, and gnawing the clams until her teeth had worried all but the last shred of meat from the tough, black necks. She and Grammer tossed the chewed necks of clams into a dish on the table so that Hipper could use the necks, each with its bright edge of yellow meat, as baits to catch sunfish.

'I do make a fine broth,' Gathy said. 'People have heard tell of my broths in all Seabrook, and in Newbury.'

'Ay,' Grammer Weare said. She sat watching Doll, who lay with her body quiet and her arms straight by her sides, with each fist clenched so that a crest of white bone gleamed through the cracked red flesh of her knuckles.

'We'll want to keep the girl all mobled now,' Grammer said. 'She'll need her gown now.'

Gathy rose and walked to a low chest of fine brown wood, whose slender brass handles had grown dull and green in the sea's air. She took a white woolen gown out of a drawer and held it up, showing it to Grammer.

'It's fresh washed this day,' Gathy said proudly.

Grammer walked over to Doll and stood above her.

'Then lay it by the fire,' Grammer said. She leaned over Doll and opened the buttons on her dress. 'Come, girl, you'll want these off now,' she said.

Doll opened her eyes.

'Is it time now, Grammer Weare?' she said. 'My hands are cold.'

'I'll not need to tell you when it's time,' said Grammer, drawing Doll's arms out of her clothing.

'My hands are cold as paddocks,' Doll said; and Grammer began to take her out of her dress.

Doll's body was not a good body; the sun and the winds off the sea had beaten and blown upon her flesh until it was creased and brown on the arms and neck, and on the legs even to the thighs. And her body had not been made shapely by bending knee-deep in the cold mud-flats seeking clam holes after the run of tide, or by rowing to the buoys of lobster-pots in the calm tides at daybreak, or by stilting up salt hay to dry upon clustered poles driven into the marshes. The food she had eaten had not always been good food, being chiefly fish and shell-fish and potatoes and the other things most easily taken from the sea or the land. Grammer eased Doll upwards on the bed, taking off her under-clothing. Her breasts, even heavy as they were with milk, sagged across her armpits, letting the nipples, swollen and cracked and stained purple and dark brown, rest upon the flesh of her arms. Already upon the inner sides of her thighs, below the dark matting at her groins, a fine lacework of blue veins had begun to spread; and the smooth white skin of her belly was now drawn tight, and made ugly by the child within her.

Doll closed her eyes and turned her head aside, and shifted one of her breasts with her hand so that it rested more easily.

'There's been milk?' Grammer Weare said.

'Yes,' Doll said. She laughed briefly. 'I'm like a freshened cow.'

Grammer Weare took one of the nipples of the girl's breasts between her fingers and bent over in the lamplight to look at the white globe of milk coming forth, marbled with yellow. Grammer laughed softly, and said: 'You'll feed him well, girl.'

Then the girl laughed again, and Grammer Weare said:

'Gathy, we'll put on her gown now.'

The two old women put Doll's arms and her head into her gown and drew it, still smelling of the fire's warmth, down over her body to her feet. They laid a tarpaulin on the bed under Doll and drew a soft blanket over it, and then another blanket over Doll. Grammer found a length of tarred rope and cut off a stretch of it and made it fast to the foot of the bed, and knotted the other end of it and gave it to Doll, saying: 'When you feel him move within you, heave on this rope. Brace your feet snug on the footboard and heave for what you're worth. It'll ease you.'

Then the women turned the light low and sat by the fire, waiting. There was no sound in the room but the snuffle of the women breathing, and sometimes a coal snapping in the fire and falling through the grate with a crackle of sparks and a soft puff into the grey powder of ashes. And focused on the girl in the bed, the silence and these small sounds turned and settled slowly in the room, like a whorl of blown fog; but outside the house there were the sounds of night and of the cold, the sea-wind falling, the slow beat of a bell in the harbour buoy, and a deep echo of the cold booming across ice on the inland ponds. Then, in a bulky shadow at one corner of the room, there was a sound of fine claws drawn over the rough grain of wood. Doll turned on her bed, laughing.

'It's a mouse there,' she cried. 'It's but a mad mouse, drunk with the heat.'

She laughed again, letting her voice rise like a wind, filling all the room with laughter. She laid her head back on the pillow, making her body rack and twist with laughter until she was weary and sobbing;

then her breath came deep and loud and Grammer Weare turned up the light, and Doll said:

'It's now, Grammer. It potches at me now, like a skewer.'

The struggle was then long, through the whole night. Sometimes the two old women could but stand watching the girl on the bed; and then they made themselves busy with the fresh white cloths, casting them into a bucket when they were sodden and heavy. Once when there was a silence the girl lay still on the bed waiting for what was left to her and Gathy sponged the girl's face with cool water, and she raised her head and cried softly:

'Grammer Weare, it was never Poll's Matt. It was never Poll's Matt but once.' She let her head rest back on the pillow and cried out: 'This thing has naught to do with Poll's Matt. It was another,' she said when she had her voice again. 'He was suthin like rain, or the sea on a fresh day.'

The girl put out her hand to Grammer Weare.

'Yes, girl,' the old woman said. 'You be one to know such things.'

Then the girl screamed once only, and the night wore on, being measured by the stretch of sinews in the girl's joints and by the quickening rhythm of pain in her body. And then Grammer Weare's hands were busy with the flesh, coaxing blind tissue, using their skill in all this ritual of agony. Sometimes Grammer Weare bent over the girl's face, trying with words to pierce the layers of ecstasy in which the girl's mind and body were muffled, trying to teach the girl that the world's reaches of time and change, men and women, trees and animals, of hills and waters still endured, and would endure without end. But the girl had been lifted apart and made too remote, she had been borne away from place on earth and away from time of night and day of year, being now sense disjoined of flesh. She was now meaning only and not substance, all the stuff of her body having vapoured away from the thing to the sense only; and anguish swelled in the room until it seemed the walls would burst with it.

So morning came slowly and the child was born. When it had been cut free of her and tied, and touched with cold water to make it breathe, and had been cleansed and swaddled in warm clothing, Gathy bent over her again and cried, 'It's me now. It's your mother now!' But Doll lay with her eyes open as if she were looking at the ceiling. Gathy bent over the face again and looked into the eyes, saying: 'Grammer, there might be aught you could do now.'

Grammer Weare left the child and walked over to the bed and sat on its edge, and began to strike the girl's face sharply with the hard palms of her hands. This sharp tempo of flesh raised and quickened in the room, and Grammer cried out: 'Bring me a bit of cold glass, Gathy!' Gathy brought a mirror and the two old women held it at Doll's mouth, peering in the lamplight at the smooth glass to see the grey smudge of the girl's breath clinging to the chill surface, and even sparkling in tiny drops in the yellow light of the room.

'She was always frail,' Gathy said. 'She'd never be a strong woman.'

'There's yet life,' Grammer Weare said.

The two old women waved the smoke of burning feathers over Doll's face, and put whiskey in her mouth, and raised her legs to pour the blood back into her brain. Grammer stopped Doll's mouth with her hand and laid her own mouth over the girl's sharpening nostrils and blew her breath into the girl's body; but the girl moved once only after the blue had come into her lips, and Gathy said: 'Ah, well.'

The two old women looked at each other, having nothing to say. At last Gathy walked over to the stove where the child lay, and began to shake down the ashes, gently.

Grammer Weare looked out of the window and said, 'You might turn down the lamp, now.'

Gathy blew down the lamp-chimney, snuffing the light, for the sun had already begun to glow red and blue at the far rim of the sea. For a moment the world seemed to hang between night and morning, like a pendulum at endswing, so still it was; and then an eddy of gulls whirled over the sea, crying; and the slow chugging of the lobster boats began to sound across the grey marshes. And Gathy said:

'You'll want to have your breakfast with Ting when he comes in?'

'I'll want but a cup of broth this morning,' Grammer said.

Then there was a rattling at the door. Grammer drew the bolt and Hipper walked in, with Poll's Matt following, carrying his lighted lantern.

'How is the girl, now?' Hipper said, swaggering. 'We've come to see.'

Grammer closed the door behind them.

'Then look for yourself,' she said.

She pointed to the bed, and Hipper and Poll's Matt looked and saw the girl under the blanket, and Hipper said, 'Ah, poor girl.' Then he looked back at the bed, and said, 'You've cut a length off the painter for my dory. Ah, well, poor thing.'

But Poll's Matt plucked at his lower lip and said, 'I'll see the babe, then.'

Grammer Weare laughed.

'You'll have naught to do with that infant, you Poll's Matt,' she said.

Poll's Matt coughed and looked about the room. Then he picked up his lantern and walked out of the door and looked back once and began to run up the road. Hipper sprang to the door after him, crying, 'Was it him, then?'

'No,' Grammer Weare said, pushing him back into the room. 'You sit down to your breakfast now.'

'He ran up the road,' Hipper said sulkily.

'You itch yourself no more of him,' Grammer Weare said. 'There's not only butter in his head, Hipper.'

Hipper blew his nose.

'He's a great fool,' Hipper said, picking up the lobster-pot and beginning to weave in the cone-shaped snare of tarred cord. 'He's not been out by night or day this nine year without he carries his lantern always with him.'

The child in the basket began to wail feebly.

'Corbey Dann's Alice is yet with milk,' Gathy said. 'We might get her to nurse this child now.'

'She'll nurse it sure,' Hipper said.

Then Ting came into the house, stamping his feet for the cold. He did not look at the bed, but cried out, 'I had it just now of Gishy Morse. Poll's Matt told him.' Ting looked at the wailing child and laid his basket down by the fire and sat at the table.

'Well, may it please God, she was a good girl when she was younger.'

He began to eat the breakfast which Gathy had laid out for him. 'I'll sleep up above in the loft this day,' he said, at last looking over at the bed.

'We'll give her tending soon,' Grammer Weare said to Gathy, who was sitting by the fire holding her palms in the warmth of the grate, as if they had been cold.

The child had stopped its crying, and already the men were walking down the road on their way to the factory, casting long shadows before them in the red sun and making their boots ring upon the frozen earth. In a few moments the whistle of the factory howled in a siren note, and then the machines set up their undersong of clatter; but inside the house there was only the sound of breathing and eating, the soft plucking of Hipper's fingers among the woven cords of his snare, the tinkle of Grammer Weare putting her instruments back into the green baize bag, and the creaking of Gathy's chair when she shifted her position at the fire.

VIRGINIA

That Woman

NANCY HALE

Men outnumber women by a considerable percentage in the United States, it is reported, and this sounds splendid except that in actual practice in many places there just aren't enough extra men, and a girl has the very devil of a time getting a beau for her exclusive use. This is particularly so in the small proud towns of the South, like Bremen, where the fact of being a woman implies a long battle to get escorted to entertainments, and getting married represents a victory over practically insuperable odds.

When I lived in Bremen there were only three unattached males you could consider having in your house, no matter how pressing the necessity to make an even number, and of these one was sixty, one was twenty-four, and the third had fits; all three were insufferably conceited. Before moving to the South I had heard that southern women were brave, capable characters while southern men were often boors; I soon found that there was truth in this allegation. The men of Bremen were a pretty infuriating lot principally because since the cradle they had known themselves to be in crying demand.

It is a beautiful, oak-shaded, graceful, honeysuckle-scented little town, Bremen. Old country houses with beautiful names—Lutesville, De Courcy, Music Hall—mark at intervals the romantic, rolling countryside. In town the houses are set back from velvet lawns; magnolias and crepe myrtles shade the porches where friends from families that have visited each other since Queen Anne's day gossip and sip juleps. The hours are gently passed in pleasant ways, as though these southerners had long ago given up thoughts of effort or strife and were making lovely each hour on the way to the grave.

If there were plenty of men, surely all would be peace in Bremen. But in Bremen an old maid is an object of pity and shudders of self-congratulation; a girl with a date is one with a considerable triumph to her credit; an engaged girl is one on tenterhooks, who will not be able to relax until the words of the marriage service have mercifully been spoken; a married woman is a successful woman; but a woman like Alida Norris, who has been married four times, is a serpent and a menace and a slur on southern womanhood and worse than that. I said a woman like Alida; there are no other women like Alida in Bremen. To find another husband after one's husband dies is a definite *coup,* and hardly to be expected. But to have the gall to divorce a perfectly good husband, and another, and another, and end up with a fourth, even if he is the town drunk, is cosmic impertinence due for punishment from the gods.

I heard about Alida soon after I moved to Bremen. Her name was not long off people's tongues. I was sitting in Sally Davis' living room drinking a highball in the late afternoon; there were four or five women sitting about having a drink, smoking lazily, unhurriedly, as if there were an eternity for seeing one's friends. The minute Alida's name came up there was a sudden edge in the air. Sally explained for my benefit.

"She was Alida Maupin—as good blood as any in Bremen. First she married Dick Wells, back up country at Perryville, owns a racing stable. We didn't know what to think when she divorced him. Thought he must have tried to kill her; the way Maizie Hankins' husband is always acting up; couldn't think of any other reason; thought she was a fool for throwing away a husband like that when heaven knew where she'd get another. She was always a right pretty girl, went to dances at the University and all when she was young and had plenty of attention; but vague; used to say the craziest things, still does. Well! If she didn't marry Duke Enters, who is, I reckon, the most famous Bremenite we've got; you know, consul or something at Paris, real distinguished man. She married him and went abroad to live, and first thing you knew she was back here in Bremen at her mother's, divorced again. She got Duke while he was young and not famous yet, but he was getting famous by the time she left him, and would you think. . . . Well! We naturally thought that finished Alida for good and all. We thought she must be just naturally crazy, throwing away husbands. And what should she do but marry again. Armistead Butts, the head of the school board and principal of the high school and a most scholarly man, really old family, never looked at a girl before, although of course every girl had been after him for years. We had to hand it to Alida," Sally said grudgingly. "She certainly fooled us. But when she divorced Armistead too we really had had enough of Alida. Didn't have any use for her. Didn't know a good thing when she had it, just flighty and unprincipled and *common,* throwing husbands around like pea pods. And so then she married again, Billy Norris, the most good-for-nothing wastrel Bremen ever had, drinks, sits around all day, not worth the powder and shot to blow him to Kingdom Come. Serves her right. What does she think she is anyway? Cleopatra? I suppose we're just jealous," Sally added to me in a tone designed to make it clear that she was not any such thing. The one thing sure was that she was good and mad just from talking about Alida.

"What has she got that we haven't got?" The question was unconscious and heartfelt; it was put by Miss Letty Coxe, who had never got married and, you could see it in her face, knew now that she never would.

"If she had gone away from here, picked herself up husbands somewhere else, it would be one thing," Virginia Staige said. "But every—single—one—of those husbands of Alida's was a Bremen boy. Now how did she do that, Sally? How do you reckon?"

"Well, she is pretty, you have to give Alida that. She's still just as pretty as she can be, though she must be forty-three, if she's a day. Maybe forty-four. She's got a right pretty figure, and she's funny to listen to sometimes, if you don't go stark staring crazy trying to follow what she's talking about. I don't know how she got them, Virginia. What is it that men want anyway?" There was real, stark tragedy in that question, I thought. There was all the long, frenzied, anxious asking of all the women of Bremen.

"Well, she can have her four husbands but she can't come into my house," Helen Randolph said, and all the women nodded. "I'm through with Alida. I don't care if her grandfather was my grandfather's colonel; she has gone too far and behaved disgracefully and I can't receive her in my house where my children are just growing up. She's a bad woman," Helen said viciously and took a big drink of highball. I suddenly saw fear in her eyes, in her voice. They were all afraid, all of these women. They were terrified of this woman, Alida Norris. She had done the impossible; she had married four separate and distinct times; surely it was not inconceivable that she might at random pluck a husband from some other woman. Terror was in their hearts and distrust in their minds, and deep down inside of all of them they hated her. They were all nice women too, but they knew what trouble was and the frantic search for a husband, and to them Alida Norris could only spell danger.

"I'd like to meet her," I said.

They all looked at me and I could see the same look in all their eyes. You haven't got a husband, they were thinking; you don't have to be afraid of her.

"You won't meet her here," Sally said firmly. "I don't know where you would meet her these days; I don't know a person that doesn't feel about Alida as I do. She just isn't received, she or Billy either, although I may say I feel sorry for him, even if he does get falling-down drunk, which my father always said no gentleman could do no matter how much whiskey he had inside him. Bad blood somewhere, that's what it is. Of course Billy, his grandmother was in Staunton and his great-grandfather went over to the Yankees." Sally looked at me sidewise. "But I don't know where it got in with the Maupins. But it's there. Bad blood. You can always tell."

"I'll point her out to you someday on Jefferson Street while we're marketing," Virginia Staige said. "Or you'll probably meet her, sooner or later, at one of the club dances. You can't keep her out of the club, after all; she is a Maupin, whatever. But I can't invite you to meet her at my house because I just won't have her in it, and that's all there is."

"Of course I understand," I said. But I was obsessed with a desire to meet Alida Norris. The potentialities were enormous. In this quiet town of conventional women, hag-ridden only by the difficulty and necessity of getting married, I had discovered the existence of what sounded like a guaranteed *femme fatale*. She must be something to see indeed, a sort of super southern belle, all beauty and lure, or else brilliant and witty, or—something. Bremen was no place to be a *femme fatale* in; there wasn't anything to work with. But here was a woman who had done it anyway.

Quite a lot of time went by after I first heard of Alida Norris and I didn't meet her. There was a real blockade against her in Bremen society. I thought of her as so fascinating that she kept her husband contented with her sole company; but I wondered, in view of her record, if she wasn't perhaps wearying of him, approaching toward the time when she would divorce him too and accomplish another impossibility, marry a fifth husband. I could not imagine what she would be like. She was my mystery woman. Someone pointed her house out to me, perfectly ordinary house in need of paint. The house told me nothing.

One day in October I went to a cocktail party a little way out in the country. Sally Davis drove me out in her car. It was a characteristic Bremen party, lots of whiskey and soda, or water, to drink, more women than men, and the men behaving the regular Bremen way. At a Bremen party all the men go off and talk among themselves, leaving the women to drink and gossip. The women don't seem to mind a bit; only the unmarried women, looking a little like anxious loose horses, keep drifting in among the men who receive them without enthusiasm. The doctors flock together and talk medicine; the lawyers form groups; the horsemen likewise. It all seemed so uncivilized and boorish of the men, and so meek and resigned of the women, that I was that day especially exasperated. One likes to see women putting out sparkle and magnetism, men making an effort to be charming to the women; here the women sat and drank together and the men stood and drank together.

I was sitting with Sally and two or three other women, when Bourne Davis, Sally's husband, walked past with a fresh drink in his hand. He did not even glance toward us; he was making for the back room and his friends, but Sally called to him, and he turned.

"The children are at Janie Bray's birthday party," she reminded him.

"You'd better go and get them. It's getting late. Come on back here for me after you've picked them up," he said and strolled off.

She began gathering her things together quite unconcernedly. I was suddenly in a rage. I was furious at Bourne's spoiled selfishness and at Sally's acceptance of it, and at the fact that men all treated their wives like this in Bremen and got away with it. The wives ate it up. It was as bad as the Middle Ages; the wives put out everything, ran everything, and the men took it as their right, and there was nothing to be done about it because of the incontrovertible fact that men were at a premium. In Bremen there seemed to be no ignominy too great for a woman to take in order to get and keep her man. I thought that southern men were even worse than I had heard. I was too mad to speak.

After Sally had left I decided to walk home alone and work off my temper. A couple of men offered to drive me home, but I wanted to walk and, besides, I knew how much my acceptance of an offer I should have once thought quite an ordinary one would disturb the wife of whoever made it.

It was exquisitely beautiful outside in the dusk and my rage evaporated almost at once in the cool exalted air. The broad land lay in the twilight, large and generous, rolling in great swells back toward the lights of occasional houses riding on the hills, toward the lights of Bremen shining up from the shallow valley ahead.

The side of the road was deep in fallen leaves and I scuffed along through them; scuffing leaves is a very soothing thing to do. At least, if the social system of Bremen was all wrong, the physical aspect of the place, its sights and smells and sounds were divinely right. I could smell apples and grapes and the indefinable sweetness of the fields, and I could hear cow bells from the pastures and the sound of a church bell tolling the hour faintly, away in the town.

I rounded a curve and there was a car standing on the side of the road. As I got nearer I saw that there was a woman sitting on the running board. I came abreast of her.

"Hello," she said, in one of the most beautiful, liquid voices I have ever heard.

"Hello," I said.

"Isn't it lovely this time of day?" she remarked casually. "I've been sitting here for hours looking at that hillside. It turns a different color every few minutes. It's been orange and then yellow and then blue and now it's dark purple."

This was a most unusual way for anybody to talk in Bremen. You felt that everyone loved the beauty of the country passionately but quite inarticulately; it was a part of their blood, their bone, that they felt without outwardly perceiving.

"I don't think I ever saw such lovely country," I said. I could not see the woman's face clearly. She just sat there, leaning forward with her arms crossed over her knees.

"I'd like to stay here all night," she said.

"It would be fun," I said. I started to walk on. I wanted to talk to the woman, but she seemed so absorbed, so really unconscious of my presence and talking almost as if to herself, that I had a feeling of intrusion. I had got a little way down the road when she called after me.

"I forgot. Do you know anything about cars?"

I walked back.

"Not much," I said. "Is something the matter?"

The woman got up from the running board.

"I was forgetting why I stayed here," she said, and laughed a laugh as lovely and musical as her speaking voice. "I stopped the car to look at the view and then I couldn't get it started again. So I just got out and enjoyed myself."

She got back into the driver's seat and I got in beside her. In the glow from the dashlight I looked at her profile. It was innocent and like a child's, although I could see now that she was in middle age; she had a tipped-up nose and a high smooth forehead. She put her foot on the starter and the engine whirred.

"You see?" she asked triumphantly. "It just won't go. I'd better walk back to town with you. My husband will do something about it. He knows all about cars."

"You haven't got the ignition turned on," I said.

"Oh." She sounded slightly crestfallen. She turned on the switch and the car started at once. I thought of Mrs. Peterkin and all the vague and impractical ladies of fiction.

"I think you'll be all right now," I said and started to get out.

"Oh, but you must let me drive you back to town," she said, and I thought of a little girl exhibiting her best company manners. "I'm Alida Norris. I'm Mrs. William Norris. You must let me take you home."

Wild horses could not have dragged me from that car. I introduced myself.

"You're from the North," she said. "Mr. Wilson at the drugstore told me all about you. He says you buy lots of sodium bicarbonate. I hope you don't have stomach-aches. You live in the Marbin house, don't you?"

I have never felt such tangible, irresistible charm radiating from anyone. She was facing me now eagerly, and I could see her face. It was a child's face, alive, unconscious. Its most beautiful feature was the mouth. The mouth was large and soft and mobile and as delicate and sensitive as a young girl's.

As we drove into the outskirts of town she suddenly turned to me, breaking off a conversation in the middle; it was a charming, impulsive turning, but it nearly killed us because two cars were passing just at that moment, and as Alida Norris turned her body she turned the wheel too. I did a moment's intensive praying.

"My," she remarked when the bad moment was over. "There are so many crazy drivers, aren't there? I was going to say: don't go home, come and meet my husband. He'd just love to meet you. You aren't a bit northern and I'd like to prove it to him northern women can be real nice. You see, I know it anyway. I've traveled. I've lived in Paris, Le Havre, New York and Washington, D. C.," she added.

"I'd love to come," I said fervently.

"I want you to see Billy. Billy's wonderful. He could be anything he wanted to. He can fix cars and electric lights and plumbing, and even the stove. I never knew anyone like Billy. And I ought to know; I've been married three times before. I suppose you've heard that," she said, more mournfully than anything else. "They were all perfectly wonderful men. *Wonderful* men. But there's never been anybody like Billy. He's so nice to me," she said in an ecstatic voice. I could not imagine anyone not being nice to her. Also my preconceived ideas of Bremen's *femme fatale,* the caster-off of husbands, were being badly confused by this ingenuous, enthusiastic, affectionate creature. She was more a mystery woman than ever to me.

She stopped the car.

"This isn't the house," she said. "The house is three houses back. But I always stop the car here. It spoils the view out of my front windows, and I'm perfectly sure the Carters—they live in this house—don't mind having their view spoiled."

We got out and walked back. We went up an untidy front walk and through a front door that opened directly into a large shabby living room. Although it was in disorder, the room had charm. It looked like a room in an antique store. Nothing was in place; a pile of Wedgwood plates stood on the floor under a Hepplewhite desk; a lovely old flower print lay flat, face up, on an end table; a screen that looked like a Coromandel stood meaninglessly in the middle of the room. There was a man sitting by the open fire with a glass in his hand; he got up as we came in.

"This is Billy. He's just having a drink. He drinks too much," Alida Norris said proudly. Again I thought of a little girl, this time showing off.

The man laughed and shook hands. He was not an attractive man. He was short and sloppily dressed and he had a bad, grayish complexion. But he had gentle, intelligent eyes. Alida put her arms around him and kissed him. It was quite obvious that they were both very much in love with each other.

"You'll have a drink, won't you?" she said to me. "We'll all have a drink. Billy, you get them."

"There aren't any more of the glasses," he said, getting up.

"Oh, gosh. So there aren't. Well, there are the other glasses in a basket under the table in the hall, darling. They're awfully dirty. But alcohol sterilizes things," she said to me.

Billy Norris got us drinks and we all sat around the fire. It was somehow very happy. You feel it when you are with happy people. We were all rather childish and laughed a lot. I liked them both enormously. They were both absolutely simple.

Alida with her charm and beauty was perfectly irresistible. Her violently illogical remarks, her trains of thought made me laugh and they made her husband laugh too. He was the first man I had met in Bremen who didn't act like a lord of creation. He was just himself. He was extremely pleasant to me and attentive to his wife. I never saw a man with better married manners. But there was no two ways about it, he was a nondescript, unimpressive little man. As time went on it was apparent that he was feeling his liquor.

"Billy's getting drunk," Alida said to me. "Aren't you, Billy?"

"Unh-hunh. Gettin' drunk now," he said cheerfully.

To someone who does not know Bremen this interchange of remarks may not seem significant, but I had been living in Bremen for some time by then, and I had seen too many husbands asserting with a proud and didactic air that they never got drunk when they were obviously reeling, and too many wives not daring to take the wheel of the car when their husbands were quite incompetent to drive safely, not to realize that in the South ability to hold his liquor is almost the ultimate point of a man's pride, and that wives are taken to task for far less than questioning that point.

I thought it was time for me to leave, and I said good-by to Alida. I asked her if she would not come in to lunch on the following Tuesday.

"Tuesday," she said reflectively. "Tuesday—let's see, that's Thursday. Yes, I'd love to."

God knew what she meant. I left. When I got to know Alida better I realized that in her funny mind were all sorts of special systems for things. Tuesday unquestionably was Thursday by some personal mathematics of her own, and black was white and the moon was green cheese.

I thought, in view of the opinions I had heard expressed, I should tell the women I invited to lunch on Tuesday that Alida was coming. As soon as they knew that they promptly declined in no uncertain terms. Sally Davis hauled me over the coals for even suggesting that she come to lunch with that woman.

"You might as well understand that none of us are going to tolerate Alida for one moment," she said over the telephone. "She's ostracized herself permanently in Bremen by her carryings on. I won't come to lunch with a woman who's been married four times, and that's that. And I'm surprised at you asking her. But of course, you're a Yankee," she said condescendingly. "I know people are right broadminded up North. But you can't be too broadminded down here. I'm just warning you, darlin'. I mean people just aren't going to put up with Alida. You can't have her and us. She's a hardhearted, fickle, common woman. Four husbands!" Sally went on about it for some time; people talk for hours on the telephone in the South.

And so Alida and I had lunch alone on Tuesday. By the time we left the dining room it was impossible not to feel that I had known Alida long and well. She had the gift of intimacy without effrontery. She had charm and style and a wit of her own. She was by far the most attractive woman in Bremen. I understood, all right, about how she found herself four husbands, and why the hand of every woman in Bremen was against her. She was a real honest-to-God charmer.

We sat in the little drawing-room. Over the mantel was a painting by a friend of mine of the Ile St. Louis.

"I know that place!" Alida explained. "I told you I'd lived in Paris. That was when I was married to my second husband. He was a vice-consul. Named Duke Enters. My, he was handsome." She said it with frank admiration.

"Duke was the handsomest man I ever saw, ever. I used to love his ears. I remember I told the consul to look and see how beautiful Duke's ears were. He was awful mad at me that time. I wish you could have seen him then! You've probably seen his picture. But then! Oh, he was so tall and dark and kind of American looking, it gave you a thrill to look at him. Like looking at the American flag. He looked so handsome in his clothes. He looked handsome out of them too but he never liked me to say that. He liked his clothes himself, I do think. Liked to have them kept pressed and all that. I was so awful, I never remembered. Somehow I never can remember about clothes. Once we were staying at the George V and I threw his tailcoat out of the window. He was good and mad that time."

The picture she was calling up of herself was irresistible to me. I could see why men would be mad about her, even more than I had before. A young Alida, fresh and gay and irresponsible, as natural as the wind, vague and bat-brained and lovely—no wonder she had had a success with men. But with her outspoken admiration of Enters I wondered what had made her divorce him. There are some things one can't ask, and since she was so frank about everything else and volunteered no information on that point I concluded that it must have been for a very good and very personal reason. Perhaps her third husband had won her away from her second. I asked about the third husband—what was he like?

"Armistead? Now, you would have adored Armistead. I did. Except I wasn't good enough for him; I mean I don't know anything and Armistead knew everything. I guess Armistead had read every book that ever got printed. He loved books. Really loved them. It used honestly to hurt him when I did awful things, like leave books open face down, or bend the corners of pages back. I ought to have learned but I never could somehow. And when I was cross one morning and threw a lot of books around the room it just about killed him. I used to feel so guilty. Afterward. It used to humiliate him awfully how dumb I was when we went out. I never knew what he was talking about and he did talk about such fancy things."

I thought I could guess why Alida had divorced that one. The pedantic grade had been one she couldn't make and I didn't blame her. Armistead sounded terrible to me. One of the most disarming things about Alida, I thought, was the way she always told the bad tales on herself and never blamed anyone else. She hadn't said a critical or unchivalrous word about either of the husbands she had discussed; she had loudly sung their praises, and, seeing that she had found it necessary to get rid of them, I thought it was very sporting of her.

A few days later I went to see Alida at her house, stopped in on my way back from a luncheon party. As I walked up to the house I saw a man in painter's overalls sitting on the doorstep, occupied in some curious way not connected with painting. Alida came running out.

"Hi! I'm so glad to see you!"

"Would you mind telling me what that man is doing?" I asked. I could see what he was doing now. He was picking up silk stockings from a pile of them next to him, running his hand up each one and scrutinizing it, then rolling them up in pairs into neat little balls.

"Oh. He's the man who's painting the kitchen. I asked him if he'd mind sorting my stockings and he said he'd love to. I can't see why. I just hate to sort stockings. They accumulate for months in my bureau drawer."

She led the way into that strange antique shop of a living-room. We sat and smoked together in the pleasant atmosphere of being old friends. Alida looked perfectly lovely. Her soft, red, sweet mouth was all quivering with smiles and her eyes beamed. She sat at the end of a sofa with her pretty legs hanging over the arm, playing with a china zebra that stood among green china glasses.

"I was married to a horseman first, you know," she said. "This zebra makes me think of it. I guess that would make Dick pretty mad if he heard me say it, as if zebras had anything to do with horses. But they have, haven't they? I don't know why horsemen are so fussy about names. You mustn't call hounds dogs, you know," she said like a little girl repeating a lesson. She sighed. "Dick was my first love. I fell in love with him while my hair was still down my back. He was such a marvelous horseman and he looked so wonderful in his pink coat—you mustn't say red—and his top hat when he was out hunting. I was just crazy about him.

"I used to try so hard to get interested in horses because he wanted me to. But I just *can't* make myself get so excited about an animal. I mean that way. Of course I always was interested in the wrong animal. The fox. I used to feel sorry for the fox, and you mustn't feel sorry for the fox; it kills chickens or something. I hate chickens. Once I was out in the pony cart when they were hunting and the hunt came by me and the huntsmen asked me which way the fox had gone and I told them the opposite way. Wasn't that awful? I don't think Dick ever forgave me. He was good and ashamed of me. I couldn't seem to learn to ride right. I fell off so much. My, I hated it! But I did try. Honestly I did. But I've always been scared of horses. They look like wild animals to me, with those big mouths, and I always feel as if they were going to put their heads round and bite me when I'm on top of one. I mean mounted. I always think a horse would look better behind bars—like a lion—than out loose there in the fields, don't you? Dick used to tell me that they were scared of me, but I didn't believe him for a minute. I was awful. I don't blame Dick for being mad at me most of the time."

I had come to deliver an invitation. I wanted Alida and Billy to have dinner with me at the dance at the club next Saturday. Alida said they'd love to.

"But you ought not to be seen with me," she said quite cheerfully. "People think I'm awful, you know, on account of all those husbands and everything. You mustn't get criticized for going around with me."

Her humility, her gentleness and frankness touched me deeply.

"I like you better than anyone I've met in Bremen," I said. "And I'll see you all you'll let me."

She gave me a beautiful smile.

When I first came to Bremen I thought perhaps club dances would be a cut above ordinary parties—that the men would stay with the women perforce, since surely a dance is designed for the glorification of the female. But they were only a little bit better, or, rather, better for only part of the time. People sat in parties at tables and danced during the early evening. The music was rather good, and everyone of course knew everyone else, and the stage seemed set for gaiety. But along about eleven or midnight the blight would strike. The men would drift off into the smoking room and the bar, to talk to one another, and the women would be left high and dry at the tables to twiddle their thumbs. I had grown increasingly enraged at a succession of these dances, and it was a relief at this one to have my own table which I hoped to be able to run as I pleased. It was a table for four—the Norrises and one of the three extra men—I think it was the old one—and myself.

The extra man, I remember, annoyed me by acting as if he were seated at table with the Scarlet Woman of Babylon. He kept his eyes downcast and replied to Alida's amusing sallies in mumbles, or else leered at her in a manner I considered offensive and which she ignored. She was at her most dazzling that night. She had on a gold dress that showed her pretty shoulders, and if ever I saw a woman intended to be surrounded by adoring and competitive admirers, she was the woman.

Her husband was not much of a conversational addition but he did seem to appreciate Alida. It was plain that he was crazy about her. When he danced with her he looked down at her with the look that men have for women who enchant them utterly. He was a funny, drab little man for Alida to be married to, I thought, especially after the romantic or impressive characters she had described her other husbands as. But she loved him, you saw that. She seemed perfectly satisfied with him, and with his drinking, of which he was doing plenty that evening.

Alida had hardly anything to drink, but she seemed more than ever intoxicated with the fact of being alive. She played absurd games with the silverware on the table, a sort of involved tiddlywinks to pop a spoon into a glass of water. I was aware of disapproving glances thrown at our table, but either she did not see them or did not care.

"There are a lot of the horsy people here tonight," I said at one point.

"These ones are mostly Yankees," Alida said, squinting her eyes up and looking round the room. "That's the way to get somewhere down here. Buy a big place and a lot of horses and then climb the social ladder dung by dung."

Billy Norris laughed uproariously. The extra man looked a little shocked and I could have slapped him. The hour was growing later and the men in the room were beginning their customary thinning out. More and more women sat unattended at their tables, gossiping of this and that and of, no doubt, us. Billy Norris was getting good and drunk. The fact seemed to amuse both him and Alida. Billy kept propping his elbow on the table and letting it drop off, at which both of them would laugh.

Finally he got up in a sort of diagonal way and excused himself. We waited, and he did not come back. It was well on to two o'clock.

"I suppose he's joined the masculine circles in the bar," I said bitterly.

"I don't think so," Alida said. "They bore Billy. He's probably just off finishing up his drinking."

We waited for awhile longer and still he did not come. My earlier approval of him was being dissolved by annoyance at this treatment of Alida.

"Do you think we ought to send someone to look for him?" I asked her, glancing meaningly at the extra man who had been looking wretched for hours. I knew he wanted to get away and I was not going to let him go.

"All right. Go and look for Billy," Alida said to the extra man.

He went and he did not come back. Nobody came back.

"Well, what do we do now?" I said after a long time.

Alida looked quite happy. She was drawing a picture on the tablecloth. It seemed to be some cats with their tails curled under them sitting on top of an elephant seen rear to.

"You take me home," she said. "What's-his-name will never turn up if he hasn't turned up now. And Billy's probably gone long ago and taken our car."

"And left you here?"

"He likes to go back in the mountains toward Sugar Hollow and wake up the mountaineers and drink with them," she explained. "It reminds him of his youth in Prohibition when he had to buy corn liquor back up there. He's all right."

We left and I drove her back into town to her house. I waited while she went up the path, for her to get in safely. But she turned and came back to me.

"I forgot. Billy's got the key. I can't get in. It just shows how silly it is to lock doors anyway. You just lock yourself out."

"You come right home with me and spend the night," I said.

"That's right sweet of you. I'd love to," she said contentedly, and climbed back into the front seat.

But I was really indignant now. Billy Norris was just another insufferable male with no consideration for his wife. Leaving her stranded at a party, and going off with the key so that she couldn't even go home. . . .

When we got back to my house I showed Alida her room and got her a nightgown and a toothbrush.

She curled up on the bed; so many of the things she did reminded me of a very small girl.

"Don't go away yet," she said, smiling coaxingly. "Let's talk. It's fun spending the night out."

I sat down in the armchair and put my feet up. The feeling of intimacy and affection I had for Alida was extraordinary; she gave out warmth and friendliness and love.

"I'm beginning to feel like one of those women with a Cause," I said. "All I do is get madder and madder at the men down here in the South. I think they really do behave too abominably. Billy just going off and leaving you in the lurch is the last straw. I should think you would be furious."

Alida lay on her back with her hands behind her head and looked at the ceiling.

"I don't mind one bit. Billy really loves me. And I just love to be loved. I don't mind anything as long as I'm loved. I like to love people and have them love me back. Billy loves me back, lots, and he doesn't mind the awful things I do. He thinks I'm funny."

"Well, who would mind? You know you're a perfectly fascinating woman and your vagueness just makes you more amusing."

"My other husbands minded," Alida said mildly. "They minded terribly. I made them just as mad as the devil."

"The saps. I suppose that was why you had to divorce them."

"Oh, I didn't divorce them!" Alida said in a tone of childlike surprise. "They asked me for a divorce, all three of them. They couldn't stand me. Billy is the only man who has ever been able to stand me."

I have never been more astonished.

"You mean to tell me those men *wanted* to be divorced from you?" The whole picture was changing violently.

"They certainly did want to be divorced from me. I reckon people fall in love with me sometimes, but nobody except Billy has ever been able to stay married to me."

"But . . . why? You're the most attractive woman in Bremen."

"You're sweet to say so. But I haven't any whatyoumaycallit, dignity, *you* know. I spoiled their dignity. Bremen men have an awful lot of dignity. They want their wives to reflect to their credit, and I was so undignified. They all ended by being ashamed of the things I did, ashamed of me. I loved all of them, you know; I guess I would have been happy with any one of them. But they just couldn't keep on loving me after the way I would disgrace them. You know the way I act. I can't seem to help it. Billy loves me the way I am. Billy doesn't worry about dignity."

"It's the most preposterous thing I ever heard. Why, in the North the amusing things you do and say would just make you all the more sought after, would make a northern man all the crazier about you. It's just these damned, pompous, spoiled southerners . . ."

"Oh, but I love it here down home. I like it lazy, living."

"I suppose you know everyone thinks you just tossed your husbands aside. Nobody has the faintest idea, nobody could have the faintest idea, that they were the ones who wanted a divorce," I said finally.

"Honestly?" Alida's childlike eyes were large and astonished. "Isn't that funny! Imagine anyone thinking I would want to divorce wonderful, attractive men like that! Aren't people funny?" she said.

NEW YORK

Search Through the Streets of the City

IRWIN SHAW

When he finally saw her, he nearly failed to recognize her. He walked behind her for a half block, vaguely noticing that the woman in front of him had long legs and was wearing a loose, college-girl polo coat and a plain brown felt hat.

Suddenly something about the way she walked made him remember —the almost affected rigidity of her back and straightness of throat and head, with all the movement of walking, flowing up to the hips and stopping there, like Negro women in the South and Mexican and Spanish women carrying baskets on their heads.

For a moment, silently, he watched her walk down Twelfth Street, on the sunny side of the street, in front of the little tired gardens behind which lay the quiet, pleasantly run-down old houses. Then he walked up to her and touched her arm.

"Low heels," he said. "I never thought I'd live to see the day."

She looked around in surprise, then smiled widely, took his arm.

"Hello, Paul," she said. "I've gone in for health."

"Whenever I think of you," he said, "I think of the highest heels in New York City."

"The old days," Harriet said. They walked slowly down the sunny street, arm in arm, toward Sixth Avenue. "I was a frivolous creature."

"You still walk the same way. As though you ought to have a basket of laundry on your head."

"I practiced walking like that for six months. You'd be surprised how much attention I get walking into a room that way."

Originally published in *The New Yorker,* August 2, 1942. Used by permission of the author.

"I wouldn't be surprised," Paul said, looking at her. She had black hair and pale clear skin and a long, full body, and her eyes were deep gray and always brilliant, even after she'd been drinking for three days in a row.

Harriet closed her coat quickly and walked a little faster. "I'm going to Wanamaker's," she said. "There're a couple of things I have to buy. Where are you going?"

"Wanamaker's," Paul said. "I've been dying to go to Wanamaker's for three years."

They walked slowly, in silence, Harriet's arm in his.

"Casual," Paul said. "I bet to the naked eye we look casual as hell. How do you feel?"

Harriet took her arm away. "Casual."

"O.K. Then that's how I feel, too." Paul whistled coldly to himself. He stopped and looked critically at her and she stopped, too, and turned toward him, a slight puzzled smile on her face. "What makes you dress that way?" he asked. "You look like Monday morning in Northampton."

"I just threw on whatever was nearest," Harriet said. "I'm just going to be out about an hour.

"You used to look like a nice big box of candy in your clothes." Paul took her arm again and they started off. "Viennese bonbons. Every indentation carefully exploited in silk and satin. Even if you were just going down to the corner for a pint of gin, you'd look like something that ought to be eaten for dessert. This is no improvement."

"A girl has different periods in clothes. Like Picasso," Harriet said. "And if I'd known I was going to meet you, I'd've dressed differently."

Paul patted her arm. "That's better."

Paul eyed her obliquely as they walked: the familiar, long face, the well-known wide mouth with always a little too much lipstick on it, the little teeth that made her face, when she smiled, looked suddenly like a little girl's in Sunday school.

"You're getting skinny, Paul," Harriet said.

Paul nodded. "I'm as lean as a herring. I've been leading a fevered and ascetic life. What sort of life have you been leading?"

"I got married." Harriet paused a moment. "Did you hear I got married?"

"I heard," Paul said. "The last time we crossed Sixth Avenue together the L was still up. I feel a nostalgic twinge for the Sixth Avenue L."

They hurried as the light changed. "On the night of January ninth, 1940," Paul said, holding her elbow, "you were not home."

"Possible," Harriet said. "I'm a big girl now; I go out at night."

"I happened to pass your house, and I noticed that the light wasn't on." They turned down toward Ninth Street. "I remembered how hot you kept that apartment—like the dahlia greenhouse in the Botanical Gardens."

"I have thin blood," Harriet said gravely. "Long years of inbreeding in Massachusetts."

"The nicest thing about you," Paul said, "was you never went to sleep."

"Every lady to her own virtue," Harriet said. "Some women're beautiful, some're smart—me—I never went to sleep. The secret of my great popularity. . . ."

Paul grinned. "Shut up."

Harriet smiled back at him and they chuckled together. "You know what I mean," he said. "Any time I called you up, two, three in the morning, you'd come right over, lively and bright-eyed, all the rouge and mascara in the right places. . . ."

"In my youth," said Harriet, "I had great powers of resistance."

"In the morning we'd eat breakfast to Beethoven. The Masterwork Hour. WNYC. Beethoven, by special permission of His Honor, the Mayor, from nine to ten." Paul closed his eyes for a moment. "The Little Flower, Mayor For Lovers."

Paul opened his eyes and looked at the half-strange, half-familiar woman walking lightly at his side. He remembered lying close to her, dreamily watching the few lights of the towers of the night-time city, framed by the big window of his bedroom against the black sky, and one night when she moved sleepily against him and rubbed the back of his neck where the hair was sticking up in sharp little bristles because he had had his hair cut that afternoon. Harriet had rubbed them the wrong way, smiling, dreamily, without opening her eyes. "What a delicious thing a man is . . ." she'd murmured. And she'd sighed, then chuckled a little and fallen asleep, her hand still on the shaven back of his neck.

Paul smiled, remembering.

"You still laughing at my clothes?" Harriet asked.

"I remember something I heard some place . . ." Paul said. " 'What a delicious thing a man is . . .' "

Harriet looked at him coldly. "Who said that?"

Paul squinted suspiciously at her. "Oswald Spengler."

"Uhuh," Harriet said soberly. "It's a famous quotation."

"It's a well-turned phrase," said Paul.

"That's what I think, too." Harriet nodded agreeably and walked a little faster.

They passed the little run-down bar where'd they'd sat afternoons all winter drinking martinis and talking and talking, and laughing so loud the people at the other tables would turn and smile. Paul waited for Harriet to say something about the bar, but she didn't even seem to notice it. "There's Eddie's Bar," Paul said.

"Uhuh." Harriet nodded briskly.

"He's going to start making his martinis with sherry when all the French vermouth runs out," Paul said.

"It sounds horrible." Harriet made a face.

"Is that all you have to say?" Paul said loudly, remembering all the times he'd looked in to see if she was there.

"What do you want me to say?" Harriet looked honestly puzzled, but Paul had never known when she was lying to him or telling the truth, anyway, and he hadn't improved in the two years, he discovered.

"I don't want you to say anything. I'll take you in and buy you a drink."

"No, thanks. I've really got to get to Wanamaker's and back home in a hurry. Give me a raincheck."

"Yeah," Paul said sourly.

They turned up Ninth Street toward Fifth Avenue.

"I knew I'd meet you some place, finally," Paul said. "I was curious to see what would happen."

Harriet didn't say anything. She was looking absently at the buildings across the street.

"Don't you ever talk any more?" Paul asked.

"What *did* happen?"

"Every once in a while," he started, "I meet some girl I used to know . . ."

"I bet the country's full of them," Harriet said.

"The country's full of everybody's ex-girls."

Harriet nodded. "I never thought of it that way, but you're right."

"Most of the time I think, isn't she a nice, decent person? Isn't it wonderful I'm no longer attached to her? The first girl I ever had," Paul said, "is a policewoman now. She subdued a gangster singlehanded in Coney Island last summer. Her mother won't let her go out of the house in her uniform. She's ashamed for the neighbors."

"Naturally," Harriet said.

"Another girl I used to know changed her name and dances in the Russian Ballet. I went to see her dance the other night. She has legs like a Fordham tackle. I used to think she was beautiful. I used to think you were beautiful, too."

"We were a handsome couple," Harriet said. "Except you always needed a shave. That electric razor . . ."

"I've given it up."

They were passing his old house now and he looked at the doorway and remembered all the times he and Harriet had gone in and come out, the rainy days and the early snowy mornings with the milkman's horse silent on the white street behind them. They stopped and looked at the old red house with the shabby shutters and the window on the fourth floor they had both looked out of time and time again to see what the weather was and Paul remembered the first time, on a winter's night, when he and Harriet had gone through that door together.

"I was so damn polite," Paul said softly.

Harriet smiled, knowing what he was talking about. "You kept dropping the key and saying, 'Lord, Lord,' under your breath while you were looking for it."

"I was nervous. I wanted to make sure you knew exactly how matters stood—no illusions. Good friends, everybody understanding everybody else, another girl coming in from Detroit in six weeks, no claims on me, no claims on you . . ." Paul looked at the window on the fourth floor and smiled. "What a fool!"

"It's a nice, quiet street," Harriet said, looking up at the window on the fourth floor, too. She shook her head, took Paul's arm again. "I've got to get to Wanamaker's."

They started off.

"What're you buying at Wanamaker's?" Paul asked.

Harriet hesitated for a moment. "Nothing much. I'm looking at some baby clothes. I'm going to have a baby." They crowded over to one side to let a little woman with four dachshunds pass them in a busy tangle. "Isn't it funny—me with a baby?" Harriet smiled. "I lie around all day and try to imagine what it's going to be like. In between, I sleep and drink beer to nourish us. I've never had such a good time in all my life."

"Well," said Paul, "at least it'll keep your husband out of the army."

"Maybe. He's a raging patriot."

"Good. When he's at Fort Dix I'll meet you in Washington Square Park when you take the baby out for an airing in its perambulator. I'll put on a policeman's uniform to make it proper. I'm not such a raging patriot."

"They'll get you anyway, won't they?"

"Sure. I'll send you my picture in a lieutenant's suit. From Bulgaria. I have a premonition I'm going to be called on to defend a strategic point in Bulgaria."

"How do you feel about it?" For the first time Harriet looked squarely and searchingly at him.

Paul shrugged. "It's going to happen. It's all damned silly, but it isn't as silly now as it was ten years ago."

Suddenly Harriet laughed.

"What's so funny?" Paul demanded.

"My asking you how you felt about something. I never used to have a chance . . . You'd let me know how you felt about everything. Roosevelt, James Joyce, Jesus Christ, Gypsy Rose Lee, Matisse, Yogi, liquor, sex, architecture . . ."

"I was full of opinions in those days." Paul smiled a little regretfully. "Lust and conversation. The firm foundations of civilized relations between the sexes."

He turned and looked back at the window on the fourth floor. "That was a nice apartment," he said softly. "Lust and conversation . . ."

"Come on, Paul," Harriet said. "Wanamaker's isn't going to stay open all night."

Paul turned up his collar because the wind was getting stronger as they neared Fifth Avenue. "You were the only girl I ever knew I could sleep in the same bed with."

"That's a hell of a thing to say to a girl." Harriet laughed. "Is that your notion of a compliment?"

Paul shrugged. "It's an irrelevant fact. Or a relevant fact. Is it polite to talk to a married lady this way?"

"No."

Paul walked along with her. "What do you think of when you look at me?" he asked.

"Nothing much," Harriet said carefully.

"What're you lying about?"

"Nothing much," Harriet said flatly.

"Don't you even think, 'What in the name of God did I ever see in him?' "

"No." Harriet put her hands deep in her pockets and walked quickly along the railings.

"Should I tell you what I think of when I look at you?"

"No."

"I've been looking for you for two years," Paul said.

"My name's been in the telephone book." Harriet hurried even more, wrapping her coat tightly around her.

"I didn't realize I was looking for you until I saw you."

"Please, Paul . . ."

"I would walk along the street and I'd pass a bar we'd been in together and I'd go in and sit there, even though I didn't want a drink, not knowing why I was sitting there. Now I know. I was waiting for you to come in. I didn't pass your house by accident."

"Look, Paul," Harriet pleaded. "It was a long time ago and it was fine and it ended. . . ."

"I was wrong," Paul said. "Do you like hearing that? I was wrong. You know, I never did get married, after all."

"I know," Harriet said. "Please shut up."

"I walk along Fifth Avenue and every time I pass St. Patrick's I half look up to see if you're passing, because I met you that day right after you'd had a tooth pulled, and it was cold; you were walking along with the tears streaming from your eyes and your eyes red and that was the only time I ever met you by accident any place . . ."

Harriet smiled. "That certainly sounds like a beautiful memory."

"Two years . . ." Paul said. "I've gone out with a lot of girls in the last two years." He shrugged. "They've bored me and I've bored them. I keep looking at every woman who passes to see if it's you. All the girls I go out with bawl the hell out of me for it. I've been walking around, following girls with dark hair to see if it'll turn out to be you, and girls with a fur jacket like that old one you had and girls that walk in that silly, beautiful way you walk. . . . I've been searching the streets of the city for you for two years and this is the first time I've admitted it even to myself. That little Spanish joint we went the first time. Every time I pass it I remember everything—how many drinks we had and what the band played and what we said and the fat Cuban who kept winking at you from the bar and the very delicate way we landed up in my apartment . . ."

They were both walking swiftly now, Harriet holding her hands stiffly down at her sides.

"There is a particular wonderful way you are joined together . . ."

"Paul, stop it." Harriet's voice was flat but loud.

"Two years. In two years the edge should be dulled off things like that. Instead . . ." How can you make a mistake as big as that? Paul thought, how can you deliberately be as wrong as that. And no remedy. So long as you live, no remedy. He looked harshly at Harriet. Her face was set, as though she weren't listening to him and only intent on getting across the street as quickly as possible. "How about you?" he asked. "Don't you remember . . . ?"

"I don't remember anything," she said. And then, suddenly, the tears sprang up in her eyes and streamed down the tight, distorted cheeks. "I don't remember a goddamn thing!" she wept. "I'm not going to Wanamaker's. I'm going home! Good-bye!" She ran over to a cab that was parked at the corner and opened the door and sprang in. The cab spurted past Paul and he had a glimpse of Harriet sitting stiffly upright the tears bitter and unheeded in her eyes.

He watched the cab go down Fifth Avenue until it turned. Then he turned the other way and started walking, thinking, I must move away from this neighborhood. I've lived here long enough.

NORTH CAROLINA

A Tempered Fellow

PAUL GREEN

All day long he hoed among his cotton. Row by row, and round by round he travelled, the rhythmic hanh, hanh, of his hoe keeping time to the turmoil of hurt and anger within him. It was near night, with the sun hanging low in the tops of the pines by Little Bethel Church. When he reached the fence he stopped and surveyed his handiwork behind him.

'Aih!' he said with grim exultation, 'three acres chopped and a hour to go yit.'

Turning sharply, he spat upon his hands and fell to thinning another row.

Ah, but he was a worker. Let it be rolling logs, splitting rails, or cutting with a cradle, he stood above them all. And many a hot August day, when 'the monkey was riding' old man McLaughlin's hands in the bottom, Eddie's loud halloo could be heard among them, urging them on to their fodder-pulling.—But he had a bad temper.—Three hundred bundles a day was easy for him. Yea, he could pull five stacks in a week; had done it all right. And today he had set a new mark. Three acres of grassy cotton chopped out by one man was a record. He thought about it. Who could equal it? But on this day he was mad, mad to the bottom. Mad and hurt. And his hurt and anger drove him, beat on him like a flail. He had quarrelled with Ola. Aih, worse than that, he had slapped her. A little slap, not much—he glanced at his heavy hands.

But he had stood enough to make any man mad. What had got into her nohow? Here he was with the grass eating his cotton up and he hoeing his liver out trying to save it. So much rainy weather. And she.

From *Salvation on a String and Other Tales of the South* by Paul Green. Published by Harper & Brothers. Used by permission of the author.

—Lying up in the house down there in the field, doing nothing—ready to spend every cent she could get, buying lace and jewelry from the peddlers who passed in the lane. 'Says she's done working in the fields, she does,' he muttered wrathfully. 'Yea, but I'll see!' And his hoe flew over the ground. He had had no dinner, his stomach was empty. Evening was coming on. Everything looked gray, lonesome, it shore did. And now he'd have to go on home. The mule and cow had to be fed and there were the shoats too. 'Dang, I didn't never plan on things like this!'

He loved Ola, always had.—Temper it was. Too much temper. His mother used to say it would bring him trouble. He'd ought to be patient. Still, she had tried him—worried him nigh to death it seemed. And now he remembered that in their courting days old man McLaughlin had warned him of Ola's dressing and finery. Her pappy and mammy couldn't satisfy her. They were too poor. Take a bank to hold her, he had said. That's right, she didn't treat him decent, and he slaving day in and day out to get ready and buy a piece of land of their own. They were both the children of tenant farmers, the grandchildren of tenant farmers, the great-grandchildren, and on back. But he'd change it for himself. He'd pay taxes on his own land before he died, he would. Aih, she knew it when she married him and seemed glad. He stamped and spat upon the ground.

He tore through a dozen more rows before the dusk came down. And when the moon had begun to shine up in the middle of the sky, he laid his hoe down and stood gazing over the wide rich fields. He would make big cotton here, a bale and a half to the acre and more maybe. And over there towards the hollow was his corn, popping with strength and as green as poison. He was a farmer and this was his, the earth was his. It was fine, aye, it was, bless God. This level forty acres would be his in a year or two. McLaughlin had promised it as soon as he could pay a thousand down. Money. Ola would have to quit spending his money. Not another cent to waste, not another damn red. It was foolish. It was foolish for her always to be looking through Sears-Roebuck's catalogue, picking out lace curtains and tablecloths and window shades. He'd told her a thousand times. And then this morning —yes, God!—With a muttered oath, he turned and went off through the darkness home.

He fed the mule and cow and the clamorous pigs. As he came up the walk to the house where Ola had wasted a lot of good guano planting a border of cannas, he saw her sitting on the porch in a cool white dress. His heart softened towards her and he could have taken her in his arms. She was sweet. She was always clean and cool and sweet. He stopped before the steps embarrassed, trying to think of something to say. The lamp was lighted on the table in the room, and he saw the waiting supper spread out on a new white tablecloth. Aih, that was it —finery! She would ruin him yet. His heart hardened again.

'Supper's ready,' she said. 'I got tired of waiting and had mine.'

He went on into the kitchen, soused his face and arms in a pan of water and dried them hurriedly on a fresh towel, then seated himself to his meal.

'Don't you want nothing more, Ola?' he called.

'I've et,' she answered.

He leaned over the table eating in huge mouthfuls. He fed his hunger with beans, side-meat, corn-bread, preserves, and a few pieces of fried chicken, washing it all down with great gulps of black coffee. His sweaty arms made streaks on the new cloth, but what did he care, consumed as he was by hunger and the thoughts within?

When he had finished, he sat picking bits of meat from his teeth with his finger-nails. Now and then he could hear Ola stirring in her chair on the porch. He was tired and sleepy, and if all was right he might go happily to bed against the next day's labor. But now—— No, he was too worried to sleep. She was out there thinking things. He would go out and talk to her.

Sitting down on the steps, he took off his shoes and stretched his feet in the soft sand of the walk. He waited, hoping she would say something, for he could find no words. But she held her peace. Time went by and drowsiness began to steal over him. Like a dream he heard the frogs creaking down near the mill-pond, and an owl screaming farther in the swamp beyond.

'You're sweaty. The tub's by the well there.' Her words startled him. He fumbled with his shoes and made no answer. Presently she went into the house and brought him some soap and a rag. As she came near him the odor of sweet cologne entered his nostrils. She was sweet enough to eat—sweet—

'Peddler been by today?' he asked quietly, choking down his anger.

'No,' she answered coldly, 'no.'

'Looks like a new tablecloth. Thought maybe you'd been a-buying.'

'Your money didn't buy it. It was brung to me.' She turned sharply and sat again in her chair.

'Who brung it?'

'Ella and her friend from Raleigh. They et dinner here.'

'A high-collared dude, riding round this busy time of the year. He'd better stay away from here. I could take him in my two hands and break him like a dead dog-fennel.' Ola laughed softly. 'Now what do you mean by that?'

'I'm going to Raleigh tomorrow with him to visit Ella awhile.'

'And the grass eating up our crop!' he cried incredulously.

'Yes.'

'By God, you won't!' he roared wrathfully as he got up and began walking back and forth in the yard.

'I'm going, I tell you,' and her voice quavered. 'I'm gonna get a rest from your slaving and sweating and your dirt and all.'

'Well, for God's sakes, listen at her!'

'I won't be run to death. Pa didn't run me to death.'

'And look at him. He's gonna die in the pore-house. And I ain't, I tell you.' He slumped down on the steps, hugging his knees in anger.

'And this morning you hit me. If Pa knowed it, he'd come over here with his gun and shoot you down like a dog.' Now she began sobbing.

'Dry up, dry up, I tell you.—Hanh!' He snorted scornfully. 'I'd grab him up and bust his brains out ag'in the ground.' He got to his feet and slammed his way into the house. 'All right,' he called back. 'Go on if you wish. You'll be back in a week.' And he went to bed.

All night she sat on the porch, listening to his heavy snores coming from the little back room. When the dawn broke beyond the old mill and chickens flew out of the china tree with a clatter, she got up and started breakfast. While the biscuits were baking, she went out and milked the cow for the last time.

Ed rose and ate his meal in silence. When he'd filed his hoe and started into the fields, he stopped and called. 'Going, are you?'

'I am,' she said.

'Well, go and be damned!' he shouted, and off he went up the path, kicking the dust before him.

Again a second day he hoed from morn till evening. The fiery sun burned down upon his back, drying up the sweat and leaving splotches of salt upon his shirt. When night came he had another three acres hoed clean and standing up for the siding plow. Again he went home under the moon, devoured by hunger and thoughts within.

The house was closed and there was no light. He found a note stuck in the door. 'I am gone. Don't look for me till you see me coming,' it said. He could read the clear letters in the moonlight. Tearing the paper into bits, he made his way to the lot to feed. When he had cooked his supper, he gorged himself and lay down in his clothes on the bed. Soon again his snores echoed through the house.

The next morning he awoke and called her. And then he remembered that she had left him. It seemed as if his head flew all to pieces, for he began cursing in loud oaths, cursing her trimmings, and he even seized one of her flower-pots and hurled it into the yard. The calendars and magazine covers shook on the wall with the violence of his voice. He cooked his breakfast in the same unwashed pans and ate out of the same dirty plate of the night before. Why should he clean up now? Let the house rot down. Let the maggots work in the dishes. God knows, he didn't care.

All that week he did mountains of work. He hoed and ploughed and ploughed and hoed, driving his mule up and down the windy fields like one possessed. Old McLaughlin came and tried to commiserate with him, but grief and anger were eating in his heart like lye. He said, 'Please let me alone.' The loneliness of the house, aih, that harried him to death. He became restless and unable to sleep at night. And on Sunday morning when he had shaved himself and sat alone on the porch staring across the wide burning fields, he gave in. Fishing out a stub of a pencil, he wrote; 'Deer Ola,' he said, 'Won't you come back? i speck i done you wrong. Ill do better, honest i will. the crop is in good shape. and there ain't so much to do. there ain't nobody to churn and theys a pile of eggs i caint eat. Im well and hope the same.—Ed.' He set off up the road, dropped it in the mail-box and waited.

The next week he worked, worked and waited. The grass was killed, the cotton sided, and all looked fine. Then came a note from Ola saying: 'I am having a good time. Please look in the top bureau drawer and send me my white slippers.—Ola.' He was stupefied with rage. All that afternoon he sat on the porch unmindful of his crops and the world about him. Near night he rushed into the house and began putting on his store-bought suit. 'I'll go get her! I'll go get her!' he kept shouting to himself. Hurrying to the barn, he hitched the mule to the buggy and went driving away in a cloud of dust to the north.

Late that night he drove up the shining main street of the capital city. The bright lights astonished, even frightened him. But he held his way. Turning to the right near the middle of the town, he went several blocks eastward and stopped before a small frame house. There was a stir inside and a light came on as he hammered on the door.

'Who's that, who's that?' Ella's sleepy voice called.

'It's me,' he cried, pushing his way into the hall. 'And I want Ola.'

A door opened in the hall and Ola came out.

'Ola, Ola,' he said, 'come home.'

'Maybe next year,' she said, and gave a little laugh.

Ella went away and left them alone.

'Git your things, I tell you,' he almost whispered.

'I ain't going. Good night. You're crazy as a fool, Ed.'

—Temper, temper, that was it. For he couldn't keep his hands off her—hands that could lift a bale of cotton.—She couldn't make a whisper, not a sound.

Then he stumbled down the walk to his buggy. He'd done it all right. He'd killed her all right. He knew all the time, every long mile to Raleigh, that's the way it'd be. He'd choke her to death.—Temper, temper. With a clatter of blows, he urged his mule towards the south. A big star was shining above the road he travelled. It caught his eye as he drove, and he rocked his head in grief. 'I wisht I was where that star is, clean away. Oh, I do!—' And he sobbed as he passed the moonlit hedges.

When the sheriff came for him in his little house, he was quiet and dignified. Poor fool, he was sitting on the porch dressed in his Sunday best with his head bent over in his hands. The dishes were washed, the floor swept, the flowers watered, and all in order. He went away like a child and stayed so till the last day.

RHODE ISLAND

Embarkation Point

VICTORIA LINCOLN

That summer, vacationing alone at the Knights' farmhouse, Mrs. Calhoun began again to wake early for the first time in years. She would lie in bed, rested and expectant, listening to the conversation of orioles and catbirds outside the window, fully conscious from the first opening of her eyes, and no longer huddling backwards from the pressure of morning into the comfortable ambiguities of her dream.

Now, too, she smiled all the time she was dressing. She would spend a comfortable ten or fifteen minutes at the mirror as she had used to do, five years ago, brushing her soft, light hair, noticing happily how her skin, darkening with the sun, made it even blonder. She would take her lipstick and fill the natural outline of her pretty mouth with care, and sit, idly happy, waiting for the color to set before she kissed the blotting tissues and smiled once more at the print she left upon them. Then she would touch her hair again, with the natural grace of a happy woman, a gesture of infinite promise, and go down to breakfast singing. For on the table by her bed, was the picture of Captain Sherry Calhoun, now overseas.

Thus, circled in heavy silver, the deliberate charm of his one-sided smile fixed unchanging under glass, Sherry Calhoun fulfilled his husbandly duties as he had never done in the flesh. It had been a bad match.

"Oh, that's Sherry Calhoun's wife," they had said for five years, now, "that's poor little Mrs. Calhoun." Sitting in a corner through countless gay country weekends, she had been poor little Mrs. Calhoun, colorless, conveniently forgotten much of the time, but still there, to be stumbled over occasionally, embarrassing as an unspoken reproach.

She had been little Ginny Tuckerman, a small town belle on her first thrilling visit to New York when she met and married wayward, graceless, philandering, cold-hearted Sherry Calhoun. The marriage was a source of irritated bewilderment to Sherry's friends, and, indeed, after the first few weeks of it, to Sherry himself. She had a small trust fund, certainly not enough to interest a man who lived on his friends as easily as Sherry did. And her soft, inconsequential beauty fed on admiration. You have all known these gentle, pastel women who are so easily quenched.

But even in the simplest creatures, the individual life dies hard. In Sherry's world she had been defeated and destroyed daily; but the deathless center of personality that is in all of us had continued to put out its dogged, unknowing shoots, to live unrecognized behind the soft, neglected face, in the chair at the rainy window out of the contract players' way, in the quiet, unending shame.

Indeed, she had grown into a certain distinction. Love and the slow death of love, never put into words or clearly realized, a marriage that had meant the loss of her young girl's narcissistic happiness and the shame of disappointed womanhood at one blow, these odd and unhappy advantages had carried her, somehow, past her mark. And now, this summer, she was beginning to catch up with herself.

She began to wake early, and with that waking a new quality touched Mrs. Calhoun's manner. It became relaxed and aware at once. There was nothing in it so coarse or simple as invitation, yet, seeing her, a man of experience might have surmised that it could do no harm to throw out a little discreet feeler or so—nothing that could startle or offend her, but an experimental word, a lingering pressure of the hand—on the chance, you know, just on the outside chance.

"I tell you," said Miss Knight to her brother, "I'm glad that picture of her husband shows he's such a terrible handsome feller, or I'd feel that girl needed watching."

"She seems a quiet, well-mannered enough young woman to me," replied her brother, slowly.

As he went out into the cow barn he kept on thinking of Mrs. Calhoun, kindly and seriously. It had been quite clear to him from the minute he helped her into the house with her coats and luggage that she was essentially unattached. The picture in the frame might be as handsome as all get-out, but Mrs. Calhoun was quite alone, and he knew it. And with the profound gentleness which was Mr. Knight's peculiar gift and wisdom, he hoped that she was going to be happy.

He watched her now, as she came out into the farmyard after breakfast, red sandals on her feet, a huge red-and-white striped purse under her arm. Her appearance pleased him impersonally, just as you might be delighted with the feast-day finery of a peasant. It was unfamiliar to him, with the gay clothes, the professionally arranged hair, the painted nails, the delicate, artificial make-up, so citified and different from the appearance of both kinds of country girls—the good ones and the bad ones. But to Mr. Knight the unfamiliar was not, automatically, either suspect or ludicrous. He was by nature a highly civilized person.

"Morning, Mrs. Calhoun," he said. "Headin' for the bus?"

"Good morning, Mr. Knight. Yes, I am."

"Could drive you down to the bus stop, if you want to set on the steps and wait a little spell, maybe five minutes. I'm takin' some eggs over to Wes Parker's."

"Thank you, I'd like to." But she did not sit down to wait. She stood, watching Mr. Knight pour water from the yard pump into the radiator of his car. She followed him through the wide door of the barn and watched him stoop to read the thermometer on the incubator in the old harness room, watched him sweep down three empty cow stalls, and fork fresh straw on their floors, watched him return to the pump to wash his face and hands and dry them on a blue bandanna from his hip pocket, produce a tie and tie clip from a compartment of the car and make himself smart.

"There," said Mr. Knight. "Now I'm fitter to drive a lady down to the Four Corners. All set, egg crates all in the back. Hop in, now, and we'll get going."

They rolled down the drive and into the deep-rutted white dust lane, towards the state highway. Sumac and flowering elderberries flanked the road, chickory, Queen Anne's lace and bouncing Bet stood in the ditches. The air above their heads was laced with the bright, bounding passage of goldfinches.

The ocean was to the left of them, hidden now by the lie of the land, but there, filling the air, making it at one time lively and soft. The knowledge of its presence changed the point of view, one interpreted the landscape in the consciousness of the sea, so that the dusty lane, the sumac and the elderberries, the bounding flight of the goldfinches and the charming uncharactered blue and pink sprawl of summer ditch flowers were not only themselves of themselves, but they were also the scream of a gull, the corded tangle of wrack at high-water mark, the child, barefoot, wet fingered, pocketing shells, smooth glass, the lucky stone; it was the scream of the foghorn in the night, and death by drowning, the rocking buoy, the hidden mine, the lobsterman pulling in his pots, the unending tides that cover and possess the greater surface of our earth, making us shine in the heavens brightest of the planets, the watery star.

"I love it here," said Mrs. Calhoun. "I love being near the ocean."

"Yep," said Mr. Knight. "Good for folks."

He turned down U. S. Route 1.

"This street goes all the way to Floridy," he said. "Know that?"

Mrs. Calhoun laughed, nodded her bright head.

"When the war's over, Mr. Knight, suppose you drive me the whole length of the street."

"Weather like this, there's nothing I'd like better." He paused and added gallantly, "Or any weather."

She smiled at him, enjoying the comfort of his impersonal male kindness, as she had enjoyed the sun and the feeling of the sea. She did not feel that she had to answer him and there was a long, relaxed silence before he spoke again.

"First Christian Church is having a bazaar this afternoon," he said. "The summer folks always take it in. I'd go if I was you. Nice way to get acquainted."

"I don't care much about seeing people."

"You would, if they was the right kind. Everyone needs friends. You go."

She turned in her seat and looked at him with childish directness. His long, plain face was turned straight ahead, his blue eyes on the road, but the smile was meant for her, the encouraging nod.

"You go on," he said again. "You're too young not to be doing more for people than you are, and being more mixed up with them." He paused and grinned, suddenly. "And old enough not to make a fool of yourself, I guess."

But it was just of this that Mrs. Calhoun was not at all sure.

"Mr. Knight," she said, abruptly, "I have the funniest feeling about this summer. As if I never noticed how I felt, or even acted like myself, till now. I'm very happy all the time, but I feel sort of queer and new. I've been wanting to tell someone that. Do you think I'm crazy?"

They were approaching the four-corners. Mr. Knight slowed down the machine.

"Well, now," he said, "don't know's I see what you're talking about, to tell you the truth. You don't appear to be crazy, though." He laughed. "Anyways, if I was you, I'd go to that bazaar. Real nice class of folks there, make you real nice friends."

He opened the door and helped her out, smiling at her red sandals, her striped bag, her pretty hair, fixed up so fancy and citified.

"Poor girl," he thought, suddenly, "if her husband had been a good man, she'd have loved him. She's the kind."

"Now you go," he said again, smiling seriously. The bus was visible down the road, and he got back into the car and drove off, taking the eggs to Wes Parker's.

Mrs. Calhoun got into the bus oddly flattered and excited. She felt important, not as she had when she was a young girl with beaux, but as she had felt in school when the English teacher had called her up to his desk after class, and laying his hand on the theme she had written, had talked to her about going to college, telling her that she was college material, that she must not waste her capabilities. She had not gone; but it had been lovely, lovely, standing by the teacher's desk, hearing his voice that was grave with the consciousness of her, Ginny's, own importance. His name was Mr. Mathewson.

"I guess maybe I will go to that bazaar for a while after the show," thought Mrs. Calhoun. "Not that I'm likely to get talking to any people. But it sounds sort of attractive. I should have worn my hat. Out here, though, I guess it won't matter much."

The day, once this decision was taken, became unlike other days, vivid and simple, slanting towards its objective. In the ten-cent store she bought shoe white, nail polish, two sample sized lipsticks. Then, filled with an unfamiliar longing to communicate with friends, with women, she bought post cards and took them to the post office where she wrote to hostesses she had barely known.

"Dear Lora," she wrote, "I wish you were here to smell this nice salt air, it is lovely here, best ever, Ginny," and, "Dear Alice, This is the First Christian Church where I am going to a Bazaar this afternoon, best wishes, Ginny Calhoun."

Coming out of the post office, she found herself face to face on the steps with a very young man in army uniform. He was a big, handsome boy, with a blond, heavy-featured face, and he looked at her closely, his clear, rather blank eyes widening and then drooping in an admiring calculation which he lacked either the manner or the self-consciousness to conceal. If she had smiled, if her eyes had shown the least recognition, he would have spoken to her. Unexpectedly, she blushed like a girl and hurried down the steps, studying her wrist watch with an intentness that could have deceived no one.

With a look of surprise, of flattered amusement, the big young soldier swaggered into the building. He looked over his shoulder as he pushed through the door, but Ginny had hurried out of sight.

The encounter, slight as it was, heightened the feeling of the day, the importance it had assumed with Mr. Knight's repeated, "Now you go."

She ate an early lunch, earlier than she had planned. The movie opened at one, and she had decided, suddenly, that she had better be there right at the start, so that she wouldn't be late, too late, for the bazaar. Too late to see it all and be back at Knight's for supper. That she might leave the movie before it was over did not occur to Ginny. For years she had been dragged into expensive openings late, and out early, following at the heels of Sherry's high-strung pack. But Sherry never went to movies, and towards them Ginny preserved her girlhood habit of mind: the whole show through once, including both features, the newsreels, the previews and the shorts. It didn't matter much where you broke in on the cycle, but you sat until you could say, "This is where we came in." By getting to the show when it opened, then, she could be free by half-past four.

It was a good show, and she enjoyed it, but through it all there was a sense of waiting. She was glad when the first title came around again, and she could go to the ladies' room to wash and powder, freshen her lipstick and comb her hair, and then start out towards the First Christian Church.

"You go," Mr. Knight had said.

She hurried out through the little lobby and up the main street, past the library and the post office, past the hardware store and Woolworth's and the A. and P. She came to the village green, and saw the white wooden tower of the church, the small smooth lawn in front, hung with paper lanterns, the wide lawn at the side, sloping down to the estuary, dotted all over with little booths, bright with crepe-paper trellises, with strings of signal flags, with the bright summer dresses of women and little girls.

"There it is," she said to herself, like a child, "that's the bazaar."

Immediately, an unfamiliar and wholly unreasonable shyness came upon her, veiling her eyes, heightening the color in her cheeks, making her feet heavy and her hands unsure. It was a public place, she told herself, sharply, like a store or a show, and there were other strangers there, too. Those people didn't all know each other. And still the childish shyness persisted, the impulse to flight, and she approached with downcast eyes, remembering for the first time in twenty years a summer hotel veranda, a group of dressed-up, laughing children at one end of it, and her mother's voice urging her briskly to run down there where that bunch of nice little kids were and play.

Nice way to get acquainted. You go.

She walked into the grounds very rapidly, with the look of a woman about to do two or three brisk errands before train time. All around her were pink paper trellises, little tables covered with pot-holders, aprons, layer-cakes, hand-decorated bridge scores, the classic rubble of countless bazaars on the lawns of countless little white churches all over America. Why, she had worked with the Camp Fire Girls in Belleville to make things like these for the Congregational Church Festival, year after year! When she was eleven she had made beadwork bookmarks that brought a better price than anything on her mother's handwork table. Mrs. Appleton, who was rich, had bought half-a-dozen of them for Christmas presents and said that she was a real little artist.

Suddenly, Mrs. Calhoun found that she was smiling and at ease. Why, these people were the kind she knew, the only kind, really, she had ever known. A wonderful sense of well-being came over Mrs. Calhoun, a complete assurance. She began to stroll, to smile.

The clink of teacups arrested her pleasantly. She sat down at a little table, ordered tea, homemade vanilla ice cream and walnut drop-cakes from a woman who looked and sounded like Mrs. Weatherby, Phyllis Weatherby's mother. What ever had happened to Phyllis? Funny how Sherry had cut her right off from Belleville like that. Of course, she never had been much of a one to write letters, which made it worse.

When the woman came back with the tea, Mrs. Calhoun looked at the lovely soft-boiled frosting dented with walnuts and exclaimed, "My, how good that looks!"

"Now, my new little daughter-in-law made them. Going to tell her what you said. She just values every word of praise she gets so. Youngest in the family and never set out to do things like this till she got married this June."

"Is he in the Army?"

"No, truck and potato farmer. Makes it nice for me, having him near. The two youngest boys are in the Coast Guard."

"My husband is in the Air Corps."

"Near here?"

"Out of the country."

Two more women came to the table and sat down. The woman who waited on her said, "Mrs. Greene, Mrs. Tyler, this is a stranger here, you ought to help her get acquainted. Mrs. er . . . my name's Cutler, by the way."

"Mine's Mrs. Calhoun. I'm very pleased to make your acquaintance, all."

Had she been speaking a foreign language for five years, too?

"Summer visitor?"

"I'm boarding at the Knights' farm."

They were acquainted. They had looked askance at her bright, smartly arranged hair when they sat down, at her bare, lotion-darkened legs, at her town-in-the-country clothes. They did not dislike city women, who were usually good contributors to the church and the library fund, and pleasant enough; but they were awkward with them, they found conversation difficult. But at the first word Mrs. Calhoun had spoken, they were at ease. They had recognized her as she recognized them, giving her immediate credit for those beaded bookends, for the church suppers she had served with Phyllis, for her parents' nicely kept house on Church Street, with the big veranda.

"Knights said they had a young lady from New York," said Mrs. Greene, as if she were penetrating an unconvincing disguise.

"Well, that's right," said Mrs. Calhoun. "But I come originally from Belleville, Maine. This lawn party puts me so much in mind of it, I was almost homesick when you ladies sat down."

"There," said Mrs. Tyler with brisk satisfaction. "I said to myself the minute you opened your mouth, you didn't sound like no New Yorker to me!"

They all laughed together, eating Mrs. Cutler's daughter-in-law's rich, delicious cup-cakes.

"Now say," said Mrs. Greene, struck by a thought, "they were wanting someone to help with the flower table about ten-fifteen minutes ago. Little Mrs. Ames got a sick headache (bet anything she's expecting, Bessie, want to bet?) and Mrs. Polk's got to get home before six to do for her mother and make sure their new boy sees to the stock right. You take over for Mrs. Ames, now, Mrs. Calhoun, why don't you? You just stay behind the counter till after the suppers are served, and then, when Mrs. Polk gets back and the menfolks begin to get here you take a basket of boutoneers and go round selling them. A pretty young woman, and a new face, too—my, I bet you could sell them like hot cakes!"

"Oh, I couldn't do *that* part of it!"

That was what Clarisse Howland had done. She was the prettiest senior. Phyllis and she had watched Clarisse, wishing that they had picture hats instead of beaded headbands, wishing that they were seventeen, or anyway, fifteen, with rouge on their cheeks and flowers to sell.

"Well, honestly," she said, as if she were making a sudden confession, "I'd love it."

"That's the stuff," exclaimed Mrs. Tyler. And Mrs. Greene wiped her lips and got up, saying, "Now you come right along before you change your mind, while I take you over to Mrs. Polk and make you acquainted."

And fifty-five minutes after Mrs. Calhoun had stopped, rigid with terror, on High Street, looking at the gay lawn, the strange people, she stood behind the table at the flower booth, helping Mrs. Polk lift the big, bright double-dahlias from the pails of water to refill the emptying vases; she was mixing a few sprays of gypsophila with the glads; she was leaning across the table eagerly to explain to a prospective customer how the hanging moss-balls would grow.

"Why, I've seen one that filled a whole bay window, the loveliest thing! If you have a southern exposure, and keep them moist to begin with and then not too moist the rest of the time, why they'll amaze you, they grow so pretty. Jerusalem Wonder is what my grandma always called them. I don't know the right name. What's the right name of these moss-balls, Mrs. Polk?"

It was fun to fix the flowers, to sell them, to hear Mrs. Polk's comfortable, half-laughing words of praise. "Now, Mrs. Calhoun, that's real artistic. I never could fix flowers any way artistic like that." And, "Say, we got a real little high-powered salesman. Go it, Mrs. Calhoun, you're good!"

The smiles and obvious appreciation fell on Mrs. Calhoun like warm spring rain. She could hardly remember when she had been so happy and relaxed. She thought of her mother, who had died the year she was married; and she saw her, waving from her booth across the grounds to Phyllis and herself in the Camp Fire wigwam, selling their lemonade.

"I bet I look a lot like she did then," thought Mrs. Calhoun. "Mama was blond as I am. She'd be tickled to see me now."

The thought, without sadness, gave a depth and gravity to Mrs. Calhoun's pleasure. "My, I'm enjoying myself," she said to Mrs. Polk. "Isn't it lucky Mr. Knight thought to tell me about this party!"

The long supper tables had been set out, the first contingent served and the second were finding their places, when Mrs. Polk returned from seeing to her mother and the new hired boy, and Mrs. Calhoun was free to take her own place at supper. With surprise she realized that she was hungry and that her arches ached a little. She had been enjoying herself far too much to notice the flight of time.

She was slightly embarrassed to discover that the only vacant chair left at the long table (and she must eat now, and not delay; she'd be needed soon to sell those "boutoneers") was the single one at the head. She looked at it, laughing and blushing a little. An elderly man with a large yellowish moustache and a shiny high collar, evidently the town wag, jumped up from his seat next to the end of the table and drew the chair for her with a flourish.

She sat down, blushing deeper and smiling with more determination. Raising her voice a little for the people on both sides of her, she said, "This makes me feel almost as if I was giving a party."

And the large wife of the man with the shiny collar said firmly, "Now Ned Ebberley, don't you go trying to fluster this little lady. She's pitching right in tonight to help us out, and she deserves our thanks." The kind words embarrassed Mrs. Calhoun even more than the pleasantry, but they heightened her happiness, too, and she smiled warmly at both big Mrs. Ebberley and her husband before she lowered her eyes and took a sip of water from her glass.

Then she looked up and along the length of the table. Sitting in the end chair opposite and facing her was the big young soldier, she had met on the steps of the post office. Mrs. Calhoun started sharply, catching her breath as if she had received a physical blow.

This hard start of emotion, of unwilling interest and irrational fear, was a discord, unpleasant in itself and wholly out of keeping with the occasion. She saw the half smile, the recognition, in the heavy, attractive young face, and she made her eyes cold and blank. Then with casual slowness she moved her head, bringing her attention back to her own end of the table.

On both sides of her, everyone had begun to talk, in a shouting, bantering, neighborly fashion. Gratefully she joined in.

It was Mr. Ebberley, the old man with the shiny collar and the drooping yellow moustache, with his flamboyant mock-gallantry, she soon realized, who made things really easy for her.

"Now you stop kidding me," she would say to him, laughing. "You're just trying to make me blush, isn't he, Mrs. Ebberley?"

And Mrs. Ebberley would nod at her, laughing too, and say, "She's too smart for you, Ned! No flies on her! I'll say you're one good little sport, Mrs. Calhoun, isn't she all? Now Ned, you quit teasing this little lady!" And Mr. Ebberley's persistent attentions, and her protests, and Mrs. Ebberley's motherly protection enlisted the amused attention, the affections, of everyone at her end of the table.

Suddenly the situation was familiar and delicious. It was as if Sherry Calhoun's poor little wife had never been, or Mrs. Calhoun, the Knights' boarder with "something about her." It was if there had never been anyone but Ginny Tuckerman, the small town belle. She was arch and innocent at once, she bridled sweetly, her lashes fluttered but her eyes were clear and happy. She was the prettiest girl at the table and she knew it, and knew that it didn't matter the least bit if she was sort of dumb and never said things that were clever or unusual. She was little Ginny Tuckerman, and people would always love her for her fair hair and her easy disposition.

She was full of joyful self-confidence and eager, now, for dessert to be over so that she could begin to sell her flowers.

"Mr. Ebberley," she said, "you're going to be the very first one to buy a boutonniere from me, and you're going to give me a nice big price for it, too, just to pay me back for all the awful things you've been saying, isn't he, Mrs. Ebberley?"

I feel, she thought, as if I'd never been away from home, only happier, because I had to go away to know how happy I used to be. It's almost scarey to feel so much at home again and be so happy.

When she got back to the flower stand, Mrs. Polk had nearly finished filling the little flat basket of boutonnieres that Ginny was to carry on her arm.

"Say," she said, "I was watching you at supper. You were the life of the party. Never saw such a one to make friends."

"It was that Mr. Ebberley. He just wouldn't stop kidding me."

"That's Ned Ebberley! Full of it, he is, and always was. Listen, did you notice a young service man down to the end of the table?"

Ginny was fingering the flowers in the basket, making room for one or two more, very intent.

"Down in the end seat right across from me, wasn't he? Yes, I did."

"Well, that's my nephew. Orphan. He was making his home with me before he enlisted. He's here on a furlough, and what I'm going to do is, I'm going to ask you to stay till the bazaar's over—that may be later than the last bus out Knights' way, they don't run real late—and then I'll get Jerry to run you out home, he's the boy, you know. He'd be glad to."

Mrs. Calhoun stood still, her head bent over the flowers.

" 'Twon't be *real* late," she heard Mrs. Polk assuring her. "You can rest up tomorrow. Come on, Mrs. Calhoun, you be a sport and stay."

"All right," she said. She made herself smile and spoke again, getting her voice back into the words. "All right."

She was angry with herself because she could not understand or control the excitement of the panic breaking in her.

"Guess I'd better get started on the job," she said, brightly, swinging the basket. But Mrs. Polk said, "Wait. I'll go with you. Want to make you acquainted with Jerry."

"Does he know what you want him to do?"

"Sure he does. Told him when he got through his supper. He said, fine."

"Then look, Mrs. Polk, you just stay here with the flowers and we won't waste the time hunting him up. Sooner or later I'll run across him and then I'll just make myself known to him. All right?"

"Why, thank you, dear, that's real thoughtful. Sure you don't mind?"

Mrs. Calhoun smiled down at the little knots of sweet William and clove pink. "Mrs. Polk, don't you think an old married lady like me would look sort of foolish, being shy?"

And she started out, hearing the good-natured approving laughter behind her, feeling like a pickpocket.

But she went directly to Mr. Ebberley, as if she knew that he could give her back everything that she had momentarily lost, Belleville, and the lovely self-confident simplicity of Ginny Tuckerman, the small town darling. She nearly ran to him, as if he were Jacob's angel with a blessing in his gift, and she said, "Now, hold still while I fix it straight. The first one of all goes to you, because you're my best beau, aren't you? He is, isn't he, Mrs. Ebberley? You heard him tell me so himself."

And in their warm laughter, their affectionate admiration, their acceptance, she was comforted, almost as assured and gay, almost as deliciously at home as she had been at the supper table.

She started out, happily, going to the older men first, letting their flattered delight consolidate her sense of security. By the time her basket was empty and she had brought it back to Mrs. Polk, her color was high, her eyes shining; you would have taken her for a girl of twenty. And indeed she was twenty again, with all the prancing egotism, the chaste, unconquerable vanity of a girl. She did not understand her happiness. But she said over and over to Mrs. Polk and the Ebberleys, "Why, I don't know when I've had so much fun. Just you watch me. I'm behaving like a regular kid!"

Mrs. Polk's nephew, who had developed in the army a taste for the world beyond the scope of a church bazaar without dancing, strolled down to the Poland House for a beer, played a pin-ball machine for some time, wandered to the Welcome Inn Tavern for another beer, explained the situation of our forces in Europe and in the Far East to a respectful knot of sixteen-year-olds, put a penny in a small counter gambling machine marked "Stud Poker," won, to his considerable surprise and the delight of the hangers-on, a pack of Camels, looked at his watch, and wandered back to the bazaar, having good-naturedly promised his aunt to see one of the ladies home. A boarder at Knights', Mrs. Something-or-other.

So the evening was nearly over before Ginny walked up to him and said firmly, "You're Mrs. Polk's nephew, aren't you? I'm Virginia Calhoun. She says that you'll be good enough to drive me out to Knights'."

The boy was startled. A lady, his aunt had said, Mrs. Calhoun. How could he have guessed it was this one, the one he gave the eye to outside the post office, the one who gave him that look to put him in his place at the table. The calculating admiration, the unconscious effrontery of his glance was gone, and in its place was a sort of apology, an unhappy confusion.

"That's right," he said. "Please to meet you, Ma'am."

Heavens, she thought. I've been an awful fool. Why I'm years older than this kid. Why, I'm practically his mother. I'm just crazy, these days, like I told Mr. Knight. I'm getting like old maids that take notions.

"I certainly appreciate it," she said. "I guess we'll meet by the stand. Come around when I get through helping Mrs. Polk clear away."

And she left him quickly. An odd sort of irritated disappointment, a tired feeling of humiliation was pulling her down. She was glad that the strings of electric lanterns had begun to blink, that the giggling group at the Girl Scout booth, excited by their late hours, had begun to sing, "Good-night, Ladies," that Mrs. Polk, beaming over the denuded counter, was beckoning her in. There was one boutonniere left. She took it out of the basket and loosened the sweet blossoms of clove pink a little, and set it high in her hair.

"See, my wages," she said, laughing, to Mrs. Polk.

"You look a mite tired," said Mrs. Polk. "My, but we certainly appreciate all you've done. Never let down one minute. We sure appreciate it."

"I loved it," said Mrs. Calhoun. "It was just like being home again."

Everyone was quiet now, a little let down. No one expected her to make an effort. She could work at the clearing away in silence, and then shake hands again, and again disclaim politely any especial virtue, and promise to come in to church Sunday morning, and laugh a little more, and let Mrs. Polk's nephew lead her out to the parked car.

But as she sat down on the seat and leaned back, she felt a heavy wave of weariness overpower her. The boy came around the car, got in beside her and started the motor. They turned in a half circle and headed out High Street away from the center of town. Mrs. Calhoun let her eyelids fall, her lips droop half open; in the dark, confident of the young man's total indifference, she let her face sag, her body slouch heavily, her hands lie open on her thighs. You have seen tired, discouraged old cleaning-women sitting like that in the streetcars, heading home to their own background of squalid troubles after a day of bearing some other woman's drudgery.

The lawn party was over. She could tell Mr. Knight that she had gone, that she had mixed right in, that, yes, she had a fine time, and yes, everybody was lovely to her. Especially the year-round people. Except to sell them flowers, she hadn't had so much to do with the strangers.

Yes, she would thank him for telling her to go. And she wouldn't tell him how she felt when it was over, as if she hadn't slept for very long, and then, finally, dozed a little in exhaustion, and dreamed that she was still a girl, and wakened to the hopeless weariness again.

It was a peculiar pleasure to yield to this awful heaviness. It was almost like dying.

"Oh, I'm so tired," her mind repeated, again and again, in a sort of luxury; "I'm so tired."

Her absolute immobility, her absolute silence, frightened the young man beside her. He was not imaginative, but he had seen how lively she was at the bazaar, and his simple mind leapt to the guilty conclusion that he had offended her. Doubtless his look, this past morning on the steps, had been more of a give-away than he had intended. He had been sizing her up, true enough, but he had never intended to give her the come-on.

"Listen," he blurted suddenly, "I didn't mean to be fresh this morning. You know, giving you the once-over like that out in front of the post office."

Through the heaviness, through the weight of exhaustion, the young man's words struck sharply. Mrs. Calhoun pulled herself erect, she tightened and moistened her lips. But she could think of nothing to say.

The young man blundered wretchedly on.

"You know how it is, on a furlough in a little place," he said. "Maybe I was hoping for some fun, well, isn't that natural? And you think you got the whole place sized up and then you see some cute little number that ain't . . . isn't . . . anyone you know, and still it isn't one of those summer people either, with their damned dogs and beach wagons and stiff faces. Oh, Gloria dawling, are you going to the dawnce at the Casino tonight? . . .

"Look, here you are, all dressed up to go to town, and a blonde, and well, see, naturally I looked at you as much as to say how's chances? But I didn't mean to be fresh."

Oh, thought Mrs. Calhoun, I'm going to cry. Oh, I mustn't cry.

"Listen," he said. "You see how it is, don't you? Don't be sore. Look, say you aren't sore."

"No," said Mrs. Calhoun. She turned her head and looked at him in the light from the dashboard, the big-featured, handsome, rather stupid young face, the disciplined shoulders, the wide, coarse hands on the wheel. "No," she said, "I'm not sore." As she heard her own words, all the tiredness left her as quickly as it had come, but in its place was a sensation of hurry that she understood less. A compulsive quality came into her words as if she could neither foresee nor prevent them.

"I'm not sore," she said. "I wasn't then."

He was relieved. "You didn't think I was fresh, then? You didn't notice me?"

"Yes, I did. I could see you sort of guessing. That's why I hurried off so fast. But I wasn't sore. I loved it."

The words startled her. They bewildered the young man who was without subtlety.

"I don't get you," he said flatly, his voice almost resentful.

"I mean, I was glad you looked at me as if I was a pretty woman and you were interested in me. I thought at the fair, when you were different, that I'd been imagining it. Like old maids."

"I don't get you," he repeated. "You aren't what I thought. You're a married woman with a husband in the service like me. Are you trying to start something? You can't be."

The brutal words, the baffled half-angry voice broke her compulsion, penetrated her to an unfamiliar depth of reality.

"I don't know," she said. "I don't want you to do anything you don't want to do, though. I'm certainly not asking for anything."

The soldier whistled, a short, exasperated sound.

"Miss your husband, hey?" he said. His voice was cold with disgust.

"No," she said, and she was surprised at her lucidity. "I don't and he doesn't miss me. I'm not the kind of person that gets missed. I don't even get noticed. I didn't even get in the way enough to make him ask me to divorce him and get out. I've been nothing for years, and I'm still nothing. Tonight it was like five years ago, when I was still a kid and stuck on myself and happy, before I married him. It wasn't like that when you looked at me. It made me happy, but not like a kid."

He listened patiently, not understanding, yet seeing that something serious was happening to the woman beside him, seeing that it was not a crass seduction as he had thought at first.

"I still don't get you," he said, more gently. "But I'm sorry I spoke to you like that. I guess I'm just dumb."

"Never mind," she said. "Look at it like this. You gave me back something I lost when I found out I was no good to Sherry. That's my husband. Just for a minute, I mean. Just then, this morning. And don't feel bad about this, now, or worry, or think I'm nuts or something. Just forget it."

She made herself smile at him, and she bowed her head while the tears flowed over her cheeks.

"What are you crying for?" he said. "Don't cry. Listen, don't cry."

"Look," she said. "Don't pay any attention to me. I can't stop, but please don't mind. It hasn't got anything to do with you."

But he had drawn over to the side of the road.

"Don't cry," he said again. He put out the lights. "Here," he said, "here."

After a long time she sighed, turning her head on his shoulder. She spoke, and he bent his head to hear her words.

"Thank you," she said. "Oh, thank you."

He laughed.

"Listen," he said. "Kissing you isn't the hardest chore I ever did." And then, the hard note coming back into his voice, "Look, a girl who can kiss like that never spent all that time in the back seat the way you were making out. Not that I care now, you little devil."

She closed her eyes in the dark.

"It doesn't matter," she said. "And you won't believe me. But I've got to tell you just the same. I never kissed anyone like that before."

Then she felt his warm hands on her again.

"The funny thing is," he said, "I believe you. I believe you."

When they moved apart he turned on the lights and drove her the rest of the way to the Knights' farm without talking.

He helped her out of the car and led her to the door. There was still a light burning in the parlor. Miss Knight had asked her to turn it out if she was the last one to come in.

The soldier looked at the window.

"Folks still waiting up for you?" he said.

She shook her head.

"I guess not. They leave the light for the last one in."

"Let me come in for a minute. I want to look at you again in the light."

"I sort of wish you wouldn't," she said.

"Why not?" he said. "I'm leaving tomorrow. I won't bother you any more."

"It isn't that."

"Well, why not?"

But she couldn't tell him that she did not want him to see her looking tired and disheveled, so much older than he, not as he had found her in the dark, beautiful.

"All right," she said. "For a minute. Come in."

She walked ahead of him into the parlor, her head hanging, the big striped bag dangling at her side. Her hair was loosened from its crisp waves, her lips were no longer bright, and her nose was a little shiny. She looked as the boy had hoped she would look, good and gentle, open, a tender, honest woman. He was still, after a year in the Army, a strictly raised boy from the state of Maine, and the situation troubled him.

She turned and raised her head, looking at him.

"Well, good-night," she said.

Suddenly his face broke up, and he caught his breath.

"Oh, you're sweet," he said. "I wish you weren't married."

"It wouldn't make any difference anyway," she said, quietly. "I'm a lot too old for you."

That was not what he had meant, but he could not explain himself to her, explain the scruple that marred his happiness in her.

"I guess so," he said, awkwardly. Then he crossed the room to her. "Let me kiss you again for good-night," he said, "in here where I can see you. And for good-by." She was smaller than he had thought in the car. He could feel her lifting herself to him. "That's right, dear. That's right. Like that. Again."

Then he moved his head away from her, and looked down, his heavy features suffused, his eyes like a sleepwalker's, unfocussed.

"Don't make me go away now," he said, very low. "Don't make me go. They're all asleep, now. You want me to stay, too. You want me to."

The powerful tide of his feeling blinded him so that it was some seconds before he actually saw her face. She was looking towards the door of the room, and his slow eyes followed her look. Miss Knight was standing in the doorway, watching them. As he looked at her, she turned and walked up the stairs.

Mrs. Calhoun and the boy moved apart.

"I guess I've messed things up for you," he said, heavily.

"No," she answered, "you mustn't ever think that. No."

She took his hand and led him to the door.

"Good-night," she said. "Thank you for . . . for bringing me home."

"Good-night," he said. He hesitated, as if he wanted to say something else, but no words came. After a minute he turned and ran down the walk to the car.

She shut the door and went upstairs. She finished packing her bag before she went to bed.

She did not see Miss Knight in the morning. The thirteen-year-old hired girl waited on her at breakfast. The girl always looked shy and ill-at-ease. It was likely, thought Mrs. Calhoun, that she only imagined a difference in her manner.

Mr. Knight drove her to the station. He was grave and quiet, helping her into the car, but she could feel his kindness as she had felt it yesterday.

"We'll go by the back road," he said, "for a change. It's real pretty."

The briar roses were flowering by the stone wall, and he drove slowly for her to see them. The field opposite bore a tangle of cow-vetch, the clear blue-purple pea-blossoms that love spare soil and salt air. Down the slope, east to the distant blue line of the ocean, the poverty grass, iridescent and lovely, blew in long waves.

"I hate to leave this place," said Mrs. Calhoun, suddenly.

"I'm sorry you got to go."

"Mr. Knight," she said, "those people were so good to me, they took me in, and now they wouldn't speak a word for me. And still, I'm their kind. I belong with them."

"You mean, you used to be. You did, once, you mean."

"I guess that's right."

She bent her head, silent for a while. When she looked up at him he was watching the road, but she knew that he was thinking about her, and kindly, and in so far as she understood herself she wanted him to understand her, too.

"Mr. Knight," she said, "about that boy. I never did anything like that before."

"I guessed that, Mrs. Calhoun."

"He's a very nice boy. Plain, somehow, and good. I . . . I hope it didn't mix him up or anything. For long, I mean."

She wanted to be reassured, but Mr. Knight shook his head.

"Well, now," he said, "I don't much expect it did. Hard to tell, though, about kids. Big responsibility."

She hung her head, looking at the stitched backs of her blue traveling gloves, the big, transparent clasp on her blue purse.

"He thought I was . . . well . . . bad, at first. But then he was kind to me, the way you are kind. Only now I don't know what to do."

"About the boy?"

"No, about me."

They had come to the station. Mr. Knight checked her bag and stood beside her on the station platform.

"Suppose you'll go back to that nice little apartment you were telling my sister about?"

She shook her head.

"No," she said. "I can't do that."

He waited, not asking her why.

"I don't know what it will be," she said, "but whatever I do it won't just be something I used to want, or something I don't dare look close at. I've been that way too long. I've got to get going."

"You ought to have a job," said Mr. Knight.

"Yes," she said.

"And a home, and children."

"Yes," she said again, but less confidently.

"And a good husband," he said.

She could not speak. The train came in. He took her hand, shaking it hard, smiling at her with his ageless, blue, sailor's eyes.

"You'll make out," said Mr. Knight.

The words were ordinary enough, but Mrs. Calhoun heard them for what they were, a farewell and a blessing. She got into the train. She was not altogether sure of her destination, and she was making a late start, but she was on her way.

VERMONT

The Murder on Jefferson Street

DOROTHY CANFIELD

I

With its low, bungalow-style, stucco cottages, and its few high old-fashioned clapboarded houses, Jefferson Street looked like any side street in the less expensive part of any American large town, small city. And it was like any one of them. Like all collections of human habitations everywhere, its roofs sheltered complex and unstable beings, perilously feeling their way, step by step, along the knife-edge narrow path of equilibrium that winds across the morasses and clings to the precipitous cliffs of life.

Mrs. Benson, the slender, middle-aged, well-bred widow who had moved to Jefferson Street because it was cheap, was the only one of them—as yet—whose foot had slipped too far from that path for recovery. With her every breath since her husband's death, she had slid down toward that gray limbo of indifference in which all things look alike. She was lost and she knew it; but as she fell, she grasped at anything that could hold her for a little longer; till her daughter grew up. At fourteen, Helen, plain, virtuous, intelligent, charmless, needed all the help she could get, if she were to have even a small share of the world's satisfaction.

Although Mrs. Benson went through the normal maneuvers of life, speaking, smiling, asking and answering questions, her secret aloofness from what other people prized was, of course, obscurely felt by the people around her. It was both felt and feared by the Warders, who were her nextdoor neighbors. It was one of the many things that made them feel insecure in Jefferson Street life. They felt everything, feared everything, started back at the snapping of a twig, all their senses

---

strained like those of nervous explorers cautiously advancing, hand on cocked trigger, into an unknown jungle. For they were undertaking a hazardous feat compared to which hunting big game or living among hostile savages is sport for children. They were moving from one social class to the one above it.

Their family (as far as Jefferson Street knew it) was made up of Bert Warder, his wife, their daughter Imogene and a brother Don, employed in a bank in Huntsville. But this presentable floe, visible above the white-collar surface, was the smallest part of the tribe. Below it was a great substructure, sunk deep in the ocean of manual work—overalled uncles who were factory hands, drab, stringy-necked aunts who 'worked out,' brothers who were garage mechanics, sisters who sold over the counters of ten-cent stores. Only Bert and his bank-clerk brother Don sat at desks with pens in their hands. Bert, like most of the men who lived on Jefferson Street, was an employee of the great Stott McDevitt Electric Company. His desk there felt to him like a pedestal. His bungalow home was another. To the occasional Packard car which, trying to locate a dressmaker or a trained nurse, sometimes purred into it and rolled noiselessly out, Jefferson Street looked plebian and small-employeeish enough. For Bert Warder and his wife, brought up in tenement houses in a black brutally industrial city, Jefferson Street was patrician with its small lawns, its shade trees, its occasional flowerbeds, above all, its leisure-class tennis courts on the two vacant lots at the end. They could hardly believe that Bert's night-school-educated brains had lifted them to such a height. The watchful tips of their antennae soon told them that in the class into which they were transferring themselves it was considered no notable feat to live in a home with a yard, so they took care to speak of the street as other people did, with amused condescension for its humbleness; but in reality they all three worshiped it, admired, feared, and tried to imitate its inhabitants, lived in dread that something from their past might cast them out from it, and did what we all do, passionately collected their neighbors' weak points as potential ammunition with which to resist attacks on their own. They would have fought to the death against a threat to their social standing on the street—as indeed they did, quite literally, when they felt themselves so threatened.

Tautly on the lookout as they were, they naturally felt that Mrs. Benson's preoccupied good manners might be intended as a reflection on their own, and suspected that the Tuttles (neighbors on the other side) looked down on them and on Jefferson Street. There was nothing definite in Francis and Mary Tuttle around which this suspicion could crystallize. It was everything. In their every contact with the Tuttles, the Warders uneasily felt the need to make an effort toward more ease, pleasantness, reticence, and quietness than was natural to them. It was fatiguing. And they were never sure they had quite caught the new tune.

Yet, as a matter of fact, the Tuttles did not look down on Jefferson Street, but were as glad to live there as the Warders. And, exactly like the Warders, had escaped to it from a life they shuddered to look back on. It was true, as Bert Warder's quiveringly suspicious nose for class differences told him, that both Francis and Mary his wife had been brought up in a house grander than any Bert had ever set foot in, and that Francis' youth (which he mentioned as little as Bert mentioned his) had been spent, not with hired girls and factory hands, but with senators and bank presidents. But his past had something else in it—misery and failure, and a period of total black eclipse such as the vigorous Bert had never dreamed of. Francis thought of his past as seldom as possible. Till Mary had dragged him up out of the morass of self-contempt in which he lay, already half drowned, and set his feet beside hers on the knife-edge narrow path of equilibrium, he had taken for granted that his failure in life was inevitable, was because he was an all-around misfit. Living with her he had begun to hope that perhaps it was only his family he did not fit. He said—he thought—'family.' What he meant was 'brother.' Away from Roger there might be a place for him in the world, after all, he began to hope.

When Mary thought of that past, as wretched for her as for Francis, it was to Francis' mother, not his brothers, she cried, 'Shame on you! Shame!' His mother had long been dead, but no tombstone could hide her from Mary's wrath. In the old bad days when both sons were little boys, and the mother's favoritism was at its maddest worst, people used to say, if they noticed Francis at all, 'It's hard on an ordinary boy, and rather a weakling at that, to have such a successful older brother. Doesn't give him a chance, really.' But Mary knew that Roger was not the one to blame for the tragedy of their relation. She had thought him stub-fingered and tiresome, the sort of successful person who bores sensitive and intelligent ones; but living as she did—mouselike invisible poor relative—close to both of them, she had always known that Roger felt wistful and clumsy beside Francis' accurate rightness of taste, and that he had even a dim divination of Francis' exquisite undeveloped gift. No, part of Roger's exasperating rightness was that he had never accepted his mother's overvaluation. The older brother had steadily tried to be friendly; but Francis' mother had early conditioned the younger to see in any friendliness from anyone only a contemptuous pity for his own ineptitude.

'You, *you!*' cried Mary ragingly to the woman in her grave. 'Before your little poet-son could walk alone, you had shut him into the black vault with your stupid admiration of Roger's commonplace successes, your stupid notion that Francis' fineness was weakness. And every year you added another padlock to the door. What strange hateful mania possessed you, you wicked woman with your mean perverted bullying . . .' Whenever another bitter adjective came into her mind, she said all this and more to Francis' dead mother, ending triumphantly: 'But *I* know what he is and I've always known—a poet, a spirit so fine and true that just to breathe the air with him lifts an ordinary human being to nobility! I, the little poor young cousin-drudge you never noticed, I married a broken man, and he's a whole man now—or will be soon. I've given him children who adore him, *who depend on him!* And I depend on him. He earns their living and mine. He's escaped from the rôle of defeated weakling you bullied him into. He creates happiness and knows it! He's coming to life! And every day I bury *you* a little deeper, thank God!'

Never a word of this did she say to Francis. He did not recognize personal resentment as one of the permissible elements in life. Not in his life. It belonged in a lower, meaner world than his. Mary had climbed through the keyhole of his vault, had triumphantly thrown open the door and led him out to happiness, without letting him hear a single reproach to his mother or brother at which his magnanimity could take fright. She knew magnanimity to be the air he must breathe or die. It was part of what she adored in him, part of what she loved in the world he shared with her. But she did not practice it in her own thoughts. Francis, she knew, would have cut his hand off before he would have admitted even to himself that the smallest part of his passionate delight in the twins came from the knowledge that Roger's brilliant marriage was childless, and that he had—at last—something that Roger envied. She felt no such scruples. Hugging her babies to her, she often reveled, unabashed, in happy savagery, 'You dumb conspicuous go-getter, you haven't anything like *this* in your expensive empty house!' Sometimes in reaction from the loftiness of Francis' ideals she thought: 'Why can't he *be* unfair like anybody, and hate Roger, even if Roger's not to blame? It's nature. Who but Francis could feel guilty—not over *being* unfair, but over the mere temptation to be not angelically just. It'd do him good to let himself go.'

But she did not believe this. 'He couldn't let himself go into unfairness like just anybody,' she thought, 'for he's not just anybody. He's a poet with a poet's fineness of fiber. And about the only civilized being on the globe.'

So there was Jefferson Street; its low bungalows, its awkward high older houses with their jigsaw ornamentation filled with people who, day by day, set one foot before the other along the knife-edge narrow path that ran—for the Warders across a treacherous black bog, for the Tuttles along the face of a cliff with crashing breakers below, for the others here and there, high and low, as Fate decreed. Nothing happened. Mrs. Benson was the only one who had lost the path. And she sank but slowly toward her final fall. Three years went by. Her daughter was a senior, getting high marks; unnoticed by the boys. Bert Warder had held his job, not yet realizing that he would never do more than hold it, would never get any higher; only beginning to feel aggrieved because other men were stepped up over his head. He had also, with what sweating pains and secret study nobody would know, learned to play tennis without betraying that he had never before held a racket in his hand. Imogene Warder had passed her examinations—well, nearly all—and was, with some conditions, a senior in the high school, intensively noticed by a certain kind of boy. Francis Tuttle had not only held his job and had had two raises in salary, but had learned to grow roses. His June garden now made him catch his breath. And he had written a little shy and beautiful poetry. Poetry not verse.

'Give me three years more,' cried Mary his wife to Fate. 'Give me only *two* more, and he'll be safe.' The exquisite happiness Francis gave her and gave their children even softened her heart toward his mother. Once she thought—just once!—'Why, perhaps she was a victim too. Someone may have hurt her in childhood as she hurt Francis, hurt her desperately, so that her will to live was all warped into the impulse to hurt back.'

Yes, just once, Mary had a moment of divination and guessed that the will to hurt comes by subterranean ways from pain and fear, not from malignancy.

It was but a flash. A partial guess, so weak and newborn a beginning of understanding, that it had no more than an instant's universal life before Mary, frightened by a glimpse at the vicious circle of the human generations, seized it and made it personal, 'Oh, yes—horrors!—of course, if Francis were still sick with that self-hating Roger-obsession, he couldn't help making the children wretched with it, one way or another. And when they grew up, they would pass it on to *their* children . . .'

She looked across the room at Francis and the twins, wrestling together on the couch, wildly, happily, breathlessly laughing, and thought contentedly, 'Well, there's *one* misery that won't be handed on. His hurt is all but healed.'

Leaning on her sword she stood, negligently smiling, at the gate of the garden where Francis grew poetry and roses, from which she had walled his demon out.

II

And then, one day four years after the Warders had moved to Jefferson Street, Fate, unheeding Mary's appeal for only a little longer respite, rode in on the bicycle of the evening newspaper boy, flinging up on each front porch the usual hard-twisted roll of trivial and ugly news. But this time, among the ugly items was a headlined statement about the arrest of one Donald Warder in Huntsville. He had been stealing from the bank he worked for, it seemed; had been playing the races; spending money on fancy women; he would probably get a long term in the penitentiary.

When Bert Warder walked across his front porch on his way home from the office that April afternoon, he was wondering resentfully why dumb-bells like Frankie Tuttle got one raise after another, while he with three times Frankie's pep just barely held his own, with frequent callings-down. 'But I can beat hell out of him at tennis, anyhow.' He applied his tried-and-true old remedy to his soreness and felt the pain abating. The evening paper was still lying in front of the screen door. He stooped, picked it up, glanced at the headlines.

Although the news took him so by surprise as to leave him stunned, his body acted as bodies do when left to themselves, in obedience to the nature of the soul dwelling in them. He rushed into the house, shut the front door, locked it and jerked down the shades of the front windows. His wife and daughter stared at him surprised. 'Look here! Look here!' he said in a strangled voice, and beckoned them to read the headlines.

They read the news together, dropped the paper, looked at each other in despair. The same thought was in them all—if only they need never open that door, if only they could leave town that night, never again be seen by anybody on Jefferson Street. For they knew that as they stood there, all their neighbors up and down the street were opening screen doors, taking in the paper. And, knowing what their own exclamations would have been, had those headlines referred to someone's else brother, they cowered before the gloating, zestful comments they could almost literally hear, 'Say, that must be Bert Warder's brother, Don. What-do-you-know-about-that? Well, *well*—maybe we'll have a little less kidding from Bert about our Harvey's being suspended from high school.' 'Why, look here, I see in the paper where Bert Warder's brother is jailed for stealing. What kind of low-down folks are they anyhow? And Bert so high and mighty about your mother's being divorced.'

Imogene drowned out the twanging of these poisoned arrows by a sudden outcry: 'I can't *ever* go back to school. Those mean kids'll just razz me to death. Helen Benson's so jealous of me about the boys, she'll be tickled pink to have something terrible like this on me. Oh, I think Uncle Don ought to be *shot!*'

Her father and mother, too, had been thinking that Don deserved to be shot for wrecking their lives. For of course they could not run away from this disgrace. Of course they must, and the very next morning, appear before their neighbors with a break in their armor far worse than anybody's. Harvey Starr's suspension from high school, Joe Crosby's not getting his raise, Mary Seabury's divorced mother, Frankie Tuttle's weak tennis, Helen Benson's unattractiveness to boys—they had been held up by the Warders as shields against possible criticism of slips in their manners. But against the positive disgrace of a brother in the penitentiary! And, of course, now everybody would find out about their folks—the aunt who was somebody's hired girl, the old grandmother who couldn't write her name. All that would be in the newspapers, now. 'If I had Don Warder here, I'd . . .' thought his sister-in-law vindictively. But Don, of course, was in jail. 'Safe in jail!' thought his brother bitterly. '*He* won't have to walk into an office tomorrow morning, and all the mornings, and face a bunch of guys that'll . . .' Like his wife, his mind was full of foreseen descriptions by newspaper reporters of his illiterate tenement-house relatives. He held the newspaper up to go on reading it. It rattled in his shaking hands. Imogene flung herself on her mother's shoulder, sobbing, 'Mamma, you *got* to send me to boarding-school. Every kid in school will be picking on me.'

Behind the newspaper her father gave a choked roar of rage. Lowering the sheet, he showed a congested face. His jaws were set. 'Boarding-school! More likely you'll have to get out of high school and go to work.' They looked at him, too stunned to ask what he meant. Still speaking between clenched teeth he told them, 'Our savings were in Don's bank and I see in the paper here where it says the bank's on the rocks because of the money he stole.'

With a wringing motion of his hands as if they had a neck between them, he crushed the paper, flung it to the floor, and turned on his weeping wife and daughter as if he would like to wring their necks too.

'What's the good of standing there hollering?' he shouted at them. 'Haven't you got any guts? Don't take it lying down like that! Stand up to them! Get back at them before they begin!'

He tramped into the next room and they heard him locking doors and windows.

It was true, just as the Warders thought, that the neighbors began to talk about them as soon as the headlines were read. Helen Benson had taken her mother over to the Tuttles' garden to look at the newly opened tulips. Mrs. Tuttle, newspaper in hand, came out of their shabby tall old house, read out the news to them and they all said how hard it was on the Warders.

'Oh, I bet there's some mistake,' said Francis Tuttle. 'The paper just says he's accused of it. There's no proof he's done it, you notice. I remember Don Warder very well, the time he came to visit Bert, last summer. He's not that kind at all. I bet when they get to the bottom of it that they'll find somebody's double-crossed him. Maybe one of the other men in the bank. I'm going to tell Bert Warder I bet that's what happened, the first time I see him.'

Thinking intently of the accused man's probable innocence, he was absent-mindedly fingering his sandy hair which, he had noticed for the first time that morning, had begun to thin a little.

Mrs. Benson said: 'It'll be a terrible blow to the Warders. We must be sure to show our sympathy for them. Helen, it'd be nice if you could think of something specially nice to do for Imogene.' She had by now slipped so far from the narrow path trod by those who still cared what happened, that this like all news was no more than a murmur in her ears. But, that Helen might learn what is correct, she brought out the right formula in the right voice.

'Yes, indeed,' said Mary Tuttle, in her warm eager way. 'People's friends ought to stand close around them when trouble comes.'

Mrs. Murray across the street, seeing the four of them standing close together, not looking at the flowers, knew what they were talking about and came over to say compassionately, 'I could cry when I think of poor Emma Warder! She'll take this hard.'

Helen Benson was awed by her first contact with drama. 'My! Imogene must be feeling simply terrible,' she said. 'I wonder if she wouldn't like to be vice-president of our class. I'd just as soon resign. Mother, how would it be if I went right up now to the Warders and told Imogene . . .'

But Helen's mother said, her sorrow salt in her heart, 'No, when people have had a blow it's better to leave them to themselves a little, at first. Don't you think so, Mrs. Tuttle?'

Mary, annoyed to see Francis once more passed over as if he were not present, said resolutely in a formula she often used, 'Yes, that is what my husband always advises in such cases, and I have great confidence in his judgment.'

But Francis had turned away. How like Mary it was to try even in little things to make it up to him for being a nonentity! But sometimes he thought she but pointed out the fact that he was. A little nettled, as any man might be (no, considerably more than a man who had had in his past no nightmare nervous collapse), he walked along in the twilight toward the house. On the other side of Mary's wall his exiled demon kept pace with him, trying hard to reach him with old dark associations of ideas, thinking longingly how easy it would be to tear open that nearly healed wound if only these passing relapses could be prolonged. He succeeded in starting a familiar train of thought in Francis' mind, like a brackish taste in his mouth.

'And now to grow bald!' he meditated moodily. 'What Bert Warder calls my "moth-eaten" look will be complete.' His fingers strayed up to his head again to explore the thinning hair. Deep under the healthy scar-tissue forming over his inner wound, an old pulse of pain began to throb. Roger was getting bald, too, he remembered, but of course baldness gave Roger dignity and authority, would actually add to his prestige. Francis, bald, would drop to a lower insignificance. 'To him that hath, and from him that hath not—the motto of my life,' thought Francis. His demon's eyes glittered redly in hope.

But Mary had built her wall high and strong. And inside its safe protection Francis' roses had struck down deep roots. The gardener came to himself with a smile at his absurdity that sent his demon scurrying away into outer darkness.

'Good gosh, only a thin place in my hair, and seeing myself bald a'ready!' he thought, amused. It had been through that mental habit as through a secret back door, he reflected, that many a dose of poison had been smuggled into his life. He stooped to straighten a drooping tulip. As he stood up, the evening star shone brightly pale in the eastern sky. The inner eye of his intelligence focused itself to a finer accuracy: the world stood before him in its true, reassuring proportions. 'Suppose I do get bald—bald as an egg—what of it!' he thought; and, loose, at ease, forgot himself to admire a young pear tree, its myriad swelling buds proclaiming with pride that, mere humble living cellulose that it was, its roots had found the universal source of growth. 'And all amid them stood The Tree of Life,' thought Francis, his eyes deeply on the miracle.

'Da-d-d-dy,' came cautiously from the sleeping porch. The bars of the railing there were high and set close together because of the dangerous three-story drop to the cement-floored basement entrance below, but Francis could make out the twins in their pajamas like little bears in a cage. 'How about a sto-o-ory?' they called down.

'With you in a sec,' called Francis, running into the house.

The twins rushed out on the landing to meet him, hopping, twittering, and as he snatched them up, planting loud kisses on his cheeks, his ears, his nose. 'Praise be to God who gave me life!' sang Francis' heart as he had never dreamed it could. On the swelling tide of this joy, this thankfulness, he rode up with a surge to the highest point—but one—of his long struggle with himself. Quite effortlessly, quite naturally, he thought, 'Too bad that Roger's wife can never give him children,' and went warm with delight that he had wished his brother well.

III

Francis had meant to tell Bert Warder when he next saw him that he was sure Don had never stolen a cent, that somebody had double-crossed him. But the next time he saw Warder, he did not tell him that or anything else.

The morning after the newspapers had announced the arrest of Bert's brother, Francis stepped out to the border along his front-yard path to get some tulips for Mary to take to Emma Warder, Bert's wife. But there was something so beautiful on the first one he cut that he stood still to look at it, marveling, forgetting the errand his sympathy had sent him on. Dew-drops clung to the flower, every tiny globe a magic mirror reflecting all the visible universe. Francis smiled dreamily down on the extravagance of this beauty. At first he remembered with amusement that he was the man who only last night had thought life hard to bear because his hair was getting thin. Then he forgot himself in contemplation of the divine playfulness that shrinks the great far blueness of the sky, the nearby intricacy of trees, immeasurable space itself, to ornament the white perfection of a flower. The doors of his heart swung softly open, as they do when a poem knocks and asks to be written.

Another door opened, the door of the next house. Through it—because he must—Bert Warder came resolutely out from the safety of his home to face the arena full of enemies waiting to spring upon him. The odds were against him now. He knew that. But he was no coward. He was no man to take things lying down. He was worn with sleeplessness, and half sick with dread of this first impact with a world echoing to his disgrace. But he did not lose his head. He remembered the plan for defense he had worked out in the long dark; he tried to keep clearly in mind the old rule of warfare that the way to head off attack is to attack first. But would he be able to carry out this plan? Cornered by Fate as he was, how could he reach anyone with a first thrust? He had no hope that he could, no hope at all; but he bared his teeth savagely with the desperation of the trapped, and would not give up. The instinct of self-preservation, feeling him appeal as if for his very life, responded with a wild rush of its inordinate stimulants to action. His eyes fell on Frankie Tuttle in the garden next door. He was mooning over a flower he held in one hand, while the other hand in a mechanical gesture drew up the sandy hair over a spot at the top of his head. When a man's hand does that without his realizing it, he fears baldness. The instinct of self-preservation, as it can when driven hard by fear, rose to genius, and showed the endangered man how to strike, in all safety, a first blow to ward off the attack he could not parry. He took off his hat, put his hand up to his head and walked rapidly along the sidewalk toward the Avenue, keeping his eyes on Frankie.

When Francis, his heart still unguardedly opened to its very depths by ecstasy, looked up from his tulip, he saw Bert Warder passing by on his way to the trolley, holding his hat in one hand. With the other he was ostentatiously patting and ruffling his abundant dark hair in uncouth caricature of Francis' unconscious fumble. As their eyes met, Bert let fly his arrow with all his might. His words were but trivial and a little common, but his panic tipped them well with the poison of the wish to hurt, and he put his back into the bending of his bow, his broad beefy back. Long before the meaning of the vapid pleasantry had penetrated to Francis' mind, the malignity of its intention was quivering deep in his opened, softened heart. 'That's the way to do it, Frankie!' called Bert in a loud, coarse tone, his fingers leaping about grotesquely in his hair. 'You've *got* a clearing up there. Scratch 'em up into it where you can get at 'em. Scratch 'em up into the clearing.'

For a nightmare second, Francis, like a man who dreams he sees a friend run on him sword in hand, felt not pain so much as a wild incredulity. His eyes widened, his dumbfounded face was blank, his upraised arm and fumbling fingers froze foolishly where they were. From his confusion a gleam of light shone into the other's darkness. The constriction around Bert's heart loosened. It might really work, then, the system of attacking first. He'd sure knocked old Frankie cold, his first try. No man who looked like that could collect his wits for taunts about jail-bird brothers. After the hours of helpless dread that lay back of Bert, his relief was exquisite. And the hope it gave! Hope! He might, after all, be able to defend himself. Drinking in greedily Francis' stunned expression and grotesque attitude, he burst into a yelling haw! haw! of triumph and clutching hope to his breast, ran on courageously to where a fellow worker stood waiting for the trolley.

By that time the meaning of his words reached Francis' mind. He snatched his hand down from his thinning hair with a betraying jerk. Through the quiet morning air Bert's voice came, loudly repeating his joke to Joe Crosby, who remarked, turning back to look at Francis, 'Why, I never noticed he has a bald spot.' The trolley roared along the tracks and carried the two men away to the office where Francis was at once to follow them.

By the end of that day everybody over in the Stott McDevitt Works and out on Jefferson Street knew that the Warders didn't want to have anything said to them about this trouble. 'Some folks take trouble that way,' said their neighbors with sympathy.

So, since that was the way the Warders took it, nobody did say anything about it to them. And since it was never mentioned, nobody knew exactly what was happening. People naturally took for granted that Bert's first thought had been of his brother's innocence, and that, like Joe Crosby at the time of his sister's divorce, he was spending his last cent to pay defending lawyers. Since his face grew steadily more haggardly anxious, they supposed that his efforts were all in vain. They sympathized silently, and read without comment day after day the abbreviated accounts of his brother's trial in the local newspapers.

For they were both brief and colorless. Huntsville was far away in another State; one more revelation of the doings of a dishonest bank employee was hardly news; the reporters apparently found Don too obscure a thief to be interesting. No revelations about a grubby working-class family were ever printed. But the Warders saw in every newspaper mention of Don's trial plenty of other material for malicious satisfaction on the part of their neighbors. When finally Don was found guilty and sentenced to fifteen years in prison, Bert Warder said wildly to his wife, 'Nobody need tell *me* what they're saying to each other. By God! I'd like to knock the words down their dirty throats.'

Drunk first with shame and then with anger—for two weeks after Don's conviction, the bank did fail and the Warders did lose their savings—he had a drunken man's glowering readiness to take offense at nothing. He snarled and hit out in response to harmless greetings; he started every conversation with an unprovoked verbal aggression; he protested every decision made against him at the North Side Tennis Club—as Jefferson Street people called the two vacant-lot courts; he took every happening in the office as flagrant and unfair discrimination against him. His neighbors, his fellow workers knew that his snarls were cries of pain, and for a time—a short time—said to each other tolerantly, 'Poor old Bert, no wonder he's got a grouch.' But they had tempers of their own, grievances of their own, their tolerance soon wore thin, his unprovoked attacks began to strike sparks. Two could play as well as one, they reminded him forcibly, at being offensively personal. He was not the only one who knew how to give a nasty dig. Nobody, of course, dreamed of sinking so low as to throw his brother up to him, Don now in stripes behind prison bars. In fact that story soon passed out of their minds. They had seen Don only once or twice. They were full of their own affairs, their own secret troubles and hidden disgraces. They did not mention the convicted thief, or remember him. But the convict's brother had not forgotten. He imagined in the turn of every exasperated retort a reminder that they had something on him, a threat that he would hear a thing or two about jail-birds if he went too far. So he did not go too far—with them. Every rough rejoinder to a brutal sally from him frightened him into choking down his ill-nature. A sort of approximate balance was found. After a week or so, a Jefferson Street maxim ran, 'Anybody can get along with Bert Warder—all you got to do is to tell him to go to hell once in so often.'

But there was one among them foolishly unable to return evil for evil. Or to defend himself from boorishness by being boorish. And Bert's first handful of mud had told him where he could fling more without having it flung back on him. Mary, annoyed to have Bert's ragging increasingly center on Francis, used to think, 'If Francis only had more vanity! He'd get mad then at teasing instead of feeling ashamed that he's bothered by it; and he'd defend himself.' But she was wrong. Against the blackguardism of the wish to cause pain, Francis now as in his youth could devise no defense that he was willing to use. The others on Jefferson Street and in the office snatched up whatever weapon came to hand, dirty or not. If a hit below the belt was what reached Bert's sensibilities most sharply, all right—sure—they'd hit below the belt—why not? But to Francis a choice between committing an ignoble act of suffering from one was no choice at all. For him only one of those two alternatives was conceivable.

When in an idiotic pleasantry that became threadbare that summer, Bert came suddenly behind him, blew hard on the thinning spot in Francis' hair, rattling off with a noisy laugh, 'Let-the-air-*blow*-on-the-head-the-hair-will-*grow*-on-the-head,' Francis only jerked away in a gesture of nervous annoyance, and then grinned apologetically for feeling sore. He was incapable of hitting back as the others did, with a gibe about Bert's pendulous paunch any mention of which, it was an open secret, made him wince, or about his big flat feet, or his bulging eyes, or his occasional bad grammar. He could not understand the idea the men around him had that hurting Bert Warder's feelings eased their own. Rather the contrary, it seemed to him. To find a festering wound in Bert's life and to press on it hard with a word well chosen for its power to cause him pain—how could that do anything but make a bad matter worse? A good deal worse. For Bert's uncouth tormenting caused him only discomfort and annoyance. But it would be shame, as at a real disgrace, which he would feel, to spy upon another's unhealed sores and dash his fist into the one that looked as though it would hurt the most. From his shadowed childhood on, Francis Tuttle had never understood why, with all the unavoidable pain in the world, anyone could wish to add to it.

So he could do no more than try to hide under an apologetic grin the annoyance he could not help feeling when week after week Bert rang the changes about his looking moth-eaten, twitted him with his poor tennis, his mistakes in gardening, his inability to carry a tune. He even managed a grin, though a faint and weary one over a new stunt of Bert's which emerged in June, a strenuous imitation of Francis' tennis serve, winding up with grotesquely strenuous contortions to deliver at the end a ball of a lamentable young-ladyish feebleness.

But it was his watchful demon not he who grinned, when Bert, in a chance remark, stumbled on one of the two secrets in Francis' life he was ashamed of. This was the lesser secret, the one he had thought he had quite outgrown. One Saturday afternoon in June, at the end of some doubles, as they were pulling on their sweaters, Bert Warder chanced to comment on the election of his daughter Imogene to be vice-president of her class in the high school—'. . . right over the head of Helen Benson, I understand. She's all right, Helen is, but kind o' slow. No S. A. as the boys say.' The other men all knew that Helen had resigned to make place for the Warder girl and had insisted on her election. A self-conscious silence fell on the group. Sensitive to silences as a sick man to draughts, Bert went hot and cold with his usual reflex of panic—were they thinking that because Imogene was a convict's niece—he backed into his corner and bared his teeth.

But Joe Crosby thought of something to turn the conversation. 'I never heard that sex appeal is what swings elections,' he said.

The casual quality of the remark blew away Bert's suspicion. But his nerves had been shaken. They needed an outlet. A safe one. His eyes fell on Francis Tuttle. 'Sure, S. A. is what settles elections!' he cried at random, giving Francis a great dig in the ribs. 'That's why our own Valentino gets elected to all the fat offices in town.'

Francis was astonished to feel a sharp twinge from old bitterness. He had not then, not even yet, left behind the boyish chagrin over all those elections in school, in college, when Roger again and again had been chosen to any office he would accept, and Roger's dead loss of a brother had never been so much as thought of. It was absurd that he still cared anything about that. But an involuntary quiver had passed over his face, just one. It was enough for his tormentor. 'Why, for fair! Frankie, there's more truth than poetry in what I say. You never do get elected to anything, do you? Were you *ever?*'

This was the time, of course, for Francis to tell him to mind his own damn business. But he could never tell anybody that, and now could think of nothing but a sorry shame that he felt even a last throb of that trivial adolescent hurt. He kept his eyes on the racket he was putting into its case; he fumbled with its fastenings; he was silent. He felt diminished and looked it.

As half-asphyxiated lungs strain joyfully to draw in a life-giving gush of fresh air, Bert felt his own painfully diminished self expanding in the other's discomfort. What suffocating man would hold his hand from the one window he can open?

'Poor old Frankie!' he cried gloatingly. 'Never had no luck with 'lections. Let's 'lect him to something right now. I nominate him to be Honorary Fly-Swatter to the Ladies' Aid Society. Haw! Haw!'

As they walked down the street together, he composed variations on this new theme. Mary, coming out to meet Francis, heard his horse-laugh, heard him as he turned in at his front walk bawl out, 'I nominate Mr. Francis Tuttle to be scorekeeper in the One-Legged Men's Athletic Meet. Who will second my motion?'

'What's he talking about?' she asked.

Francis answered, 'Oh, nothing.'

Sitting that evening over her accounts, Mary chanced to glance up at Francis, reading, and was startled to see an old shadow on his face. He wore the shrunken look that had always frightened her. She had not seen it for a long time now. His relapses in the last years had come seldom and were short; but they still made her almost as miserable as he. Adding up a total and transferring it to the next page she thought: 'It is like an old tubercular lesion. Doctors tell you that even when they are healed—or almost—they feel strains that are nothing to normal tissue.' Looking down fixedly at her column of figures but not seeing it, she fell for the hundredth time into a puzzled wonder at the inexplicable difference between what people feel about bodily and mental sickness. 'If it had been a temporary breakdown in a normal lung, acquired in childhood by direct infection from the outside, now almost but not quite healed—why, we'd have told everybody about it, sure of their sympathy. We'd have given it as the natural explanation for the things Francis isn't quite well enough to do yet. There'd have been nothing to hide. Everybody would be interested, and sort of proud and encouraged when Francis recovered. But because it's a temporary breakdown of a normal personality he's recovering from—and yet that was forced on a sensitive mind by a direct infection from the outside as much as any disease germ!—we have to hide it as though it were a disgrace. We can't even talk it over together, and plan what's best to do.'

More than by anything else, she was worn by the need to appear unconscious of what was the center of her thoughts. Now, for instance, to be forced to cast about in the dark for a possible explanation of the recurrence on Francis' face of that old look of sickness. Not even to be sure she was not imagining it. What strain could have come into their safe Jefferson Street refuge that was just the same now as ever? Nothing had happened there to change anything. She did give one fleeting thought to Bert Warder's joshing. But he had always been a boor. And anyhow, he was only teasing. Teasing! The word brought up recollections of child play. And child play was always unimportant. The thought reassured her. She began to emerge from her concentration, set her pen down to the paper again, added 23 to 44, and thought in the phrase she had heard her elders let drop so often, 'Oh, teasing's nothing.' She shot a sidelong look at Francis again. He was reading. His face looked quiet. Yes, she must have been mistaken. It could be no recurrence of his old trouble, vague and dimmed as that was now. Perhaps his tennis had tired him. Presently the idea occurred to her that he might have a real worry, a present one, something at the office, perhaps. No matter how bad that was, it would be less dangerous.

IV

She was right. It was a present worry. About a real danger. But not in the office. In his past, close to the foolish weakness uncovered by Bert's random thrust lay his other secret—the base and bad one. The two were woven together by a thousand connecting nerves. Bert's hammering on one had set the other a-quiver. Suppose—he thought, horrified, that some day, with a reflex reaction like this, some involuntary quiver of his face should betray his feeling about Roger. That he had such a secret to hide was his shame. That Mary might learn it was his terror. Great-hearted as she was, she would never go on sharing life with him if she knew of his mean jealousy of Roger—fiercely suppressed, always festering in the dark hollow of his heart. He thought, as he had a thousand times in his boyhood, that there could be no depravity so low as this vicious ill-will toward his unconscious, blameless brother. He told himself once again that he was cheating Mary—he knew why she overlooked his personal insignificance, his poverty—it was because she had the illusion that he was true-hearted, above baseness. If she should learn that he was capable of this obscene resentment of the kind and generous Roger's superiority—she would turn away from him forever. Was there any real difference—no, there was not—between such a feeling toward a brother and the upraised arm of Cain?

But Mary was looking at him! She had lifted her eyes from her account book! He had not seen when. How long had she been watching him? A man with a guilty secret is always terrified to be watched. Had she guessed? Had she read this thought in his face? He froze. And waited.

But Mary smiled. The room shone. The golden light around him brought Francis with a start out of his nightmare.

'Why, you've been asleep,' said Mary.

'Yes, I must have dropped off for a moment.' He thought he had been having a bad dream. What a relief to be waked up!

Before he lay down to sleep that night, he stepped over to the twins' little cribs. Through the high railing of the sleeping-porch the barred moonlight shone on their round faces, bland in sleep. How safe they looked! And it was he who made them safe, their father. His heart grew great with love.

But after he was in bed Mary heard him draw the long sighing breath of disheartenment. 'What is it, dear?' she murmured. He did not answer. Probably he was already asleep, she thought.

He was awake. His sigh had been of disheartenment. He had perceived that his love for his little boys was tarnished and sullied by satisfaction in his brother's childlessness.

The tide that had been sweeping in so strongly had begun to ebb.

The two vacant-lot courts had never been so busy as that summer. Bert Warder made them the center of Jefferson Street life as much as he could. For there he knew success. By concentrating fiercely on his game, he had made himself one of the best players, and looked forward all through his uneasy days to the hour with his racket at the end, which was almost his only respite from misery. His big unused workingman's body grunted with satisfaction in the hard physical effort and the copious sweat: the strain of his fixed idea relaxed in a momentary forgetfulness of Don in jail: and his perpetual doubt of his equality with those about him fell with the ravening zest of starvation on the chance to inflict defeat.

He steered clear cunningly of the two or three men who could beat him. And naturally played a good deal with Frankie Tuttle. They did not work in the same department of Stott McDevitt, but he scarcely let a day go by without hunting up Francis, inviting him to play, and saying facetiously that he did hope *this* time he might get by Francis' cannon-ball serve and maybe score a few points against him: promising, if he did, to campaign for Frankie's election to be town dog-catcher, or chief reader-aloud at the Sewing Society. Day by day he scored more points.

Mary went up to watch the play once, and afterwards said, 'See here, Francis, why don't you give up tennis for the rest of the summer? You're wearing yourself out.' But the turn of her phrase, the quality of her voice showed Francis how pitiful he looked on the courts, going to pieces under Bert's ragging, trotting about, broken-kneed, like a futile old woman, unstrung, unable to command even his usual modestly competent strokes. If he stopped playing now after such exhibitions of feebleness, there would be no limit to the joshing he would get at Bert's hands.

And by this time Bert's joshing did not so much annoy as frighten him. He was terrified at the thought that another chance lunge in the dark might lay open to Bert's rough handling the secret shame he was trying to leave behind. Bert had, so far, never twitted him with Roger, but at any moment he might try that line; certainly would if he guessed that to be a sore point. Francis' nerves tautened in vigilance if he even caught sight of Bert from afar. He seemed to feel Roger in the air, whenever Bert was present.

He was right in feeling that Roger's name was often in Bert's mind. The contrast between Francis' brother, distinguished, wealthy, well-known, and his disgraced convict brother was one of the sorest of Bert's stripes, the worst of all his envies. Glaring across the net at Francis, going forlornly and hopelessly through the complicated wind-up for his serve, he often thought (as he called out in his witty way, 'Play ball, bald head!'), 'There's one sure thing, 'bo . . . you'll never know from *me* I ever heard of that big stiff!'

Mary was rather troubled by the way Francis seemed to feel the heat that summer. But the hot weather would soon be gone. And wasn't he growing thinner? She'd have to start the evening hot chocolate and crackers again. He didn't seem to have the interest in his garden of other summers. Perhaps only that he hadn't much time left over from tennis. He hadn't written a line of poetry for weeks. But of course the wind of poetry blew fitfully. Was he enjoying the twins as much as he did? Or was that only a fancy of hers?

It was no fancy of hers. Coming in to his children after his daily defeat in tennis, worn out with standing guard over his threatened secret, it was soon borne in on him that he had been in a fool's paradise. Now, while his little sons were babies, yes, of course, they were his, as other men's children were theirs. But they grew so fast. Over and over he lived helplessly through in imagination, as if it had already happened, how they would turn from him. They would soon naturally be asked to visit their Uncle Roger. They could not but be struck by the difference between the two homes. They would begin to compare their father with his brother. And then they would see how their father always took a back seat, never was consulted, never elected to any office, had no influence. As they grew, they would note people's surprise that a senator—Roger would probably be a senator by that time—had such a queer singed-cat of a brother . . . 'And now,' Francis often thought, his fingers fumbling with his thinning hair, 'now a mangy singed-cat.'

Twenty times a day, it seemed to him, he was startled to find that without his knowing it, he was nervously drawing his hair up over the crown of his head.

He was even more startled to discover that he was not the only one to notice this involuntary reflex. 'Have you hurt the top of your head lately, Mr. Tuttle?' Mrs. Benson once asked him. He was shocked and turned on her such a darkening face that she hurriedly excused herself, 'I just noticed that you often put your hand up to it.'

He snatched down his hand—to his amazement it was once more lifted to his head—and told her shortly, 'No, I'm all right.' As he moved away a strong thought came to him, one that soon became familiar by repetition. 'It would be better if all the hair on my head would come out. And have it over with!' Sometimes he imagined for an instant between sleep and waking that this had happened. And it was a relief. He was sickened to find that he could not control himself even in such a little matter as fumbling with that thin place. How could he hope to hide his secret vice? Every time he found his fingers in his hair he thought anew, disheartened at his own weakness, that he would never be quick enough to hide what would come leaping up to his eyes at a mention of Roger.

V

But until now he had had Mary. As long as Mary was there . . .

Then early in August a tragic telegram took Mary away for a time. Her delicate sister, now a young wife, was lying at the point of death, her baby prematurely born. 'Come at once. Florence calling for you,' the telegram read. She telephoned the news to Francis, who looked up the hour of the next train for her and hurried to draw the money from the savings bank to cover her expenses. Mary, wild with sorrow and alarm, began to pack, interrupted herself to run over to ask Mrs. Benson to keep a neighborly eye on Francis while she was away, tried to think what clothes the twins would need, stopped to telephone the cleaning-woman about getting Francis' meals, stood still in the middle of the floor and wrung her hands.

When Francis came with the money, he was startled to see her so distraught. 'If it were only time for my vacation, so I could go along to take care of the twins,' he said.

'Oh, if you only could be there to take care of *me!*' cried poor Mary, weeping on his shoulder. 'I'm scared to death to go by myself. I don't know how to face *any*thing without you now!'

The memory of this cry of Mary's, the thought of her need for him, Mary's real and actual need for *him* hung like incense around Francis as he stood on the station platform that evening looking after the train from which the twins' handkerchiefs still fluttered. It was a sweetness in the night air as he let himself into the empty house. He was breathing it in as he fell asleep, his arm on the pillow sacred to Mary's dear head. Mary had not yet wholly gone.

The next day, the first day since his marriage that he had wakened alone, he arrived early at the office. To his surprise Bert Warder was at a desk farther down the same room, among the apprentices. Francis wondered if this meant that Bert had been definitely put out of the drafting-room. There had been some gossip about his mistakes there. Bert's eyes were roving about unhappily. He saw the surprise in Francis' glance. 'You, damn you, with your rich brother and your pull! Of course you get on!' he thought, savage over the injustice of the world. To say something he called out foolishly, 'Hey, there, Francis, I got special orders to report here to keep the air blowing through your clearing.' As Francis took out the papers from his drawer he heard Bert's loud, unmodulated voice explaining the joke about 'the clearing.' 'Have I got to go all through that again?' thought Francis shrugging his shoulders wearily. But the men near Bert thought the joke a flat one, found Bert's noise about it tiresome, and took no pains to conceal their impression. Smarting, humiliated, apprehensive, resentful, Bert drew glumly back into himself, waiting bodefully for a chance to pay Francis out for his rebuff.

At lunch he went out of his way in the cafeteria to sit at the same table with Francis, ostentatiously familiar with him, and after work he let trolley after trolley go by the corner where he waited till Francis arrived. Knowing that he had been punished for being too fresh, he was impelled, by the fatality that hangs over people who have struck a false note, to strike it yet more loudly.

Francis had never found him harder to endure. As they walked up Jefferson Street together, he said peremptorily: 'Run on in and get your tennis things on, Frankie. We'll have a set before supper. Maybe if I try *hard,* I can score a point or two on you.'

'It's gosh-awful hot for tennis,' protested Francis.

Bert's heavy eyebrows lifted ironically over his bulging eyes, he began a certain menacing one-sided smile which was the introduction to his worst joshing. It was uglier than usual, ominous and threatening.

There was but one threat that Francis feared. It came instantly into his mind. He lost his head, 'This is the time he is going to bring Roger up—and I have not yet thought what to say or how to look!' and said in a hurried panic: 'All right, all right. Yes, let's play. It may do us good.'

A couple of hours later he came in. He had lost one love set after another to Bert. Too tired to bathe and change, he sank down in a chair. The cold supper that was to be left for him every evening by Mary's cleaning-woman, faced him on the table. After a time he ate a little of it, and went stiffly to bed. But for a long time not to sleep. Out of the darkness white balls hurtled toward him. Every time he began to doze, he saw one, like a bullet, driving straight toward his eyes, and starting to one side to avoid it woke up to find himself sweating, his heart beating fast, all his muscles taut.

The cleaning-woman, come in early by Mary's instructions to get Mr. Tuttle's breakfast, told him, 'You don't look so good, Mr. Tuttle.'

'It was hot last night,' he told her, pushing his uneaten breakfast away.

It was hot all that day too. But in spite of it he lingered in the furnace-like office till the five-twenty trolley. To no avail. As soon as he stepped off the trolley, Bert and a couple of others shouted at him to come and make a fourth at doubles. They played set after set, shifting partners in all the possible combinations. But defeat always came to the side that Francis was on. He could have told them that beforehand, he thought, playing more and more feebly.

When he went home he found two letters waiting for him in the hot shut-up living-room. One from Mary. One from Roger. What could Roger be writing for? Looking at that letter with apprehension, he opened Mary's. The twins were well, she wrote, her sister had recognized her, but was not expected to live. The rest was love. '. . . take care of yourself, darling, *darling!* I miss you so! I need you, dearest. I love you. I love you.' A murmur as from Mary's voice rose faintly from the paper. But died away in the silence coldly breathed out from the letter he had not read. He sat a long time looking at it, forgetting his dinner. But it had to be read. He tore it open.

Roger wrote to give Francis the news everybody was to see in the newspaper the next day, that through a new business combine he was now one of the vice-presidents of the Stott McDevitt Company, as well as of his own. 'We'll see to it that this means some well-deserved advancement for you too, Francis, old man,' wrote Roger pleasantly. His letters were always kind. 'It'll be fine to see more of you and Mary. We may even decide to become neighbors of yours. Nothing holds us here. And I certainly would enjoy getting acquainted with my splendid little nephews.'

The darkness fell slowly around Francis holding the letter in a clutch he could not relax. He had not eaten since noon. His old inner wound opened slowly, gaping here and there, and began to bleed. No, no, he told himself, shamed to the heart, it was nothing so clean and wholesome as bleeding; it was the drip of pus from a foul old ulcer. Well, a man was a leper who could feel nothing but mortal sickness over his own brother's success.

The blackness deepened. Out of it, one after another, there hurtled toward him bullet-like revelations of his own pitiful abjectness. He had always known he was a dub at business, a dub at tennis, a dub at life—everybody's inferior in everything! But till now he had hoped he might at least grow into a harmless dub. But he was not even that. He was incurably vicious, with the mean vice of feebleness. The beast in his heart would not die, starve it though he might. It snarled and gnashed its teeth over every new triumph of Roger's and sprang up from its lair, rattling its chain in sordid hope every time a faint shadow came over Roger's life. He would rather die, oh, infinitely rather die, than have Mary learn that her husband could not kill that hope tighten his hold as he might around its filthy throat.

Through the darkness a voice in a loud snarl came to Francis' ears, 'He'll never have any children. And I have two sons.' Francis leaped to his feet. Who was there in the dark with him? He had thought he was alone. He snapped on a light and looked wildly around the empty room. He was alone.

Had *he* said that? Or had he only thought it so fiercely that it rang in his ears like a cry? His knees shook. Suppose Mary had been there? Suppose Bert Warder had heard him? Why, he was likely to betray himself wholly at any moment, even without the dreaded mention of Roger's name. How it would be mentioned tomorrow at the office, after everyone had seen the announcement in the morning paper! And he who could control his voice no more than his fingers—he found them again fumbling involuntarily at the crown of his head!

He turned off the light, undressed, and sat down on the edge of his bed to think, to plan, to prepare himself for tomorrow's ordeal. Everyone would speak of Roger to him, not Bert only, everybody. And he had only this one night in which to find the right look, the right intonations, the right answers.

Yet when it happened he was somehow equal to it. Tense and careful as a man handling a bomb, he thought he had come through safely. Everybody had said the proper thing about what good luck it was to have his brother one of the company's vice-presidents, and he had made the proper answers. At least they had sounded all right when he said them. Why did he still have this terrified uneasiness?

Then he realized that his apprehension came from the fact that Bert Warder alone had not said a word to him. He, alone of all the men, had only nodded with a sardonic smile, and sat down silently to work. Francis' heart gave a frightened leap. Bert knew something. Somehow he had found out. Perhaps spying on him from a distance as he had doggedly answered the congratulations of the other men, Bert had seen through the mask he had tried to keep closely clamped over his face.

All that morning Bert stuck closely to his desk. But Francis knew that he was not thinking of his work. As the hot morning went on, and Bert said nothing, did not so much as look at him, Francis was surer and surer that somehow he knew. But how could he have found out?

A few moments before lunch time, Bert took his hat and without a word went out by himself. He was not at the cafeteria at all. In the alarm over this inexplicable variation from routine, Francis suddenly knew how Bert had found out. He had been standing outside the open windows last night listening in the dark, and had heard that cry of evil joy in Roger's childlessness. Yes, of course, that was what had happened.

All that afternoon Francis covertly watched Bert. It was strange how easy it was to watch him without seeming to. Even when his back was squarely turned, he could see Bert continually leaving his desk to go from one man to another, whispering in their ears. And then not knowing that Francis could see them even though his back was turned, the listener would stare at him, nodding, nodding his head with pursed-up lips, as Bert went on whispering, whispering, telling about the shameful secret he had heard as he stood listening in the dark.

Through the breach in Mary's wall the demon had stepped softly in, bringing blackness with him.

VI

Bert said nothing about tennis that day and went home early. Francis got off the trolley at Jefferson Street alone. Forgetting to look in the mailbox he let himself into the unaired, empty house. He did not go about to open windows. He sat down heavily, alarmed to feel his legs shaking under him. He could not afford to be agitated. He must collect himself. His only hope lay in not losing his head. The situation was grave. Bert might even now be coming up the walk to . . . He looked out to reassure himself, and saw not Bert, but a shining limousine drawing up in front of the house.

Before he knew that he had recognized it was Roger's, his trembling legs had carried him in a wild rush of panic to the back of the house. The locked kitchen door halted him. If he went out there he would be seen. Where could he hide? Glaring around, he saw the closet where the mops and cleaning-cloths were kept. He flung himself into it. He was just in time. He had no more than drawn the door shut when the front doorbell rang, and it came to him sickeningly that he could not remember whether he had locked the front door when he came in. He had not breathed till now, when, his lungs almost collapsing, he gasped deeply and drew into his last capillary the stench from the dirt on the damp mops, decomposing in the heat. The bell rang again. The noise found out his hiding-place so accurately that for an instant he felt he was discovered, and gave up hope. He tightened his clutch on the doorknob. Even if they found him out, he would hold the door shut, no matter how they pulled on it. He braced himself. A long silence. Had they stepped into the house? He tried to listen. The drumming of his pulse was the only sound. He stood rigid, clutching the doorknob to him, breathing the fetid air deeply in and out of his lungs. Presently from the street the sound of a starting motor came dimly through the closed door.

He waited a long time before he ventured to come out. This might be a trap to make him think they had gone. If he opened the door, he might see someone's cold, contemptuous eyes fixed on the door, waiting for him. But when he finally did cautiously turn the knob and look out, the kitchen was empty. He tiptoed to the front door, found he had locked it, that he had been safe all the time.

And then, coming to himself for a moment's respite, he turned so faint in a revulsion of feeling that he could not stand. What in God's name had he been doing? But was it *possible!* It was so remote from anything he wished that he thought for an instant he must have dreamed it. He, Francis, had had no intention of hiding from Roger! Why should he? There was no reason. Suppose Mary had been there? What possible reason could he have given her?

The respite was over . . . *suppose someone had seen him!* A cold sweat drenched him. Someone had seen him, of course. Everyone! They all must have known what he had done. Everyone on the street must have seen him leave the trolley and go into the house. They all knew Roger by sight. They must all have been looking from their windows, saying to each other, 'But he's there. I saw him go in just now.' Perhaps they had gone out to the street to tell Roger that. Tomorrow they would say to him, suspicious eyes boring into his, 'Why in the world didn't you let your brother in yesterday?' What could he say?

He wrung his hands. 'What can I say? What can I say?' Then he thought of a way out. It was simple. He could say he had gone at once to sleep, that he had not heard the bell. He would hurry up to the sleeping-porch now and lie down so that if anyone came in he would be found there, his eyes closed. He raced up the stairs and flung himself down on the bed, clenching his eyelids shut. It was essential that he should seem to be asleep. Then he remembered that nobody could come in because the doors were locked. He opened his eyes. He tried to get up.

But he was by now exhausted. He fell back, his wide-open eyes facing a new danger. He imagined Bert Warder asking him the next morning, 'What were you up to yesterday that you didn't want your brother to catch you at?' He must think of an answer to that question. Perhaps if he went over it all now in anticipation, question and answer, he might be able to . . . Suppose Bert said suddenly, 'What did you get into the mop-closet for yesterday, when your brother . . .'

Oh horror! He had forgotten to keep his eyes shut to prove to people who came in to spy on him that he really had been asleep when Roger rang the bell. He shut them hard. Then slowly remembered, no, no, that was not necessary. The front door was locked. No one could come in. He opened them again and stared out through the high railing of the sleeping-porch.

He had been trying to think what he could answer Bert Warder tomorrow. But how could he hope to control his face to hide his secret when he had no control over his fingers—he snatched his fumbling hand down from his head—over his body—he felt himself cowering again in front of the foul-smelling mop. His desperate thoughts of how to ward off tomorrow's danger were cut short by a sudden cold divination of the present peril. Danger was stealthily closing in on him now, this instant. He felt it creeping up on him from behind. He had known what that danger was. He tried wildly to remember. Oh, yes. He was to keep his eyes closed so that people would think him asleep. He had forgotten that. He shut them tightly, and weak with relief, felt that he had been just in time.

He opened them in the morning, rose and under the cleaning-woman's eyes went through the motions of eating breakfast. He and Bert happened to walk into the office together. He was incapable of speech, all his vitality concentrated on being on his guard. Bert looked pale and out of sorts and said he hadn't been feeling very well yesterday. But he was all right today, he said, goggling his eyes, 'And how about some tennis?'

Francis saw through this trick instantly. He knew Bert was lying, and why he was lying . . . to throw Francis off his guard. His plan was to wait till Francis was exhausted at the end of the tennis that afternoon and then suddenly to shoot his question like one of his cannon-ball serves . . . *'Why didn't you let your brother in yesterday?'* Yes, it would come to him like one of those fiercely driven balls he could not return.

All day he tried to invent a way out of the trap laid for him. But it was not till he was on the trolley with Bert that his inspiration came to him. The ride home was triumphal. He told Bert with a happy smile that he was going to change his clothes for tennis, and ran into the empty house. He stepped lightly, exultantly, into the kitchen and putting all his weight against it, tipped the heavy refrigerator to one side. As it toppled he stooped, still smiling, and held his right hand under it.

VII

But of course the bandaged hand that could not hold a racket could not hold a pen or run a typewriter either. When he went to the office, he was sent home on sick-leave. This pleased him. It meant he could lie on the bed all day, his eyes tightly shut to prevent the discovery that threatened him, that threatened Mary through him. The moment he opened them—as he must if he went downstairs to eat—Mary was in danger again, might at any moment be dragged in the filth of knowing what kind of man her husband was. But he had grown very clever in thinking of ways to protect Mary from that discovery. 'I seem to be very sleepy,' he said cunningly to the cleaning-woman. 'The doctor who took care of my hand told me the accident might have that effect and wanted me to sleep as much as I could. Just keep some food on a tray for me, will you, outside the door. When I wake up I will eat it.'

After this he need not open his eyes. He could lie, hour after hour, reveling in the pain of his mangled hand, glorious anguish with which he was buying security for Mary. He could, waiting till black night, grope his way into the bathroom, find scissors and razor blades by feel, and use them without looking. Without opening those tightly shut eyelids he could find the food left for him on the tray, and empty it out in the corner of his closet so that the cleaning-woman would think he ate it. Mostly he lay rigidly still, as still as if he were in his coffin. Now that there was no reason to raise his hand to his head, his arms lay quiet at his side. What a heavenly rest! He was resting almost as well as if he were dead. And Mary was as safe as if he were dead. He was very tired, but infinitely proud of knowing how to protect Mary.

Sometimes his tense eyelids relaxed and he really slept. That was the best. Oh, that was the best . . .

VIII

Since he no longer knew whether it were night or day he could not judge of time. How long had he lain there keeping Mary safe? A day . . . a week . . . a year? The silence of the empty house seemed to be broken by voices. The cleaning-woman's. And—could it be—it sounded like Mary's! It *couldn't* be Mary's, could it, come back into danger when he was so sure he had made her safe? Not *Mary!* This must be a ruse of his enemies to frighten him into opening his eyes.

He sat up in bed, staring into the red blackness of his closed lids. Horrified, he strained his ears and recognized the children's voices. And that was Mary's step in the hall downstairs. His heart beat in time with it as with no other. Mary had come back, walking straight into mortal peril.

Once more he had failed. He had not saved her after all. For a moment he was undone with defeat, and trembling from head to foot sat dumb with stupid panic.

He heard the dear remembered step start up the stairs. With an effort greater than any in all his life, he summoned his soul to rise on the wings of love and be strong. And saw how even now it was not too late. Even now, though Mary's dear step was mounting the stairs, unsuspecting . . . Now, now was the time to play the man, once for all.

He flung himself on his love for Mary, and with one beat of its mighty wings it bore him beyond Destiny that thought to have him vanquished. Weak he might be—his love, immortal and divine, made him, at the last, mightier than Fate.

IX

Only after the excitement of the clearing of Don's name was all over, when the Warders were on the train going home from their exhausting week in Huntsville, did they begin to understand all that the proving of Don's innocence meant to them. Their days in Huntsville, after the melodramatic discovery of the real thief, were so crammed with raw emotion they had been bewildered. They had passed without a pause from their first incredulous excitement to incredulous joy and then indignant sympathy for their brother with all those months of undeserved wretchedness back of him. What a nightmare they had all lived through, they said over and over to each other. They had wept together, and the tears had washed the poison out of their wounds so that now, in the train on their way home, they were faint in the sweet weakness of convalescence. Bert's heart, that had been crushed shut by shame and fear, softened, opened, and let him out from the bitter desolation of self-pity. His imagination that had been smothered under the consciousness of disgrace drew breath again. He forgot what he had suffered; his thoughts were for his brother. 'Poor Don!' he said over and over. 'Poor *Don!*' After what he had lived through, it was like dying and going to heaven, to feel love and compassion. He was proud with a noble and new pride that the loss of all his savings weighed as nothing with him compared to his brother's vindication.

The news had been in the newspapers. With headlines. Everybody must have read it. The Warders almost expected a congratulating delegation of neighbors to meet them at the station. But when they climbed heavily down from the dusty train and saw that the platform was empty, they thought at once that it was only uneducated working-class people who made a fuss in public, and laid the lesson humbly to heart.

There was no one to be seen on Jefferson Street when they stepped from the trolley at the home corner. They set their suitcases down with a long breath, to look. There was their street! It was theirs, with its genteel lawns, its ornamental useless flower-gardens, its dignified park-like shade trees. There it stood brooding dreamily in the blue summer twilight, and welcomed them back.

'I'll carry the bags, both of them,' said Bert to his wife, chivalrously.

They trudged along toward their home, their own home, redeemed, shining, safe. They belonged here, they thought, with deep content. They were accepted by these refined people who took lawns and trees and flowers for granted. Their purged hearts swelled with thankfulness, with friendliness, with good resolutions. They must be worthy of their good fortune.

As they approached the Benson house, they saw that Helen was standing on the front porch, looking at the newspaper. What a nice girl Helen was, they thought fondly. Imogene called, '*Ooh*-hoo, Nellie!' and skipped up the front walk. Stricken by Helen's face she fell back, shocked. 'Oh . . . why . . . what's the *matter?*'

Two or three short sentences were all Helen had to say. Her news, whining ominously like a loaded shell, flew over her listeners' blanched faces, not exploding till long after it had passed.

They stood like stocks, stupidly listening to the sound of the words they could not understand. Then Bert said in a flat voice, 'Not Frankie Tuttle! You didn't say it was *Frankie Tuttle!*' He took the newspaper from Helen's hand. Through the brooding summer twilight the headlines shrieked.

JEFFERSON STREET MAN
GOES SUDDENLY INSANE
LEAPS FROM THIRD STORY
TO DEATH.

The paper fell from his hand.

'This very morning,' said Helen.

'That deep cement-covered entrance to the basement,' began Mrs. Benson. 'Right over the high railing around the sleeping-porch. Mary had come home—you knew she'd been away with a sick sister—and she had just started up the stairs.'

The Warders, stunned, sank down on their suitcases. Bert's mouth hung slackly open.

Joe Crosby came over from across the street. His lips twitched. His eyes were red. He shook Bert's hand without a word. The Warders had been but bludgeoned into stupefaction by the headlines. They had not believed them. But this silence told them what had happened. Mrs. Warder and Imogene began to cry. A film came over Bert's bulging eyes. He got out his handkerchief, blew his nose, and took his hat off, holding it on his knee and looking fixedly down at it.

After a time, when they could, they asked the usual questions. And had the usual answers. No imaginable explanation. His accounts in perfect order. His health all right—he'd hurt his hand, of course, but that was not serious; the doctor said it was healing without any sign of infection. And everything going extra well with him, seems though—his brother just made vice-president of the company, the luckiest kind of a break, his brother thinking the world and all of him—came right over the minute he heard of this and took Mary and the children back. To make their home with him. Always. Said he'd always wanted children in his home. No, everything in the business end of his life was fine, couldn't be better. His brother kept saying there wasn't *any*thing he wouldn't have done for him. And no trouble at home, Lord, *no!* He and Mary were the happiest couple on the street. Suspicious of their good faith, Bert said it seemed as if there *must* have been some warning. 'No, there wasn't. He was just exactly the same as ever, the last time anybody saw him. He'd hurt his hand, you know—was that before you went to Huntsville? No, I guess it was afterwards—and that kept him away from the office for a while. It must have been while he was at home with that, that he . . .'

Bert Warder was shocked at a glimpsed possibility of unneighborly neglect. 'For the Lord's sake, hadn't anybody gone in to see that he was all right?' he asked sternly.

Mrs. Benson defended herself hastily. 'Oh, yes, yes. Before she left, Mary had asked me to look after him, and I went over there every day. Sometimes twice. But the cleaning-woman always said he was asleep. She told me the doctor had given him something to deaden the pain in his hand and make him drowsy.'

Joe Crosby confirmed this. 'Yes, every time I went in, too, he was asleep. I went clear up to his room, several times. The shades were pulled down and it was dark. But I could see he was asleep all right.' He answered the stubborn question in the other's face. 'Yes, I know, Bert, I felt just the way you do, as if we might have done *some*thing, if we'd been any good. But you know there isn't anything *any*body can do when it's a case of'—he drew in a long breath before he could pronounce the word—'it was just plain insanity, Bert.'

'Frankie wasn't insane!' rapped out Bert, indignant. 'He was a *swell* fellow!'

Joe lowered his voice and, with a dark, shamed intonation and yet with a certain relish of the enormity he was reporting, said: 'Bert, when they picked up his body they found he'd shaved his head. All over. Every spear of hair shaved off. Down to the skin. The way you shave your face.'

This did stagger the questioner. He said feebly: 'You don't *say* . . . ! Good gosh, his *head!* Why, what in the . . . whatever would make anybody do *that?'* and fell back into his stockish, uncomprehending blankness.

Mrs. Benson murmured an explanation. 'The doctors told his brother that's one of the signs of religious mania—the tonsure, you know. They told his brother that sometimes insane . . .'

'Oh, they make me tired!' cried Joe Crosby in angry sorrow. 'They don't know anything about it. Why don't they keep still!'

Bert Warder agreed sadly. 'I guess nobody knows anything about what causes insanity.'

It came over him that this was no waking nightmare, was fact. But he could not admit it as fact. 'It just don't seem *possible* to me!' he told them, his voice breaking grotesquely in his pain. 'Why, Frankie and me . . . why, I never *had* a better pal than Frankie Tuttle!'

KENTUCKY

Dawn of Remembered Spring

JESSE STUART

'Be careful, Shan,' Mom said. 'I'm afraid if you wade that creek that a water moccasin will bite you.'

'All right, Mom.'

'You know what happened to Roy Deer last Sunday!'

'Yes, Mom!'

'He's nigh at the point of death,' she said. 'I'm going over there now to see him. His leg's swelled hard as a rock and it's turned black as black-oak bark. They're not looking for Roy to live until midnight tonight.'

'All water moccasins ought to be killed, hadn't they, Mom?'

'Yes, they're pizen things, but you can't kill them,' Mom said. 'They're in all of these creeks around here. There's so many of them we can't kill 'em all.'

Mom stood at the foot-log that crossed the creek in front of our house. Her white apron was starched stiff; I heard it rustle when Mom put her hands in the little pocket in the right upper corner to get tobacco crumbs for her pipe. Mom wore her slat bonnet that shaded her sun-tanned face—a bonnet with strings that came under her chin and tied in a bowknot.

'I feel uneasy,' Mom said as she filled her long-stemmed clay-stone pipe with bright-burley crumbs, tamped them down with her index finger, and struck a match on the rough bark of an apple tree that grew on the creek bank by the foot-log.

'Don't feel uneasy about me,' I said.

From *Tales from the Plum Grove Hills*. Published by E. P. Dutton & Co., Inc. Used by permission of the author.

'But I do,' Mom said. 'Your Pa out groundhog huntin' and I'll be away at Deers'—nobody at home but you, and so many pizen snakes around this house.'

Mom blew a cloud of blue smoke from her pipe. She walked across the foot-log—her long clean dress sweeping the weed stubble where Pa had mown the weeds along the path with a scythe so we could leave the house without getting our legs wet by the dew-covered weeds.

When Mom walked out of sight around the turn of the pasture hill and the trail of smoke that she left behind her had disappeared into the light blue April air, I crossed the garden fence at the wild-plum thicket.

Everybody gone, I thought. I am left alone. I'll do as I please. A water moccasin bit Roy Deer but a water moccasin will never bite me. I'll get me a club from this wild-plum thicket and I'll wade up the creek killing water moccasins.

There was a dead wild-plum sprout standing among the thicket of living sprouts. It was about the size of a tobacco stick. I stepped out of my path into the wild-plum thicket. Barefooted, I walked among the wild-plum thorns. I uprooted the dead wild-plum sprout. There was a bulge on it where roots had once been—now the roots had rooted in the earth. It was like a maul with this big bulge on the end of it. It would be good to hit water moccasins with.

The mules played in the pasture. It was Sunday—their day of rest. And the mules knew it. This was Sunday and it was my day of rest. It was my one day of freedom, too, when Mom and Pa were gone and I was left alone. I would like to be a man now, I thought, I'd love to plow the mules, run a farm, and kill snakes. A water moccasin bit Roy Deer but one would never bite me.

The bright sunlight of April played over the green Kentucky hills. Sunlight fell onto the creek of blue water that twisted like a crawling snake around the high bluffs and between the high rocks. In many places dwarf willows, horse-weeds, iron weeds, and wild grapevines shut away the sunlight and the creek waters stood in quiet cool puddles. These little puddles under the shade of weeds, vines, and willows were the places where the water moccasins lived.

I rolled my overall legs above my knees so I wouldn't wet them and Mom wouldn't know I'd been wading the creek. I started wading up the creek toward the head of the hollow. I carried my wild-plum club across my shoulder with both hands gripped tightly around the small end of it. I was ready to maul the first water moccasin I saw.

'One of you old water moccasins bit Roy Deer,' I said bravely, clinching my grip tighter around my club, 'but you won't bite me.'

As I waded the cool creek waters, my bare feet touched gravel on the creek bottom. When I touched a wet water-soaked stick on the bottom of the creek bed, I'd think it was a snake and I'd jump. I'd wade into banks of quicksand. I'd sink into the sand above my knees. It was hard to pull my legs out of this quicksand and when I pulled them out they'd be covered with thin quicky mud that the next puddle of water would wash away.

'A water moccasin,' I said to myself. I was scared to look at him. He was wrapped around a willow that was bent over the creek. He was sleeping in the sun. I slipped toward him quietly—step by step—with my club drawn over my shoulder. Soon as I got close enough to reach him, I came over my shoulder with the club. I hit the water moccasin a powerful blow that mashed its head flat against the willow. It fell dead into the water. I picked it up by the tail and threw it upon the bank.

'One gone,' I said to myself.

The water was warm around my feet and legs. The sharp-edged gravels hurt the bottoms of my feet but the soft sand soothed them. Butterflies swarmed over my head and around me—alighting on the wild pink phlox that grew in clusters along the creek bank. Wild honey bees, bumble bees, and butterflies worked on the elder blossoms, the shoe-make blossoms and the beet-red finger-long blossoms of the iron weed and the whitish pink covered smart-weed blossoms. Birds sang among the willows and flew up and down the creek with four-winged snakefeeders in their bills.

This is what I like to do, I thought. I love to kill snakes. I'm not afraid of snakes. I laughed to think how afraid of snakes Mom was—how she struck a potato-digger tine through a big rusty-golden copperhead's skin just enough to pin him to the earth and hold him so he couldn't get under our floor. He fought the potato-digger handle until Pa came home from work and killed him. Where he'd thrown poison over the ground it killed the weeds and weeds didn't grow on this spot again for four years.

Once when Mom was making my bed upstairs, she heard a noise of something running behind the paper that was pasted over the cracks between the logs—the paper split and a house snake six feet long fell onto the floor with a mouse in his mouth. Mom killed him with a bed slat. She called me once to bring her a goose-neck hoe upstairs quickly. I ran upstairs and killed two cow snakes restin' on the wall plate. And Pa killed twenty-eight copperheads out of a two-acre oat field in the hollow above the house one spring season.

'Snakes—snakes,' Mom used to say, 'are goin' to run us out'n this Hollow.'

'It's because these woods ain't been burnt out in years,' Pa'd always answer. 'Back when I's a boy the old people burnt the woods out every spring to kill the snakes. Got so anymore there ain't enough good timber for a board tree and people have had to quit burning up the good timber. Snakes are about to take the woods again.'

I thought about the snakes Pa had killed in the cornfield and the tobacco patch and how nearly copperheads had come to biting me and how I'd always seen the snake in time to cut his head off with a hoe or get out of his way. I thought of the times I had heard a rattlesnake's warning and how I'd run when I hadn't seen the snake. As I thought these thoughts, plop a big water moccasin fell from the creek bank into a puddle of water.

'I'll get you,' I said. 'You can't fool me! You can't stand muddy water.'

I stirred the water until it was muddy with my wild-plum club. I waited for the water moccasin to stick his head above the water. Where wild ferns dipped down from the bank's edge and touched the water, I saw the snake's head rise slowly above the water—watchin' me with his lidless eyes. I swung sidewise with my club like batting at a ball. I couldn't swing over my shoulder, for there were willow limbs above my head.

I surely got him, I thought. I waited to see. Soon, something like milk spread over the water. 'I got 'im.' I raked in the water with my club and lifted from the bottom of the creek bed a water moccasin long as my club. It was longer than I was tall. I threw him upon the bank and moved slowly up the creek—looking on every drift, stump, log, and sunny spot. I looked for a snake's head along the edges of the creek bank where ferns dipped over and touched the water.

I waded up the creek all day killing water moccasins. If one were asleep on the bank, I slipped upon him quietly as a cat. I mauled him with the big end of my wild-plum club. I killed him in his sleep. He never knew what struck him. If a brush caught the end of my club and caused me to miss and let the snake get into a puddle of water, I muddied the water and waited for him to stick his head above the water. When he stuck his head above the water, I got him. Not one water moccasin got away from me. It was four o'clock when I stepped from the creek onto the bank. I'd killed fifty-three water moccasins.

Water moccasins are not half as dangerous as turtles, I thought. A water moccasin can't bite you under the water for he gets his mouth full of water. A turtle can bite you under water and when one bites you he won't let lose until it thunders, unless you cut his head off. I'd been afraid of turtles all day because I didn't have a knife in my pocket to cut one's head off if it grabbed my foot and held it.

When I left the creek, I was afraid of the snakes I'd killed. I didn't throw my club away. I gripped the club until my hands hurt. I looked below my path, above my path, and in front of me. When I saw a stick on the ground, I thought it was a snake. I eased up to it quietly as a cat trying to catch a bird. I was ready to hit it with my club.

What will Mom think when I tell her I've killed fifty-three water moccasins? I thought. A water moccasin bit Roy Deer but one's not going to bite me. I paid the snakes back for biting him. It was good enough for them. Roy wasn't bothering the water moccasin that bit him. He was just crossing the creek at the foot-log and it jumped from the grass and bit him.

Shadows lengthened from the tall trees. The Hollow was deep and the creek flowed softly in the cool recesses of evening shadows. There was one patch of sunlight. It was upon the steep broomsedge-covered bluff above the path.

'Snakes,' I cried, 'snakes a-fightin' and they're not water moccasins! They're copperheads!'

They were wrapped around each other. Their lidless eyes looked into each other's eyes. Their hard lips touched each other's lips. They did not move. They did not pay any attention to me. They looked at one another.

I'll kill 'em, I thought, if they don't kill one another in this fight. I stood in the path with my club ready. I had heard snakes fought each other but I'd never seen them fight.

'What're you lookin' at, Shan?' Uncle Alf Skinner asked. He walked up the path with a cane in his hand.

'Snakes a-fightin'.'

'Snakes a-fightin'?'

'Yes.'

'I never saw it in my life.'

'I'll kill 'em both if they don't finish the fight,' I said. 'I'll club 'em to death.'

'Snakes a-fightin', Shan,' he shouted, 'you are too young to know! It's snakes in love! Snakes in love! Don't kill 'em—just keep your eye on 'em until I bring Martha over here! She's never seen snakes in love!'

Uncle Alf ran around the turn of the hill. He brought Aunt Martha back with him. She was carrying a basket of greens on her arm and the case knife that she'd been cutting greens with in her hand.

'See 'em, Martha,' Uncle Alf said. 'Look up there in that broom-sedge!'

'I'll declare,' she said. 'I've lived all my life and I never saw this. I've wondered about snakes!'

She stood with a smile on her wrinkled lips. Uncle Alf stood with a wide smile on his deep-lined face. I looked at them and wondered why they looked at these copperheads and smiled. Uncle Alf looked at Aunt Martha. They smiled at each other.

'Shan! Shan!' I heard Mom calling.

'I'm here,' I shouted.

'Where've you been?' she asked as she turned around the bend of the hill with a switch in her hand.

'Be quiet, Sall," Uncle Alf said. 'Come here and look for yourself!'

'What is it?' Mom asked.

'Snakes in love,' Uncle Alf said.

Mom was mad. 'Shan, I feel like limbing you,' she said. 'I've hunted every place for you! Where've you been?'

'Killin' snakes,' I answered.

'Roy Deer is dead," she said. 'That's how dangerous it is to fool with snakes.'

'I paid the snakes back for him,' I said. 'I've killed fifty-three water moccasins!'

'Look, Sall!'

'Yes, Alf, I see,' Mom said.

Mom threw her switch on the ground. Her eyes were wide apart. The frowns left her face.

'It's the first time I ever saw snakes in love,' Aunt Martha said to Mom.

'It's the first time I ever saw anything like this,' Mom said. 'Shan, you go tell your Pa to come and look at this.'

I was glad to do anything for Mom. I was afraid of her switch. When I brought Pa back to the sunny bank where the copperheads were loving, Art and Sadie Baker were there and Tom and Ethel Riggs—and there were a lot of strangers there. They were looking at the copperheads wrapped around each other with their eyes looking into each other's eyes and their hard lips touching each other's lips.

'You hurry to the house, Shan,' Pa said, 'and cut your stove wood for tonight.'

'I'd like to kill these copperheads,' I said.

'Why?' Pa asked.

'Fightin',' I said.

Uncle Alf and Aunt Martha laughed as I walked down the path carrying my club. It was something—I didn't know what—all the crowd watching the snakes were smiling. Their faces were made over new. The snakes had done something to them. Their wrinkled faces were as bright as the spring sunlight on the bluff; their eyes were shiny as the creek was in the noonday sunlight. And they laughed and talked to one another. I heard their laughter grow fainter as I walked down the path toward the house. Their laughter was louder than the wild honey bees I had heard swarming over the shoe-make, alderberry, and wild phlox blossoms along the creek.

TENNESSEE

Bright and Morning Star

RICHARD WRIGHT

She stood with her black face some six inches from the moist window-pane and wondered when on earth would it ever stop raining. It might keep up like this all week, she thought. She heard rain droning upon the roof, and high up in the wet sky her eyes followed the silent rush of a bright shaft of yellow that swung from the airplane beacon in far-off Memphis. Momently she could see it cutting through the rainy dark; it would hover a second like a gleaming sword above her head, then vanish. She sighed, troubling, Johnny-Boys been trampin in this slop all day wid no decent shoes on his feet. . . . Through the window she could see the rich black earth sprawling outside in the night. There was more rain than the clay could soak up; pools stood everywhere. She yawned and mumbled: 'Rains good n bad. It kin make seeds bus up thu the groun, er it kin bog things down lika watah-soaked coffin.' Her hands were folded loosely over her stomach and the hot air of the kitchen traced a filmy veil of sweat on her forehead. From the cook-stove came the soft singing of burning wood and now and then a throaty bubble rose from a pot of simmering greens.

'Shucks, Johnny-Boy coulda let somebody else do all tha runnin in the rain. Theres others bettah fixed fer it than he is. But, naw! Johnny-Boy ain the one t trust nobody t do nothin. Hes gotta do it *all* hissef. . . .'

She glanced at a pile of damp clothes in a zinc tub. Waal, Ah bettah git to work. She turned, lifted a smoothing iron with a thick pad of cloth, touched a spit-wet finger to it with a quick, jerking motion: *smiiitz!* Yeah; its hot! Stooping, she took a blue work-shirt from

---

the tub and shook it out. With a deft twist of her shoulder she caught the iron in her right hand; the fingers of her left hand took a piece of wax from a tin box and a frying sizzle came as she smeared the bottom. She was thinking of nothing now; her hands followed a life-long ritual of toil. Spreading a sleeve, she ran the hot iron to and fro until the wet cloth became stiff. She was deep in the midst of her work when a song rose out of the far off days of her childhood and broke through half-parted lips:

Hes the Lily of the Valley, the Bright n Mawnin Star
Hes the Fairest of Ten Thousan t mah soul . . .

A gust of wind dashed rain against the window. Johnny-Boy oughta c mon home n eat his suppah. Aw Lawd! Itd be fine ef Sug could eat wid us tonight! Itd be like ol times! Mabbe aftah all it wont be long fo he'll be back. Tha lettah Ah got from im las week said *Don give up hope. . . .* Yeah; we gotta live in hope. Then both of her sons, Sug and Johnny-Boy, would be back with her.

With an involuntary nervous gesture, she stopped and stood still, listening. But the only sound was the lulling fall of rain. Shucks, ain no usa me ackin this way, she thought. Ever time they gits ready to hol them meetings Ah gits jumpity. Ah been a lil scared ever since Sug went t jail. She heard the clock ticking and looked. Johnny-Boys a *hour* late! He sho mus be havin a time doin all tha trampin, trampin thu the mud. . . . But her fear was a quiet one; it was more like an intense brooding than a fear; it was a sort of hugging of hated facts so closely that she could feel their grain, like letting cold water run over her hand from a faucet on a winter morning.

She ironed again, faster now, as if the more she engaged her body in work the less she would think. But how could she forget Johnny-Boy out there on those wet fields rounding up white and black Communists for a meeting tomorrow? And that was just what Sug had been doing when the sheriff had caught him, beat him, and tried to make him tell who and where his comrades were. Po Sug! They sho musta beat tha boy something awful! But, thank Gawd, he didnt talk! He ain no weaklin' Sug ain! Hes been lion-hearted all his life long.

That had happened a year ago. And now each time those meetings came around the old terror surged back. While shoving the iron a cluster of toiling days returned; days of washing and ironing to feed

Johnny-Boy and Sug so they could do party work; days of carrying a hundred pounds of white folks' clothes upon her head across fields sometimes wet and sometimes dry. But in those days a hundred pounds was nothing to carry carefully balanced upon her head while stepping by instinct over the corn and cotton rows. The only time it had seemed heavy was when she had heard of Sug's arrest. She had been coming home one morning with a bundle upon her head, her hands swinging idly by her sides, walking slowly with her eyes in front of her, when Bob, Johnny-Boy's pal, had called from across the fields and had come and told her that the sheriff had got Sug. That morning the bundle had become heavier than she could ever remember.

And with each passing week now, though she spoke of it to no one, things were becoming heavier. The tubs of water and the smoothing iron and the bundle of clothes were becoming harder to lift, her with her back aching so, and her work was taking longer, all because Sug was gone and she didn't know just when Johnny-Boy would be taken too. To ease the ache of anxiety that was swelling her heart, she hummed, then sang softly:

> He walks wid me, He talks wid me
> He tells me Ahm His own. . . .

Guiltily, she stopped and smiled. Looks like Ah jus cant seem t fergit them ol songs, no mattah how hard Ah tries. . . . She had learned them when she was a little girl living and working on a farm. Every Monday morning from the corn and cotton fields the slow strains had floated from her mother's lips, lonely and haunting; and later, as the years had filled with gall, she had learned their deep meaning. Long hours of scrubbing floors for a few cents a day had taught her who Jesus was, what a great boon it was to cling to Him, to be like Him and suffer without a mumbling word. She had poured the yearning of her life into the songs, feeling buoyed with a faith beyond this world. The figure of the Man nailed in agony to the Cross, His burial in a cold grave, His transfigured Resurrection, His being breath and clay, God and Man—all had focused her feelings upon an imagery which had swept her life into a wondrous vision.

But as she had grown older, a cold white mountain, the white folks and their laws, had swum into her vision and shattered her songs and their spell of peace. To her that white mountain was temptation, something to lure her from her Lord, a part of the world God had made in order that she might endure it and come through all the stronger, just as Christ had risen with greater glory from the tomb. The days crowded with trouble had enhanced her faith and she had grown to love hardship with a bitter pride; she had obeyed the laws of the white folks with a soft smile of secret knowing.

After her mother had been snatched up to heaven in a chariot of fire, the years had brought her a rough workingman and two black babies, Sug and Johnny-Boy, all three of whom she had wrapped in the charm and magic of her vision. Then she was tested by no less than God; her man died, a trial which she bore with the strength shed by the grace of her vision; finally even the memory of her man faded into the vision itself, leaving her with two black boys growing tall, slowly into manhood.

Then one day grief had come to her heart when Johnny-Boy and Sug had walked forth demanding their lives. She had sought to fill their eyes with her vision, but they would have none of it. And she had wept when they began to boast of the strength shed by a new and terrible vision.

But she had loved them, even as she loved them now; bleeding, her heart had followed them. She could have done no less, being an old woman in a strange world. And day by day her sons had ripped from her startled eyes her old vision; and image by image had given her a new one, different, but great and strong enough to fling her into the light of another grace. The wrongs and sufferings of black men had taken the place of Him nailed to the Cross; the meager beginnings of the party had become another Resurrection; and the hate of those who would destroy her new faith had quickened in her a hunger to feel how deeply her strength went.

'Lawd, Johnny-Boy,' she would sometimes say, 'Ah jus wan them white folks t try t make me tell *who* is *in* the party n who *ain!* Ah jus wan em t try, n Ahll show em something they never thought a black woman could have!'

But sometimes like tonight, while lost in the forgetfulness of work, the past and the present would become mixed in her; while toiling under a strange star for a new freedom the old songs would slip from her lips with their beguiling sweetness.

The iron was getting cold. She put more wood into the fire, stood again at the window and watched the yellow blade of light cut through the wet darkness. Johnny-Boy ain here yit. . . . Then, before she was aware of it, she was still, listening for sounds. Under the drone of rain she heard the slosh of feet in mud. Tha ain Johnny-Boy. She knew his long, heavy footsteps in a million. She heard feet come on the porch. Some woman. . . . She heard bare knuckles knock three times, then once. Thas some of them comrades! She unbarred the door, cracked it a few inches, and flinched from the cold rush of damp wind.

'Whos tha?'

'Its me!'

'Who?'

'Me, Reva!'

She flung the door open.

'Lawd, chile, c mon in!'

She stepped to one side and a thin, blonde-haired white girl ran through the door; as she slid the bolt she heard the girl gasping and shaking her wet clothes. Somethings wrong! Riva wouldna walked a mile t mah mouse in all this slop fer nothin! Tha gals stuck onto Johnny-Boy; Ah wondah ef anything happened t im?

'Git on inter the kitchen, Reva, where its warm.'

'Lawd, Ah sho is wet!'

'How yuh reckon yuhd be, in all tha rain?'

'Johnny-Boy ain here *yit?*' asked Reva.

'Naw! N ain no use yuh worrying bout im. Jus yuh git them shoes off! Yuh wanna ketch yo deatha col?' She stood looking absently. Yeah; its something bout the party er Johnny-Boy thas gone wrong. Lawd, Ah wondah ef her pa knows how she feels bout Johnny-Boy? 'Honey, yuh hadnt oughta come out in sloppy weather like this.'

'Ah had t come, An Sue.'

She led Reva to the kitchen.

'Git them shoes off an git close t the stove so yuhll git dry!'

'An Sue, Ah got something to tell yuh . . .'

The words made her hold her breath. Ah bet its something bout Johnny-Boy!

'Whut, honey?'

'The sheriff wuz by our house tonight. He come see pa.'

'Yeah?'

'He done got word from somewheres bout tha meetin tomorrow.'

'Is it Johnny-Boy, Reva?'

'Aw, naw, An Sue! Ah ain hearda word bout im. Ain yuh seen im tonight?'

'He ain come home t eat yit.'

'Where kin he be?'

'Lawd knows, chile.'

'Somebodys gotta tell them comrades tha meetings off,' said Reva. 'The sheriffs got men watchin our house. Ah had t slip out t git here widout em followin me.'

'Reva?'

'Hunh?'

'Ahma ol woman n Ah wans yuh t tell me the truth.'

'Whut, An Sue?'

'Yuh ain tryin t fool me, is yuh?'

'*Fool* yuh?'

'Bout Johnny-Boy?'

'Lawd, naw, An Sue!'

'Ef theres anything wrong jus tell me, chile. Ah kin stan it.'

She stood by the ironing board, her hands as usual folded loosely over her stomach, watching Reva pull off her waterclogged shoes. She was feeling that Johnny-Boy was already lost to her; she was feeling the pain that would come when she knew it for certain; and she was feeling that she would have to be brave and bear it. She was like a person caught in a swift current of water and knew where the water was sweeping her and did not want to go on but had to go on to the end.

'It ain nothin bout Johnny-Boy, An Sue,' said Reva. 'But we gotta do something er we'll all git inter trouble.'

'How the sheriff know bout tha meetin?'

'Thas whut pa wans t know.'

'Somebody done turned Judas.'

'Sho looks like it.'

'Ah bet it wuz some of them new ones,' she said.

'Its hard to tell,' said Reva.

'Lissen, Reva, yuh oughta stay here n git dry, but yuh bettah git back n tell yo pa Johnny-Boy ain here n Ah don know when hes gonna show up. *Some*bodys gotta tell them comrades t stay erway from yo pas house.'

She stood with her back to the window, looking at Reva's wide, blue eyes. Po critter! Gotta go back thu all tha slop! Though she felt sorry for Reva, not once did she think that it would not have to be done. Being a woman, Reva was not suspect; she would have to go. It was just as natural for Reva to go back through the cold rain as it was for her to iron night and day or for Sug to be in jail. Right now, Johnny-Boy was out there on those dark fields trying to get home. Lawd, don let em git im tonight! In spite of herself her feelings became torn. She loved her son and, loving him, she loved what he was trying to do. Johnny-Boy was happiest when he was working for the party, and her love for him was for his happiness. She frowned, trying hard to fit something together in her feelings: for her to try to stop Johnny-Boy was to admit that all the toil of years meant nothing; and to let him go meant that sometime or other he would be caught, like Sug. In facing it this way she felt a little stunned, as though she had come suddenly upon a blank wall in the dark. But outside in the rain were people, white and black, whom she had known all her life. Those people depended upon Johnny-Boy, loved him and looked to him as a man and leader. Yeah; hes gotta keep on; he cant stop now. . . . She looked at Reva; she was crying and pulling her shoes back on with reluctant fingers.

'Whut yuh carryin on tha way fer, chile?'

'Yuh done los Sug, now yuh sendin Johnny-Boy . . .'

'Ah got t, honey.'

She was glad she could say that. Reva believed in black folks and not for anything in the world would she falter before her. In Reva's trust and acceptance of her she had found her first feelings of humanity; Reva's love was her refuge from shame and degradation. If in the early days of her life the white mountain had driven her back from the earth, then in her last days Reva's love was drawing her toward it, like the beacon that swung through the night outside. She heard Reva sobbing.

'Hush, honey!'

'Mah brothers in jail too! Ma cries every day . . .'

'Ah know, honey.'

She helped Reva with her coat; her fingers felt the scant flesh of the girl's shoulders. She don git ernuff t eat, she thought. She slipped her arms around Reva's waist and held her close for a moment.

'Now, yuh stop tha cryin.'

'A-a-ah c-c-cant hep it. . . .'

'Every thingll be awright; Johnny-Boyll be back.'

'Yuh think so?'

'Sho, chile. Cos he will.'

Neither of them spoke again until they stood in the doorway. Outside they could hear water washing through the ruts of the street.

'Be sho n send Johnny-Boy t tell the folks t stay erway from pas house,' said Reva.

'Ahll tell im. Don yuh worry.'

'Good-bye!'

'Good-bye!'

Leaning against the door jamb, she shook her head slowly and watched Reva vanish through the falling rain.

II

She was back at her board, ironing, when she heard feet sucking in the mud of the back yard; feet she knew from long years of listening were Johnny-Boy's. But tonight with all the rain and fear his coming was like a leaving, was almost more than she could bear. Tears welled to her eyes and she blinked them away. She felt that he was coming so that she could give him up; to see him now was to say good-bye. But it was a good-bye she knew she could never say; they were not that way toward each other. All day long they could sit in the same room and not speak; she was his mother and he was her son; most of the time a nod or a grunt would carry all the meaning that she wanted to say to him, or he to her.

She did not even turn her head when she heard him come stomping into the kitchen. She heard him pull up a chair, sit, sigh, and draw off his muddy shoes; they fell to the floor with heavy thuds. Soon the kitchen was full of the scent of his drying socks and his burning pipe. Tha boys hongry! She paused and looked at him over her shoulder; he was puffing at his pipe with his head tilted back and his feet propped up on the edge of the stove; his eyelids drooped and his wet clothes steamed from the heat of the fire. Lawd, tha boy gits mo like his pa ever day he lives, she mused, her lips breaking in a faint smile. Hols tha pipe in his mouth jus like his pa usta hol his. Wondah how they woulda got erlong ef his pa hada lived? They oughta liked each other, they so mucha like. She wished there could have been other children besides Sug, so Johnny-Boy would not have to be so much alone. A man needs a woman by his side. . . . She thought of Reva; she liked Reva; the brightest glow her heart had ever known was when she had learned that Reva loved Johnny-Boy. But beyond Reva were cold white faces. Ef theys caught it means *death*. . . . She jerked around when she heard Johnny-Boy's pipe clatter to the floor. She saw him pick it up, smile sheepishly at her, and wag his head.

'Gawd, Ahm sleepy,' he mumbled.

She got a pillow from her room and gave it to him.

'Here,' she said.

'Hunh,' he said, putting the pillow between his head and the back of the chair.

They were silent again. Yes, she would have to tell him to go back out into the cold rain and slop; maybe to get caught; maybe for the last time; she didn't know. But she would let him eat and get dry before telling him that the sheriff knew of the meeting to be held at Lem's tomorrow. And she would make him take a big dose of soda before he went out; soda always helped to stave off a cold. She looked at the clock. It was eleven. Theres time yit. Spreading a newspaper on the apron of the stove, she placed a heaping plate of greens upon it, a knife, a fork, a cup of coffee, a slab of cornbread, and a dish of peach cobbler.

'Yo suppahs ready,' she said.

'Yeah,' he said.

He did not move. She ironed again. Presently, she heard him eating. When she could no longer hear his knife tinkling against the edge of the plate, she knew he was through. It was almost twelve now. She would let him rest a little while longer before she told him. Till one er'clock, mabbe. Hes so tired. . . . She finished her ironing, put away the board, and stacked the clothes in her dresser drawer. She poured herself a cup of coffee, drew up a chair, sat, and drank.

'Yuh almos dry,' she said, not looking around.

'Yeah,' he said, turning sharply to her.

The tone of voice in which she had spoken let him know that more was coming. She drained her cup and waited a moment longer.

'Reva wuz here.'

'Yeah?'

'She lef bout a hour ergo.'

'Whut she say?'

'She said ol man Lem hada visit from the sheriff today.'

'Bout the meetin?'

'Yeah.'

She saw him stare at the coals glowing red through the crevices of the stove and run his fingers nervously through his hair. She knew he was wondering how the sheriff had found out. In the silence he would ask a wordless question and in the silence she would answer wordlessly. Johnny-Boys too trustin, she thought. Hes tryin t make the party big n hes takin in folks fastern he kin git t know em. You cant trust ever white man yuh meet. . . .

'Yuh know, Johnny-Boy, yuh been takin in a lotta them white folks lately . . .'

'Aw, ma!'

'But, Johnny-Boy . . .'

'Please, don talk t me bout tha now, ma.'

'Yuh ain t ol t lissen n learn, son,' she said.

'Ah know whut yuh gonna say, ma. N yuh wrong. Yuh cant judge folks jus by how yuh feel bout em n by how long yuh done knowed em. Ef we start tha we wouldnt have *no*body in the party. When folks pledge they word t be with us, then we gotta take em in. Wes too weak t be choosy.'

He rose abruptly, rammed his hands into his pockets, and stood facing the window; she looked at his back in a long silence. She knew his faith; it was deep. He had always said that black men could not fight the rich bosses alone; a man could not fight with every hand against him. But he believes so hard hes blind, she thought. At odd times they had had these arguments before; always she would be pitting her feelings against the hard necessity of his thinking, and always she would lose. She shook her head. Po Johnny-Boy; he don know. . . .

'But ain nona our folks tol, Johnny-Boy,' she said.

'How yuh know?' he asked. His voice came low and with a tinge of anger. He still faced the window and now and then the yellow blade of light flicked across the sharp outline of his black face.

'Cause Ah know em,' she said.

'*Any*body mighta tol,' he said.

'It wuznt nona *our* folks,' she said again.

She saw his hand sweep in a swift arc of disgust.

'*Our* folks! Ma, who in Gawds name is *our* folks?'

'The folks we wuz born n raised wid, son. The folks we *know!*'

'We cant make the party grow tha way, ma.'

'It mighta been Booker,' she said.

'Yuh don know.'

'. . . er Blattberg . . .'

'Fer Chrissakes!'

' . . . er any of the fo-five others whut joined las week.'

'Ma, yuh jus don wan me t go out tonight,' he said.

'Yo ol ma wans yuh t be carcful, son.'

'Ma, when yuh start doubtin folks in the party, then there ain no end.'

'Son, Ah knows ever black man n woman in this parta the county,' she said, standing too. 'Ah watched em grow up; Ah even heped birth n nurse some of em; Ah knows em *all* from way back. There ain none of em tha *coulda* tol! The folks Ah know jus don open they dos n ast death t walk in! Son, it wuz some of them white folks! Yuh jus mark mah word!'

'Why is it gotta be *white* folks?' he asked. 'Ef they tol, then theys jus Judases, thas all.'

'Son, look at whuts befo yuh.'

He shook his head and sighed.

'Ma, Ah done tol yuh a hundred times Ah cant see white an Ah cant see black,' he said. 'Ah sees rich men an Ah sees po men.'

She picked up his dirty dishes and piled them in a pan. Out of the corners of her eyes she saw him sit and pull on his wet shoes. Hes goin! When she put the last dish away he was standing fully dressed, warming his hands over the stove. Just a few mo minutes now n he'll be gone, like Sug, mabbe. Her throat swelled. This black mans fight takes *ever*thing! Looks like Gawd puts us in this worl jus t beat us down!

'Keep this, ma,' he said.

She saw a crumpled wad of money in his outstretched fingers.

'Naw; yuh keep it. Yuh might need it.'

'It ain mine, ma. It berlongs t the party.'

'But, Johnny-Boy, yuh might hafta go erway!'

'Ah kin make out.'

'Don fergit yosef too much, son.'

'Ef Ah don come back theyll need it.'

He was looking at her face and she was looking at the money.

'Yuh keep tha,' she said slowly. 'Ahll give em the money.'

'From where?'

'Ah got some.'

'Where yuh git it from?'

She sighed.

'Ah been savin a dollah a week fer Sug ever since hes been in jail.'

'Lawd, ma!'

She saw the look of puzzled love and wonder in his eyes. Clumsily, he put the money back into his pocket.

'Ahm gone,' he said.

'Here; drink this glass of soda watah.'

She watched him drink, then put the glass away.

'Waal,' he said.

'Take the stuff outta yo pockets!'

She lifted the lid of the stove and he dumped all the papers from his pocket into the hole. She followed him to the door and made him turn round.

'Lawd, yuh tryin to maka revolution n yuh cant even keep yo coat buttoned.' Her nimble fingers fastened his collar high around his throat. 'There!'

He pulled the brim of his hat low over his eyes. She opened the door and with the suddenness of the cold gust of wind that struck her face, he was gone. She watched the black fields and the rain take him, her eyes burning. When the last faint footstep could no longer be heard, she closed the door, went to her bed, lay down, and pulled the cover over her while fully dressed. Her feelings coursed with the rhythm of the rain: Hes gone! Lawd, Ah *know* hes gone! Her blood felt cold.

III

She was floating in a gray void somewhere between sleeping and dreaming and then suddenly she was wide awake, hearing and feeling in the same instant the thunder of the door crashing in and a cold wind filling the room. It was pitch black and she stared, resting on her elbows, her mouth open, not breathing, her ears full of the sound of tramping feet and booming voices. She knew at once: They lookin fer im! Then, filled with her will, she was on her feet, rigid, waiting, listening.

'The lamps burnin!'

'Yuh see her?'

'Naw!'

'Look in the kitchen!'

'Gee, this place smells like niggers!'

'Say, somebodys here er been here!'

'Yeah; theres fire in the stove!'

'Mabbe hes been here n gone?'

'Boy, look at these jars of jam!'

'Niggers make good jam!'

'Git some bread!'

'Heres some cornbread!'

'Say, lemme git some!'

'Take it easy! Theres plenty here!'

'Ahma take some of this stuff home!'

'Look, heres a pota greens!'

'N some hot cawffee!'

'Say, yuh guys! C mon! Cut it out! We didnt come here fer a feas!'

She walked slowly down the hall. They lookin fer im, but they ain got im yit! She stopped in the doorway, her gnarled, black hands as always folded over her stomach, but tight now, so tightly the veins bulged. The kitchen was crowded with white men in glistening raincoats. Though the lamp burned, their flashlights still glowed in red fists. Across her floor she saw the muddy tracks of their boots.

'Yuh white folks git outta mah house!'

There was quick silence; every face turned toward her. She saw a sudden movement, but did not know what it meant until something hot and wet slammed her squarely in the face. She gasped, but did not move. Calmly, she wiped the warm, greasy liquor of greens from her eyes with her left hand. One of the white men had thrown a handful of greens out of the pot at her.

'How they taste, ol bitch?'

'Ah ast yuh t git outta mah house!'

She saw the sheriff detach himself from the crowd and walk toward her.

'Now Anty . . .'

'White man, don yuh *Anty* me!'

'Yuh ain got the right sperit!'

'Sperit hell! Yuh git these men outta mah house!'

'Yuh ack like yuh don like it!'

'Naw, Ah don like it, n yuh knows dam waal Ah don!'

'What yuh gonna do about it?'

'Ahm tellin yuh t git outta mah house!'

'Gittin sassy?'

'Ef tellin yuh t git outta mah house is sass, then Ahm sassy!'

Her words came in a tense whisper; but beyond, back of them, she was watching, thinking, and judging the men.

•

'Listen, Anty,' the sheriff's voice came soft and low. 'Ahm here t hep yuh. How come yuh wanna ack this way?'

'Yuh ain never heped yo *own* sef since yuh been born,' she flared. 'How kin the likes of yuh hep me?'

One of the white men came forward and stood directly in front of her.

'Lissen, nigger woman, yuh talkin t *white* men!'

'Ah don care who Ahm talkin t!'

'Yuhll wish some day yuh did!'

'Not t the likes of yuh!'

'Yuh need somebody t teach yuh how t be a good nigger!'

'*Yuh* cant teach it t me!'

'Yuh gonna change yo tune.'

'Not longs mah bloods warm!'

'Don git smart now!'

'Yuh git outta mah house!'

'Spose we don go?' the sheriff asked.

They were crowded around her. She had not moved since she had taken her place in the doorway. She was thinking only of Johnny-Boy as she stood there giving and taking words; and she knew that they, too, were thinking of Johnny-Boy. She knew they wanted him, and her heart was daring them to take him from her.

'Spose we don go?' the sheriff asked again.

'Twenty of yuh runnin over one ol woman! Now, ain yuh white men glad yuh so brave?'

The sheriff grabbed her arm.

'C mon, now! Yuh done did ernuff sass fer one night. Wheres tha nigger son of yos?'

'Don yuh wished yuh knowed?'

'Yuh wanna git slapped?'

'Ah ain never seen one of yo kind tha wuznt too low fer . . .'

The sheriff slapped her straight across her face with his open palm. She fell back against a wall and sank to her knees.

'Is tha whut white men do t nigger women?'

She rose slowly and stood again, not even touching the place that ached from his blow, her hands folded over her stomach.

'Ah ain never seen one of yo kind that wuznt too low fer . . .'

He slapped her again; she reeled backward several feet and fell on her side.

'Is tha whut we too low t do?'

She stood before him again, dry-eyed, as though she had not been struck. Her lips were numb and her chin was wet with blood.

'Aw, let her go! Its the nigger we wan!' said one.

'Wheres that nigger son of yos?' the sheriff asked.

'Find im,' she said.

'By Gawd, ef we hafta find im we'll kill im!'

'He wont be the only nigger yuh ever killed,' she said.

She was consumed with a bitter pride. There was nothing on this earth, she felt then, that they could not do to her but that she could take. She stood on a narrow plot of ground from which she would die before she was pushed. And then it was, while standing there feeling warm blood seeping down her throat, that she gave up Johnny-Boy, gave him up to the white folks. She gave him up because they had come tramping into her heart demanding him, thinking they could get him by beating her, thinking they could scare her into making her tell where he was. She gave him up because she wanted them to know that they could not get what they wanted by bluffing and killing.

'Wheres this meetin gonna be?' the sheriff asked.

'Don yuh wish yuh knowed?'

'Ain there gonna be a meetin?'

'How come yuh astin me?'

'There *is* gonna be a meetin,' said the sheriff.

'Is it?'

'Ah gotta great mind t choke it outta yuh!'

'Yuh so smart,' she said.

'We ain playin wid yuh!'

'Did Ah say yuh wuz?'

'Tha nigger son of yos is erroun here somewheres an we aim t find im,' said the sheriff. 'Ef yuh tell us where he is n ef he talks, mabbe he'll git off easy. But ef we hafta find im, we'll kill im! Ef we hafta find im, then yuh git a sheet t put over im in the mawnin, see? Git yuh a sheet, cause hes gonna be dead!'

'He wont be the only nigger yuh ever killed,' she said again.

The sheriff walked past her. The others followed. Yuh didnt git whut yuh wanted! she thought exultingly. N yuh ain gonna *never* git it! Hotly something ached in her to make them feel the intensity of her pride and freedom; her heart groped to turn the bitter hours of her life into words of a kind that would make them feel that she had taken all they had done to her in her stride and could still take more. Her faith surged so strongly in her she was all but blinded. She walked behind them to the door, knotting and twisting her fingers. She saw them step to the muddy ground. Each whirl of the yellow beacon revealed glimpses of slanting rain. Her lips moved, then she shouted:

'Yuh didn't git whut yuh wanted! N yuh ain gonna nevah git it!'

The sheriff stopped and turned; his voice came low and hard.

'Now, by Gawd, thas ernuff outta yuh!'

'Ah know when Ah done said ernuff!'

'Aw, naw, yuh don!' he said. 'Yuh don know when yuh done said ernuff, but Ahma teach yuh ternight!'

He was up the steps and across the porch with one bound. She backed into the hall, her eyes full on his face.

'Tell me when yuh gonna stop talkin!' he said, swinging his fist.

The blow caught her high on the cheek; her eyes went blank; she fell flat on her face. She felt the hard heel of his wet shoes coming into her temple and stomach.

'Lemme hear yuh talk some mo!'

She wanted to, but could not; pain numbed and choked her. She lay still and somewhere out of the gray void of unconsciousness she heard someone say: *Aw fer chrissakes leave her erlone its the nigger we wan. . . .*

IV

She never knew how long she had lain huddled in the dark hallway. Her first returning feeling was of a nameless fear crowding the inside of her, then a deep pain spreading from her temple downward over her body. Her ears were filled with the drone of rain and she shuddered from the cold wind blowing through the door. She opened her eyes and at first saw nothing. As if she were imagining it, she knew she was half-lying and half-sitting in a corner against a wall. With difficulty she twisted her neck, and what she saw made her hold her breath—a vast white blur was suspended directly above her. For a moment she could not tell if her fear was from the blur or if the blur was from her fear. Gradually the blur resolved itself into a huge white face that slowly filled her vision. She was stone still, conscious really of the effort to breathe, feeling somehow that she existed only by the mercy of that white face. She had seen it before; its fear had gripped her many times; it had for her the fear of all the white faces she had ever seen in her life.

Sue . . . As from a great distance, she heard her name being called. She was regaining consciousness now, but the fear was coming with her. She looked into the face of a white man, wanting to scream out for him to go; yet accepting his presence because she felt she had to. Though some remote part of her mind was active, her limbs were powerless. It was as if an invisible knife had split her in two, leaving one half of her lying there helpless, while the other half shrank in dread from a forgotten but familiar enemy. *Sue its me Sue its me . . .* Then all at once the voice came clearly.

'Sue, its me! Its Booker!'

And she heard an answering voice speaking inside of her, Yeah, its Booker . . . The one whut jus joined . . . She roused herself, struggling for full consciousness; and as she did so she transferred to the person of Booker the nameless fear she felt. It seemed that Booker towered above her as a challenge to her right to exist upon the earth.

'Yuh awright?'

She did not answer; she started violently to her feet and fell.

'Sue, yuh hurt!'

'Yeah,' she breathed.

'Where they hit yuh?'

'Its mah head,' she whispered.

She was speaking even though she did not want to; the fear that had hold of her compelled her.

'They beat yuh?'

'Yeah.'

'Them bastards! Them Gawddam bastards!'

She heard him saying it over and over; then she felt herself being lifted.

'Naw!' she gasped.

'Ahma take yuh t the kitchen!'

'Put me down!'

'But yuh cant stay here like this!'

She shrank in his arms and pushed her hands against his body; when she was in the kitchen she freed herself, sank into a chair, and held tightly to its back. She looked wonderingly at Booker; there was nothing about him that should frighten her so; but even that did not ease her tension. She saw him go to the water bucket, wet his handkerchief, wring it, and offer it to her. Distrustfully, she stared at the damp cloth.

'Here; put this on yo fohead . . .'

'Naw!'

'C mon; itll make yuh feel bettah!'

She hesitated in confusion; what right had she to be afraid when someone was acting as kindly as this toward her? Reluctantly, she leaned forward and pressed the damp cloth to her head. It helped. With each passing minute she was catching hold of herself, yet wondering why she felt as she did.

'Whut happened?'

'Ah don know.'

'Yuh feel bettah?'

'Yeah.'

'Who all wuz here?'

'Ah don know,' she said again.

'Yo head still hurt?'

'Yeah.'

'Gee, Ahm sorry.'

'Ahm awright,' she sighed and buried her face in her hands.

She felt him touch her shoulder.

'Sue, Ah got some bad news fer yuh . . .'

She knew; she stiffened and grew cold. It had happened; she stared dry-eyed with compressed lips.

'Its mah Johnny-Boy,' she said.

'Yeah; Ahm awful sorry t hafta tell yuh this way. But Ah thought yuh oughta know . . .'

Her tension eased and a vacant place opened up inside of her. A voice whispered, Jesus, hep me!

'W-w-where is he?'

'They got im out t Foleys Woods tryin t make im tell who the others is.'

'He ain gonna tell,' she said. 'They just as waal kill im, cause he ain gonna nevah tell.'

'Ah hope he don,' said Booker. 'But he didn't have chance t tell the others. They grabbed im just as he got t the woods.'

Then all the horror of it flashed upon her; she saw flung out over the rainy countryside an array of shacks where white and black comrades were sleeping; in the morning they would be rising and going to Lem's; then they would be caught. And that meant terror, prison, and death. The comrades would have to be told; she would have to tell them; she could not entrust Johnny-Boy's work to another, and especially not to Booker as long as she felt toward him as she did. Gripping the bottom of the chair with both hands, she tried to rise; the room blurred and she swayed. She found herself resting in Booker's arms.

'Lemme go!'

'Sue, yuh too weak t walk!'

'Ah gotta tell em!' she said.

'Set down, Sue! Yuh hurt; yuh sick!'

When seated she looked at him helplessly.

'Sue, lissen! Johnny-Boys caught. Ahm here. Yuh tell me who they is n Ahll tell em.'

She stared at the floor and did not answer. Yes; she was too weak to go. There was no way for her to tramp all those miles through the rain tonight. But should she tell Booker? If only she had somebody like Reva to talk to. She did not want to decide alone; she must make no mistake about this. She felt Booker's fingers pressing on her arm and it was as though the white mountain was pushing her to the edge of a sheer height; she again exclaimed inwardly, Jesus, hep me! Booker's white face was at her side, waiting. Would she be doing right to tell him? Suppose she did not tell and then the comrades were caught? She could not ever forgive herself for doing a thing like that. But maybe she was wrong; maybe her fear was what Johnny-Boy had always called 'jus foolishness.' She remembered his saying, Ma we cant make the party ef we start doubtin everybody. . . .

'Tell me who they is, Sue, n Ahll tell em. Ah just joined n Ah don know who they is.'

'Ah don know who they is,' she said.

'Yuh *gotta* tell me who they is, Sue!'

'Ah tol yuh Ah don know!'

'Yuh *do* know! C mon! Set up n talk!'

'Naw!'

'Yuh wan em all t git *killed?'*

She shook her head and swallowed. Lawd, Ah don blieve in this man!

'Lissen, Ahll call the names n yuh tell me which ones is in the party n which ones ain, see?'

'Naw!'

'Please, Sue!'

'Ah don know,' she said.

'Sue, yuh ain doin right by em. Johnny-Boy wouldnt wan yuh t be this way. Hes out there holdin up his end. Les hol up ours. . . .'

'Lawd, Ah don know. . . .'

'Is yuh scareda me cause Ahm *white?* Johnny-Boy ain like tha. Don let all the work we done go fer nothin.'

She gave up and bowed her head in her hands.

'Is it Johnson? Tell me, Sue?'

'Yeah,' she whispered in horror; a mounting horror of feeling herself being undone.

'Is it Green?'

'Yeah.'

'Murphy?'

'Lawd, Ah don know!'

'Yuh gotta tell me, Sue!'

'Mistah Booker, please leave me erlone. . . .'

'Is it Murphy?'

She answered yes to the names of Johnny-Boy's comrades; she answered until he asked her no more. Then she thought, How he know the sheriffs men is watchin Lems house? She stood up and held onto her chair, feeling something sure and firm within her.

'How yuh know bout Lem?'

'Why . . . How Ah know?'

'Whut yuh doin here this tima night? How yuh know the sheriff got Johnny-Boy?'

'Sue, don yuh blieve in me?'

She did not, but she could not answer. She stared at him until her lips hung open; she was searching deep within herself for certainty.

'You meet Reva?' she asked.

'Reva?'

'Yeah; Lems gal?'

'Oh, yeah. Sho, Ah met Reva.'

'She tell yuh?'

She asked the question more of herself than of him; she longed to believe.

'Yeah,' he said softly. 'Ah reckon Ah oughta be goin t tell em now.'

'Who?' she asked. 'Tell *who?*'

The muscles of her body were stiff as she waited for his answer; she felt as though life depended upon it.

'The comrades,' he said.

'Yeah,' she sighed.

She did not know when he left; she was not looking or listening. She just suddenly saw the room empty, and from her the thing that had made her fearful was gone.

V

For a space of time that seemed to her as long as she had been upon the earth, she sat huddled over the cold stove. One minute she would say to herself, They both gone now; Johnny-Boy n Sug . . . Mabbe Ahll never see em ergin. Then a surge of guilt would blot out her longing. 'Lawd, Ah shouldna tol!' she mumbled. 'But no man kin be so lowdown as t do a thing like tha . . .' Several times she had an impulse to try to tell the comrades herself; she was feeling a little better now. But what good would that do? She had told Booker the names. He just couldnt be a Judas t po folks like us . . . He *couldnt!*

'An Sue!'

Thas Reva! Her heart leaped with an anxious gladness. She rose without answering and limped down the dark hallway. Through the open door, against the background of rain, she saw Reva's face lit now and then to whiteness by the whirling beams of the beacon. She was about to call, but a thought checked her. Jesus, hep me! Ah gotta tell her bout Johnny-Boy . . . Lawd, Ah cant!

'An Sue, yuh there?'

'C mon in, chile!'

She caught Reva and held her close for a moment without speaking.

'Lawd, Ahm sho glad yuh here,' she said at last.

'Ah thought something had happened t yuh,' said Reva, pulling away. 'Ah saw the do open . . . Pa tol me to come back n stay wid yuh tonight . . .' Reva paused and stared. 'W-w-whuts the mattah?'

She was so full of having Reva with her that she did not understand what the question meant.

'Hunh?'

'Yo neck . . .'

'Aw, it ain nothin, chile. C mon in the kitchen.'

'But theres blood on yo neck!'

'The sheriff wuz here . . .'

'Them fools! Whut they wanna bother yuh fer? Ah could kill em! So hep me Gawd, Ah could!'

'It ain nothin,' she said.

She was wondering how to tell Reva about Johnny-Boy and Booker. Ahll wait a lil while longer, she thought. Now that Reva was here, her fear did not seem as awful as before.

'C mon, lemme fix yo head, An Sue. Yuh hurt.'

They went to the kitchen. She sat silent while Reva dressed her scalp. She was feeling better now; in just a little while she would tell Reva. She felt the girl's finger pressing gently upon her head.

'Tha hurt?'

'A lil, chile.'

'Yuh po thing.'

'It ain nothin.'

'Did Johnny-Boy come?'

She hesitated.

'Yeah.'

'He done gone t tell the others?'

Reva's voice sounded so clear and confident that it mocked her. Lawd, Ah cant tell this chile . . .

'Yuh tol im, didnt yuh, An Sue?'

'Y-y-yeah . . .'

'Gee! Thas good! Ah tol pa he didnt hafta worry ef Johnny-Boy got the news. Mabbe thingsll come out awright.'

'Ah hope . . .'

She could not go on; she had gone as far as she could; for the first time that night she began to cry.

'Hush, An Sue! Yuh awways been brave. Itll be awright!'

'Ain nothin awright, chile. The worls just too much fer us, Ah reckon.'

'Ef yuh cry that way itll make me cry.'

She forced herself to stop. Naw; Ah cant carry on this way in fronta Reva . . . Right now she had a deep need for Reva to believe in her. She watched the girl get pine-knots from behind the stove, rekindle the fire, and put on the coffee pot.

'Yuh wan some cawffee?' Reva asked.

'Naw, honey.'

'Aw, c mon, An Sue.'

'Jusa lil, honey.'

'Thas the way t be. Oh, say, Ah fergot,' said Reva, measuring out spoonfuls of coffee. 'Pa tol me t tell yuh t watch out fer tha Bookerman. Hes a stool.'

She showed not one sign of outward movement or expression, but as the words fell from Reva's lips she went limp inside.

'Pa tol me soon as Ah got back home. He got word from town . . .'

She stopped listening. She felt as though she had been slapped to the extreme outer edge of life, into a cold darkness. She knew now what she had felt when she had looked up out of her fog of pain and had seen Booker. It was the image of all the white folks, and the fear that went with them, that she had seen and felt during her lifetime. And again, for the second time that night, something she had felt had come true. All she could say to herself was, Ah didnt like im! Gawd knows, Ah didnt! Ah tol Johnny-Boy it wuz some of them white folks . . .

'Here; drink yo cawffee . . .'

She took the cup; her fingers trembled, and the steaming liquid spilt onto her dress and leg.

'Ahm sorry, An Sue!'

Her leg was scalded, but the pain did not bother her.

'Its awright,' she said.

'Wait; lemme put something on tha burn!'

'It don hurt.'

'Yuh worried bout something.'

'Naw, honey.'

'Lemme fix yuh so mo cawffee.'

'Ah don wan nothin now, Reva.'

'Waal, buck up. Don be tha way . . .'

They were silent. She heard Reva drinking. No; she would not tell Reva; Reva was all she had left. But she had to do something, some way, somehow. She was undone too much as it was; and to tell Reva about Booker or Johnny-Boy was more than she was equal to; it would be too coldly shameful. She wanted to be alone and fight this thing out with herself.

'Go t bed, honey. Yuh tired.'

'Naw; Ahm awright, An Sue.'

She heard the bottom of Reva's empty cup clank against the top of the stove. Ah *got* t make her go t bed! Yes; Booker would tell the names of the comrades to the sheriff. If she could only stop him some way! That was the answer, the point, the star that grew bright in the morning of new hope. Soon, maybe half an hour from now, Booker would reach Foley's Woods. Hes boun t go the long way, cause he don know no short cut, she thought. Ah could wade the creek n beat im there . . . But what would she do after that?

'Reva, honey, go t bed. Ahm awright. Yuh need res.'

'Ah ain sleepy, An Sue.'

'Ah knows whuts bes fer yuh, chile. Yuh tired n wet.'

'Ah wanna stay up wid yuh.'

She forced a smile and said:

'Ah don think they gonna hurt Johnny-Boy . . .'

'Fer *real,* An Sue?'

'Sho, honey.'

'But Ah wanna wait up wid yuh.'

'Thas mah job, honey. Thas whut a mas fer, t wait up fer her chullun.'

'Good night, An Sue.'

'Good night, honey.'

She watched Reva pull up and leave the kitchen; presently she heard the shucks in the mattress whispering, and she knew that Reva had gone to bed. She was alone. Through the cracks of the stove she saw the fire dying to grey ashes; the room was growing cold again. The yellow beacon continued to flit past the window and the rain still drummed. Yes; she was alone; she had done this awful thing alone; she must find some way out, alone. Like touching a festering sore, she put her finger upon that moment when she had shouted her defiance to the sheriff, when she had shouted to feel her strength. She had lost Sug to save others; she had let Johnny-Boy go to save others; and then in a moment of weakness that came from too much strength she had lost all. If she had not shouted to the sheriff, she would have been strong enough to have resisted Booker; she would have been able to tell the comrades herself. Something tightened in her as she remembered and understood the fit of fear she had felt on coming to herself in the dark hallway. A part of her life she thought she had done away with forever had had hold of her then. She had thought the soft, warm past was over; she had thought that it did not mean much when now she sang: 'Hes the Lily of the Valley, the Bright n Mawnin Star.' . . . The days when she had sung that song were the days when she had not hoped for anything on this earth, the days when the cold mountain had driven her into the arms of Jesus. She had thought that Sug and Johnny-Boy had taught her to forget Him, to fix her hope upon the fight of black men for freedom. Through the gradual years she had believed and worked with them, had felt strength shed from the grace of their terrible vision. That grace had been upon her when she had let the sheriff slap her down; it had been upon her when she had risen time and again from the floor and faced him. But she had trapped herself with her own hunger; to water the long dry thirst of her faith her pride had made a bargain which her flesh could not keep. Her having told the names of Johnny-Boy's comrades was but an incident in a deeper horror. She stood up and looked at the floor while call and counter-call, loyalty and counter-loyalty struggled in her soul. Mired she was between two abandoned worlds, living, dying without the strength of the grace that either gave. The clearer she felt it the fuller did something well up from the depths of her for release; the more urgent did she feel the need to fling into her black sky another star, another hope, one more terrible vision to give her the strength to live and act. Softly and restlessly she walked about the kitchen, feeling herself naked against night, the rain, the world; and shamed whenever the thought of Reva's love crossed her mind. She lifted her empty hands and looked at her writhing fingers. Lawd, whut kin Ah do now? She could still wade the creek and get to Foley's Woods before Booker. And then what? How could she manage to see Johnny-Boy or Booker? Again she heard the sheriff's threatening voice: Git yuh a sheet, cause hes gonna be dead! The sheet! Thas it, the sheet! Her whole being leaped with will; the long years of her life bent toward a moment of focus, a point. Ah kin go wid mah sheet! Ahll be doin whut he said! Lawd Gawd in Heaven, Ahma go lika nigger woman wid mah windin sheet t git mah dead son! But then what? She stood straight and smiled grimly; she had in her heart the whole meaning of her life; her entire personality was poised on the brink of a total act. Ah know! Ah know! She thought of Johnny-Boy's gun in the dresser drawer. Ahll hide the gun in the sheet n go aftah Johnny-Boys body. . . . She tiptoed to her room, eased out the dresser drawer, and got a sheet. Reva was sleeping; the darkness was filled with her quiet breathing. She groped in the drawer and found the gun. She wound the gun in the sheet and held them both under her apron. Then she stole to the bedside and watched Reva. Lawd, hep her! But mabbe shes bettah off. This had t happen sometimes . . . She n Johnny-Boy couldna been together in this here South . . . N Ah couldnt tell her bout Booker. Itll come out awright n she wont nevah know. Reva's trust would never be shaken. She caught her breath as the shucks in the mattress rustled dryly; then all was quiet and she breathed easily again. She tiptoed to the door, down the hall, and stood on the porch. Above her the yellow beacon whirled through the rain. She went over muddy ground, mounted a slope, stopped and looked back at her house. The lamp glowed in her window, and the yellow beacon that swung every few seconds seemed to feed it with light. She turned and started across the fields, holding the gun and sheet tightly, thinking, Po Reva . . . Po critter . . . Shes fas ersleep . . .

VI

For the most part she walked with her eyes half shut, her lips tightly compressed, leaning her body against the wind and the slanting rain, feeling the pistol in the sheet sagging cold and heavy in her fingers. Already she was getting wet; it seemed that her feet found every puddle of water that stood between the corn rows.

She came to the edge of the creek and paused, wondering at what point was it low. Taking the sheet from under her apron, she wrapped the gun in it so that her finger could be upon the trigger. Ahll cross here, she thought. At first she did not feel the water; her feet were already wet. But the water grew cold as it came up to her knees; she gasped when it reached her waist. Lawd, this creeks high! When she had passed the middle, she knew that she was out of danger. She came out of the water, climbed a grassy hill, walked on, turned a bend and saw the lights of autos gleaming ahead. Yeah; theys still there! She hurried with her head down. Wondah did Ah beat im here? Lawd, Ah hope so! A vivid image of Booker's white face hovered a moment before her eyes and a driving will surged up in her so hard and strong that it vanished. She was among the autos now. From nearby came the hoarse voices of the men.

'Hey, yuh!'

She stopped, nervously clutching the sheet. Two white men with shotguns came toward her.

'Whut in hell yuh doin out here?'

She did not answer.

'Didnt yuh hear somebody speak t yuh?'

'Ahm comin aftah mah son,' she said humbly.

'Yo *son?*'

'Yessuh.'

'Whut yo son doin out here?'

'The sheriffs got im.'

'Holy Scott! Jim, its the niggers ma!'

'Whut yuh got there?' asked one.

'A sheet.'

'A *sheet?*'

'Yessuh.'

'Fer whut?'

'The sheriff tol me t bring a sheet t git his body.'

'Waal, waal . . .'

'Now, ain tha something?'

The white men looked at each other.

'These niggers sho love one ernother,' said one.

'N tha ain no lie,' said the other.

'Take me t the sheriff,' she begged.

'Yuh ain givin us *orders,* is yuh?'

'Nawsuh.'

'We'll take yuh when wes good n ready.'

'Yessuh.'

'So yuh wan his body?'

'Yessuh.'

'Waal, he ain dead yit.'

'They gonna kill im,' she said.

'Ef he talks they wont.'

'He ain gonna talk,' she said.

'How yuh know?'

'Cause he ain.'

'We got ways of makin niggers talk.'

'Yuh ain got no way fer im.'

'Yuh thinka lot of tha black Red, don yuh?'

'Hes mah son.'

'Why don yuh teach im some sense?'

'Hes mah son,' she said again.

'Lissen, old nigger woman, yuh stan there wid yo hair white. Yuh got bettah sense than t blieve tha niggers kin make a revolution . . .'

'A black republic,' said the other one, laughing.

'Take me t the sheriff,' she begged.

'Yuh his ma,' said one. 'Yuh kin make im talk n tell whos in this thing wid im.'

'He ain gonna talk,' she said.

'Don yuh wan im t live?'

She did not answer.

'C mon, les take her t Bradley.'

They grabbed her arms and she clutched hard at the sheet and gun; they led her toward the crowd in the woods. Her feelings were simple; Booker would not tell; she was there with the gun to see to that. The louder became the voices of the men the deeper became her feeling of wanting to right the mistake she had made; of wanting to fight her way back to solid ground. She would stall for time until Booker showed up. Oh, ef theyll only lemme git close t Johnny-Boy! As they led her near the crowd she saw white faces turning and looking at her and heard a rising clamor of voices.

'Whos tha?'

'A nigger woman!'

'Whut she doin out here?'

'This is his ma!' called one of the men.

'Whut she wans?'

'She brought a sheet t cover his body!'

'He ain dead yit!'

'They tryin t make im talk!'

'But he will be dead soon ef he don open up!'

'Say, look! The niggers ma brought a sheet t cover up his body!'

'Now, ain tha sweet?'

'Mabbe she wans hol a prayer meetin!'

'Did she git a preacher?'

'Say, go git Bradley!'

'O.K.!'

The crowd grew quiet. They looked at her curiously; she felt their cold eyes trying to detect some weakness in her. Humbly she stood with the sheet covering the gun. She had already accepted all that they could do to her.

The sheriff came.

'So yuh brought yo sheet, hunh?'

'Yessuh,' she whispered.

'Looks like them slaps we gave yuh learned yuh some sense, didnt they?'

She did not answer.

'Yuh don need tha sheet. Yo son ain dead yit,' he said, reaching.

She backed away, her eyes wide.

'Naw!'

'Now, lissen, Anty!' he said. 'There ain no use in yuh ackin a fool! Go in there n tell tha nigger son of yos t tell us whos in this wid im, see? Ah promise we wont kill im eff he talks. We'll let im git outta town.'

'There ain nothin Ah kin tell im,' she said.

'Yuh wan us t kill im?'

She did not answer. She saw someone lean toward the sheriff and whisper.

'Bring her erlong,' the sheriff said.

They led her to a muddy clearing. The rain streamed down through the ghostly glare of the flashlights. As the men formed a semi-circle she saw Johnny-Boy lying in a trough of mud. He was tied with rope; he lay hunched, one side of his face resting in a pool of black water. His eyes were staring questioningly at her.

'Speak t im,' said the sheriff.

If she could only tell him why she was there! But that was impossible; she was close to what she wanted and she stared straight before her with compressed lips.

'Say, nigger!' called the sheriff, kicking Johnny-Boy. 'Here's yo ma!'

Johnny-Boy did not move or speak. The sheriff faced her again.

'Lissen, Anty,' he said. 'Yuh got mo say wid im than anybody. Tell im t talk n hava chance. Whut he wanna pertect the other niggers n white folks fer?'

She slid her finger about the trigger of the gun and looked stonily at the mud.

'Go t him,' said the sheriff.

She did not move. Her heart was crying out to answer the amazed question in Johnny-Boy's eyes. But there was no way now.

'Waal, yuhre astin fer it. By Gawd, we gotta way to *make* yuh talk t im,' he said, turning away. 'Say, Tim, git one of them logs n turn tha nigger upsidedown n put his legs on it!'

A murmur of assent ran through the crowd. She bit her lips; she knew what that meant.

'Yuh wan yo nigger son crippled?' she heard the sheriff ask.

She did not answer. She saw them roll the log up; they lifted Johnny-Boy and laid him on his face and stomach, then they pulled his legs over the log. His knee-caps rested on the sheer top of the log's back, the toes of his shoes pointing groundward. So absorbed was she in watching that she felt that it was she that was being lifted and made ready for torture.

'Git a crowbar!' said the sheriff.

A tall, lank man got a crowbar from a near-by auto and stood over the log. His jaws worked slowly on a wad of tobacco.

'Now, its up t yuh, Anty,' the sheriff said. 'Tell the man whut t do!'

She looked into the rain. The sheriff turned.

'Mabbe she think wes playin. Ef she don say nothin, then break em at the knee-caps!'

'O.K., Sheriff!'

She stood waiting for Booker. Her legs felt weak; she wondered if she would be able to wait much longer. Over and over she said to herself, Ef he came now Ahd kill em both!

'She ain sayin nothin, Sheriff!'

'Waal, Gawddammit, let im have it!'

The crowbar came down and Johnny-Boy's body lunged in the mud and water. There was a scream. She swayed, holding tight to the gun and sheet.

'Hol im! Git the other leg!'

The crowbar fell again. There was another scream.

'Yuh break em?' asked the sheriff.

The tall man lifted Johnny-Boy's legs and let them drop limply again, dropping rearward from the knee-caps. Johnny-Boy's body lay still. His head had rolled to one side and she could not see his face.

'Just lika broke sparrow wing,' said the man, laughing softly.

Then Johnny-Boy's face turned to her; he screamed.

'Go way, ma! Go way!'

It was the first time she had heard his voice since she had come out to the woods; she all but lost control of herself. She started violently forward, but the sheriff's arm checked her.

'Aw, naw! Yuh had yo chance!' He turned to Johnny-Boy. 'She kin go ef yuh talk.'

'Mistah, he ain gonna talk,' she said.

'Go way, ma!' said Johnny-Boy.

'Shoot im! Don make im suffah so,' she begged.

'He'll either talk or he'll never hear yuh ergin,' the sheriff said. 'Theres other things we kin do t im.'

She said nothing.

'Whut yuh come here fer, ma?' Johnny-Boy sobbed.

'Ahm gonna split his eardrums,' the sheriff said. 'Ef yuh got anything t say t im yuh bettah say it *now!*'

She closed her eyes. She heard the sheriff's feet sucking in mud. Ah could save im! She opened her eyes; there were shouts of eagerness from the crowd as it pushed in closer.

'Bus em, Sheriff!'

'Fix im so he cant hear!'

'He knows how t do it, too!'

'He busted a Jew boy tha way once!'

She saw the sheriff stoop over Johnny-Boy, place his flat palm over one ear and strike his fist against it with all his might. He placed his palm over the other ear and struck again. Johnny-Boy moaned, his head rolling from side to side, his eyes showing white amazement in a world without sound.

'Yuh wouldn't talk t im when yuh had the chance,' said the sheriff. 'Try n talk now.'

She felt warm tears on her cheeks. She longed to shoot Johnny-Boy and let him go. But if she did that they would take the gun from her, and Booker would tell who the others were. Lawd, hep me! The men were talking loudly now, as though the main business was over. It seemed ages that she stood there watching Johnny-Boy roll and whimper in his world of silence.

'Say, Sheriff, heres somebody lookin fer yuh!'

'Who is it?'

'Ah don know!'

'Bring em in!'

She stiffened and looked around wildly, holding the gun tight. Is tha Booker? Then she held still, feeling that her excitement might betray her. Mabbe Ah kin shoot em both! Mabbe Ah kin shoot twice! The sheriff stood in front of her, waiting. The crowd parted and she saw Booker hurrying forward.

'Ah know em all, Sheriff!' he called.

He came full into the muddy clearing where Johnny-Boy lay.

'Yuh mean yuh got the names?'

'Sho! The ol nigger . . .'

She saw his lips hang open and silent when he saw her. She stepped forward and raised the sheet.

'Whut . . .'

She fired, once; then, without pausing, she turned, hearing them yell.

She aimed at Johnny-Boy, but they had their arms around her, bearing her to the ground, clawing at the sheet in her hand. She glimpsed Booker lying sprawled in the mud, on his face, his hands stretched out before him; then a cluster of yelling men blotted him out. She lay without struggling, looking upward through the rain at the white faces above her. And she was suddenly at peace; they were not a white mountain now; they were not pushing her any longer to the edge of life. Its awright . . .

'She shot Booker!'

'She hada gun in the sheet!'

'She shot im right thu the head!'

'Whut she shoot im fer?'

'Kill the bitch!'

'Ah *thought* something wuz wrong bout her!'

'Ah wuz fer givin it t her from the firs!'

'Thas whut yuh git fer treatin a nigger nice!'

'Say, Bookers dead!'

She stopped looking into the white faces, stopped listening. She waited, giving up her life before they took it from her; she had done what she wanted. Ef only Johnny-Boy . . . She looked at him; he lay looking at her with tired eyes. Ef she could only tell im!

'Whut yuh kill im fer, hunh?'

It was the sheriff's voice; she did not answer.

'Mabbe she wuz shootin at yuh, Sheriff?'

'Whut yuh kill im fer?'

She felt the sheriff's foot come into her side; she closed her eyes.

'Yuh black bitch!'

'Let her have it!'

'Yuh reckon she foun out bout Booker?'

'She mighta.'

'Jesus Christ, whut yuh dummies *waitin* on!'

'Yeah; kill her!'

'Kill em *both!*'

'Let her know her nigger sons dead firs!'

She turned her head toward Johnny-Boy; he lay looking puzzled in a world beyond the reach of voices. At leas he cant hear, she thought.

'C mon, let im have it!'

She listened to hear what Johnny-Boy could not. They came, two of them, one right behind the other; so close together that they sounded like one shot. She did not look at Johnny-Boy now; she looked at the white faces of the men, hard and wet in the glare of the flashlights.

'Yuh hear tha, nigger woman?'

'Did tha surprise im? Hes in hell now wonderin whut hit im!'

'C mon! Give it t her, Sheriff!'

'Lemme shoot her, Sheriff! It wuz mah pal she shot!'

'Awright, Pete! Thas fair ernuff!'

She gave up as much of her life as she could before they took it from her. But the sound of the shot and the streak of fire that tore its way through her chest forced her to live again, intensely. She had not moved, save for the slight jarring impact of the bullet. She felt the heat of her own blood warming her cold, wet back. She yearned suddenly to talk. 'Yuh didnt git whut yuh wanted! N yuh ain gonna nevah git it! Yuh didnt kill me; Ah come here by mahsef . . .' She felt rain falling into her wide-open, dimming eyes and heard faint voices. Her lips moved soundlessly. *Yuh didnt git yuh didnt yuh didnt* . . . Focused and pointed she was, buried in the depths of her star, swallowed in its peace and strength; and not feeling her flesh growing cold, cold as the rain that fell from the invisible sky upon the doomed living and the dead that never dies.

OHIO

★

The Strength of God and *The Teacher*

SHERWOOD ANDERSON

The Strength of God

The Reverend Curtis Hartman was pastor of the Presbyterian Church of Winesburg, and had been in that position ten years. He was forty years old, and by his nature very silent and reticent. To preach, standing in the pulpit before the people, was always a hardship for him and from Wednesday morning until Saturday evening he thought of nothing but the two sermons that must be preached on Sunday. Early on Sunday morning he went into a little room called a study in the bell tower of the church and prayed. In his prayers there was one note that always predominated. "Give me strength and courage for Thy work, O Lord!" he plead, kneeling on the bare floor and bowing his head in the presence of the task that lay before him.

The Reverend Hartman was a tall man with a brown beard. His wife, a stout, nervous woman, was the daughter of a manufacturer of underwear at Cleveland, Ohio. The minister himself was rather a favorite in the town. The elders of the church liked him because he was quiet and unpretentious and Mrs. White, the banker's wife, thought him scholarly and refined.

The Presbyterian Church held itself somewhat aloof from the other churches of Winesburg. It was larger and more imposing and its minister was better paid. He even had a carriage of his own and on summer evenings sometimes drove about town with his wife. Through Main Street and up and down Buckeye Street he went, bowing gravely to the people, while his wife, afire with secret pride, looked at him out of the corners of her eyes and worried lest the horse become frightened and run away.

For a good many years after he came to Winesburg things went well with Curtis Hartman. He was not one to arouse keen enthusiasm among the worshippers in his church but on the other hand he made no enemies. In reality he was much in earnest and sometimes suffered prolonged periods of remorse because he could not go crying the word of God in the highways and byways of the town. He wondered if the flame of the spirit really burned in him and dreamed of a day when a strong sweet new current of power would come like a great wind into his voice and his soul and the people would tremble before the spirit of God made manifest in him. "I am a poor stick and that will never really happen to me," he mused dejectedly and then a patient smile lit up his features. "Oh well, I suppose I'm doing well enough," he added philosophically.

The room in the bell tower of the church, where on Sunday mornings the minister prayed for an increase in him of the power of God, had but one window. It was long and narrow and swung outward on a hinge like a door. On the window, made of little leaded panes, was a design showing the Christ laying his hand upon the head of a child. One Sunday morning in the summer as he sat by his desk in the room with a large Bible opened before him, and the sheets of his sermon scattered about, the minister was shocked to see, in the upper room of the house next door, a woman lying in her bed and smoking a cigarette while she read a book. Curtis Hartman went on tiptoe to the window and closed it softly. He was horror stricken at the thought of a woman smoking and trembled also to think that his eyes, just raised from the pages of the book of God, had looked upon the bare shoulders and white throat of a woman. With his brain in a whirl he went down into the pulpit and preached a long sermon without once thinking of his gestures or his voice. The sermon attracted unusual attention because of its power and clearness. "I wonder if she is listening, if my voice is carrying a message into her soul," he thought and began to hope that on future Sunday mornings he might be able to say words that would touch and awaken the woman apparently far gone in secret sin.

The house next door to the Prebysterian Church, through the windows of which the minister had seen the sight that had so upset him, was occupied by two women. Aunt Elizabeth Swift, a grey competent-looking widow with money in the Winesburg National Bank, lived there with her daughter Kate Swift, a school teacher. The school teacher was thirty years old and had a neat trim-looking figure. She had few friends and bore a reputation of having a sharp tongue. When he began to think about her, Curtis Hartman remembered that she had been to Europe and had lived for two years in New York City. "Perhaps after all her smoking means nothing," he thought. He began to remember that when he was a student in college and occasionally read novels, good, although somewhat worldly women, had smoked through the pages of a book that had once fallen into his hands. With a rush of new determination he worked on his sermons all through the week and forgot, in his zeal to reach the ears and the soul of this new listener, both his embarrassment in the pulpit and the necessity of prayer in the study on Sunday mornings.

Reverend Hartman's experience with women had been somewhat limited. He was the son of a wagon maker from Muncie, Indiana, and had worked his way through college. The daughter of the underwear manufacturer had boarded in a house where he lived during his school days and he had married her after a formal and prolonged courtship, carried on for the most part by the girl herself. On his marriage day the underwear manufacturer had given his daughter five thousand dollars and he promised to leave her at least twice that amount in his will. The minister had thought himself fortunate in marriage and had never permitted himself to think of other women. He did not want to think of other women. What he wanted was to do the work of God quietly and earnestly.

In the soul of the minister a struggle awoke. From wanting to reach the ears of Kate Swift, and through his sermons to delve into her soul, he began to want also to look again at the figure lying white and quiet in the bed. On a Sunday morning when he could not sleep because of his thoughts he arose and went to walk in the streets. When he had gone along Main Street almost to the old Richmond place he stopped and picking up a stone rushed off to the room in the bell tower. With the stone he broke out a corner of the window and then locked the door and sat down at the desk before the open Bible to wait. When the shade of the window to Kate Swift's room was raised he could see, through the hole, directly into her bed, but she was not there. She also had arisen and had gone for a walk and the hand that raised the shade was the hand of Aunt Elizabeth Swift.

The minister almost wept with joy at this deliverance from the carnal desire to "peep" and went back to his own house praising God. In an ill moment he forgot, however, to stop the hole in the window. The piece of glass broken out at the corner of the window just nipped off the bare heel of the boy standing motionless and looking with rapt eyes into the face of the Christ.

Curtis Hartman forgot his sermon on that Sunday morning. He talked to his congregation and in his talk said that it was a mistake for people to think of their minister as a man set aside and intended by nature to lead a blameless life. "Out of my own experience I know that we, who are the ministers of God's word, are beset by the same temptations that assail you," he declared. "I have been tempted and have surrendered to temptation. It is only the hand of God, placed beneath my head, that has raised me up. As he has raised me so also will he raise you. Do not despair. In your hour of sin raise your eyes to the skies and you will be again and again saved."

Resolutely the minister put the thoughts of the woman in the bed out of his mind and began to be something like a lover in the presence of his wife. One evening when they drove out together he turned the horse out of Buckeye Street and in the darkness on Gospel Hill, above Waterworks Pond, put his arm about Sarah Hartman's waist. When he had eaten breakfast in the morning and was ready to retire to his study at the back of his house he went around the table and kissed his wife on the cheek. When thoughts of Kate Swift came into his head, he smiled and raised his eyes to the skies. "Intercede for me, Master," he muttered, "keep me in the narrow path intent on Thy work."

And now began the real struggle in the soul of the brown-bearded minister. By chance he discovered that Kate Swift was in the habit of lying in her bed in the evenings and reading a book. A lamp stood on a table by the side of the bed and the light streamed down upon her white shoulders and bare throat. On the evening when he made the discovery the minister sat at the desk in the study from nine until after eleven and when her light was put out stumbled out of the church to spend two more hours walking and praying in the streets. He did not want to kiss the shoulders and the throat of Kate Swift and had not allowed his mind to dwell on such thoughts. He did not know what he wanted. "I am God's child and he must save me from myself," he cried, in the darkness under the trees as he wandered in the streets. By a tree he stood and looked at the sky that was covered with hurrying clouds. He began to talk to God intimately and closely. "Please, Father, do not forget me. Give me power to go to-morrow and repair the hole in the window. Lift my eyes again to the skies. Stay with me, Thy servant, in his hour of need."

Up and down through the silent streets walked the minister and for days and weeks his soul was troubled. He could not understand the temptation that had come to him nor could he fathom the reason for its coming. In a way he began to blame God, saying to himself that he had tried to keep his feet in the true path and had not run about seeking sin. "Through my days as a young man and all through my life here I have gone quietly about my work," he declared. "Why now should I be tempted? What have I done that this burden should be laid on me?"

Three times during the early fall and winter of that year Curtis Hartman crept out of his house to the room in the bell tower to sit in the darkness looking at the figure of Kate Swift lying in her bed and later went to walk and pray in the streets. He could not understand himself. For weeks he would go along scarcely thinking of the school teacher and telling himself that he had conquered the carnal desire to look at her body. And then something would happen. As he sat in the study of his own house, hard at work on a sermon, he would become nervous and begin to walk up and down the room. "I will go out into the streets," he told himself and even as he let himself in at the church door he persistently denied to himself the cause of his being there. "I will not repair the hole in the window and I will train myself to come here at night and sit in the presence of this woman without raising my eyes. I will not be defeated in this thing. The Lord has devised this temptation as a test of my soul and I will grope my way out of darkness into the light of righteousness."

One night in January when it was bitter cold and snow lay deep on the streets of Winesburg Curtis Hartman paid his last visit to the room in the bell tower of the church. It was past nine o'clock when he left his own house and he set out so hurriedly that he forgot to put on his overshoes. In Main Street no one was abroad but Hop Higgins the night watchman and in the whole town no one was awake but the watchman and young George Willard, who sat in the office of the *Winesburg Eagle* trying to write a story. Along the street to the church went the minister, plowing through the drifts and thinking that this time he would utterly give way to sin. "I want to look at the woman and to think of kissing her shoulders and I am going to let myself think what I choose," he declared bitterly and tears came into his eyes. He began to think that he would get out of the ministry and try some other way of life. "I shall go to some city and get into business," he declared. "If my nature is such that I cannot resist sin, I shall give myself over to sin. At least I shall not be a hypocrite, preaching the word of God with my mind thinking of the shoulders and neck of a woman who does not belong to me." It was cold in the room of the bell tower of the church on that January night and almost as soon as he came into the room Curtis Hartman knew that if he stayed he would be ill. His feet were wet from tramping in the snow and there was no fire. In the room in the house next door Kate Swift had not yet appeared. With grim determination the man sat down to wait. Sitting in the chair and gripping the edge of the desk on which lay the Bible he stared into the darkness thinking the blackest thoughts of his life. He thought of his wife and for the moment almost hated her. "She has always been ashamed of passion and has cheated me," he thought. "Man has a right to expect living passion and beauty in a woman. He has no right to forget that he is an animal and in me there is something that is Greek. I will throw off the woman of my bosom and seek other women. I will besiege this school teacher. I will fly in the face of all men and if I am a creature of carnal lusts I will live then for my lusts."

The distracted man trembled from head to foot, partly from cold, partly from the struggle in which he was engaged. Hours passed and a fever assailed his body. His throat began to hurt and his teeth chattered. His feet on the study floor felt two cakes of ice. Still he would not give up. "I will see this woman and will think the thoughts I have never dared to think," he told himself, gripping the edge of the desk and waiting.

Curtis Hartman came near dying from the effects of that night of waiting in the church, and also he found in the thing that happened what he took to be the way of life for him. On other evenings when he had waited he had not been able to see, through the little hole in the glass, any part of the school teacher's room except that occupied by her bed. In the darkness he had waited until the woman suddenly appeared sitting in the bed in her white nightrobe. When the light was turned up she propped herself up among the pillows and read a book. Sometimes she smoked one of the cigarettes. Only her bare shoulders and throat were visible.

On the January night, after he had come near dying with cold and after his mind had two or three times actually slipped away into an odd land of fantasy so that he had by an exercise of will power to force himself back into consciousness, Kate Swift appeared. In the room next door a lamp was lighted and the waiting man stared into an empty bed. Then upon the bed before his eyes a naked woman threw herself. Lying face downward she wept and beat with her fists upon the pillow. With a final outburst of weeping she half arose, and in the presence of the man who had waited to look and to think thoughts the woman of sin began to pray. In the lamplight her figure, slim and strong, looked like the figure of the boy in the presence of the Christ on the leaded window.

Curtis Hartman never remembered how he got out of the church. With a cry he arose, dragging the heavy desk along the floor. The Bible fell, making a great clatter in the silence. When the light in the house next door went out he stumbled down the stairway and into the street. Along the street he went and ran in at the door of the *Winesburg Eagle*. To George Willard, who was tramping up and down in the office undergoing a struggle of his own, he began to talk incoherently. "The ways of God are beyond human understanding," he cried, running in quickly and closing the door. He began to advance upon the young man, his eyes glowing and his voice ringing with fervor. "I have found the light," he cried. "After ten years in this town, God has manifested himself to me in the body of a woman." His voice dropped and he began to whisper. "I did not understand," he said. "What I took to be a trial of my soul was only a preparation for a new and more beautiful fervor of the spirit. God has appeared to me in the person of Kate Swift, the school teacher, kneeling naked on a bed. Do you know Kate Swift? Although she may not be aware of it, she is an instrument of God, bearing the message of truth."

Reverend Curtis Hartman turned and ran out of the office. At the door he stopped, and after looking up and down the deserted street, turned again to George Willard. "I am delivered. Have no fear." He held up a bleeding fist for the young man to see. "I smashed the glass of the window," he cried. "Now it will have to be wholly replaced. The strength of God was in me and I broke it with my fist."

The Teacher

Snow lay deep in the streets of Winesburg. It had begun to snow about ten o'clock in the morning and a wind sprang up and blew the snow in clouds along Main Street. The frozen mud roads that led into town were fairly smooth and in places ice covered the mud. "There will be good sleighing," said Will Henderson, standing by the bar in Ed Griffith's saloon. Out of the saloon he went and met Sylvester West the druggist stumbling along in the kind of heavy overshoes called arctics. "Snow will bring the people into town on Saturday," said the druggist. The two men stopped and discussed their affairs. Will Henderson, who had on a light overcoat and no overshoes, kicked the heel of his left foot with the toe of the right. "Snow will be good for the wheat," observed the druggist sagely.

Young George Willard, who had nothing to do, was glad because he did not feel like working that day. The weekly paper had been printed and taken to the post office on Wednesday evening and the snow began to fall on Thursday. At eight o'clock, after the morning train had passed, he put a pair of skates in his pocket and went up to Waterworks Pond but did not go skating. Past the pond and along a path that followed Wine Creek he went until he came to a grove of beech trees. There he built a fire against the side of a log and sat down at the end of the log to think. When the snow began to fall and the wind to blow he hurried about getting fuel for the fire.

The young reporter was thinking of Kate Swift who had once been his school teacher. On the evening before he had gone to her house to get a book she wanted him to read and had been alone with her for an hour. For the fourth or fifth time the woman had talked to him with great earnestness and he could not make out what she meant by her talk. He began to believe she might be in love with him and the thought was both pleasing and annoying.

Up from the log he sprang and began to pile sticks on the fire. Looking about to be sure he was alone he talked aloud pretending he was in the presence of the woman. "Oh, you're just letting on, you know you are," he declared. "I am going to find out about you. You wait and see."

The young man got up and went back along the path toward town leaving the fire blazing in the wood. As he went through the streets the skates clanked in his pocket. In his own room in the New Willard House he built a fire in the stove and lay down on top of the bed. He began to have lustful thoughts and pulling down the shade of the window closed his eyes and turned his face to the wall. He took a pillow into his arms and embraced it thinking first of the school teacher, who by her words had stirred something within him and later of Helen

White, the slim daughter of the town banker, with whom he had been a long time half in love.

By nine o'clock of that evening snow lay deep in the streets and the weather had become bitter cold. It was difficult to walk about. The stores were dark and the people had crawled away to their houses. The evening train from Cleveland was very late but nobody was interested in its arrival. By ten o'clock all but four of the eighteen hundred citizens of the town were in bed.

Hop Higgins, the night watchman, was partially awake. He was lame and carried a heavy stick. On dark nights he carried a lantern. Between nine and ten o'clock he went his rounds. Up and down Main Street he stumbled through the drifts trying the doors of the stores. Then he went into alleyways and tried the back doors. Finding all tight he hurried around the corner to the New Willard House and beat on the door. Through the rest of the night he intended to stay by the stove. "You go to bed. I'll keep the stove going," he said to the boy who slept on a cot in the hotel office.

Hop Higgins sat down by the stove and took off his shoes. When the boy had gone to sleep he began to think of his own affairs. He intended to paint his house in the spring and sat by the stove calculating the cost of paint and labor. That led him into other calculations. The night watchman was sixty years old and wanted to retire. He had been soldier in the Civil War and drew a small pension. He hoped to find some new method of making a living and aspired to become a professional breeder of ferrets. Already he had four of the strangely shaped savage little creatures, that are used by sportsmen in the pursuit of rabbits, in the cellar of his house. "Now I have one male and three females," he mused. "If I am lucky by spring I shall have twelve or fifteen. In another year I shall be able to begin advertising ferrets for sale in the sporting papers."

The night watchman settled into his chair and his mind became a blank. He did not sleep. By years of practice he had trained himself to sit for hours through the long nights neither asleep nor awake. In the morning he was almost as refreshed as though he had slept.

With Hop Higgins safely stowed away in the chair behind the stove only three people were awake in Winesburg. George Willard was in the office of the *Eagle* pretending to be at work on the writing of a story but in reality continuing the mood of the morning by the fire in the wood. In the bell tower of the Presbyterian Church the Reverend

Curtis Hartman was sitting in the darkness preparing himself for a revelation from God, and Kate Swift, the school teacher, was leaving her house for a walk in the storm.

It was past ten o'clock when Kate Swift set out and the walk was unpremeditated. It was as though the man and the boy, by thinking of her, had driven her forth into the wintry streets. Aunt Elizabeth Swift had gone to the county seat concerning some business in connection with mortgages in which she had money invested and would not be back until the next day. By a huge stove, called a base burner, in the living room of the house sat the daughter reading a book. Suddenly she sprang to her feet and, snatching a cloak from a rack by the front door, ran out of the house.

At the age of thirty Kate Swift was not known in Winesburg as a pretty woman. Her complexion was not good and her face was covered with blotches that indicated ill health. Alone in the night in the winter streets she was lovely. Her back was straight, her shoulders square and her features were as the features of a tiny goddess on a pedestal in a garden in the dim light of a summer evening.

During the afternoon the school teacher had been to see Dr. Welling concerning her health. The doctor had scolded her and had declared she was in danger of losing her hearing. It was foolish for Kate Swift to be abroad in the storm, foolish and perhaps dangerous.

The woman in the streets did not remember the words of the doctor and would not have turned back had she remembered. She was very cold but after walking for five minutes no longer minded the cold. First she went to the end of her own street and then across a pair of hay scales set in the ground before a feed barn and into Trunion Pike. Along Trunion Pike she went to Ned Winter's barn and turning east followed a street of low frame houses that led over Gospel Hill and into Sucker Road that ran down a shallow valley past Ike Smead's chicken farm to Waterworks Pond. As she went along, the bold, excited mood that had driven her out of doors passed and then returned again.

There was something biting and forbidding in the character of Kate Swift. Everyone felt it. In the schoolroom she was silent, cold, and stern, and yet in an odd way very close to her pupils. Once in a long while something seemed to have come over her and she was happy. All of the children in the schoolroom felt the effect of her happiness. For a time they did not work but sat back in their chairs and looked at her.

With hands clasped behind her back the school teacher walked up and down in the schoolroom and talked very rapidly. It did not seem to matter what subject came into her mind. Once she talked to the children of Charles Lamb and made up strange intimate little stories concerning the life of the dead writer. The stories were told with the air of one who had lived in a house with Charles Lamb and knew all the secrets of his private life. The children were somewhat confused, thinking Charles Lamb must be someone who had once lived in Winesburg.

On another occasion the teacher talked to the children of Benvenuto Cellini. That time they laughed. What a bragging, blustering, brave, lovable fellow she made of the old artist! Concerning him also she invented anecdotes. There was one of a German music teacher who had a room above Cellini's lodgings in the city of Milan that made the boys guffaw. Sugars McNutts, a fat boy with red cheeks, laughed so hard that he became dizzy and fell off his seat and Kate Swift laughed with him. Then suddenly she became again old and stern.

On the winter night when she walked through the deserted snow-covered streets, a crisis had come into the life of the school teacher. Although no one in Winesburg would have suspected it, her life had been very adventurous. It was still adventurous. Day by day as she worked in the schoolroom or walked in the streets, grief, hope, and desire fought within her. Behind a cold exterior the most extraordinary events transpired in her mind. The people of the town thought of her as a confirmed old maid and because she spoke sharply and went her own way thought her lacking in all the human feeling that did so much to make and mar their own lives. In reality she was the most eagerly passionate soul among them, and more than once, in the five years since she had come back from her travels to settle in Winesburg and become a school teacher, had been compelled to go out of the house and walk half through the night fighting out some battle raging within. Once on a night when it rained she had stayed out six hours and when she came home had a quarrel with Aunt Elizabeth Swift. "I am glad you're not a man," said the mother sharply. "More than once I've waited for your father to come home, not knowing what new mess he had got into. I've had my share of uncertainty and you cannot blame me if I do not want to see the worst side of him reproduced in you."

Kate Swift's mind was ablaze with thoughts of George Willard. In something he had written as a school boy she thought she had recognized the spark of genius and wanted to blow on the spark. One day in the summer she had gone to the *Eagle* office and finding the boy unoccupied had taken him out Main Street to the fair ground, where the two sat on a grassy bank and talked. The school teacher tried to bring home to the mind of the boy some conception of the difficulties he would have to face as a writer. "You will have to know life," she declared, and her voice trembled with earnestness. She took hold of George Willard's shoulders and turned him about so that she could look into his eyes. A passer-by might have thought them about to embrace. "If you are to become a writer you'll have to stop fooling with words," she explained. "It would be better to give up the notion of writing until you are better prepared. Now it's time to be living. I don't want to frighten you, but I would like to make you understand the import of what you think of attempting. You must not become a mere peddler of words. The thing to learn is to know what people are thinking about, not what they say."

On the evening before that stormy Thursday night, when the Reverend Curtis Hartman sat in the bell tower of the church waiting to look at her body, young Willard had gone to visit the teacher and to borrow a book. It was then the thing happened that confused and puzzled the boy. He had the book under his arm and was preparing to depart. Again Kate Swift talked with great earnestness. Night was coming on and the light in the room grew dim. As he turned to go she spoke his name softly and with an impulsive movement took hold of his hand. Because the reporter was rapidly becoming a man something of his man's appeal, combined with the winsomeness of the boy, stirred the heart of the lonely woman. A passionate desire to have him understand the import of life, to learn to interpret it truly and honestly, swept over her. Leaning forward, her lips brushed his cheek. At the same moment he for the first time became aware of the marked beauty of her features. They were both embarrassed, and to relieve her feeling she became harsh and domineering. "What's the use? It will be ten years before you begin to understand what I mean when I talk to you," she cried passionately.

On the night of the storm and while the minister sat in the church waiting for her Kate Swift went to the office of the *Winesburg Eagle,* intending to have another talk with the boy. After the long walk in the snow she was cold, lonely, and tired. As she came through Main Street she saw the light from the print shop window shining on the snow and on an impulse opened the door and went in. For an hour she sat by the stove in the office talking of life. She talked with passionate earnestness. The impulse that had driven her out into the snow poured itself out into talk. She became inspired as she sometimes did in the presence of the children in school. A great eagerness to open the door of life to the boy, who had been her pupil and who she thought might possess a talent for the understanding of life, had possession of her. So strong was her passion that it became something physical. Again her hands took hold of his shoulders and she turned him about. In the dim light her eyes blazed. She arose and laughed, not sharply as was customary with her, but in a queer, hesitating way. "I must be going," she said. "In a moment, if I stay, I'll be wanting to kiss you."

In the newspaper office a confusion arose. Kate Swift turned and walked to the door. She was a teacher but she was also a woman. As she looked at George Willard, the passionate desire to be loved by a man, that had a thousand times before swept like a storm over her body, took possession of her. In the lamplight George Willard looked no longer a boy, but a man ready to play the part of a man.

The school teacher let George Willard take her into his arms. In the warm little office the air became suddenly heavy and the strength went out of her body. Leaning against a low counter by the door she waited. When he came and put a hand on her shoulder she turned and let her body fall heavily against him. For George Willard the confusion was immediately increased. For a moment he held the body of the woman tightly against his body and then it stiffened. Two sharp little fists began to beat on his face. When the school teacher had run away and left him alone, he walked up and down in the office swearing furiously.

It was into this confusion that the Reverend Curtis Hartman protruded himself. When he came in George Willard thought the town had gone mad. Shaking a bleeding fist in the air, the minister proclaimed the woman George had only a moment before held in his arms an instrument of God bearing a message of truth.

George blew out the lamp by the window and locking the door of the print shop went home. Through the hotel office, past Hop Higgins lost in his dreams of the raising of ferrets, he went and up into his own room. The fire in the stove had gone out and he undressed in the cold. When he got into bed the sheets were like blankets of dry snow.

George Willard rolled about in the bed on which he had lain in the afternoon hugging the pillow and thinking thoughts of Kate Swift. The words of the minister, who he thought had gone suddenly insane, rang in his ears. His eyes stared about the room. The resentment, natural to the baffled male, passed and he tried to understand what had happened. He could not make it out. Over and over he turned the matter in his mind. Hours passed and he began to think it must be time for another day to come. At four o'clock he pulled the covers up about his neck and tried to sleep. When he became drowsy and closed his eyes, he raised a hand and with it groped about in the darkness. "I have missed something. I have missed something Kate Swift was trying to tell me," he muttered sleepily. Then he slept and in all Winesburg he was the last soul on that winter night to go to sleep.

LOUISIANA

Cold Death

ROARK BRADFORD

Mammy Clo grumbled and fussed when Babe lifted her, chair, crutch, and all, and carried her from the dinner table to the shade in front of the cabin. But her protesting, 'I kin wawk, gal; don't go totin' me round like I was a baby' lacked some of its usual vigor.

Mammy Clo, chair and crutch, weighed less than a hundred pounds. Years—so many of them that no one remembered the exact number—had toughened and dried the split-hickory chair, the leather-tipped crutch, and Mammy Clo.

'You's awright, mammy, hunh?' Babe asked as she placed the chair in the shade. 'You's feelin' awright?' Babe was Mammy Clo's granddaughter, and Babe herself was a grandmother since Little Henry's baby had come.

'Cou'se I's awright, gal,' declared Mammy Clo. 'Ain't nothin' de matter wid me. You totin' me round! I swear! Whyn't you git yo' hoe and git out yonder in de field? I ain't rose you up to stay round de house axin' me is I awright. I swear, gal!'

'Yeah, you's awright,' grinned Babe. 'Long as you kin grumble, well you's bound to be awright. Now d's you want anything befo' I goes to de field?'

Mammy Clo considered. The cedar bucket with its gourd dipper had been filled with cool water and was setting within easy reach of her chair. 'Bring me out dat quilt I been piecin',' she decided. 'De Star er Bet-ly-ham. In dat big box. On top.'

The quilt was brought and spread in the old woman's lap. 'You sho' you's awright now, mammy?' Babe pressed.

'Don't I look awright?' demanded Mammy Clo. 'Gawd er mighty, gal! Whyn't you git to de field?'

From *Let the Band Play Dixie* by Roark Bradford, copyright 1934 by Roark Bradford. Published by Harper & Brothers. Used by permission of the author.

As soon as Babe disappeared down the path Mammy Clo grinned proudly. 'Dat chile jest won't do,' she chuckled. 'I sho' rose her up right.' She laughed softly. 'Waitin' on me like I was de Lawd, or somebody!'

A robin, playing among the moss tufts in the live oak, broke into a saucy little song, and Mammy Clo hummed a wordless accompaniment to it as she sat with half-closed eyes, enjoying the peaceful rest that follows a wholesome meal. Time slipped by so easily, these nice clear days when she sat in the shade. The first thing she knew the 'cool of the evening' would be upon her, and with it would come Rucker to read his Bible and discuss the works of the Lord.

Day after day Mammy Clo had spent in the shade in just such idleness. Day after day she had planned to 'hitch her crutch under her arm' and work about the house while Babe was in the field. But mid-afternoon breezes and Rucker slipped up on her.

Rucker was the preacher. Mammy Clo had 'raised' him. She did not remember, offhand, whether he was her own child or the child of some other woman about the place. It did not matter, however. All the Negroes and half the whites in that part of the country she counted among her children. And none of them ever grew up, white or black. She helped them into the world and nursed them through the dangerous months of infancy. Parentage and race meant nothing to her. A baby was a baby and had to be treated just so. 'And hit ain't a natchal one of 'em,' she declared proudly, 'which wan't riz up right. Don't mind de work. Love de Lawd, and ain't skeered er nothin' but sin.'

She sat in idle reverie for another minute and then she remembered the quilt. 'And hyar me,' she reproached, 'lazin' round and dis quilt ain't done yit. Rucker'll be hyar terrackly and when he gits to argyin' 'bout how skeered he is to die, well I might jest as well lay hit down and quit, cause I can't sew and listen at Rucker argy.'

She spread the quilt, untied a bundle of cloth scraps, and began piecing them into a general pattern. Her fingers, old and stiff, wriggled and twisted, and the needle went back and forth with lightning speed, making fine, even stitches.

The quilt was Mammy Clo's masterpiece—no less. In the center was a large star fashioned from white silk. Around that star, stitched with cunning neatness and prim accuracy, were smaller stars of various colors and sizes. It was a difficult design and had to be executed exactly right or it would be a failure. And it took time, Lord, a long time.

Mammy had hoped to have it completed in time to give it as a 'cradle present' to Little Henry's baby, her great-great-grandchild. But time slipped up on her, and Little Henry's baby received a Paul and Silas in Prison quilt instead. Not that the Paul and Silas designs were not beautiful and appropriate cradle gifts. Mammy Clo's old fingers had stitched hundreds of them while sitting by the cradles of fretful babies, and had brought them to other babies as cradle presents. White and black babies, grown old by now, treasured Mammy Clo's Paul and Silas quilts as they treasured the love of the old nursewoman herself.

But this Star of Bethlehem was to be a very special quilt. Mammy Clo had conceived it and started it in time, she hoped, to have it ready for the arrival of Babe, her first grandchild. But it proved tedious work, and then too, there were babies to be brought into the world and nursed to health and strength. The quilt was not finished. Babe got a Paul and Silas quilt for a cradle present.

Then, when Babe married, Mammy Clo took out the unfinished quilt and set to work again, getting ready for Babe's first child. She got considerable work done on it, but about that time Rucker began preaching and he took up much of her time, discussing the Scriptures and going over his sermons with her. Time slipped by, and a Paul and Silas quilt went to Babe's baby, Little Henry.

The quilt was almost forgotten until suddenly Little Henry grew up and married. The very day he married Mammy Clo got out the quilt and set to work, determined to have it ready for Little Henry's first baby. But it seemed like she would no more then get settled down in her chair before here came Rucker to talk about the ways of the Lord. She tried to work while Rucker talked, but Rucker was so interested and argumentative over his own ideas that her stitches were bad and had to be removed. Nothing but a perfect stitch could stay in that quilt.

'Whyn't you quit wearyin' me wid dat tawk about cold death?' she complained. 'I ain't studdin' cold death. I ain't studdin' nothin' but de Promise' Land.'

'Dat's jest yo' trouble,' Rucker replied. 'You got yo' haid in de air and yo' eye on Glory. But yo' foots still is on de ground. You knows all about livin' hyar on de yearth and you knows all about how you gonter live when you gits to heab'm. But you got to grabble wid Cold Death befo' you gits dar. And what er you know 'bout dyin'?'

'I don't know nothin' 'bout dyin', and I don't keer nothin' 'bout dyin',' Mammy Clo retorted. 'All I know is——'

'Well,' interrupted Rucker, 'you got to die. I don't keer how much you don't keer. When you quits livin' you got to die befo' you kin git Over Yonder.'

'Dat's all right,' Mammy Clo assured him. 'De Lawd gonter take keer of all er dat. Me and de Lawd been wawkin' side by side for goin' on I don't know how long and de Lawd love me too good. I ain't wearied. I been too good to de Lawd.'

Rucker accused her of being proud and the argument waged—for months.

And then, before she knew it, Babe told her Little Henry and his wife had a baby.

There was nothing else for Mammy Clo to do. The Star of Bethlehem quilt was not completed, and when they placed her chair in the spring wagon for the ride over to Little Henry's, she carried a Paul and Silas quilt on her arm for the cradle gift.

'And hit ain't done ontwell yit!' she chided herself. 'Me settin' hyar dozin' like a preacher full er possum ain't gonter git hit done, too.' Her bony old fingers moved faster and faster, and star after star was woven into the mosaic of varicolored cloths.

She worked diligently for what seemed to her a very short time. Then she heard the hinges on the picket gate squawk, and she knew without turning her head that it was Rucker. In a minute they were exchanging their habitual greetings.

'Hy-dy, mammy. How you comin' 'long?'

'Po'ly, thank Gawd. And you, son?'

'Tole'ble. Jest tole'ble.'

Rucker seated himself in the shade near Mammy Clo and began fanning himself with his old woolen hat.

'What you doin', mammy? Makin' a quilt?'

'Yeah,' said Mammy Clo. 'Ain't hit purty?'

'Mighty,' agreed Rucker. 'Got stars and things in hit, ain't hit?'

'Don't dey look like stars and things?' demanded Mammy Clo.

Instead of replying, Rucker fanned himself vigorously.

'And don't come botherin' me wid fool tawk,' added Mammy Clo. 'I got to git dis quilt done, and I can't work wid you settin' round hyar, droolin' at me.'

'Yeah?' grinned Rucker. 'Well, ef'n I didn't drool at you, well, you wouldn't have nothin' to grumble about. Den whar'd you been?' He chuckled with the old woman at his retort. Then he added seriously, 'Mammy, you needs tawkin' to about yo' proudfulness. I aims to change yo' mind befo' you has to grabble wid Cold Death.'

'Hyar you goes!' exclaimed Mammy Clo. 'Shet up till I gits dis quilt done, will you? I ain't got no time to listen at you now.'

'How come you so sot on gittin' dat quilt done?' Rucker wanted to know. 'You got mo' quilts made up now den you kin shake a stick at.'

'I needs dis quilt in my business,' she explained. 'I got somethin' to do wid hit.'

'Which is——?'

Mammy Clo stopped sewing and looked at Rucker.

'Son,' she said, solemnly, 'I'm gittin' along in de years. My time is mighty nigh out.'

'You ain't so young,' Rucker agreed.

'Well,' the old woman continued, 'seein' how dis is a mighty purty quilt, I kind er counted on takin' hit to Glory wid me and givin' hit to the Po' Little Jesus for a cradle present.'

'Humph!' snorted Rucker. 'Don't you know dey got all de quilts dey needs Up Yonder?'

'I don't keer how many quilts dey got,' defended Mammy Clo. 'I got some manners. And hit ain't manners to go nowhar empty-handed. I ain't gonter put up on de Lawd and not bring a little somethin' along for manners.' She fingered the fine stitches lovingly. 'And dis is a fine quilt too.' She hesitated dubiously and then continued defiantly, "I don't speck dey got no quilts in heab'n any purtier den dis. And maybe not as purty!'

For a moment Rucker was shocked beyond speech.

'Proud-tawkin'!' he exclaimed finally. 'And you wid one foot in de grave, right now. Mammy, dat ain't no way for a good woman to tawk!'

'Hit's de natchal truf,' defended Mammy Clo, doggedly. 'I seed a heap er quilts in my time and I ain't never yit seed one no purtier den dis.'

'I don't keer what you ain't never seed!' Rucker's amazement was giving way to indignation. 'You ain't got no call to go braggin' 'bout yo' quilts and proud-tawkin' de Lawd when ole Cold Death ready to grab you ev'y minute. Braggin' ain't humble, I don't keer how purty de quilt is. And you got to be humble do you want to die right.' Rucker paused in his outburst and calmed. 'De Book say so,' he added.

'Humph!' snorted Mammy Clo.

'Don't go humphin' de Book,' cautioned Rucker. 'De Book——'

'I ain't humphin' de Book,' Mammy Clo corrected. 'I'm humphin' yo' fool tawk. Cause you know I ain't studdin' 'bout dying. De Lawd gonter look after me when my time is out. I ain't wearied. De Lawd love me too good.'

Rucker was puzzled. Mammy Clo always had been a contradiction—to him and to the Scriptures. He could not understand her attitude. 'Mammy,' he said gently, 'you's a mighty good woman but you's a mighty proud woman.'

'Proud in de Lawd, yes,' she agreed.

'But proud,' insisted Rucker. 'And proudfulness is a sin. De Book say. And de proud die hard.'

Mammy Clo stitched nervously for several minutes. The last star on the quilt took shape under her flying needle. Rucker had told her virtually the same thing a thousand times, and she never had paid any attention to him. But as the last stitch was made she was seized with a strange feeling. It was as though Rucker at last had unsettled her peaceful mind.

'Rucker,' she said, 'what do you know 'bout dis cold death you been carryin' on about?'

Rucker considered for a minute. 'Nothin',' he admitted. 'Not nothin'.' He sat in serious, silent study for a while. 'And dat's de p'int,' he added. 'Hit's a mystery. A mighty mystery.' Rucker's words agitated the strange feeling that was upon Mammy Clo. It was as though she were standing in sand and the sand were giving way from under her feet.

'What do de Scriptures say about hit?' she pressed.

Rucker cast about uncertainly in his mind. 'De ole song,' he explained, 'say, "Death ain't nothin' but a robber in dis land." Dat what de ole song say. But de chune don't say dat. De chune say like a nigger in de graveyard. De nigger say, "Dem ha'nts ain't nothin' but de tombstones." But whilst de nigger sayin' dat, de chune say, "Maybe not, but all de same, I'm gonter reach up and git my hat and git along down de road." '

'Unhunh,' agreed Mammy Clo. 'De chune don't say what de words say.'

'Now,' continued Rucker, tackling it from another angle. 'Dat "Deep River" song don't say so much, but de chune say a heap. De song say, "Deep River. My home is over Jurdin." But de chune say, "Yeah? I know yo' home is over Jurdin, All Right. But what about dat deep river? You got to cross dat river befo' you kin git home. Deep river!"'

Mammy Clo shivered. Something like a panic was taking place within her. 'But de Scriptures, Rucker?' she pressed. 'What do de Scriptures 'low?'

'De Scriptures,' Rucker explained in a hushed voice, 'don't 'low. Dat's what makes hit a mighty mystery.'

Mammy Clo clutched desperately at one straw of hope. 'Maybe hit ain't——'

'Oh, yes, hit is,' Rucker interrupted. 'Dat's de p'int. De Scriptures allows by a parable. De Scriptures allows dat de Lawd led de Hebrews round de wilderness fawty years gittin' 'em humble so dey c'd git to de Promise' Land, and de ones which wouldn't git, well de Lawd struck 'em down.'

'Hmmm,' groaned Mammy Clo. 'Hmmm, hmmm.'

'And when de Lawd got 'em humbled,' continued Rucker, 'well, he led 'em to Jurdin and *showed* 'em de Promise' Land on de yuther side.' He paused dramatically and repeated, '*Showed* 'em de Promise' Land. And den, de Scriptures say, *dey crossed over*. De Lawd didn't cross 'em over, like at de Red Sea. Dey done dey own crossin'.'

Mammy Clo's head bobbed from side to side. Her eyes closed, and weird, twitchy whines came from her troubled lips.

'And,' continued Rucker, 'dat's de mystery of Cold Death. De Lawd lead you round hyar on de yearth, and he show you de Promise' Land. But you got to do yo' own dyin' . . . and de Scripture say de proud die hard.'

Mammy Clo's hands shook as if in palsy and she tried to speak. Her mouth opened, but only a dry rattle came from her throat. For a moment she was terrified. Then, as suddenly as it had come, the feeling of terror left her and she was calm and serene. She grinned. 'Rucker ain't nothin' but a chile wid a heap er tawk in his mouf,' she told herself, 'and hyar me listenin' at his fool tawk. Humph!'

Even as the realization came to her she vaguely heard Rucker calling nervously 'Mammy Clo! Mammy Clo!' and she vaguely felt him tugging at her arm. Some childish prank of his, no doubt. Well, Rucker was such a child, anyway. He never would grow up!

While the thoughts moved gently and comfortably through her mind she heard the hinges on the yard gate creak again, and she turned to see who could be coming in at that time in the afternoon. It was a tall straight man with a horn in his hand.

'Looks like Ole Gab'l, hisself,' she commented.

'Dat's zackly who he is, too,' the tall man grinned.

'Well, drag up a cheer and set,' invited Mammy Clo. 'Hit's cool water in de bucket and de gou'd is handy.'

Gabriel helped himself to a drink of water and drew up a chair. 'I'm kind er in a hurry, Clo,' he said, seating himself comfortably. 'I ain't got much time. I jest drapped by to——'

'Sh-h-h-h-h,' interrupted Mammy Clo, raising her finger for silence and cupping her hand to her ear. Sh-h-h-h-h.'

'I jest drapped by to——' Gabriel started again, but Mammy Clo's old ear caught the sound distinctly. It was the cry of a tiny baby.

'Hand me my crutch,' she ordered briskly and, without waiting for Gabriel to explain his business, she adjusted the crutch under her arm and hobbled toward the house.

Mammy Clo was not surprised when she walked into the room where the baby lay in its crib. Rather, she was disgusted.

The room was big and richly furnished. A huge table heavily laden with fine cradle gifts stood at the side of the cradle. But Mammy Clo was accustomed to going into fine houses. The big mansions of rich white folks and the lowliest cabins of the poorest Negroes all looked alike to her. A baby was a baby—white or black. The surroundings did not matter.

The first thing that caught her eye was a woman dressed in white. A white cap, white apron, white stockings, white shoes. The garments were stiffly starched, and shining where the iron had passed over them too many times. Mammy Clo knew exactly what she was up against. She had encountered trained nurses before. 'Too much starch and not enough brains,' was her estimate.

The nurse was heating milk over an alcohol stove and toying with a thermometer. Meanwhile the baby was crying pitifully in the crib.

The cradle was a fine one—made of solid gold laths joined together an inch apart. The head and foot boards were set with a huge star of clustered diamonds. But the baby lay writhing in pain on the bare slats of the crib.

'Well, befo' Gawd!' exclaimed Mammy Clo. 'Layin' hyar naked as a jaybird! And no mattress! And in a cradle built like a jackass ought to be eatin' hay out'n!' She turned threateningly to the nurse. 'Gal!' she exploded. 'How come diserway?'

'Now, aunty,' protested the nurse. 'The doctor has everything exactly as he wants it. The baby must have ventilation, and the doctor——'

'De doctor, hunh?' snorted Mammy Clo. 'Well, I ain't studdin' what de doctor say de baby got to have. What I'm studdin' 'bout is what de baby got. He got de colic. Dat's what he got!'

The nurse tried to interrupt, but Mammy Clo drowned her out. 'Now drag yo'se'f on out in de gyarden and bring me some catnip. Dis baby need some catnip tea.'

'But the doctor——'

'I ain't studdin' de doctor,' Mammy Clo broke in. 'And you too! Dis chile got de bellyache and he got hit bad. Now git out and git dat catnip! You hyar me! And some hot water!' She unhitched her crutch menacingly. 'And make tracks,' she added, 'befo' I wrops dis cretch 'round you!'

The nurse left and Mammy Clo lifted the baby tenderly from its crib, holding it in one arm while she adjusted the Star of Bethlehem quilt into a pillowy mattress with her free hand.

'Now you git back in dar, suh,' she said, placing the infant tenderly in the cradle. 'De doctor, hunh? And you mighty nigh got de epizoodics right now!'

The baby continued to cry, but its cries were softer, and soon they were little more than troubled whimpers that fitted into the wordless tune which Mammy Clo hummed.

Presently the nurse returned with the herb and water, and the baby was given the tea.

'The doctor will be awfully put out about this,' the nurse declared.

'Listen, honey,' said Mammy Clo, 'lemme ax you a question: Did de doctor ever had a baby?'

The nurse snickered at the idea.

'And you neither, I bet,' grinned Mammy Clo. 'Now you git over yonder by de lamp and jest let me alone.' And the nurse surrendered.

The baby, soothed by the tea, slept peacefully. Mammy Clo sat by the cradle, rocking back and forth, watching every move of the child. Toward morning the expression of pain faded from its face and the baby opened its big, round, blue eyes. There seemed to be a knowing, understanding glance in them as it saw the old woman, sitting with head bent, at the side of the cradle.

'You rascal you!' she accused fondly. 'You jest puttin' off on me! Dat's what you doin' suh!' She shook her tightly braided head close to the baby's face and gurgled, 'Goodly-goodly-goodly-goo,' and the baby's face muscles contorted in a manner that only Mammy Clo could have interpreted as an expression of merriment. She beamed.

'You scound'el, you,' she said. 'Look at you laughin' at ole mammy! Jest as mannish! I swear! Laughin' right out loud like a grown-up man! I bet you gonter be raisin' up and axin' me to please give you a chaw er 'backer, fust thing I know!' She smoothed the quilt gently and added, 'Now you git to sleep, suh, and rest dem purty eyes some mo'. And de next time you wakes up mamm' gonter have a sugar tit for dat boy to suck on. Now, git to sleepy!'

The baby soon was in a quiet, peaceful sleep, and Mammy Clo instructed the nurse to bring a piece of clean, white cloth and some sugar. Then she fell asleep in the chair by the cradle.

When she woke it was light and she was quite rested. Both the baby and the nurse still were asleep, but Mammy Clo noticed the 'sugar tit' had been knotted properly and placed on the table near the cradle.

After a few minutes Gabriel opened the door wide, holding it back and bowing low. Almost immediately the Lord walked in.

The Lord looked exactly as Clo imagined he would look—exactly six feet tall and straight as a ramrod. And proud, too. With his shoulder drawn back and a heavy crown on his head. His stride was majestic—just short of a swagger. The sight of him was enough to fill one with awe.

Clo got up immediately and bowed, and the Lord opened his mouth as though to speak. But Clo interrupted him just in time. 'Sh-h-h-h, Lawd,' she whispered. 'De baby's sleepin' now, and he need dat sleep powerful bad. He was mighty sick last night. Mighty nigh had de cholly-mawbuses.'

The Lord looked shocked for an instant and then he smiled indulgently. 'That's mighty fine, Clo,' he said in a surprisingly soft whisper.

'Yeah, Lawd,' put in Gabriel. 'Clo do ack mighty handy around de babies.'

Clo was embarrassed by the bald praise. 'He jest need sleep,' she repeated, 'and some tea and stuff. He's awright, now.'

The Lord turned and tiptoed out of the room, and Gabriel and Clo followed. Outside Gabriel began talking, apparently resuming a conversation that had been started before he and the Lord entered the room.

‘ ’Bout dat time,’ he said, ‘she hyared de baby cry and she lit out twarge de cradle like a hawg after cawn.’

‘What! And you didn’t explain, suh?’ The Lord thundered the question more like an accusation.

‘Explain?’ repeated Gabriel. ‘Lawd, how anybody gonter explain anything at her when she hyars a baby squallin’? Me and you bofe couldn’t explain her nothin’ when she hyars a young ’un holler.’

Clo did not understand exactly what they were talking about, but she knew it had to do with Gabriel’s arrival the afternoon before, and that the Lord was displeased with it. She hastened to Gabriel’s rescue.

‘You see, Lawd,’ she amplified, ‘I and Gab’l was jest fixin’ to pass de time er day and I didn’t no mo’n give him howdy, to I hyared de baby squallin’. And quick as I hyared dat, I knowed hit wan’t nothin’ but de bellyache make a baby holler like dat. So I jest lit out.’

‘Yeah,’ supplemented Gabriel. ‘She been tawkin’ to Rucker, and Rucker, he say Clo ain’t humble enough.’

‘Rucker,’ put in Clo, ‘don’t think my Star er Bet-ly-ham quilt is purty, and Lawd, dat is a mighty purty quilt.’

They had been walking along, Gabriel and Clo slightly in rear of the Lord, who was swinging his arms and stepping higher with his left foot so that his stride was one of majesty. Clo paid no attention to where they were going until suddenly she realized that she was in the box elder grove back of the orchard, where she used to come to funerals.

‘Dog gone!’ she exclaimed. ‘Hit’s de fust time I been hyar since I don’t know when. I used to never miss a funeral, but lately hit’s been hard to git around. . . .’ She looked about and saw a pile of freshly dug earth, just off to the left. ‘Look like a new grave, too!’ she exclaimed. ‘Must gonter be a funeral today.’

‘A big’n too,’ Gabriel assured her, with a knowing grin.

‘Well, I be dad blame!’ Mammy Clo’s old eyes sparkled. ‘I ain’t been to a funeral in a month er Sundays! Le’s watch hit!’

‘You’re mighty right, we’ll watch it,’ the Lord declared importantly. ‘That’s what I had in my mind when I led you out here. I want you to watch, and listen too. Gabriel got to drinking water and chinning with you and forgot to . . .’

'Aw, Lawd,' protested Gabriel, 'don't be so hard on me. I done tole you she hyared dat baby yellin' before I c'd git my mouf open to tell her.'

Before the Lord had time to reply the procession came into view. Rucker, Bible in hand and head bowed, walked in front.

'Rucker gonter preach, too,' Clo explained. 'Rucker preaches a powerful good funeral, too, Lawd. I rose him up to be a preacher.'

Behind Rucker six husky Negroes carried a rosewood casket that was banked high with flowers. Then came more than a hundred men, women, and children—white and black. They were straggling slowly, singing in ragged time, 'When the Saints Go Marchin' On.'

'Ev'y last'n one of 'em is my chilluns, Lawd,' Mammy Clo explained proudly. 'Love de Lawd. Don't mind de work. And ain't skeered er nothin' but sin. Dat de way I rose dem chilluns.'

The casket was rested by the side of the grave. Rucker took a position at the head and the others formed a semicircle at the foot. Rucker raised his hand and a hushed silence fell.

'People,' he said huskily, 'most generally when I preaches a funeral, well I preaches hit. But I don't feel like preachin' much today. So we gonter sing dis funeral.'

'Now jest watch, Lawd!' Mammy Clo explained jubilantly. 'Rucker do git right at a singin' funeral. When his wife died and he didn't feel like preachin', well, we sung de funeral. Den all at once ole Rucker got hot and he got up and whupped de devil to he wan't no bigger'n a gnat!'

Rucker raised his hand again. 'Somebody h'ist a chune,' he commanded, 'while de body er dis cawpse is bein' lowered in de grave.'

An uncertain baritone voice began tunelessly:

'Befo' dis time another year, I may be gone——'

The others straggled along after the baritone. When time came for the second line, a shrill—too shrill—soprano had seized the lead:

'And er my body a-layin' in de ground,
Lawd knows how long.'

Rucker shook his head. 'Dat's rotten,' he declared.

'Well, I believe you,' Mammy Clo agreed heartily. 'Plum rotten.'

There was a moment of tense silence and then a rumbling bass began:

'Deep river! My home is over Jurdin.
Deep river, Lawd! I want to cross over into Camp Ground.'

'Dat's mo' better,' Rucker admitted, and soon the song was rolling along, now gently and soothingly, now wild and rumbling.

'Oh, won't you come to de Gospel Feast,
In de Promise' Land whar all is peace?
Deep river! My home is over Jurdin.
Deep river, Lawd! I want to cross over into Camp Ground.'

The pall bearers placed cotton ropes under the casket and lifted it over the gaping hole. The song droned weirdly, wistfully. Rucker addressed the casket as it was being lowered into the grave:

'Ashes might be unto ashes and dust might be unto dust, but hit ain't a natchal man kin put you in de ground. And dat's a fack.'

'Deep river, Lawd! I want to cross over——'

The song rose higher and higher while Rucker struggled not only with words to express his feeling, but against the din of wailing voices. Then, when the last note of a line was dying out, he raised his own voice with the swing of the song and led the next verse himself:

'Oh, de news f'm heab'm which is gone around,
She crossed over Jurdin on dusty ground.'

Gabriel leaped excitedly to his feet. 'I be dag gone, Lawd!' he exclaimed, 'listen at Rucker!'

'I made him say that,' said the Lord. 'I wanted Clo to hear from Rucker's own lips that she was dead. Now, listen at this one, Clo, and you'll find out all about that mystery!' But Clo was not there.

She was hurrying away, grumbling to herself. 'I ain't got no time to pleasure myse'f at nobody's funeral,' she was saying. 'I got to mine dat baby. Dat sassy scound'el! All r'ared back on my fine quilt, jest as buckish! I swear!' She giggled deep down in her throat. 'He gonter git dat sugar tit de minute he open dem purty eyes er his'n. R'ared back, laughin' at me! He jest won't do!' And she hurried on to the side of the cradle.

INDIANA

First Day Finish

JESSAMYN WEST

I

'Thee's home, Lady,' Jess told his mare.

They had made the trip in jig time. The sun was still up, catalpa shadows long across the grass, and mud daubers still busy about the horse trough, gathering a few last loads before nightfall, when Lady turned in the home driveway.

Jess loosened the reins, so that on their first homecoming together they could round the curve to the barn with a little flourish of arrival. It was a short-lived flourish, quickly subsiding when Jess caught sight of the Reverend Marcus Augustus Godley's Black Prince tied to the hitching rack.

'Look who's here,' Jess told his mare and they came in slow and seemly as befitted travelers with forty weary miles behind them.

The Reverend Godley himself, shading his eyes from the low sun, stepped to the barn door when his Black Prince nickered.

Jess lit stiffly down and was standing at Lady's head when the Reverend Marcus Augustus reached them.

'Good evening, Marcus,' said Jess. 'Thee run short of something over at thy place?'

'Welcome home,' said the Reverend Godley, never flinching. 'I was hunting, with Enoch's help, a bolt to fit my seeder,' he told Jess, but he never took his eyes off Lady.

He was a big man, fat but not pursy, with a full red face preaching had kept supple and limber. A variety of feelings, mostly painful, flickered across it now as he gazed at Jess's mare.

He opened and shut his mouth a couple of times, but all he managed to say was, 'Where'd you come across that animal, Friend Birdwell?'

'Kentucky,' Jess said shortly.

'I'm a Kentuckian myself.' The Reverend Godley marveled that the state that had fathered him could have produced such horseflesh.

'You trade Red Rover for this?' he asked.

Jess rubbed his hand along Lady's neck. 'The mare's name is Lady,' he said.

'Lady!' The preacher gulped, then threw back his big head and disturbed the evening air with laughter.

'Friend,' Jess said, watching the big bulk heave, 'thy risibilities are mighty near the surface this evening.'

The Reverend Godley wiped the tears from his face and ventured another look. 'It's just the cleavage,' he said. 'The rift between the name and looks.'

'That's a matter of opinion,' Jess told him, 'but Lady is the name.'

The preacher stepped off a pace or two as if to try the advantage of a new perspective on the mare's appearance, clapped a handful of Sen-sen into his mouth, and chewed reflectively.

'I figure it this way,' he told Jess. 'You bought that animal Red Rover. Flashy as sin and twice as unreliable. First little brush you have with me and my cob, Red Rover curdles on you—goes sourer than a crock of cream in a June storm. What's the natural thing to do?'

The Reverend Godley gave his talk a pulpit pause and rested his big thumbs in his curving watch chain.

'The natural thing to do? Why, just what you done. Give speed the go-by. Say farewell to looks. Get yourself a beast sound in wind and limb and at home behind a plow. Friend,' he commended Jess, 'you done the right thing, though I'm free to admit I never laid eyes before on a beast of such dimensions.

'Have some Sen-sen?' he asked amiably. 'Does wonders for the breath.' Jess shook his head.

'Well,' he continued, 'I want you to know—Sunday mornings on the way to church, when I pass you, there's nothing personal in it. That morning when I went round you and Red Rover, I somehow got the idea you's taking it personal. Speed's an eternal verity, friend, an eternal verity. Nothing personal. Rain falls. The stars shine. The grass withereth. The race is to the swift. A fast horse passes a slow one. An eternal verity, Friend Birdwell. You're no preacher, but your wife is. She understands these things. Nothing personal. Like gravitation, like life, like death. A law of God. Nothing personal.

'The good woman will be halloing for me,' he said, gazing up the pike toward his own farm a quarter of a mile away. He took another look at Jess's new mare.

'Name's Lady,' he said, as if reminding himself. 'Much obliged for the bolt, Friend Birdwell. Me and my cob'll see you Sunday.'

2

Enoch stepped out from the barn door as the Reverend Godley turned down the driveway.

'Figure I heard my sermon for the week,' he said.

'He's got an endurin' flock,' Jess told his hired man.

'Cob?' Enoch asked. 'What's he mean always calling that animal of his a cob? He ignorant?'

'Not ignorant—smooth,' Jess said. 'Cob's just his way of saying Black Prince's no ordinary beast without coming straight out with so undraped a word as stallion.'

The two men turned with one accord from Godley's cob to Jess's Lady. Enoch's green eyes flickered knowingly; his long freckled hand touched Lady's muscled shoulder lightly, ran down the powerful legs, explored the deep chest.

'There's more here, Mr. Birdwell, than meets the eye?'

Jess nodded.

'As far as looks goes,' Enoch said, 'the Reverend called the turn.'

'As far as looks goes,' Jess agreed.

'She part Morgan?'

'Half,' Jess said proudly.

Enoch swallowed. 'How'd you swing it?'

'Providence,' Jess said. 'Pure Providence. Widow woman wanted a pretty horse and one that could be passed.'

'Red Rover,' Enoch agreed and added softly, 'The Reverend was took in.'

'He's a smart man,' said Jess. 'We'd best not bank on it. But by sugar, Enoch, I tell thee I was getting tired of taking Eliza down the pike to Meeting every First Day like a tail to Godley's comet. Have him start late, go round me, then slow down so's we'd eat dust. Riled me so I was arriving at Meeting in no fit state to worship.'

'You give her a tryout—coming home?' Enoch asked guardedly.

'I did, Enoch,' Jess said solemnly. 'This horse, this Morgan mare named Lady, got the heart of a lion and the wings of a bird. Nothing without pinfeathers is going to pass her.'

'It's like Mr. Emerson says,' said Enoch earnestly.

Jess nodded. 'Compensation,' he agreed. 'A clear case of it and her pure due considering the looks she's got.'

'You figure on this Sunday?' Enoch asked.

'Well,' Jess said, 'I plan to figure on nothing. Thee heard the Reverend Marcus Augustus. A fast horse goes round a slow one. Eternal law. If Black Prince tries to pass us First Day—and don't—it's just a law, just something eternal. And mighty pretty, Enoch, like the stars.'

'A pity,' Enoch said reflecting, 'the Reverend's young'uns all so piddling and yours such busters. It'll tell on your mare.'

'A pity,' Jess acquiesced, 'but there it is. Eliza'd never agree to leave the children home from Meeting.'

Enoch ruminated, his fingers busy with Lady's harness.

'What'll your wife say to this mare? Been a considerable amount of trading lately.'

'Say?' said Jess. 'Thee heard her. "Exchange Red Rover for a horse not racy-looking." This mare racy-looking?'

'You have to look twice to see it,' Enoch admitted.

'Eliza don't look twice at a horse. I'll just lead Lady up now for Eliza to see. She don't hold with coming down to the barn while men's about.'

Jess took Lady from the shafts and led her between the rows of currant bushes up to the house. Dusk was come now, lamps were lit. Inside, Eliza and the children were waiting for their greeting until the men had had their talk.

'Lady,' Jess said fondly, 'I want thee to see thy mistress.'

3

The rest of the week went by, mild and very fair, one of those spells in autumn when time seems to stand still. Clear days with a wind which would die down by afternoon. The faraway Sandusky ridges seemed to have moved up to the orchard's edge. The purple ironweed, the farewell summer, the goldenrod, stood untrembling beneath an unclouded sky. Onto the corn standing shocked in the fields, gold light softer than arrows, but as pointed, fell. A single crow at dusk would drop in a slow arc against the distant wood to show that not all had died. Indian summer can be a time of great content.

First Day turned up pretty. Just before the start for Meeting, Jess discovered a hub cap missing off the surrey.

'Lost?' asked Eliza.

'I wouldn't say lost,' Jess told her. 'Missing.'

Odd thing, a pity to be sure, but there it was. Nothing for it but for him and Eliza to ride to Meeting in the cut-down buggy and leave the children behind. Great pity, but there it was.

Eliza stood in the yard in her First Day silk. 'Jess,' she said in a balky voice, 'this isn't my idea of what's seemly. A preacher going to Meeting in a cut-down rig like this. Looks more like heading for the trotting races at the county fair than preaching.'

Jess said, 'Thee surprises me, Eliza. Thee was used to put duty before appearance. Friend Fox was content to tramp the roads to reach his people. Thee asks for thy surrey, fresh blacking on the dashboard and a new whip in the socket.'

He turned away sadly. 'The Lord's people are everywhere grown more worldly,' he said, looking dismally at the ground.

It didn't set good with Jess, pushing Eliza against her will that way—and he wasn't any too sure it was going to work. But the name Fox got her. When she was a girl she'd set out to bring the Word to people, the way Fox had done, and he'd have gone, she knew, to Meeting in a barrow, if need be.

So that's the way they started out, and in spite of the rig, Eliza was lighthearted and holy-feeling. When they pulled out on the pike, she was pleased to note the mare's gait was better than her looks. Lady picked up her feet like she knew what to do with them.

'Thee's got a good-pulling mare, Jess,' she said kindly.

'She'll get us there, I don't misdoubt,' Jess said.

They'd rounded the first curve below the clump of maples that gave the Maple Grove Nursery its name when the Reverend Godley bore down upon them. Neither bothered to look back; both knew the heavy, steady beat of Black Prince's hoofs.

Eliza settled herself in the cut-down rig, her Bible held comfortably in her lap. 'It taxes the imagination,' she said, 'how a man church-bound can have his mind so set on besting another. Don't thee think so, Jess?'

'It don't tax mine,' Jess said, thinking honesty might be the only virtue he'd get credit for that day.

Eliza was surprised not to see Black Prince pulling abreast them. It was here on the long stretch of level road that Black Prince usually showed them his heels.

'Thee'd best pull over, Jess,' she said.

'I got no call to pull out in the ditch,' Jess said. 'The law allows me half the road.'

4

The mare hadn't made any fuss about it—no head-shaking, no fancy footwork—but she'd settled down in her harness, she was traveling. It was plain to Eliza they were eating up the road.

'Don't thee think we'd better pull up, Jess?' Eliza said it easy, so as not to stir up the contrary streak that wasn't buried very deep in her husband.

'By sugar,' Jess said, 'I don't see why.'

As soon as Eliza heard that 'by sugar' spoken as bold-faced as if it were a weekday, she knew it was too late for soft words. 'By sugar,' Jess said again, 'I don't see why. The Reverend Godley's got half the road and I ain't urging my mare.'

It depended on what you called urging. He hadn't taken to lambasting Lady with his hat yet, the way he had Red Rover, but he was sitting on the edge of the seat—and sitting mighty light, it was plain to see—driving the mare with an easy rein and talking to her like a weanling.

'Thee's a fine mare. Thee's a tryer. Thee's a credit to thy dam. Never have to think twice about thy looks again.'

Maybe, strictly speaking, that was just encouraging, not urging, but Eliza wasn't in a hairsplitting mood.

She looked back at the Reverend Marcus Augustus, and no two ways about it: he *was* urging Black Prince. The Reverend Godley's cob wasn't a length behind them and the Reverend himself was half standing, slapping the reins across Black Prince's rump and exhorting him like a sinner newly come to the mourner's bench.

This was a pass to which Eliza hadn't thought to come twice in a lifetime—twice in a lifetime to be heading for Meeting like a county fair racer in a checkered shirt.

'Nothing lacking now,' she thought bitterly, 'but for bets to be laid on us.'

That wasn't lacking either, if Eliza had only known it. They'd come in view of the Bethel Church now, and more than one of Godley's flock had got so carried away by the race as to try for odds on their own preacher. It didn't seem loyal not to back up their Kentucky brother with hard cash. Two to one the odds were—with no takers.

The Bethel Church sat atop a long, low rise, not much to the eye—but it told on a light mare pulling against a heavy stallion, and it was here Black Prince began to close in; before the rise was half covered, the stallion's nose was pressing toward the buggy's back near wheel.

Jess had given up encouraging. He was urging now. Eliza lifted the hat off his head. Come what might, there wasn't going to be any more hat-whacking if she could help it—but Jess was beyond knowing whether his head was bare or covered. He was pulling with his mare now, sweating with her, sucking the air into scalding lungs with her. Lady had slowed on the rise—she'd have been dead if she hadn't—but she was still a-going, still trying hard. Only the Quaker blood in Jess's veins kept him from shouting with pride at his mare's performance.

The Reverend Godley didn't have Quaker blood in his veins. What he had was Kentucky horse-racing blood, and when Black Prince got his nose opposite Lady's rump Godley's racing blood got the best of him. He began to talk to his cob in a voice that got its volume from camp-meeting practice—and its vocabulary, too, as a matter of fact—but he was using it in a fashion his camp-meeting congregations had never heard.

They were almost opposite the Bethel Church now; Black Prince had nosed up an inch or two more on Lady and the Reverend Godley was still strongly exhorting—getting mighty personal, for a man of his convictions.

But Lady was a stayer and so was Jess. And Eliza, too, for that matter. Jess spared her a glance out of the corner of his eye to see how she was faring. She was faring mighty well—sitting bolt upright, her Bible tightly clasped, and clucking to the mare. Jess couldn't credit what he heard. But there was no doubt about it—Eliza was counseling Lady. 'Thee keep a-going, Lady,' she called. Eliza hadn't camp-meeting experience, but she had a good clear pulpit voice and Lady heard her.

She kept a-going. She did better. She unloosed a spurt of speed Jess hadn't known was in her. Lady was used to being held back, not yelled at in a brush. Yelling got her dander up. She stretched out her long neck, lengthened her powerful stride, and pulled away from Black Prince just as they reached the Bethel Church grounds.

Jess thought the race was won and over, that from here on the pace to Meeting could be more suitable to First Day travel. But the Reverend Godley had no mind to stop at so critical a juncture. He'd wrestled with sinners too long to give up at the first setback. He figured the mare was weakening. He figured that with a strong stayer like his Black Prince he'd settle the matter easy in the half mile that lay between the Bethel Church and the Quaker Meetinghouse at Rush Branch. He kept a-coming.

But one thing he didn't figure—that was that the slope from Bethel to Rush Branch was against him. Lady had a downhill grade now. It was all she needed. She didn't pull away from Black Prince in any whirlwind style, but stride by stride she pulled away.

It was a great pity Jess's joy in that brush had to be marred. He'd eaten humble pie some time now, and he was pleasured through and through to be doing the dishing up himself. And he was pleasured for the mare's sake.

5

But neither winning nor his mare's pleasure was first with Jess. Eliza was. There she sat, white and suffering, holding her Bible like it was the Rock of Ages from which she'd come mighty near to clean slipping off. Jess knew Eliza had a forgiving heart when it came to others—but whether she could forgive herself for getting heated over a horse race the way she'd done, he couldn't say.

And the worst for Eliza was yet to come. Jess saw that clear enough. When Lady and Black Prince had pounded past Godley's church, a number of the Bethel brethren, who had arrived early and were still in their rigs, set out behind the Reverend Marcus Augustus to be in at the finish. And they were going to be. Their brother was losing, but they were for him still, close behind and encouraging him in a wholehearted way. The whole caboodle was going to sweep behind Jess and Eliza into the Quaker churchyard. They wouldn't linger, but Jess feared they'd turn around there before heading back again. And that's the way it was.

Lady was three lengths ahead of Black Prince when they reached the Rush Branch Meetinghouse. Jess eased her for the turn, made it on two wheels, and drew in close to the church. The Bethelites swooped in behind him and on out—plainly beat but not subdued.

The Reverend Marcus Augustus was the only man among them without a word to say. He was as silent as a tombstone and considerably grimmer. Even his fancy vest looked to have faded.

The Quakers waiting in the yard for Meeting to begin were quiet, too. Jess couldn't tell from their faces what they were feeling; but there was no use thinking that they considered what they'd just witnessed an edifying sight. Not for a weekday even, that mess of rigs hitting it down the pike with all that hullabaloo—let alone to First Day and their preacher up front, leading it.

Jess asked a boy to look after Lady. He was so taken up with Eliza he no more than laid a fond hand on Lady's hot flank in passing. He helped Eliza light down, and set his hat on his head when she handed it to him. Eliza looked mighty peaked and withdrawn, like a woman communing with the Lord.

She bowed to her congregation and they bowed back and she led them out of the sunshine into the Meetinghouse with no word being spoken on either side. She walked to the preacher's bench, laid her Bible quietly down, and untied her bonnet strings.

Jess sat rigid in his seat among the men. Jess was a birthright Quaker—and his father and grandfathers before him—and he'd known Quakers to be read out of Meeting for less.

Eliza laid her little plump hands on her Bible and bowed her head in silent prayer. Jess didn't know how long it lasted—sometimes it seemed stretching out into eternity, but Quakers were used to silent worship and he was the only one who seemed restive. About the time the ice round Jess's heart was hardening past his enduring, Eliza's sweet, cool, carrying voice said, 'If the spirit leads any of thee to speak, will thee speak now?'

Then Eliza lowered her head again—but Jess peered round the Meetinghouse. He thought he saw a contented look on most of the faces—nothing that went so far as to warm into a smile, but a look that said they were satisfied the way the Lord had handled things. And the spirit didn't move any member of the congregation to speak that day except for the prayers of two elderly Friends in closing.

6

The ride home was mighty quiet. They drove past the Bethel Church, where the sermon had been short—for all the hitching racks were empty. Lady carried them along proud and untired. Enoch and the children met them down the pike a ways from home and Jess nodded the good news to Enoch—but he couldn't glory in it the way he'd like because of Eliza.

Eliza was kind, but silent. Very silent. She spoke when spoken to, did her whole duty by the children and Jess, but in all the ways that made Eliza most herself, she was absent and withdrawn.

Toward evening Jess felt a little dauncy—a pain beneath the ribs, heart, or stomach, he couldn't say which. He thought he'd brew himself a cup of sassafras tea, take it to bed and drink it there, and maybe find a little ease.

It was past nightfall when Jess entered his and Eliza's chamber, but there was a full moon and by its light he saw Eliza sitting at the east window in her white nightdress, plaiting her black hair.

'Jess,' asked Eliza, noting the cup he carried, 'has thee been taken ill?'

'No,' Jess said, 'no,' his pain easing off of itself when he heard by the tones of Eliza's voice that she was restored to him—forgiving and gentle, letting bygones be bygones.

'Eliza,' he asked, 'wouldn't thee like a nice hot cup of sassafras tea?'

'Why, yes, Jess,' Eliza said. 'That'd be real refreshing.'

Jess carried Eliza her cup of tea walking down a path of roses the moon had lit up in the ingrain carpet.

He stood, while she drank it, with his hand on her chair, gazing out the window: the whole upcurve and embowered sweep of the earth soaked in moonlight—hill and wood lot, orchard and silent river. And beneath that sheen his own rooftree, and all beneath *it,* peaceful and at rest. Lady in her stall, Enoch reading Emerson, the children long abed.

' "Sweet day," ' he said, ' "so cool, so calm, so bright, The bridal of the earth and sky." '

And though he felt so pensive and reposeful, still the bridge of his big nose wrinkled up, his ribs shook with laughter.

Eliza felt the movement of his laughing in her chair. 'What is it, Jess?' she asked.

Jess stopped laughing, but said nothing. He figured Eliza had gone about as far in one day as a woman could in enlarging her appreciation of horseflesh; still he couldn't help smiling when he thought of the sermon that might have been preached that morning in the Bethel Church upon the eternal verities.

MISSISSIPPI

That Evening Sun Go Down

WILLIAM FAULKNER

Monday is no different from any other week day in Jefferson now. The streets are paved now, and the telephone and the electric companies are cutting down more and more of the shade trees—the water oaks, the maples and locusts and elms—to make room for iron poles bearing clusters of bloated and ghostly and bloodless grapes, and we have a city laundry which makes the rounds on Monday morning, gathering the bundles of clothes into bright-colored, specially made motor-cars: the soiled wearing of a whole week now flees apparition-like behind alert and irritable electric horns, with a long diminishing noise of rubber and asphalt like a tearing of silk, and even the Negro women who still take in white peoples' washing after the old custom, fetch and deliver it in automobiles.

But fifteen years ago, on Monday morning the quiet, dusty, shady streets would be full of Negro women with, balanced on their steady turbaned heads, bundles of clothes tied up in sheets, almost as large as cotton bales, carried so without touch of hand between the kitchen door of the white house and the blackened wash-pot beside a cabin door in Negro Hollow.

Nancy would set her bundle on the top of her head, then upon the bundle in turn she would set the black straw sailor hat which she wore Winter and Summer. She was tall, with a high, sad face sunken a little where her teeth were missing. Sometimes we would go a part of the way down the lane and across the pasture with her, to watch the balanced bundle and the hat that never bobbed nor wavered, even when she walked down into the ditch and climbed out again and stooped through the fence. She would go down on her hands and knees and crawl through the gap, her head rigid, up-tilted, the bundle steady as a rock or a balloon, and rise to her feet and go on.

Sometimes the husbands of the washing women would fetch and deliver the clothes, but Jubah never did that for Nancy, even before father told him to stay away from our house, even when Dilsey was sick and Nancy would come to cook for us.

And then about half the time we'd have to go down the lane to Nancy's house and tell her to come on and get breakfast. We would stop at the ditch, because father told us to not have anything to do with Jubah—he was a short black man, with a razor scar down his face—and we would throw rocks at Nancy's house until she came to the door, leaning her head around it without any clothes on.

"What yawl mean, chunking my house?" Nancy said. "What you little devils mean?"

"Father says for you to come and get breakfast," Caddy said. "Father says it's over a half an hour now, and you've got to come this minute."

"I ain't studying no breakfast," Nancy said. "I going to get my sleep out."

"I bet you're drunk," Jason said. "Father says you're drunk. Are you drunk, Nancy?"

"Who says I is?" Nancy said. "I got to get my sleep out. I ain't studying no breakfast."

So after a while we quit chunking the house and went back home. When she finally came, it was too late for me to go to school. So we thought it was whiskey until that day when they arrested her again and they were taking her to jail and they passed Mr. Stovall. He was the cashier in the bank and a deacon in the Baptist church, and Nancy began to say:

"When you going to pay me, white man? When you going to pay me, white man? It's been three times now since you paid me a cent——" Mr. Stovall knocked her down, but she kept on saying, "When you going to pay me, white man? It's been three times now since——" until Mr. Stovall kicked her in the mouth with his heel and the marshal caught Mr. Stovall back, and Nancy lying in the street, laughing. She turned her head and spat out some blood and teeth and said, "It's been three times now since he paid me a cent."

That was how she lost her teeth, and all that day they told about Nancy and Mr. Stovall, and all that night the ones that passed the jail could hear Nancy singing and yelling. They could see her hands holding to the window bars, and a lot of them stopped along the fence, listening to her and to the jailer trying to make her shut up. She didn't shut up until just before daylight, when the jailer began to hear a bumping and scraping upstairs and he went up there and found Nancy hanging from the window bar. He said that it was cocaine and not whiskey, because no nigger would try to commit suicide unless he was full of cocaine, because a nigger full of cocaine was not a nigger any longer.

The jailer cut her down and revived her; then he beat her, whipped her. She had hung herself with her dress. She had fixed it all right, but when they arrested her she didn't have on anything except a dress and so she didn't have anything to tie her hands with and she couldn't make her hands let go of the window ledge. So the jailer heard the noise and ran up there and found Nancy hanging from the window, stark naked.

When Dilsey was sick in her cabin and Nancy was cooking for us, we could see her apron swelling out; that was before father told Jubah to stay away from the house. Jubah was in the kitchen, sitting behind the stove, with his razor scar on his black face like a piece of dirty string. He said it was a watermelon that Nancy had under her dress. And it was Winter, too.

"Where did you get a watermelon in the Winter?" Caddy said.

"I didn't," Jubah said. "It wasn't me that give it to her. But I can cut it down, same as if it was."

"What makes you want to talk that way before these chillen?" Nancy said. "Whyn't you go on to work? You done et. You want Mr. Jason to catch you hanging around his kitchen, talking that way before these chillen?"

"Talking what way, Nancy?" Caddy said.

"I can't hang around white man's kitchen," Jubah said. "But white man can hang around mine. White man can come in my house, but I can't stop him. When white man want to come in my house, I ain't got no house. I can't stop him, but he can't kick me outen it. He can't do that."

Dilsey was still sick in her cabin. Father told Jubah to stay off our place. Dilsey was still sick. It was a long time. We were in the library after supper.

"Isn't Nancy through yet?" mother said. "It seems to me that she has had plenty of time to have finished the dishes."

"Let Quentin go and see," father said. "Go and see if Nancy is through, Quentin. Tell her she can go on home."

I went to the kitchen. Nancy was through. The dishes were put away and the fire was out. Nancy was sitting in a chair, close to the cold stove. She looked at me.

"Mother wants to know if you are through," I said.

"Yes," Nancy said. She looked at me. "I done finished." She looked at me.

"What is it?" I said. "What is it?"

"I ain't nothing but a nigger," Nancy said. "It ain't none of my fault."

She looked at me, sitting in the chair before the cold stove, the sailor hat on her head. I went back to the library. It was the cold stove and all, when you think of a kitchen being warm and busy and cheerful. And with a cold stove and the dishes all put away, and nobody wanting to eat at that hour.

"Is she through?" mother said.

"Yessum," I said.

"What is she doing?" mother said.

"She's not doing anything. She's through."

"I'll go and see," father said.

"Maybe she's waiting for Jubah to come and take her home," Caddy said.

"Jubah is gone," I said. Nancy told us how one morning she woke up and Jubah was gone.

"He quit me," Nancy said. "Done gone to Memphis, I reckon. Dodging them city *po*-lice for a while, I reckon."

"And a good riddance," father said. "I hope he stays there."

"Nancy's scaired of the dark," Jason said.

"So are you," Caddy said.

"I'm not," Jason said.

"Scairy cat," Caddy said.

"I'm not," Jason said.

"You, Candace!" mother said. Father came back.

"I am going to walk down the lane with Nancy," he said. "She says Jubah is back."

"Has she seen him?" mother said.

"No. Some Negro sent her word that he was back in town. I won't be long."

"You'll leave me alone, to take Nancy home?" mother said. "Is her safety more precious to you than mine?"

"I won't be long," father said.

"You'll leave these children unprotected, with that Negro about?"

"I'm going too," Caddy said. "Let me go, father."

"What would he do with them, if he were unfortunate enough to have them?" father said.

"I want to go, too," Jason said.

"Jason!" mother said. She was speaking to father. You could tell that by the way she said it. Like she believed that all day father had been trying to think of doing the thing that she wouldn't like the most, and that she knew all the time that after a while he would think of it. I stayed quiet, because father and I both knew that mother would want him to make me stay with her, if she just thought of it in time. So father didn't look at me. I was the oldest. I was nine and Caddy was seven and Jason was five.

"Nonsense," father said. "We won't be long."

Nancy had her hat on. We came to the lane. "Jubah always been good to me," Nancy said. "Whenever he had two dollars, one of them was mine." We walked in the lane. "If I can just get through the lane," Nancy said, "I be all right then."

The lane was always dark. "This is where Jason got scared on Hallowe'en," Caddy said.

"I didn't," Jason said.

"Can't Aunt Rachel do anything with him?" father said. Aunt Rachel was old. She lived in a cabin beyond Nancy's, by herself. She had white hair and she smoked a pipe in the door, all day long; she didn't work any more. They said she was Jubah's mother. Sometimes she said she was and sometimes she said she wasn't any kin to Jubah.

"Yes you did," Caddy said. "You were scairder than Frony. You were scairder than T. P. even. Scairder than niggers."

"Can't nobody do nothing with him," Nancy said. "He say I done woke up the devil in him, and ain't but one thing going to lay it again."

"Well, he's gone now," father said. "There's nothing for you to be afraid of now. And if you'd just let white men alone."

"Let what white men alone?" Caddy said. "How let them alone?"

"He ain't gone nowhere," Nancy said. "I can feel him. I can feel him now, in this lane. He hearing us talk, every word, hid somewhere, waiting. I ain't seen him, and I ain't going to see him again but once more, with that razor. That razor on that string down his back, inside his shirt. And then I ain't going to be even surprised."

"I wasn't scaired," Jason said.

"If you'd behave yourself, you'd have kept out of this," father said. "But it's all right now. He's probably in St. Louis now. Probably got another wife by now and forgot all about you."

"If he has, I better not find out about it," Nancy said. "I'd stand there and every time he wropped her, I'd cut that arm off. I'd cut his head off and I'd slit her belly and I'd shove——"

"Hush," father said.

"Slit whose belly, Nancy?" Caddy said.

"I wasn't scared," Jason said. "I'd walk right down this lane by myself."

"Yah," Caddy said. "You wouldn't dare to put your foot in it if we were not with you."

Dilsey was still sick, and so we took Nancy home every night until mother said, "How much longer is this going to go on? I to be left alone in this big house while you take home a frightened Negro?"

We fixed a pallet in the kitchen for Nancy. One night we waked up, hearing the sound. It was not singing and it was not crying, coming up the dark stairs. There was a light in mother's room and we heard father going down the hall, down the back stairs, and Caddy and I went into the hall. The floor was cold. Our toes curled away from the floor while we listened to the sound. It was like singing and it wasn't like singing, like the sounds that Negroes make.

Then it stopped and we heard father going down the back stairs, and we went to the head of the stairs. Then the sound began again, in the stairway, not loud, and we could see Nancy's eyes half way up the stairs, against the wall. They looked like cat's eyes do, like a big cat against the wall, watching us. When we come down the steps to where she was she quit making the sound again, and we stood there until father came back up from the kitchen, with his pistol in his hand. He went back down with Nancy and they came back with Nancy's pallet.

We spread the pallet in our room. After the light in mother's room went off, we could see Nancy's eyes again. "Nancy," Caddy whispered, "are you asleep, Nancy?"

Nancy whispered something. It was oh or no, I don't know which. Like nobody had made it, like it came from nowhere and went nowhere, until it was like Nancy was not there at all; that I had looked so hard at her eyes on the stair that they had got printed on my eyelids, like the sun does when you have closed your eyes and there is no sun. "Jesus," Nancy whispered. "Jesus."

"Was it Jubah?" Caddy whispered. "Did he try to come into the kitchen?"

"Jesus," Nancy said. Like this: Jeeeeeeeeeeeeeesus, until the sound went out like a match or a candle does.

"Can you see us, Nancy?" Caddy whispered. "Can you see our eyes too?"

"I ain't nothing but a nigger," Nancy said. "God knows. God knows."

"What did you see down there in the kitchen?" Caddy whispered. "What tried to get in?"

"God knows," Nancy said. We could see her eyes. "God knows."

Dilsey got well. She cooked dinner. "You'd better stay in bed a day or two longer," father said.

"What for?" Dilsey said. "If I had been a day later, this place would be to rack and ruin. Get on out of here, now, and let me get my kitchen straight again."

Dilsey cooked supper, too. And that night, just before dark, Nancy came into the kitchen.

"How do you know he's back?" Dilsey said. "You ain't seen him."

"Jubah is a nigger," Jason said.

"I can feel him," Nancy said. "I can feel him laying yonder in the ditch."

"Tonight?" Dilsey said. "Is he there tonight?"

"Dilsey's a nigger too," Jason said.

"You try to eat something," Dilsey said.

"I don't want nothing," Nancy said.

"I ain't a nigger," Jason said.

"Drink some coffee," Dilsey said. She poured a cup of coffee for Nancy. "Do you know he's out there tonight? How come you know it's tonight?"

"I know," Nancy said. "He's there, waiting. I know. I done lived with him too long. I know what he fixing to do fore he knows it himself."

"Drink some coffee," Dilsey said. Nancy held the cup to her mouth and blew into the cup. Her mouth pursed out like a spreading adder's, like a rubber mouth, like she had blown all the color out of her lips with blowing the coffee.

"I ain't a nigger," Jason said. "Are you a nigger, Nancy?"

"I hell-born, child," Nancy said. "I won't be nothing soon. I going back where I come from soon."

She began to drink the coffee. While she was drinking, holding the cup in both hands, she began to make the sound again. She made the sound into the cup and the coffee sploshed out on to her hands and her dress. Her eyes looked at us and she sat there, her elbows on her knees, holding the cup in both hands, looking at us across the wet cup, making the sound.

"Look at Nancy," Jason said. "Nancy can't cook for us now. Dilsey's got well now."

"You hush up," Dilsey said. Nancy held the cup in both hands, looking at us, making the sound, like there were two of them: one looking at us and the other making the sound. "Whyn't you let Mr. Jason telefoam the marshal?" Dilsey said. Nancy stopped then, holding the cup in her long brown hands. She tried to drink some coffee again, but it sploshed out of the cup, on to her hands and her dress, and she put the cup down. Jason watched her.

"I can't swallow it," Nancy said. "I swallows but it won't go down me."

"You go down to the cabin," Dilsey said. "Frony will fix you a pallet and I'll be there soon."

"Won't no nigger stop him," Nancy said.

"I ain't a nigger," Jason said. "Am I, Dilsey?"

"I reckon not," Dilsey said. She looked at Nancy. "I don't reckon so. What you going to do, then?"

Nancy looked at us. Her eyes went fast, like she was afraid there wasn't time to look, without hardly moving at all. She looked at us, at all three of us at one time. "You member that night I stayed in yawls' room?" she said. She told about how we waked up early the next morning, and played. We had to play quiet, on her pallet, until father woke and it was time for her to go down and get breakfast. "Go and ask you maw to let me stay here tonight," Nancy said. "I won't need no pallet. We can play some more," she said.

Caddy asked mother. Jason went too. "I can't have Negroes sleeping in the house," mother said. Jason cried. He cried until mother said he couldn't have any dessert for three days if he didn't stop. Then Jason said he would stop if Dilsey would make a chocolate cake. Father was there.

"Why don't you do something about it?" mother said. "What do we have officers for?"

"Why is Nancy afraid of Jubah?" Caddy said. "Are you afraid of father, mother?"

"What could they do?" father said. "If Nancy hasn't seen him, how could the officers find him?"

"Then why is she afraid?" mother said.

"She says he is there. She says she knows he is there tonight."

"Yet we pay taxes," mother said. "I must wait here alone in this big house while you take a Negro woman home."

"You know that I am not lying outside with a razor," father said.

"I'll stop if Dilsey will make a chocolate cake," Jason said. Mother told us to go out and father said he didn't know if Jason would get a chocolate cake or not, but he knew what Jason was going to get in about a minute.We went back to the kitchen and told Nancy.

"Father said for you to go home and lock the door, and you'll be all right," Caddy said. "All right from what, Nancy? Is Jubah mad at you?" Nancy was holding the coffee cup in her hands, her elbow on her knees and her hands holding the cup between her knees. She was looking into the cup. "What have you done that made Jubah mad?" Caddy said. Nancy let the cup go. It didn't break on the floor, but the coffee spilled out, and Nancy sat there with her hands making the shape of the cup. She began to make the sound again, not loud. Not singing and not un-singing. We watched her.

"Here," Dilsey said. "You quit that, now. You get a-holt of yourself. You wait here. I going to get Versh to walk home with you." Dilsey went out.

We looked at Nancy. Her shoulders kept shaking, but she had quit making the sound. We watched her. "What's Jubah going to do to you?" Caddy said. "He went away."

Nancy looked at us. "We had fun that night I stayed in yawl's room, didn't we?"

"I didn't," Jason said. "I didn't have any fun."

"You were asleep," Caddy said. "You were not there."

"Let's go down to my house and have some more fun," Nancy said.

"Mother won't let us," I said. "It's too late now."

"Don't bother her," Nancy said. "We can tell her in the morning. She won't mind."

"She wouldn't let us," I said.

"Don't ask her now," Nancy said. "Don't bother her now."

"They didn't say we couldn't go," Caddy said.

"We didn't ask," I said.

"If you go, I'll tell," Jason said.

"We'll have fun," Nancy said. "They won't mind, just to my house. I been working for yawl a long time. They won't mind."

"I'm not afraid to go," Caddy said. "Jason is the one that's afraid. He'll tell."

"I'm not," Jason said.

"Yes you are," Caddy said. "You'll tell."

"I won't tell," Jason said. "I'm not afraid."

"Jason ain't afraid to go with me," Nancy said. "Is you, Jason?"

"Jason is going to tell," Caddy said. The lane was dark. We passed the pasture gate. "I bet if something was to jump out from behind that gate, Jason would holler."

"I wouldn't," Jason said. We walked down the lane. Nancy was talking loud.

"What are you talking so loud for, Nancy?" Caddy said.

"Who; me?" Nancy said. "Listen at Quentin and Caddy and Jason saying I'm talking loud."

"You talk like there was four of us here," Caddy said. "You talk like father was here too."

"Who; me talking loud, Mr. Jason?" Nancy said.

"Nancy called Jason 'Mister,'" Caddy said.

"Listen how Caddy and Quentin and Jason talk," Nancy said.

"We're not talking loud," Caddy said. "You're the one that's talking like father——"

"Hush," Nancy said; "hush, Mr. Jason."

"Nancy called Jason 'Mister' aguh——"

"Hush," Nancy said. She was talking loud when we crossed the ditch and stooped through the fence where she used to stoop through with the clothes on her head. Then we came to her house. We were going fast then. She opened the door. The smell of the house was like the lamp and the smell of Nancy was like the wick, like they were waiting for one another to smell. She lit the lamp and closed the door and put the bar up. Then she quit talking loud, looking at us.

"What're we going to do?" Caddy said.

"What you all want to do?" Nancy said.

"You said we would have some fun," Caddy said.

There was something about Nancy's house; something you could smell. Jason smelled it, even. "I don't want to stay here," he said. "I want to go home."

"Go home, then," Caddy said.

"I don't want to go by myself," Jason said.

"We're going to have some fun," Nancy said.

"How?" Caddy said.

Nancy stood by the door. She was looking at us, only it was like she had emptied her eyes, like she had quit using them.

"What do you want to do?" she said.

"Tell us a story," Caddy said. "Can you tell a story?"

"Yes," Nancy said.

"Tell it," Caddy said. We looked at Nancy. "You don't know any stories," Caddy said.

"Yes," Nancy said. "Yes I do."

She came and sat down in a chair before the hearth. There was some fire there; she built it up; it was already hot. You didn't need a fire. She built a good blaze. She told a story. She talked like her eyes looked, like her eyes watching us and her voice talking to us did not belong to her. Like she was living somewhere else, waiting somewhere else. She was outside the house. Her voice was there and the shape of her, the Nancy that could stoop under the fence with the bundle of clothes balanced as though without weight, like a balloon, on her head, was there. But that was all. "And so this here queen come walking up to the ditch, where that bad man was hiding. She was walking up the ditch, and she say, 'If I can just get past this here ditch,' was what she say. . . ."

"What ditch?" Caddy said. "A ditch like that one out there? Why did the queen go into the ditch?"

"To get to her house," Nancy said. She looked at us. "She had to cross that ditch to get home."

"Why did she want to go home?" Caddy said.

Nancy looked at us. She quit talking. She looked at us. Jason's legs stuck straight out of his pants, because he was little. "I don't think that's a good story," he said. "I want to go home."

"Maybe we had better," Caddy said. She got up from the floor. "I bet they are looking for us right now." She went toward the door.

"No," Nancy said. "Don't open it." She got up quick and passed Caddy. She didn't touch the door, the wooden bar.

"Why not?" Caddy said.

"Come back to the lamp," Nancy said. "We'll have fun. You don't have to go."

"We ought to go," Caddy said. "Unless we have a lot of fun." She and Nancy came back to the fire, the lamp.

"I want to go home," Jason said. "I'm going to tell."

"I know another story," Nancy said. She stood close to the lamp. She looked at Caddy, like when your eyes look up at a stick balanced on your nose. She had to look down to see Caddy, but her eyes looked like that, like when you are balancing a stick.

"I won't listen to it," Jason said. "I'll bang on the floor."

"It's a good one," Nancy said. "It's better than the other one."

"What's it about?" Caddy said. Nancy was standing by the lamp. Her hand was on the lamp, against the light, long and brown.

"Your hand is on that hot globe," Caddy said. "Don't it feel hot to your hand?"

Nancy looked at her hand on the lamp chimney. She took her hand away, slow. She stood there, looking at Caddy, wringing her long hand as though it were tied to her wrist with a string.

"Let's do something else," Caddy said.

"I want to go home," Jason said.

"I got some popcorn," Nancy said. She looked at Caddy and then at Jason and then at me and then at Caddy again. "I got some popcorn."

"I don't like popcorn," Jason said. "I'd rather have candy."

Nancy looked at Jason. "You can hold the popper." She was still wringing her hand; it was long and limp and brown.

"All right," Jason said. "I'll stay a while if I can do that. Caddy can't hold it. I'll want to go home, if Caddy holds the popper."

Nancy built up the fire. "Look at Nancy putting her hands in the fire," Caddy said. "What's the matter with you, Nancy?"

"I got popcorn," Nancy said. "I got some." She took the popper from under the bed. It was broken. Jason began to cry.

"We can't have any popcorn," he said.

"We ought to go home, anyway," Caddy said. "Come on, Quentin."

"Wait," Nancy said; "wait. I can fix it. Don't you want to help me fix it?"

"I don't think I want any," Caddy said. "It's too late now."

"You help me, Jason," Nancy said. "Don't you want to help me?"

"No," Jason said. "I want to go home."

"Hush," Nancy said; "hush. Watch. Watch me. I can fix it so Jason can hold it and pop the corn." She got a piece of wire and fixed the popper.

"It won't hold good," Caddy said.

"Yes it will," Nancy said. "Yawl watch. Yawl help me shell the corn."

The corn was under the bed too. We shelled it into the popper and Nancy helped Jason hold the popper over the fire.

"It's not popping," Jason said. "I want to go home."

"You wait," Nancy said. "It'll begin to pop. We'll have fun then." She was sitting close to the fire. The lamp was turned up so high it was beginning to smoke.

"Why don't you turn it down some?" I said.

"It's all right," Nancy said. "I'll clean it. Yawl wait. The popcorn will start in a minute."

"I don't believe it's going to start," Caddy said. "We ought to go home, anyway. They'll be worried."

"No," Nancy said. "It's going to pop. Dilsey will tell um yawl with me. I been working for yawl long time. They won't mind if you at my house. You wait, now. It'll start popping in a minute."

Then Jason got some smoke in his eyes and he began to cry. He dropped the popper into the fire. Nancy got a wet rag and wiped Jason's face, but he didn't stop crying.

"Hush," she said. "Hush." He didn't hush. Caddy took the popper out of the fire.

"It's burned up," she said. "You'll have to get some more popcorn, Nancy."

"Did you put all of it in?" Nancy said.

"Yes," Caddy said. Nancy looked at Caddy. Then she took the popper and opened it and poured the blackened popcorn into her apron and began to sort the grains, her hands long and brown, and we watching her.

"Haven't you got any more?" Caddy said.

"Yes," Nancy said; "yes. Look. This here ain't burnt. All we need to do is——"

"I want to go home," Jason said. "I'm going to tell."

"Hush," Caddy said. We all listened. Nancy's head was already turned toward the barred door, her eyes filled with red lamplight. "Somebody is coming," Caddy said.

Then Nancy began to make that sound again, not loud, sitting there above the fire, her long hands dangling between her knees; all of a sudden water began to come out on her face in big drops, running down her face, carrying in each one a little turning ball of firelight until it dropped off her chin.

"She's not crying," I said.

"I ain't crying," Nancy said. Her eyes were closed. "I ain't crying. Who is it?"

"I don't know," Caddy said. She went to the door and looked out. "We've got to go home now," she said. "Here comes father."

"I'm going to tell," Jason said. "You all made me come."

The water still ran down Nancy's face. She turned in her chair. "Listen. Tell him. Tell him we going to have fun. Tell him I take good care of yawl until in the morning. Tell him to let me come home with yawl and sleep on the floor. Tell him I won't need no pallet. We'll have fun. You remember last time how we had so much fun?"

"I didn't have any fun," Jason said. "You hurt me. You put smoke in my eyes."

Father came in. He looked at us. Nancy did not get up.

"Tell him," she said.

"Caddy made us come down here," Jason said. "I didn't want to."

Father came to the fire. Nancy looked up at him. "Can't you go to Aunt Rachel's and stay?" he said. Nancy looked up at father, her hands between her knees. "He's not here," father said. "I would have seen. There wasn't a soul in sight."

"He in the ditch," Nancy said. "He waiting in the ditch yonder."

"Nonsense," father said. He looked at Nancy. "Do you know he's there?"

"I got the sign," Nancy said.

"What sign?"

"I got it. It was on the table when I come in. It was a hog bone, with blood meat still on it, laying by the lamp. He's out there. When yawl walk out that door, I gone."

"Who's gone, Nancy?" Caddy said.

"I'm not a tattletale," Jason said.

"Nonsense," father said.

"He out there," Nancy said. "He looking through that window this minute, waiting for yawl to go. Then I gone."

"Nonsense," father said. "Lock up your house and we'll take you on to Aunt Rachel's."

" 'Twon't do no good," Nancy said. She didn't look at father now, but he looked down at her, at her long, limp, moving hands. "Putting it off won't do no good."

"Then what do you want do do?" father said.

"I don't know," Nancy said. "I can't do nothing. Just put it off. And that don't do no good. I reckon it belong to me. I reckon what I going to get ain't no more than mine."

"Get what?" Caddy said. "What's yours?"

"Nothing," father said. "You all must go to bed."

"Caddy made me come," Jason said.

"Go on to Aunt Rachel's," father said.

"It won't do no good," Nancy said. She sat before the fire, her elbows on her knees, her long hands between her knees. "When even your own kitchen wouldn't do no good. When even if I was sleeping on the floor in the room with your own children, and the next morning there I am, and blood all——"

"Hush," father said. "Lock the door and put the lamp out and go to bed."

"I scared of the dark," Nancy said. "I scared for it to happen in the dark."

"You mean you're going to sit right here, with the lamp lighted?" father said. Then Nancy began to make the sound again, sitting before the fire, her long hands between her knees. "Ah, damnation," father said. "Come along, chillen. It's bedtime."

"When yawl go, I gone," Nancy said. "I be dead tomorrow. I done have saved up the coffin money with Mr. Lovelady——"

Mr. Lovelady was a short, dirty man who collected the Negro insurance, coming around to the cabins and the kitchen every Saturday morning, to collect fifteen cents. He and his wife lived in the hotel. One morning his wife committed suicide. They had a child, a little girl. After his wife committed suicide Mr. Lovelady and the child went away. After a while Mr. Lovelady came back. We could see him going down the lanes on Saturday morning. He went to the Baptist church.

Father carried Jason on his back. We went out Nancy's door; she was sitting before the fire. "Come and put the bar up," father said. Nancy didn't move. She didn't look at us again. We left her there, sitting before the fire with the door opened, so that it wouldn't happen in the dark.

"What, father?" Caddy said. "Why is Nancy scared of Jubah? What is Jubah going to do to her?"

"Jubah wasn't there," Jason said.

"No," father said. "He's not there. He's gone away."

"Who is it that's waiting in the ditch?" Caddy said. We looked at the ditch. We came to it, where the path went down into the thick vines and went up again.

"Nobody," father said. There was just enough moon to see by. The ditch was vague, thick, quiet. "If he's there, he can see us, can't he?" Caddy said.

"You made me come," Jason said on father's back. "I didn't want to."

The ditch was quite still, quite empty, massed with honeysuckle. We couldn't see Jubah, any more than we could see Nancy sitting there in her house, with the door open and the lamp burning, because she didn't want it to happen in the dark. "I just done got tired, Nancy said. "I just a nigger. It ain't no fault of mine."

But we could still hear her. She began as soon as we were out of the house, sitting there above the fire, her long brown hands between her knees. We could still hear her when we had crossed the ditch, Jason high and close and little about father's head.

Then we had crossed the ditch, walking out of Nancy's life. Then her life was sitting there with the door open and the lamp lit, waiting, and the ditch between us and us going on, the white people going on, dividing the impinged lives of us and Nancy.

"Who will do our washing now, father?" I said.

"I'm not a nigger," Jason said on father's shoulders.

"You're worse," Caddy said, "you are a tattletale. If something was to jump out, you'd be scairder than a nigger."

"I wouldn't," Jason said.

"You'd cry," Caddy said.

"Caddy!" father said.

"I wouldn't," Jason said.

"Scairy cat," Caddy said.

"Candace!" father said.

ILLINOIS

★

How the Devil Came Down Division Street

NELSON ALGREN

Last Saturday Evening there was a great argument in the Polonia Bar. All the biggest drunks on Division were there, trying to decide who the biggest drunk of them was. Symanski said he was, and Oljiec said he was, and Koncel said he was, and Czechowski said he was.

Then Roman Orlov came in and the argument was decided. For Poor Roman has been drunk so long, night and day, that when we remember living men we almost forget Poor Roman, as though he were no longer really among the living at all.

'The devil lives in a double-shot,' Roman explains himself obscurely. 'I got a great worm inside. Gnaws and gnaws. Every day I drown him and every day he gnaws. Help me drown the worm, fellas.'

So I bought Poor Roman a double-shot and asked him frankly how, before he was thirty, he had become the biggest drunk on Division.

It took a long time, and many double-shots, for him to tell. But tell it he did, between curses and sobs, and I tell it now as closely to what he told as I can. Without the sobs, of course. And of course without any cursing.

When Roman was thirteen, it seems, the Orlovs moved into three stove-heated rooms in the rear of a lopsided tenement on Noble Street. Mama O. cooked in a Division Street restaurant by day and cooked in her own home by night.

Papa O. played an accordion for pennies in Division Street taverns by night and slept alone in the rooms by day.

There were only two beds in the tiny flat, so nobody encouraged Papa O. to come home at all.

Because he was the oldest, Roman slept between the twins, on the

---

bed set up in the front room, to keep the pair from fighting during the night as they did during the day. Every day, Teresa, who was eleven and could not learn her lessons as well as some of her classmates, slept with Mama O. in the windowless back bedroom; under a bleeding heart in a gilded oval frame.

If Papa O. got in before light, as happened occasionally early in the week he crawled uncomplainingly under Roman's bed until Roman rose and got the twins, who were seven, up with him in time for Mass.

If Udo, who was something between a collie and a St. Bernard and as big as both together, was already curled up beneath the front-room bed, Papa O. slugged him with the accordion in friendly reproach—and went on into the back bedroom to crawl under Mama O.'s bed. In such an event he slept under a bed all day. For he never crawled, even with daylight, into Mama O.'s bed. Empty or not. As though he did not feel himself worthy to sleep there even when she was gone.

It was as though, having given himself all night to his accordion, he must remain true to it during the day.

For all manner of strange things went on in Papa O.'s head, as even the twins had become aware. Things so strange that Teresa was made ashamed of them by her school mates, whenever they wanted someone to tease.

This, too, was why no one, not even the twins, paid Papa O. any heed when the family returned from Mass one Sunday forenoon and he told them someone had been knocking while they were away.

'Some*body* was by door,' he insisted. 'I say "Hallo." Was no*body*.' He looked slyly about him at the children. 'Who plays tricks by Papa?'

'Maybe was the Zolewitzes,' Mama O. suggested indifferently. 'Mama Z. comes perhaps to borrow.'

That Sunday night it was cold in all the corners. Papa O. was gone to play for pennies and drinks, Mama O. was frying *pierogi,* the twins were in bed and Teresa was studying her catechism across the table from Roman, when someone knocked lightly twice.

To Roman it sounded like someone at the clothes-closet door; but that was foolish to think, since the twins were in bed. Yet, when he opened the hall door, only a cold wind came into the room from the long gaslit passage.

Roman, being only thirteen, did not dare look behind the door. Far less to speak of the clothes closet.

All that night a light snow fell, while Roman O. lay wakeful, fancying he saw it falling on darkened streets all over the mysterious earth, on the pointing rooftops of old world cities, on mountain-high waves of the mid-Atlantic, and in the leaning eaves of Noble Street. He was just falling off to sleep when the knocking came again. Three times, like a measured warning. The boy stiffened under the covers, listening with his fear. Heard the hall door squeak softly, as though Papa O. were sneaking in. But Papa O. never knocked, and Papa O. never sneaked. Papa O. came home with the accordion banging against buildings all down Noble Street, jingling his pennies proudly, singing off-key bravely, mumbling and laughing and stumbling. Papa O. never knocked. He kicked the door in happily and shouted cheerfully, 'What you say, all peoples? How's t'ings, ever-body?' Papa O. pulled people out of bed and rattled pans and laughed at nothing and argued with unseen bartenders until somebody gave him sausage and eggs and coffee and bread and hung the accordion safely away.

Roman crept, barefooted, in the long underwear Mama O. had sewed on him in the early fall, to the hallway door.

The whole house slept. The windows were frosted and a thin line of ice had edged up under the front window and along the pane. The family slept. Roman shoved the door open gently. The tenement slept. Down the hall the single gas jet flickered feebly. No one. Nothing. The people slept.

Roman looked behind the door, shivering now with more than cold.

No one. Nothing. All night long.

He returned to bed and prayed quietly, until he heard Mama O. rise; waited till he knew she had the fire going in the big kitchen stove. Then, dressing with his back to the heat, he told Mama O. what he had heard. Mama O. said nothing.

Two mornings later, Papa O. came home without the accordion. It did not matter then to Mama O. whether he had sold it or lost it or loaned it: she knew it at last for a sign, she had felt the change coming, she said, in her blood. For she had dreamed a dream, all night, of a stranger waiting in the hall: a young man, drunken, leaning against the gaslit wall for support, with blood down the front of his shirt and drying on his hands. She knew, as all the Orlovs knew, that the unhappy dead return to warn or comfort, to plead or repent, to gain peace or to avenge.

That day, standing over steaming kettles, Mama O. went back in her mind to all those dear to her of earth who had died: the cousin drowned at sea, the brother returned from the war to die, the mother and father gone from their fields before she had married.

That night she knocked on Mama Zolewitz's door. Mama Z. sat silently, as though she had been expecting Mama O. for many evenings.

'Landlord doesn't like we should tell new tenants too soon,' Mama Z. explained even before being told of the knocking, 'so you shouldn't say it, I told. It was a young man lived in this place, in your very rooms. A strong young man, and good to look at. But sick, sick in the head from the drink. A sinner certainly. For here he lived with his lady without being wed, and she worked and he did not. That he did not work had little to do with what happened, and the drink had little to do. For it was being unwed that brought it on, at night, on the New Year. He returned from the taverns that night and beat her till her screams were a whimpering. Till her whimpering became nothing. A strong young man, like a bull, made violent by the drink. When the whimpering ceased, there was no sound at all. No sound until noon, when the police came with shouting.

'What was there to shout about? I could have told them before they came. The young man had hanged himself in the bedroom closet. Thus it is that one sin leads to another and both were buried together. In unsanctified ground, with no priest near.'

Mama O. grew pale. Her very clothes closet.

'It is nothing to worry,' Mama Z. told her neighbor sagely, 'he does not knock to do harm. He comes only to gain a little peace that good Christian prayer for him may give. Pray for the young man, Mama O. He wishes peace.'

That night after supper the Orlovs gathered in prayer about the front-room stove, and Papa O. prayed also. For now that the accordion was gone, the taverns must do without him. When the prayer was done, he went to bed with Mama O. like a good husband, and the knocking did not come again.

Each night the Orlovs prayed for the poor young man. And each night Papa O. went to bed with Mama O. for lack of his accordion.

Mama O. knew then that the knocking had been a sign of good omen and told the priest, and the priest blessed her for a Christian. He said it was the will of God that the Orlovs should redeem the young man by prayer and that Papa O. should have a wife instead of an accordion.

Papa O. stayed at home until, for lack of music, he became the best janitor in the 800 block on Noble Street. Mama Z. went to the priest and told of her part in the miracle of the poor young man, and the priest blessed Mama Z. also.

When the landlord learned that his house was no longer haunted, he brought the Orlovs gifts; and when the rent was late, he said nothing. So the priest blessed him equally, and in time the Orlovs paid no rent at all, but prayed for the landlord instead.

Teresa became the most important person in her class, for it became known that a miracle had been done in the Orlov home. Sister Mary Ursula said the child looked more like a little saint every day. And no other child in the room ever had her lessons as well as Teresa thereafter.

The twins sensed the miracle, and grew up to be fast friends, doing all things together, even to wearing the same clothes and reading the same catechism. Udo, too, knew that the home was blessed. For he received no more blows from the accordion.

Only one sad aspect shadowed this great and happy change: Poor Roman was left bedless. For with Papa O. home every night like a good husband, Teresa must sleep between the twins.

Thus it came about that the nights of Roman Orlov became fitful and restless, first under the front-room bed and then under the back-room bed. With the springs overhead squeaking half the night as likely as not. The nights of Roman's boyhood were thereafter passed beneath one bed or the other, with no bed of his own at all. Until, attaining his young manhood and his seventeenth year, he took at last to sleeping during the day in order to have no need for sleep at night.

And at night, as everyone knows, there is no place to go but the taverns.

So it was, being abroad with no place to go and the whole night to kill, that Roman took his father's place. He had no accordion for excuse —only lack of a bed. He came to think of the dawn, when the taverns closed and he must go home, as the bitterest hour of the day.

This is why he still calls the dawn the bitterest hour: he must go home though he has no home.

Is this a drunkard's tale or sober truth? I can only say he told it like the truth, drinking double-shots all the while. I only know that no one argues about who the biggest drunk on Division is if Roman O. is around.

I only know what Mama O. now tells, after many years and Papa O.

in his grave and the twins scattered: that the young man who knocked was in truth the devil. For did she not give, without knowing what she did, a good son in return for a worthless husband?

'I'm drownin' the worm t'night,' Poor Roman explains, talking to his double-shot. 'Help me drown the worm t'night, fellas.'

Does the devil live in a double-shot? Or is he the one who gnaws, all night, within?

Or is he the one who knocks on winter nights with blood drying on his knuckles, in the gaslit passages of our dreams?

ALABAMA

Alabama Sketches

RUBY PICKENS TARTT

RICHARD, THE TALL-HEARTED

It had rained just enough to make the red clay roads slippery and to give the Negroes an excuse to quit work. Near the base of a sprawling hill wooded with loblolly pine and young cane my Ford slipped off into the ditch. Close by a group of Negroes had congregated in a small log cabin. They were singing and I sat for a while and listened.

> Joshua was de son of Nun,
> God was wid him 'til his work was done;
> God open de window and begin to look out
> And de ram horn blowed an' de chillun did shout.

Standing in the dog-trot of the cabin was a huge Negro man with solid sloping shoulders and a wide mouth held tight at the corners. His fiery eyes were set in a long curiously modeled head covered with kinky hair. A scrawny dog, the kind that almost all country Negroes have, cringed and fixed his eyes on him as if he saw things invisible to me.

I walked up to the house. The man looked for all the world like he might be in league with the devil, and but for a slow confident smile which was a trifle belated for my comfort, I might have sought help elsewhere. While the other men pushed my car back on the road, he just watched and talked.

'You see, Miss, I didn't come up 'round here in dese red hills, an' I ain't no help in dis sort of mud. Ole Marster used to say, red clay was a sign of po' white trash an' I b'lieve him. Dis here ain't nothin' but a old throwed-away road nohow. Don't nobody never work hit no more.

From Winter, 1944, *Southwest Review*, Southern Methodist University, Dallas, Texas. Permission for its use granted by Allen Maxwell, Editor.

'You see I come from 'round Brown's Chapel, an' I come up de hard way, what I mean I jes' had a hard time a eatin' and a wearin', too. Does you know, Miss, dat de first greens I ever et was wild pepper grass outer de field? An' de first milk I ever drunk come from a deer my mammy raised when old man Boyd killed hits mammy? First cornbread I ever et was a ash cake made in a pone an' put on de brick 'fore de fire an' my mammy knock ashes over hit like roastin' 'taters? First pants I ever wore to church was made out of burlap dat Mammy dyed with red oak bark. First hat I ever put on my kinky head was made out of pasteboard an' she dyed hit too. An' man was I dressed up!

'And my shoes?

'Us pappy killed a yearlin' an' all us little chilluns wore shoes made out of de hide from de small part of de yearlin's legs, de middle size chilluns' shoes was made from de hide in the middle of de yearlin's leg, an' Mammy's an' Pappy's shoes was made from de thigh. But I had a uncle an' there warn't no part of dat yearlin's hide what was big enough to make him no shoes. Yes, ma'am, dat Nigger had de biggest feet I ever is seen on nobody. Why his feet was so big once when de back water come up 'round his house an' his skiff got loose, an' hit look like him an' his whole family going to drown in spite of everything, he jes' put his ten chilluns an' his wife in one of his shoes, then got in hisself an' rowed 'em all to de bank.

'Dat same Nigger had de biggest teeth I ever seen in all my life. One day he was jes' settin' down on de gallery, idle like, doin' nothin' when he heard a mighty roarin'.

'"What's dat?" he asked.

'One of de chillun hollered back, "Hit's a storm."

'"Don't get skeered," he told 'em. "Jes' you an' your mammy an' all de rest crawl in dis here hollow tooth 'til hit blow over. Ain't nothin' goin' to hurt you." An' in dey got, den he crawled in with 'em, an' soon as de wind an' de rain ceasted, dey all come crawlin' out dry as a bone.

'I tell you there warn't nothin' that Nigger couldn't settle, an' when he come to die the Society had to buy him three coffins. Dey buried his body in one, an' his feet in de other two.

'He sho' was a right smart size Nigger. He's dead now, but before dey buried him his folks put a chain 'round one of his teeth an' hitched the other end to a mule, Old Dolly, an' de 'lasses mill, an', Miss, I never seed such a tooth in all my born days as come out dat Nigger's mouth.

Hit was mighty nigh dusk 'fore dey got to de end of de roots, an' dey started pullin' 'bout sun up. I wants to tell you there was enough of dem dere roots to put posts 'round a ten-acre field.

'When dey all seed dat, dey decided to pull some more. Well, Miss, dey made house blocks out of some of de smallest ones, took some more an' made de sills, took his jawbone an' made walls, took de top of his skull an' made a roof, split open his nose and used one nostril for a stove pipe an' one for a chimney, took his neck an' stuck hit in de groun' for a well, made windows out of his ears an' used his eye balls for de window panes to see out of. Den him an' his whole family moved back in de house an' hit hadn't cost him a cent.

'Yes, ma'am, dat was 'bout as talented a job as I ever seed. Jes' shows you what a man can do if he uses his head. I forgot about de paint he made out of de rest of dem teeth. He dried 'em in de sun an' beat 'em up an' made de prettiest white paint you ever seed. Painted de house inside an' out, an' hit sho' was a pretty thing if I do say so myself.

'He's de sensiblist Nigger I ever knowed, an' was he stout! Dey tells me hit took three women to nurse him when he was a baby. His mammy nursed him 'til she went blind, his auntie nursed him 'til she went crazy, an' he give his grandmother fits.

' 'Course I didn't know him den so I can't say 'bout dat, but I sho' knowed 'bout all dat other. Yes, ma'am, God moves in his misery, His wonders to perform, an' I 'spect hit am true.

'Oh, yes, I left out of dere after my uncle died, hit was so lonesome like, an' I went a ramblin'. Dat's how come I'm down here.'

By now my car was back on the road but I was not ready to leave.

'I'd like to hear some more of your experiences,' I said to the Negro.

'Jes' call me Rich,' he said. 'I'm Richard Amason, but don't nobody call me dat. Mostly dey say I'm frenzy-minded, but I ain't, but dat gal of mine settin' yonder by dat sweet gum is. She calls herself Ophely King Jesus, but dat ain't her name. Hits Lucile. I don't know how come she say Ophely, 'less hits whiskey. She was a mighty midnight rambler an' whiskey drinker, an' 'fore dat she was fat an' fine an' muffle-jawed. White folks want to put her in jail, but bein' shut up like dat'll aggravate anybody. Whiskey done hit, but now she done come back home where she can get back to drinkin' pot licker an' eatin' heavy greens. An' she gettin' healthy an' fat again. You see if you is brought up on branch water, you better continue on in prayer an' drink branch water, 'cause cistern water will kill you sho' as you's born. Take a mule off grass an' feed him heavy corn an' you'll kill him sho'. Folks ain't no different from animals, jes' harder headed.

'No, ma'am, I ain't frenzy-minded, 'cause I ain't never had a lick on my head to give me hit, or no sprung ankle, no mashed toe or nothin' to make me crazy. I jes' cross-talks folks, an' my brain dances, but I ain't told you 'bout dat turkey my uncle had is I? Miss, dat turkey was so tall he could reach de throne of God an' get a biscuit an' put hit in his lef' hind pocket.'

Rich stopped. I looked at him inquiringly. He held out his hand.

'The Bible say praise de bridge what puts you safely 'cross, Miss, and it's sho'ly right dat you help dem what put your car back on de road. But hit also say dat a Nigger in hand is worth ten in de field, and I sho' is done help you. Help dis old frenzy-minded Nigger, please, Miss.'

I had long ago learned the magic-like results of a dime or so on a Negro, but I had given all of my change to the men who had helped with the car.

'Come over to town,' I said to Rich. 'I have some clothes which may fit you, and a pair of shoes which I believe you can wear.'

'Hush yo' mouth, White Folks, an' me barefooted. I'll sho' be dere. 'Sides I got a good job over in town, when I takes a notion to do hit. Mister Simpson done wants me to dig him a well. Hit pays thirty-five cents a foot, and left to *my* jedgment. 'Twixt dat foot [he held up a foot about fifteen inches long] an' *my* jedgment, ain't no tellin' how deep dat well goin' to be.'

At five o'clock the next morning Rich was at my back door. From appearances he had again 'come up de hard way.' His clothes were torn and his legs and face badly scratched.

' 'Twarn't quite daybreak, Miss,' he mumbled, 'so I reckon I must of went to de wrong house an' dem folks must of thought I was stealin' 'cause dey sicked dat big brindle dog what I didn't know dey had on me, an' I took out through de brier patch.

'Kin dis old critter run?

'I tells you, Miss, I ain't askin' nothin' to wait on me. I jes' ducked my head an' sailed through dat kitchen window same as if hit had been left open. I must of been flyin' but I felt like I was stayin' where I was at. Dats how come I don't like red clay mud. Lawd Jesus, I says, when I got in dat road, please up dis old Nigger's feet out of dis here clay, 'cause if you does he kin sho' put 'em down again. 'Bout dat time I pass Yellow Creek an' dere was Simmy, de one what helped you with de car when you was stuck, ridin' little Dolly to de lodge. Dat boy left me at home in de field before sun down, an' he hadn't got dere yet. I sho' was glad I warn't bothered with no mule. Simmy, he hollers at me an' wants to know where I's goin'.

'"Ain't goin' no place, I's comin' from somewhere," I says.

'Dat was de truth, ma'am, 'cause I was flyin' from dat dog an' comin' to you for protection. If dat brindle dog had ever put dem teeth in me, I wouldn't need but one more clean shirt.'

Rich glanced around cautiously.

'Miss, in case dat man was to overtake me somewhere and put me in jail, please, ma'am, come an' get dis old Nigger, all bent with rheumatiz and can't hardly move, an' bail him out of dere. An' if he asks you where you reckon I got dat chicken I put under your step . . . but, shucks, ain't no white man goin' to ask where no Nigger got no chicken. I hope hit ain't dead, but I specks I held him a little too tight 'round de neck.'

Rich sniffed and wiggled his nose.

'Yes, Miss, de chillun of de darkness is wiser den de chillun of de light. Ain't dat de truth, Miss? I ain't never felt so good nor had so less in my life, an' if I could get a cup of coffee with some future to hit, an' dem clothes you said you had, I wouldn't feel so exasperated inside. I done decided hits a good idea to put 'em on over dese here, hits safer dat way, for ain't nobody goin' pick up dis Nigger's tracks, an' if I meets dat man what sicked dat brindle dog on me, all he goin' be doing is jes' fallin' behind, 'cause de Lawd done heard me once an' de Bible says He will again.

'Miss, I feels sad about not helpin' you yesterday with yo' car, but, Miss, I's got rheumatiz, an' all I needs is jes' some inspiration like dis here brindle dog, den can't nobody beat Old Rich.'

Bing Oliver Is a Pushing Man

Bing, an Elder in the Sinner's Friend Colored Baptist Church, lives near the line between Sumter and Narketa counties, close to a fellow elder, Dink Yarborough. Last summer the Baptist Association met above Narketa at Electric Springs, Mississippi. Bing was lamenting his lack of a way to go when Dink told him that his brother, Shug, had a car and would take them for two dollars. Bing told Dink to have the car at his house by five the next morning so that they could be at the meeting by nine; it closed at two and he wanted a chance to talk with the brethren and sisters. Bing was in Livingston recently and told me about the trip.

'Well, Miss Ruby, dey got to my house a little late dat mornin', which I sorter 'spected an' allowed for. When I went to de car and started to get in, Shug, he say,

' "Y'all have to push me off."

'Me an' Dink started pushin' an' dat car shot off liken a fire cracker, an' I asks why. Dey say hit back-firin'. An' I told 'em I didn't like a car which back-fired, but us'd push an' hit would back-fire, an' us'd jump, den push some more. After while I got tired pushin', an' I 'cided I'd go back home, but when I looked round, 'twas so far back I allowed I'd push some more. Den on de front seat I seed a chair, an' I asks Shug what was de chair for? An' he say for to sit on when us fixes punctures. An' I asks if he 'specs to have punctures, an' den he say,

' " 'Spec? Hell, I knows we will."

' 'Twan't no use to ask, for 'bout dat time us had four punctures at one time, an' Shug, he got out an' Dink an' me pulled off an' pumped up de tires, whilst Shug was a-settin' down fixin' de punctures. Den us push to 'long 'bout two-fifteen, when de 'Sociation is done broke up an' folks was leavin'. Shug he say,

' "Well, us is here, so pay me."

'An' I say, "Pay, hell, nobody ride but you."

'Just here I 'minded Shug that the road from Narketa to Electric Mills was pretty hilly and asked if we couldn't ride down the hill, and he say,

' "Hell, no, dis car ain't got no brakes."

'So us had to hold her back goin' downhill.'

Remembering that the main road to Electric Mills ran through the business section of Narketa and that a longer road circled the town and rejoined the highway, I asked,

'Bing, how did you go through Narketa?'

And the spontaneous reply was, 'Miss Ruby, us went through a-pushin'.'

A Pair of Blue Stockings

I never was in debt but once in my life. I come over to de sto' ever once in a while, an' I always made enough to pay up. Mr. McMillan at de bank say,

'Josh, yo' cotton shine mighty bright on yo' debt this year, an' I believe you's goin' pay out.'

An' I always did 'cept once. But it's another time what I's goin' tell you 'bout, when I come over to town to have a settlement. An' I paid out all right; but I didn't clear but a nickel. I never will forget it. I sorter hated to go home. Alice was a good woman an' mothered my sixteen chillun, an' us never had a cross word. She told me to fetch her some snuff when I left that mornin', an' I jes' natcherly hated to face her.

Dere was a clearin' 'bout a quarter of a mile (fur as from here to de long bridge down dere); an' dat mornin' I seed Alice come out de door an' shut it an' come on down de road to meet me. She met me right at de little plum thicket, with two or three new plum toothbrushes in her mouth jes' ready for that snuff. An' de fust thing she asked was,

'Josh, is you made dat settlement all right?'

'Yes,' I say, 'I made de settlement all right.'

She stopped me right dere. 'Don't tell me nuthin' else,' she said. 'Jes' git down off'n dat hoss.'

She could jes' taste de snuff, look like. So I got down off my hoss an' I told her 'bout how we jes' cleared a nickel. I didn't look up, but I knowed she was upset. Then she say,

'Did you get me some snuff?'

An' I told her no; then she wanted to know if I got me some tobacco; an' I told her no, that she couldn't chew tobacco an' I couldn't dip snuff, so I didn't get nothin', I jes' brought her de nickel and she could say what to do wid it.

So she say, 'Give it to me, an' I won't spend it till you say so, and you don't spend it till I say so.' An' I handed her de nickel an' she say, 'Come on an' we'll go to de house an' I'll get you some breakfast.' (I come to town early dat mornin' to make de settlement.)

While we was walkin' to de house she say, 'I'll fix a way to get you some tobacco an' me some snuff. Jes' put de hoss in de stable but don't take de saddle off; jes' take de bridle off.'

She got some corn an' called de chickens. I did what she said. I hung de bridle on de horn of de saddle an' I et my breakfast, an' she caught eight old hens. I brought dem here to town an' sold 'em to Mr. Dick Arrington for two-bits apiece. Den I took dat money an' got two-bits of flour and a dime's worth of coffee; an' got me a plug of tobacco, an' got her some snuff. In dem days dey had snuff in big old jars, an' you could buy a nickel or a dime's worth. An' I got Alice a dime's worth. Den I went back home.

De next week dey summons'd me to come to court. Dat day I sold de fust cotton seed I ever sold or saw sold to Mr. Dick Arrington. He give me a pair of plow shoes, an' give me a pair for Alice. Dat's what he give me for de cotton seed.

Durin' de next week dey summons me to court again. It was mighty cold. It looked like de cold wind would cut my shanks off when my britches leg come up, ridin' dat hoss. I had good shoes (dem plow shoes what Mr. Dick give me), but you see I didn't have no socks.

Dere was a merchant here named Mr. Zimmons, an' I went in his sto' an' bought me a pair of socks. Dat was de last of de hens. I went 'round back of de sto' an' put on one of de socks. An' it come to me dat Alice was out home an' didn't have no stockin's, an' me here puttin' on socks. I jes' took dat sock off. You know people wore long blue coarse socks in dem days. I went back in de sto' an' asked Mr. Zimmons would he swap me a pair of stockin's for de socks, an' he say,

'Yes, I'll do dat.'

An' he took de socks an' throwed dem under de counter an' give me de stockin's. Dis is a fact Miss Ruby, an' if you ever heard de truth, I'm givin' you de truth now. I put de stockin's on an' come on back to de stove to get my feet warm. An' dat evenin' when I went on back home I put my foot out thiser way for Alice to see my stockin's on, an' she looked at dem an' say,

'You bought you some stockin's, didn't you?'

An' I say, 'Yes,' an' stuck my other foot out.

An' she say, 'Pull 'em off, Josh.' An' I took de stockin's off. An' Alice say, 'Sunday is my meetin' day.'

You see I belongs to de church here in town but she belonged to de Christian Valley church. An' I handed her de stockin's. An' she didn't put 'em on, she put 'em up. Sunday come an' she went to church an' wore de stockin's. Next Sunday was my Sunday here in town. So I put de stockin's on an' wore 'em over here. Fust an' third Sundays was my days to wear 'em, an' second an' fourth was hers down to Christian Valley. An' we wore dem stockin's all dat whole year, Miss Ruby, an' when she would come back from church she took 'em off, an' when I come home on my Sundays I took 'em off. Us jes' wore 'em on Sundays.

Well, we worked it all dat year till one day we had a mix-up. Dey had de annual joint meetin', an' everybody come to Christian Valley church to divide up an' separate, or join up together. Well, dat fixed it. Me an' Alice both knowed us both couldn't go. So I went, an' dat lef' Alice at home an' without no stockin's. We had a good meetin' dat day, singin' an' tellin' what de Lord done for us. An' I forgot 'bout Alice till us was leavin'. 'Bout dat time de preacher steps up to me an' asks how was she. So I told him she warn't doin' so well. Den he says he believed he'd jes' drop by an' see 'bout her. You see, he was her preacher, he warn't mine. Well, warn't nothin' I could think of to do but jes' let him go. But all de way home I was worried mightily.

De house warn't no piece off de road an' Alice seen us comin'. Hit had two doors in front an' Alice was standin' in one of 'em; but when us turned in off de big road, I see her go to de back. We had a little center table in dem days settin' in de front room, holdin' de hymn books. So I jes' told de preacher to go in dere an' make hisself satisfied, an' I'd go an' help de old lady. An' dere was Alice, jes' standin' in de kitchen door beckonin' to me like dis. An' I knowed what she wanted. I pulled off de stockin's an' Alice put 'em on. I reckon he wondered what took her so long. I told her jes' tell him I'm out in de barn feedin' his hoss. An' to dis day he don't know we jes' had dat one pair of stockin's 'twixt us, an' we was changin' 'em.

We ginned our cotton dat fall, an' I went to de trunk an' got out dat nickel. I never seed one turn black befo'. Alice took it, an' I put two bales of cotton in de wagon, an' Alice climbed on top of de cotton an' us come to town. We sold de cotton, put dat nickel wid it an' had a settlement. Dis time de good Lord favored us, an' we had enough to pay out of debt an' get me some long blue coarse socks an' Alice some pretty stockin's. Yes, Miss Ruby, de Lord been mighty good to me an' Alice. We both is had a pair of socks an' stockin's apiece since dat year.

MAINE

So Clyde Was Born

GLADYS HASTY CARROLL

I think very well of God. At least, of whatever One it is who will sometimes take hold with gentle, unseen hands upon nothing, cupping and turning and shaping it until it takes form. He is not always about, not even when He is desperately needed; but sometimes He stops by, a wandering craftsman, and fashions most curious things—a vessel to bear water to a parched mouth, a still space in the midst of pain, a sweet memory where everything good has long been forgotten. Whatever His gift, it is more than it would have occurred to anyone to ask for, and what no one but He could have brought.

It must have been He who gave Clyde to Min Dailey. That is, who planted the seed in her heart. Min herself, alone, gave birth to Clyde on Tower Hill one night in the fall, with that blinding hurt of flesh and spirit which every mother knows, and the incredible moment of utter bliss and beauty in the end. Nor was it a matter for shock to her that she found her newborn child to be a man. God, or whatever One it is who does these things, had known well enough which seed to choose for the planting. . . .

During the years when I lived as a boy in Deepside, Min was one of the characters of the village. Her father's name was painted on the sign nailed above her door—ALBERT DAILEY, GROCERIES AND HARDWARE—but Albert liked best to sit in one of the rows of chairs under the window and be ready to exchange as many words as possible with anyone who happened along. He was an old man, frail, querulous, half blind; the weather was never right for him, nor the times, nor the local government. It was Min who waited on us when we went in to buy.

"Oh, hello," she would say, jumping up from her chair behind the counter and thrusting a bit of sewing out of sight. "My goodness! Who would have thought to see you! Well, how are you? Good as you look?"

She was tall and thin, with narrow shoulders and wide hips. All her joints were prominent, her knuckles, ankles, elbows; her shoulders bulged at the points as if she had them stuffed a bit, like a man's coat. Her face was older than thirty-two or three, and yet in a way ageless, as if the years tramped rudely across but left no definite mark on her, nor ever would; her cheeks must always have been broad, hard, too red; her eyes small, black, and leaping; her hair heavy and without luster, seeming to hang there asleep. She was in no way beautiful.

But she was not ugly enough to arouse comment. If she had looked just as she did, and behaved differently, no one would have especially noticed her. She might have hidden behind her homeliness and never revealed that she knew it was a prison, as other women have. But this was not like Min.

"Hey, everybody!" she would shout, bursting in, all abeam, upon a church supper. Her dresses were always aflutter with scallops and ruffles on these occasions; in a close, warm room she reeked of perfume. "I guess you thought I'd never get here, didn't you? Well, I was kept late. My business is picking up, as they say. Mostly picking up after Pa. . . . Move over, Mr. Pease, and I'll set down aside of you. Don't be skeart, even if I am an old maid; I won't bite you. . . . Well, here I am. My, the victuals look awful good. I'll take some beans. You got to pie already, Benny Strout? You had any of mine? It's apple. It's good. I can cook as good as any of them. . . . What are them boys making such a piece of work about over there? Are they laughing at me?"

Here she might spring up from her chair, big, menacing.

"Then they can stop it! . . . You can stop it, I say! You're always at it. I'm sick of it. Nothing funny about me. I'm sick of it, I tell you. Your mothers ought to—your mothers ought to see after you. If I was your mother—"

If Min Dailey were our mother! Old Min Dailey, our mother! We ached with wanting to abandon ourselves to the humor of it, as we should have, freely, in any other place, trusting to our legs to carry us beyond the reach of Min's loosed fury. But the church women were kind to her, as kind as they knew how to be. They lectured her upon her loudness, sometimes, telling her ladies did not behave so; and worried her by praying she be helped to control her temper; but they learned how to soothe her, too, and prevented us from doing our worst. It was in other places than the church that she could sometimes, often very easily, be reduced to tears. It was in the grandstand at a ball game that she was heckled until, when a ball fell into her lap, she rose from her hunched smoldering and threw the weapon with accurate aim and murderous intent at Shorty Drew's head.

These things did not happen to her among the church women; and this was the reason that she was willing to wash the dishes after their suppers, change beds and scrub stained linen for the sick poor, grit her teeth and tear her nails and rub her knees raw over jobs no other member of the Ladies' Aid cared to undertake. She clung to these people out of gratitude, and for the sake of their protection, not suspecting that the One whom they were always importuning for favors would come to her, unasked, one night and bring deliverance.

It was said she reached out with her hands and her smile for every man who entered the store, touching him whenever she could make excuse, talking until even the most polite must be rude to save his dignity from her. This was true.

It was said she had in so many words invited every elder of the church to come and stay with her in her rooms over the store. This was not true. It was women who befriended Min; men had no patience with her, and none needed so much excuse as such an invitation to insist that she leave the church. Whatever she might have liked to be, she was not "bad."

It was said the sewing she was so often found with by a customer went to swell the contents of an old green box which stood in the back of the store—that this was Min's hope chest. But as long as I lived in Deepside, nobody knew whether it was or not, for it never stood open. The night four of us jimmied a window and scrambled in to turn it out, hoping to decorate the Square with Min Dailey's bridal nightgowns and lengths of lace and bits of linen, to celebrate a hockey victory, we found the chest fastened with a lock beyond all our skill of breakage.

Min Dailey was no fool; nor was she insensitive, as I have shown. She not only understood the full significance of what the cruel young were doing, but she knew quite well that the warmest feeling anyone had for her was one of patronage. Now, looking at a crucifix, I invariably think of Min. Then, at nine and twelve and fifteen, I did my full share of spitting and dragging on of thorns. Yet she lived, and met every new encounter with a friendly hail, a spring forward, a sudden flaming up of hope and confidence.

"Oh, hello!" she would say whenever one of us sidled in. "What can I do for you? I live in a house by the side of the road, you know. How are you, anyway, Bub? Good as you look?"

It must have been so that she met Douglas Paul when he came to Deepside. Douglas Paul was a man who did radio repair work, a war veteran, about forty years old, a lean fellow with slightly stooped shoulders, a long, silent face, quiet, full blue eyes, and a scar on his chin. Nobody knew where he had been before this, except to the war, nor why he had come to Deepside instead of to some other town. Probably there was no reason, or perhaps he had had enough of the other towns. He did not talk much; there seemed to be no need of it in his work. He came, hired the cupboard-like shop next to Dailey's store, placed his bench in the one window, and began repairing radios.

He slept in the room above his store, as Min and her father lived in the rooms over theirs; and he took his meals at the lunchroom down the street. In the evenings he sat on one of Albert Dailey's chairs, pulling hard at his pipe, looking at the sky, saying little or nothing to the old man and not appearing to listen to his grumbling chatter. Of course Min sat near too, whenever she was not busy. He drew her like a magnet. Other men noticed it, and chuckled, wondering how long it would be before Douglas Paul would see fit to move his shop to a more congenial neighborhood.

But he stayed on there all through the summer and fall; and when it grew too cold for sitting outdoors, he took his pipe in beside the rosy stove of the grocery store; it was not possible to keep his cubbyhole warm enough for anything but work. Every evening when the Daileys came downstairs from their supper, the radio repair man would be sitting there on a bench, his legs crossed, the thick soles of his shoes resting on the grate, his head lounging forward, his collar unbuttoned and turned in.

"Seems like it used to," the old man said bitterly, grudging himself the pleasure of company. "I used to have somebody or other in night after night when I first kept store. Lots of times, four or five. It's just since Min's growed up that nobody's come around here to set. She scares 'em off. Flies at 'em so. Can't let anybody rest."

"There, Father," Min told him cheerfully, "you ain't happy unless you're finding fault with something. It might as well be me. I don't seem to bother Mr. Paul, anyway. You ain't so easy scared, are you, Mr. Paul? I don't believe that chair's very easy for you. You'd better take this rocker. Here, we had some apple pie for supper. I brought you down a piece. And a cup of coffee. I don't make bad apple pie, do I?"

"Good enough," Douglas Paul answered, remaining on the bench, but taking the pie in both hands and eating it down in great bites. He gulped coffee from her mug now and then, lifting it from beside him with a thumb thrust through the handle, his fingers long and brown against the white earthenware.

Min stood watching him with radiant face, her hands on her hips. He did not lift his head, but sat eating and drinking what she had brought. At the point of his turned-in collar a few crisp hairs grew.

"Good coffee, too," he sometimes added evenly, passing back the cup to her, slapping his pockets in search of his pipe.

After this he smoked until an early bedtime. Whether Min or her father talked, he only sat there smoking; if they asked him a direct question, there was an instant's silence, as if his mind looked over its shoulder, and then he slowly answered "Yes," or "No," or "Well," in his toneless voice.

It was not much, but it was more than Min had ever had. More than the cruel young of the village could allow her. It occurred now to the girls of Deepside to take their turn at the torture.

"What do you think, has Min Dailey got a man at last?" they asked one another. "Has he swallowed her, hook, line and sinker?"

"Such a sweet man, too," they said. "Really, you know, Douglas Paul is a perfectly nice man."

"And scarce they are in this town. He isn't so terribly old, either. Did you hear he was publicly commended by the Secretary of War when he got his discharge from the army?"

"Well, it's no use any of us going out for him, anyway," another laughed. "Min's in on the ground floor, weaving her fatal web of fascination."

"It isn't fair to him, though," Milly Bridges said. "It's leaving him stuck."

"Christian Endeavor is going to give a play," my sister announced at supper one night. "All the trouble is getting men to take part. We think we'll ask that Douglas Paul to try out—the radio repair man.

He ought to associate with some church. Don't you think so, Mother?"

Mother said yes, certainly; we are expressly directed to go into the byways and hedges; she was glad to see Christian Endeavor awake to its responsibilities.

Once persuaded to join the little group in the vestry, Douglas Paul proved himself a natural comedian; the type of grave-eyed, lean-jawed man, cadaverous, who can upon demand play the clown and be the funnier because of the complete reversal. He took the comedy part in the play, became the auctioneer at box parties and ice-cream socials, and within a month was teaching a class of small boys in the Sunday school. Friendly, respectful young girls can do these things to a lonely man. Min, full of pride and noisy delight, beamed on him from a distance at all his appearances; but she saw far less of him at close range now. Often they walked up to the church together; but when the evening was over, however long she waited by the door, he did not come back to her. There was money to be taken care of, or borrowed furniture to be returned. . . . Douglas Paul, abroad again after many years of blinking in a tomb, worked soberly, faithfully, absorbed in this new demand on him.

It may have been his age. It may have been his reputation as a hero, the scar on his chin, his success on the stage, his steady reliability, or the way he listened to a girl quietly, and, after she had finished, did what she asked. Whatever the reason, Milly Bridges, small, with fair hair, and eyes like blue-painted clothespin heads, counted herself in love with him before Thanksgiving. And it was the same with Dorris Evanston, a tall girl with a hard, crimson mouth. The two eyed each other grimly for a week or two. Then the day after Douglas took Milly with him to return a farmer's radio, and break off branches of yellow leaves along the roadside, a little story started, like a new brook after a rain, through the church.

Douglas Paul, it was said, had come from Concord, New Hampshire, to Deepside. Before Concord, he had lived in Tiverton, Rhode Island, and before that somewhere in Illinois. In Illinois he had grown up, and he had a wife there and five children. Since the war he had never returned home to see them, and they had no idea where he was. The wife advertised in the Boston papers, saying: "All is forgiven. Please come home. No questions asked. Children need you." His real name, it was added with significant looks, was not Douglas Paul, but something quite different.

"Oh, is it true?" Milly begged, feverishly. "Is it true, do you think?"

"I don't know, I'm sure," Dorris told her. "One thing I *do* know—I'm glad *I* never went out with him. If he's *that* kind—"

"Well, of course we have to admit he's been very tight-lipped ever since he came here," said my sister Jane with relish, swinging in the hammock between our maple trees.

"But I can't believe it's true," faltered Milly.

She looked frightened and bewildered, hurrying out of the yard. It was from her, later, that we heard enough to understand what happened.

Douglas Paul stopped at her house that night and asked her to walk up Tower Hill, behind the stores, with him. It was a place where lovers went; there were ledges to sit on, and groves of little firs in which to hide. Milly, suddenly cool and quiet, was not sure she wished to go; then, relenting, she went along, holding aloof from him, saying nothing.

Up on the Hill, looking down on the lights of the village at their feet, he tried to kiss Milly, and she struck him.

"Don't you dare!" she cried. "You've done enough. You've—you've spoiled my life; that's what you've done, Douglas Paul—or whatever your name is! Go way. Go right down off the Hill. I wish I wouldn't ever see you again as long as I live. I wish you'd go back to your—your wife and children, where you belong!"

Being Douglas Paul, he went away from Milly at once.

Outside his shop he walked up and down in the dark, finally pushing open the door into the grocery, seeing Min's light was on. She looked up from her sewing.

"Well, Mr. Paul! Who'd have thought to see you this time of night? What is it—you hungry?"

He had only thrust in his head and was not listening.

"You'd better go up on the Hill," he told her. "I left Milly Bridges on the Hill. Over at this end where the ledge juts out. I don't know but she's sick. She was talking strange."

Min sat and looked at him. So, he was taking Milly Bridges on the Hill. It was a place where Min had never been after dark. The Hill was for lovers.

"You'd better go along," he urged her.

The new little story had not escaped Min. Slowly she rose, folding her sewing.

"You'd better come in and shut the door," she said. "It's getting pretty cold lately. What was this strange talk Milly Bridges had over?"

"Something or other," Douglas Paul said in bewilderment. "I don't know exactly. Sounded like she thought I had a wife and children."

"Yes," Min answered bitterly. "That's what everybody thinks. There's some gossip going around the church to that effect. Is it true? Have you got a wife and five young ones out in Illinois?"

Douglas Paul stared at her.

"God help me," he said. "No—I was never married."

"No; well, I didn't suppose so," Min told him. "But some of them that looked to be such fine friends to you started the yarn; and now every man-jack of the rest is going to believe it. That don't surprise you, does it? You didn't suppose them little young girls like Milly Bridges cared anything about you but what they could get out of you, did you?"

There was a silence, and then Douglas Paul said, "You'd better go up. She hadn't ought to be alone up there."

"Oh, I'll go," Min answered darkly. "I'll go up, all right. And I'll tell her what I think of her goings-on. But it won't do any good. Only thing, if this will open your eyes to what she is—"

She shrugged into a big double-breasted coat and went out into the dark, her step heavy like a man's, crunching the frozen grass. Through the field and up the Hill her feet found their way surely, for she had traveled this steep path to school, as a child, and gone sliding here on Saturdays. But she had never been here at night before, and even now she came alone. The little fir trees pointed their green fingers. Here was a woman who had no lover. . . . Here was a woman who came alone. . . .

Milly Bridges sat up from lying flat on the moonlit ledge. Her face was silvered, her body a child's body, round and soft under her leather jacket and plaid skirt. She was frightened. Min could hear her choked breath. She tried to crawl away among the junipers. Min tramped on doggedly into the light.

"Oh—oh, it's Min Dailey!"

Milly scarcely sounded reassured.

"Yes," Min said, looming dark above her. "It's Min Dailey. Douglas Paul sent me up here to see after you. What's the matter with you, anyway? What've you been saying to him? Can't you treat a decent man decent? What's the reason men can't take to any woman except the kind that's willing to knife them in the back? A tormented wretch like Dorris Evanston wouldn't flick an eyelash about making up a lie to serve her purposes; and you'd as quick believe it as not! That's the kind you are!"

Milly sat quivering. This was a new Min Dailey. This was a sudden straw to which to cling. In a swift movement she was on her feet, standing wind-whipped and white with cold and moonlight.

"You don't believe it, then?" she asked.

It was not a voice to be expected of Milly or of any girl.

"That's all I need," came from Milly's mouth. "I'm *not* that kind, Min Dailey! It's just—I'm not so old as you are! I haven't—been—been through what you have!"

The words fathered the realization of what she meant. Something in her met the soul of Min, and saw how bruised it was. She was no longer one of the Deepside young. Min's eyes fell. It was the first time understanding had ever come to her, and she found it almost too much to bear.

"But I've been through enough. All day, and here tonight," Milly was going on. "I didn't believe it. You can say it till you die, but it'll never be true, Min Dailey. I did not believe it. Only, everybody else did. Everybody I knew. Mother does. I don't know how I'll dare go home tonight, after coming out with him. . . . You know how it will be. I can't stand by him, now, and stay at home. We couldn't live here. It wouldn't ever be right for us. We're marked. . . . But I will stand by him if you'll say you don't believe it, either. That's all I need. That's how much I care about him."

She pulled out a blue ribbon from under her dress.

"He gave me this little ring on here," she said. "He gave it to me the day we went into the country. That was a lovely day. . . . I'd been wondering if I should wear it; and tonight I meant to give it back to him. I thought I had to. . . . But if you'll swear you don't believe it about him, I'll put the ring on my finger before I go back down the Hill!"

They stood there together in the wind and moonlight, and it was Min's hour. It did not seem long to Milly, only a few breaths, a minute's hesitation; but for Min it was the time of being shut away interminably from every thing and everyone but herself, of fighting and rending and casting out all that had troubled her so long, of coming back from a great distance, quietly, sweetly, peacefully, and finding to her surprise that she had brought something new and beautiful with her.

She said, then, with difficulty: "I swear it with a will, Milly Bridges. Douglas Paul himself told me it was a lie. I guess that's proof enough. Put your ring on your finger. You've got you a good man."

Yes, Milly had him. He was gone from Min, for good and all. But it did not matter, for who was Douglas Paul? Only the radio repair man, forty and gaunt, who had sat beside her stove a few evenings.

"I'll tell you something, Milly," Min said. Her words were coming surely now, exultant and strong, but quiet. She drew strength and calm from this new thing which lay beside her. "I'll tell you something you ought to know. . . . I wasn't always the kind of woman I've been lately! Once, before I was twenty, I spent a summer with my aunt out in Montana. And out there I got engaged to a man. . . . He was twenty-two—twenty-two and a half. Tall and square-shouldered. Oh, a nice one to look at. . . .

"I might have married him. Clyde, his name was—Clyde Harrison. Minnie Harrison, my name might have been. We used to ride and talk together just like you and Douglas Paul. We had great times. . . . I can see him now, thin face, gray eyes. . . .

"But they got a story going about him, too. I don't doubt it started from some jealous one, just like Dorris Evanston. There always is that kind. And they made me believe it, so I give him up. I come home without marrying him. . . . And that winter out there *he died*. . . .

"That's what happened to me. . . . I guess you don't want to be another Min Dailey, do you? . . . We even had the house in mind we meant to buy. Why, I've got that green chest down at the store full of stuff I was making to keep house with. . . . I had my ring on a ribbon around my neck, too. . . . But I took it off and give it back to him. Now all I've got left is the ribbon.

"So you see what happened to me, Milly, and it ought to make you have a little more courage. . . . That's foolish, thinking you can't stay in Deepside with him if you want to. You can stare 'em all down, so in six months they won't even remember it. You'll make out—"

Her words wandered now, her mind remaining with difficulty on Milly. She did not hear what Milly said, nor see her motion clearly when she snatched out the ring and put it on her finger. When Milly went running ahead down the Hill to Douglas Paul, Min lingered. This was what she wanted, for Milly to go, and the wind to die down, and the moon to drop behind the trees; she wanted, above all things, to be alone in her incredible peace with this small, beautiful thing she had created—this Clyde Harrison that never was, but always would be twenty-two and a half, tall and broad and good to see, with the collar of his shirt turned in.

Sitting on the ledge in the cold, Min reached down absently, fingering the creased ribbon Milly had let fall and catch on a bush, and finally tying it, blue, about her own brown neck.

The next spring Milly Bridges was married to Douglas Paul, and they went to Illinois on their wedding trip to visit his relatives. Nobody believed the foolish story any longer. Dorris Evanston had a new man now, a government surveyor who wore a uniform.

The only real change was in Min. Here nothing was as it had been. Already she was ceasing to be a village character, had become quiet, pleasant, and proud. She was safe, cheerful, gentle, like a widow who has been left an ample legacy of love and worldly goods, so that she need ask nothing more of anyone as long as she lives. Gradually the nature of her church work changed. She waited on tables oftener than she washed dishes. She was welcome to sew with the best of women. It was said that the chest of linens she gave Milly Bridges for a wedding gift had the finest stitches ever set in Deepside. . . .

Last summer, when I was at home for a few days and went to Dailey's on errands for my mother, I found Min getting old; a tall, very neat woman with white hair and a pleasant mouth, always wearing plain dark blue or black, with a little white about her neck. "To lie against the blue ribbon," I thought. Or didn't she take that ribbon? But Milly and Douglas had never found it, though they went back to look.

Old Albert is dead. Min's grocery store is modern and spotless, with glass cases for all her wares. Deepside boys call her Miss Dailey; and when they go in she says, friendly and reserved: "What can I do for you?" She no longer talks of living in a house by the side of the road. She lives at home up a little lane; roses climb over her gate; her lamp is lighted, but her shades are properly drawn.

I think very well of God.

MISSOURI

Weed Sack

JOSEPHINE JOHNSON

Seeds of the cockle, dry-burred and rough. Dangerous seeds which, ground-up, might poison. . . . Seeds of the quack grass, slippery and straw-colored. . . . False oat seeds that take good soil or bad, flourish in rain or drouth, and ruin land. . . . Grooved seeds of the daisy—black and white seeds that make a farmer swear.

Old Kale Brian went stooping along the pasture path, and the dust came up in a gray smoke around his feet and sank back in still air. He stooped from side to side along the path and moved out a way into the pasture where a drying clump of thistles was broken on the ground. He pulled off the gray thistle-flowers and shoved them down, dry seeding fluff in his sack. Thistle seed ruined land fast. Thistle seed, and cockle with its green and flabby leaves. No matter how good this Warren Nickels' land, thistle seed would take it in the end. "Let him sweat to dig and knife it," the old man mumbled. "Let him have sun on his head, Lord, and the salt in his teeth. Let him work as I've worked. Let him feel sky swimming in his head, and his stomach heave. Let him know noon sun on his head, O Lord!"

It would be rich land this Warren Nickels owned. Rich bottom land, and level. Fall-plowed and waiting for the seed. And there would be high land and slopes where the winter wheat came green in long even rows. No man with money would work hill country—gravel ground and mullein-rooted. Mullein; there was the one weed he'd forgotten. *Mulleins had a pretty flower, yellow and cup-shaped, and the big woolly leaves were like giant rabbit ears, but the seed—ah God! the seeds were like rabbit teeth, gnawing at the land. Hand-rooting you'll have to do, Warren Nickels, each giant plant rooted out by hand (in the sun, Lord,—make him do it in the sun), and the sly seeds burrowing where the stalk falls.* Kale shook the high stalks down in the dark mouth of his sack, and they fell with a dry rustling quiet in among the other seeds. Then he picked up the long sack, wide and stuffed, but curiously light, bobbing on his shoulder like a little mound of straw. He peered around him once more, searching with his pale old eyes.

All about him the pasture stretched for acres, dry and dusty, with white stones cropping from the earth and the asters dead as hay. The path was soft with dust from grinding of the cows' feet, but the other earth cracked and hard as stone. Drouth land. Hill country, and no rain for three months. He looked down where the steers moved along the dry creek-bed, switching at flies and hunting for the stale pools. Their bones jutted out sharp enough to cut the hide and the skin fell in wrinkled folds where the flesh was parched away. Dust powdered all weeds along the path.

Down at the hill foot, where the house was, he could see Wolf moving around in the potato field, hacking the dead and shriveled plants in a wandering way, or stopping to rest his hands on the hoe; Jamie crawled after him between the potato stalks, and dragged his cracked little feet in the dust. Jamie was five, brown and skinny as a beagle, with his spine showing twisted in hard buttons down his back. Brian heard his shrill child-voice come up through the air. "Where's Grampaw?" he heard Jamie ask, and Wolf answer, "I dunno," in a mumble. "Gone wandering. Picking things. Up to something."

"I seen a white bug walking on the ellum leaf, Pop,—a white bug like a flour-pinch. What would make a white bug like that, huh, Pop?"

"I dunno," Wolf answered. "It was a mealy bug maybe."

"Could you eat a mealy bug baked, Pop?"

Wolf shook his head. "Go ask your grampaw. He'll make you up an answer. Grampaw'll answer anything you want to know."

"Grampaw ain't here," Jamie said. "He's gone off pickin' things . . .
Old Grampaw Brian, crazy as a loon,
Gone pickin' cherries,
Huntin' for the moon. . . . I found a tater, Pop." He held up a shrunken brown knob and Wolf stooped down, peering at the warped root. Then he picked Jamie up and threw the hoe away. "Twenty big

sacks out empty in the shed, Jamie. That'll go a far way—that runt potater!" He burst out laughing; and at first the little boy laughed too, and then began to cry at the sound. All around them was a field of brown char, and nothing alive but the crawling little stink-bugs and late white butterflies.

Brian strained his sight down, holding his hand up to shield his eyes, and saw Wolf go back up to the house carrying Jamie; but could see Kate nowhere, and thought of her lying on the hot sheets inside, waiting for the black suns to stop dancing in her head and the pain let loose of her cheeks again. They seemed to him, unseen above them, watching down, little jointed wood things—his son and his son's wife and Jamie; and himself too a little wooden moving man, cracking in the sun and rain-warped . . . always going on, one farm to the next farm . . . moving on, moving on . . . a year in one place, two years in another, drouth following in their wagon tracks like a big dry dog. Always the crop failing, the rent money swallowed up in the mouth of other debts.

Two years in one place, three years in another. Where were they last year and the year before that? Calhoun . . . Clay . . . Cedar County . . . Prayerville . . . Omarston . . . the names marched and faded through his mind and dwindled in a fog. Wolf always managed, asked and arranged. And he followed where Wolf went, and stayed wherever there was place to stay. Sometimes it was rent down and half the crop, and sometimes, like now, just the rent alone to pay. Once it had been half a crop and no rent in money, and once, a long time ago, when his wife was living, they'd found a place that paid *them* instead; but the farmer had gone broke himself and moved away, and they had to get out and travel on again, creaking through the cold dust of an early autumn.—He tried to reckon up how long it was since Winnie died back in Cedar County, but the time was lost in the long fog of years and days.

Wolf managed somehow. Sour and sullen and kind as any man ever born. Always tired now even in the mornings, and Kate with her neuralgy-pains in the face that were like fire-fingers half the time. She wanted a place to live, a home to rest down and sit in, where she could always stay; but there was never any staying when the rent-month came. Wolf had been a strong fellow once, a tough, grinning boy with an inside fire. "This ain't the same one," Brian thought sometimes—"this stiff old wood-stick ain't no son of mine!" And he would try to recall if Wolf had died some place back in Cherryville or Newstead, and if this was some new man Kate had picked up in their wandering. But even in his fuddled mind he could bring up nothing that was like a funeral for his son.

Now they had come here, two years or so gone, and rented twenty acres from this Warren Nickels man. One year they'd paid by squeezing earth till it was nearly strangled, and themselves about willing to lie heavy and dead as a potato in earth; but still not utterly black of hope until this drouth had come. Now, in a month, they'd be moving on again, houseless and acreless, and the autumn rains—come too late to save even pastures—sluicing down their necks in some nameless county a dozen miles away.

Brian shook his fist up at the dusty sky and swept his arm around in a wild feeble flapping, as though he would point out to God some place of whose whereabouts he was not sure himself, but which was most certainly not far. "I'll find out where he lives, Lord, and sow his fields by night. Jimson weed and dodder and broomsedge in his hay. We'll sweat all the meanness and the stone out his hide. We'll grind him till he howls like a beagle hunting. We'll stoop him till he knows what stooping means!" He lifted up his fierce, muddled face and grinned at the drying land around him. "We may take it long, Ol' Warren Nickels, we may take it long and quiet, but we ain't going to take it lying down. The Lord moves in a mysterious way, Warren Nickels, but He moves—He moves!" The old man picked up the great sack again and moved on down the path, calm and cunning, and a holy hate taking place of the mild maze in his eyes.

Wolf was sitting quiet on the porch when Brian came up stealthily from the woodshed and sat down by him. For a while they were there without speaking, and watched the red light wash over the fields and the dead potato stalks, and a pinkness come over the rock ledges like a stain off the hot unclouded sky. The old man crouched in his chair, excited, not willing yet to speak. He opened and shut his mouth, and Wolf turned toward him, inviting his father by the question in his face.

"What say, Pop?" he asked when Brian opened his mouth again, but still held back the words.

"I didn't say nothin'," Brian answered. "I was just long thinkin'."

"What didja think about?" Wolf asked. He talked only to be kind, and hardly ever listened to what the old man said.

I ain't goin' to tell him, Brian thought. *I'll ask him round.*

"I was thinking this Mister Nickels must own wide land," he said aloud. "Wide, rich land." . . . *Rich valley acres, ripe for the fall seed, river-land where the rains came. . . . Seeds of the dodder falling on the ripe earth . . . seeds of burdock falling . . . poison-burrs falling on the pastures . . . thistle seed and mustard . . . hawkweed and plantain . . . seeds of the morning-glory and pearly everlasting—foul weeds with pretty names, choking Nickels' pastures . . . corn cockle, snakeroot. . . . And then this Nickels, this rich man, down on his knees, knifing at the daisy roots, hacking the plantain flowers, snarling in an August sun . . . grubbing at the dodder vines, the love-vines that strangled all his wheat stalks, wound around his alfalfa, smothering with its skinny arms, sucking all the green life. . . . Ah, God! that was a sight for a tired man to see!—Old Warren Nickels with the sweat in his eye-corners, down on his knees, hacking at the weed-roots, hunting through his pastures for poison plants of snakeroot, lying without sleep at night, thistles in his fingers. Then, by God, he'd know what paying meant!—then he'd know what two bushels meant, when there was only four!—he'd see how it felt to split a jack-bean and give the bigger half away!*

So lost he was and wandering in his own thoughts that Brian hardly noticed when his son answered.

"Nickels is a wide land-owner, all right," Wolf said. "He owns fifteen farms around about here. Fifteen farmers paying rent money out of half their crop."

"Where's his own farm at, Wolf? Where's he live himself, this Mister Nickels? I'll bet it's rich land, ain't it?—not like this, or these around. Rich river-bottom land, eh, Wolf? With fat pastures? Good corn land, easy to plow. I'll bet he has orchards, too—young ones with no scale or borers—clean orchards with bluegrass, eh, Wolf?"

Wolf moved uneasily and looked at the old man's rapt and eager face, and his hands clenched together with their thick veins swollen out. "What's this you're saying, Pop? What land's this you're telling me about?"

Brian sat up and smiled patiently. Now it was Wolf being the dumb one. Wolf being the one who didn't understand. Muck-headed and wandering in his thoughts.

"I mean Mister Nickels' land," he explained very slowly. "The land he lives on hisself, not renting out to other folks." He could see it so plainly in his own mind. All he wanted Wolf to tell him was the road. He'd know it by dark or moon when he got there. *Black soil, marly and full of nourishment, corn stalks wide and juicy green, come up with sun on their blades—green glittering above the dark soil. . . . And then the morning vines creeping up from the cast seeds, twining round the green stalks, crushing all the bright blades, and Nickels standing there cursing and mourning, with the cockle in his pastures, thistle and the poison oat in his wheat, shaking his fist up at God—"What've I done, Lord, to be so afflicted?" and the Lord answering in the one flesh corner of Nickels' heart, shouting in the rock shell of his heart, "You've been blind and deaf, Nickels. You've been hard and cheating. You ain't never understood and you ain't never tried. You've made pinching, sour little slaves of my people, and called yourself a man.—Now get down and pull. Get down and yank up the bitter weeds. Sift out the wild oat and plantain. Twist up iron earth and squeeze out the stones. . . ."*

Wolf looked at his father and asked again his question. "What land, Pop? What land of Nickels'? Nickels don't live on land himself. Warren Nickels is a corporation; it's a company that owns. Mister Nickels ain't a farmer, he's a man at the business head. The Warren Nickels Company rents out land."

Old Kale Brian stared at his son.

"Warren Nickels ain't a farmer?" he repeated. "He don't live on no land? He rents out land, and don't live on none hisself?"

"That's how it is," Wolf said, "they rent out land.—What makes you stare so Pop? How's that change things any?"

"Nothin'. It ain't nothin'," Brian mumbled. "I walked too far and too much today, I guess. . . . It jus' seems queer, a person not living on no land. Ain't he even got a bean-patch to weed, Wolf? Not even a little melon-bed, maybe?"

"He don't grow nothin'," Wolf said. "He ain't no ground at all. He lives in a house without space around for grass. He don't need no melon-patch. He can buy all his melons without growing."

Old Brian sat very still, then he got up and shuffled off toward the shed.

"Where you goin', Pop?" Wolf called after him. The old man looked so doused out and tired all of a sudden that it made him afraid.

"Nowhere," Brian said. "I ain't goin' nowhere special. I just got some trash I wanter burn." Then Wolf, watching, saw him come out the shed and go down the ditch-patch with a big sack bobbing on his shoulder; and he looked like a shrunken gnome against the sky.

ARKANSAS

A Woman Like Dilsie

DAVID THIBAULT

On a Saturday in June, Easter, George and John were walking home from the commissary, each with his rations slung in a gunny sack upon his back. Now and then a wagon passed them, going toward town. In one of these sat Aunt Minnie Graves, with her husband and the girl whom Easter had seen at the revival the August before.

George pleasantly called the old man by name.

"So dat's Peter Graves," commented Easter. "I know Mis' Minnie since I wuz 'bout seventeen."

"Don't you know 'im?" George asked.

"I seed 'im at chu'ch wid Mis' Minnie. I figgered who 'twas. But I ain't to say knowed 'im."

John laughed his slow, provoking laugh. "Now you done ax 'bout all of 'em but de onliest one you thinkin' 'bout."

"Who dat?" demanded George, smiling. "Dilsie?"

"Who you think East been stud'in'? Not de team of mules."

"Shucks!" said Easter. "I ain't even knowed her name till now."

"She a fine gal, East." For once George was not ribald. "Her ol' folks is fine too. You heahed of de Peter Graves Lake? A big cyp'us brake ovah across de bottoms?"

"Co'se I is."

"Hit named fo' him. He homesteaded fawty acres ovah dare. Good lan' as a crow ever flew ocross. He got nigh twenty acres cleared."

"Dat's all he *kin* clear," said John, "lessen he hires catfishes an' mud turkles to roll de logs. De rest of it runs out in de lake."

But George pointed out that this was no tragedy, because the pond acres bore a good stand of big cypresses. These Peter Graves felled and rived into boards and pickets. Everyone knew that Peter Graves kept

Originally published in *Harper's* Magazine, April, 1937. Used by permission of David Thibault, Jr.

a stock of clear, air-dried boards on hand, and that his count and his price were fair.

"He done well 'fore he got agable," George concluded. "Now he got to hire de timberin' done."

Easter said no more. Here, after nearly a year, he was tapping information he had longed for since his first sight of Dilsie. It was a part of her peculiar effect on Easter that he had asked no one about her, not even her name or where she lived. He had been afraid of this girl, and then there was Annie C., the kind of woman to occupy any hard-working man's spare time completely. Annie had comfortable ways, she was cheerful and not at all terrifying. Once or twice a year she might fly off the handle and mark you with a bed slat or a poker, but she never hit as hard as she could, and ten minutes afterward she would be laughing and joking and comfortable. Easter could take a rest from her, and she could take a rest from him, and when they came back together it was as though all were new.

Easter left George and John at his own turnrow and tramped on alone to his cabin. He unlocked the door, stored his rations and brought out a chair, which he tilted back against the walnut tree. Then he thought about marriage. It must be a good thing, after a man has run round over the bottoms like a stray boar shoat, to marry a woman like Dilsie Graves. A man should do this in time to have his children coming up ready to lend a hand in the field when he began to fail and lose his teeth and get old. He wondered if Annie C. could have children even if she wanted to; and he wondered why he thought of Dilsie, whom he had seen twice, in connection with marriage, and not of the comfortable Annie. "Annie, she jest ain't de marryin' kind," Easter muttered half aloud.

Today's encounter with the Graveses had focused the dream of Dilsie which Easter had entertained since the revival. While he kept this dream vague, and played it against the immediate and usable flesh of Annie C., his emotional setup was ideal. He could not have explained it, but that was why he had not sought to know more of Dilsie. Knowing her better, he might have needed her, and the things she meant to him, intolerably. As it was, he had of her all that he needed. Dilsie was merely a tenuous memory made into a beautiful dream which Easter delighted to evoke when, as now, he sat with his eyes half shut, his thoughts turned to pasture. This dream could not displace the grappling realities of Annie's breasts and thighs. But neither could poor, everyday flesh, frankly real, obviously limited, destroy the dream.

That afternoon Easter took his gun and struck out through the bottoms toward the Peter Graves Lake. "I needs to kill me a squirrel fo' some freshenin'," he told himself. "H'm," said Double-Actin'. "De squirrel you is atter wears a blue calico dress." Easter resentfully denied it, a course always dangerous, because his conscience was irascible in argument, personal, and sometimes vile. "I *is* gwinna hunt me some squirrels!" he insisted and put a cap on each nipple of his gun. "Sho'!" jeered Double-Actin'. "Sho'! But dis squirrel ain't got no bush tail." Stung and disgusted, Easter crossed half a dozen narrow straits between cypress ponds, skirted two fair-sized lakes, and came to the Graveses' clearing. The double log house was locked and still.

Knowing the family was in town, Easter boldly approached the house. There was a front gallery and a water shelf loaded with cans and buckets and broken crocks full of moss roses. The unfenced yard was clean swept, the sizable woodpile was neat, and a sound wooden tub stood under the spout of the pitcher pump. Between woodpile and pump, handy to chips and to water, two big washpots stood, each with its three legs resting upon half bricks. Look at the crops and you know the man. The front gallery, the yard, and the wash place tell you about his womenfolks. True as a mirror, everything here reflected Aunt Minnie Graves—brisk, clean, kindly. Easter turned back to the house. Against the house, under the gallery roof, hung festoons of red peppers, bunches of herbs, and loops of well-roped onions. On a tiny three-legged stand stood a handleless earthenware pitcher filled with old-fashioned cabbage roses. At this Easter looked long. He was sure Dilsie had placed those flowers there.

He crossed the lead between the lake and a smaller pond adjoining it and plunged into the thick woods beyond. For two hours he hunted squirrels as he never hunted them before. By late afternoon he had killed eight. He tied their necks together with a strip of elm bark and returned to the Graveses' clearing. The place was still deserted. Easter ambushed himself near the foot log across the lead and waited. It was nearing sunset, and the mosquitoes were about him in booming clouds when he heard the wagon approaching. When Peter Graves stopped his team in front of the house, Easter crossed the foot log and walked briskly forward, perfect picture of a belated hunter hurrying homeward.

Peter had helped his womenfolk out of the wagon and they were all three busy with their packages when Easter came up to them.

"Well, Lawd bless my heart!" cried Minnie Graves. "It's Easter, dat Malissa Thomas raised. How is you, honey?"

"I's all right, Mis' Minnie." Then to Peter. "Kin I he'p you wid de team, Mistuh Graves?"

"Glad to see you," said the old man. "Dems some fine squirrels you got. I kin unhitch. You go in an' take a cheer."

Easter insisted on helping with the team. It staved off by so long the beatific terror of looking at Dilsie. But for all that, the corners of his eyes saw her demurely attending to her own business, helping her ma the way a gal does who is used to it. Easter was miserably afraid. He presented Peter Graves with all the squirrels and prepared to bolt. The old man herded him with difficulty to the front gallery, calling cheerily to the women, "Dis boy done gimme *all* his squirrels. I's gwinna make 'im stay an' he'p eat 'em."

"Sho'!—course he is!" Minnie followed her voice through the door. "Come in an' have a cheer, Easter."

But the stiffening had gone from Easter's bones. He reeled off lie after lie to get out of doing what he had schemed and worked half a day to do, rejecting the fruits of the victory he had not even dared to hope for.

"Den effen you *got* to go," said Minnie, disappearing inside, "wait jes' a minute." She returned with a pie tin piled full of something over which a clean white cloth was tied. "Heah you some beef we bought in town. You kin bring back de pan sometime."

"Sho'," said Peter Graves. "Now you know de way, come an' visit. Don't many come across dese bottoms—'cepen a lot of boys dats a-settin' up to Dilsie." What barbed information for Easter to pack home across the swamps!

Easter cooked his supper and ate it, washed the skillet, pans and cups, and then sat down on his door block under June stars to think of Dilsie; and he came to the image of her in his mind as a famished man faces manna. Not even old Peter's mention of many rivals hurt him now. When at last he went to bed he was convinced that just thinking about a woman like Dilsie was more exciting than possessing any other woman he had ever known, except Annie C. Here he was thinking of those two at the same time again. He wished to goodness he could keep his thoughts about them separated. But it wasn't his fault, he maintained to his vision of Dilsie. Thoughts of those two girls ought to be more alike than they were different, or more different than they were alike.

Sunday, Easter attended meeting at Zion Wheel, hoping and fearing the Graveses would be there. They were not. He saw Loda Green, Annie and Elsie in the congregation. How had he ever come to marry Loda? Elsie's remembered fascination was nearly as incredible. He studied her face as the sermon thundered on: a tired, leanish woman of forty, with one eye. . . . When his meditative glance fell on Annie C. she flashed her wide smile, and his lips flashed an answer; but he was thinking of that broken pitcher full of pink cabbage roses on Peter Graves's gallery.

Monday morning Easter hoed in his own crop. Between quartering time and noon it showered; so little that he had trouble convincing himself that it would be too wet to work in the afternoon. However, he managed it and was just ready to set out across the swamps to return Aunt Minnie's pan and cloth when Mr Henry rode up.

"Easter," said Mr Henry, "I want you to help us out this afternoon. We're chopping the upper eighty." It had not occurred to Mr Henry that it was too wet to work, and Easter didn't argue the point this time.

That was the heartbreaking pattern of events for three weeks of grinding work. On the first Saturday following his visit to Graveses' clearing he had to drive the wagon to town for rations, substituting for Pink Dawson, who was down with chills and fever. Sunday, dressed in his best, he crossed the bottoms to find the Graveses' house locked and silent. He learned later that they had attended meeting. The following week his own crop needed him. A blessed thunderstorm halted field work Friday, but Mr Henry sent Easter to town again, and on Saturday had him help issue rations in the commissary. Sunday Easter was at meeting again—and the Graveses were not. But Annie C. was there.

"How come you ain't been down to see me?" she asked.

"Gal," said Easter, "dey is tryin' to work me down. W'en nighttime come, I jes' falls on de bed."

"I b'lieves you, East. Whut I wants to know is *who wid?*"

Easter had been thinking so often of Dilsie and so seldom of Annie that he looked half guilty, but Annie's laugh made him comfortable again. "East"—she was solicitous now—"you is lookin' kinda ganted, sho' nuff. Whatever you is doin', you better not do much of it as you is."

Wednesday of the next week he met Aunt Minnie Graves herself in the big road. "Easter, boy, why ain't you been to see us?"

"I's been layin' off to come, Mis' Minnie. I sho' is. I ain't forgot yo' pan an' de cloth. I washed 'em *good.*"

"I done forgot 'em myself! I don't need 'em, honey. When you gwinna come see us?"

"You-all be dare Sadday?"

"We'll be dare all day Sadday."

"Den effen I lives an' nothin' happens, I's sho' gwinna come."

Seedy though he had felt for days past, Easter did strike out for the Graveses' clearing Saturday morning. Every step he took increased his lassitude. He began to feel a shiveriness despite the June sunshine, and every fifty yards he yawned. With about half his journey done, Easter was seized with nausea. Afterward he lay on the ground on the sunny side of a log and shivered. He and malaria were old acquaintances. He lay in the sun until the dumb ague passed; afterward, when his fever mounted, he crawled into the shade and slept. It was noon when he awoke. No visiting that day. He knew he would feel comparatively well until next "chill time": the same hour tomorrow or the next day. But right now it would be well to get on up to the big house and ask Mr Henry for quinine.

For a week Easter wrestled with malaria. Mr Henry knew the malady thoroughly and fought it with broken doses of calomel and six ten-grain doses of quinine daily.

By the middle of the following week Easter reported for work. He was still a bit "ganted," but the hoe gang was busy again, and hoeing was child's play to him. Easter finished next the leader, Flint, and, resting on his hoe, turned toward the gang which was strung out for a hundred and fifty yards back along the rows. When you finish your own row it is your privilege to rest until the others "cut out"; but seemly conduct requires that you rest only a moment and then turn back and "he'p out" some slower hand. You pick a friend's row or that of some woman whose favor you seek. It is an orthodox means of sparking as well as a gesture of friendliness. Also it is a point of honor for the leader not to start ahead of the gang but give everyone an even chance to displace him each round.

Easter turned to the row next his own, without noting who carried it. As he began chopping, three other men chopped out and hastened to that same row. But Easter was ahead of them, already several yards along the row. Astonished that so many should rush to a row far from the stragglers where most of the women worked, he looked for the first time at the hand he was helping out. It was a girl . . . Dilsie Graves. For the moment Easter lost his awe of her in amazement and admiration. A gal carrying third from lead in a gang of fifty hoes!

When he and Dilsie met, the girl gave him a tiny scared smile. "Thank you," she said, and they walked back to the end together.

"How you been?" Easter ventured.

"I's been well. Dey says you been sick. I hopes you is better."

"I is," Easter mumbled.

It was well that he was better, for that was the fastest day's hoeing Easter ever put in. There were three or four of the best hands who raced him for the privilege of helping out Dilsie. He held his own and thanked his stars that the lead row was carried by Flint Winfrey, the best hoe hand in the bottoms.

"Don't let 'em git de inturn on you, East!" Flint would chuckle. "I sho' never saw so many lazy niggers hoein' dis fast befo' in my bawn days. Jes' look at 'em! Dey's kicking up dust like a cow a-runnin' in de road." Flint weighed close to three hundred. He moved his body as clumsily as an erect bear, but in his thick hands an eight-inch hoe became a rapier-like thing.

Easter had time for no more than a quick grin acknowledging Flint's banter. Nathan Grant, Dick Mickings, and others pushed him hard. Once or twice Nathan finished a stroke or two before Easter, and the latter was saved only because his place in the gang was next Dilsie's. By quartering time that afternoon Easter knew he was slipping, though his performance gave no sign of it.

"You is sweatin' too free, East," said Flint. "Hit ain't *dat* hot, boy."

"I kin hol' it."

Easter was in the grip of one of his fits of bullheaded stubbornness, and he would have hoed until he dropped. Dilsie saved him on the very next round. When they met in finishing her row she said to Easter in a rush, frightened: "You mind he'pin' out my mommer 'stead of me? It shames her so to be behin' all de time."

Thereafter Easter helped out Aunt Minnie Graves, and Nathan Grant, swiftest of the remaining rivals, got Dilsie's shy, stimulating thanks.

However much this stung Easter, there was balm in Aunt Minnie's good nature, her appreciation of his help, and her evident liking for him. He refused to consider another palliating circumstance: he would surely have "fallen out" had he kept to the racing clip.

That same afternoon he learned of another of Dilsie's accomplishments. The squad of women had begun to hum. Often an hour of this precedes actual articulate song. Finally, when even the men were leavened with harmony, one of the elder women called across to Dilsie, "Pitch it, gal!" Clear and true Dilsie's voice rose across the perfect accompaniment of their humming:

" 'Oh, Cav-a-reee! Hit's a mighty high mountain!' "

They all swung in with the mellow antiphony:

" 'Look how He died! Look how He died!' "

Then Dilsie's voice, alone as one star at nightfall:

" 'Oh, Cav-a-reee! Hit's a mighty high mountain!' "

And their response, deep from the men, wailing as Rachael's own from the women:

" 'Oh, don't you hate dem cruel, cruel Jews!' "

That carried them half down the field.

That night Easter, loose limbed with fatigue and the weakness of his convalescence, sat on his chair under the walnut tree and thought of Dilsie. The day's scenes flickered through his head: Dilsie's hand on her hoe handle; Dilsie's figure with the wind molding her skirts about her. He thought, too, of the girl's popularity with all manner of folks. He had seen men race to "he'p out" gals before . . . but these wenches were of a pattern flamingly different from Dilsie's. For the first time Easter stood Dilsie and Annie C. side by side in his mind and examined them without flinching; he realized with joyous amazement that, after just one day's association with Dilsie, it was Annie C. who was now the tenuous dream. "An' Dilsie, she got good hips an' breastes her own self," said Double-Actin'. "I wasn't stud'in' 'bout dat!" cried Easter, perhaps aloud. "H'm," grunted Double-Actin'. "Dat how come you sees 'em in yo' haid so strong now?"

There was another glorious day with the hoe gang; then a thunderstorm split open the skies to soaking rain, and work ceased. That was on Thursday. Friday morning Easter shouldered his ax and tramped across the bottoms to the Graveses' clearing. Long before he reached it the sound of three busy axes rang in his ears. Aunt Minnie had told him that Peter would be at work in the timber and that he had no one hired to help him. Easter was puzzled, chagrined, at the sound of the axes. His own purposed offer of help would depreciate if two hirelings were already employed, and the hirelings would not be pleased by it.

But he found Peter Graves's helpers were two young men with motives as high perhaps as his own: Nathan Grant and Dick Mickings. Easter had liked these boys before they had raced him in the hoe gang for Dilsie's favor. Since then he had marveled at the faults with which they suddenly bristled. Nathan was plump and aggressive and biggity. Dick smiled to himself all the time, like a possum, making everybody round him uncomfortable.

Easter saw the three men at work in the timber before he himself was seen and he came within an ace of turning back. His feet, more than his volition, carried him toward them.

"Hello, East," called Dick Mickings.

"Good mawnin', Easter," said Peter Graves.

"Whut you doin' ovah dis way?" Nathan Grant asked, pleasantly enough, but with point that stung Easter to the quick.

"I come ovah to he'p Mistuh Peter—same as you."

"He got he'p enough," said Nathan, eying the slight-built Easter less pleasantly.

"Dat fo' him to say." Easter knew Nathan could lick him, but he would hold his ground.

"We all done done 'nuff to earn a cold drink ob water," said Peter Graves. "You-all come up to de house."

The three young men shouldered their axes and followed their host to the pump.

"Dilsie!" called Peter. "Bring us out de drinkin' gourd, gal! Dis rain," he continued conversationally, "done made my turnip groun' just right to turn, but heah I is: Mistuh Keatts a-callin' fo' boards. Mistuh Mitchell a-callin' fo' two hundred posties, an'——"

Here Aunt Minnie came out with the dipper. "Mawnin', Easter. Boy, you got no business ovah heah wid no ax. You been sick."

"I's well now, Mis' Minnie."

"Dat's zackly whut I tole 'im," said Nathan Grant. "A man whut is too light fo' timber work when he is well ain't got to be tryin' it when he under de weather."

"You *is* been sick." Peter Graves turned his kind old eyes on Easter.

"I ain't gwinna have you swingin' no ax." Easter protested, begged, became nearly eloquent. Peter and Minnie were too much for him. Finally Peter said, "Effen you is *bleedged* to he'p, you kin ketch up de team an' turn ovah my turnip lan'."

Easter preferred any field work to timbering, but under the circumstances this was defeat; bitterly he hitched Peter's team to the twelve-inch turnplow. Peter and his volunteer woodsmen prepared to return to their work. Minnie Graves stood on the gallery, the gourd dipper in her hand. "Easter, boy," she called. "I'll send Dilsie down wid some fresh water fo' noon."

The turnip patch was stumpy, half-subdued new ground, but Easter never knew the day when plowing was not fun to him. Now, besides this workday satisfaction in it, he could hope for Dilsie's coming. But hours went by and she didn't come. Finally he was sure she wouldn't, and he spoke sharply to the astonished mules.

Easter stopped his team, swung them left in a right-angle turn, and started the new furrow. This brought him facing toward the house, which was invisible behind an angle of a dense thicket of second-growth ash. The mules set their ears forward and slowed up; Easter followed their gaze, knowing a mule is harder to surprise than a watchdog. "Whoa!" said he, and he stopped without knowing why. A moment later Dilsie came into view round the thicket. She wore a sunbonnet and dress of crisp blue, and she had a tin bucket in her hand.

"Don't you walk 'cross de plowed groun'," Easter called to her. "I'll come git it." He tied the lines to the plow handle, and stalked across his furrows toward Dilsie. "I ain't scairt of her no mo'," he thought. "Didn't I call out loud and tell her not to walk in de plow dirt?" "H'm," said Double-Actin'. "Dat wuz jes' part of yo' plowin' sense. Effen you ain't scairt, how come yo' heart pattin' juber?"

Easter took the tin bucket from Dilsie, and their eyes met in quick frightened acknowledgment.

"You jes' keep de bucket," said Dilsie, beginning to go away. "Effen you don't mind you kin bring it up at noon."

"Dis groun' turns *good*—after de rain," muttered Easter.

"It sho' do." Dilsie neither stopped nor continued her flight. She merely half turned, pausing like a swamp blackbird alighting on a swaying willow, wings still a-flutter. Easter's craven tongue found no further words. He watched the blue figure recede across the clearing. When it vanished behind the thicket Easter uttered an impatient oath and dashed the untasted water to the ground.

Through that summer and fall Peter Graves had no labor problem. Five or six stalwart young men placed their spare time at his command. Of these Nathan Grant, Dick Mickings, and Easter were most constant. And with the tactlessness of their kind, the old couple showed their strong partiality for Easter. The rivals must have felt it, since it was meant to be felt; Dilsie undoubtedly knew of it for the same reason. Easter sensed it, even through the wistful panics and jealousies of his condition. He could turn the advantage to no use. He worked the harder with plow, hoe and cotton sack, winning golden opinions from the old folks, while bolder blades found the opportunities for laughing words with Dilsie which he was too fearful to engineer. And along another march circumstances built a wall against him: none of his serious rivals lived on Mr Henry's plantation. If he had been thrown with them anywhere but at the Graveses' clearing, Nathan's biggitiness, Dick's possum grin, would have bred trouble, from which, since he had the lasting rage of a man of slow anger, Easter would have emerged perhaps badly beaten but with his emotions unshackled. Not even this doubtful solution was possible. The boys, for all they thought of one another, were average good field boys. They were not bloodthirsty enough to seek out one another for a quarrel, and they met only at Peter Graves's.

Through that winter Easter kept up his own work and managed to help Peter Graves lay in wood, pick cotton, and pull corn. There were beautiful days when no other suitor was there—when Dilsie, her parents, and Easter were snug round the table at noontime. Peter Graves even let Easter build up the fire; and any man who relinquishes that function in his own home expresses complete confidence in the one to whom he grants the privilege. Easter couldn't think of any person in the whole world whom he would want tampering with his own fire; not even Dilsie. God made men to build fires, and He made women to put them out. Those winter days were good days, and the clearing became home to Easter; but he got no mastery over the panic that sparkled through his soul when he and Dilsie were alone together; and in so far as he knew, he drew no step nearer to her.

April came, and there was no change, and Easter was gaunt and lean faced with protracted anxiety and ecstasy. May boomed in, with trees full leafed, the bottoms full of water and roaring with life. It seemed to Easter that folks meeting him on the road grinned a Dick Mickings grin at him. But he couldn't help it; he had lived so long with his cowardice now that he knew which was master. If Dilsie had once made him angry, slighted him, or showed marked favor for a rival, the proper mechanism within Easter might have clicked; but the girl minded her own business and dealt with her suitors with appalling equity.

One day in mid-May he met Annie C. in the big road. Neither of them smiled. Annie spoke first. "East, you gwinna wanna take me to de dance week atter next?"

"Whut dance?"

"You knows. Dey is givin' a frolic at de Tom Brown schoolhouse Thursday atter dis nex' one comin'."

"Gal, I's workin' so hard——"

"I knows whut you workin' at. Dat ain't none of my business. But I's been axed plenty fo' dis frolic——"

"Den go ahaid on! Who's a-stoppin' you?"

"Ain't nobody," said Annie musingly. "East, you ain't got much sense, but I sho' is liked you, boy, you long, rusty, no-'count black-snake!"

"Who is no 'count, gal?"

"I's done said." Annie had to smile. She could go just so long with out it. "Now git on. You'll see me at de Tom Brown schoolhouse wid some low-down mink whut ain't no better dan you is. An' me, I'll see you a-buggin' yo' eyes at Nathan Grant a-dancin' wid Dilsie Graves."

"Dilsie don't dance! She in de chu'ch."

"Well, git on down de road." Annie smiled mysteriously and walked away. "You know how long it's been gone since you been to see me, East?"

"Two-three weeks. I's been——"

"Six months, East. Effen you wuz a ol' sow, you could a-done drapped two litters ob pigs in dat time!" Screaming with laughter, Annie C. swung away. Easter felt down in himself the full gallantry of her; but there was nothing he could do about it. In five minutes he was absorbed in her news of the party and had forgotten Annie. Would Dilsie go? Would her ma and pa let her go? Could he find courage to ask her to go with him? He side-stepped that last by a craven inspiration: he would not ask Dilsie to go with him; he would ask her parents, of whom he had no fear at all.

Whether he could have carried through even that anemic campaign was in doubt until he met Elsie Lewis in the big road. He would have grumbled a greeting and trudged on, but Elsie stopped him peremptorily.

"Whar you gwine—shovin' along de road wid yo' head down, like a sow in heat? Answer me, boy!"

"Nowhar. Jes' down to George's."

"Nowhar. You is right! East, I couldn't believe it till I seed you. Now I knows you is even a bigger fool dan dey says." Elsie's lean face was kind. She tilted back her head and looked steadily at Easter with her one eye.

"East," she said briskly, "I ain't whut I wuz onct, but I knows wimmins. Now listen at me: you standin' off, an' you standin' on. But a woman want to be stood on all de time. You is he'pin' her paw, an you's he'pin' her maw. But whut you doin' 'bout Dilsie *her own self?'* Git busy, boy! Work like a red sow rustlin' overcup acrosn in deep leaves! . . . How is crops up dis way?"

They exchanged the universal shoptalk of earth. When they parted Elsie called, "Don't forgit whut I done tole you!"

Easter found George Mack sitting on his door block. The two men walked to the rear to look at the frame of seed sweet potatoes George had bedded.

"I ain't bedded me out none," said Easter. "I'll have to buy me some slips, 'gin time to set 'em out."

"You knows you can git all de slips you needs heah. You been busy crossin' de bottoms," laughed George.

"Ev'ybody I sees, dey got to talk 'bout dat same ol' subject."

"Well, don't git mad at *me,* East. Git mad at yo'self. East, is dese damn blacks like Nathan an' Dick makin' you stan' back? You scairt—or is dat gal done tamed you?"

It takes a man to lay a man's wound wide to the beginnings of healing.

"She done tamed me, George. I can't lay a finger on her. I done lost my rabbit-foot on Dilsie. All I kin do is jes' *want* her like you needs vittles at noon when you ain't et since sunup. My belly's weak right across de middle—jes' de same way."

"East," said George, "you is ridin' fo' yourself a fall effen you don't make 'ase. Too many good mens is around atter dat gal. She sho' a fine 'un too. But, East, 'tain't but one way to git any of 'em. You got to go atter 'em like guttin' a dawg."

That night Easter recalled Elsie's and George's words with the wholesome resentment recipients of good advice should feel.

"One thing"—he was near bitterness as he crawled into bed—"dey is sho' plenty folks to tell you whut to do in dis yearth. An' plenty misery." He believed that summed up and dismissed these two encounters. But back in his rational years he had regarded Elsie and George as experts. Doubtless what they had said worked deep down in him, unknown to himself.

It didn't work hard enough to pump his courage up to the point of asking Dilsie to go to the frolic with him. He put that request to Minnie and Peter. Peter promptly side-stepped, leaving the decision with Minnie.

"Dilsie *wants* to go," said Minnie; "an' two-three done axed her. I didn't want any gal of mine traipsin' round wid jes' *anybody*. But I do want her to have her pleasure. You won't make her dance, will you, East?"

"No ma'am! I sho' won't." He meant it.

"Den you kin take her."

The horrible swiftness, the dazzling sweet torture, of the days and nights which followed! Finally the revolving earth turned up that particular Thursday morning, dealt out a day of May with soft clouds and slow wind, folded the clouds and put them away at sunset, and then—night.

When they set out together through the young night and entered the path which tunneled the purple tree-shadows, Easter turned and saw Minnie Graves silhouetted against the gleam from the open cabin door, and it turned him weak; he longed to run back there, to seek the peace of which that light and Minnie's blurred figure were symbols. But life had him by the hind leg. He walked silently beside the silent girl, too afraid of the inexorable events which lay coiled in the hours ahead. Then, in crossing a foot log, he took her by the hand—for the first time; and the stark business that had laid so heavy upon Easter broke up, leavened with light. But his warmed and glowing panic was still panic, and when he spoke to Dilsie his voice was oppressed.

"Dem stars is a-winkin' like mo' rain."

"Sho' is. An' we don't need none, does we?"

"Sho' don't. We needs choppin' weather."

"Mr Henry hirin' any choppin'?"

"He ain't dis last past week." Easter was nearly at ease; agriculture was always his tutelary deity.

They came to the next foot log, and the recurrent thrill of touching Dilsie's hand swept Easter to new boldness.

"We been choppin' de lower field. It's so fur a man can't go home at noon to cook himse'f suthin' t'eat."

"Does you fix up a bucket at breakfus time?" Dilsie's own voice was stronger; here was her province.

"Naw. When my belly's full of breakfus seem like I can't bother my haid 'bout lunch—wid it so fur off."

"Umph! Dat jes' like a man!" murmured Dilsie, and then her lips seemed to freeze at her own boldness, her panic swept through herself to Easter, and they walked on in silence. Without words and with no contact Easter knew, with swelling heart, that Dilsie loved him; it made a white light of the gloom under the trees to know it; but the surging lift of this realization brought with it new fears. If he could take Dilsie in his arms he was sure the thin, strong barrier that held them apart would dissolve. But he could no more raise his two arms and put them about this girl than he could have plucked up one of the trees that made a leaky roof against the sprinkle of May stars. Each time their hands touched, whenever they were close together in the narrow path, Easter felt a warm, triumphant flood rise up inside him. And when it rose, and receded and came again, it came stronger and higher. When its heartening current flooded over, beyond his control, he could take this girl—this woman Dilsie—in his arms; but not before then. Shakily his mind compounded his vigorous strength, her slenderness, and the lonely dark into a compelling reason, a divine compulsion; but reason and experience were no helps for him with a woman like Dilsie. The rising of the tide inside him was his only hope, and it receded after each intoxicating surge.

They had traversed the woods; an open plantation road lay before them with the feel of wide fields about. Easter knew every step of the way as well as he knew the gear for his own mule, but tonight it was like walking out into a world remembered from a dream. He lifted his face to the night sky and got strength. Now he knew that the next wave of courage would sweep him out of his shackles. He wanted to sing his triumph as he walked, and he drew close to Dilsie in the path; and she seemed to shrink away, without actually moving off—while leaning closer.

They turned the angle of a dense thicket. Laughter floated through the warm air. A dim light glowed ahead. They had come to the Tom Brown schoolhouse.

It stood at the edge of the fields. It had only one room, with windows three to a side. There were two kerosene ceiling lamps, but only the one farthest from the door was lighted. The rough school benches were lined up along the walls; the tiny rostrum had been converted into a refreshment stand. From Ziek Bell the revelers could buy hard candies at ten cents a pound, a plate or sandwich of barbecued pork, coffee hot but tenuous, and lemonade mixed in a wooden tub.

Easter and Dilsie were early, and with others they sat uneasily on the benches, waiting until numbers gave them courage to be gay. In the field, at work, that faculty never failed them. Stalking fun purposefully, focusing gaiety in time and space, and going at it like laying rails require more practice than they could ever acquire. For that reason parties were oftener matters of excitement, hilarity and brawl than events of carefree pleasure. But sitting here in the dim schoolhouse, Easter could not imagine any event more exhilarating. His eyes shone; he felt his lips stiff with involuntary smiling. He felt as though he had taken three fingers of whisky.

Later, when others had arrived and noise had warmed them, when they had begun to stamp and clap rhythmically, and the more sinful felt their feet tingling, Easter saw Dick Mickings come in with Annie C. Behind them, towering above the crowd, was Nathan Grant.

The clapping and stamping settled into an even, compelling roar. Now and then a woman's voice keened an excited "E-e-e-e Yah! E-e-e-e Yah!" in time to the jungle beat of it. It was not gay—it was as deadly solemn as lust itself.

"Lemme at dat flo'!" yelled Hezekiah.

They pressed back, walling an oval opening with their heated bodies, and in this space Hezekiah capered. John Mack followed, then George, Nathan and half a dozen others. Only sinners will dance, and this being a respectable party no women joined in; but the boldest of them clapped and stamped, and when the rhythm drummed irresistible compulsion, they shouted an excited accompaniment to the clapping.

The first mechanical austerities of the dance flowed off and into the grace of primitive abandon. They leaped and whirled, they shuffled and swayed, they wiggled out the full repertory of sound, earthy obscenities, interpreting that universal essence of rhythm as it has shaken the cypresses of Mylitta's groves and the spotted canvas of revival tents. Easter did not dance; he was too clumsy, and tonight he would have been too self-conscious. He clapped and stamped with glowing eyes. Sweat stood on his forehead. The women shrieked their high-pitched triple "E-e-e-e Yah!" and the schoolhouse quivered. Ziek Bell suddenly struck the bottom of a dishpan with his huge iron spoon.

"Time t'eat! Time t'eat!" he bawled.

The dancers stood, the clapping died a fluttering death like the stopping of a furious machine, the crowd broke, and the first gay shouts and genuine laughter of the evening swept through it.

Ziek Bell's hospitality was mercenary but hearty. Opulent couples crowded up to his table. Thoughtful men fingered through their jumper pockets under the intent, encouraging smiles of their womenfolk.

Easter led Dilsie to Ziek Bell's table as soon as he had located the errant six bits among his pockets. Dilsie would have taken only coffee, but Easter pressed a sandwich and lemonade upon her; he also bought a bag of hard candy for them to eat on the way home. The other women greeted Dilsie pleasantly—until their men began offering to buy things for her.

"I's buyin' fo' Dilsie," Easter stated boldly, and they desisted. The code was simple and plain. But this was a challenge Easter's rivals could not ignore completely.

"I b'lieves I'll take Dilsie home my ownself," said Nathan Grant genially. "I kin jes' tuck her under one arm an' East under de yuther."

"You can't make no crop wid one arm," retorted John Mack loyally; "an' you'd be sho' to git *one* of 'em gnawed off."

When the laughter eased up, Dick Mickings said, smiling his dead-possum smile, "Whut effen Brother Nathan an' me double-teams an' *bofe* takes her home? Would he gnaw us bofe, Brother Johnnie?"

"Naw! East is got good toofs, but dey couldn't stan' up to dat."

The crowd howled, Nathan and Dick with the rest. They were fairly routed; they knew, besides, that Easter was fully backed by his friends and by the approval of Dilsie's parents.

"Tell you whut us *kin* do!" cried George Mack. "All de mens heah kin make a congregation an' walk home wid Dilsie an' East—t'keep de snakes off."

"Sho'!" they shouted, and John added good-naturedly, "East, he kinda timid anyhow."

"It ain't only snakes he's scairt of—round wimmins," laughed Hezekiah Jones.

Easter's lips rolled out and his eyes blazed. The jest had been harmless in the hands of his two rivals. It was rapidly becoming fatal now that his friends had taken it up: there were so many of them.

"Hot dawg! Dats de thing!" said Hezekiah. "East can't do nuthin' wid *all* of us!" As the effects registered on Easter the others increased their efforts. George Mack silenced them to explain more fully the perfections of the scheme. "Effen jes' *some* of us tries it, East mout kill us dead. But effen *all* of us——"

They cut him short with shouts of acquiescence. The party had focus now, and a butt whom everyone liked and nobody feared. The ring formed again, the dance thundered into full fury. But now it was lightsome. The dancers would shout, "Who gwinna take her home, Lawd, who gwinna take her home?" And the triple response came spontaneously, shouted to the accompaniment of redoubled clapping and stamping: "*I* is! *I* is! *I* is!"

Easter looked at Dilsie. She was frightened and she tried to smile back at him. Suddenly a red wave inside Easter rose up behind his eyeballs, and he turned and plowed his way to the door.

The old Tom Brown house which had stood a hundred yards from the school, had been destroyed by fire years before. Easter knew he could find brickbats on the house site and he steered for the weedy ruins like a serpent for its hole. Where the old blacksmith had stood he saw the spread fingers of a ruined wagon wheel. The tire and felloe were gone. He laid hold of one of the spokes and wrenched it from its mortise in the hub. The spoke was sound oak, twenty inches long, tapered, and had the perfect balance of a war mace. It could crack a man's skull like a walnut, but it was as handy as a rapier.

Without haste, because the full flavor of his dish of martyrdom lay before him with no check and hindrance of sanity, Easter turned and stalked back toward the lighted door.

"Whut you up to, East?" demanded a voice at his shoulder.

"Watch an' see."

"Wait, East!" Easter had not even recognized George Mack.

"I ain't waitin'!"

"Stop, you damn fool,—listen! I wants t'help you."

"Don't need none."

"You'l git kilt fo' nuthin'! Some of dem boys is got guns on 'em."

"I'll gun 'em!"

George sprang from behind and pinned Easter's arms to his sides. "I wants to *he'p* you, you mule-headed fool! Listen . . ."

They wrestled, and despite George's advantage of hold and greater strength, Easter's madness would have prevailed if George had not pleaded and cursed.

"I wants to he'p! Listen, East, I knows how we kin do it!"

"Talk in a hurry den."

Easter rested, panting. George did not relax his grip. "East, effen you starts a rookus dey'll lay you out——"

"I don't care!"

"—an' effen dey don't, somebody 'll pull a knife or a gun——"

"I don't care!"

"You *will* care—wid a bullet in yo' guts! Lemme tell you whut us kin do——"

"I ain't gwinna leave. I's gwinna——"

"All right! All right, boy! But listen at me *fust."*

"Talk fast, George."

"I's got my gun on me. You stan' by de do'. I'll shoot out de light through one of dem back windows. Dese damn blacks'll run. I knows 'em! Dey'll run. You stan' at de do'. 'Tain't but one do', an' de windows is nailed shut. When dey comes out——"

"Come on!"

"Wait!" George released Easter now, sure of him. "Be sho' you lays yo' mark on all de men—not 'scusin' Nathan an' Dick."

"Come on!"

"Wait, fool! Now listen at me *good*; effen you jes' scares a nigger or jes' lashes him, he mout bust you from behin' a bush someday. But effen you makes yo' mark on him wid suthin' like a wagon spoke, he know who de boss is. Now git to de do'. Don't show yourself till dey starts out. Dey'll run! I knows dese damn blacks."

George vanished and Easter moved to the door. He spat generously into his palm and sunk his fingers into the wagon spoke.

Almost at once George fired through the rear window nearest the lamp, and the party exploded with the noise and velocity of shrapnel. It took the third shot to fetch the lamp and bring it crashing down. By that time the door was vomiting a screaming tangle of bodies, and Easter's right arm rose and fell with mechanical regularity.

Now and again he recognized a friend or a woman in the struggling mass and tried to hold his hand with an effort that nearly stood him on his head. Mercy was impossible; too many got by unmarked. He abandoned discrimination and went to work with grim thoroughness. Even when the frame of the glutted door fell down among them he missed no lick, and the clear crack of oak on skull beat on. Five or six lay on the ground, heaped up. Those inside dived over the rampart of bodies. While fresh victims still fell, some of the first revived enough to stagger up, and these followed the impulse to run which had been interrupted by Easter's wagon spoke. When the supply slackened, George's pistol roared again, and stragglers who had huddled inside plunged out, often cheating Easter by tripping on the wrecked doorframe and stunning themselves on the ground.

Finally after a quick eternity of bliss Easter found no fugitives under his club. The last of the fallen had made off. George's pistol shots could evict no more. Only the shrieks of the women responded. They had not run with the men. Easter could see them in his mind's eye: a pile of them, hugging one another, burrowing under one another's bodies, kicking and scratching to crawl under, to put bodies between their own bodies and the terror—like a clot of lively fishing worms in a tin can.

George came to the door. "Heah—dese is matches. Go in an' git her."

Easter snatched the matches. He was already going in.

He dropped the wagon spoke and cupped his hands round a lighted match. The women had crammed themselves under benches and in corners. A dozen were stuffed like tattered, shameless rag dolls under the teacher's table on the little rostrum. Their struggles had spilled Ziek Bell's edibles over the floor. Wild eyes caught the gleam of Easter's match.

"I wants Dilsie!" Easter called. His match flared and died, and while he lighted another he wondered how he could ever have been afraid of that girl. "Dilsie!" he called, and the next match blazed up.

"I's comin'," she quavered.

Easter blew out his match. He did not wish to see her untangle herself from the mass of frightened flesh. He walked to the door and stood just outside in the starlight. When the girl came out to him he curved his right arm round her shoulders and led her through the fields toward the level shadow that marked the edge of the woods.

"My first wife," said Easter, "lemme go hongry in de field. Whut you think of a woman like dat?"

"She ain't hardly no woman—she jes' a mess!"

"Effen a man make de money an' bring home de rations of a Sadday, he got a right to find cooked grub in de house, come time t'eat."

"He sho' is."

"An'—Dilsie"—Easter made the name precious in the saying—"I wants me some chullens."

"Don't—don't *ev'ybody* want 'em, Easter?"

It was enough now to walk under the trees side by side. When they came to the edge of the Graveses' clearing, Easter drew Dilsie off the path toward a new, clean log. "Not *on* it!" he breathed when, half hesitating, she sat down upon it. "We kin sit on de groun' an' lean our backs again' de log." He drew her down beside him on the short grass, which was cool with dew.

The stars had steadied to the unshaken air of deep night, and quiet lay on the wide bottom lands. A cock crowed, and the sound came to them as strained silver through the miles of sweet air.

"Don't!—not t'night, Easter!" Dilsie murmured, but she clung the closer as his arms, suddenly harsh and hurried with his long hunger for her, bent her down.

MICHIGAN

This Town and Salamanca

ALLAN SEAGER

So when he returned, we asked him why had he gone to live there and he said he'd just heard of it and thought it might be a nice place to live in for a while. He had lived in an old house built around a court. The walls were four feet thick and the windows were larger on the inside than they were on the outside; the sills slanted. They kept goats' milk there on the window-sills because the stone made the air cool. You could see the sticks of a hawk's nest hanging over one corner of the roof, and Jesus the landlady's son—he looked up here to see if we thought it was funny that a man should be named Jesus, but none of us said anything. We read a great deal—he often whistled to it evenings. Yes, the food was good. They had a sausage with tomatoes in it that was very good and the wine was not like French wine, it was heavier and sweeter. And there were no fireplaces for heating but things they called braseros. They were big pans like that with his arms stretched and on cold mornings they set it alight and covered the flame with ashes. They would put the brasero under a big table. The table had a sort of plush cover to it that hung down to the floor with slits in it. You put your feet through the slits and wrapped the cover around your waist. Then although your feet roasted, you could still see your breath and you couldn't stay in the room long because of the fumes, and sitting by the brasero gave you chilblains but they were a common thing and no one minded. Klug asked him about the women. Were they—you know? The women were all right he said. The peasant girls were very pretty but they faded early and got fat. Yes, but, Klug said impatiently, but he was talking then about the riots, how they used beer bottles full of black powder for bombs and when they bombed the convent, the nuns all ran out crying and waving their arms after the explosion and some fell on their knees and prayed in the midst of the rioters but the bomb had not even chipped the wall, it was four feet thick. All the houses were like that with big thick walls and the streets were narrow and the town was quiet. They could not hang the washing in the courtyards because it was too cool for it to dry, so they spread it on rocks beside the river when they finished. It was a very old town and they lived in the same way year after year. Gordon asked him about the spiritual remnants of medievalism. He answered that the people were very pious and went to the cathedral to pray for everything, even lost articles. The cathedral had small windows and the light was yellow inside not like the gray light inside the cathedrals in Ile de France.

Well, I thought, as they talked on into the evening, it is not anything like that here. You see I remember this particular evening very clearly and all that we said, because it was the last time John had anything new to tell us, and from that time on, he has lived here with us in this town. We never thought he would settle here. It is a good enough town but nothing to the places he has seen, not even the kind of place you would close your book to watch if you went through on the train. First there are the ball-bearing factory and the electric bell factory, with the other factories hidden behind them; then there are trees hiding the houses with their backs turned toward you and vegetable gardens beside the tracks; and then you would see the spire, not of a cathedral, but of the Methodist church, and the town would soon dwindle away into the cornfields and just after that you could look at your watch to see how long before Chicago. It is not like Salamanca, but the four of us were born and grew up here and only John had gone away. And when he came home to see his mother, he would tell us these things that made us seem fools to ourselves for having stayed but we were busy with our work and could not follow him. There are maple trees on both sides of the streets and in summer it is like driving through a tunnel of green leaves.

You see he never answered Gordon's intelligent questions and he always disappointed Klug who thinks that all the women in foreign countries wait on street corners after dark winking and motioning yonder with their heads. John seldom was an actor in his own play—he merely looked, it seemed, and told us what he saw. It was the best way, keeping himself out, but they would not admit it, so they kept on with the questions. They admitted it to themselves though. Klug said he thought of the peasant girls with their ankles shining under their tucked-up skirts doing the washing by the river bank when he was scrubbing his hands after taking the cancer out of Mrs. Gira, the Polish washwoman, and the nurse was counting the used wet sponges and the hospital smell made his stomach turn. And when the aldermen brought the plans of the new railroad station to Gordon and sat down to talk and object for hours, he saw the smoke drifting from where the bomb exploded and the nuns praying in the confusion and one of the aldermen had spots on his waistcoat that he kept picking at. Though we had nothing but questions when he came, we all knew that the questions were merely little signs to show that we too might very well have been there and seen these things, and that it was nothing more important than chance that we had stayed here. He talked late and I remember there was a bat lurching to and fro under a light down the street.

Mrs. Gira got well though and it is a fine new railroad station.

II

He was in an old boat-house whistling. We heard him when we came down the path. The boat-house was so old the shingles curled and weeds grew on the roof, and we used to tell him that some day the whole thing would give way with him in it and he would have to swim out with the rafters round his neck. He had borrowed the use of it from Old Man Suggs who hadn't kept a boat in years. When we were kids I remember seeing it when we went to the river-flats to look for dog-tooth violets. It was a motor launch and he sold it when the tomato cannery started up. Every summer the river is full of blobs of red tomato pulp and no one wants to go out in a boat then. But John was building a sail boat. It was May then and he had worked all his spare time on it since the August before; every Saturday afternoon, and nights after supper he would go down and work by the light of three oil lamps he got from his mother. That was the winter we played so much poker and sometimes we would go to the boat-house at midnight and ask John to take a hand. He was always pleasant about it, without any scruples against gambling, but he never stopped working and we would shout above the hammer blows, "Where do you think you're going in this boat when it's finished? Going to haul tomatoes for the cannery?" He would laugh and say that a good many waters would wet this hull before she was much older. We would laugh because we knew he had got the phrase out of some book, and we would start up the path. The ripples on the water always shone in the lamplight and we could hear this hammer as far as the dirt road where we turned to Klug's house. Often we played till midnight. I won a lot of money that winter.

When we entered the boat-house we could see it was nearly finished. It looked very big and white and seemed not too much to have put a winter's work into. He was planing some teak for the deck, and when we came near there was the acrid leathery odor of the fresh shavings. We had seen pictures of yachts, and once or twice the ore boats on the big lakes, but the things we saw every day, the houses, trees and grain elevators, went straight up from the ground. They had roots. If they had not, as they seemed, been always in one place, they always would be. John's boat was a strange shape, curved for the water. Even in the dim boat-house, propped up with blocks, she seemed ready for movement. I looked at John with the handle of the plane easy in his hand, a carpenter's tool, and we were going to be "professional" men, and I knew he would go away. The boat had sprung from some matrix within him that we would never understand, just as he was puzzled when Gordon asked him how long she was and how many tons weight as if she were a heifer fattened for market. When we went out of the boat-house, Klug said, "So long, skipper."

He went away in the boat as I had thought he would and after this he never came back for long at a time. God knows how he got the blocks from under her without any help, but one afternoon he launched her all by himself, and in ten days he had her rigged and the galley full of stores. He sailed away without saying anything to anyone, down our little river into the Ohio and then into the Mississippi and out into the Gulf below New Orleans. He was gone all summer into October. I saw him on the street when he returned. He was tanned almost black. We shook hands and I said:

"Where did you go? Did you have a good trip?"

He looked at me a moment before answering. "Trip" means a journey you take in a car during your two-weeks' vacation in the summer, maybe to Yellowstone or the Grand Canyon or Niagara. It is a relaxation from your work. I could see as I said it that "trip" was the wrong word, but just how far wrong, it took me years to find out and then I never was certain. I thought of his boat, a strange and unfamiliar shape, and how he, whom we had seen unsuspectingly every day through his boyhood, had made it.

"Yes, I had a good time."

"Where did you go?"

"Well, down into the Gulf and around."

"Cuba?"

"Yes, I put in at Havana," and then as if he had at last found something he could tell me, "you know, Klug would like that place—they've got a park there where you can get free beer. It's owned by a brewing company and you can go there and drink all you want, free."

"Where else did you go?"

"Oh, the Tortugas, Hayti, Vera Cruz."

He showed me a gold piece he had got off a pawnbroker in Port-au-Prince. He said it was a moidore. He was nineteen then.

III

When he returned next time, he was less reticent. It was not because he was proud of being a traveler but more, I think, that he saw we really wanted to hear about the distant places he had been. When his boat was coming into the harbor of Singapore, he said you could see the junks waiting with their crinkled sails. And when the ship came near, they sailed right in front of the bow as close as they could. Sometimes they didn't make it and they all smashed up and drowned. He said they did it to cut off the devils following behind. The day after he told us that Gordon asked Tom Sing, who runs the chop suey joint, if he believed in devils but Tom only grinned. Gordon said it was the oriental inscrutability. Gordon is quite serious.

During the next ten years John did all the things we said we'd do that time in the apple orchard. He joined the army to fly and left the army after a time and went to Italy. I went to his house from the office the day he got home. He was dressed in white, lunging at himself in a long mirror with a foil in his hand. The French held their foils this way with the thumb so, but the Italians that way. After that he was a sailor on one of the crack clippers that still bring the wheat up from Australia, and from Liverpool I had a postcard with a picture of Aintree race-course on the back. It said, "Give Gordon my congratulations." Gordon had been elected mayor and we were very proud of him. How John heard of it we couldn't figure out.

One time there was a card from Aden and another from Helsingfors.

You can see he traveled. No one in the town had ever gone so far and people used to stop his mother on the street to ask where he was then, not that they really cared but because the thread that tied them to him as a local boy tied them also to the strange name his mother answered when they asked.

When he was a sailor in the Pacific, spinal meningitis broke out on board. Eighteen people died and they put the bodies down in the hold. The ship's doctor examined all the crew and said John was the healthiest and the captain ordered him to go below and sew up the bodies in shrouds and heave them overboard.

John got a roll of canvas, a reel of pack-thread, a leather palmguard and a needle and went down into the hold. He rigged up an electric light in a wire cage and swung it from a hook over his head. The eighteen lay there in a row. They were quite stiff, and when the ship rolled, sometimes an arm would come up and pause until the ship rolled back. But they were in the shadow and he did not watch them much because the sewing was hard work about an hour to each one. He jabbed his finger with the needle three or four times and that made it harder. When he got one ready, he would put it over his shoulder and stagger up the companionway to the deck.

High up above him beside the funnel, to escape the risk of infection, stood an Anglican parson, one of the passengers. He had an open prayer book and said the service very quickly, the leaves fluttering in the wind. Then John would pick up the corpse again and heave it over the side. Sometimes a shark ripped the shroud almost as it hit the water; others he could see jerked from the ring of foam of their impact and carried quickly below. There were at least a dozen sharks and John said he knew his work was useless and he took bigger and bigger stitches in the canvas. There was quite a wind and John could never hear the whole service because the wind blew the words away but a few snatches would come down to him. He and the parson were all alone, the other people having hidden from fear; and they did not speak to each other. When John brought up the last corpse, it had been a Portuguese merchant from Manila on his way to Goa to see his daughter, the wind stopped suddenly and there was a moment of calm. ". . . to the deep to be turned into corruption," the parson said. John picked up the merchant, balanced him on the rail and shoved him over and the sharks came.

IV

"And Eloise said it was when she was getting the coffee after dinner. Mr. and Mrs. Booth were setting in the parlor and Mr. Booth was drinking brandy like he always does and both of them quiet as mutes at a funeral when all at once the door bell rang and Eloise answered it and there stood John Baldwin. My, I think he's handsome. Oh, he's much better looking than him. And he asked could he see Mr. Booth and Eloise said he could; he was right in the parlor. So Mr. Baldwin come in but he wouldn't give Eloise his hat. He kept it and said he was only staying a minute. Well Eloise said she went to the kitchen to get another cup naturally expecting Mr. Baldwin would have some coffee and when she come back through the dining-room she was so surprised she nearly dropped it.

"She said Mr. Baldwin was standing right in front of Mr. Booth and he says, 'Dennis, I've come for your wife.' Just like that. And Mr. Booth says, 'What do you mean—you've come for my wife?' Eloise said she got behind the window drapes so they wouldn't see her and Mr. Baldwin says, 'Frances loves me. I want you to divorce her.' Mr. Booth was drunk on all that brandy and he jumped up and began to shout that it was damned cool and a lot of things about throwing Mr. Baldwin out of the house only Eloise don't think for a minute he could have even if he was sober. Why, John Baldwin's way over six feet and a sailor and always fighting with them little swords and all, but Mr. Booth got white, he was so mad, and Mrs. Booth she didn't say anything. She just sat there and looked at them and Eloise said it was like Mr. Baldwin didn't hear a word Mr. Booth said because he was looking at Mrs. Booth all the time and when Mr. Booth stopped talking Mr. Baldwin looked up at him quick like you do when a clock stops. Then he just says, 'Well, Dennis,' and Mr. Booth began to swear something terrible but he didn't try to throw him out, he didn't even come close to him. Then Mr. Baldwin looked at Mrs. Booth and smiled and says, 'Come along, Frances,' and Mrs. Booth smiled back and they walked right out of the house without her even packing any clothes. And that's all there was to it. Eloise says Mrs. Booth walked right out of her house into a new life, never to return. And Mrs. Booth they say has gone to Paris to get a divorce from Mr. Booth. Well, all I got to say is, it serves him right—he was always running around after them dirty little factory girls. Certainly he was. Everybody knows it. Why you know that little Muller girl, the one with the fox fur. Why Eloise says that. . . ."

I stopped listening then. I always liked to look even at the Italian flags on bottles of olive oil when I was a kid. I had the same feeling then: no one does things like that here, walking into a man's house and taking his wife. If you want a man's wife, you meet her by chance in Chicago and she goes on being his wife afterwards. Or maybe it was like the boat. We hadn't lived with him. He was only the things he had done and those at a distance. Now that he had begun his marriage this way I did not think he would change the pattern, but that was before I knew he intended to settle here.

He was, I thought then, rootless and invincible. He didn't seem to want what we had, what we had remained here and worked for. Which comes down to this, I suppose, and little more: the same trees every day when you go to work, in summer hanging over the lawns beside the walks, and bare with snow at the forks of the limbs and the sound of snow shovels scraping the walks; and when you look up, the line of the roof of the house next door against the sky. You could call it peace. It is just peace with no brilliance. I remembered how bright the gold piece was in his hand.

But he didn't go away again. He settled here very quietly and took a nice little house. He and Frances were very happy, and we all used to say how glad we were that they were so happy. We used to say it very loudly to ourselves and sometimes to him, and we put ourselves out to help him meet people. He had been away so long that he had forgot or never had known them. We got him into the golf club the first week he was in the bank. Everything we could show him about the town we did gladly.

After he had been married a year, we all came to Gordon's one night to drink beer. Most of the evening we taught John poker, and after that we just sat around and talked. John said:

"You know Roy Curtis from out Fruit Ridge way? Well, he came in today and wanted to borrow ten thousand dollars to buy another hundred acres. That piece there by the bridge. Belongs to Dick Sheppard."

"He'll raise wheat. There's no money in wheat now," we said.

"That's what I told him, but he wants to have a shot at it just the same. He offered a second mortgage. I don't know though. What do you think?"

We told him that Roy Curtis was a fool if he thought he could make money in wheat at fifty-six cents a bushel.

"He's got a combine you know. He says he'll have five hundred acres in wheat, and he and his boy can work it all by themselves."

We remembered when he'd bought the combine. Five hundred acres is too small for a combine. This isn't Dakota.

"You wouldn't lend him the money, then? He's coming in Thursday. It's good security, a second mortgage on his place."

We told him that we wouldn't lend the money, but John had drunk a lot of beer. He kept on talking about it.

"He's a smart farmer, Roy. Look at that house he's got there. It's a fine place, as good as any of these here in town. Got a Packard and a big radio. Why, he said he got Rome on that radio the other night. He didn't make his money doing foolish things. I don't know about the loan."

Roy's aunt had left him money, but that was while John was away. We didn't tell him. I said:

"Do you fence any now, John?"

He got up laughing and went out into the hall and got a mashie out of Gordon's golf bag and came in with it. He began standing with a bent leg and one hand flung up behind him. He went through the lunges and parries laughing.

"Getting fat," he said, "I can't do 'em any more."

I had to leave then because I had to be at the office early next day. John was still talking about the loan when I left. It had been raining and the wind had blown down leaves from the maples. The evening had been unsatisfactory and I thought about it as I walked along. I was in sight of my house before I thought why, and I stopped to pick off the red leaves stuck to my shoes.

I remembered him in white with his face grave. "You see, the French hold a foil this way. It's not like the Italians. I learned in Marseilles." That was the way he used to talk. We knew all about loans; we knew all about him now. Of course I could never do more than just remind him of these things because he was so happy. But I did not think he would ever go away again to return and tell us these things, because of his happiness. Suddenly I felt old. It was as if we had trusted him to keep our youth for us and he had let it go. But our youth only.

FLORIDA

Benny and the Bird-Dogs

MARJORIE KINNAN RAWLINGS

You can't change a man, no-ways. By the time his mammy turns him loose and he takes up with some innocent woman and marries her, he's what he is. If it's his nature to set by the hearthfire and scratch hisself, you just as good to let him set and scratch. If it's his nature, like Will Dover, my man, to go to the garage in his Sunday clothes and lay down under some backwoods Cracker's old greasy Ford and tinker with it, you just as good to let him lay and tinker. And if it's his nature to cut the fool, why, it's interfering in the ways of Providence even to stop to quarrel with him about it. Some women is born knowing that. Sometimes a woman, like the Old Hen (Uncle Benny's wife, poor soul!), has to quarrel a lifetime before she learns it. Then when it does come to her, she's like a cow has tried to jump a high fence and has got hung up on it—she's hornswoggled.

The Old Hen's a mighty fine woman—one of the finest I know. She looks just the way she did when she married Uncle Benny Mathers thirty years ago, except her hair has turned gray, like the feathers on a Gray Hackle game hen. She's plump and pretty and kind of pale from thirty years' fretting about Uncle Benny. She had a disposition, by nature, as sweet as a new cane syrup. When she settled down for a lifetime's quarrelling at him, it was for the same reason syrup sours—the heat had just been put to her too long.

I can't remember a time when the Old Hen wasn't quarrelling at Uncle Benny. It begun a week after they was married. He went off prowling by hisself, to a frolic or such as that, and didn't come home until four o'clock in the morning. She was setting up waiting for him. When she crawled him about it, he said, 'Bless Katy, wife, let's sleep now and quarrel in the morning.' So she quarrelled in the morning and just kept it up. For thirty years. Not for meanness—she just kept hoping she could change him.

Change him? When he had takened notice of the way she was fussing and clucking and ruffing her feathers, he quit calling her by her given name and begun calling her the Old Hen. That's all I could ever see she changed him.

Uncle Benny's a sight. He's been constable here at Oak Bluff, Florida, for twenty years. We figure it keeps him out of worse trouble to let him be constable. He's the quickest shot in three counties and the colored folks is all as superstitious of him as if he was the devil hisself. He's a comical-appearing somebody. He's small and quick and he don't move—he prances. He has a little bald sun-tanned head with a rim of white hair around the back of it. Where the hair ends at the sides of his head, it sticks straight up over his ears in two little white tufts like goat horns. He's got bright blue eyes that look at you quick and wicked, the way a goat looks. That's exactly what he looks and acts like—a mischievous little old billy-goat. And he's been popping up under folks' noses and playing tricks on them as long as Oak Bluff has knowed him. Doc in particular. He loved to torment Doc.

And stay home? Uncle Benny don't know what it is to stay home. The Old Hen'll cook hot dinner for him and he won't come. She'll start another fire in the range and warm it up for him about dusk-dark and he won't come. She'll set up till midnight, times till daybreak, and maybe just about the time the east lightens and the birds gets to whistling good, he'll come home. Where's he been? He's been with somebody 'gatoring, or with somebody catching crabs to Salt Springs; he's been to a square-dance twenty miles away in the flat-woods; he's been on the highway in that Ford car, just rambling as long as his gas held out—and them seven pieded bird-dogs setting up in the back keeping him company.

It was seven years ago, during the Boom, that he bought the Model-T and begun collecting bird-dogs. Everybody in Florida was rich for a while, selling gopher holes to the Yankees. Now putting an automobile under Uncle Benny was like putting wings on a wild-cat—it just opened up new territory. Instead of rambling over one county, he could ramble over ten. And the way he drove—like a bat out of Torment. He's one of them men just loves to cover ground. And that car and all them bird-dogs worked on the Old Hen like a quart of gasoline on a campfire. She really went to raring. I tried to tell her then 'twasn't no use to pay him no mind, but she wouldn't listen.

I said, 'It's just his nature. You can' do a thing about it but take it for your share and go on. You and Uncle Benny is just made different. You want him home and he don't want to be home. You're a barnyard fowl and he's a wild fowl.'

'Mis' Dover,' she said, 'it's easy for you to talk. Your man runs a garage and comes home nights. You don't know how terrible it is to have a man that prowls.'

I said, 'Leave him prowl.'

She said, 'Yes, but when he's on the prowl, I don't know no more where to look for him than somebody's tom-cat.'

I said, 'If 'twas me, I wouldn't look for him.'

She said, 'Moonlight nights he's the worst. Just like the varmints.'

I said, 'Don't that tell you nothing?'

She said, 'If he'd content hisself with prowling—but he ain't content until he cuts the fool. He takes that Ford car and them seven bird-dogs and maybe a pint of moonshine, and maybe picks up Doc to prowl with him, and he don't rest until he's done something crazy. What I keep figuring is, he'll kill hisself in that Ford car, cutting the fool.'

I said, 'You don't need to fret about him and that Ford. What's unnatural for one man is plumb natural for another. And cutting the fool is so natural for Uncle Benny, it's like a bird in the air or a fish in water—there won't no harm come to him from it.'

She said, 'Mis' Dover, what the devil throws over his back has got to come down under his belly.'

I said, 'Uncle Benny Mathers is beyond rules and sayings. I know men-folks, and if you'll listen to me, you'll settle down and quit quarrelling and leave him go his way in quiet.'

I happened to be in on it this spring, the last time the Old Hen ever quarrelled at Uncle Benny. Me and Doc was both in on it. It was the day of old lady Weller's burying. Doc carried me in his car to the cemetery. My Will couldn't leave the garage, because the trucks hauling the Florida oranges north was bringing in pretty good business. Doc felt obliged to go to the burying. He's a patent-medicine salesman—a big fat fellow with a red face and yellow hair. He sells the Little Giant line of remedies. Old lady Weller had been one of his best customers.

She'd taken no nourishment the last week of her life except them remedies, and Doc figured he ought to pay her the proper respect and show everybody he was a man was always grateful to his customers.

Uncle Benny and the Old Hen went to the burying in the Model-T. And the seven bird-dogs went, setting up in the back seat. They always went to the buryings.

Uncle Benny said, 'Walls nor chains won't hold 'em. Better to have 'em go along riding decent and quiet, than to bust loose and foller the Model-T like a daggone pack of bloodhounds.'

That was true enough. Those bird-dogs could hear that old Ford crank up and go off in low gear, clear across the town. They'd always hope it was time to go bird-hunting again, and here they'd come, trailing it. So there were the bird-dogs riding along to old lady Weller's burying, with their ears flopping and their noses in the air for quail. As constable, Uncle Benny sort of represented the town, and he was right in behind the hearse. I mean, that car was a pain, to be part of a funeral procession. In the seven years he'd had it, he'd all but drove it to pieces, and it looked like a rusty, mangy razor-back hog. The hood was thin and narrow, like a shoat's nose—you remember the way all Model-T Fords were built. It had no top to it, nor no doors to the front seat, and the back seat rose up in a hump where the bird-dogs had squeezed the excelsior chitlin's out of it.

The Old Hen sat up stiff and proud, not letting on she minded. Doc and I figured she'd been quarrelling at Uncle Benny about the bird-dogs, because when one of them put his paws on her shoulders and begun licking around her ears, she turned and smacked the breath out of him.

The funeral procession had just left the Oak Bluff dirt road and turned onto No. 9 Highway, when the garage-keeper at the bend ran out.

He hollered, 'I just got a 'phone call for Uncle Benny Mathers from the high sheriff!'

So Uncle Benny cut out of the procession and drove over to the pay station by the kerosene tank to take the message. He caught up again in a minute and called to Doc, 'A drunken nigger is headed this way in a Chevrolet and the sheriff wants I should stop him.'

About that time here come the Chevrolet and started to pass the procession, wobbling back and forth as if it had the blind staggers. You may well know the nigger was drunk or he wouldn't have passed a funeral. Uncle Benny cut out of line and took out after him. When he saw who was chasing him, the nigger turned around and headed back the way he'd come from. Uncle Benny was gaining on him when they passed the hearse. The bird-dogs begun to take an interest and rared up, barking. What does Uncle Benny do but go to the side of the Chevrolet so the nigger turns around—and then Uncle Benny crowded him so all he could do was to shoot into line in the funeral procession. Uncle Benny cut right in after him and the nigger shot out of the line and Uncle Benny crowded him in again.

I'll declare, I was glad old lady Weller wasn't alive to see it. She'd had no use for Uncle Benny, she'd hated a nigger, and she'd despised dogs so to where she kept a shotgun by her door to shoot at them if one so much as crossed her cornfield. And here on the way to her burying where you'd figure she was entitled to have things the way she liked them, here was Uncle Benny chasing a nigger in and out of line, and seven bird-dogs were going Ki-yippity-yi! Ki-yippity-yi! Ki-yippity-yi! I was mighty proud the corpse was no kin to me.

The Old Hen was plumb mortified. She put her hands over her face and when the Ford would swerve by or cut in ahead of us, Doc and me could see her swaying back and forth and suffering. I don't scarcely need to say Uncle Benny was enjoying hisself. If he'd looked sorrowful-like, as if he was just doing his duty, you could of forgive him. Near a filling-station the Chevrolet shot ahead and stopped and the nigger jumped out and started to run. Uncle Benny stopped and climbed out of the Ford and drew his pistol and called 'Stop!' The nigger kept on going.

Now Uncle Benny claims that shooting at niggers in the line of duty is what keeps him in practice for bird-shooting. He dropped a ball to the right of the nigger's heel and he dropped a ball to the left of it. He called 'Stop!' and the nigger kept on going. Then Uncle Benny took his pistol in both hands and took a slow aim and he laid the third ball against the nigger's shin-bone. He dropped like a string-halted mule.

Uncle Benny said to the man that ran the filling-station, 'Get your gun. That there nigger is under arrest and I deputize you to keep him that-a-way. The sheriff'll be along to pick him up direckly.'

He cut back into the funeral procession between us and the hearse, and we could tell by them wicked blue eyes he didn't know when he'd enjoyed a burying like the old lady Weller's. When we got back from the burying, he stopped by Will's garage. The Old Hen was giving him down-the-country.

She said, 'That was the most scandalous thing I've ever knowed you to do, chasing that nigger in and out of Mis' Weller's funeral.'

Uncle Benny's eyes begun to dance and he said, 'I know it, wife, but I couldn't help it. 'Twasn't me done the chasing—it was the Model-T.'

Doc got into it then and sided with the Old Hen. He gets excited, the way fat men do, and he swelled up like a spreading adder.

'Benny,' he said, 'you shock my modesty. This ain't no occasion for laughing nor lying.'

Uncle Benny said, 'I know it, Doc. I wouldn't think of laughing nor lying. You didn't know I've got that Ford trained, I've got it trained to where it'll do two things. It's helped me chase so many niggers, I've got it to where it just naturally takes out after 'em by itself.'

Doc got red in the face and asked, real sarcastic, 'And what's the other piece of training?'

Uncle Benny said, 'Doc, that Ford has carried me home drunk so many times, I've got it trained to where it'll take care of me and carry me home safe when I ain't fitten.'

Doc spit half-way across the road and he said, 'You lying old jay-bird.'

Uncle Benny said, 'Doc, I've got a pint of moonshine, and if you'll come go camping with me to Salt Springs this evening, I'll prove it.'

The Old Hen spoke up and she said, 'Benny, Heaven forgive you for I won't if you go on the prowl again before you've cleared the weeds out of my old pindar field. I'm a month late now, getting it planted.'

Doc loves Salt Springs crab and mullet as good as Uncle Benny does, and I could see he was tempted.

But he said, 'Benny, you go along home and do what your wife wants, and when you're done—when she says you're done—then we'll go to Salt Springs.'

So Uncle Benny and the Old Hen drove off. Doc watched after them.

He said, 'Anyways, cutting the fool at a burying had ought to last Benny quite a while.'

I said, 'You don't know him. Cutting the fool don't last him no time at all.'

I was right. I ain't no special wise a woman, but if I once know a man, I can come right close to telling you what he'll do. Uncle Benny hadn't been gone hardly no time, when somebody come by the garage hollering that he'd done set the Old Hen's pindar field on fire.

I said to Doc, 'What did I tell you? The last thing in the world was safe for that woman to do, was to turn him loose on them weeds. He figured firing was the quickest way to get shut of them.'

Doc said, 'Let's go see.'

We got in his car and drove out to Uncle Benny's place. Here was smoke rolling up back of the house, and the big live oak in the yard was black with soldier blackbirds the grass fire had drove out of the pindar field. The field hadn't had peanuts in it since fall, but bless Katy, it was full of something else. Uncle Benny's wife had it plumb full of setting guinea-hens. She hadn't told him, because he didn't like guineas.

Far off to the west corner of the field was the Old Hen, trying to run the guineas into a coop. They were flying every which-a-way and hollering *Po-drac!* Pod-rac! the way guineas holler. All the young uns in the neighborhood were in the middle of the field, beating out the grass fire with palmettos. And setting up on top of the east gate, just as unconcerned, was Uncle Benny, with them two little horns of white hair curling in the heat. Now what do you reckon he was doing? He had all seven of them bird-dogs running back and forth retrieving guinea eggs. He'd say now and again, 'Dead—fetch!' and they'd wag their tails and go hunt up another nest and here they'd come, with guinea eggs carried gentle in their mouths. He was putting the eggs in a basket.

When the commotion was over, and the fire out, and everybody gone but Doc and Me, we went to the front porch to set down and rest. The Old Hen was wore out. She admitted it was her fault not letting Uncle Benny know about the setting guinea-hens. She was about to forgive him setting the field afire, because him and the bird-dogs had saved the guinea eggs. But when we got to the porch, here lay the bird-dogs in the rocking-chairs. There was one to every chair, rocking away and cutting their eyes at her. Their coats and paws were smuttied from the burnt grass—and the Old Hen had put clean sugar-sacking covers on every blessed chair that morning. That settled it. She was stirred up anyway about the way he'd cut the fool at the burying, and she really set in to quarrel at Uncle Benny. And like I say, it turned out to be the last piece of quarrelling she ever done.

She said to him, 'You taught them bird-dogs to rock in a rocking-chair just to torment me. Ever' beast or varmint you've brought home, you've learned to cut the fool as bad as you do.'

'Now wife, what beast or varmint did I ever learn to cut the fool?'

'You learned the 'coon to screw the tops of my syrup cans. You learned the 'possum to hang upside down in my cupboard, and I'd go for a jar of maybe pepper relish and put my hand on him. . . . There's been plenty of such as that. I've raised ever'thing in the world for you but a stallion horse.'

Doc said, 'Give him time, he'll have one of them stabled in the kitchen.'

'Bird-dogs is natural to have around,' she said. 'I was raised to bird-dogs. But it ain't natural for 'em to rock in a rocking-chair. There's so terrible many of them, and when they put in the night on the porch laying in the rocking-chairs and rocking, I don't close my eyes for the fuss.'

Uncle Benny said, 'You see, Doc? You see, Mis' Dover? She's always quarrelling that me and the dogs ain't never home at night. Then when we do come in, she ain't willing we should all be comf'table.

'We just as good to go on to Salt Springs, Doc. Wait while I go in the house and get my camping outfit and we'll set out.'

He went in the house and came out with his camping stuff. She knowed he was gone for nobody knew how long.

We walked on down to the gate and the Old Hen followed, sniffling a little and twisting the corner of her apron.

'Benny,' she said, 'please don't go to Salt Springs. You always lose your teeth in the Boil.'

'I ain't lost 'em but three times,' he said, and he cranked up the Model-T and climbed in. 'I couldn't help losing 'em the first time. That was when I was laughing at the Yankee casting for bass, and his plug caught me in the open mouth and lifted my teeth out. Nor I couldn't help it the second time, when Doc and me was rassling in the rowboat and he pushed me in.'

'Yes,' she said, 'and how'd you lose 'em the third time?'

His eyes twinkled and he shoved the Ford in low. 'Cuttin' the fool,' he said.

'That's just it,' she said, and the tears begun to roll out of her eyes. 'Anybody with false teeth hadn't ought to cut the fool!'

Now I always thought it was right cute, the way Uncle Benny fooled Doc about the trained Ford. You know how the old-timey Fords get the gas—it feeds from the hand-trottle on the wheel. Well, Uncle Benny had spent the day before old lady Weller's funeral at Will's garage, putting in a foot accelerator. He didn't say a word to anybody, and Will and me was the only ones knowed he had it. Doc and Uncle Benny stayed three-four days camping at Salt Springs. Now the night they decided to come home, they'd both had something to drink, but Uncle Benny let on like he was in worse shape than he was.

Doc said, 'Benny, you better leave me drive.'

Uncle Benny pretended to rock on his feet and roll his head and he said, 'I've got that Model-T trained to carry me home, drunk or sober.'

Doc said, 'Never mind that lie again. You get up there in the seat and whistle in the dogs. I'm fixing to drive us home.'

Well I'd of give a pretty to of been in the back seat with them bird-dogs that night when Doc drove the Ford back to Oak Bluff. It's a treat, anyways, to see a fat man get excited. The first thing Doc knowed, the Ford was running away with him. The Ford lights were none too good, and Doc just did clear a stump by the roadside, and he run clean over a black-jack sapling. He looked at the hand trottle on the wheel, and here it was where the car had ought to be going about twenty miles an hour and it was going forty-five. That rascal of an Uncle Benny had his foot on the foot accelerator.

Doc shut off the gas altogether and the Ford kept right on going. He said, 'Something's the matter.'

Uncle Benny seemed to be dozing and didn't pay no mind. The Ford whipped back and forth in the sand road like a 'gator's tail. Directly they got on to the hard road and the Model-T put on speed. They begun to get near a curve. It was a dark night and the carlights wobbling, but Doc could see it coming. He took a tight holt of the wheel and begun to sweat. He felt for the brakes, but Uncle Benny never did have any.

He said, 'We'll all be kilt.'

When they started to take the curve, the Model-T was going nearly fifty-five—and then just as they got there, all of a sudden it slowed down as if it knowed what it was doing, and went around the curve as gentle as a day-old kitten. Uncle Benny had eased his foot off the accelerator. Doc drawed a breath again.

It's a wonder to me that trip didn't make Doc a nervous wreck. On every straightaway the Ford would rare back on its haunches and stretch out like a gray hound. Every curve they come to, it would go to it like a jack-rabbit. Then just as the sweat would pour down Doc's face and the drops would splash on the wheel, and he'd gather hisself together to jump, the Ford would slow down. It was a hot spring night, but Uncle Benny says Doc's teeth were chattering. The Model-T made the last mile lickety-brindle with the gas at the hand-trottle shut off entirely—and it coasted down in front of Will's garage and of its own free will come to a dead stop.

It was nine o'clock at night. Will was just closing up and I had locked the candy and cigarette counter and was waiting for him. There was a whole bunch of the men and boys around, like always, because the garage is the last place in Oak Bluff to put the lights out. Doc climbed out of the Ford trembling like a dish of custard. Uncle Benny eased out after him and I looked at him and right away I knowed he'd been up to mischief.

Doc said, 'I don't know how he done it—but dogged if he wasn't telling the truth when he said he had that blankety-blank Model-T trained to carry him home when he ain't fitten.'

Will asked, 'How come?' and Doc told us. Will looked at me and begun to chuckle and we knowed what Uncle Benny had done to him. I think maybe I would of let Uncle Benny get away with it, but Will couldn't keep it.

'Come here, Doc,' he said. 'Here's your training.'

I thought the bunch would laugh Doc out of town. He swelled up like a toad-fish and he got in his car without a word and drove away.

It's a wonderful thing just to set down and figure out how many different ways there are to be crazy. We never thought of Uncle Benny as being really crazy. We'd say, 'Uncle Benny's cutting the fool again,' and we'd mean he was just messing around some sort of foolishness like a daggone young un. We figured his was what you might call the bottom kind of craziness. The next would be the half-witted. The next would be the senseless. The next would be what the colored folks call 'mindless.' And clear up at the top would be what you'd call cold-out crazy. With all his foolishness, we never figured Uncle Benny was cold-out crazy.

Well, we missed Uncle Benny from Oak Bluff a day or two. When I came to ask questions, I found he'd gone on a long prowl and was over on the Withlacoochie River camping with some oyster fishermen. I didn't think much about it, because he was liable to stay off that-a-way. But time rocked on and he didn't show up. I dropped by his house to ask the Old Hen about him. She didn't know a blessed thing.

She said, 'Ain't it God's mercy we've got no young uns? The pore things would be as good as fatherless.'

And then a few days later Doc came driving up to the garage. He got out and blew his nose and we could see his eyes were red.

He said, 'Ain't it awful! I can't hardly bear to think about it.'

Will said, 'Doc, if you know bad news, you must be carrying it. Ain't nothing sorrowful I know of, except the Prohi's have found Philbin's still.'

Doc said, 'Don't talk about such little accidents at a time like this. You don't mean you ain't heard about Benny?'

The bunch was there and they all perked up, interested. They know if it was Uncle Benny, they could expect 'most any news.

I said, 'We ain't heard a word since he went off to the west coast.'

'You ain't heard about him going crazy?'

I said, 'Doc, you mean being crazy. He's always been that-a-way.'

'I mean being crazy and going crazy. Pore ol' Benny Mathers has gone really cold-out crazy.'

Well, we all just looked at him and we looked at one another. And it came over the whole bunch of us that we weren't surprised. A nigger setting by the free air hose said, 'Do, Jesus!' and eased away to tell the others.

Doc blew his nose and wiped his eyes and he said, 'I'm sure we all forgive the pore ol' feller all the things he done. He wasn't responsible. I feel mighty bad, to think the hard way I've often spoke to him.'

Will asked, 'How come it to finally happen?'

Doc said, 'He'd been up to some foolishness all night, raring through some of them Gulf coast flat-woods. Him and the fellers he was camping with was setting on the steps of the camp-house after breakfast. All of a sudden Uncle Benny goes to whistling, loud and shrill like a jay-bird. Then he says, "I'm Samson," and he begun to tear down the camp-house.'

Will asked, 'What'd they do with him?'

Doc said, 'You really ain't heard? I declare, I can't believe the news has come so slow. They had a terrible time holding him and tying him. They got in the doctors and the sheriff and they takened pore ol' Uncle Benny to the lunatic asylum at Chattahoochie.'

Doc wiped his eyes and we all begun to sniffle and our eyes to burn. I declare, it was just as if Uncle Benny Mathers had died on us.

I said, 'Oh, his pore wife——'

Will said, 'We'll have to be good to him and go see him and take him cigarettes and maybe slip him a pint of 'shine now and again.'

I said, 'The way he loved his freedom—shutting him up in the crazy-house will be like putting a wildcat in a crocus sack.'

Doc said, 'Oh, he ain't in the asylum right now. He's broke loose. That's what makes me feel so bad. He's headed this way, and no telling the harm he'll do before he's ketched again.'

Everybody jumped up and begun feeling in their hip pockets for their guns.

Doc said, 'No use to try to put no guns on him. He's got his'n, and they say he's shooting just as accurate as ever.'

That was enough for me. I ran back of the counter at the garage and begun locking up.

I said, 'Doc, you're a sight. 'Tain't no time to go to feeling sorry for Uncle Benny and our lives and property in danger.'

Doc said, 'I know, but I knowed him so long and I knowed him so good. I can't help feeling bad about it.'

I said, 'Do something about it. Don't just set there, and him liable to come shooting his way in any minute.'

Doc said, 'I know, but what can anybody do to stop him? Pore man, with all them deputies after him.'

Will said, 'Deputies?'

Doc said, 'Why, yes. The sheriff at Ocala asked me would I stop along the road and leave word for all the deputies to try and ketch him. Pore ol' Benny, I'll swear. I hated doing it the worst way.'

I scooped the money out of the cash register and I told them, 'Now, men, I'm leaving. I've put up with Uncle Benny Mathers when he was drunk and I've put up with him when he was cutting the fool. But the reckless way he drives that Ford and the way he shoots a pistol, I ain't studying on messing up around him and him gone cold-out crazy.'

Doc said, 'Ain't a thing in the world would stop him when he goes by, and all them deputies after him, but a barricade acrost the road.'

I said, 'Then for goodness' sake, you sorry, low-down, no-account, varminty white men tear down the wire fence around my chicken yard and fix Uncle Benny a barricade.'

Doc said, 'I just hated to suggest it.'

Will said, 'He'd slow down for the barricade and we could come in from behind and hem him in.'

Doc said, 'It'll be an awful thing to hem him in and have to see him sent back to Chattahoochie.'

Will said, 'I'll commence pulling out the posts and you-all can wind up the fencing.'

They worked fast and I went out and looked up the road now and again to see if Uncle Benny was coming. Doc had stopped at the Standard filling-station on his way, to leave the news, and we could see the people stirring around and going out to look, the same as we were doing. When we dragged the roll of wire fencing out into the road we hollered to them so they could see what we were doing and they all cheered and waved their hats. The word had spread, and the young uns begun traipsing bare-footed down to the road, until some of their mammies ran down and cuffed them and hurried them back home out of the way of Uncle Benny. The men strung the fencing tight across the road between the garage on one side and our smoke-house on the other. They nailed it firm at both ends.

Doc said, 'Leave me drive the last nail, men—it may be the last thing I can do for Benny this side of Chattahoochie.'

I talked the men into unloading their guns.

'He'll have to stop when he sees the barricade,' I said, 'and then you can all go in on him with your guns drawed and capture him. I just can't hear to a loaded gun being drawed on him, for fear of somebody getting excited and shooting him.'

Doc wiped the sweat off his forehead and he said, 'Men, this is a mighty serious occasion. I'd be mighty proud if you'd all have a little snort on me,' and he passed the bottle.

'Here's to Uncle Benny, the way we all knowed him before he went cold-out crazy,' he said.

And then we heard a shouting up the dirt road and young uns whistling and women and girls screaming and chickens scattering.

'Yonder comes Uncle Benny!'

And yonder he came.

The Model-T was swooping down like a bull-bat after a mosquito. The water was boiling up out of the radiator in a foot-high stream. The seven pieded bird-dogs were hanging out of the back seat and trembling as if they craved to tell the things they'd seen. And behind Uncle Benny was a string of deputy sheriffs in Fords and Chevrolets and motorcycles that had gathered together from every town between Oak Bluff and Ocala. And Uncle Benny was hunched over the steering wheel with them two tufts of goat-horn hair sticking up in the breeze—and the minute I laid eyes on him I knowed he wasn't one mite crazier than he ever had been. I knowed right then Doc had laid out to get even with him and had lied on him all the way down the road.

It was too late then. I knowed, whatever happened, there'd be people to the end of his life would always believe it. I knowed there'd be young uns running from him and niggers hiding. And I knowed there wasn't a thing in the world now could keep him out of Chattahoochie for the time being. I knowed he'd fight when he was taken, and all them mad and hot and dusty deputies would get him to the lunatic asylum quicker than a black snake can cross hot ashes. And once a man that has cut the fool all his life, like Uncle Benny, is in the crazy house, there'll be plenty of folks to say to keep him there.

It was too late. Uncle Benny was bearing down toward the garage and right in front of him was the barricade.

Doc hollered, 'Be ready to jump on him when he stops!'

Stop? Uncle Benny stop? He kept right on coming. The sight of that chicken-wire barricade was no more to him than an aggravation. Uncle Benny and the Model-T dived into the barricade like a water-turkey into a pool. The barricade held. And the next thing we knowed, the Ford had somersaulted over the fencing and crumpled up like a paper shoebox and scattered bird-dogs over ten acres and laid Uncle Benny in a heap over against the wall of the smoke-house. I was raised to use the language of a lady, but I couldn't hold in.

'Doc,' I said, 'you low-down son of a ——'

He said, 'Mis' Dover, the name's too good. I've killed my friend.'

Killed him? Killed Uncle Benny? It can't be done until the Almighty Hisself hollers 'Sooey!' Uncle Benny was messed up considerable, but him nor none of the bird-dogs was dead.

The doctor took a few stitches in him at the garage before he come to, and tied up his head right pretty in a white bandage. We left Will to quiet the deputies and we put Uncle Benny in Doc's car and carried him home to the Old Hen. Naturally, I figured it would set her to quarrelling. Instead, it just brought out all her sweetness. I can guess a man, but I can't guess another woman.

'The pore ol' feller,' she said. 'I knowed he had it coming to him. What the devil throws over his back——. I knowed he'd kill hisself in that Ford car, cutting the fool and prowling. The biggest load is off my mind. Now,' she said, 'now, by God's mercy, when it did come to him, he got out alive.'

She began fanning him with a palmetto fan where he lay on the bed, and Doc poured out a drink of 'shine to have ready for him when he come to. Doc's hand was trembling. Uncle Benny opened his eyes. He eased one hand up to the bandage across his head and he groaned and grunted. He looked at Doc as if he couldn't make up his mind whether or not to reach for his pistol. Doc put the 'shine to his mouth and Uncle Benny swallowed. Them wicked blue eyes begun to dance.

'Doc,' he said, 'how will I get home when I'm drunk, now you've tore up my trained Ford?'

Doc broke down and cried like a little baby.

'I ain't got the money to replace it,' he said, 'but I'll give you my car. I'll carry the Little Giant line of remedies on foot.'

Uncle Benny said, 'I don't want your car. It ain't trained.'

Doc said, 'Then I'll tote you on my back, anywheres you say.'

The Old Hen let in the bird-dogs, some of them limping a little, and they climbed on the bed and beat their tails on the counterpane and licked Uncle Benny. We felt mighty relieved things had come out that way.

Uncle Benny was up and around in a few days, with his head bandaged, and him as pert as a woodpecker. He just about owned Oak Bluff —all except the people that did like I figured, never did get over the idea he'd gone really crazy. Most people figured he'd had a mighty good lesson and it would learn him not to cut the fool. The Old Hen was happy as a bride. She was so proud to have the Ford torn up, and no money to get another, that she'd even now and again pet one of the bird-dogs. She waited on Uncle Benny hand and foot and couldn't do enough to please him.

She said to me, 'The pore ol' feller sure stays home nights now.'

Stay home? Uncle Benny stay home? Two weeks after the accident the wreck of the Model-T disappeared from behind the garage where Will had dragged it. The next day the seven bird-dogs disappeared. The day after that Doc and Uncle Benny went to Ocala in Doc's car. Will wouldn't answer me when I asked him questions. The Old Hen stopped by the garage and got a Coca-Cola and she didn't know any more than I did. Then Will pointed down the road.

He said, 'Yonder he comes.'

And yonder he came. You could tell him way off by the white bandage with the tufts of hair sticking up over it. He was scrooched down behind the wheel of what looked like a brand-new automobile. Doc was following behind him. They swooped into the garage.

Will said, 'It's a new second-hand body put on the chassis and around the engine of the old Ford.'

Uncle Benny got out and he greeted us.

He said, 'Will, it's just possible it was the motor of the Model-T that had takened the training. The motor ain't hurt, and me and Doc are real hopeful.'

The Old Hen said, 'Benny, where'd you get the money to pay for it?'

He said, 'Why, a daggone bootlegger in a truck going from Miami to New York bought the bird-dogs for twenty-five dollars apiece. The low-down rascal knowed good and well they was worth seventy-five.'

She brightened some. Getting shut of the bird-dogs was a little progress. She walked over to the car and began looking around it.

'Benny,' she said, and her voice come kind of faintified, 'if you sold the bird-dogs, what's this place back here looks like it was fixed for 'em?'

We all looked, and here was a open compartment-like in the back, fixed up with seven crocus sacks stuffed with corn-shucks. About that time here come a cloud of dust down the road. It was the seven bird-dogs. They were about to give out. Their tongues were hanging out and their feet looked blistered.

Uncle Benny said, 'I knowed they'd jump out of that bootlegger's truck. I told him so.'

I tell you, what's in a man's nature you can't change. It takened the Old Hen thirty years and all them goings-on to learn it. She went and climbed in the front seat of the car and just sat there waiting for Uncle Benny to drive home for his dinner. He lifted the bird-dogs up and set them down to rest on the cornshucks cushions, and he brought them a pan of water.

He said, 'I figure they busted loose just above Lawtey.'

The Old Hen never opened her mouth. She hasn't quarrelled at him from that day to this. She was hornswoggled.

TEXAS

"—Neber Said a Mumblin' Word"

VERNON LOGGINS

Tom Whittleton, his red face gleaming, his thick blue shirt splotched with patches dark in the wet of perspiration, stalked up his back-gallery steps. When he reached the top, he kicked off his heavy brogans—hurled them bang against the wall, leaned his shotgun in the corner next to the kitchen door, and patted over to the wooden water bucket, which was hanging on a wire fastened to a rafter. "This stuff was drawed yestiddy mornin'!" Nevertheless, he drank three full gourds of it, dipping each time right down to the yellow slimy bottom of the bucket.

His thirst slackened, he slapped his hands against his breast, sent tiny squirts of perspiration darting out from between his fingers. He was satisfied with himself. Hunting rabbits on an April afternoon when the cotton was in the grass and needed plowing wasn't exactly work, and yet it was useful. The long-eared, white-tailed little pests were fine in corn dumplings, just the right sort of grub to make kids grow. It wasn't his fault if the Lord didn't scare up any of the animals for him to take a crack at. He had rambled down the gullies and in the woods looking for them—harder work than following a lazy mule along a furrow. "In the sweat of thy face shalt thou eat bread." God had said that to Adam; and he was Adam's son, sweating. Yes, he was satisfied with himself.

"Mama!" he called.

"I'm fixin' the boys' breeches, Papa. Come on out here an' blow a minute," reeled the whining reply of his wife, Maude, from the front gallery.

From *Opportunity,* April, 1928. Used by permission of Vernon Loggins and *Opportunity.*

He slipped into the hall, his gray-stockinged feet dragging along the smooth pine floor, scoured that morning and still not dry in places. As he passed the parlor door, a nice inspiration came to him. Since he was an elder, blessed with the ceremony of the laying on of hands only the summer before, he could well give the rest of the afternoon to a reading of the Word. He turned and eased into the room, where there was bright-colored straw matting on the floor, over the windows long trailing lace curtains dotted with last year's Sunday school Christmas tree ornaments, and in the most prominent corner a golden-oak what-not adorned with home-made paper flowers, more and more of them and brighter and gayer as he looked from the top to the bottom. Too fancy. He had always felt out of place here, ever since he was a boy and his oldest sister had threatened him with a spanking if he came prowling around where she was entertaining her beaux. Ugh. Hadn't all this been his own for years now, the pretty as well as the homely? Why, before very long beaux would come courting his own daughter. Addie Bird was thirteen her last birthday, and soon there would be plenty of boys setting their caps for her.

Reassured and proud and master-like, he strode over to the center table and picked up a much-worn Bible, with a limp cover projecting into a skimpy ruffle around the edges. The touch of the Book in his hands gave him a feeling of righteousness, and he walked out on the front gallery and sat down in a rocking chair near his wife, who was in the act of putting the finishing touches to a neat pair of patches on the seat of their son Bob's pants.

"You needn' be readin' for prayer meetin' tonight, Papa. Alice was here right after dinner, an' she said that ol' Brother Cooke come ridin' up to her gate this mornin' 'bout leben o'clock. I 'low he'll be holdin' preachin' tonight."

"Ol' Brother Cooke? He ain't been in this neighborhood in fifteen year! What'd he go to Alice an' Ned's for? Why didn' he come here?"

"She didn' tell me that." Silence—during which Mrs. Whittleton took off her spectacles and looked down the road. "Them chillun's late gittin' from school." More silence—except for a nimble needle making little fine stitches in tough cotton cloth and Tom Whittleton's big gnarled thumb following clumsily the lines of the Forty-sixth Psalm. "Any way 't ain't any o' us what needs a preacher's company. An' as for Alice—she's lived a faithful Christian ever since she come through. But Ned, even if he is y'r brother—well, back-slidin' like he does, I'd hate to be in his shoes when he gits up to the judgment house on the streets o' pearl."

She might have been saying, "Scat, Jack Robinson!" so far as her husband was concerned. "There is a river, the streams whereof shall make glad the city of God, the holy place of the tabernacle of the Most High." He was on the banks of that wondrous river, in company with a host of saints, all of them with their wings lowered in humble and comely manner. The waters were sparkling with the brilliance of the July sun, but his eyes, transfigured by the grace of Jesus Christ, were not dazzled. Transfigured by the grace of Jesus Christ, he had a pretty way of reasoning things out, even when his mind was in the ecstasy of a heavenly vision.

"Papa, here comes them two boys, an' Addie Bird ain't with 'em!" Maude Whittleton sighed, dropped her sewing in her lap, and looked up anxiously.

Bob and Marvin, aged fifteen and fourteen respectively, leaped over the board fence separating the yard from the open horse lot, wheeled around the flower beds—phlox and verbenas blooming—sprang up to the front gallery, and threw down their dirty oilcloth book satchels and dinner pails. They were in a feverish hurry about something.

"What's the matter with you two youngsters?" snarled their mother. "Ain't I done tol' you not to leave Addie Bird come home by herself, with all these black bucks doin' nothin' but traipse up an' down the road day an' night?"

"Augh—she had to stay in. She don't never know her spellin'," retorted Bob, who had inherited his mother's peculiar whine. "An' we couldn' wait. There's a crowd cuttin' a bee tree over in the Henson pasture, an' we're goin' to git some honey."

"Wanta come, Papa?" suggested Marvin, who had examined his father's expression and had decided that Bob was too sure.

"You ain't goin' to take a step to the Henson pasture," said Tom Whittleton, patriarchal. He had laid his Bible down on the floor by his chair, and was standing up straight. "You're goin' with me to the cotton patch. Git y'r hoes."

His sons hung their heads, muttered something about "never havin' no fun," and moped around the house in the direction of the log crib where the farming tools were stored.

"You're too easy on them boys, Tom," explained Mrs. Whittleton, her apprehensive eyes fixed on the road. "They oughta be whipped. I don't have a minute's peace when Addie Bird is out of my sight. I've felt that way ever since what happen to that po' girl up in the Cedar Creek neighborhood las' fall."

"Ain't you never goin' to git through talkin' about that? The niggers aroun' here know their place. I ain't the deputy sheriff o' this beat for nothin'."

The sharp grinding noise of hoes being filed came from the back yard, and Mr. Whittleton, content that he was training his offspring to know the blessings of such honest toil as Moses had enjoined upon the children of Israel, started for his shoes. Just as he was entering the hall door, piercing shrieks, repeated screams, broke the afternoon stillness of the oak-bordered road.

"It's Addie Bird, Tom! My God!"

One glance at the anguish in his wife's ashen stupefied face,—and he dashed off the gallery, down the front walk, pushed the yard gate open with such force that a hinge was wrenched split, and ran madly towards the frenzied screams. Around the bend by the duck pond he rushed, and there was his little daughter flying up the middle of the sandy road, her long yellow hair in a straight stream behind her, her hands jerking furiously, her short skirt worked up above her knees by her fast-moving legs.

"Papa! Papa!" she cried, in a spasm of relief, as he sped on to meet her. Soon her palpitating body was folded in his arms.

"What's happened, my chil'? Tell me!"

But her breath was wheezing in quick nervous pants, and she was speechless. He nestled her hot head against his bosom, and turned to retrace his steps back to the house, carrying her along as though she were still a baby.

"Tom! Tom! Is she dead?" called Mrs. Whittleton, just on the other side of the duck pond.

"No, Mama!" cried the girl, relaxed enough now to break into a fit of tears.

The dread-driven woman, followed by her two boys, appeared from around the bend. She came on desperately, clutched the sobbing child, and held her tightly.

"It's y'r kind ol' mother that's got you now, sweetie! Don' cry no mo'. Come, an' say what made the lil angel lamb holler like that!"

The father and sons looked on in a passive wonder. There was more coaxing, and soon Addie Bird was in condition to speak.

"I stopped at the bendin' oak," she said, in a shambling voice, "an' put down my things to pull some violets. I heard somep'n in the woods, an' I was scared it was a mad dog, an' when I looked up a nigger was crawlin' through the fence. He come runnin' towards me, an' when I started away he whistled an' said for me to wait an' he wouldn' hurt me, jus' like that nigger done up on Cedar Creek."

"God protect us po' women! It's right in our own home at last! I knew it! I felt it comin'!"

"Where's he went, Addie Bird? Had you ever seen 'im befo'? Go on an' tell me everything. I'm y'r Papa, an' have got to know!"

"I looked back once, an' he was wavin' his han' at me to foller 'im up the Gladish road, an'—"

The horrified faces of her mother and father and brothers threw the child into another terror, and her words were lost in a fresh paroxysm of screams.

Tom Whittleton, his brow stern and dreadful with determination, fixed his eyes on Bob and Marvin.

"Go to them fellows cuttin' that bee tree in the Henson pasture, an' tell 'em what's happen. Run every step o' the way. Come on, Mama."

His sons darted into the woods to obey his command, and he snatched his daughter into his arms again and ran to the house with her. His wife, sobbing and crying more violently than the child, struggled along in the sand behind him.

He put Addie Bird down on his own bed, left her in the care of her frantic mother, and made for the telephone in the hall.

Four short rings—his brother's store, opposite Hopewell Church, where the Gladish and Rock Island bottom roads crossed. Curious ears, at least a dozen of them, followed the custom of the party line and clicked receivers off the hooks. "Stay on, all o' you. I wants you to hear what I got to say to Ned." "H'lo," came his brother's deep-bassed voice. "Ned, this is Tom. A nigger attacked Addie Bird when she was comin' home from school. He was last seen turnin' up the Gladish road. Stir everybody up. We've got to find 'im."

Without waiting for a word of reply, he thrust the receiver roughly on its resting place, hurried to the back gallery for his shoes and shotgun, came back to the trunk in the hall for his revolver—emblem of his distinction as an officer of the law—and rushed to the stables and threw a saddle on his red mule. God was on his side, for he had kept that mule from her pasture that afternoon with the vague feeling that he might take a notion to plow a little.

Twenty minutes later, a crowd of men, forty or fifty in number, on foot, mounted on horses and mules, in automobiles, were gathered around the bending oak where Addie Bird had stopped to cull violets. It was a stately and magnificent tree, with its great deep trunk slanting gracefully towards the east. It had bowed before a hundred years of beautiful dawns, and yet it was youthful. Parasitic gray moss and white-berried mistletoe and sapping ivy had made no inroads on its vigorous vitality. Free and strong, it projected its straight rich branches out over the road, on the most shapely of which a long heavy rope was now strung.

One end of it was held in the hands of three men, Tom Whittleton's brother Ned among them; and the other end was being tied around the neck of a tall black Negro, perhaps twenty years old. He was straight and rigid, his bare feet imbedded in the sand, his head thrust back slightly by the knots in the rope under his chin. His awful rolling eyes seemed to stare without seeing the glowering faces about him. His fingers were twitching strangely, making little circles and figures, as though they would in some way exorcise the steel hand-cuffs that bound his wrists.

"For the las' time I asks you," fiercely rang the voice of Tom Whittleton, who was standing just at the foot of the tree, his two young sons near him. "to confess y'r crime."

The Negro remained fixed, a statue of terror. No movement, except in the twirling black fingers.

"This'll make 'im talk," growled Ned Whittleton, and straightway a pocket-knife was stuck deep in the victim's leg. There was a faint moan of pain, and blood oozed through the rough denim trousers and trickled down. The sight of it set the gloating onlookers on fire. Grim oaths and hideous curses rumbled, thundered, and more pocket-knives were whisked out and hurled into the body of the Negro.

Still he did not speak.

"He's guilty!" shouted Tom Whittleton above the passionate uproar. "He'd howl out if he was innocent. Pull 'im up, boys!"

Silence speaks in the affirmative—nothing declared is always yes.

The officer of the law reasoned that since he had heard this saying so many times it must be in the Bible, and therefore infallible. Yes, God was on his side, making the path of his duty clear to him.

The deed was done. The tall black body hung stiff and stark in the air. For a few moments there was stillness, broken only by the blood dripping down the dangling legs and sinking heavily into the loose sand below.

Then conversation arose, talk quiet and casual, about the wisdom of keeping niggers in their places, and crops, and mares that were going to foal, and the June elections. Contented, sated, the lynchers dispersed.

Tom Whittleton, leading his submissive red mule, walked slowly up the road in the company of his two boys. When they reached the open place, where his field began, the sun, no more than a half hour high, was shooting wide bands of yellow light right down the cotton rows.

"Didn' he never say a single word, Papa?" asked Marvin.

"Narry a word," answered the father. "He was shakin' like a ague when Ned an' them fellows found 'im runnin' through that hump o' woods at the cross-roads. Nobody couldn' git nothin' out o' him, excep' a few grunts. They always acts like that when they's guilty."

"Didn' nobody know who he was?"

"No. He was a strange nigger. Musta come from across the river some'rs."

"Who's goin' to cut 'im down?"

"Ned's goin' to git ol' Uncle Jerry an' his boys to take 'im to the Rock Island bottom an' bury 'im."

"I thought he'd dance when they pulled 'im up," interposed Bob, who had the habit of going about with his head dropped and was not so inquisitive as his brother. "He didn' do nothin' but hang up there straight."

"I saw his neck gittin' longer. I bet it's more'n two feet by this time," added Marvin.

When they got into the house, they found Addie Bird and her mother in the parlor. The girl had all of her dolls sitting up in a row on the sofa and was pinning paper flowers on them, playing like a child of six, to the delight of her doting mama, who had listened over the telephone and had already heard in detail the relieving tidings of the hanging.

At supper, when a sweet-potato pudding was served because Addie Bird was very fond of it, Tom Whittleton reminded himself and his hungry family that old Brother Cooke would no doubt preach at the prayer meeting at Hopewell Church that night. It was out of the question to think of the baby girl leaving the house after the nerve-racking experience which she had undergone in the afternoon. Maude ought to stay with her. The boys must work their sums, for a man could never know too much arithmetic. Anyway, every blessed soul under Tom Whittleton's roof-tree had confessed Jesus Christ as a personal saviour, and it wasn't a sin if a meeting was missed occasionally, when there was a real excuse. But, as for the father himself, he was an elder and must always go, rain or shine, sickness or health.

Thus the matter was beautifully reasoned out while he and his wife and children ate sweet-potato pudding. When the last morsel was devoured, he got up, emitted a puffed grunt of satisfaction, and then went to comb at his hair and put on a gray coat over his blue shirt, which had been wet with sweat twice that day and was still a little damp. Armed with his Bible and a lantern, he set out, with that sacred feeling which always came over him when he was going to church. The dew hadn't fallen yet, so he took the short cut through the cotton patch and the stretch of woods up by old Aunt Dora's house.

There was a waning glow of red in the west but the stars were out in all their numbers and a full moon swung tranquilly against the milky sky over towards Gladish. Frogs had set up a merry questioning and answering in the duck pond, and whip-poor-wills called playfully to each other along the edge of the woods. The smell of growing April was in the air. The elder, unconscious of his surroundings, left the cotton field and entered the trail leading through the woods. He was thinking hard, trying to decide whether it really would be his duty to run for sheriff when Bill Perry did finally retire. There was nothing to do but trust to God to give him a sign. He passed on by Aunt Dora's house, a hundred yards in front of it, and saw the old woman sitting on her door-step with the light of the moon falling directly on her round black face.

As he neared the church, the singing started, all the congregation, and a big one too, repeating lustily—

When the roll is called up yonder I'll be there!

He loved the songs that told about heaven—his inheritance as a child of God, and the inheritance of Maude and the three kids also. Listening intently, he stole up to the little porch at the entrance of the church, and slipped his lantern which he had not lighted, under the steps. He would not go in until the chorus was ended, since it was as bad to interrupt a hymn of praise as it was to walk into a sanctuary while a preacher or elder was leading a prayer.

"Tom," spoke his brother just behind him.

"Hello, Ned. You here?"

"Yep. I wanted to fin' out what ol' man Cooke had to say tonight. He's all shook up over what happened this evenin'. Alice said he come pretty near faintin' when he foun' out that there'd been a hangin' right under his nose. He went in the front room an' got down on his knees an' prayed for hours, didn' eat no supper."

"Well, I do declare. That's funny."

"I think the ol' man must be kinda crazy."

"He was a rip-roarin' soul-winner in his day. Let's go in befo' another song starts. There's Alice over next to the front window holdin' a place for you."

"Wait a minute. There's somep'n else I wanted to tell y'u. Uncle Jerry an' his boys cut down that nigger, an' the ol' man sent 'em on to Rock Island bottom with 'im an' come back home to do the feedin'. The blamed fools got it into their heads that it'd bring bad luck to touch a hangin' tree an' they lef' the rope there. Couldn't you git it when you go by on your way home? We oughtn' not to leave it there."

"Sho, I'll git it. It'll make a good pair o' tetherin' ropes for the cows."

The two brothers entered the church. Ned did not join his wife, but slouched down in the first vacant seat he came to in the back. Tom, setting a good example by holding his Bible so that everybody could see it, made straight for his accustomed place in the amen corner.

If they expected anything exciting from the visiting preacher, they were to be disappointed. The old man might have come into the church with a special message, but now that he faced his hearers he was afraid to voice it. For an hour he talked vaguely and incomprehensibly about Christians keeping the peace of God in their hearts. The congregation, among whom Tom Whittleton counted twenty who had helped at the hanging, grew fidgety. Nobody seemed to be touched except Sister Henson, who kept putting her handkerchief to her eyes. It didn't take much to make that woman cry. Ned left before the sermon was half over, and Tom was disgusted that such a weak-voiced preacher was not put on the superannuated list. What sinners and back-sliders needed was to be scared out of their skins by thundering stories of hell-fire and brimstone, like the tale of the jay bird and eternity.

But at the conclusion of the service something really did happen. "Let us lift our hearts to God in a prayer of silence, and go meditating on Him to our homes," said the old man, supporting himself on the pulpit. Tom Whittleton got on his knees and closed his eyes to pray. The church was still, like death. Then, across the fields and through the woods, came the sound of a ringing bell, intermittent peals, louder and clearer after each interval. It was in the direction of Rock Island bottom. God! Those dirty niggers were burying that black beast in the nighttime, and were bold enough to toll a funeral knell for him. Every last one of the brutes ought to be wiped out of existence for the outrage.

The officer of the law straightened up from his knees, looked about, and saw that heads were being raised and necks craned all over the house. Then for one long moment his eyes were fixed on the unearthly, bowed face of the aged preacher. There was a look in that wizened countenance which he didn't understand, which all his reason couldn't for the time explain. It was like a ghost. With the image of it glaring clear in his mind, he broke up the prayer of silence by shuffling roughly out the back door. From there he rushed around to the front for his lantern and was gone before any one else left the church. He must see Ned, for something had to be done about that infernal bell, the inevitable tolling of which was still sounding.

But the knell had ceased before he reached his brother's yard. Leaning up against the gate post, he lighted his lantern and waited, terrified lest the frightful ringing would set in again. Voices came from the foot of the lane leading up to the house—Alice and the kids and old Brother Cooke. A cold shiver throbbed through him at the thought of looking upon that strange and ghastly countenance again. He ran across the vegetable garden and crawled through a barbed-wire fence out into the main road, and started rapidly towards the bending oak. He wanted to get that rope and be through with this business.

At last he reached the tree, looming up in the silent moonlight, with its great spreading limbs, and broad folding leaves, and new acorns sticking around like little balls. He had always liked this oak. When he and Ned were boys, they used to race and see which one could climb it first. They would crawl up high, straddle their legs across a branch, take hickory nuts from their pockets and crack them between two rocks, making believe that they were squirrels. Thank God that niggers thought there was a curse on it and would let it alone. But would it ever again be the same to him, now that his little daughter had happened to stop there to gather flowers?

He unwound the rope from the trunk of the tree, stepped back to pull down the end that was suspended above, and his foot struck something solid. It was Addie Bird's book satchel, buried in the sand, and on one side of it there was a splotch of dried blood as big as his hand. He would bury the things somewhere. No. Mama could wash off that stain and the satchel would be as good as new.

Burdened with the Bible, the lantern, the satchel, and the rope, now made into a neat roll, he trudged on towards home. When he reached the duck pond, a strange uncanny sound came to him from somewhere in the woods. That bell was tolling again. No, it was somebody singing—a nigger woman—old Aunt Dora. He stood still and listened. She must be on her doorstep, where he had seen her two hours before, with the moon shining right down on her black face. The words fell distinctly on his ears.

Dey pierced Him in de side,
An' He neber said a mumblin' word.
Dey pierced Him in de side,
An' He neber said a mumblin' word—
Not a word—not a word—not a word.

De blood come twinklin' down,
An' He neber said a mumblin' word.
De blood come twinklin' down,
An' He neber said a mumblin' word—
Not a word—not a word—not a word.

Held as though charmed, he heard the song to the end. Then, in no way aware of what he was doing, he impulsively hurled the book satchel and the bundle of rope into the pond. The loud splashes in the water brought him back to himself. That old woman had no right to make him destroy things. A farmer worth his salt never knew what it was to have too much rope, and it would take five dollars to replace those school books. He would show her who could pay for them. She mustn't forget that she was working a few acres of his land on halves, and that next fall when the year's profits were divided he would do the figuring. Her half wouldn't amount to more than a gourd.

He went on, and did not stop again until he reached his house, where everything was dark and silent. He flopped down in his rocking chair, set his lantern up on the arm of the swing, and opened his Bible to read. A few verses here and there would calm his mind, get him ready for a good night's sleep. "The heavens declare the glory of God: and the firmament showeth his handiwork." No. He could see nothing in the heavens but the yellowish sickly moon—like the countenance of old man Cooke, staring at him. And something was holding him down—the weight of that cursed rope and blood-stained book satchel. And there was a continual ringing in his ears—that funeral bell, and old Aunt Dora's song—

Dey pierced Him in de side,
An' He neber said a mumblin' word.

He turned the leaves, and a trembling terror gripped him as he read: "Thou shalt not kill." But a soldier who had fought in France had explained to him what that commandment really meant. The chaplains always read it, "Thou shalt do no murder," and that was the way God meant it when he handed it down to Moses. Germans had to be killed during the war, beeves and hogs had to be slaughtered, fryers had to have their necks wrung, rats had to be choked in traps, and sometimes niggers had to be hung. It was easy to see how clear that was.

But maybe the nigger whom he had sent to death that afternoon had meant no harm to Addie Bird, and shouldn't have been killed. Could niggers possibly have souls? He would open the Bible just anywhere and what his eyes fell upon would give him light on an answer to that question. God had helped him solve many a problem in this way. He turned the pages again, and saw: "Blessed are the meek, for they shall inherit the earth." The meek?

Dey pierced Him in de side,
An' He neber said a mumblin' word.

Cowering in horror, seeing the finger of a wrathful God pointed at him and directing him to that hell of flames which he had so many times warned sinners against, Tom Whittleton dropped his Bible to the floor and covered his face with his rough hands. He was aroused from his agonizing reverie by a horse galloping up the road towards his house. From the hind feet dragging in the sand, he recognized it as Ned's mare, and he was waiting at the gate when his brother arrived.

"Tom," began Ned, anxiety in his voice, "have you heard anything about Sheriff Perry resignin'? I think you'd better go to West Falls in the mornin' an' see 'im."

"Didn' I tell you about that?" replied Tom somewhat relieved. "There ain't nothin' to it. He's jus' puttin' out that rumor in case anybody runs again' him in the primary. Then he could use it in his campaign that he wanted to quit an' the people wouldn' let 'im. I had dinner with 'im las' Sa'day, an' we talked it all over. He wants me to keep on as deputy in this beat."

"Well, that takes a load off'n my mind. I heard it from Luke Wallis tonight, an' if Perry'd git out an' the wrong sort o' man'd git in befo' the grand jury meets, you an' me an' some more fellows aroun' here might be in for it."

"What do yo' mean?"

"That nigger we hung this evenin' was innocent."

"Innocent? Don' say that! How do y'u know?"

"Ol' Jerry's boys foun' out who he was when they got down to Rock Island with 'im. He'd been plowin' for Luke Wallis a week or two, an' I rode down to see Luke to git things straight. He was a West Falls nigger, an' this evenin' a telephone message come for 'im that his mammy was sick, about to die. When we caught 'im he was hurryin' to Gladish to ketch the train to go to her."

"But why didn' he explain things to us?"

"There was a mighty good reason," Ned went on, half laughing. "He couldn', 'cause he was deaf and dumb."

"It's a lie! He hollered to Addie Bird to wait!"

"Augh—Maude has spoiled that kid so that she's scared o' her shadow an' is likely to imagine anything."

"You're jokin' with me! Tell me 'tain't so! Tell me that that nigger wasn' deaf an' dumb!" Tom Whittleton's whole body was shaking, and he had caught hold of the palings to steady himself. "Ned, do you believe niggers is got souls?"

"My God, Tom!" exclaimed Ned, disgusted. "Are you goin' crazy? Since you been an elder you ain't like yourself. I'm jus' as good a Christian as you, but I'll be damned if religion has made me a chicken-hearted fool. Of course niggers ain't got no souls! I'd rather hang a real brute any day, but one that's deaf an' dumb is better'n none at all. Here. Take a swig o' this white-mule an' brace up."

Tom Whittleton took the opened bottle which his brother was holding out to him. "Look not upon the wine when it is red." But it wasn't red. It was watery. Color! He held the bottle to his lips and took a long draft of the fiery liquid. Color! Why, everything depended upon color! A mule often lost her hearing when she strained herself in pulling a heavy load up a hill, and he had a cow once so dumb she couldn't utter a sound. Her durned calf would see her shaking her head and wagging her tail and understand her just as though she were mooing. Color and souls and brutes. Why hadn't he used that head which God had given him? Things were so simple when a man reasoned a little.

"I don' like ol' man Cooke's way o' actin'," Ned was saying. "I'm goin' to give 'im a strong hint in the mornin' to be pushin' on. We want a preacher in here like that fellow Graham over in Montgomery County. By golly, he led a lynchin' hisself not long ago. What do y'u think about an intimidatin' raid? Luke Wallis says he'll see that there ain't no talk among his niggers about this hangin', but I think we ought to scare the res' of 'em up a little too. They didn' have no business to toll that bell tonight."

"Intimidatin' raid?" answered Tom enthusiastic. "Sho. Make it tomorrow night. I'll tell all the fellows I see to meet at the bendin' oak at ten o'clock. We'll tackle ol' Dora first o' all. I wants to see that ol' woman shake till she coughs her gills up so's she can never sing no mo'. An' say, Ned. Bring along a quart or two o' that white-mule if y'u got it to spare."

"All right. It's good stuff, ain't it? So long. See you tomorrow."

He rode away, and Tom Whittleton walked heavily upon his gallery. Since God had given him peace of heart, what would the Word say to him now? He picked up his Bible, opened it at random, and held it in the light of the lantern to read: "For rulers are not a terror to the good works, but to the evil." Rulers? That was simple enough. It was what he had been looking for, the sign, direct from heaven, that he should run for sheriff when Bill Perry retired. Yes, the Lord was on his side.

Glowing with satisfaction, he took his Bible into the fancy parlor, placed it reverently on the center table, and blundered into his bedroom without waking his wife. Ugh. Mama had Addie Bird in bed with her. He'd rather sleep on the cot in the boys' room anyway, for Maude's snoring was getting to be something terrible.

IOWA

★

A Jury of Her Peers

SUSAN GLASPELL

When Martha Hale opened the storm door and got a cut of the north wind she ran back for her big woolen scarf. As she hurriedly wound that round her head her eye made a scandalized sweep of her kitchen. It was no ordinary thing that called her away; it was probably further from ordinary than anything that had ever happened in Dickson County. But what her eye took in was that her kitchen was in no shape for leaving: her bread all ready for mixing, half the flour sifted and half unsifted.

She hated to see things half done, but she had been at that when the team from town stopped to get Mr. Hale, and then the sheriff came running in to say his wife wished Mrs. Hale would come too, adding, with a grin, that he guessed she was getting scary and wanted another woman along. So she had dropped everything right where it was.

"Martha!" now came her husband's impatient voice. "Don't keep folks waiting out here in the cold."

She again opened the storm door, and this time joined the three men and the one woman waiting for her in the big two-seated buggy.

After she had the robes tucked around her she took another look at the woman who sat beside her on the back seat. She had met Mrs. Peters the year before at the county fair, and the thing she remembered about her was that she didn't seem like a sheriff's wife. She was small and thin and didn't have a strong voice. Mrs. Gorman, sheriff's wife before Gorman went out and Peters came in, had a voice that somehow seemed to be backing up the law with every word. But if Mrs. Peters didn't look like a sheriff's wife, Peters made it up in looking like a sheriff. He was

---

to a dot the kind of man who could get himself elected sheriff, a heavy man with a big voice, who was particularly genial with the law-abiding, as if to make it plain that he knew the difference between criminals and non-criminals. And right there it came into Mrs. Hale's mind, with a stab, that this man who was so pleasant and lively with all of them was going to the Wrights' now as a sheriff.

"The country's not very pleasant this time of year," Mrs. Peters at last ventured, as if she felt they ought to be talking as well as the men.

Mrs. Hale scarcely finished her reply, for they had gone up a little hill and could see the Wright place now, and seeing it did not make her feel like talking. It looked very lonesome this cold March morning. It had always been a lonesome-looking place. It was down in a hollow, and the poplar trees around it were lonesome-looking trees. The men were looking at it and talking about what had happened. The county attorney was bending to one side of the buggy and kept looking steadily at the place as they drew up to it.

"I'm glad you came with me," Mrs. Peters said nervously, as the two women were about to follow the men in through the kitchen door.

Even after she had her foot on the door-step, her hand on the knob, Martha Hale had a moment of feeling she could not cross that threshold. And the reason it seemed she couldn't cross it now was simply because she hadn't crossed it before. Time and time again it had been in her mind, *I ought to go over and see Minnie Foster*—she still thought of her as Minnie Foster, though for twenty years she had been Mrs. Wright. And then there was always something to do and Minnie Foster would go from her mind. But now she could come.

The men went over to the stove. The women stood close together by the door. Young Henderson, the county attorney, turned around and said, "Come up to the fire, ladies."

Mrs. Peters took a step forward, then stopped. "I'm not—cold," she said.

And so the two women stood by the door, at first not even so much as looking around the kitchen.

The men talked for a minute about what a good thing it was the sheriff had sent his deputy out that morning to make a fire for them, and then Sheriff Peters stepped back from the stove, unbuttoned his outer coat, and leaned on the kitchen table in a way that seemed to mark the beginning of official business. "Now, Mr. Hale," he said in a sort of semi-official voice, "before we move things about, you tell Mr.

Henderson just what it was you saw when you came here yesterday morning."

The county attorney was looking around the kitchen.

"By the way," he said, "has anything been moved?" He turned to the sheriff. "Are things just as you left them yesterday?"

Peters looked from cupboard to sink; from that to a small worn rocker a little to one side of the kitchen table.

"It's just the same."

"Somebody should have been left here yesterday," said the county attorney.

"Oh—yesterday," returned the sheriff, with a little gesture as of yesterday having been more than he could bear to think of. "When I had to send Frank to Morris Center for that man who went crazy; let me tell you, I had my hands full yesterday. I knew you could get back from Omaha by today, George, and as long as I went over everything here myself—"

"Well, Mr. Hale," said the county attorney, in a way of letting what was past and gone go, "tell just what happened when you came here yesterday morning."

Mrs. Hale, still leaning against the door, had that sinking feeling of the mother whose child is about to speak a piece. Lewis often wandered along and got things mixed up in a story. She hoped he would tell this straight and plain, and not say unnecessary things that would just make things harder for Minnie Foster. He didn't begin at once and she noticed that he looked queer, as if standing in that kitchen and having to tell what he had seen there yesterday morning made him almost sick.

"Yes, Mr. Hale?" the county attorney reminded.

"Harry and I had started to town with a load of potatoes," Mrs. Hale's husband began.

Harry was Mrs. Hale's oldest boy. He wasn't with them now, for the very good reason that those potatoes never got to town yesterday and he was taking them this morning, so he hadn't been home when the sheriff stopped to say he wanted Mr. Hale to come over to the Wright place and tell the county attorney his story there, where he could point it all out. With all Mrs. Hale's other emotions came the fear now that maybe Harry wasn't dressed warm enough; they hadn't any of them realized how that north wind did bite.

"We came along this road," Hale was going on, with a motion of his hand to the road over which they had just come, "and as we got in sight of the house I says to Harry, 'I'm goin' to see if I can't get John Wright to take a telephone.' You see," he explained to Henderson, "unless I can get somebody to go in with me they won't come out this branch road except for a price I can't pay. I'd spoke to Wright about it once before; but he put me off, saying folks talked too much anyway, and all he asked was peace and quiet—guess you know about how much he talked himself. But I thought maybe if I went to the house and talked about it before his wife, and said all the women-folks liked the telephones, and that in this lonesome stretch of road it would be a good thing—well, I said to Harry that that was what I was going to say—though I said at the same time that I didn't know what his wife wanted made much difference to John—"

Now there he was, saying things he didn't need to say! Mrs. Hale tried to catch her husband's eye, but fortunately the county attorney interrupted with:

"Let's talk about that a little later, Mr. Hale. I do want to talk about that, but I'm anxious now to get along to what happened when you got here."

When he began this time, it was very deliberately and carefully:

"I didn't see or hear anything. I knocked at the door. And still it was all quiet inside. I knew they must be up—it was past eight o'clock. So I knocked again, louder, and I thought I heard somebody say, 'Come in.' I wasn't sure, I'm not sure yet. But I opened the door, this door—" jerking a hand toward the door by which the two women stood—"and there, in that rocker—" pointing to it—"sat Mrs. Wright."

Everyone in the kitchen looked at the rocker. It came into Mrs. Hale's mind that that rocker didn't look in the least like Minnie Foster, the Minnie Foster of twenty years before. It was a dingy red, with wooden rungs up the back, and the middle rung was gone, and the chair sagged to one side.

"How did she—look?" the county attorney was inquiring.

"She looked queer," said Hale.

"How do you mean, queer?"

As he asked it he took out a notebook and pencil. Mrs. Hale did not like the sight of that pencil. She kept her eyes fixed on her husband, as if to keep him from saying unnecessary things that would go into that notebook and make trouble.

Hale did speak guardedly, as if the pencil had affected him too.

"Well, as if she didn't know what she was going to do next. And kind of—done up."

"How did she seem to feel about your coming?"

"Why, I don't think she minded one way or other. She didn't pay much attention. I said, 'Ho' do, Mrs. Wright? It's cold, ain't it?' and she said, 'Is it?' and went on pleatin' at her apron.

"Well, I was surprised. She didn't ask me to come up to the stove or to sit down, but just set there, not even lookin' at me. And so I said: 'I want to see John.'

"And then she laughed. I guess you would call it a laugh.

"I thought of Harry and the team outside, so I said, a little sharp, 'Can I see John?' 'No,' says she kind of dull like. 'Ain't he home?' says I. Then she looked at me. 'Yes,' says she, 'he's home.' 'Then why can't I see him?' I asked her, out of patience with her now. ''Cause he's dead,' says she, just as quiet and dull, and fell to pleatin' her apron. 'Dead?' says I, like you do when you can't take in what you've heard.

"She just nodded her head, not getting a bit excited, but rocking back and forth.

"'Why—where is he?' says I, not knowing what to say.

"She just pointed upstairs—like this," pointing to the room above.

"I got up, with the idea of going up there myself. By this time I didn't know what to do. I walked from there to here; then I says: 'Why, what did he die of?'

"'He died of a rope round his neck,' says she; and just went on pleatin' at her apron."

Hale stopped speaking and stood staring at the rocker, as if he were still seeing the woman who had sat there the morning before. Nobody spoke; it was as if everyone were seeing the woman who had sat there the morning before.

"And what did you do then?" the county attorney broke the silence.

"I went out and called Harry. I thought I might need help. I got Harry in and we went upstairs." His voice fell almost to a whisper. "There he was—lying over the—"

"I think I'd rather have you go into that upstairs," the county attorney interrupted, "where you can point it all out. Just go on now with the rest of the story."

"Well, my first thought was to get that rope off. It looked—"

He stopped, his face twitching. "But Harry, he went up to him, and he said, 'No, he's dead all right and we'd better not touch anything.' So we went downstairs.

"She was still sitting that same way. 'Has anybody been notified?' I asked. 'No,' says she, unconcerned.

"'Who did this, Mrs. Wright?' said Harry. He said it businesslike, and she stopped pleatin' her apron. 'I don't know,' she says. 'You don't know?' says Harry. 'Weren't you sleepin' in the bed with him?' 'Yes,' says she, 'but I was on the inside.' 'Somebody slipped a rope round his neck and strangled him and you didn't wake up?' says Harry. 'I didn't wake up,' she said after him.

"We may have looked as if we didn't see how that could be, for after a minute she said, 'I sleep sound.'

"Harry was going to ask her more questions, but I said maybe that weren't our business; maybe we ought to let her tell her story first to the coroner or the sheriff. So Harry went fast as he could over to High Road, the Rivers' place, where there's a phone."

"And what did she do when she knew you had gone for the coroner?" The attorney got his pencil in his hand all ready for writing.

"She moved from that chair to this one over here," Hale pointed to a small chair in the corner, "and just sat there with her hands held together and looking down. I got a feeling that I ought to make some conversation, so I said I had come in to see if John wanted to put in a telephone; and at that she started to laugh, and then she stopped and looked at me, scared."

At sound of a moving pencil the man who was telling the story looked up.

"I dunno, maybe it wasn't scared," he hastened; "I wouldn't like to say it was. Soon Harry got back, and then Dr. Lloyd came, and you, Mr. Peters, and so I guess that's all I know that you don't."

He said that last with relief and moved a little, as if relaxing. Everyone moved a little. The county attorney walked toward the stair door.

"I guess we'll go upstairs first, then out to the barn and around there."

He paused and looked around the kitchen.

"You're convinced there was nothing important here?" he asked the sheriff. "Nothing that would—point to any motive?"

The sheriff too looked all around, as if to reconvince himself.

"Nothing here but kitchen things," he said, with a little laugh for the insignificance of kitchen things.

The county attorney was looking at the cupboard, a peculiar, ungainly structure, half closet and half cupboard, the upper part of it being built in the wall, and the lower part just the old-fashioned kitchen cupboard. As if its queerness attracted him, he got a chair and opened the upper part and looked in. After a moment he drew his hand away sticky.

"Here's a nice mess," he said resentfully.

The two women had drawn nearer and now the sheriff's wife spoke.

"Oh, her fruit," she said, looking to Mrs. Hale for sympathetic understanding. She turned back to the county attorney and explained: "She worried about that when it turned so cold last night. She said the fire would go out and her jars might burst."

Mrs. Peters' husband broke into a laugh.

"Well, can you beat the women! Held for murder and worrying about her preserves!"

The young attorney set his lips.

"I guess before we're through with her she may have something more serious than preserves to worry about."

"Oh, well," said Mrs. Hale's husband, with good natured superiority, "women are used to worrying over trifles."

The two women moved a little closer together. Neither of them spoke. The county attorney seemed suddenly to remember his manners and think of his future.

"And yet," said he, with the gallantry of a young politician, "for all their worries, what would we do without the ladies?"

The women did not speak, did not unbend. He went to the sink and began washing his hands. He turned to wipe them on the roller towel; whirled it for a cleaner place.

"Dirty towels! Not much of a housekeeper, would you say, ladies?"

He kicked his foot against some dirty pans under the sink.

"There's a great deal of work to be done on a farm," said Mrs. Hale stiffly.

"To be sure. And yet," with a little bow to her, "I know there are some Dickson County farmhouses that do not have such roller towels." He gave it a pull to expose its full length again.

"Those towels get dirty awful quick. Men's hands aren't always as clean as they might be."

"Ah, loyal to your sex, I see," he laughed. He stopped and gave her a keen look. "But you and Mrs. Wright were neighbors. I suppose you were friends too."

Martha Hale shook her head.

"I've seen little enough of her of late years. I've not been in this house —it's more than a year."

"Why was that? You didn't like her?"

"I liked her well enough," she replied with spirit. "Farmers' wives have their hands full, Mr. Henderson. And then—" She looked around the kitchen.

"Yes?" he encouraged.

"It never seemed a cheerful place," said she, more to herself than to him.

"No," he agreed, "I don't think anyone would call it cheerful. I shouldn't say she had the homemaking instinct."

"Well, I don't know as Wright had, either," she muttered.

"You mean they didn't get on very well?" he was quick to ask.

"No, I don't mean anything," she answered with decision. As she turned a little away from him, she added, "But I don't think a place would be any the cheerfuller for John Wright bein' in it."

"I'd like to talk to you about that a little later, Mrs. Hale," he said. "I'm anxious to get the lay of things upstairs now."

He moved toward the stair door, followed by the two men.

"I suppose anything Mrs. Peters does'll be all right?" the sheriff inquired. "She was to take in some clothes for her, you know, and a few little things. We left in such a hurry yesterday."

The county attorney looked at the two women they were leaving alone there among the kitchen things.

"Yes—Mrs. Peters," he said, his glance resting on the woman who was not Mrs. Peters, the big farmer woman who stood behind the sheriff's wife. "Of course Mrs. Peters is one of us," he said, in a manner of entrusting responsibility. "And keep your eye out, Mrs. Peters, for anything that might be of use. No telling; you women might come upon a clue to the motive and that's the thing we need."

Mr. Hale rubbed his face after the fashion of a showman getting ready for a pleasantry.

"But would the women know a clue if they did come upon it?" he said; and, having delivered himself of this, he followed the others through the stair door.

The women stood motionless and silent, listening to the footsteps, first upon the stairs, then in the room above.

Then, as if releasing herself from something strange, Mrs. Hale began to arrange the dirty pans under the sink, which the county attorney's disdainful push of the root had deranged.

"I'd hate to have men comin' into my kitchen," she said testily, "snoopin' round and criticizin'."

"Of course it's no more than their duty," said the sheriff's wife, in her manner of timid acquiescence.

"Duty's all right," replied Mrs. Hale bluffly, "but I guess that deputy sheriff that come out to make the fire might have got a little of this on." She gave the roller towel a pull. "Wish I'd thought of that sooner! Seems mean to talk about her for not having things slicked up when she had to come away in such a hurry."

She looked around the kitchen. Certainly it was not "slicked up." Her eye was held by a bucket of sugar on a low shelf. The cover was off the bucket and beside it was a paper bag, half full.

Mrs. Hale moved toward it.

"She was putting this in there," she said to herself slowly.

She thought of the flour in her kitchen at home, half sifted, half not sifted. She had been interrupted, and had left things half done. What had interrupted Minnie Foster? Why had that work been left half done? She made a move as if to finish it; unfinished things always bothered her; and she didn't want Mrs. Peters to get that feeling she had got of work begun and then for some reason not finished.

"It's a shame about her fruit," she said and walked toward the cupboard that the county attorney had opened, and got on the chair, murmuring: "I wonder if it's all gone."

It was a sorry enough looking sight, but, "Here's one that's all right," she said at last. She held it toward the light. "This is cherries, too." She looked again. "I declare, I believe that's the only one."

With a sigh, she got down from the chair, went to the sink and wiped off the bottle.

"She'll feel awful bad, after all her hard work in the hot weather. I remember the afternoon I put up my cherries last summer."

She set the bottle on the table and, with another sigh, started to sit down in the rocker. But she did not sit down. Something kept her from sitting down in that chair. She straightened, stepped back and, half turned away, stood looking at it, seeing the woman who had sat there "pleatin' at her apron."

The thin voice of the sheriff's wife broke in upon her: "I must be getting those things from the front-room closet." She opened the door into the other room, started in, stepped back. "You coming with me, Mrs. Hale?" she asked nervously. "You—you could help me get them."

They were soon back; the stark coldness of that shut-up room was not a thing to linger in.

"My!" said Mrs. Peters, dropping the things on the table and hurrying to the stove.

Mrs. Hale stood examining the clothes the woman who was being detained in town had said she wanted.

"Wright was close!" she exclaimed, holding up a shabby black skirt that bore the marks of much making over. "I think maybe that's why she kept so much to herself. I s'pose she felt she couldn't do her part; and then, you don't enjoy things when you feel shabby. She used to wear pretty clothes and be lively when she was Minnie Foster, one of the town's girls, singing in the choir. But that—oh, that was twenty years ago."

With a carefulness in which there was something tender, she folded the shabby clothes and piled them at one corner of the table. She looked up at Mrs. Peters, and there was something in the other woman's look that irritated her.

"She don't care," she said to herself. "Much difference it makes to her whether Minnie Foster had pretty clothes when she was a girl."

Then she looked again and she wasn't so sure; in fact, she hadn't at any time been perfectly sure about Mrs. Peters. She had that shrinking manner, and yet her eyes looked as if they could see a long way into things.

"This all you was to take in?" asked Mrs. Hale.

"No," said the sheriff's wife, "she said she wanted an apron. Funny thing to want," she ventured in her nervous way, "for there's not much to get you dirty in jail, goodness knows. But I suppose just to make her feel more natural. If you're used to wearing an apron— She said they were in the bottom drawer of this cupboard. Yes, here they are. And then her little shawl that always hung on the stair door."

She took the small gray shawl from behind the door leading upstairs and stood a minute looking at it.

Suddenly Mrs. Hale took a quick step toward the other woman.

"Mrs. Peters!"

"Yes, Mrs. Hale?"

"Do you think she—did it?"

A frightened look blurred the other thing in Mrs. Peters' eyes.

"Oh, I don't know," she said in a voice that seemed to shrink away from the subject.

"Well, I don't think she did," affirmed Mrs. Hale stoutly. "Asking for an apron and her little shawl. Worryin' about her fruit."

"Mr. Peters says—" Footsteps were heard in the room above; she stopped, looked up, then went on in a lowered voice, "Mr. Peters says—it looks bad for her. Mr. Henderson is awful sarcastic in a speech and he's going to make fun of her saying she didn't—wake up."

For a moment Mrs. Hale had no answer. Then, "Well, I guess John Wright didn't wake up when they was slippin' that rope under his neck," she muttered.

"No, it's *strange,"* breathed Mrs. Peters. "They think it was such a funny way to kill a man."

She began to laugh; at sound of the laugh, abruptly stopped.

"That's just what Mr. Hale said," said Mrs. Hale, in a resolutely natural voice. "There was a gun in the house. He says that's what he can't understand."

"Mr. Henderson said, coming out, that what was needed for the case was a motive. Something to show anger—or sudden feeling."

"Well, I don't see any signs of anger around here," said Mrs. Hale. "I don't—"

She stopped. It was as if her mind tripped on something. Her eye was caught by a dishtowel in the middle of the kitchen table. Slowly she moved toward the table. One half of it was wiped clean, the other half messy. Her eyes made a slow, almost unwilling turn to the bucket of sugar and the half empty bag beside it. Things begun and not finished.

After a moment she stepped back and said, in that manner of releasing herself:

"Wonder how they're finding things upstairs? I hope she had it a little more red up up there. You know," she paused, and feeling gathered, "it seems kind of sneaking: locking her up in town and coming out here to get her own house to turn against her!"

"But, Mrs. Hale," said the sheriff's wife, "the law is the law."

"I s'pose 'tis," answered Mrs. Hale shortly.

She turned to the stove, saying something about that fire not being much to brag of. She worked with it a minute and when she straightened up she said aggressively:

"The law is the law and a bad stove is a bad stove. How'd you like to cook on this?"—pointing with the poker to the broken lining. She opened the oven door and started to express her opinion of the oven; but she was swept into her own thoughts, thinking of what it could mean, year after year, to have that stove to wrestle with. The thought of Minnie Foster trying to bake in that oven and the thought of her never going over to see Minnie Foster—

She was startled by hearing Mrs. Peters say: "A person gets discouraged and loses heart."

The sheriff's wife had looked from the stove to the sink, to the pail of water which had been carried in from outside. The two women stood there silent, above them the footsteps of the men who were looking for evidence against the woman who had worked in that kitchen. That look of seeing into things, of seeing through a thing to something else, was in the eyes of the sheriff's wife now. When Mrs. Hale next spoke to her, it was gently.

"Better loosen up your things, Mrs. Peters. We'll not feel them when we go out."

Mrs. Peters went to the back of the room to hang up the fur tippet she was wearing. A moment later she exclaimed, "Why, she was piecing a quilt," and held up a large sewing basket piled high with quilt pieces.

Mrs. Hale spread some of the blocks on the table.

"It's a log-cabin pattern," she said, putting several of them together. "Pretty, isn't it?"

They were so engaged with the quilt that they did not hear the footsteps on the stairs. Just as the stair door opened Mrs. Hale was saying:

"Do you suppose she was going to quilt it or just knot it?"

The sheriff threw up his hands.

"They wonder whether she was going to quilt it or just knot it!"

There was a laugh for the ways of women, a warming of hands over the stove, and then the county attorney said briskly:

"Well, let's go right out to the barn and get that cleared up."

"I don't see as there's anything so strange," Mrs. Hale said resentfully, after the outside door had closed on the three men, "our taking up our time with little things while we're waiting for them to get the evidence. I don't see as it's anything to laugh about."

"Of course they've got awful important things on their minds," said the sheriff's wife apologetically.

They returned to an inspection of the block for the quilt. Mrs. Hale was looking at the fine, even sewing, and preoccupied with thoughts of the woman who had done that sewing, when she heard the sheriff's wife say in a queer tone:

"Why, look at this one."

She turned to take the block held out to her.

"The sewing," said Mrs. Peters, in a troubled way. "All the rest of them have been so nice and even—but—this one. Why, it looks as if she didn't know what she was about!"

Their eyes met, something flashed to life, passed between them; then, as if with an effort, they seemed to pull away from each other. A moment Mrs. Hale sat there, her hands folded over that sewing which was so unlike all the rest of the sewing. Then she had pulled a knot and drawn the threads.

"Oh, what are you doing, Mrs. Hale?" asked the sheriff's wife, startled.

"Just pulling out a stitch or two that's not sewed very good," said Mrs. Hale mildly.

"I don't think we ought to touch things," Mrs. Peters said a little helplessly.

"I'll just finish up this end," answered Mrs. Hale, still in that mild, matter-of-fact fashion.

She threaded a needle and started to replace bad sewing with good. For a little while she sewed in silence. Then, in that thin, timid voice, she heard:

"Mrs. Hale!"

"Yes, Mrs. Peters?"

"What do you suppose she was so—nervous about?"

"Oh, I don't know," said Mrs. Hale, as if dismissing a thing not important enough to spend much time on. "I don't know as she was—nervous. I sew awful queer sometimes when I'm just tired."

She cut a thread and out of the corner of her eye looked up at Mrs. Peters. The small, lean face of the sheriff's wife seemed to have tightened up. Her eyes had that look of peering into something. But next moment she moved and said in her thin, indecisive way:

"Well, I must get those clothes wrapped. They may be through sooner than we think. I wonder where I could find a piece of paper and string."

"In that cupboard, maybe," suggested Mrs. Hale, after a glance around.

One piece of the crazy sewing remained unripped. Mrs. Peters' back turned, Martha Hale now scrutinized that piece, compared it with the dainty, accurate sewing of the other blocks.

The difference was startling. Holding this block made her feel queer, as if the distracted thoughts of the woman who had perhaps turned to it to try and quiet herself were communicating themselves to her.

Mrs. Peters' voice roused her.

"Here's a bird cage," she said. "Did she have a bird, Mrs. Hale?"

"Why, I don't know whether she did or not." She turned to look at the cage Mrs. Peters was holding up. "I've not been here in so long." She sighed. "There was a man round last year selling canaries cheap but I don't know as she took one. Maybe she did. She used to sing real pretty herself."

Mrs. Peters looked around the kitchen.

"Seems kind of funny to think of a bird here." She half laughed, an attempt to put up a barrier. "But she must have had one or why would she have a cage? I wonder what happened to it."

"I suppose maybe the cat got it," suggested Mrs. Hale, resuming her sewing.

"No; she didn't have a cat. She's got that feeling some people have about cats, being afraid of them. When they brought her to our house yesterday, my cat got in the room and she was real upset and asked me to take it out."

"My sister Bessie was like that," laughed Mrs. Hale.

The sheriff's wife did not reply. The silence made Mrs. Hale turn around. Mrs. Peters was examining the bird cage.

"Look at this door," she said slowly. "It's broke. One hinge has been pulled apart."

Mrs. Hale came nearer.

"Looks as if someone must have been rough with it."

Again their eyes met, startled, questioning, apprehensive. For a moment neither spoke nor stirred. Then Mrs. Hale, turning away, said brusquely:

"If they're going to find any evidence, I wish they'd be about it. I don't like this place."

"But I'm awful glad you came with me, Mrs. Hale." Mrs. Peters put the bird cage on the table and sat down. "It would be lonesome for me sitting here alone."

"Yes—it would, wouldn't it?" agreed Mrs. Hale, a certain determined naturalness in her voice. She had picked up the sewing, but now it dropped in her lap and she murmured in a different voice: "But I tell you what I do wish, Mrs. Peters. I wish I had come over sometimes when she was here. I wish I had."

"But of course you were awful busy, Mrs. Hale. Your house and your children."

"I could've come," retorted Mrs. Hale shortly. "I stayed away because it weren't cheerful and that's why I ought to have come. I—" she looked around—"I've never liked this place. Maybe because it's down in a hollow and you don't see the road. I don't know what it is, but it's a lonesome place and always was. I wish I had come over to see Minnie Foster sometimes. I can see now—" She did not put it into words.

"Well, you mustn't reproach yourself," counseled Mrs. Peters. "Somehow, we just don't see how it is with other folks till something comes up."

"Not having children makes less work," mused Mrs. Hale, after a silence, "but it makes a quiet house, and Wright out to work all day, and no company when he did come in. Did you know John Wright, Mrs. Peters?"

"Not to know him. I've seen him in town. They say he was a good man."

"Yes—good," conceded John Wright's neighbor grimly. "He didn't drink and kept his word as well as most, I guess, and paid his debts. But he was a hard man, Mrs. Peters. Just to pass the time of day with him—" She stopped, shivered a little. "Like a raw wind that gets to the bone." Her eye fell upon the cage on the table before her, and she added, almost bitterly: "I should think she would've wanted a bird!"

Suddenly she leaned forward, looking intently at the cage. "But what do you s'pose went wrong with it?"

"I don't know," returned Mrs. Peters, "unless it got sick and died."

But after she said it she reached over and swung the broken door. Both women watched it as if somehow held by it.

"You didn't know her?" Mrs. Hale asked, a gentler note in her voice.

"Not till they brought her yesterday," said the sheriff's wife.

"She—come to think of it, she was kind of like a bird herself. Real sweet and pretty, but kind of timid and—fluttery. How she did change."

That held her for a long time. Finally, as if struck with a happy thought and relieved to get back to everyday things, she exclaimed:

"Tell you what, Mrs. Peters, why don't you take the quilt in with you? It might take up her mind."

"Why, I think that's a real nice idea, Mrs. Hale," agreed the sheriff's wife, as if she too were glad to come into the atmosphere of a simple kindness. "There couldn't possibly be any objection to that, could there? Now, just what will I take? I wonder if her patches are in here and her things."

They turned to the sewing basket.

"Here's some red," said Mrs. Hale, bringing out a roll of cloth. Underneath that was a box. "Here, maybe her scissors are in here and her things." She held it up. "What a pretty box! I'll warrant that was something she had when she was a girl."

She held it in her hand a moment; then, with a little sigh, opened it. Instantly her hand went to her nose.

"Why—!"

Mrs. Peters drew nearer, then turned away.

"There's something wrapped up in this piece of silk," faltered Mrs. Hale.

"This isn't her scissors," said Mrs. Peters in a shrinking voice.

Her hand not steady, Mrs. Hale raised the piece of silk. "Oh, Mrs. Peters!" she cried. "It's—"

Mrs. Peters bent closer.

"It's the bird," she whispered.

"But, Mrs. Peters!" cried Mrs. Hale. "Look at it! Its neck—look at its neck! It's all—other side too."

She held the box away from her.

The sheriff's wife again bent closer.

"Somebody wrung its neck," said she in a voice that was slow and deep.

And then again the eyes of the two women met, this time clung together in a look of dawning comprehension, of growing horror. Mrs. Peters looked from the dead bird to the broken door of the cage. Again their eyes met. And just then there was a sound at the outside door.

Mrs. Hale slipped the box under the quilt pieces in the basket and sank into the chair before it. Mrs. Peters stood holding to the table. The county attorney and the sheriff came in from outside.

"Well, ladies," said the county attorney, as one turning from serious things to little pleasantries, "have you decided whether she was going to quilt it or knot it?"

"We think," began the sheriff's wife in a flurried voice, "that she was going to—knot it."

He was too preoccupied to notice the change in her voice.

"Well, that's very interesting, I'm sure," he said tolerantly. He caught sight of the bird cage. "Has the bird flown?"

"We think the cat got it," said Mrs. Hale in a voice curiously even.

He was walking up and down, as if thinking something out.

"Is there a cat?" he asked absently.

Mrs. Hale shot a look up at the sheriff's wife.

"Well, not now," said Mrs. Peters. "They're superstitious, you know; they leave."

She sank into her chair.

The county attorney did not heed her. "No sign at all of anyone having come in from the outside," he said to Peters in the manner of continuing an interrupted conversation. "Their own rope. Now let's go upstairs again and go over it, piece by piece. It would have to have been someone who knew the—"

The stair door closed behind them.

The two women sat motionless, not looking at each other, but as if peering into something and at the same time holding back. When they spoke now it was as if they were afraid of what they were saying, but as if they could not help saying it.

"She liked the bird," said Martha Hale, low and slowly. "She was going to bury it in that pretty box."

"When I was a girl," said Mrs. Peters, under her breath, "my kitten—there was a boy took a hatchet, and before my eyes—before I could get there—" She covered her face an instant. "If they hadn't held me back I would have" she caught herself, looked upstairs where footsteps were heard, and finished weakly—"hurt him."

"I wonder how it would seem," Mrs. Hale at last began, as if feeling her way over strange ground, "never to have had any children around?" Her eyes made a slow sweep of the kitchen, as if seeing what that kitchen had meant through all the years. "No, Wright wouldn't like the bird," she said after that, "a thing that sang. She used to sing. He killed that too."

Mrs. Peters moved uneasily.

"Of course we don't know who killed the bird."

"I knew John Wright," was Mrs. Hale's answer.

"It was an awful thing was done in this house that night, Mrs. Hale," said the sheriff's wife. "Killing a man while he slept, slipping a thing round his neck that choked the life out of him."

Mrs. Hale's hand went out to the bird cage.

"His neck. Choked the life out of him."

"We don't know who killed him," whispered Mrs. Peters wildly.

Mrs. Hale had not moved. "If there had been years and years of—nothing, then a bird to sing to you, it would be awful—still—after the bird was still."

It was as if something within her not herself had spoken and it found in Mrs. Peters something she did not know as herself.

"I know what stillness is," she said, in a queer, monotonous voice. "When we homesteaded in Dakota and my first baby died and me with no other—"

Mrs. Hale stirred.

"How soon do you suppose they'll be through looking for evidence?"

"I know what stillness is," repeated Mrs. Peters in just the same way. Then she too pulled back. "The law has got to punish crime, Mrs. Hale," she said in her tight little way.

"I wish you'd seen Minnie Foster," was the answer, "when she wore a white dress with blue ribbons and stood up there in the choir and sang."

The picture of that girl, the fact that she had lived neighbor to that girl for twenty years and had let her die for lack of life, was suddenly more than she could bear.

"Oh, I wish I'd come over here once in awhile!" she cried. "That was a crime! Who's going to punish that?"

"We mustn't take on," said Mrs. Peters with a frightened look.

"I might 'a' known she needed help! I tell you, it's queer, Mrs. Peters. We live close together and we lived far apart. We all go through the same things, it's all just a different kind of the same thing! If it weren't—why do you and I understand? Why do we know what we know this minute?"

She dashed her hand across her eyes. Then, seeing the jar of fruit on the table, she reached for it.

"If I was you I wouldn't tell her her fruit was gone! Tell her it ain't. Tell her it's all right—all of it. Here, I take this in to prove it to her! She—she may never know it was broke."

She turned away.

Mrs. Peters reached out for the bottle of fruit as if she were glad to take it, as if touching a familiar thing, having something to do, could keep her from something else. She got up, looked about for something to wrap the fruit in, took a petticoat from the pile of clothes she had brought from the front room and nervously started winding that round the bottle.

"My!" she began in a high, false voice, "it's a good thing the men couldn't hear us! Getting all stirred up over a little thing like a—dead canary." She hurried over that. "My wouldn't they laugh?"

Footsteps were heard on the stairs.

"Maybe they would," muttered Mrs. Hale, "maybe they wouldn't."

"No, Peters," said the county attorney incisively, "it's all perfectly clear, except the reason for doing it. But you know juries when it comes to women. If there was some definite thing, something to show—"

In a covert way Mrs. Hale looked at Mrs. Peters. Mrs. Peters was looking at her. Quickly they looked away from each other. The outer door opened and Mr. Hale came in.

"I've got the team round now," he said. "Pretty cold out there."

"I'm going to stay here awhile by myself," the county attorney suddenly announced. "You can send Frank out for me, can't you?" he asked the sheriff. "I'm not satisfied we can't do better."

Again, for one brief moment, the two women's eyes found one another.

The sheriff came up to the table.

"Did you want to see what Mrs. Peters was going to take in?"

The county attorney picked up the apron. He laughed.

"Oh, I guess they're not very dangerous things the ladies have picked out."

Mrs. Hale's hand was on the sewing basket in which the box was concealed. She felt that she ought to take her hand off the basket. She did not seem able to. He picked up one of the quilt blocks which she had piled on to cover the box. Her eyes felt like fire. She had a feeling that if he took up the basket she would snatch it from him.

But he did not take it up. With another little laugh, he turned away, saying:

"No, Mrs. Peters doesn't need supervising. For that matter, a sheriff's wife is married to the law. Ever think of it that way, Mrs. Peters?"

Mrs. Peters was standing beside the table. Mrs. Hale shot a look up at her, but she could not see her face. Mrs. Peters had turned away. When she spoke, her voice was muffled.

"Not—just that way," she said.

"Married to the law!" chuckled Mrs. Peters' husband. He moved toward the door into the front room, and said to the county attorney:

"I just want you to come in here a minute, George. We ought to take a look at these windows."

"Oh, windows," said the county attorney scoffingly.

"We'll be right out, Mr. Hale," said the sheriff to the farmer, who was still waiting by the door.

Hale went to look after the horses. The sheriff followed the county attorney into the other room. Again, for one final moment, the two women were alone in that kitchen.

Martha Hale sprang up, her hands tight together, looking at that other woman, with whom it rested. At first she could not see her eyes, for the sheriff's wife had not turned back since she turned away at that suggestion of being married to the law. But now Mrs. Hale made her turn back. Her eyes made her turn back. Slowly, unwillingly, Mrs. Peters turned her head until her eyes met the eyes of the other woman. There was a moment when they held each other in a steady, burning look in which there was no evasion nor flinching. Then Martha Hale's eyes pointed the way to the basket in which was hidden the thing that would make certain the conviction of the other woman—that woman who was not there and yet who had been there with them all through that hour.

For a moment Mrs. Peters did not move. And then she did it. With a rush forward, she threw back the quilt pieces, got the box, tried to put it in her handbag. It was too big. Desperately she opened it, started to take the bird out. But there she broke, she could not touch the bird. She stood there helpless, foolish.

There was the sound of a knob turning in the inner door. Martha Hale snatched the box from the sheriff's wife and got it in the pocket of her big coat just as the sheriff and the county attorney came back into the kitchen.

"Well, Henry," said the county attorney facetiously, "at least we found out that she was not going to quilt it. She was going to—what is it you call it, ladies?"

Mrs. Hale's hand was against the pocket of her coat.

"We call it—knot it, Mr. Henderson."

WISCONSIN

The Cobweb

ZONA GALE

Evenings, at seven o'clock, the new Timber Library opened for an hour. Unless there was a band concert, or a moving-picture show, or a night that Timber called "real bad and sloppy out," Emmons's store, for that hour, was the center of village life. A corner of the store was the City Library. There, Bathany Emmons kept sacred to books a section of shelves, beyond the canned goods and above the salt-fish barrel. The top shelf, too high to be reached by Lissa Bard, the librarian, held the dried-fruit boxes. The grocery was not large; and by seven o'clock, one winter Saturday night, it was filled with women borrowers.

Lissa Bard had not come in. It not infrequently happened, however, that, by the newness of her duties or by her nature, Lissa was late at her post. And of this and of other things about her, three women, standing near the threshold of the little dark coffee-smelling back room of the store, talked enjoyably while they waited.

"It's often that way with sister," Mrs. Hibbard observed. (Mrs. Hibbard always set the "t" in "often," and the "u" in "column," "because," she defended, "there they are, all ready to say. It isn't like the psalm p—that's Bible, and old-fashioned, and not a real necessary word anyway. But 'often' and 'column' you hear every day, and that's all the more reason to take pains with them."

"Yes, you look at the Clark girls," Mrs. Arthur, with her challenging emphasis, agreed; "one is light skin and no life, and the other one's black hair and goes like the wind. And the Mosses; one of them like real folks, and the other one just kind of big and in the way. But the two Bards: they're more different than it's possible to be."

"Lissy always was a real scholar," Mrs. Main said, sighing, "and real intelligent too. But of the two, poor Kate is the only housekeeper."

Mrs. Arthur nodded, tapping an emphasis on the cookbook she was returning.

"Well," she said, "if you're not a good housekeeper, with all that means, what are you? And Kate is. The run of books is all very well, and nobody likes to see them in anybody's parlor more than our family, but there's no contradicting: they're not to eat nor drink, nor sweep the floor with. Kate Bard keeps house like waxworks, if Lissy has got the brains."

In the moment of strained silence that fell as the three women became aware of her presence, Kate Bard, who had entered the store through the little dark back room, stood at their elbows, nodded to them all, and looked elaborately as if she had not heard. But they all knew that she must have heard.

Mrs. Arthur, as culprit, did her part, and laughed out, heartily and guiltily.

"Lawsey, Kate," she said, "are you listening? Well, nobody born keeps house any neater than you do, and you know it."

Little, flat-waisted, her pointed face held slightly down, her large eyes raised, the gray shawl about her head caught tightly beneath her chin, Kate Bard looked at the three with a faint twist of smile and briefly closed lids.

"Shucks," she said, and passed them.

Seeing her, Bathany Emmons took down the lamp from its bracket above his desk, and set it on the deal table of the City Library.

"Lissa's late getting started," Kate explained to everyone, throwing off her shawl, with a stiff swing of her head to keep her hair free of it. "She wanted I should come on ahead and say she'd be right over. She was afraid somebody might get tired waiting, an' try to go off."

She sat at the table awkwardly; the librarianship was new to Lissa, and Kate had not before been asked to take her sister's place. She fell to rearranging the little articles: the petrified potato inkwell, the pretty stone, the smart plush case of the thermometer.

Mrs. Arthur, who had followed her to the table, laid down the cookbook.

"I've got to get back home and hunt up the clean clothes," Mrs. Arthur said, "so mebbe you could give me some book yourself, Kate. I thought of The Pathfinder. I've been reading that all my life, off and on. I guess I'll get it out and read a couple or two more chapters on it."

Kate rose and took up the lamp and held it in both hands while she looked along the lowest shelf, squinting in the light, her lips moving as she read the titles. The lowest shelf held the set of Dickens, bound in four volumes, and that of Scott, in eight, and of Dumas in eight: tall, startled-looking tomes, each appearing to wonder at itself for being so many books in one. Halfway across the row Kate turned, frowning a little.

"Know who wrote it?" she inquired.

"Wasn't his name Cooper, or like that?" Mrs. Arthur hesitated. "I've got that name in my head."

"Is it poetry or reading?" Kate demanded.

"Oh, reading," Mrs. Arthur said hastily. "Land! It's for myself."

"Anybody got it out?" Kate called in a moment. "Anybody got out a book called Pathfinder?" she repeated over-shoulder.

"I've read it," "I've read it twice," several volunteered. And, "I've never read it, but I've heard of it," offered Mrs. Hibbard pleasantly. "I dunno but what you're looking at the wrong writers," she added to Kate. "Mr. Cooper isn't a set. He's just that one."

And now Kate's search was extending laboriously over the titles on the histories and lives. And at last it touched at a big, black book without a binding, and she set down the lamp to take the volume from the shelf. But when it was in her hands, she did not see the title.

"My soul," she said, "look at the dust."

From the top of the black book she blew a fine, quite visible cloud, in evidence for one full breath; and at one more breath there was a little second cloud. And from the book's edge fine tentacles of cobweb clung and outwavered and caught at Kate's hands and drew about her wrists like airy manacles. Quite instinctively she turned to the side of the shelves, where a dust-cloth might be native; and, the cloth not being there, she opened the table-drawer and reached capably back among its tumbled papers. Evidently Lissa had no dust-cloth, and Kate glanced perplexedly about. "I never come out without my handkerchief that I'm not sure to need it for something," she observed, and caught up a corner of her dressing-sack and dusted the black book. Then she took down another book and another—the histories and the lives—and from each she blew fine, condemnatory dust, and each she carefully brushed with the dressing-sack until the blue cloth, like her hands, was cobweb-covered.

She was still at her task when the bell above the store's front door jingled noisily, much as if a gay little wind had prevailed against it. The wind—that one or another—entering with the opening of the door, breathed on a kerosene lamp aswing from the ceiling, and momentarily it flared up and brightened all the store. Then the door was smartly shut, and Lissa Bard came down the room, a blown leaf of a figure, wind still in her strayed hair, brightness in her face. She was tiny, frail of waist and wrist, evidently unable to undertake tasks of the hand, but armored with the disinction of her book-craft and with mere charm; so that whatever was her excuse—and no one quite caught it—seemed admirably to answer, and no one seemed really to care that when the librarian reached the City Library, the clock above the cheese pointed to fifteen past seven.

Kate stood hitching her shawl from side to side, upward from waist to shoulder.

"Have you got Cooper's Pathfinder in the library?" she asked, and, intent on her shawl, missed the shade of amused surprise in Lissa's look.

"Why yes!" Lissa said. "Don't you know—"

"Well, somebody must have it out," Kate went on. "It isn't on the shelves. I've read through almost every name."

Lissa's eyes danced.

"Why, we've got it out!" she cried. "I read it aloud to you last night."

At that the women about the table laughed, frankly and unrestrainedly. Kate Bard colored slowly, her thin cheeks burning in two high, bright spots. Then she made her twisted smile and closed her eyes momentarily.

"I'm no hand to look at the name of a book I'm interested in," she said. "Every man's name that writes them sounds just alike to me, anyhow. Good night, all."

But as she crossed the alley from the store to the house where, until Lissa's recent home-coming, she had lived alone, Kate's smile went out. She fumbled in the pump-spout for the key, stepped into the chill cheer of the kitchen, went about the unimportant offices of her return; and in her breast something hurt and seemed heavy, so that she felt a sickness almost physical. But then for days she had not been well—"a peaked feelin'," she had described her state to Lissa—and now she tried to think that this was the weakness that she felt. She knew better than that, however; and when she had turned up the wick and poked at the fire in the cooking-stove, she sat down before the open oven door, her skirt turned back to dry its hem, and tried to brave the thing that hurt. And what she had to brave were Lissa's eyes, dancing to her own reply, and Lissa's light laughter threading the inadvertent, wounding mockery of the women.

From her school Lissa had lately come into Kate's orderly life and home and quite casually had accepted both. Kate's surprise, first amused, then grieved, grew to an understanding that her own talent in what she called "flying round the house" was to Lissa a matter of course, as spring must be a matter of course to a tributary wind. Kate observed that Lissa at her "book-reading" quickened as she never quickened in the presence of that vague spirit of home to which Kate sacrificed with her housewifery. And of all this the older sister had come to think with tender tolerance for the child ill equipped for home-craft, and promptness, and all exactitudes. Yet this child and the women had laughed at her for not knowing about Pathfinder, and nobody had laughed at the dust on the City Library books. And Mrs. Arthur had used a kind of defense in: "Kate Bard keeps house like wax-works, if Lissy has got all the brains."

Her resentment toward Lissa could not all have come in that hour, for now it was big in her, a living thing. Lissa had laughed with the rest; and since her return home there must have been other things at which she had laughed, secretly. In spite of Kate's own chieftainship in the home, Lissa all this time must have been making allowance for her—Lissa, who always had been auxiliary in the household and not a burdenbearer, who was temperamentally alien to responsibility, who was of those who never turn the soil for a garden, but merely drop in the seeds. "She's a poor little stick of a housekeeper and always will be," Kate thought miserably, "and everybody in Timber knows that. And yet they'll bow down to her, knee to dust, because she knows a few funny names." So she thought about it, burning, resolutely overcoming her own tenderness.

After a time, as she tended her skirt's hem in the growing warmth, her look fell on her cooking-stove oven, from which she had drawn thousands of loaves and cakes. Behind the sink looking-glass there was a paper on which she had once tried to compute these loaves and to reckon how many times she had turned the clock-key. And by the wood-box stood the little toy broom that she used for sweeping the top of the long stovepipe, where dust and cobwebs never gathered, and of the cupboard, where no spider ever lived a day. The cupboards locked away the dishes which she knew; as Lissa knew the City Library books, Kate knew those dishes, line and crack and nick; knew what should be piled in what on the ordered shelves; knew every stain and knothole of the unpainted floor; and the look of the other rooms, lying beyond in the dark—spotless, dustless, their parts adjusted in all the scrupulous nicety with which men should legislate a nation. It was the work of her hands, and her glow was that of the creator who greets his achievement and his waiting material, and lords it over them, and in them passionately sees, for his spirit, the way out. All this was hers, as peculiarly hers as Lissa's little toy kingdom of funny names. Here she was mistress, here her skill was of importance, here—she sank in the consciousness as into cherishing arms—Lissa could never enter.

And there isn't a housekeeper in Timber but what knows that! Kate thought, with her little twisted smile.

When her sister came from the library, Kate still sat by the open oven door. Unaccustomed to fathom mood, to divine the tentacle-like, waving things that web it round, Lissa, bright and uncorrelated, chattered while her wraps came off.

"So many books went out! I haven't started keeping the cards yet, but I guess Bathany could tell how many. Everybody who took a book bought something: Kenilworth and ten cents' worth of crackers; David Copperfield and a jug of vinegar; Vanity Fair and a pound of prunes. We had to stop the whole circulating department while Bathany climbed the library desk to get those prunes down. Oh, Kate! And little Aggie Ellsworth asked me for thweet pickelth, and I reached for the catalogue before I saw the tin pail and sent her across to Bathany!"

Kate did not laugh.

"Been me," she said somberly, "I'd have been hunting along the shelves for it yet. Unless," she added, "Aggie'd spoken the pickle man's name. The pickle authors I can seem to keep pretty straight in my head."

Something in her sister's attitude arrested Lissa's look as she came to the stove.

"Are you cold?" she inquired.

"No," Kate answered listlessly. "I feel some chilly—on my shoulders. But I guess I just like to be warm."

"You aren't well," Lissa said with decision. "You haven't felt well for days. I'll put a flatiron on. You sit there and toast your feet and I'll read to you while the iron heats."

Without waiting for assent, Lissa brought The Pathfinder from the "other" room and set the table-lamp on a wooden-bottomed chair drawn to the hearth. She herself sat on the braided hearth-rug. As she read, Kate looked down at her—a frail little figure whose bent head showed her fair curls at their best. The warm light from the open draft fell on the small-featured face, no longer in its first youth, but having that perennial youth of a body remote from the activities that age, of a spirit without flight, but perpetually fanning certain wings. And as Kate looked, for the first time she became conscious of, say, these wings. Maybe Lissa's "book-reading" was a kingdom of more than funny names. Maybe it was as real a comfort to her as "flying round the house" to Kate herself. Maybe it was a bigger, better place to be, and this the women in the store knew, and that was why they had laughed. The perception came to the older woman in an impression as sharp and as wordless as a wound. And the conviction possessed her the more that her perceptions could not be ordered or explained by her, but merely suffered.

It's something inside of her that I haven't got and never did have, Kate thought. We're different, but it isn't the same kind of different as her liking her bread thin and me liking mine thick; or her opening her window nights and me shutting mine almost down; or her turning the lamp-wick down and me blazing it away up. She's to some woke-up thing in her that bites down on i-dees the way I spy on to dust and cobwebs. She's more than different. She's the otherest from me that a person can be.

And as the understanding grew upon her, Kate turned the more passionately to her own place, as if her way of skill were a pleasance where she might have her ease, take her way out. Lissa might have some dimly guessed better kingdom, but Kate's kingdom was her own. She was like a word, envious of an idea, but glorying in the certainty that the idea could not be spelled without her.

Until Lissa had finished a chapter and had gone away to iron the chill sheets of her sister's bedroom, Kate brooded and burned. Then she rose and took the book from the wing of the stove where Lissa had slid it, and turned to the title-page. So many books! So many different names! But it would not be a disgrace not to remember who had been president of the United States in a certain year, and that was far more important than book names. Yet all those women had laughed at her, and Lissa's eyes had laughed. If only Lissa would laugh at her now for that blunder in the library! No need of her keeping such a nasty, delicate silence, Kate thought.

"The bed's all ready when you are," Lissa called.

Kate closed the book and spoke over-shoulder to the open door.

"I'm nowhere near ready," she said tartly. "Lissa Bard! You've let the books down to the City Library get a perfect sight. There's dust on them like feathers, and cobwebs a regular fringe. And now you've laid Mr. Cooper's book on the stove-wing out here and it'll get all splattered with grease. If I was so crazy about book-reading, I declare if I wouldn't do different."

In Lissa's amazed silence, away there in the bedroom, Kate looked about the kitchen. Then she opened the cupboard door, and, tiptoe, laid the book on the top shelf. There, with the toy broom kept for stovepipe cobwebs, she thrust The Pathfinder far back, beside the cherry-pitter.

Her chilliness and weariness had foretold the illness which seized Kate that night, and when the Sunday morning came, she was hot with fever and throbbing with pain. Lissa woke, vaguely alarmed not to hear her sister already astir, and for a little lay listening, then went to her door.

"I don't want a doctor," Kate observed weakly. "I'd just as lief have a cat open the door and walk around the bed. You heat me a cup of hot water."

Lissa hurried her dressing, built a fire in the frosty kitchen, waited interminably for the kettle to boil. Kate's silence and her inability to drink even the water terrified the girl as if in the little house some sinister presence had appeared. And when it was church time, and from the kitchen window she saw Mrs. Arthur and Mrs. Hibbard coming down the street, she ran outside and, not to pass Kate's window, stumbled through the deep snow on the side of the yard that was pathless.

"Oh," she told them, "I don't know what's the matter with Kate! She's sick and in the bed."

The women, accustomed to treat all crises as their own, followed Lissa to the house, accepting the pathless way as a matter of course, and briskly questioning. Was Kate conscious? When was she taken? There were colds everywhere and it was real pneumonia weather. Had she had her sister's hands and feet in good hot water? They laid their hymn-books by the unwashed dishes and stalked through the cold dining-room to Kate's little grave of a chamber.

"Lawsey, Kate Bard, you thought you'd take down to relieve the monotony, did you?" one of them greeted her.

Kate, opening her eyes, saw them standing in a place without walls and from which she was infinitely remote. She knew them, but instantly she was aware that they were allied against her, and with them was Lissa. Secure in some friendly and infinitely companionable understanding to which she was alien, they were all laughing at her. And so thought drifted out, without her power to grasp at one association to stay its drifting.

In the weeks that followed, her wandering look often rested unseeingly on one or the other of those two faces, or on the face of Mrs. Main, who forever crossed the alley from her home to bring a covered bowl of something steaming. Sometimes Kate saw them quite clearly; sometimes the faces blurred and flickered, the better to menace her; always they were quick with an understanding of something that she did not know. But even a greater vexation was the face which hovered constantly above her—that of Lissa. The stricken brain, become a thing of sick impressions that outwavered and clung and fled, lay as if webbed about by its last sane sensation.

They were all persistently "against her," they all knew something that she did not know—and with them was Lissa, who could not even take care of her books. Lissa's books were all dust and cobwebs. The dust and cobwebs were what shut away the meaning in the books so that she could not know all about them, as Lissa knew. And before she too could know, the dust and cobwebs must all be swept away with the toy broom.

Dust and cobwebs, dust and cobwebs. In her fever this became to her a kind of refrain. And it was no great gulf to have bridged from fantasy to faculty when at last one day Kate lay quiet, listening to what the women were saying, and realized that she had been listening for some moments before she was self-conscious.

". . . awful. I donno how it is folks can do as they *do* do. Some seems just bent on getting along any way they can. Shouldn't you think she'd have noticed it by now if she was calculating to do any noticing?"

It was Mrs. Hibbard's voice; without lifting her tired lids Kate knew that. Mrs. Arthur's emphasis seemed as usual to make a kind of groove for her own reply.

"Well," Mrs. Arthur put it, "if ever I saw anybody no hand to take notice, it's her. She doesn't seem to go by rhyme nor rule. If she was a clock, you couldn't tell the time by her no more than you could tell time by a wild duck. She just sort of goes along, and goes along . . ."

Kate's little figure lay tense. They meant her!

". . . for eight days, hand-running," Mrs. Main was saying. "And there it is, full the way it was when I first laid look to it—floating away as hard as it could float, and just like it was made for floating."

And "It doesn't seem," Mrs. Arthur said, "as if two sisters could be so opposite. Do you suppose Kate Bard, in her well days, would ever leave a cobweb swinging that long?"

At that a pang of fierce delight shot through Kate's whole body. It was not she that they meant. It was not she!

"The idea," the hushed voices went on, "of taking no more responsibility. It's plumb over Kate's head when she lies on the back pillow. It might drop on her any minute."

"The only wonder is it hasn't fallen on her long before now. But it's a good strong cobweb—it's old enough to have body to it, the dear land knows. How long do you suppose Lissy'll let it be there?"

"I've sat here and watched her when she dusts, and she goes right past it as if it had been a wreath in the border. I suppose it's mean, but I declare I've got interested seeing how long it'll stay there. Why, Kate Bard would die rather than to have a cobweb in the family that long."

When the women, still talking, had left the room, Kate lay for a long time without opening her eyes. Like a warm lapping bath it rested her, this indignant praise of her, yes, and this arraignment of Lissa. She lay, luxuriously glad, smiling a little, alive and praised. And after a very long time she languidly opened her eyes and, almost with a sense of gratitude, looked about for the cobweb.

In all Kate's lifetime there had never been, in the bare little room, a cobweb like that. It hung from the corner above the bed, attached just where the eagle on the side-wall border met the stars on the ceiling. To eagle and stars it clung by many a visible filament, and, escaping these, it floated, in vagrant currents, its full yard length. It was, Kate thought, like an attic cobweb, a cobweb behind the store-room blinds in house-cleaning. But a house cobweb, a bedroom cobweb like that—her head drooped sidewise on its pillow, and her eyes fell on the little toy broom in a corner—she must have brought the little broom in with her from the kitchen on the night of her illness, and Lissa had left it there. Its uselessness and isolation in the face of so obvious a task moved her to laughter. She lay for a little, shaken with silent mirth, until from weakness she fell asleep.

When she awoke, Lissa sat by the bed with a book. If only Lissa had been sewing, the return to life would have been a simpler matter; but Lissa was reading. For some time she did not lift her eyes from the page, and Kate lay watching her. The girl's face was pleased and quiet, and it shut Kate out.

"What you reading?" Kate demanded abruptly.

Lissa started, tossed aside the book, hung above her sister with little happy exclamations; but these and the many questions Kate passed impatiently.

"What you reading?" she persisted. "Pathfinder?"

"No," Lissa said. "Kate, I found The Pathfinder away on the top shelf of the cupboard, when I was looking for the potato-masher. How do you suppose it ever got up there?"

To which, with closed eyes and a mere shadow of her twisted smile, Kate responded: "Who ever heard of keeping anybody's potato-masher on the *top* shelf? What you reading?"

In some wonder Lissa named her book, a strange, singing name that told Kate nothing.

"Read some out loud," she commanded; and, at Lissa's look, "Go on!" she added. "I'm not out of my head. I feel just like life."

So Lissa read to her at random, wondering, secretly simplifying, or making in her voice little shallows of shadow and crests of clearness, more safely to bear meaning. But she knew that she was alone as she read, and that it was Kate who could not come to her.

When the reading paused, "Keep it up," Kate said; I donno what it means, but it rubs around nice on the outside of my brain."

But, Kate was brooding, Lissa did know what it meant. Lissa knew, not just with her brain, outside or inside, but with the "woke-up thing" in her, the thing that somehow could "bite a-hold of life." She could not have told why she had wanted Lissa to read, whether in some wistfulness to try to share whatever Lissa had, or whether for a kind of dogged strengthening of her own resentment. As she lay listening, her thought returned and beat upon Lissa, and her own irritation increased and mounted and possessed her. So then she turned passionately to the warm spot in her consciousness, the certainty, unformulated but secure, that for her the way of "biting a-hold of life" lay in manipulating those little engineries of home, in that which she called "flying round the house."

She moved her head and lay looking up where the eagle met the stars, above the back pillow. It was thick and gray and dusty, that cobweb. And all this time, in spite of that mysterious, wise, "woke-up thing" within her, Lissa had missed the cobweb—as of course Lissa would miss it! A glow crept and warmed Kate. Poor Lissa! she thought. She said it over and over, luxuriously; and, lulled by the singing things freed from the book, she fell asleep.

The four o'clock sun streamed across the blue coverlet, illumining the blossoms of a begonia on the window-sill, wakening Kate. In the bedroom it was deliciously quiet. A wood-fire was crackling in the parlor stove. On the table a napkin-covered dish awaited her mood. Murmur of voices penetrated the closed kitchen door, eloquent of the gentleness that tended her. The convalescent's sense of well-being filled Kate.

In a week, she thought, she would be about again—flying round the house. How long it had been since she had seen her oven! It would be good to shut the hot door on a batch of bread, a tin of cake, a pan of cookies. She must get at her cupboards and give them "a good going-over." Lissa never could remember what was to be piled in what.

She found herself even wanting to wind the clock—Lissa had probably let it run down and, when she set it, had guessed at the time. Poor Lissa! she thought pleasurably.

Yes, the whole house must be gone over thoroughly, must be swept and dusted and rid of its cobwebs; the very first day that she was about again, down should come that cobweb wavering there over her head. Then, when Mrs. Hibbard and Mrs. Arthur and Mrs. Main dropped in, she would make excuse to lead them into the bedroom. She would pretend not to see them exchange glances of approval of her and of her housekeeping, which was so much better than Lissa's. Poor Lissa!

On that, as at a motif, Lissa came into the room, in her hand a blue dust-cloth and a feather-duster. From the kitchen still sounded the voices, and Lissa answered Kate's questioning look.

"I was just coming to wipe up the dust a little, if you were awake," she explained, "when Mrs. Hibbard and Mrs. Arthur and Mrs. Main came in. They'd heard you were conscious. They told me to go right ahead, I'd had to neglect this room so long, and they'd sit there and get warm and come in here afterward."

"Oh," said Kate, "*that's* how they did it."

She lay still while Lissa dusted. When she was well, it had immeasurably irritated Kate to see Lissa dust. To all wide, flat, horizontal surfaces the girl gave the prettiest attention, bending to her task till the curls in her neck were at their best. But all narrow edges, the tops of chairs, of splashers, of pictures, she neglected as if they were in another dimension, and flat vertical surfaces she treated as if they were in no dimension at all. For Lissa, dust that was immaterial was non-existent. For Kate, even if dust were non-existent, dusting was dusting. Yet that day it was with definite enjoyment that Kate lay with half-closed eyes and watched.

A gay little wind would have dusted a room much as did Lissa. The wind—that one or another—would have entered and breathed on this and that, touching and lifting, rearranging a disorder rather than ordering. And so Lissa did, omitting needs in all the pretty complaisance with which a housekeeper divines them.

Ordinarily Kate would have crashed down on the process with the finality of a drawn blind. Now she lay benignly indulgent—as spring at the gaucheries of some faint tributary wind.

But always there had been in Kate's attitude to Lissa much of the attitude of motherhood. Lissa's body had constantly demanded the guardianship of which her mind was childishly impatient. This late resentment of Kate's was wholly toward that mysterious "woke-up thing," unfostered of her, which made Lissa remote, versed in baffling matters. Yet now, as she worked, these matters were no longer evident. Instead, in her own unwonted leisure and supineness, Kate was immeasurably struck with the littleness of her sister, with her physical unfitness for tasks of the hand. Her slenderness of throat, of waist, of wrist, her narrowness of shoulder and thigh—these smote Kate with a pitying sense of the girl's utter inadequacy for her woman's work. Poor little Lissa—poor little Lissa! That was it: poor little Lissa!

Lissa came, in her dusting, to the bed's head, and this, presumably because of Kate's presence, she did not touch at all. Lying so that she could see the cobweb, Kate held her breath as Lissa moved about its corner. Because of her long habit of getting good things for her, almost Kate wished that Lissa would look up toward the spot where it hung.

There came a stillborn impulse to tell her. But Kate watched her turn away without an upward glance toward eagles and stars, and then, when the impulse to tell her had not yet wholly passed, the girl serenely shook the dust-cloth in the room, in the mere general direction of the paper-basket.

"Shall I have Mrs. Hibbard and Mrs. Arthur and Mrs. Main come in for a minute?" she asked.

"Yes!" Kate burst out. "My land, yes. Have them in here! And you get back to your book."

Lissa looked at her inquiringly. "I've got the supper to get pretty soon now," she said.

As one divining tentacle-like things that web one round, Kate heard the undernote of weariness in the girl's voice. Her fragility had always made Kate fear that she might be tired or ill or even merely cold. The older sister threw out her hand on the coverlet.

"Well, you keep them out there a minute or two," she said irresolutely. "I'll pound on the wall with the little broom there—you set it by the bed—in just a minute. Then you let them come in."

Left alone, Kate shut her eyes tightly, grotesquely, in her unwonted will to think swiftly and to a purpose. And in that troubled darkness she visualized the faces of the three women, looking her over sympathetically enough, asking their intimate questions, honestly glad of her recovery, but all the while waiting for a chance to peer up in that cobwebbed corner and then to look at one another, moving confirmatory eyebrows or lids or lips. It all came to Kate as a picture only, but she knew its truth. She knew how they would go away telling scornfully about Lissa Bard's housekeeping, and praising her—Kate—in the comparison; these very women who had laughed at her, as Lissa had laughed. But they must not laugh at Lissa too, poor little Lissa!

Kate lifted her head tentatively from the pillow and then drew herself to sit erect, a scant, gaunt figure in its outing flannel, with a tight braid of gray hair reaching hardly half-way down the gown's yoke. Something seemed tipping her dizzy head like a weight when, with infinite difficulty, she groped out for the toy broom. In the faintness that seized her as she pulled herself to her knees on the bed, then unsteadily to her feet, the darkness within her closed lids changed to a glow of red. She saw nothing of what she was doing as she laboriously lifted the little broom up the wall and swept long, random strokes about the corner, freeing from its hold the flaunting filaments that clung and wavered very near her hair, as if they would have webbed her about. Then she sank, her head jarred to dull aching, throbbing and chill in all her body. So she lay, huddled outside the covers until, hearing some stir in the kitchen, she crept into her place, and the toy broom slipped behind the bed to the floor.

Mrs. Hibbard and Mrs. Arthur and Mrs. Main came tiptoeing through the parlor, and pushed at the bedroom door.

"We'll just peek in and see if she's awake," they said to Lissa, who had thought to wait the summons. "You awake, Kate?" one put it fairly.

In the whimsical, faint answer there was all the old vitality. "If you're the nightmare, I'm not," she said; "but if you're a call, I am. Come along in, why don't you?"

They came to the bedside.

"Showed the sense to get well, didn't you, Kate?" said one. "Well said. I'm real pleased you've come to."

"Maybe you think we haven't danced round lively over you while you've been lazing here in the bed," said another. "If you're threatening well, I donno who's got the biggest chore done, you or us."

"Lawsey, Kate Bard," said the third, "I thought one while your coffin was cut, but I guess it's green wood yet awhile, and mebbe growing."

Having told her like this of their genuine gladness at her recovery, they all three, with one accord, looked up at the corner of the room, where the eagle met the stars. Kate saw them look, and look again, and risk peering this way and that. Mrs. Hibbard stepped about the foot of the bed to try a new light, Mrs. Arthur came close to Kate's head, as if her assurance were almost reluctant. Then, certainty being fully established, they glanced at one another and moved surprised commendatory heads.

Lissa, tying on her big gingham apron, came to the bedroom door.

"Well, sir, Kate," Mrs. Hibbard said, "I tell you, Lissy's getting to be quite a first-class housekeeper. She'll beat you at it if you don't look out."

In Kate's unimportant reply they could not divine the leaping exultation, as it were the very romance of renunciation. Nor did they understand her twisted smile.

CALIFORNIA

The Red Pony

JOHN STEINBECK

At daybreak Billy Buck emerged from the bunkhouse and stood for a moment on the porch looking up at the sky. He was a broad, bandy-legged little man with a walrus mustache, with square hands, puffed and muscled on the palms. His eyes were a contemplative, watery gray and the hair which protruded from under his Stetson hat was spiky and weathered. Billy was still stuffing his shirt into his blue jeans as he stood on the porch. He unbuckled his belt and tightened it again. The belt showed, by the worn shiny places opposite each hole, the gradual increase of Billy's middle over a period of years. When he had seen to the weather, Billy cleared each nostril by holding its mate closed with his forefinger and blowing fiercely. Then he walked down to the barn, rubbing his hands together. He curried and brushed two saddle horses in the stalls, talking quietly to them all the time; and he had hardly finished when the iron triangle started ringing at the ranch house. Billy stuck the brush and currycomb together and laid them on the rail, and went up to breakfast. His action had been so deliberate and yet so waste-less of time that he came to the house while Mrs. Tiflin was still ringing the triangle. She nodded her gray head to him and withdrew into the kitchen. Billy Buck sat down on the steps, because he was a cow-hand, and it wouldn't be fitting that he should go first into the dining-room. He heard Mr. Tiflin in the house, stamping his feet into his boots.

The high jangling note of the triangle put the boy Jody in motion. He was only a little boy, ten years old, with hair like dusty yellow grass and with shy polite gray eyes, and with a mouth that worked when he thought. The triangle picked him up out of sleep. It didn't occur to

---

him to disobey the harsh note. He never had; no one he knew ever had. He brushed the tangled hair out of his eyes and skinned his nightgown off. In a moment he was dressed—blue chambray shirt and overalls. It was late in the summer, so of course there were no shoes to bother with. In the kitchen he waited until his mother got from in front of the sink and went back to the stove. Then he washed himself and brushed back his wet hair with his fingers. His mother turned sharply on him as he left the sink. Jody looked shyly away.

"I've got to cut your hair before long," his mother said. "Breakfast's on the table. Go on in, so Billy can come."

Jody sat at the long table which was covered with white oilcloth washed through to the fabric in some places. The fried eggs lay in rows on their platter. Jody took three eggs on his plate and followed with three thick slices of crisp bacon. He carefully scraped a spot of blood from one of the egg yolks.

Billy Buck clumped in. "That won't hurt you," Billy explained. "That's only a sign the rooster leaves."

Jody's tall stern father came in then and Jody knew from the noise on the floor that he was wearing boots, but he looked under the table anyway, to make sure. His father turned off the oil lamp over the table, for plenty of morning light now came through the windows.

Jody did not ask where his father and Billy Buck were riding that day, but he wished he might go along. His father was a disciplinarian. Jody obeyed him in everything without questions of any kind. Now, Carl Tiflin sat down and reached for the egg platter.

"Got the cows ready to go, Billy?" he asked.

"In the lower corral," Billy said. "I could just as well take them in alone."

"Sure you could. But a man needs company. Besides your throat gets pretty dry." Carl Tiflin was jovial this morning.

Jody's mother put her head in the door. "What time do you think to be back, Carl?"

"I can't tell. I've got to see some men in Salinas. Might be gone till dark."

The eggs and coffee and big biscuits disappeared rapidly. Jody followed the two men out of the house. He watched them mount their horses and drive six old milk cows out of the corral and start over the hill toward Salinas. They were going to sell the old cows to the butcher.

When they had disappeared over the crown of the ridge Jody walked up the hill in back of the house. The dogs trotted around the house corner, hunching their shoulders and grinning horribly with pleasure. Jody patted their heads—Doubletree Mutt with the big thick tail and yellow eyes, and Smasher, the shepherd, who had killed a coyote and lost an ear in doing it. Smasher's one good ear stood up higher than a collie's ear should. Billy Buck said that always happened. After the frenzied greeting the dogs lowered their noses to the ground in a business-like way and went ahead, looking back now and then to make sure that the boy was coming. They walked up through the chicken yard and saw the quail eating with the chickens. Smasher chased the chickens a little to keep in practice in case there should ever be sheep to herd.

Jody continued on through the large vegetable patch where the green corn was higher than his head. The cow-pumpkins were green and small yet. He went on to the sagebrush line where the cold spring ran out of its pipe and fell into a round wooden tub. He leaned over and drank close to the green mossy wood where the water tasted best. Then he turned and looked back on the ranch, on the low, whitewashed house girded with red geraniums, and on the long bunk-house by the cypress tree where Billy Buck lived alone. Jody could see the great black kettle under the cypress tree. That was where the pigs were scalded. The sun was coming over the ridge now, glaring on the whitewash of the houses and barns, making the wet grass blaze softly. Behind him, in the tall sage-brush, the birds were scampering on the ground, making a great noise among the dry leaves; the squirrels piped shrilly on the side-hills. Jody looked along at the farm buildings. He felt an uncertainty in the air, a feeling of change and of loss and of the gain of new and unfamiliar things. Over the hillside two big black buzzards sailed low to the ground and their shadows slipped smoothly and quickly ahead of them. Some animal had died in the vicinity. Jody knew it. It might be a cow or it might be the remains of a rabbit. The buzzards overlooked nothing. Jody hated them as all decent things hate them, but they could not be hurt because they made away with carrion.

After awhile the boy sauntered down hill again. The dogs had long ago given him up and gone into the brush to do things in their own way. Back through the vegetable garden he went, and he paused for a moment to smash a green musk-melon with his heel, but he was not happy about it. It was a bad thing to do, he knew perfectly well. He kicked dirt over the ruined melon to conceal it.

Back at the house his mother bent over his rough hands, inspecting his fingers and nails. It did little good to start him clean to school for too many things could happen on the way. She sighed over the black cracks on his fingers, and then gave him his books and his lunch and started him on the mile walk to school. She noticed that his mouth was working a good deal this morning.

Jody started his journey. He filled his pockets with little pieces of white quartz that lay in the road, and every so often he took a shot at a bird or at some rabbit that had stayed sunning itself in the road too long. At the crossroads over the bridge he met two friends and the three of them walked to school together, making ridiculous strides and being rather silly. School had just opened two weeks before. There was still a spirit of revolt among the pupils.

It was four o'clock in the afternoon when Jody topped the hill and looked down on the ranch again. He looked for the saddle horses, but the corral was empty. His father was not back yet. He went slowly, then, toward the afternoon chores. At the ranch house, he found his mother sitting on the porch, mending socks.

"There's two doughnuts in the kitchen for you," she said. Jody slid to the kitchen, and returned with half of one of the doughnuts already eaten and his mouth full. His mother asked him what he had learned in school that day, but she didn't listen to his doughnut-muffled answer. She interrupted, "Jody, tonight see you fill the wood-box clear full. Last night you crossed the sticks and it wasn't only about half full. Lay the sticks flat tonight. And Jody, some of the hens are hiding eggs, or else the dogs are eating them. Look about in the grass and see if you can find any nests."

Jody, still eating, went out and did his chores. He saw the quail come down to eat with the chickens when he threw out the grain. For some reason his father was proud to have them come. He never allowed any shooting near the house for fear the quail might go away.

When the wood-box was full, Jody took his twenty-two rifle up to the cold spring at the brush line. He drank again and then aimed the gun at all manner of things, at rocks, at birds on the wing, at the big black pig kettle under the cypress tree, but he didn't shoot for he had no cartridges and wouldn't have until he was twelve. If his father had seen him aim the rifle in the direction of the house he would have put the cartridges off another year. Jody remembered this and did not point the rifle down the hill again. Two years were enough to wait for cartridges. Nearly all of his father's presents were given with reservations which hampered their value somewhat. It was good discipline.

The supper waited until dark for his father to return. When at last he came in with Billy Buck, Jody could smell the delicious brandy on their breaths. Inwardly he rejoiced, for his father sometimes talked to him when he smelled of brandy, sometimes even told things he had done in the wild days when he was a boy.

After supper, Jody sat by the fireplace and his shy polite eyes sought the room corners, and he waited for his father to tell what it was he contained, for Jody knew he had news of some sort. But he was disappointed. His father pointed a stern finger at him.

"You'd better go to bed, Jody. I'm going to need you in the morning."

That wasn't so bad. Jody liked to do things he had to do as long as they weren't routine things. He looked at the floor and his mouth worked out a question before he spoke it. "What are we going to do in the morning, kill a pig?" he asked softly.

"Never you mind. You better get to bed."

When the door was closed behind him, Jody heard his father and Billy Buck chuckling and he knew it was a joke of some kind. And later, when he lay in bed, trying to make words out of the murmurs in the other room, he heard his father protest, "But, Ruth, I didn't give much for him."

Jody heard the hoot-owls hunting mice down by the barn, and he heard a fruit tree limb tap-tapping against the house. A cow was lowing when he went to sleep.

When the triangle sounded in the morning, Jody dressed more quickly than usual. In the kitchen, while he washed his face and combed back his hair, his mother addressed him irritably. "Don't you go out until you get a good breakfast in you."

He went into the dining room and sat at the long white table. He took a steaming hotcake from the platter, arranged two fried eggs on it, covered them with another hotcake and squashed the whole thing with his fork.

His father and Billy Buck came in. Jody knew from the sound on the floor that both of them were wearing flat-heeled shoes, but he peered under the table to make sure. His father turned off the oil lamp, for the day had arrived, and he looked stern and disciplinary, but Billy

Buck didn't look at Jody at all. He avoided the shy questioning eyes of the boy and soaked a whole piece of toast in his coffee.

Carl Tiflin said crossly, "You come with us after breakfast!"

Jody had trouble with his food then, for he felt a kind of doom in the air. After Billy had tilted his saucer and drained the coffee which had slopped into it, and had wiped his hands on his jeans, the two men stood up from the table and went out into the morning light together, and Jody respectfully followed a little behind them. He tried to keep his mind from running ahead, tried to keep it absolutely motionless.

His mother called, "Carl! Don't you let it keep him from school."

They marched past the cypress, where a singletree hung from a limb to butcher the pigs on, and past the black iron kettle, so it was not a pig killing. The sun shone over the hill and threw long, dark shadows of the trees and buildings. They crossed a stubble-field to shortcut to the barn. Jody's father unhooked the door and they went in. They had been walking toward the sun on the way down. The barn was black as night in contrast and warm from the hay and from the beasts. Jody's father moved over toward the one box stall. "Come here!" he ordered. Jody could begin to see things now. He looked into the box stall and then stepped back quickly.

A red pony colt was looking at him out of the stall. Its tense ears were forward and a light of disobedience was in its eyes. Its coat was rough and thick as an airedale's fur and its mane was long and tangled. Jody's throat collapsed in on itself and cut his breath short.

"He needs a good currying," his father said, "and if I ever hear of you not feeding him or leaving his stall dirty, I'll sell him off in a minute."

Jody couldn't bear to look at the pony's eyes any more. He gazed down at his hands for a moment, and he asked very shyly, "Mine?" No one answered him. He put his hand out toward the pony. Its gray nose came close, sniffing loudly, and then the lips drew back and the strong teeth closed on Jody's fingers. The pony shook its head up and down and seemed to laugh with amusement. Jody regarded his bruised fingers. "Well," he said with pride—"Well, I guess he can bite all right." The two men laughed, somewhat in relief. Carl Tiflin went out of the barn and walked up a side hill to be by himself, for he was embarrassed, but Billy Buck stayed. It was easier to talk to Billy Buck. Jody asked again—"Mine?"

Billy became professional in tone. "Sure! That is, if you look out for him and break him right. I'll show you how. He's just a colt. You can't ride him for some time."

Jody put out his bruised hand again, and this time the red pony let his nose be rubbed. "I ought to have a carrot," Jody said. "Where'd we get him, Billy?"

"Bought him at a sheriff's auction," Billy explained. "A show went broke in Salinas and had debts. The sheriff was selling off their stuff."

The pony stretched out his nose and shook the forelock from his wild eyes. Jody stroked the nose a little. He said softly, "There isn't a—saddle?"

Billy Buck laughed. "I'd forgot. Come along."

In the harness room he lifted down a little saddle of red morocco leather. "It's just a show saddle," Billy Buck said disparagingly. "It isn't practical for the brush, but it was cheap at the sale."

Jody couldn't trust himself to look at the saddle either, and he couldn't speak at all. He brushed the shining red leather with his fingertips, and after a long time he said, "It'll look pretty on him though." He thought of the grandest and prettiest things he knew. "If he hasn't a name already, I think I'll call him Gabilan Mountains," he said.

Billy Buck knew how he felt. "It's a pretty long name. Why don't you just call him Gabilan? That means hawk. That would be a fine name for him." Billy felt glad. "If you will collect tail hair, I might be able to make a hair rope for you some time. You could use it for a hackamore."

Jody wanted to go back to the box stall. "Could I lead him to school, do you think—to show the kids?"

But Billy shook his head. "He's not even halter-broke yet. We had a time getting him here. Had to almost drag him. You better be starting for school though."

"I'll bring the kids to see him here this afternoon," Jody said.

Six boys came over the hill half an hour early that afternoon, running hard, their heads down, their forearms working, their breath whistling. They swept by the house and cut across the stubble-field to the barn. And then they stood self-consciously before the pony, and then they looked at Jody with eyes in which there was a new admiration and a new respect. Before today Jody had been a boy, dressed in overalls and a blue shirt—quieter than most, even suspected of being a little cowardly. And now he was different. Out of a thousand centuries they drew the ancient admiration of the footman for the horseman. They knew instinctively that a man on a horse is spiritually as well as physically bigger than a man on foot. They knew that Jody had been miraculously lifted out of equality with them, and had been placed over them. Gabilan put his head out of the stall and sniffed them.

"Why'n't you ride him?" the boys cried. "Why'n't you braid his tail with ribbons like in the fair?" "When you going to ride him?"

Jody's courage was up. He too felt the superiority of the horseman. "He's not old enough. Nobody can ride him for a long time. I'm going to train him on the long halter. Billy Buck is going to show me how."

"Well, can't we even lead him around a little?"

"He isn't even halter-broke," Jody said. He wanted to be completely alone when he took the pony out the first time. "Come and see the saddle."

They were speechless at the red morocco saddle, completely shocked out of comment. "It isn't much use in the brush," Jody explained. "It'll look pretty on him, though. Maybe I'll ride bareback when I go into the brush."

"How you going to rope a cow without a saddle horn?"

"Maybe I'll get another saddle for every day. My father might want me to help him with the stock." He let them feel the red saddle, and showed them the brass chain throat-latch on the bridle and the big brass buttons at each temple where the headstall and brow band crossed. The whole thing was too wonderful. They had to go away after a little while, and each boy, in his mind, searched among his possessions for a bribe worthy of offering in return for a ride on the red pony when the time should come.

Jody was glad when they had gone. He took brush and currycomb from the wall, took down the barrier of the box stall and stepped cautiously in. The pony's eyes glittered, and he edged around in kicking position. But Jody touched him on the shoulder and rubbed his high arched neck as he had always seen Billy Buck do, and he crooned, "So-o-o Boy," in a deep voice. The pony gradually relaxed his tenseness. Jody curried and brushed until a pile of dead hair lay in the stall and until the pony's coat had taken on a deep red shine. Each time he finished he thought it might have been done better. He braided the mane into a dozen little pigtails, and he braided the forelock, and then he undid them and brushed the hair out straight again.

Jody did not hear his mother enter the barn. She was angry when she came, but when she looked in at the pony and at Jody working over him, she felt a curious pride rise up in her. "Have you forgot the woodbox?" she asked gently. "It's not far off from dark and there's not a stick of wood in the house, and the chickens aren't fed."

Jody quickly put up his tools. "I forgot, ma'am."

"Well, after this do your chores first. Then you won't forget. I expect you'll forget lots of things now if I don't keep an eye on you."

"Can I have carrots from the garden for him, ma'am?"

She had to think about that. "Oh, I guess so, if you only take the big tough ones."

"Carrots keep the coat good," he said, and again she felt the curious rush of pride.

Jody never waited for the triangle to get him out of bed after the coming of the pony. It became his habit to creep out of bed even before his mother was awake, to slip into his clothes and to go quietly down to the barn to see Gabilan. In the gray quiet mornings when the land and the brush and the houses and the trees were silver-gray and black like a photograph negative, he stole toward the barn, past the sleeping stones and the sleeping cypress tree. The turkeys, roosting in the tree out of coyotes' reach, clicked drowsily. The fields glowed with a gray frost-like light and in the dew the tracks of rabbits and of field mice stood out sharply. The good dogs came stiffly out of their little houses, hackles up and deep growls in their throats. Then they caught Jody's scent, and their stiff tails rose up and waved a greeting—Doubletree Mutt with the big thick tail, and Smasher, the incipient shepherd—then went lazily back to their warm beds.

It was a strange time and a mysterious journey to Jody—an extension of a dream. When he first had the pony he liked to torture himself during the trip by thinking Gabilan would not be in his stall, and worse, would never have been there. And he had other delicious little self-induced pains. He thought how the rats had gnawed ragged holes in the red saddle, and how the mice had nibbled Gabilan's tail until it was stringy and thin. He usually ran the last little way to the barn. He unlatched the rusty hasp of the barn door and stepped in, and no matter how quietly he opened the door, Gabilan was always looking at him over the barrier of the box stall and Gabilan whinnied softly and stamped his front foot, and his eyes had big sparks of red fire in them like oakwood embers.

Sometimes, if the work horses were to be used that day, Jody found Billy Buck in the barn harnessing and currying. Billy stood with him and looked long at Gabilan and he told Jody a great many things about horses. He explained that they were terribly afraid for their feet, so that one must make a practice of lifting the legs and patting the hoofs and ankles to remove their terror. He told Jody how horses love conversation. He must talk to the pony all the time, and tell him the reasons for everything. Billy wasn't sure a horse could understand everything that was said to him, but it was impossible to say how much was understood. A horse never kicked up a fuss if someone he liked explained things to him. Billy could give examples too. He had known, for instance, a horse nearly dead beat with fatigue to perk up when told it was only a little farther to his destination. And he had known a horse paralyzed with fright to come out of it when his rider told him what it was that was frightening him. While he talked in the mornings, Billy Buck cut twenty or thirty straws into neat three-inch lengths and stuck them into his hatband. Then during the whole day, if he wanted to pick his teeth or merely to chew on something, he had only to reach up for one of them.

Jody listened carefully, for he knew and the whole country knew that Billy Buck was a fine hand with horses. Billy's own horse was a stringy cayuse with a hammer head, but he nearly always won the first prizes at the stock trials. Billy could rope a steer, take a double half-hitch about the horn with his riata, and dismount, and his horse would play the steer as an angler plays a fish, keeping a tight rope until the steer was down or beaten.

Every morning, after Jody had curried and brushed the pony, he let down the barrier of the stall, and Gabilan thrust past him and raced down the barn and into the corral. Around and around he galloped, and sometimes he jumped forward and landed on stiff legs. He stood quivering, stiff ears forward, eyes rolling so that the whites showed, pretending to be frightened. At last he walked snorting to the water-trough and buried his nose in the water up to the nostrils. Jody was proud then, for he knew that was the way to judge a horse. Poor horses only touched their lips to the water, but a fine spirited beast put his whole nose and mouth under, and only left room to breathe.

Then Jody stood and watched the pony, and he saw things he had never noticed about any other horse, the sleek, sliding flank muscles and the cords of the buttocks, which flexed like a closing fist, and the shine the sun put on the red coat. Having seen horses all his life, Jody had never looked at them very closely before. But now he noticed the moving ears which gave expression and even inflection of expression to the face. The pony talked with his ears. You could tell exactly how he felt about everything by the way his ears pointed. Sometimes they were stiff and upright and sometimes lax and sagging. They went back when he was angry or fearful, and forward when he was anxious and curious and pleased; and their exact position indicated which emotion he had.

Billy Buck kept his word. In the early fall the training began. First there was the halter-breaking, and that was the hardest because it was the first thing. Jody held a carrot and coaxed and promised and pulled on the rope. The pony set his feet like a burrow when he felt the strain. But before long he learned. Jody walked all over the ranch leading him. Gradually he took to dropping the rope until the pony followed him unled wherever he went.

And then came the training on the long halter. That was slower work. Jody stood in the middle of a circle, holding the long halter. He clucked with his tongue and the pony started to walk in a big circle, held in by the long rope. He clucked again to make the pony trot, and again to make him gallop.

Around and around Gabilan went thundering and enjoying it immensely. Then he called, "Whoa," and the pony stopped. It was not long until Gabilan was perfect at it. But in many ways he was a bad pony. He bit Jody in the pants and stomped on Jody's feet. Now and then his ears went back and he aimed a tremendous kick at the boy. Every time he did one of these bad things, Gabilan settled back and seemed to laugh to himself.

Billy Buck worked at the hair rope in the evenings before the fireplace. Jody collected tail hair in a bag, and he sat and watched Billy slowly constructing the rope, twisting a few hairs to make a string and rolling two strings together for a cord, and then braiding a number of cords to make the rope. Billy rolled the finished rope on the floor under his foot to make it round and hard.

The long halter work rapidly approached perfection. Jody's father, watching the pony stop and start and trot and gallop, was a little bothered by it.

"He's getting to be almost a trick pony," he complained. "I don't like trick horses. It takes all the—dignity out of a horse to make him do tricks. Why, a trick horse is kind of like an actor—no dignity, no character of his own." And his father said, "I guess you better be getting him used to the saddle pretty soon."

Jody rushed for the harness-room. For some time he had been riding the saddle on a sawhorse. He changed the stirrup length over and over, and could never get it just right. Sometimes, mounted on the sawhorse in the harness-room, with collars and hames and tugs hung all about him, Jody rode out beyond the room. He carried his rifle across the pommel. He saw the fields go flying by, and he heard the beat of the galloping hoofs.

It was a ticklish job, saddling the pony the first time. Gabilan hunched and reared and threw the saddle off before the cinch could be tightened. It had to be replaced again and again until at last the pony let it stay. And the cinching was difficult too. Day by day Jody tightened the girth a little more until at last the pony didn't mind the saddle at all.

Then there was the bridle. Billy explained how to use a stick of licorice for a bit until Gabilan was used to having something in his mouth. Billy explained, "Of course we could force-break him to everything, but he wouldn't be as good a horse if we did. He'd always be a little bit afraid, and he wouldn't mind because he wanted to."

The first time the pony wore the bridle he whipped his head about and worked his tongue against the bit until the blood oozed from the corners of his mouth. He tried to rub the headstall off on the manger. His ears pivoted about and his eyes turned red with fear and with general rambunctiousness. Jody rejoiced, for he knew that only a mean-souled horse does not resent training.

And Jody trembled when he thought of the time when he would first sit in the saddle. The pony would probably throw him off. There was no disgrace in that. The disgrace would come if he did not get right up and mount again. Sometimes he dreamed that he lay in the dirt and cried and couldn't make himself mount again. The shame of the dream lasted until the middle of the day.

Gabilan was growing fast. Already he had lost the long-leggedness of the colt; his mane was getting longer and blacker. Under the constant currying and brushing his coat lay as smooth and gleaming as orange-red lacquer, Jody oiled the hoofs and kept them carefully trimmed so they would not crack.

The hair rope was nearly finished. Jody's father gave him an old pair of spurs and bent in the side bars and cut down the strap and took up the chainlets until they fitted. And then one day Carl Tiflin said:

"The pony's growing faster than I thought. I guess you can ride him by Thanksgiving. Think you can stick on?"

"I don't know," Jody said shyly. Thanksgiving was only three weeks off. He hoped it wouldn't rain, for rain would spot the red saddle.

Gabilan knew and liked Jody by now. He nickered when Jody came across the stubble-field, and in the pasture he came running when his master whistled for him. There was always a carrot for him every time.

Billy Buck gave him riding instructions over and over. "Now when you get up there, just grab tight with your knees and keep your hands away from the saddle, and if you get throwed, don't let that stop you. No matter how good a man is, there's always some horse can pitch him. You just climb up again before he gets to feeling smart about it. Pretty soon, he won't throw you no more, and pretty soon he *can't* throw you no more. That's the way to do it."

"I hope it don't rain before," Jody said.

"Why not? Don't want to get throwed in the mud?"

That was partly it, and also he was afraid that in the flurry of bucking Gabilan might slip and fall on him and break his leg or his hip. He had seen that happen to men before, had seen how they writhed on the ground like squashed bugs, and he was afraid of it.

He practiced on the sawhorse how he would hold the reins in his left hand and a hat in his right hand. If he kept his hands thus busy, he couldn't grab the horn if he felt himself going off. He didn't like to think of what would happen if he did grab the horn. Perhaps his father and Billy Buck would never speak to him again, they would be so ashamed. The news would get about and his mother would be ashamed too. And in the school yard—it was too awful to contemplate.

He began putting his weight in a stirrup when Gabilan was saddled, but he didn't throw his leg over the pony's back. That was forbidden until Thanksgiving.

Every afternoon he put the red saddle on the pony and cinched it tight. The pony was learning already to fill his stomach out unnaturally large while the cinching was going on, and then to let it down when the straps were fixed. Sometimes Jody led him up to the brush line and let him drink from the round green tub, and sometimes he led him up through the stubble-field to the hilltop from which it was possible to see the white town of Salinas and the geometric fields of the great valley, and the oak trees clipped by the sheep. Now and then they broke through the brush and came to little cleared circles so hedged in that the world was gone and only the sky and the circle of brush were left from the old life. Gabilan liked these trips and showed it by keeping his head very high and by quivering his nostrils with interest. When the two came back from an expedition they smelled of the sweet sage they had forced through.

Time dragged on toward Thanksgiving, but winter came fast. The clouds swept down and hung all day over the land and brushed the hilltops, and the winds blew shrilly at night. All day the leaves drifted down from the trees until they covered the ground, and yet the trees were unchanged.

Jody had wished it might not rain before Thanksgiving, but it did. The brown earth turned dark and the trees glistened. The cut ends of the stubble turned black with mildew; the haystacks grayed from exposure to the damp, and on the roofs the moss, which had been all summer as gray as lizards, turned a brilliant yellow-green. During the week of rain, Jody kept the pony in the box stall out of the dampness, except for a little time after school when he took him out for exercise and to drink at the water-trough in the upper corral. Not once did Gabilan get wet.

The wet weather continued until little new grass appeared. Jody walked to school dressed in a slicker and short rubber boots. At length one morning the sun came out brightly. Jody, at his work in the box stall, said to Billy Buck, "Maybe I'll leave Gabilan in the corral when I go to school today."

"Be good for him to be out in the sun," Billy assured him. "No animal likes to be cooped up too long. Your father and me are going back on the hill to clean the leaves out of the spring." Billy nodded and picked his teeth with one of his little straws.

"If the rain comes, though—" Jody suggested.

"Not likely to rain today. She's rained herself out." Billy pulled up his sleeves and snapped his arm bands. "If it comes on to rain—why, a little rain don't hurt a horse."

"Well, if it does come on to rain, you put him in, will you, Billy? I'm scared he might get cold so I couldn't ride him when the time comes."

"Oh, sure! I'll watch out for him if we get back in time. But it won't rain today."

And so Jody, when he went to school, left Gabilan standing out in the corral.

Billy Buck wasn't wrong about many things. He couldn't be. But he was wrong about the weather that day, for a little after noon the clouds pushed over the hills and the rain began to pour down. Jody heard it start on the schoolhouse roof. He considered holding up one finger for permission to go to the outhouse and, once outside, running for home to put the pony in. Punishment would be prompt both at school and at home. He gave it up and took ease from Billy's assurance that rain couldn't hurt a horse. When school was finally out, he hurried home through the dark rain. The banks at the sides of the road spouted little jets of muddy water. The rain slanted and swirled under a cold and gusty wind. Jody dog-trotted home, slopping through the gravelly mud of the road.

From the top of the ridge he could see Gabilan standing miserably in the corral. The red coat was almost black, and streaked with water. He stood head down with his rump to the rain and wind. Jody arrived running and threw open the barn door and led the wet pony in by his forelock. Then he found a gunny sack and rubbed the soaked hair and rubbed the legs and ankles. Gabilan stood patiently, but he trembled in gusts like the wind.

When he had dried the pony as well as he could, Jody went up to the house and brought hot water down to the barn and soaked the grain in it. Gabilan was not very hungry. He nibbled at the hot mash, but he was not very much interested in it, and he still shivered now and then. A little steam rose from his damp back.

It was almost dark when Billy Buck and Carl Tiflin came home. "When the rain started we put up at Ben Herche's place, and the rain never let up all afternoon," Carl Tiflin explained. Jody looked reproachfully at Billy Buck, and Billy felt guilty.

"You said it wouldn't rain," Jody accused him.

Billy looked away. "It's hard to tell, this time of year," he said, but his excuse was lame. He had no right to be fallible and he knew it.

"The pony got wet, got soaked through."

"Did you dry him off?"

"I rubbed him with a sack and I gave him hot grain."

Billy nodded in agreement.

"Do you think he'll take cold, Billy?"

"A little rain never hurt anything," Billy assured him.

Jody's father joined the conversation then and lectured the boy a little. "A horse," he said, "isn't any lap-dog kind of thing." Carl Tiflin hated weakness and sickness, and he held a violent contempt for helplessness.

Jody's mother put a platter of steaks on the table and boiled potatoes and boiled squash, which clouded the room with their steam. They sat down to eat. Carl Tiflin still grumbled about weakness put into animals and men by too much coddling.

Billy Buck felt bad about his mistake. "Did you blanket him?" he asked.

"No. I couldn't find any blanket. I laid some sacks over his back."

"We'll go down and cover him up after we eat, then." Billy felt better about it then. When Jody's father had gone in to the fire and his mother was washing dishes, Billy found and lighted a lantern. He and Jody walked through the mud to the barn. The barn was dark and warm and sweet. The horses still munched their evening hay. "You hold the lantern!" Billy ordered. And he felt the pony's legs and tested the heat of the flanks. He put his cheek against the pony's gray muzzle and then he rolled up the eyelids to look at the eyeballs and he lifted the lips to see the gums, and he put his fingers inside the ears. "He don't seem so chipper," Billy said. "I'll give him a rubdown."

Then Billy found a sack and rubbed the pony's legs violently and he rubbed the chest and the withers. Gabilan was strangely spiritless. He submitted patiently to the rubbing. At last Billy brought an old cotton comforter from the saddle-room, and threw it over the pony's back and tied it at neck and chest with string.

"Now he'll be all right in the morning," Billy said.

Jody's mother looked up when he got back to the house. "You're late up from bed," she said. She held his chin in her hard hand and brushed the tangled hair out of his eyes and she said, "Don't worry about the pony. He'll be all right. Bill's as good as any horse doctor in the country."

Jody hadn't known she could see his worry. He pulled gently away from her and knelt down in front of the fireplace until it burned his stomach. He scorched himself through and then went into bed, but it was a hard thing to go to sleep. He awakened after what seemed a long time. The room was dark but there was a grayness in the window like that which precedes the dawn. He got up and found his overalls and searched for the legs, and then the clock in the other room struck two. He laid his clothes down and got back into bed. It was broad daylight when he awakened again. For the first time he had slept through the ringing of the triangle. He leaped up, flung on his clothes and went out of the door still buttoning his shirt. His mother looked after him for a moment and then went quietly back to her work. Her eyes were brooding and kind. Now and then her mouth smiled a little but without changing her eyes at all.

Jody ran on toward the barn. Halfway there he heard the sound he dreaded, the hollow rasping cough of a horse. He broke into a sprint then. In the barn he found Billy Buck with the pony. Billy was rubbing its legs with his strong thick hands. He looked up and smiled gaily. "He just took a little cold," Billy said. "We'll have him out of it in a couple of days."

Jody looked at the pony's face. The eyes were half closed and the lids thick and dry. In the eye corners a crust of hard mucus stuck. Gabilan's ears hung loosely sideways and his head was low. Jody put out his hand, but the pony did not move close to it. He coughed again and his whole body constricted with the effort. A little stream of thin fluid ran from his nostrils.

Jody looked back at Billy Buck. "He's awful sick, Billy."

"Just a little cold, like I said," Billy insisted. "You go get some breakfast and then go back to school. I'll take care of him."

"But you might have to do something else. You might leave him."

"No, I won't. I won't leave him at all. Tomorrow's Saturday. Then you can stay with him all day." Billy had failed again, and he felt badly about it. He had to cure the pony now.

Jody walked up to the house and took his place listlessly at the table. The eggs and bacon were cold and greasy, but he didn't notice it. He ate his usual amount. He didn't even ask to stay home from school. His mother pushed his hair back when she took his plate. "Billy'll take care of the pony," she assured him.

He moped through the whole day at school. He couldn't answer any questions nor read any words. He couldn't even tell anyone the pony was sick, for that might make him sicker. And when school was finally out he started home in dread. He walked slowly and let the other boys leave him. He wished he might continue walking and never arrive at the ranch.

Billy was in the barn, as he had promised, and the pony was worse. His eyes were almost closed now, and his breath whistled shrilly past an obstruction in his nose. A film covered that part of the eyes that was visible at all. Now and then he snorted, to clear his nose, and by the action seemed to plug it tighter. Jody looked dispiritedly at the pony's coat. The hair lay rough and unkempt and seemed to have lost all of its old luster. Billy stood quietly beside the stall. Jody hated to ask, but he had to know.

"Billy, is he—is he going to get well?"

Billy put his fingers between the bars under the pony's jaw and felt about. "Feel here," he said and he guided Jody's fingers to a large lump under the jaw. "When that gets bigger, I'll open it up and then he'll get better."

Jody looked quickly away, for he had heard about that lump. "What is it the matter with him?"

Billy didn't want to answer, but he had to. He couldn't be wrong three times. "Strangles," he said shortly, "but don't you worry about that. I'll pull him out of it. I've seen them get well when they were worse than Gabilan is. I'm going to steam him now. You can help."

"Yes," Jody said miserably. He followed Billy into the grain room and watched him make the steaming bag ready. It was a long canvas nose bag with straps to go over a horse's ears. Billy filled it one-third full of bran and then he added a couple of handfuls of dried hops. On top of the dry substance he poured a little carbolic acid and a little turpentine. "I'll be mixing it all up while you run to the house for a kettle of boiling water," Billy said.

When Jody came back with the steaming kettle, Billy buckled the straps over Gabilan's head and fitted the bag tightly around his nose. Then through a little hole in the side of the bag he poured the boiling water on the mixture. The pony started away as a cloud of strong steam rose up, but then the soothing fumes crept through his nose and into his lungs, and the sharp steam began to clear out the nasal passages. He breathed loudly. His legs trembled in an ague, and his eyes closed against the biting cloud. Billy poured in more water and kept the steam rising for fifteen minutes. At last he set down the kettle and took the bag from Gabilan's nose. The pony looked better. He breathed freely, and his eyes were open wider than they had been.

"See how good it makes him feel," Billy said. "Now we'll wrap him up in the blanket again. Maybe he'll be nearly well by morning."

"I'll stay with him tonight," Jody suggested.

"No. Don't you do it. I'll bring my blankets down here and put them in the hay. You can stay tomorrow and steam him if he needs it."

The evening was falling when they went to the house for their supper. Jody didn't even realize that someone else had fed the chickens and filled the wood-box. He walked up past the house to the dark brush line and took a drink of water from the tub. The spring water was so cold that it stung his mouth and drove a shiver through him. The sky above the hills was still light. He saw a hawk flying so high that it caught the sun on its breast and shone like a spark. Two blackbirds were driving him down the sky, glittering as they attacked their enemy. In the west, the clouds were moving in to rain again.

Jody's father didn't speak at all while the family ate supper, but after Billy Buck had taken his blankets and gone to sleep in the barn, Carl Tiflin built a high fire in the fireplace and told stories. He told about the wild man who ran naked through the country and had a tail and ears like a horse, and he told about the rabbit-cats of Moro Cojo that hopped into the trees for birds. He revived the famous Maxwell brothers who found a vein of gold and hid the traces of it so carefully that they could never find it again.

Jody sat with his chin in his hands; his mouth worked nervously, and his father gradually became aware that he wasn't listening very carefully. "Isn't that funny?" he asked.

Jody laughed politely and said, "Yes, sir." His father was angry and hurt, then. He didn't tell any more stories. After awhile, Jody took a lantern and went down to the barn. Billy Buck was asleep in the hay, and, except that his breath rasped a little in his lungs, the pony seemed to be much better. Jody stayed a little while, running his fingers over the red rough coat, and then he took up the lantern and went back to the house. When he was in bed, his mother came into the room.

"Have you enough covers on? It's getting winter."

"Yes, ma'am."

"Well, get some rest tonight." She hesitated to go out, stood uncertainly. "The pony will be all right," she said.

Jody was tired. He went to sleep quickly and didn't awaken until dawn. The triangle sounded, and Billy Buck came up from the barn before Jody could get out of the house.

"How is he?" Jody demanded.

Billy always wolfed his breakfast. "Pretty good. I'm going to open that lump this morning. Then he'll be better maybe."

After breakfast, Billy got out his best knife, one with a needle point. He whetted the shining blade a long time on a little carborundum stone. He tried the point and the blade again and again on his callused thumb-ball, and at last he tried it on his upper lip.

On the way to the barn, Jody noticed how the young grass was up and how the stubble was melting day by day into the new green crop of volunteer. It was a cold sunny morning.

As soon as he saw the pony, Jody knew he was worse. His eyes were closed and sealed shut with dried mucus. His head hung so low that his nose almost touched the straw of his bed. There was a little groan in each breath, a deep-seated, patient groan.

Billy lifted the weak head and made a quick slash with the knife. Jody saw the yellow pus run out. He held up the head while Billy swabbed out the wound with weak carbolic acid salve.

"Now he'll feel better," Billy assured him. "That yellow poison is what makes him sick."

Jody looked unbelieving at Billy Buck. "He's awful sick."

Billy thought a long time what to say. He nearly tossed off a careless assurance, but he saved himself in time. "Yes, he's pretty sick," he said at last. "I've seen worse ones get well. If he doesn't get pneumonia, we'll pull him through. You stay with him. If he gets worse, you can come and get me."

For a long time after Billy went away, Jody stood beside the pony, stroking him behind the ears. The pony didn't flip his head the way he had done when he was well. The groaning in his breathing was becoming more hollow.

Doubletree Mutt looked into the barn, his big tail waving provocatively, and Jody was so incensed at his health that he found a hard black clod on the floor and deliberately threw it. Doubletree Mutt went yelping away to nurse a bruised paw.

In the middle of the morning, Billy Buck came back and made another steam bag. Jody watched to see whether the pony improved this time as he had before. His breathing eased a little, but he did not raise his head.

The Saturday dragged on. Late in the afternoon Jody went to the house and brought his bedding down and made up a place to sleep in the hay. He didn't ask permission. He knew from the way his mother looked at him that she would let him do almost anything. That night he left a lantern burning on a wire over the box stall. Billy had told him to rub the pony's legs every little while.

At nine o'clock the wind sprang up and howled around the barn. And in spite of his worry, Jody grew sleepy. He got into his blankets and went to sleep, but the breathy groans of the pony sounded in his dreams. And in his sleep he heard a crashing noise which went on and on until it awakened him. The wind was rushing through the barn. He sprang up and looked down the lane of stalls. The barn door had blown open and the pony was gone.

He caught the lantern and ran outside into the gale, and he saw Gabilan weakly shambling away into the darkness, head down, legs working slowly and mechanically. When Jody ran up and caught him by the forelock, he allowed himself to be led back and put into his stall. His groans were louder, and a fierce whistling came from his nose. Jody didn't sleep any more. The hissing of the pony's breath grew louder and sharper.

He was glad when Billy buck came in at dawn. Billy looked for a time at the pony as though he had never seen him before. He felt the ears and flanks. "Jody," he said, "I've got to do something you won't want to see. You run up to the house for awhile."

Jody grabbed him fiercely by the forearm. "You're not going to shoot him?"

Billy patted his hand. "No. I'm going to open a little hole in his windpipe so he can breathe. His nose is filled up. When he gets well, we'll put a little brass button in the hole for him to breathe through."

Jody couldn't have gone away if he had wanted to. It was awful to see the red hide cut, but infinitely more terrible to know it was being cut and not to see it. "I'll stay right here," he said bitterly. "You sure you got to?"

"Yes. I'm sure. If you stay, you can hold his head. If it doesn't make you sick, that is."

The fine knife came out again and was whetted again just as carefully as it had been the first time. Jody held the pony's head up and the throat taut, while Billy felt up and down for the right place. Jody sobbed once as the bright knife point disappeared into the throat. The pony plunged weakly away and then stood still, trembling violently. The blood ran thickly out and up the knife and across Billy's hand and into his shirt-sleeve. The sure square hand sawed out a round hole in the flesh, and the breath came bursting out of the hole, throwing a fine spray of blood. With the rush of oxygen, the pony took a sudden strength. He lashed out with his hind feet and tried to rear, but Jody held his head down while Billy mopped the new wound with carbolic salve. It was a good job. The blood stopped flowing and the air puffed out the hole and sucked it in regularly with a little bubbling noise.

The rain brought in by the night wind began to fall on the barn roof. Then the triangle rang for breakfast. "You go up and eat while I wait," Billy said. "We've got to keep this hole from plugging up."

Jody walked slowly out of the barn. He was too dispirited to tell Billy how the barn door had blown open and let the pony out. He emerged into the wet gray morning and sloshed up to the house, taking a perverse pleasure in splashing through all the puddles. His mother fed him and put dry clothes on. She didn't question him. She seemed to know he couldn't answer questions. But when he was ready to go back to the barn she brought him a pan of steaming meal. "Give him this," she said.

But Jody did not take the pan. He said, "He won't eat anything," and ran out of the house. At the barn, Billy showed him how to fix a ball of cotton on a stick, with which to swab out the breathing hole when it became clogged with mucus.

Jody's father walked into the barn and stood with them in front of the stall. At length he turned to the boy. "Hadn't you better come with me? I'm going to drive over the hill." Jody shook his head. "You better come on, out of this," his father insisted.

Billy turned on him angrily. "Let him alone. It's his pony, isn't it?"

Carl Tiflin walked away without saying another word. His feelings were badly hurt.

All morning Jody kept the wound open and the air passing in and out freely. At noon the pony lay wearily down on his side and stretched his nose out.

Billy came back. "If you're going to stay with him tonight, you better take a little nap," he said. Jody went absently out of the barn. The sky had cleared to a hard thin blue. Everywhere the birds were busy with worms that had come to the damp surface of the ground.

Jody walked to the brush line and sat on the edge of the mossy tub.

He looked down at the house and at the old bunkhouse and at the dark cypress tree. The place was familiar, but curiously changed. It wasn't itself any more, but a frame for things that were happening. A cold wind blew out of the east now, signifying that the rain was over for a little while. At his feet Jody could see the little arms of new weeds spreading out over the ground.

Doubletree Mutt came sideways and embarrassed up through the vegetable patch, and Jody, remembering how he had thrown the clod, put his arm about the dog's neck and kissed him on his wide black nose. Doubletree Mutt sat still, as though he knew some solemn thing was happening. His big tail slapped the ground gravely. Jody pulled a swollen tick out of Mutt's neck and popped it dead between his thumbnails. It was a nasty thing. He washed his hands in the spring water.

Except for the steady swish of the wind, the farm was very quiet. Jody knew his mother wouldn't mind if he didn't go in to eat his lunch. After a little while he went slowly back to the barn. Mutt crept into his own little house and whined softly to himself for a long time.

Billy Buck stood up from the box and surrendered the cotton swab. The pony still lay on his side and the wound in his throat bellowsed in and out. When Jody saw how dry and dead the hair looked, he knew at last that there was no hope for the pony. He had seen the dead hair before on dogs and on cows, and it was a sure sign.

He sat heavily on the box and let down the barrier of the box stall. For a long time he kept his eyes on the moving wound, and at last he dozed, and the afternoon passed quickly. Just before dark his mother brought a deep dish of stew and left it for him and went away. Jody ate a little of it, and, when it was dark, he set the lantern on the floor by the pony's head so he could watch the wound and keep it open. And he dozed again until the night chill awakened him. The wind was blowing fiercely, bringing the north cold with it. Jody brought a blanket from his bed in the hay and wrapped himself in it. Gabilan's breathing was quiet at last; the hole in his throat moved gently. The owls flew through the hayloft, shrieking and looking for mice. Jody put his head down on his hands and slept. In his sleep he was aware that the wind had increased. He heard it slamming about the barn.

It was daylight when he awakened. The barn door had swung open. The pony was gone. He sprang up and ran out into the morning light.

The pony's tracks were plain enough, dragging through the frost-like dew on the young grass, tired tracks with little lines between them where the hoofs had dragged. They headed for the brush line halfway up the ridge. Jody broke into a run and followed them. The sun shone on the sharp white quartz that stuck through the ground here and there. As he followed the plain trail, a shadow cut across in front of him. He looked up and saw a high circle of black buzzards, and the slowly revolving circle dropped lower and lower. The solemn birds soon disappeared over the ridge. Jody ran faster then, forced on by panic and rage. The trail entered the brush at last and followed a winding route among the tall sage bushes.

At the top of the ridge Jody was winded. He paused, puffing noisily. The blood pounded in his ears. Then he saw what he was looking for. Below, in one of the little clearings in the brush, lay the red pony. In the distance, Jody could see the legs moving slowly and convulsively. And in a circle around him stood the buzzards, waiting for the moment of death they know so well.

Jody leaped forward and plunged down the hill. The wet ground muffled his steps and the brush hid him. When he arrived, it was all over. The first buzzard sat on the pony's head and its beak had just risen dripping with dark eye fluid. Jody plunged into the circle like a cat. The black brotherhood arose in a cloud, but the big one on the pony's head was too late. As it hopped along to take off, Jody caught its wing tip and pulled it down. It was nearly as big as he was. The free wing crashed into his face with the force of a club, but he hung on. The claws fastened on his leg and the wing elbows battered his head on either side. Jody groped blindly with his free hand. His fingers found the neck of the struggling bird. The red eyes looked into his face, calm and fearless and fierce; the naked head turned from side to side. Then the beak opened and vomited a stream of putrefied fluid. Jody brought up his knee and fell on the great bird. He held the neck to the ground with one hand while his other found a piece of sharp white quartz. The first blow broke the beak sideways and black blood spurted from the twisted, leathery mouth corners. He struck again and missed. The red fearless eyes still looked at him, impersonal and unafraid and detached. He struck again and again, until the buzzard lay dead, until its head was a red pulp. He was still beating the dead bird when Billy Buck pulled him off and held him tightly to calm his shaking.

Carl Tiflin wiped the blood from the boy's face with a red bandana. Jody was limp and quiet now. His father moved the buzzard with his toe. "Jody," he explained, "the buzzard didn't kill the pony. Don't you know that?"

"I know it," Jody said wearily.

It was Billy Buck who was angry. He had lifted Jody in his arms, and had turned to carry him home. But he turned back on Carl Tiflin. " 'Course he knows it," Billy said furiously. "Man, can't you see how he'd feel about it?"

MINNESOTA

God Made Little Apples

MERIDEL LESUEUR

"Yeah . . . yeah," Lars said. "Arrested . . . well, I'll be——"

"What is it?" the women clattered from the kitchen like geese.

Lord . . . so many women he had! He saw their fair fat flesh steaming in the morning kitchen, with the broth and coffee. "Well," he said, "what do you know? The old devil. That's the way for a man to act now after harvest."

"What is it?" Helga, his wife, said, turning her bright face. And the wizened face of his mother looked over the coffee pot, and there were the round laughing faces of his three big girls.

"It's Grandpa," Emily, the oldest, said. "Oh, Grandpa has spent his harvest money."

"Oh," Grandma said, "that old codger!"

"Yas," Lars said, swatting his huge thigh, "Yas, the old man's in jail in Hastings—smack in jail and wants me to come get him out. There's a man for you. First harvest in four years and there goes the harvest money! Ho, ho; ha, ha!"

"Tch, tch, tch!" Grandma said, but she couldn't help smiling.

"Now, Helga, you'd have some complaining to do proper if I did that in the fall. It's a fair day for deviltry. Got a mind to go after him and stop and see Mrs. Potter I courted forty years ago, and would have married her, too."

"Go on!" Helga said, flicking him with a towel.

"Tell us, Pa . . ."

"You're too young," he laughed, listening to the clucks, the warm

From *Prairie Schooner,* Winter 1942 issue. Published by University of Nebraska Press. Used by permission.

talk of the women. He thought, "One good season can make a man feel good. Haven't been across the river for years. Wonder what Effie Potter looks like now; she used to be a sweet apple-faced gal for certain. Suppose I had married her." But he looked at Helga, warm as bread, opulent as his fields this year, mother of his seven children. No drouth in her.

And now the land, the weather, was with you again; the barn was full of hay.

"I'll go with you," Helga said. "The canning's done; I haven't had a vacation . . ."

He didn't know why he was set against her going. He wanted to get away from her, from them all.

"I'll get my things and go along," Grandma said. "I know how to handle these things. Every year at harvest . . ."

"No, you don't!" Lars said. "This is a man's affair. I think I'll join the old coot for a nip."

"Lars!" Helga said, and he saw her anxious eyes, blue as his mother's, and the great braids wound on her head, white now, as the snow of Sweden. "Mama," Helga said, "have you got the harvest money?"

"No," the old lady said, grinning in her empty gums, "he's the man of the family . . ."

"Twice a year," Helga said, "all his life, roaring drunk at seeding, at harvest!"

"You see what I tell you," Lars said, "you don't appreciate me."

"Lars," Helga said, "you're spoiled."

"How will we get him out?" the old lady said.

"I'll go get him out; I'll go this very morning. The cows are milked; the haying's done." And he thought, "I can go across the river. Why, I haven't driven over there in nearly forty years. I haven't seen Effie since her wedding day . . ."

He felt caught inside his life, inside the warm kitchen, in the golden hair of his women, his six girls. And he felt enormous, like a man who has been sweating at fighting in too small a space, a six-room house, ninety acres, where you plowed your sweat, and thought, riding all day on the sand, that it was like the fine hair of your Scandinavian women. Suddenly, he was greatly excited.

He rose in his chair, roaring for his good shirt, his Sunday shirt. "Iron it!" he cried, and stood in the kitchen roaring.

The women scampered like geese when he roared like that. He had on his clean shirt . . . Helga cut his hair around the edges . . . He pared his big nails.

"You're dressing up like your wedding day," Helga twitted.

"Might meet a brace of apple-cheeked gals," he laughed, and she made a face at him.

Then he got into the car, without a pig to market, without a bag of grain, free to cross the river into the fair, fall, country hills. Tiny villages, bearing the mark of men like himself who had come from his own country, seamen like his ancestors, with fierce scarred faces, tight curls and earrings.

He looked back and saw the girls waving, saw Helga by the door, and her kiss had meant, Do not get drunk. For a moment he wondered what is it—good years, bad years, your life, the sun shining down, women's faces laughing, a picture of your mother in a full skirt, mortgages making a ghost of the spoons you ate off? He waved, and turned the car down the road towards the river, through the village, across the bridge, up the river road and seemed to be driving into his childhood, his mother beside him, as she clucked to the horses and held him loose in her great skirts so he wouldn't fall. In the tiny mirror of the Ford he laughed, roared with laughter, seeing his thick pelt of a neck and one eye looking from the burned laps of skin pitted like the sand from his own hills; and the eye kept looking at him and made him laugh.

Memory lay like a thick mosaic all around him, a substance sweet and heavy. The wrecked and ruined houses, and the shapes of the strong men who had lived in them, thirty years before. There was the house of Strawberry Pratt, one of the first lumbermen. The house was empty now and the shutters flapping. The sawmills gone, the villages removed, a few white houses looking like New England, and some summer tourists. You passed cars with canoes on top and motorboats in trailers, and summer bedding and cookstoves piled in them. All along the river the old men stooped in the melon patches. And there was the store of old Sam. He could beat you out of your mother-in-law. By Heavens, he remembered the time Sam beat him out of a fighting cock, and he came away without the cock and with a couple of old hens not worth the powder to blow them up! Old Sam was dead now.

As he drove into the lift of the hills toward Effie's he thought he remembered certain trees, turns in the road, and a curious excitement made him drive faster. Her husband was dead now and she lived alone on the hill, her son gone away. He saw the barns empty. What harm was there in going to see Effie? Yet he looked down the road to see if anyone was behind him. And old collie came out to meet him after he had passed the windmill and the cream house, and a big rooster strutted past the wheels, and Lars laughed as if he had nothing to do but go traipsing around the country visiting old loves.

When he stood by the door looking into the cool, dark summer kitchen, flavorsome, smelling of piccalilli, and—did he imagine it?—the lavender perfume Effie used to use, he grinned sheepishly to feel his heart hammering as he waited for an answer to his knock. But he wasn't prepared for the woman who strode from the darkness, peering at him through the sunlight as if from the grave. She was wearing an old hat and the face of Effie as he remembered her hung like a dream in the layers of old flesh.

"What do you want?" she said, peering blindly, and the dead bird, hanging with dead claws to the hat, seemed to see him more brightly.

"Howdy," Lars said, and knew that she didn't remember him nor ever would. She giggled and thrust the hat on her rats, and he smelled beer on her breath. "I thought maybe you had a calf to sell."

"No," she said, "the barn is empty. I tell you—" She went on with the garrulousness of people who live alone, as if continuing a conversation she had been having many years in a lonely house with herself. "I tell you I got my troubles. Did my only son have a right to leave his poor old mother?"

He stood awkwardly in the door, the sun shining on his back, and the odorous dark out of which the old woman loomed going over him like a litany of disaster, over everything that she had lost, remembering every lost thing, stove, chickens, child, husband, chair, cow, bird; taken by flood, famine, cholera, graft, or natural decay and rot. Her mind was like a huge and fabulous junkyard filled with the idiocy of inanimate things to be lost, maimed, forgotten, ruined, until he could stand it no longer. But she didn't want him to go now, seeing his hungry startled listening, and she followed him to the car, clinging to its side, thrusting her ruined face at him.

And when he drove away, leaving her on the stone threshold still counting up disasters, he felt sick and wanted a drink, and drove away fast to Sam's tavern and drank down two cool draughts of beer, before he felt good again, and bought two hot melons which he thought he would eat for lunch. The day was bright, lying under the prismatic glass of sky, and the blue mist fell in the shadows of the stacks and followed each fattening Thanksgiving turkey, and he filled his pipe and began to laugh, thinking of the old man in the cooler.

Afton was a village named by Scotchmen. It was a nice neat village with cows grazing in the lowlands by the river, an old hotel he had known as a child, little farms and neat English houses. Many of these people had been seamen like his own, had come at the same time, but he didn't know them or they him. Only ten miles from his house and he didn't know them from Adam. He had a feeling for going in and asking them, "What do you know? How do you find it? What's up? How's tricks?" What would you say? "Well, I've been living for sixty years ten miles from you. Ain't it time we got acquainted?"

He stopped at the lunchroom and sat on a stool. An old woman came down the steps from the kitchen. She said in a queer voice, "What do you want?" and it sounded as if it were coming from a throat caught in a noose. He looked at her and saw where her whole throat had been burned, shooting right up beneath her eyes. She brought him some home-made cake and whipped cream, and he ate, wondering how it would go with the beer. And he still felt hungry, but he paid her, said good day, and went out. The village street lay quiet, empty. He got into the car and took to the road that went now into the hills, a dirt road, lined with birches and grapevines and gold and purple flowers of harvest blooming, goldenrod and niggertoe.

He drove along slowly, smoking, putting one foot up on the door to cool it off; the lizzy got pretty warm on the hills. He drove slowly because of the love he had for looking at all the tiny farms on the hills, seeing the grains all cut, the corncribs full, everything looking neat; but he could see how they clung to the hills by the skin of their teeth, too. He could read the farms like a book. It was very interesting as he went along. He could see the signs of struggle. "Bees . . . now they are trying bees," he thought; "they think they'll make out with bees." Then someone had tried raising peanuts. "You can't do that here," he thought; "they'll find that out." And ducks and muskrats.

He knew how it was:

Always reading in some journal, that how if you got this or that you'd be sitting in clover, all your troubles over, everything hunky-dory. He'd done it himself, put in this and that, pulled it out, found the soil or the climate no good for it, that it was a racket. Ah, it was a fine thing to look at the farms when they had half a chance, when there was half a crop, and half a price. The animals looked good, too, and he passed trucks full of squealing fat hogs going to market, and saw the faces of heifers and steers looking over the laths. He stopped once and some sheep came to the fence and looked at him, and he looked at them. He knew the hills would be full of berries and grapes, but he felt too lazy to get them. He had done his harvesting. He thought he would bring the girls down some day and let them gather grapes and berries, but he knew he never would.

He stopped at another tavern at the crossroads, where an old man with a dog gave him beer, the dog walking at the old man's heels. He drank down the beer and had another. He didn't count the money spent. He was like a man at a carnival who will cheerfully spend everything he has. The old man sat down with him after the fifth beer and had one himself, and they both lighted up and talked about crops, the fishing, and the weather. And then they got to telling stories, and Lars told the story about the Negro who was going to Birmingham . . .

They both laughed and their pipes went out, and they lighted up again, and the old man brought two more beers and told another story. They laughed and looked out the window down the road where two carloads of fishermen were just coming up from the river, their poles on top of their cars. And the old man began to tell about when he was young, and Lars listened and it seemed pretty wonderful to him. And the old man got out some pictures in an old cigar box that had a picture of a chorus girl of the nineties stuck on the lid; and he showed Lars pictures of children now gone or dead, and of his wife, austere and thin.

The old man said, "Why, sir, my wife was a saint. When she had her first baby she didn't know what was ailin' her till the fourth month. I was ashamed. I had to up and tell her she was goin' to have a youngun. I felt like a goat. She was a saint if ever there was one."

Lars laughed and said, "I got to be going up the river and get my old man out of jail."

"I'd like to go with you," the bartender said. "I know a man in Hastings who could fix it up. But there's nobody to keep store. Should I shut up?"

"No," Lars said, "you shouldn't, what with hard times. Nobody can tell how many pike fishers might be in for beer between now and sundown, and want to fill up and maybe want some hard liquor." Lars winked.

And the old man said, "I'd like a snort of hard liquor myself."

Lars said, "Sure, I would too. Why didn't you come out with it sooner?" He took a snort and bought a pint bottle for himself and put it in his pocket. Then he got into his car, the old man, like a broken stick, telling him where the turn was at the brick house.

"My own grandfather laid the bricks in that house and in all the viaducts around about, one of the best masons in the country. He laid every stone and brick worth layin' and was a boozer from way back, drank hard liquor like a baby drinks milk, and lived to a hearty old age, sound as a nut."

"Yes, sir," Lars said, and drove off toward Hastings, now only a few miles away. And he turned at the brick house and came to the corkscrew bridge which he hadn't seen since he was a young man and came here for his marriage license. That's why he knew where the courthouse was, which he entered and went down to the left wing.

The jailer opened the door, grinning, and brought the old man out grumbling. "Well, you took your time about it," in Swedish, and hooked his bones onto the side of the chair, folding his old bent legs under him, then said in broken English, "I told the old woman to send for you. You got to go to Thief River and get my harvest money out of the seaman's chest in the barn, and get me out."

"Why don't she do it?" Lars said.

"She don't know where it is," the old man said cunningly, "and I won't tell her. She might spend it."

Lars laughed. "I got other things to do myself," he said.

The old man said, "You get the money and get me out. It's a hundred and ten dollars."

"A hundred and ten dollars!" Lars whistled. "That's plenty. How much did you make on your wheat?"

"A hundred and twenty. I spent ten already."

"All your harvest money," Lars said.

The old man bent his head but looked from under his shaggy brows with one cunning eye. Lars had to laugh.

"Take a snifter," he said, offering his bottle of moon.

The old man threw back his turkey-gobbler throat, and it turned red slowly from the powerful drink. He took out a half pint from his own lean pocket and filled it from Lars's bottle, quick as a wink. Lars began to laugh. There they were, sitting in the Hastings jail, as naked of worries as jays. By Heavens, he hoped he lived as long as the old man; he hoped he lived forever.

Outside the barred windows he saw the tall black trees standing in the golden day. A fiery juice of life seemed to pour through his huge and powerful frame, and he felt as if he could bend the bars back and he and the old man could climb, like youngsters, through the window and tear across the courthouse lawn, escaping down to the river where they would build a raft and float down to Natchez in the moonlight.

He became excited as if he was going to do all that, and yet he knew that he wasn't going to move. He didn't want to move, sitting on the stool opposite the crafty old man who must still feel the wild burgeoning of the young liquor in his veins; must still feel it though he must be eighty-five if he was a day. Lars suddenly loved the old man. He put his arms around him.

"Don't take any wooden nickels. I'll get the money back. I'll see if I can talk to the sheriff." He wanted to appear young and important to the old man, as if he still had some power in the world because of his physical strength, his vitality.

"Good . . . good boy," the old codger said. "Good boy." And Lars resented it.

"I'll mail the money in tomorrow; I can't waste another day," Lars said at the open door as if he moved, enormously busy, in the process of a swarming life already ghostly to the old man. But, looking back, he didn't want to leave the old man. There he stood, fragile as a cricket, his hands almost to his swollen knees, so little Lars could have picked up the strong stubborn bones and taken them with him.

The sheriff said, "But he does this every spring and fall. He's a menace—tearing down the highway."

"Did he ever kill anybody? You never heard of him having an accident, did you?"

"No," the sheriff said, taking a drink from Lars's bottle, "but that's because we always catch him in time. Danged if I ever see the beat of it."

They both grinned. "Aw, cripes," Lars said, "a man's got to have his fling; you know how it is." They both grinned and sat a while. "Have another drink," Lars said.

"Don't care if I do. Well, it's a pretty stiff fine, all right, but them fly cops . . ."

"The old man's pretty canny when he's drunk; just as a grasshopper spitting juice, he's harmless. You and I are getting on a little, Sheriff."

"Speak for yourself, Lars; I'm as chipper as I was at fifty."

"Why, Sheriff, a man wouldn't take you for a day over fifty."

"And you, Lars Larson . . . it's amazing. They must take good care of you 'cross the river there. What keeps you so young?"

"Aw, you're full of taffy."

"Well, you get me fifty and I'll just have to have another snifter."

When Lars left he looked up at the barred window. Even if the old man was looking out he knew there would be no sign of it. He would simply look out at his son and the strong blood feeling would be tender between them, strong as the sweet day. He stood in the strong light feeling that tumult in his blood caused by seeing the old man, feeling his blood kin rousing him to this wild warmth. He stood under a tree and took a swig from his bottle.

He drove back swiftly; it was getting coolish. Once he stopped and tore the melons open with his hands and ate them, and they went good with the hot corn liquor burning in him. Driving through the hills, he passed the tavern of the old man and the dog, drove into the hills where the valleys were cool and dark and the hill tips rose, catching the sunlight. Letting the old car rattle down a hill he saw a marvelous orchardful of crab apples, and his mouth watered. By Jesus, he hadn't seen such a fine orchard of crab apples in many moons, the trees were loaded, they shone red and smart.

Without even thinking, now that the liquor was warm and strong in him, he turned in, drove up a turning road to a ramshackle house in the curve, and stopped the car. It was very still. Some ducks walked across to the water trough. It didn't seem as though anybody was home. He sat there in a little doze, guessing maybe he had drunk too much, and now his bones would ache, but he didn't feel any ache yet, only pleasantness. He could hear a bull kicking the sides of the barn, a steady thud. He dozed off, seeing everything through his half-closed eyelids. It all looked warm as if swimming in a golden syrup, and he heard a woman's voice from the house say:

"Do you want something?" He opened his eyes, and saw a woman in the door, her arm lifted so he could almost see the pit. She was shading her eyes, looking at him.

He moved his limbs; they felt heavy and fine. "Yes, ma'am," he said, feeling easy and hearty. He got out of the car. "That's a fine orchard of crab apples you got here," he said, going up to her, and she put down her arm and smiled easily.

"Yes," she said, "the best in these parts, if I do say it."

"Yes, sir," he said, "it's hard to get a crop like that what with pests and drouth, and tarnation in general."

She laughed, still standing in the door. He saw what fine arms she had, burned, and he could see the strong muscle turning on the bone, yet the flesh was ripe and full.

"How's chances for getting a peck of them apples?" he said, easy and slow, looking at her. She looked right back at him.

"All right," she said; "we ain't got any in the house, though. We ain't shucked them down yet. We'll have to go out and pick them up."

"Fine!" he said. "That suits me. I haven't been turned loose in such an orchard since I was knee-high to a grasshopper."

"Well, all right," her heavy slumbrous voice said. "Wait and I'll get a basket."

He stood at the door rubbing his hands together. He felt heavy and fine. He wondered if she could tell he'd been drinking. Shucks, he hadn't been drinking much—just enough to put silk on his bones.

She came out with a bonnet on that hid her hair and face and made her body more noticeable. He walked beside her to the orchard and he could feel the strong easy swing of her legs, and her body settling down easy on each step, then rising and settling again. By God, he liked that—the way she walked. Her strong breasts hung down in her wrapper and she walked swiftly, stooping to pick up the apples in her brown talons. He picked up apples too, dropping them into the basket. On one side the apple was warm, on the ground side cool as a cucumber.

His mouth watered from touching them and he set his teeth into one, and the white crab juice sprang out on his mouth and chin, and ran into his fingers. It was a fine taste, and he looked at the woman while he was eating, and she went on swiftly scooping up the apples which she was now putting into her apron and dropping into the basket all at once. He felt like a slacker in the face of her swift voluptuous industry, and he spit out the core and began to pick again. He found himself picking close to her and he felt heady. The orchard was silent around them, and as far as he could tell, all the menfolks must be out in the fields or gone to town with hogs or steers. Apples dropped from the trees around them, or farther away in the orchard, and a strange communication was between them as they walked under the little gnarled apple trees of the orchard.

And he only half heard when she said, "I think there was a wind last night. I think enough have shaken on the ground."

He was walking powerfully beside her and he felt again that strong and terrible desire. It was mixed with the feeling of the whole day, some last redolence of the blood before winter. He felt a fright to think of his towering strength diminishing in him in ills, aches, and debility, until one morning in some fall he would be old and dying and could feel no more the plow, the hot resurgence of spring and brandy, the potent flood of desire and life.

They passed through a grove of live oaks, and hanging from the trees by their feet were two steers, freshly butchered, their entrails a-light in the sun, blood soaking into the ground.

"Sure," he heard himself saying, "a right smart wind down the valley." But all the time he felt the strong shifting of her weight in a thrust of energy, and the down-dropping relaxation of her whole body as she settled on the earth, and he saw the long sweep of her hips as her dress fell in front and slightly hitched in back.

She said, "My husband took the steers to market," and it startled him.

They were alone there then, and he felt the subtle and curious surge of her strong bending hips, the rhythmic dip toward the earth and then the slight rise as she dropped the apples in her apron, which she held up with her other hand. Then she lifted her head in the hot silence and he saw her young and burned face from within the sunbonnet, and most of all he saw her eyes looking at him as if he were a young man in his prime, and her woman's mouth slightly open and the moisture of her movement shining on her face. And then she lowered her head again and filled the basket.

He didn't move. It was very quiet with just the apples dropping. It was the moment. He knew that. The baskets were full, the sun was setting. He moved towards her and he felt her stiffen and wait. And he stood very close to her and as he reached for the basket he touched the golden down on her arms and he saw the turn of the young powerful flesh up the bone gleaming and sweating. His big brown hand tightened around the belly of her arm and she did not move. He felt her breath, odorous of apples, and the sun hot on one cheek.

Then he took the basket from her, and he knew the moment was over forever and he felt a kind of huge peace with the slanting sun. And he walked silently beside her, and it was as if she felt it too. He poured the two baskets of apples into the back seat and saw it was nearly full of the little apples, cheek by jowl. He ate another, fingering the round tiny cheek.

He turned to the woman, who stood by the well, her face half hidden and secret. He started to say, "How much?" But something in her forbade him, as she stood there, still accessible to him. And he knew he would always see her standing there in the long fingers of the sun, like the opulent earth, like the great harvest, like all of his life, openhanded, generous, sweet-smelling.

"I thank you," he said, taking off his hat and dropping it. "I surely do thank you." He felt his face reddening as he stooped to pick up his hat. And he still felt her generous silence as he started the car and called good-bye. And when he looked back at the turn of the road she was gone.

The dusk caught him before he crossed the bridge towards home. The village looked strange and neat to him, and he drove into his own yard with relief as if he had had a great adventure, gone through dangers. The lamp was lit in the kitchen and the girls' faces clustered in the door. He shouted at them, and went through, the warm hands touching him, and the bodies of the girls changing into women, and their bright tender faces towards him.

His wife stood at the stove. She turned her startled face towards him, not knowing what he felt, nettled by his absence. Supper was all ready and he washed his hands and sat down, and took a fresh piece of bread. They had baked that day, and he could see his wife at the stove looking askance, not knowing what had befallen him.

The girls at the table in the lamplight were full of questions, and he began to swing into his story, making it a fine one. He felt strange and looked at the faces around him, and they seemed almost comic. It was like some Swedish fairy tale where you leave a picnic, go around a mountain, meet a gnome, marry, live a whole life, and then come back and your mortal wife is just wiping up the dishes from the meal not half an hour ago.

His wife was frying potato pancakes; so she stood in the half dark at the stove, and he knew she was looking at him and hanging on every word he was speaking to them. Once he stopped and lifted his head. "Bet you don't believe that, Mama, eh?"

She snorted in the dark. "Bet you got drunk yourself," she said; "bet you had a girl with you."

The girls made little screams and clucks. He threw back his head and laughed and the girls laughed with him. "What do I need of a girl?" he said, looking around at the strong, gleaming daughters' flesh. "What do I need of any more girls?" And they smiled and were pleased.

He felt strong and fine. His wife sniffed at the stove, and he got up, pretending to get water, and he stopped on the dark side away from the lamp, beside her. And she kept on turning the pancakes cooking on top of the stove. The fire from the cracked iron flew over her face, and he could smell the good smell of her flesh and of her hands. He put his hand on her thigh where the children could not see, and put his wind-burned face into her warm neck.

She turned her head, laughing into her shoulder. "Lars," she said, "the children, please—" And her face was full of fright and desire and embarrassment. "Please, Lars . . ."

And from the darkness of his fields came the full rich lowing of cows.

OREGON

The Bulldogger

JAMES STEVENS

For seven days Til Allen had stuck to the bench in the employment office. From eight in the morning until six in the evening, hour by hour, the short wiry man in the ten-gallon hat sat and stared grimly at the jobs chalked on the blackboard. Whenever a new call was wired in from a sawmill or a logging camp—and that was rare in these days near to winter—Til Allen was always the first man to reach the counter.

"Ever punch a donkey engine?" the job shark would ask. Or: "Ever run an air trimmer in a sawmill?"

"You betcher!" was the snapped reply every time.

And then an experienced logger or millman would be picked from the mackinawed, calk-booted crowd that drifted in all day from the streets of Portland's skidroad.

But the short wiry man in the ten-gallon hat could not be rebuffed. He hung on. At last he got on the job shark's nerves.

"Say, you!" he exploded on the seventh day. "Say, why don't you go back where you come from? Don't you see it's no use to hang on here? Work's too tight. Too many experienced lumber rasslers and loggers lookin' for jobs. Better go back to yer cows, feller."

"Back home they call me the bulldogger," said the wiry man calmly. "Try to live up to the name. Usually do. Hangin' on. That's me, Til Allen."

"Huh!" the job shark snorted. "You'll just starve."

"Starve hangin' on then."

"Well!" The job shark's voice rose to a yell. "You think you'll get anything from me? Think I'd give a timber job to a blamed cow-hand?"

"What are you a-callin' me?" said the wiry man gently.

Originally published in *Adventure* magazine. Used by permission of the author.

"Cow-hand. Think I can't tell? That horny spike of a thumb nail shows me. A rope-burned cow-hand. Yes, sir."

"You make it sound insultin'," said Til Allen, gentler than ever.

"Meant to," growled the job shark. "Sick of lookin' at you. Get out of my office."

"Hangin' on," said Til sweetly. "Me, I'm a bulldogger."

The job shark tramped heavily around the counter. He reached out a beefy hand for the wiry man's collar. Things happened. The job shark's head split a chair bottom as he went down. When the stars faded he discovered that his arm was clamped in a hammerlock.

"Held down five hun'erd steers in my time, more or less," said Til, sweeter than ever. "Guess I can hold you, mister. How about a job now?"

"Lemme loose," whimpered the job shark. "Lemme loose. Ow! Yeah, I'll send you to a job—honest!"

"All things come to him who bulldogs on," said Til, getting up. "I know you'll give me the worst job you got, mister, but that's all right."

The job shark had thought of it first. It happened that a call had just come in for a husky and experienced lumber handler to be sent down to the McCall Lumber Company. A man was wanted for the timber chute. Scarce though jobs were, the experienced lumber handlers were passing this one up. They knew that the McCall timber chute was the toughest place to work on the Columbia River.

"You got to be half bulldog and half mule to hold down a job on that chute," said one. "Not me!"

Til Allen thought the shark was a good sport to write out a ticket for a job that paid five dollars a day, one dollar more than the going sawmill wages for common labor.

"Much obliged," said Til. "I leave you with the kindest of feelin's. This means more to me than you can know."

"There's a lot you don't know, too." The job shark said that when Til was headed for the door and out of hearing. "But you're goin' to learn, young feller, what it means for a cowhand to get fresh with the gener'l manager of a employment emporium."

On a wet and windy November morning there was an alien figure among the men in mackinaws, slickers, and calked boots who were tramping down the soggy board walks from the sawmill men's hotel to the yards of the McCall Lumber Company. Most of them were unmistakably "webfooters," as the natives of the region west of Oregon's Cascade Range are called. Their faces were red, but had no lines or tan from dry winds, dust and sunshine.

Til Allen, on the other hand, was unmistakably from "east of the mountains," the land of cattle and wheat. He wore a ten-gallon hat and a leather coat. His belt was ten inches wide and studded with brass. His laced boots came to his knees and had no calks. The legs of his overalls were not stagged; they were stuffed inside his boot tops. Til, himself, was wiry and lean, his tan was deep and as brown as the inside of fir bark, and the lines which spread from the corners of his eyes had been made by years of squinting against dust, wind, and the brilliant sunlight of an arid country. His legs were bowed, and he stalked through the yards with the stiff gait of a man more accustomed to the saddle and the wagon seat than the ground. He had but the vaguest idea of what a timber chute was like. He inquired cautiously as to its location. At last he found it, in charge of a giant of a man called Big Jess Blaney.

The timber chute worked four men, including the straw boss. It was a trestle thirty feet high and one hundred and twenty long, topped by a line of powered steel rolls, with beams sloping down to horizontal skids which were greased for the easy sliding of the rough timbers. There were eighty feet of dock floor between the chute and the river. In this space the chute men built their loads. The straw boss explained that the smaller timbers were loaded directly from the skids, while each big one was wheeled out to its load on a two-wheeled truck.

"I savvy it, I guess," said Til Allen. "Something like cuttin' out your brands in a roundup."

"What are you talkin' about?" said Big Jess Blaney, with honest curiosity.

"Cattle."

"Oh." The big webfooter nodded. "I've heard of them. You must come from east of the mountains."

"Yep."

"I'm afeard," said the straw boss, "that what you know about ranchin' won't do you much good here. Lumber is lumber, and nothin' else, and this partickler job is hell and hallelujah."

"Watch me hang on," said Til, and his mouth was a tight line.

"You seem to be one of these strong, wiry kind." But Big Jess' voice was doubtful. "If you've never rassled lumber, though—"

"I can buck wheat sacks with any man in the Grass Hills country."

Til made it sound like a plain statement and not a boast. "I can out-bulldog any man back home, too."

"Yeah? What's bulldoggin'?"

"Gosh, but you webfooters are ignorant! It's rasslin' steers down. You dive off your hoss, take your steer by the horns, twist him down and hold him."

"What in thunder you want to do that for?" The straw boss looked skeptical. "Sounds fishy to me," he went on. "What man in his right mind would go out and rassle with a cow? I ask you, now."

"What man in his right mind would go out and rassle timbers like these here?" said Til.

"Why, rasslin' lumber's a job. A trade, you might say. I've done it all my life."

"And I've rassled wheat sacks and steers the same way. But we won't argy," said Til. "I just want a chance to hang on here. Just a chance to make good."

"You'll get 'er," said the straw boss. "Just don't forget you're a greenhorn here."

"A tenderfoot." Til Allen grinned, but his jaw was set. "Watch me hang on. Got to work, Mr. Blaney. Simply got to."

Work. On the timber chute of the McCall sawmill a man soon learned what the word meant. A man soon learned there what was needed for holding down the toughest job on the Columbia River. It needed big arms and shoulders, a sound heart, a deep chest, speed in hands and feet and above all, the skill that comes from experience in handling green lumber. Til Allen excelled in none of these qualities; he was especially lacking in the last and most important. Yet he managed to hang on throughout the forenoon. And when the five o'clock whistle boomed, he was still staggering through the drizzle from the timber-burdened skids to the loads, and back again.

"Do I get another chance tomorrow?" he said weakly to the straw boss when the whistle blew.

"Bulldogger, you do," said Big Jess admiringly. "But why? It's the miserablest way of committin' suicide I know. Why don't you jump off the dock and get it over sudden?"

"Five dollars a day," said Til Allen, as much to himself as to the straw boss. "A dollar more than for a common labor job. Got to hang on. Got to."

Jess Blaney stared solemnly at him for a moment, then shook his head in a puzzled way and tramped off for the company hotel. Til Allen leaned against a load of timbers and rested. The labor of the day pounded on in his head. Boom—boom—boom! Timbers thudding down from the live rolls. A yank and a heave on his end of a leaden green stick six inches thick, sixteen wide, and sixty feet long. Rolling it away on a two-wheeled truck. Straining himself to his toes as the big stick was labored into place on a load. His partner, Ham Nelson, growling "Greenhorn!" whenever he made a miscue. Jess Blaney yelling "Big rush! Hustle!" every ten minutes, when a pile of smaller timbers or ties would crash down the skids. His fingers and thumbs pinched by his clumsiness until every one was aching and blue. Spots of fire in his elbows and shoulder blades. A catch of sharp pain in the small of his back at every strain on the muscles there. The weak trembles in his knees. Rain down his neck. Brittle fir slivers gouging through his ragged gloves. The nerve-wracking screams of the big saws in his ears.

That for a man from east of the mountains anyway. Til Allen was smitten with homesickness. He gazed out over the loads of timber at the rain-grayed surface of the great Columbia. A vision swept over the water and the dull green hedge of firs on the far shore. . . .

A vision of rolling lands. Stubble, yellow, and shining in the clear air of an Eastern Oregon autumn. The smell of black soil in fields sown to winter wheat. The sagebrush hills of the cattle range, rising in ridges toward the piney mountains. Himself trailing a bunch of beef. A pitifully small bunch—but beef. Honest, baldfaced beef, and his own. . . . Trailing along . . . Sundown . . . Moonrise . . . The keen snap of frost in the dry air . . . The home fence . . . The home gate . . . Smell of coffee boiling and bacon frying . . . A light in the window of the old ranch-house where he was born . . . A voice from an opened door—a brave woman's voice. . . .

Til Allen snapped himself erect. His eyes were steely gray again. His jaw was set in ridges of muscle.

"You'll hang on, Til Allen!" He jabbed a sore rib with a bruised thumb for emphasis. "Three months of hell ahead, but you're hangin' on!"

He felt like a soldier on a battlefield as he walked stiffly through the lumber stacks. Most of the sawmill men were waiting in the hotel lobby for the supper gong, when he entered. Jess Blaney was there, with George Paddock and Ham Nelson, the others of the timber chute crew. They were discussing the new chute hand, this lean, wiry, sunburned greenhorn from the Eastern Oregon ranch country.

"Bet he don't last another shift," said Ham Nelson, after Til had passed upstairs to his room.

"Dunno," said the boss of the timber chute. "He's got some reason for hangin' on. Some powerful reason. And he calls hisself a bulldogger. He'll drop before he'll quit, that's what I bet."

A month later Til Allen was still on the timber chute. He had not quit and he had not dropped. He was still hanging on to the toughest job. But he was wearing the marks of twenty-six days of killing labor. Lean as he had been in the first place, he had worked off six pounds of weight. The lines about his eyes had deepened. His jaw was perpetually set as he worked. The steely glitter was never gone from his eyes. By sheer nerve and determination he had hung on.

The others of the chute crew knew it. They sensed, too, that he hated the labor of handling lumber, that even the river country itself repelled him. He was an alien. Paddock and Nelson, lumber handlers all their lives, were hostile. And an instinctive hostility had developed among the other sawmill men against the bulldogger. They saw him washing his own clothes, patching his overalls, shirts, and gloves, buying the cheapest tobacco. They were aware of it when he shunned the hotel poker games.

"A swell guy, he is," they said. "Always knowed them east of the mountains ranchers was tightwads."

Til did not help matters any by his talk. Whenever he joined the lobby gang after supper, he could talk of nothing but his home country. Cattle and horses. Sunshine and dry air. Wheat and range grass. The free life of a horse riding rancher.

The webfooters snorted.

"What the hell you doin' over here, then?" George Paddock would roar. "Nobody invited you out of the sticks to a civilized country, did they?"

Til Allen never told anybody—not even Jess Blaney—why he was here. When he was questioned about it, his eyes got a bleaker look, his mouth set in a grimmer line, and he made no reply. But he hung on.

Big Jess Blaney was always sympathetic and curious. To the boss of the timber chute, Til Allen was a man from a foreign country. He himself knew nothing but sawmilling in the timberlands. He felt that the wiry little bulldogger from east of the mountains would never be a timber-country man. The heavy work was breaking him down. Why was he hanging like grim death to the toughest sawmill job on the Columbia River?

"The pore cuss must need the extra money mighty bad for some reason," said Big Jess to himself, as he sized up the bulldogger in the lobby crowd on Chistmas Eve. "Must need it mighty infernal bad. I'd think he'd go hold up a bank first."

There was some such desperate thought in Til Allen's own mind, as he sat in a corner and watched the crowd of timber-country men. Nearly all of them were rigged up in white collars, gaudy silk neckties, and tailored suits. Only their muscle-ridged necks, broad shoulders, bulging sleeves, and large red hands gave them the appearance of workingmen. Allen felt conspicuous in his patched overalls, rough boots, and faded wool shirt. It seemed that he was thousands of miles away from his own kind. The only talk here was of the woods and mills. Not a word about range lands and ranch fields. Suddenly he was dog-tired —worn out; so homesick that he was turning weak all over. It was Christmas Eve, and his first one away from the old ranch home where he was born. . . .

Had to get out of this mob. In another minute he would go wild and crack Ham Nelson between the eyes. Go up to his room. Write a letter home. . . .

Half an hour later, Til Allen was sitting on the edge of his bed. He was staring down at the lined page of a cheap tablet in his left hand. In his right, a stub of a pencil was clasped loosely in sliver-scarred fingers. He read over again all that he had written on the first page:

Dear Emmy and kids:

Well, I hope you're having as fine a Christmas eve as I am. Only wish I was with you right now. Bound to get homesick in spite of my fine job. I'm making it fine and I'll have the money by spring so don't you worry, Emmy. How is everything? You write like all was fine but I can't help but worry some. Alton, when your ma wrote me you were roping the calves and riding them I vowed I'd lick you when I was home again, but I take it back now for a Christmas present. Only don't do it any more but mind your ma. I guess, Emmy, I'll keep hanging on here unless there's a shutdown—

He had stopped there for a spell of figuring. There was to be a shutdown for repairs that would last ten days. Jess Blaney had as much as promised that the bulldogger should have a place on the dock repairing during that time. But it would be only a four-dollar job.

Ten dollars less for the period. Til filled a page with figures. He scowled at them, he swore at them, he worked them over again, but they refused to change.

He shook his head wearily and his shoulders sagged. It was no use. He had written in the letter that he was certain to have the money—but the figures disputed him. Til Allen felt the urge to fight on dying out of his heart. No use. His grip was breaking. Might as well give in now. This job would kill him off anyway. Go back home—there was a shutdown. He would not need to lie. Yeah, he could be on the old home soil by tomorrow night—and he'd have until the first of March. Might as well slide. . . .

There was a knock on his door.

"Well, come in," said Til Allen, wondering who it could be.

The door opened and the big frame of Jess Blaney seemed to fill the little room. The straw boss was embarrassed. His ears were red and his gaze roved nervously over Til's head. He cleared his throat before he spoke.

"Got a chance for—uh—somebody durin' the shutdown," he said. "A tough job. Not such a hell and hallelujah job as on the chute, but a steady grind. And twelve or sixteen hours a day. Big money—ninety cents an hour for eight, then time and a half for overtime. What say?"

"Why," said Til slowly, the vision of home still on him. "I—uh—"

Big Jess glared.

"I thought you was a bulldogger! Thought you needed money for your fambly some way. Thought I was doin' you a favor. But if you're not willin' . . ."

Til Allen shut his eyes and gave his head a fierce shake. His hands clenched. Then he growled:

"Who said I wasn't willin'? I'm mighty obliged."

"All right." Big Jess was easily mollified. "It's longshorin'. River gangs are short account of Christmas week. My brother's stevedore boss here. Got two ships comin' in. He'll put you on tomorrow. Ought to make twelve a day. It'll be just for the time of the shutdown. There's a union, you know."

Til Allen looked down at the unfinished letter and at the page of figures. His heart was still sick for home. He felt all the weariness from a month of overwork. But he had to hang on. Could not lose his grip now. He forced himself into a feeling of gratitude.

"You're mighty good, Jess Blaney," he said, looking up with a grin that was forced. "I'm just writin' my wife what a fine boss I got. Yes, sir, I'll bulldog that longshorin' job, and obliged to you."

"Forget that part." Big Jess was embarrassed again. "And now come over to my room and have a seegar and a drink and tell me some more about rasslin' cows. It shore does tickle me, that idee of cow rasslin'."

"Just as soon as I finish my letter," said Til. "But it's bulldoggin' steers, I've told you a hundred times. Not rasslin' cows."

The morning after Christmas, Til Allen was out with a longshore gang among the tall stacks of lumber on the McCall cargo dock. A huge black freighter was swinging out her yellow booms. She was to load three million feet of structural timbers for New York. The longshoremen were due to earn their big money on this timber cargo.

Now, the bulldogger from the ranch country learned a new brand of hard labor. Here were no desperate rushes of work such as were needed to keep the timber chute clean. The work was a heavy, steady grind, minute after minute, hour after hour. A rope sling was stretched away from a stack on the dock floor. Til Allen and his partner swung out the weighty timbers from the stack and piled them on the sling until a load was made. For half a minute then, they could take an easy breath, until the load was hoisted. Then they stooped to the grind again.

Bend and swing over to the stack. Grab for a timber. Watch for the feel of it in your partner's hands. Yank, heave, and steer the bulky green stick into place on the sling. Swing back to the stack. On and on. Grind away. Swing and heave. Swing and heave. Only half minute letups as you labored through the hours. That was longshoring on the cargo dock of a river mill.

The rainy season was now at its height. The sky was eternally low and gray. The thick drizzle veiled the river and grayed the forests of cedar and fir on the hills. All day little streams trickled down the oilskin backs of the men stooped at labor. Their faces were always wet and red.

Twelve hours among the timber stacks. Four in the morning. Four in the afternoon. Four after supper under arc-lights which shone with misty golden rays in the slanting lines of rain. A sagging, dragging band of brawny men shambling for the hotel when the hatches swallowed their last slingloads at ten at night.

The bulldogger was half dead at that hour of the first night. He did not wait to eat from the lunch table spread in the dining room. He dragged upstairs to bed. There was no strain in his muscles from this labor. He was simply fagged out. He got his shoes off, and that was all of his undressing. He rolled over on his bed. Tired out. But his jaw was still set hard as he went to sleep. Twelve dollars a day. . . . That was his last waking thought.

He hung to the longshoring job all through the shutdown. His tough, wiry body held up under the grueling labor, though it lost another two pounds of weight. When the ship was loaded and the mill had started again, Til Allen had one hundred and twelve dollars clear from his ten days on the cargo dock.

Again he covered a page with figures, and then he wrote to Emmy that he was certain now of having the money they needed by the first of March. He would have a chance to work overtime, he wrote, as a night shift was starting in the sawmill. Certain to make it now, with the overtime. He would hang on, he guessed.

He wrote nothing to intimate what a bulldog grip it took to hang to a job on the McCall timber chute, and to work frequent half shifts of overtime besides.

"That takes a man who is half bulldog and half mule," said Big Jess Blaney, after another month was gone. "And this feller is just *all* bulldog. Just that. Not enough mule I'm afeared."

But it was not until the first of March that Til Allen eased himself from a local passenger train in the Eastern Oregon town of Grass Hills. The station agent, trundling a truck along the platform, stared at him curiously, then let out a yell of surprise.

"Why, Til Allen! Where you been and what you been doin' to yoreself?"

"Been bulldoggin'," said Til shortly.

He tramped heavily on for the main street. The agent gazed after him, with increased curiosity. There was nothing much left of Til Allen but skin and bones. He dragged his feet. His shoulders slouched. He looked ten years older.

"Bulldoggin'!" grunted the agent. "Must of been grizzlies. Looks like he'd had the daylights licked out of him, and for good."

Til Allen tramped slowly but steadily on down the main street. He stopped at a familiar corner. The stone walls of the Grass Hills State Bank bulked before him. Behind them old Hard Cash Carlton was at his battered black desk, his eyes like gray pebbles behind their gold-rimmed glasses, his mouth a thin line. Yep, old Hard Cash was waiting there.

Til Allen's shoulders straightened as he stared at the stone wall with the eyes of a conqueror. He stared and he remembered. Word by word and act by act, he re-lived his last scene with Hard Cash Carlton. That was last fall.

His grain was hauled, his seeding done, his beef was gathered; and he had plowed eighty acres for summer fallowing this year. Then he had gone to his banker and spread out his cards.

"Mr. Carlton, I hate to beg, but I got to. Got to, yes, sir. You ain't lived in this ranch country long enough to know, to understand why I'd do anything to hang on. Well, I was born here. Out there in the hills is the only home I've ever known. Once ours was the biggest ranch in the valley. It went; all the hay lands in the bottoms, forty by forty. My dad, I don't blame him. Runnin' cattle was in his blood—strong. I know, for it's in mine. He wouldn't give up beef. Was sheeped out, and then the dry landers fenced in his summer range. Since he died I've tried to make 'er with wheat. Hung on to what was left of the old home ranch.

"You know my story well enough. Crop failures. Owe you all the ranch is worth. But I've got to hang on. Got to. The old home. Mine. Got to bring 'er back. One good year and I'll begin to pay up. Mr. Carlton, I got to beg you to see me through another year. Just got to do it."

"Business is business," said Hard Cash grimly. "But your crop's in. I aim to be fair. Have our interest—the three hundred and fifty—here by the first of March, and I'll make you out a new note."

"How can I ever get that much by then?"

"Work."

"Work? Where? Feedin' sheep at forty a month?"

"On the coast. Big wages in the timber. Best I can do."

"I'll try 'er," said Til. "Anything to hang on. . . ."

And here he was on the first of March. Here, with a crisp draft for three hundred and fifty dollars pinned in his shirt pocket. Still hanging on. Bulldogging life for another fall.

His head was up like a conqueror's as he pushed through the swinging door of the bank. He headed directly for the short counter before the president's desk. The eyes like gray pebbles gazed up at him through gold-rimmed glasses.

"Good morning, Allen. Back on time, heh?"

The bulldogger slowly drew the crisp bit of paper from the pocket of his patched shirt and as slowly slid it across the counter.

God, how it hurt him to see it go! He was caught unaware by the sudden revulsion of feeling and it hit him like a sledging body blow. All that this bit of paper meant to him, all of the straining physical labor, torment of soul, and oppression of mind that had gone into the making of it, moved in a black whirl before Til Allen's tired eyes.

The life that he had lived during this winter of exile. The misery of it all. The eternally gray sky of the timber country. The eternal rain. The everlasting smell of freshly cut lumber. Screams of saws and harsh roars of machines in his ears through all the hours of heat-breaking labor. The boom-boom-boom of timbers sliding down the skids. The strain of yanking and heaving at the sap-heavy, slivery, sharp-cornered bulks of sawed logs, hour after hour, day after day. Life away from his own soil, his own blood, his own kind. An alien. A man of the ranch country, an exile in the timberlands.

And all for this crisp bit of paper. The stubby hand of Hard Cash Carlton reached hungrily for it. It vanished from the counter, and then—

"We'll renew," the banker said.

Without another word Til Allen turned for the door. He stared into the dry, brilliant sunlight and forced the memory of the killing months out of his mind. That was done. He had bulldogged life for another fall. A new fight was ahead. Home by noon. He could get in at least five hours of plowing before dark.

His hands itched for the feel of saddle and harness leather. His heart ached for a sight of the old home hills. Yeah, home. . . .

All that the heartbreaking labor of the winter meant to Til Allen now, was the new chance it had won for him to keep his home.

"Got to hang on," he said, as he headed for the hills.

KANSAS

Kansas Afternoon

SANORA BABB

On Sundays they slept no later because the cow wanted to be milked on time, but sometimes they napped in the hot afternoons, unless they went visiting and they rarely did. The distances were far, the car was not often inclined to run, being very old and needing repair in too many parts, and they did not know many other farmers well enough to arrive without telephoning first and they had no telephone. The lines hummed along the road and Dale often placed his ear against a pole and listened to the pleasant and mysterious rhythm which he called "talking." He made a line of his own with a long wire and two tin cans, but there was no one for the other end.

This Sunday in late spring, while they were eating a breakfast of eggs and pancakes and corn syrup and coffee, a warm lonesome wind came in the window and made them all feel restless. Dale asked Homer for a spoonful of coffee in his milk and his father gave it without protest. There were only three small oranges and Betts brought one of them to the table and gave it to Dale as a surprise present. The orange made the day like Christmas, except that at Christmas they had been snowed in and had very little of anything to eat.

"Well," Homer said, winking slyly at his wife, "if you could pack up something, Betts, we might go a-visiting."

"Who'll we visit, dad!" Dale exploded, losing a piece of orange onto the oilcloth table cover.

"That depends on your mother."

"If you'll kill a chicken, Homer, I'll fry it, and make some potato salad and devilled eggs."

From *Kansas Magazine*. Used by permission.

"Who, dad?"

"Dip."

"Oh, boy! Dip!"

"We ain't visited Ol' Dip in a month o' Sundays," Homer said forlornly.

"It's a nice day for the walk," Betts said. "I ain't over missin' Dip myself."

"One thing," Homer said, "We don't have to phone up Dip. We're welcome anytime."

"That's one of the pleasures of his state," Betts said, and her slow smile sent the corners of her eyes up.

"I'd like to be excused," Dale said, crossing his knife and fork on his plate.

"You may, son. Don't be in too big a hurry to set your chair in to the table."

Dale obeyed and ran out the door letting the screen door fly back with a soft thud against the piece of rubber Homer had tacked into the jamb.

"Beats all how excited a kid can get over a small thing."

"I'll bet you're kinda excited yourself, Homer."

"I am that," he smiled at her. "Summer makes me want to ramble around."

"I'm glad to get out of the kitchen," she said, and began clearing the table. "I've got to step lively."

"Now don't get flustered. We got all day. I'll kill the chicken and pick him."

"Pick him, too?"

"I will."

"This is a rare day, Homer Delaney."

"Why, woman, I'm liable to lose my temper."

"Faunch away!" She laughed.

"No, my temper's restin' too."

"Get a move on you, Homer. Men are so slow."

"Some men and some women," he said gently and went out.

She put the potatoes and eggs on the stove and got out the old grape basket and washed it, lining it with clean paper and a tea towel. Up from the cellar she brought a jar of pickles for the salad.

"Wish I had some lemons for lemonade," she grumbled. "Reckon there'll ever be a time when we got enough of anything?"

"Not likely," said Homer, coming in after the hot water.

"Don't come in on me like that!"

"Been comin' in this door some years now. Little late to start knockin'."

"I didn't mean that."

"Then you better stop talkin' to yourself."

She flushed. "It's natural when anybody's alone so much."

"You said you didn't like to live in town."

"I don't. I just wish we had the money for a better car so we could go in oftener or go visiting."

"Well, we're going visiting today."

"And here we are, all excited. It's the limit."

He went out with the steaming tea kettle, and she moved quickly preparing the picnic lunch. When Homer came in again, he said, "I cleaned it too!"

"Well, forevermore, Homer. I believe you're right down anxious."

They stood in the treeless yard waiting for Dale, who came running.

"Get a drink first," Betts said.

"Ain't we taking water?"

"A little, but you fill up now. We don't want to load ourselves down."

"It'll be not walkin'," Homer said. "We'll take turns carryin' the basket. 'Course, since Dale's the littlest he won't have to carry it very far."

With the back of his hand, imitating his father, Dale wiped the water off his smiling face. "I'll bet Dip's been lonesome. Reckon he's changed much, Dad?"

"Not much any more. Last year was the biggest change."

The wind was pungent with the smell of sage. A row of thunderheads like a street of white mansions curved around the big blue sky to the east.

"They just lay off there and promise and threaten and don't ever rain," Homer complained. "I declare, it tries a man."

"They look like big fat white cats sound asleep," Betts said accusingly.

"When it lightnings," Dale said, "they're opening their eyes."

"Blowing and yowling when they go on the rampage."

A meadow lark flew up suddenly from the grass, and Dale ran toward it.

"Don't bother her nest, son."

"I won't, dad; I just want to look."

"Better come away; she's worryin'."

The low tough grass was springy under their feet. The sun grew warmer and they went without talking over the treeless plain. In each of their minds was an image of their dog Bounce who had just last week run off over the prairie with a queer jerking gait and a queerer bark. He had got rabies from the coyotes or wolves and gone mad. Homer had come in for the shotgun and killed him "to get him out of his misery" and that night they ate supper in silence. Homer passed word along to the neighbors for a pup. Occasionally townspeople dropped unwanted dogs on the road and they wandered to the nearest farm. Bounce had come to them like that when he was small. Maybe they would be lucky again.

"I read where some old crank," Homer said, "wants to kill off all the dogs. Says their barkin' causes eight per cent of all nervous breakdowns."

"Must be that humans cause the other ninety-two per cent," Betts said. "Does he want to kill *them* off?"

"Wouldn't be surprised, if he's sour on an animal as good as a dog."

"What's a nervous breakdown, dad?"

"I can't rightly say, son, but I reckon that was what happened to that little coyote we had chained up. Remember how he would run out to the end of the chain all the time and get jerked up short? He lost confidence in himself. He couldn't live his life the way he ought to, and finally he just crumpled up and didn't care. Couldn't care, I reckon."

"Is that all?"

"Well, you ask your mother. I may be entirely wrong. Womenfolks have more such ailments than menfolks."

"I doubt that, Homer Delaney! If men had to be women a little while they'd crumple up faster'n that poor little old coyote."

"Look out now, Betsy, we're out for a good time."

"You're a good enough man, Homer, but I declare, that humorin' won't fit down very snug over the truth of such things."

"Well, the menfolks have their troubles, too, but I ain't thinkin' of trouble today."

"I'm not either. This is a quiet and peaceful day and my heart matches it."

Homer had been walking a few steps ahead and he dropped back beside her.

They came to a hollow which Dale thought was fun. He ran down the side, lay panting at the bottom and waited.

"Haven't seen any old rattlesnakes today," he called to them.

"Well, now, it's just beyond," Homer said.

As they came out of the hollow, Betts stopped and looked round. A mirage shimmered far ahead like a new dream. "This is a lonesome land, but I like it. As far as the eye can see, just space, and the biggest sky there is. Not one tree."

"Some folks wouldn't like it," Homer said proudly, "but I can't tolerate being shut in by a lot of hills and trees."

"A tree in our yard and one at Dip's would be nice," Betts said. "That would be enough."

"There he is!" Dale shouted. "There's Dip!" He ran ahead.

Dip was easy to see on the prairie. They came up to him and stood together looking down.

"Hello, old boy. We've come to pay you a visit," Homer said cheerfully.

"Hello, Dip," Betts said.

The bleached white skeleton of the horse lay as if asleep on the prairie. The wolves had at first torn him apart, but after the flesh was gone, Homer and Dale had rearranged his bones, and now that they were dry and odorless they remained unmolested.

"He was a good worker," Homer said, "and steadied that nervous Lollie."

"I'll bet he's been lonesome, dad."

Under the great bow of his chalky ribs a bull snake stirred and moved off slowly toward a soap weed.

"He's a grand horse," Betts said. And it seemed to them all for a moment that Dip was sharing the pleasant Sunday afternoon.

A few feet away Betts spread a cloth on the grey buffalo grass and set out the lunch. Looking out for thistles they sat down. The sun was warm but the wind which would blow hot in mid-summer was now cool, and tangy with the smell of the high arid lands. They ate leisurely, speaking quietly the random thoughts of their Sunday minds.

"Supposing we were the only people left on earth," Dale said, waving his arm round at the uninhabited plain.

"It's not unlikely," Homer said drowsily.

"Supposing," Dale said, paying no attention to anything but his imagination. "Supposing—"

"Supposing we got so lonesome we went calling on the bones of people?" Betts asked.

"Naw. Just supposing we had the earth all to ourselves."

"Wouldn't do us a bit of good, son. Though I swear there's a lot of grown men with the same thought."

"Can't we just imagine we're the only ones left?"

"Sure we can, but your imagination'll die off feedin' on such as that. Folks seem bent on destruction."

"More people are bent on living, I'd say. Look how they survive," Betts said sharply.

"Aw, you won't play," and Dale got up and kicked at Dip's skull. Then he bent over curiously. "There's a little blue bell growing up near his head!"

"That's just a little reminder of the indestructibility of nature, including two-legged man. Kinda like the hope weed. Can't kill it."

"Don't break your jaw, Homer. You showin' off before Dip, here?"

"No, woman. I could as easy say the plain stubbornness of life in everything, but I've come by a few words in my time, and I mean to whet my mind."

Dale was on his knees peering into the horse's skull.

"That flower's some of Dip's immortality, son. You been askin' me what it means."

"You mean a flower can grow from a horse?"

"In a roundabout way. Everything dies and goes back in the earth and helps something new to come up. In that way we live forever, and in no other, the way I see it."

"Could I be some wheat, maybe, dad?"

"Reckon so—unbeknownst to you. In that case you'd end up as bread and keep another man alive."

"Say!" Dale said and reached toward the skull and picked the flower.

"You see, that flower puts a fine thought in us. And our thoughts, well—maybe I'm goin' a piece too far today, but it's in my mind."

"It's endless," Betts said. "One thing leads to another."

"Yes, it's endless."

"Does Dip know about the thought he gave us in the flower?"

"No, son, but it won't matter to him because he's dead and the thought is alive."

"I can't imagine dead," Dale said.

"That's because you can't imagine *nothing*. Ain't none of us can do that."

"I wonder," Betts said tartly.

"Be a better world on earth if men weren't saddled with future bliss," Homer grumbled.

"What's that, dad?"

"Well, heaven and such. It's a crime to make a mockery of life on earth. It's a good thing to feel wonder, but there's room enough for wonder in nature and man."

"Homer, ain't you sleepy?" Betts demanded.

"The thing is, son, to put your mind on your living life and other people's. I don't mean meddlin'."

Dale looked puzzled.

"What would you say to goin' round by way of the crick and all takin' a bath?"

"Whoopee!" Dale yelled, instantly shedding eternity.

"I didn't bring towels, Homer."

"Ah, we'll use the sun and the tablecloth."

The sun was halfway down the sky.

They went over to Dip and for a moment their sadness came back. Dale wore the flower in a buttonhole of his overall strap.

"Goodbye, old boy. We'll visit you again."

They started off south although there was nothing to be seen but the prairie. After two miles they came to a precipice. Far below, a small stream ran through a wide bed of sand. On the opposite shore was the pale bright green of cottonwood trees; beyond, a rise of rock and scrub to the level floor of the endless plain. They found a steep path and supporting themselves on the huge eroded stones, they reached the stream below. There a willow tree grew on the bank with part of its roots exposed. They placed their clothes on a rock and holding onto the roots waded into the shallow crystal water. Homer and Dale were naked but Betts wore her underskirt. They swam where the water was deep enough, splashed, laughed, rubbed themselves and dried in the cooling sun. Refreshed, they dressed and climbed up to the plain, starting the long walk home.

The red sun sat on the horizon and then moved slowly down, sending great colored shafts into the sky. After the long sunset, the dusk came up around their knees like the fields of night growing swiftly into a forest darkening overhead. They moved a long time through the dusk and during the last mile they came into the night, as if it had been waiting for them ahead, another place, a world of night. The sky was black and tall and wide and pointed with all the stars. No moon rose.

They walked steadily and did not speak, withdrawing into delicately defiant separateness. Now and then Dale touched the wilted tender flower in his overall strap.

Their silence was not sad although they were lonely. This was not a loneliness for anyone, because the three of them had no acute feelings for anyone else; it was merely aloneness, therefore it had a largeness, an impersonal grandeur, which caused each to feel in need of some special communication. They had felt it often, especially at night when they stood in the yard before going to bed and looked into the dark. This aloneness appealed silently and familiarly to the big sky and the stars and the moon (never to the sun), to the vast distances of the prairie, to the winds always blowing, and most of all to the night, because the night was endless, unlike the circled day, because the night contained many things: reminders of the known, urges to the unknown; smells, of living things and dead, of the weather; sounds of animals, wild and tame, of a motor on a far road, of distant thunder, of the high faint roar of an airplane, the lonely whistle of a train. The wind made sounds although it blew unrestrained across the plains over the low grass. Along the roads it sang through the wires, a weird music, it whined around the corners of farm buildings and moaned to itself. The wind of storm blasted and roared and boomed and made them afraid of its mindless fury. But the unangry wind of tonight had ears to listen to their wordlessness.

They entered the yard feeling reluctant and glad to be home. When Betts lighted the lamp, they looked sheepishly at one another and Homer said loudly, "We sure had a good time with old Dip, didn't we?"

"We sure did!" Betts and Dale spoke at once.

Betts lighted the oil stove.

"That old cow must be thinkin' hard of us," Homer said. "We're late with the milkin'!"

Betts placed the teakettle on the flame, scraping the bottom over the burner unnecessarily. Homer and Dale went out to do the chores. As she turned toward the pantry she saw Dip's flower lying crumpled on the floor.

"Wild flowers don't last," she mumbled, but she picked it up and dropped it into a jelly glass of water. She gazed at it remembering the indestructible and living day. Starting, she hurried into her tasks.

"One thing's clear," she said aloud, "I've got to put some food into our mortal stomachs."

WEST VIRGINIA

If Only

JOHN PEALE BISHOP

It was not until after the war that the Sabines moved into Mordington. The farm, always lonely, had become impossible, their father being dead, their brothers dead, and the mother blind. Remote, the stone farmhouse was set on a gusty hill and hidden from all roads by woodland. After the war they were always afraid. In the orchards the apples ripened and unpicked fell, or rotted on the branch; rank with weeds the rolling fields went down to the Shenandoah; their gardens were stolen. Once a week perhaps they heard a rickety wagon crawl down a lane. It called at the ferry and after a long time the answering halloo would come across the water. The long flat-bottomed boat was poled by a grizzled black who had been their slave. Beyond the river were the mountains. In the slave quarters a few Negroes stayed on.

They were young then, Ellen and Lou, and at night alone but for an old woman whose tears still gathered under blinded eyelids. At night the doors slammed upstairs where there was no one. Their mother sat with hands held straight on the worn arms of her chair and cried without meaning.

She had cried her eyes out, they said, weeping for one son who had lost three. Old Sabine was a Unionist. When the first two boys fell in battles that went to the Confederates, she was sarcastic and proud. When Jimmy, in the last month of the war, sank wearily, exhausted by dysentery, she could only weep. The father was silent; he had paid for his sons' uniforms and known they were ashamed of him. He walked awkwardly about the house, his strong shoulders lowered like a bull's. He could not speak without bringing on reproaches which ended still

From *Many Thousands Gone* by John Peale Bishop. Used by permission of the publishers, Charles Scribner's Sons.

in tears. Jimmy was the youngest of the boys—younger than either of the girls.

Mordington is a small county seat at the end of the Valley of the Shenandoah. From a distance, lost in leaves, nothing of the town appears but the spires of churches and the court house clock. They came in from the country to find the town already abandoned by time and since the war no longer in Virginia. But this the Sabines did not recognize. Congress might admit the treacherous western counties as a state. They could not. So for them there was no West Virginia. They continued having their mail sent to Mordingon, Virginia, and when their letters were delayed felt they had their private revenge on Abraham Lincoln, Lord John Russell, and Napoleon III—all three at once—for not having recognized the Confederacy.

They were well-off, for their father in his obstinacy had saved them from the common poverty of the time. They lived comfortably and admitted nothing that touched their pride.

The town they accepted with all its past, and each year it seemed to them a little grander. Great men had lived there, and more than once Mordington had altered the history of the country. The jail is the usual one of bricks painted a brighter red; on summer evenings the jailor's daughters sit on the narrow porch with palm-leaf fans. The Court House lifts its cupola above a cloud of trees to show a clockface to every quarter of the town; under the columns of the portico—colored a dirty serviceable yellow—the pavement is spattered with the droppings of hundreds of blackbirds that nightly roost in the yard. Yet the jail had once held a fatal prisoner, in the Court House a decision had been made that had sundered the Republic. The Sabines did not forget it, nor that afterwards, because of the old murderer whom the North had made a martyr, the town had suffered much and was poor.

I

They came down that morning to find the kitchen dark, the shutters closed, and no one there. Beside the sink, on the draining board, the cold dishes of the night's supper were stacked, scraped, but not washed. And they knew their cook was gone.

(When this was cannot be said, for the Sabines themselves could never remember—but it was on a Monday and when Ellen had thrown back the shutters the morning was warm, with murmurs of summer and the scattered shadows of leaves on the sunlit sill.)

This was the Negress' usual departure, for Selly needed no other notice than the increasing sun. Through the winter she worked, and fed the four children of her unchastity at the Sabines' larder. But with the first warm days she was gone.

After breakfast, they explored, timidly, knowing what they would find. Dust was everywhere. On top of the cupboard, it lay in a winter's thickness. The closet gave up more unwashed dishes and stale ends of food, chunks of suet, crusts of bread, a shrivelled hambone and old biscuits which the mice had not only nibbled, but completely digested. It was disgusting! From the lower doors of the cupboard, pots and skillets tumbled out, sad-irons and waffle-irons, kettles and griddles, a black and greasy confusion. They were amazed. They had not believed such filth could be in their kitchen! There were brooms worn to stubs—but not it would seem with sweeping—and rags that might have been used for scouring came out of strange hiding places, wadded in dirt and showing still the imprint of Selly's wet fingers. In the corner under the sink, cockroaches had made themselves familiar.

'I'm glad she's gone,' said Ellen. 'I'm tired of Selly. I'm tired of her trifling ways.' But she looked dismayed.

'But Ellen—Selly's our nigger!' Lou sat down.

'She's our cook,' said Ellen, 'but she's not our nigger.'

'But she should have been. By rights, all the Hannions should have been our niggers! If only——'

'And a dirty, trifling lot they were too, those Hannions. Look at this!' Ellen had found the table drawer. 'We'll have to clean the kitchen. I can't have anybody coming in here after Selly.'

They cleaned. As usual after Selly's summer departure they cleaned. For four days they swept, they scraped; they scoured with soap and polished with pumice. Ellen mounted on chairs and stepladders to wash the shelves of closet and cupboard while Lou sat at the table and from white paper cut scallops and patterns of lace to line them. Ellen bent her knees over the floor with scrubbrush and bucket; Lou washed the window and returned to her sitting. Ellen wrestled with the serious pots and kettles while Lou at the table, with short deft fingers—always a little too red, as though she had just dipped them in hot water—polished silver and glass. Applying paste, or rubbing with cloths, her bangs trembled; she talked while she worked, helping Ellen with suggestions.

Four days they cleaned, and both felt the unaccustomed labor. They had little to eat, for when Ellen was tired not much cooking was done.

Both drank more coffee than was good for them. But at the end of the day Lou had still the strength to go driving. The weather continued fine and every evening George Hite came for her. They drove off in the yellow varnished dogcart behind the docked bays and Ellen was left alone in the kitchen. Darkness fell while she washed the dishes.

Friday morning she did not come downstairs. She had found her only retreat from her sister's sweet insistence and kept her bed with a sick headache.

Lou was late with the breakfast. She came in gaily. Ellen brought up her drawn cheeks from the pillow.

'Don't you want the shade up?' Lou suggested.

'Leave it the way it is,' moaned Ellen. 'I've fixed it.'

'But, Ellen, I was only trying to make you comfortable!'

'How can I be comfortable with a sick headache?' The voice from the coverlets faintly screamed, like a parrot irritable behind its wires. She turned her face to the green-darkened window. It made her look quite ill.

'O, very well!' said Lou. She caught her breath and held it between parted teeth. Ellen's bed was wide. The posts were not high and the top of each was a pinecone cut from cherry wood. On this bed their mother had died.

Lou closed the door softly and tiptoed along the corridor, down the stairs, leaning so hard against the balustrade that it creaked. In the lower hall she let her breath come again.

She too was tired. She had dressed slowly that morning and with care; and moving through the empty rooms Lou was white and flimsy with ruffles. The loneliness was oppressing; she came into the parlor, but not even the long mirror consoled her; she saw the black moire ribbon at her throat and dangling from her ears tiny baskets of fruit, cut from coral, and thought how she had given her youth to her mother, who had taken ten years to die. She let her fingers run along the table; picked up a book which she did not read. Nothing had been touched for days, nothing was changed. Only on the surface of walnut and rosewood, in the crevices of roses carved on the backs of chairs, dust had gathered.

'What we need,' she said, 'is a man. I've always thought it.' And she went to the porch repeating, 'What we need in this house is a man.'

'She saw at once looking across the street that the colonel's horse was still there. It was earlier, then, than she thought; relieved she sat down. For every morning the great sorrel was brought by a boy, who, after making it fast to a hitching post, knocked at the Gores' back door and went away. Then at a quarter past ten the old military cloak himself would come out, mount and ride downtown for his mail. If Ellen and Lou were there, he saluted them with a grisly smile. He was a little man, but they set their clocks by him.

It was always pleasant on the porch. For though here was but one house opposite—where the Colonel Gore kept his shuttered silence—the street was long and shady and there were always people passing under the summer trees. Lou knew everybody. And of course she was herself known; it was more than a hundred years since the first Sabine had come into the county. In Mordington, she and Ellen were treated almost as natives of the town.

II

It was strange then, this morning, that Lou should be looked at so long in silence and when at last she was spoken to it was as though she had not been seen.

She sat in still fascination while the mulatto boy in front of Colonel Gore's iron gate stared at her. She had not seen him come there, though it was possible that he had come out of the alley and crossed the street without her noticing him. He was slim and swayed when he stepped down from the curb and walked about the sorrel with a litheness that was like, too like, a girl's. A hat with old tattered straw brim had been crushed into a shape that increased the likeness. And his shadowed eyes were large and dark and impudent. Mrs. Cawley went by and did not see her, and then Miss Lila Colston and Mrs. Burden, who both nodded to Lou but with such restraint that she was abashed at having called to them from the porch.

They went on, and from their backs she guessed the stiffness of their gait. She and the boy followed them with their eyes and then were left looking at each other. Colonel Gore had not come out. She tried not to see the slim mulatto, who stared at her relentlessly. She saw the rent in his white shirt and through it the dull-colored skin and one nipple and tried to look past him and into the country. For beyond this street the town stopped, and after Colonel Gore's orchard were fields of wheat, pale, and wanting only a few days of sun to ripen. There the wind was like the sorrel restless. She saw it trampling the grain and in the sunlight remembered the old abolitionist they had brought out there to die, and how he had raised his stringy neck for the last time and said that the country was beautiful.

Two more ladies passed, walking with the same decent composure, nodding as the others had done with chill restraint and like them dressed in black.

There was a wait with the yellow boy. Then the bell of the Episcopal Church began tolling. Lou heard it, and knew why the ladies had been in black, had passed her without speaking. Someone was dead. But who? Mr. Hite the night before had not told her. It was eleven o'clock, the hour of funerals. Colonel Gore had not come out. But no, it could not be the colonel. He could not be dead. She would at least have known that. But there was still the dull tolling of the bell. Then it stopped. And in the sunlight the mulatto moved on, swaying as he walked. The sorrel, restless with flies, strained his long neck. And Lou was irritable in the wind.

The sun brought the shadow of the roof on her head. And she heard the sound of distant and repeated thunder, blasts from the quarries four miles to the east, that shook the ground. She thought of the dead. The blasts would be felt in the cemetery; for there, with reiterated assaults at noon, they loosened the tombstones until often they fell and were broken.

Twelve. It was time to think of Ellen.

When she went back to the kitchen, he was there. A fine, tall, black, handsome nigger sat at the table, peeling potatoes, dropping them one by one into the water of an earthenware bowl. But Lou did not at once see him. Her eyes were dimmed by sunshine, she was overcome and downcast as though she had actually seen as she looked out over the summer of windy grain—black against the pale unripened wheat, and already like a dead man—the old abolitionist sitting up on his coffin and straining his bewildered eyes through the orchard. His fine bony black head was held sidewise, as with an expert knife he curled a long peeling from a potato and dropped it chuckling ino the water. Lou started.

Smiling, he stood up and wiped his hands on a cloth. 'This is Miss Louisa, ain't it?' She saw his knife flash in the sunlight.

'Who are you?'

'I'm the new cook. I come this morning.' Again he smiled and his voice was so polite and pleasant that she liked him at once. His eyes were straight now. 'I don't know whether I put the dishes away right. If you'd look, Miss Lou——'

'Where do you come from?'

'O, most everwhere. I been all up and down. You can 'quire 'bout me anywhere from here on goin' south. My name's Bones.'

'Bones?'

'Yes'm. They most and generally calls me Bones, nobody can't remember my Christian name, so they just calls me Bones.'

'I've always wanted a man,' she thought. And it was true. She looked at the cupboard and saw that all was clean and ordered.

'I'll have to ask my sister,' she said aloud.

'Or you can tell Miss Ellen it'll be all right, not to worry, jes' to rest herself good and stay in bed. We got lots of time, you tell her we got lots of time.'

Lou hurried upstairs.

'Ellen—' She shut the door on the darkened bedroom. 'I've got a man!'

On the bed the pale face was exposed between strands of hair. 'What did you say?'

Lou bent over her. 'How are you feeling?'

'All right, I suppose.' But Ellen let the coverlet contract with pain. 'Only I wish I knew who hitched that horse down there—he's breathing so loud!'

'A man's better, don't you think?'

'They're better. But you can't get them,' said Ellen.

'I've got one, he's in the kitchen now, and he has very nice manners and he's getting dinner.' Lou's breath was hurried. 'And I've always wanted a man.'

Ellen sat up. 'Did you ask him where he'd worked before?'

'I liked his looks,' Lou smiled assuringly.

'You'd like anything that looked like a nigger. What's his name?'

'Bones!'

'I don't know any Bones niggers,' Ellen mused. 'But it might be a Tidewater name.'

'He's very aristocratic looking,' said Lou.

'I'm getting up,' said Ellen.

'But your headache?'

'It's better.'

Ellen was curious about the new Negro. But she too was impressed by Bones. And the days that followed deepened the impression that here was a godsend. It was agreed that men were desirable, but Bones was a rarity among males. Every morning brought out new accomplishments; he seemed to have worked only in the very best families. He mentioned names, the oldest and the best, but it was his manners that proved him. In the kitchen he was easy and polite, grand in the dining room. As a polisher he shone; mahogany acquired a shimmering magnificence, floors were waxed till they were perilous, and cherry wood soon looked dark and rich as though it had grown in Campeche. Under his hand silver and gilt and glass were restored to a before-the-war splendor. They found when they came down in the morning the lower rooms aired and perfect; when they went up at night to their beds, all was in order for sleeping, with a single light and, if the nights were cool, fires laid in the grates. They had never known anything like it. 'It's just like the old days,' said Lou, 'when Mrs. Dancy had six servants for her town house and one that did nothing all day but shine brass.'

But it was Bones's cooking that most amazed them. Under his long bony fingers all the savors of the old South revived in their kitchen: Maryland chicken, Kentucky corn-dodgers, Virginia hams sprigged with cloves and spotted with pepper like leopards; ducks from the Carolinas and turkeys with stuffings of pecans, savory messes from Louisiana with odors of thyme, marjoram, and sassafras. Bones baked sweet potatoes with chestnuts as in Tennessee, his corn puddings were grated and thickened with eggs as in Alabama. He gave them shad from the Chesapeake, bass from the Shenandoah, and even made an effort to import shrimps from Barataria. Game appeared on their table for the first time in years, pheasants and partridges, once a wild turkey from the Blue Ridge. And even the ordinary and familiar dishes suddenly discovered the most unexpected qualities, due, so Bones explained, to their being prepared in the traditional manner. He could not put down an apple pie without saying that its spiciness was, in the first instance, Martha Washington's, a cream tart but he claimed that Mrs. Taylor had ordered it always done in this way for the White House. All his recipes were old, secret and derived from aristocratic kitchens; so at all events he said, and proved it to the satisfaction of everybody who tasted the concoctions.

Accustomed for years to the meagre diet of the genteel, the Sabines suffered somewhat from this new and prodigal table. They were often unpleasantly reminded of dinner about three o'clock, they frequently lay awake half the night forgetting Bones's suppers. The after taste of the Old South was acrid and distressing. They could only suffer in silence, they could neither refuse nor complain. Proudly they recalled that Jefferson Davis had also been a sufferer from dyspepsia.

Sustained by the pride of Virginia ladies, after many heartaches, they endured their heart-burn and said nothing. Bones was by now installed in the house. He had begun by asking for a room to change his clothes in, and Lou had seen no reason why he should not be given the spare bedroom on the alley. Within a week he was sleeping there—if indeed he slept! For at night, long after they had retired, they would hear him prowling, shuffling along the corridor or in the lower hall, trying the locks, sliding the bolts on the door. It gave them a feeling of security—Bones was so careful. And sometimes when supper lay heavy and they stifled in the night without sleeping, there was heard from window to window the fain playing of a banjo, alone in the bedroom on the alley. Bones was awake. Bones was singing! Yet in the morning it was clear that he had risen at dawn, had cleaned and dusted while they lay sound in their sheets.

He was really a marvel—so clean, so temperate! Moreover, he was an Episcopalian. They could ask nothing more. To be sure he was extravagant. Bones took over the marketing from Ellen and, though he could show that nothing was wasted, the bills did mount. Wines were consumed in his cooking, bottles of brandy lost in his sauces. And his wages, too, for that town, were high.

'But then,' said Ellen after her first consternation, 'we've never lived so well before.'

'It's worth it,' said Lou. 'It's the way I've always wanted to live.'

'If only we can afford it—' Ellen sighed.

Bones was worth it. They had lived so long in a dream that it was sweet to taste the reality. With this one tall, black, jovial Negro in the house it was as though the war had never been or, having been fought, had turned to a triumph for the South. The old molds were restored. It was indeed as though dead bones were alive again. And they were content. Or almost——

'If only—' said Ellen, 'Brother Jimmy were here!'

'Yes,' said Lou, 'how he would enjoy it!'

III

Snow had fallen some days before, so that when the Sabines looked out of their windows it was over ledges deeply white and into a world of winter. The lawns were snow; the dark burdened pine trees held their branches like the claws of dead birds. Days passed under one cloud.

But on Sunday all was changed. They woke to see trees brittle with light intricately over-arching the street with crystal. Morning rising unclouded after a night of sleet had cased each tiny twig in brilliant ice. The snow shone—to venture out was perilous. In that sun the air was hard and cold; the branches glittering sagged and crashed though there was no wind. To walk was to go upon flawed mirrors. Ellen came down dressed for church a little before eleven.

Lou waited for her at the foot of the stairs. 'I'm not going,' she announced. 'In the first place, it's too slippery.'

'Not with an umbrella,' Ellen said.

'Besides, I've been thinking.' In the drafty hall the little Confederate flags faintly stirred. Lou looked hard at her sister. 'I know now what was the matter with General Lee.'

'General Lee?' Ellen turned and was astonished at Lou's excitement. 'I don't know what you're talking about.'

'I do! I do! He was too kind, he was too considerate——'

'But of course,' said Ellen.

'That's just it!' Lou's voice rose and shivered in the chilly hall. 'It tamed him. That's why we lost the war!'

Ellen sought her umbrella behind the door. 'There's one thing,' she said. 'And that is, he never failed in his duty. Are you going to church?'

Lou did not at once answer. Then she said, 'I think I know my duty.'

'Very well,' said Ellen, 'then please let me go. I'm late as it is. And I hope you'll be in a better state when I get back.'

'I'll be just what I am now.'

Ellen looked at her hopelessly. She was wrapped in sealskin and veiled in green against the cold. 'Then you ought to apologize. I don't mean to me, I mean to General Lee.' The gust of her departure swept around Lou and she was left standing alone under the portrait of Light Horse Harry's son.

I do not know just when this was, or how long it had been since first black Bones took shape in the Sabine household. It may have been the winter after his coming, it may have been a year or more later. I do not know.

It is so difficult to tell time in the case of those who ignored it. It was not simply that as maiden ladies the Sabines were skittish at the mention of years. Both had a memory for dates and could tell you to the hour of the day or night when every shot was fired, every skirmish fought, at Mordington. Twenty battles are recorded under its name and they could tell you all. Then too, they were susceptible to the spring, serious when the earth was cold, for they remarked the seasons to whom time brought no other change. But of years, they were afraid; they never mentioned them.

It was so in Lou's affair with Mr. Hite. They did not withstand time, they denied it. And nothing changed.

George stayed as he had been when first she met him, and they had met at a time when the one passion left to young men was for death. Living was a shame. They had lost all faith except in a cause that was lost. Earth was shaken, since Virginia was not a state but a military district and they no longer Virginians. Lou had wanted to devote herself to her sightless mother. Young Hite had perhaps wanted nothing.

There the affair stayed. Hite was a russet-haired youth, sturdy, but strangely enervate, after five months on late and disastrous battlefields. He felt the infirmities of years, for ten summers did nothing and then bought a drugstore. He put on weight, forgot what it was that made him ill, and continued sampling all the remedies on his bottled shelves. His coach dogs died, he bought better and better horses—after the old roan salvaged from war, a pair of blacks; greys in the early eighties; then bays, and all through the nineties bays. He called on Lou and they drove out together; dogcart succeeded the discredited buggy; the courtship in the summer dusks was unending. There was always the same trembling anticipation of delight, never a conclusion. She was still the young girl to be adored and pursued but not touched, he the lover who worshipping sought and never came to hard and male possession.

George got heavier, lost his sideburns so patiently acquired. He wore checks, docked the tails of his bays and looked more and more the racing man. The veins broke in his purple cheeks, pouches of wrinkles came under his eyes, the down thickened on forearm and hand. Love did not change. They were young no longer and had long since come to the silent communication of couples who have been married for years.

Time is a dizziness, and states have been known to fall who stood too long in that element. By time we are all at last confused. Ellen and Lou did not like to think about it; they were—and not only to themselves, but to all their contemporaries—the Sabine girls. They had kept all the emotions of their youth, but were themselves conscious only of their courage. They held out against time, and were aware only of time's sensuous coloring, which we know as weather.

So, though I know the cold into which Ellen stepped that Sunday morning, veiled and huddled in sealskin, I cannot tell its date, nor even for certain in what decade it fell.

The gust from the closing door as Ellen departed fluttered the flags in the hallway. Lou stood under the engraving of the Confederate general and bit her lip. Ellen annoyed her; she had not understood, she had not even tried to understand, what she was saying.

She was still excited—it was the excitement that sent her—when she hurried upstairs to the bathroom. She opened the door and for a second saw only the little window with frosted pane, saw it (she had just come from the dusky corridor) as a white glare in which slowly the forms of frost unfolded like submarine foliage. On the floor was a strip of rag carpet plaited of many colors. She saw it so distinctly that afterwards she could recall the coarse white threads stitching together the strands of faded red and blue and grey. Then she saw Bones.

Bones was playing some sort of game with himself. Quite naked, he stood in the tub, laughing, flicking a wet towel out and back. Terrible and tall he stood, and very black; each time that his long right arm shot out he held his breath. He watched it, his wrist turned and the towel came back slapping loud and wet on his bright black body. And he chuckled. Bones stood there, all a Negro, not in the least obscured by the mists that rose from the water. He chuckled all over. Once he winked at Lou, but did not stop his game. She shut her eyes and could not move; she heard the swishing Negro and the slap and the loud blind chuckling.

How she found her way out, how she groped her way down the stairs and waited, one hand on the knob of the front door, for Ellen, how she poured out the whole excited tale to her sister and again waited trembling while Ellen went upstairs and into the dusky corridor to see for herself what had happened—all, until Ellen came slowly down and gravely stopped on the last step to say in a troubled whisper that the door was closed but there was no sound from the bathroom—all that hour and the next hour was for Lou terror and confusion. She did not know how she lived through it. One thing only was clear: she had shut her eyes and behind them there was still the sight of the black man in the white glare, standing in the tub, tall and so naked, chuckling—under his ribs, chuckling.

They sat on the parlor haircloth, thinking what to do. And Lou in the mirror saw the door open and Bones entered, an impeccable reflection, in white jacket and black trousers. She heard him say that dinner was ready. Then he went out, disappearing through a door in the long glass. She turned and saw the door into the dining room just closing.

'We can't, we can't!' She held her face crying, 'I can't go in there!'

'We must,' said Ellen. 'It's best not to anger him. I've always heard that was the only thing with crazy people, not to cross them.'

They sat stiffly, and Bones brought in the painted soup tureen, put it down before Ellen, and proudly uncovered a steaming fragrance. Its heat was comforting, the dinner that followed so calm and excellent that they lost something of terror. Whatever Bones might be, the cooking was not insane. Ellen could even whisper as they left the room, leaning toward Lou, 'You're sure you saw him?'

Lou was astonished that anyone could doubt her vision. 'But Ellen,' she said, 'I saw everything. I even saw the threads in the carpet. It was all so clear.'

'Then I don't know what we'll do,' said Ellen. 'We'll have to do something, but I don't know what.'

In Ellen's high bedroom, with the doors locked, they consulted. Both whispered, 'What can we do?' until the white glare was gone and the dark gathered, falling first in the room. They were imprisoned by winter, all their windows barred with snow. If they went out, it would only be to come back again in the night over pavements of ice. They were held. Lou suggested that they write a note and throw it down and wait for someone to pick it up. But to whom? To Mr. Hite? To the police? They saw a colored boy who stooped and picked the folded paper from the snow; he looked at it and seeing it had no address tossed it away again. Besides, it was already so dim that he could hardly have seen it even if it had been there. There was nothing to do but to let night come and hope for Mr. Hite.

In the night the snow again fell. Under the street lamps they saw it falling—waited for the ringing of the bell that would tell them Mr. Hite was at the door.

He came, as usual, for Sunday night supper. Ellen and Lou were surprised to see him, they had waited so long upstairs behind the locked doors. He stood in the hall, red and puffing, wrapped to the nose; his eyes were watery in the light and on the lashes tiny beads. He had left his galoshes outside and for some minutes walked stiffly and strangely. But he got them through supper and afterwards Ellen carefully shut the doors on the parlor and waited for Lou's confidences. Their chairs were drawn close to the grate. Mr. Hite moved easily; he watched the flames some minutes, then straightened and, as though it were a formal bouquet in lace paper, presented his gossip. So-and-so was sick, somebody else was thought to be dying; he offered illness for violets, misfortunes for jonquils, and in the center a corpse (old Mrs. Hunter from Summit Point) like a white rose. His listeners were not depressed, though their voices were serious, for this is the usual conversation in a country town when the weather is bad.

At ten o'clock he was gone. They bolted the door and Ellen turned to Lou in amazement.

'But you didn't say a word! Why didn't you? I was waiting all evening.'

'But Ellen, how could I? I couldn't tell Mr. Hite I saw a man naked.'

'No, I suppose not. And it would be worse with the police.'

'O much worse! I couldn't do it.'

Lou fluttered. As quickly as possible and with as little noise they reached Ellen's bedroom. Bones had not been there. When Ellen leaned from the window to close the frozen shutters, the snow was still falling. They barricaded the doors. Lou was first into bed in a borrowed nightgown. Ellen left the lamp burning. They lay in the great bed in which their mother had died and at last, in the silence of snow, slept. Impossible phantoms pursued Lou, and among them the great Lee, untamed and all a general, his eyes not on her but fixed afar in the very ecstasy of battle. She lost him and he came again, with drawn sword, naked steel; he did not see her, but she saw that his eyes were pale and the lashes frozen.

IV

Bones stayed on. Something of their terror communicated itself to the town, but the Sabines did nothing. They had never been able to dismiss Selly; they could hardly think of dismissing a servant so grand as Bones.

His manner was grander than ever. When the time for spring cleaning came, he rearranged the whole house; they had not believed their furniture could seem so elegant. When he had done, the rooms were a little bare downstairs and the attic was littered with rubbish. Ellen wept when she saw her mother's sad rocking chair, its arms worn where her hands had rubbed them, relegated to the refuse under the eaves. But they had to approve, for they saw that Bones had added almost a century to the house. Once you had entered the front door, it had an air and discomfort that was almost colonial.

Bones stayed on. And life was once more ordered to the calm of the past. Yet, they were not easy; those prowlings at night which once made them feel the more secure now seemed unnatural. A thing that slept so little could hardly be a man. They heard him trying the bolts and creaking along the staircase with apprehension. They slept often together, but did not sleep well. Nervousness brought loss of appetite; Ellen could not open a letter without fraying the edges, Lou started at every knock on the door and was not quite reassured when she saw who it was. Both looked like women who expected calamity and heard in every sound its coming.

It was almost with relief that Ellen, coming into her room in the dead hour of the midsummer's afternoon, found the long Negro asleep on her bed. His mouth was open and except for his breath, which was heavy, he might have been dead. Mr. Hite when he came—they sent for him at once—thought he might have been dead drunk. Ellen said 'No,' and Lou insisted that Bones never touched a drop. Happily, the sleeper was clothed, so they could speak of having seen him. And Ellen took Mr. Hite to her bedroom to show him the black smudge on the counterpane which his shoes had left.

'Well,' said Mr. Hite, 'he buys a lot of liquor. I've known that for some time. I've been meaning to speak of it.'

'We know,' said Ellen.

'It all goes into the cooking.' Lou was emphatic. 'I've seen it.'

'All?' asked Mr. Hite. 'Anyhow, I think you better let me get rid of him for you.'

'I don't think,' said Ellen, 'he'll go.'

'He'll never go,' Lou agreed.

'We'll see about that,' said Mr. Hite. 'If I tell him to go, he'll skedaddle. Let me see him.'

And before they could halt him, he had gone toward the kitchen.

'We'll never get anybody else like Bones,' said Lou.

'Yes,' said Ellen, 'and there's the garden. Without Bones, we'll never get anything done the way he wants it.'

'It's all right!' Mr. Hite shut the door behind him and looked at them beaming. 'He'll leave in the morning.'

Bones came in the next morning and Ellen sat at the high secretary and went over the accounts. He was, as always, calm, polite and ready with suggestions. But when his money had been handed to him, his eyes filled with tears. He quite broke down. He had considered them as his ladies, and then too, Mr. Hite, he had always thought him such a nice white gentleman. Then Lou began weeping, and in the sadness of disappointment Bones went off to pack.

No one ate any dinner. The sun was half-way down the sky when, surrounded by his belongings, he settled himself in the ramshackle old trap that Ellen had had brought from the livery stable and gave the word to start. His long legs were opened and bent about his trunk, propped between the two seats. He leaned back and, smiling, ran his fingers along the fringe of the black, moth-eaten top. Beside him, in the hired hack, were his banjo and a slanting pile of leathery books.

'Those are our books!' screamed Lou. The sisters were peering from an upper window, each from one side of the drawn blind.

But the coachman had already bent over the dashboard to crack his whip. The bony sorrel broke into a trot, and the last the Sabines saw as the carriage disappeared in a golden light under distant trees was Bones leaning forward to try the driver's hat on his own head.

That night they heard the banjo's tinkling begin in the bedroom on the back corridor, very softly and behind closed doors. Then it must have been that the window was opened, for the sound suddenly increased and in a moment they heard the familiar voice in wild hilarity singing, *My head got wet with the morning dew. And the morning star was a witness too.*

Half the night he sang (though it was rather shouting than singing), the banjo twanged and his mirth was wild. But when he stopped and there was an interval when they heard only the leaves, the break brought such a sense of melancholy that both the listeners trembled. And they waited for Bones and his twining strings again to begin, as he always did, with a little chuckle before each song.

'Bones, you made,' said Ellen at breakfast, 'a great deal of noise last night. Neither I nor Lou could sleep.'

'Yes'm,' Bones agreed. 'But then I just had to do something to keep my heart up.'

'You're back?' Lou asked.

'O yes'm. I'se back. I just had to come back. There ain't nobody else can look after you two ladies like I can. Miss Lou here, she don't eat more'n enough to keep a bird alive. What'd she do if I wasn't here to make these nice corn cakes for her? Then,' he said, 'I just had to come back to see 'bout my garden. I'm startin' in the mornin' on my maze.'

'Your what?'

'Didn't you all know you was going to have a maze? Just like the one at Mount Vernon.'

Already he had done marvels with the garden, which until his coming had been much like any other in the town. Lawns were made smooth. Bones had straightened paths and strewed gravel; where before were only unkempt patches of vegetables were now neat borders, marigolds and cornflowers between thyme and lavender. And following an even older tradition he had set in the midst of green a small scent garden, where in spring violets and jonquils lost their breath in the nimble air and summer nights were enriched by fragrant stocks and white tobacco flowers. It was all very old-fashioned; you had only to shut your eyes to imagine yourself at Westover or Sabine Hall (where, be it said, no Sabine had ever lived or even been invited). And now he talked, to their bewilderment, of a maze of intricate box.

'Yes'm, I got it all here—' He pointed a bony finger to his forehead. 'It'll be 'bout twenty years before I gets it out there.' He chuckled. 'Boxwood grows awful slow.'

'I'll have to have some coffee,' said Ellen. She scattered her plate and felt faint.

'Yes'm,' said Bones.

'In some ways, he's a great comfort,' said Lou. She did not look up, and both shuddered as the door on the kitchen closed. They knew Bones was there to stay.

They knew the prowling nights that were before them, the bolts that would slide, the pantings up and down the dark corridor. The nights would be worse, but the days, too, would be afraid. They would come on him, they knew, moving like a creature out of a dream and have to remember that niggers can sleep standing up, with eyelids apart and their yellow eyeballs showing.

'I can't dismiss him,' said Ellen. And Bones could not be confined. He had been their intimate so long, they could not reasonably confine him to a lunatic cell. They would feel themselves mad. Above all they could not have him declared mad in West Virginia. As Ellen said: 'A nice Virginia prison, I would consider. But as that's impossible, we must keep Bones with us.'

'I almost think I'm glad,' said Lou.

'Yes,' said Ellen, but she trembled.

They knew now what they owed him. With him they lived in terror, but in the tradition. Their digestions were destroyed, their nerves frayed, but their pride sustained. They were like that Valley in which they had been born and which they loved and which indeed, as it lies between two ridges of intensely blue hills, is a country to be loved. The richness of its soil it owes to a slow disintegration; water has worn its rocks as noiselessly as time and all underneath the dark is hollow. The Sabines were slowly decomposing, like the limestone which arched and caverned underlies the long Valley and worried by water minutely decays. With Bones gone, they felt the hollowness underground. They had contended against time, but they were growing old.

They would soon be old. But with Bones there, they could stand it. To one who looks at all the Valley and the rich yield of its seasons it is easy to ignore the caves beneath, damp, empty, impenetrable. He would stay, they knew now, to the end. They would keep him, as it were a dear obsession, till they were dead.

NEVADA

The Wind and the Snow of Winter

WALTER VAN TILBURG CLARK

It was near sunset when Mike Braneen came onto the last pitch of the old wagon road which had led into Gold Rock from the east since the Comstock days. The road was just two ruts in the hard earth, with sagebrush growing between them, and was full of steep pitches and sharp turns. From the summit it descended even more steeply into Gold Rock in a series of short switch-backs down the slope of the canyon. There was a paved highway on the other side of the pass now, but Mike never used that. Cars coming from behind made him uneasy, so that he couldn't follow his own thoughts long, but had to keep turning around every few minutes, to see that his burro, Annie, was staying out on the shoulder of the road, where she would be safe. Mike didn't like cars anyway, and on the old road he could forget about them, and feel more like himself. He could forget about Annie too, except when the light, quick tapping of her hoofs behind him stopped. Even then he didn't really break his thoughts. It was more as if the tapping were another sound from his own inner machinery, and when it stopped, he stopped too, and turned around to see what she was doing. When he began to walk ahead again at the same slow, unvarying pace, his arms scarcely swinging at all, his body bent a little forward from the waist, he would not be aware that there had been any interruption of the memory or the story that was going on in his head. Mike did not like to have his stories interrupted except by an idea of his own, something to do with his prospecting, or the arrival of his story at an actual memory which warmed him to closer recollection or led into a new and more attractive story.

An intense, golden light, almost liquid, fanned out from the peaks

From *The Yale Review,* December, 1944. Used by permission.

above him and reached eastward under the gray sky, and the snow which occasionally swarmed across this light was fine and dry. Such little squalls had been going on all day, and still there was nothing like real snow down, but only a fine powder which the wind swept along until it caught under the brush, leaving the ground bare. Yet Mike Braneen was not deceived. This was not just a flurrying day; it was the beginning of winter. If not tonight, then tomorrow, or the next day, the snow would begin which shut off the mountains, so that a man might as well be on a great plain for all he could see, perhaps even the snow which blinded a man at once and blanketed the desert in an hour. Fifty-two years in this country had made Mike Braneen sure about such things, although he didn't give much thought to them, but only to what he had to do because of them. Three nights before, he had been awakened by a change in the wind. It was no longer a wind born in the near mountains, cold with night and altitude, but a wind from far places, full of a damp chill which got through his blankets and into his bones. The stars had still been clear and close above the dark humps of the mountains, and overhead the constellations had moved slowly in full panoply, unbroken by any invisible lower darkness; yet he had lain there half awake for a few minutes, hearing the new wind beat the brush around him, hearing Annie stirring restlessly and thumping in her hobble. He had thought drowsily, 'Smells like winter this time,' and then, 'It's held off a long time this year, pretty near the end of December.' Then he had gone back to sleep, mildly happy because the change meant he would be going back to Gold Rock. Gold Rock was the other half of Mike Braneen's life. When the smell of winter came, he always started back for Gold Rock. From March or April until the smell of winter, he wandered slowly about among the mountains, anywhere between the White Pines and the Virginias, with only his burro for company. Then there would come the change, and they would head back for Gold Rock.

Mike had travelled with a good many burros during that time, eighteen or twenty, he thought, although he was not sure. He could not remember them all, but only those he had had first, when he was a young man and always thought most about seeing women when he got back to Gold Rock, or those with something queer about them, like Baldy, who'd had a great, pale patch, like a bald spot, on one side of his belly, or those who'd had something queer happen to them, like Maria. He could remember just how it had been that night. He could remember it as if it were last night. It had been in Hamilton. He had felt unhappy, because he could remember Hamilton when the whole hollow was full of people and buildings, and everything was new and active. He had gone to sleep in the hollow shell of the Wells Fargo Building, hearing an old iron shutter banging against the wall in the wind. In the morning, Maria had been gone. He had followed the scuffing track she made on account of her loose hobble, and it had led far up the old snow-gullied road to Treasure Hill, and then ended at one of the black shafts that opened like mouths right at the edge of the road. A man remembered a thing like that. There weren't many burros that foolish. But burros with nothing particular about them were hard to remember—especially those he'd had in the last twenty years or so, when he had gradually stopped feeling so personal about them, and had begun to call all the jennies Annie and all the burros Jack.

The clicking of the little hoofs behind him stopped, and Mike stopped too, and turned around. Annie was pulling at a line of yellow grass along the edge of the road.

'Come on, Maria,' Mike said, patiently. The burro at once stopped pulling at the dead grass and came on up towards him, her small black nose working, the ends of the grass standing out on each side of it like whiskers. Mike began to climb again, ahead of her.

It was a long time since he had been caught by a winter, too. He could not remember how long. All the beginnings ran together in his mind, as if they were all the beginning of one winter so far back that he had almost forgotten it. He could still remember clearly, though, the winter he had stayed out on purpose, clear into January. He had been a young man then, thirty-five or forty or forty-five, somewhere in there. He would have to stop and try to bring back a whole string of memories about what had happened just before, in order to remember just how old he had been, and it wasn't worth the trouble. Besides, sometimes even that system didn't work. It would lead him into an old camp where he had been a number of times, and the dates would get mixed up. It was impossible to remember any other way, because all his comings and goings had been so much alike. He had been young, anyhow, and not much afraid of anything except running out of water in the wrong place; not even afraid of the winter. He had stayed out because he'd thought he had a good thing, and he had wanted to prove it. He could remember how it felt to be out in the clear winter weather on the mountains, the piñon trees and the junipers weighted down with feathery snow, and making sharp, blue shadows on the white slopes. The hills had made blue shadows on one another too, and in the still air his pick had made the beginning of a sound like a bell's. He knew he had been young, because he could remember taking a day off now and then, just to go tramping around those hills, up and down the white and through the blue shadows, on a kind of holiday. He had pretended to his common sense that he was seriously prospecting, and had carried his hammer, and even his drill along, but he had really just been gallivanting, playing colt. Maybe he had been even younger than thirty-five, though he could still be stirred a little, for that matter, by the memory of the kind of weather which had sent him gallivanting. High-blue weather, he called it. There were two kinds of high-blue weather, besides the winter kind, which didn't set him off very often, spring and fall. In the spring it would have a soft, puffy wind and soft, puffy white clouds which made separate shadows that travelled silently across hills that looked soft too. In the fall it would be still, and there would be no clouds at all in the blue, but there would be something in the golden air and the soft, steady sunlight on the mountains that made a man as uneasy as the spring blowing, though in a different way, more sad and not so excited. In the spring high-blue, a man had been likely to think about women he had slept with, or wanted to sleep with, or imaginary women made up with the help of newspaper pictures of actresses or young society matrons, or of the old oil paintings in the Lucky Boy Saloon, which showed pale, almost naked women against dark, sumptuous backgrounds—women with long hair or braided hair, calm, virtuous faces, small hands and feet, and ponderous limbs, breasts, and buttocks. In the fall high-blue, though it had been much longer since he had seen a woman, or heard a woman's voice, he was more likely to think about old friends, men, or places he had heard about, or places he hadn't seen for a long time. He himself thought most often about Goldfield the way he had last seen it in the summer in 1912. That was as far south as Mike had ever been in Nevada. Since then, he had never been south of Tonopah. When the high-blue weather was past, though, and the season worked towards winter, he began to think about Gold Rock. There were only three or four winters out of the fifty-two when he hadn't gone home to Gold Rock, to his old room at Mrs. Wright's, up on Fourth Street, and to his meals in the dining room at the International House, and to the Lucky Boy, where he could talk to Tom Connover and his other friends, and play cards, or have a drink to hold in his hand while he sat and remembered.

This journey had seemed a little different from most, though. It had started the same as usual, but as he had come across the two vast valleys, and through the pass in the low range between them, he hadn't felt quite the same. He'd felt younger and more awake, it seemed to him, and yet, in a way, older too, suddenly older. He had been sure that there was plenty of time, and yet he had been a little afraid of getting caught in the storm. He had kept looking ahead to see if the mountains on the horizon were still clearly outlined, or if they had been cut off by a lowering of the clouds. He had thought more than once, how bad it would be to get caught out there when the real snow began, and he had been disturbed by the first flakes. It had seemed hard to him to have to walk so far, too. He had kept thinking about distance. Also the snowy cold had searched out the regions of his body where old injuries had healed. He had taken off his left mitten a good many times, to blow on the fingers which had been frosted the year he was sixty-three, so that now it didn't take much cold to turn them white and stiffen them. The queer tingling, partly like an itch and partly like a pain, in the patch on his back that had been burned in that old powder blast, was sharper than he could remember its ever having been before. The rheumatism in his joints, which was so old a companion that it usually made him feel no more than tight-knit and stiff, and the place where his leg had been broken and torn when that ladder broke in '97 ached, and had a pulse he could count. All this made him believe that he was walking more slowly than usual, although nothing, probably not even a deliberate attempt, could actually have changed his pace. Sometimes he even thought, with a moment of fear, that he was getting tired.

On the other hand, he felt unusually clear and strong in his mind. He remembered things with a clarity which was like living them again —nearly all of them events from many years back, from the time when he had been really active and fearless and every burro had had its own name. Some of these events, like the night he had spent in Eureka with the little, brown-haired whore, a night in the fall in 1888 or '89, somewhere in there, he had not once thought of for years. Now he could remember even her name. Armandy she had called herself: a funny name. They all picked names for their business, of course, romantic names like Cecily or Rosamunde or Belle or Claire, or hard names like Diamond Gert or Horseshoe Sal, or names that were pinned on them, like Indian Kate or Roman Mary, but Armandy was different.

He could remember Armandy as if he were with her now, not the way she had behaved in bed; he couldn't remember anything particular about that. In fact, he couldn't be sure that he remembered anything about that at all. There were others he could remember more clearly for the way they had behaved in bed, women he had been with more often. He had been with Armandy only that one night. He remembered little things about being with her, things that made it seem good to think of being with her again. Armandy had a room upstairs in a hotel. They could hear a piano playing in a club across the street. He could hear the tune, and it was one he knew, although he didn't know its name. It was a gay tune that went on and on the same, but still it sounded sad when you heard it through the hotel window, with the lights from the bars and hotels shining on the street, and the people coming and going through the lights, and then, beyond the lights, the darkness where the mountains were. Armandy wore a white silk dress with a high waist, and a locket on a gold chain. The dress made her look very brown and like a young girl. She used a white powder on her face, that smelled like violets, but this could not hide her brownness. The locket was heart-shaped, and it opened to show a cameo of a man's hand holding a woman's hand very gently, just their fingers laid out long together, and the thumbs holding, the way they were sometimes on tombstones. There were two little gold initials on each hand, but Armandy would never tell what they stood for, or even if the locket was really her own. He stood in the window, looking down at the club from which the piano music was coming, and Armandy stood beside him, with her shoulders against his arm, and a glass of wine in her hand. He could see the toe of her white satin slipper showing from under the edge of her skirt. Her big hat, loaded with black and white plumes, lay on the dresser behind him. His own leather coat, with the sheep-skin lining, lay across the foot of the bed. It was a big bed, with a knobby brass foot and head. There was one oil lamp burning in the chandelier in the middle of the room. Armandy was soft-spoken, gentle, and a little fearful, always looking at him to see what he was thinking. He stood with his arms folded. His arms felt big and strong upon his heavily muscled chest. He stood there, pretending to be in no hurry, but really thinking eagerly about what he would do with Armandy, who had something about her which tempted him to be cruel.

He stood there, with his chin down into his heavy, dark beard, and watched a man come riding down the middle of the street from the west. The horse was a fine black, which lifted its head and feet with pride. The man sat very straight, with a high rein, and something about his clothes and hat made him appear to be in uniform, although it wasn't a uniform he was wearing. The man also saluted friends upon the sidewalks like an officer, bending his head just slightly, and touching his hat instead of lifting it. Mike Braneen asked Armandy who the man was, and then felt angry because she could tell him, and because he was an important man who owned a mine that was in bonanza. He mocked the airs with which the man rode, and his princely greetings. He mocked the man cleverly, and Armandy laughed and repeated what he said, and made him drink a little of her wine as a reward. Mike had been drinking whisky, and he did not like wine anyway, but this was not the moment in which to refuse such an invitation.

Old Mike remembered all this, which had been completely forgotten for years. He could not remember what he and Armandy had said, but he remembered everything else, and he felt very lonesome for Armandy, and for the room with the red, figured carpet and the brass chandelier with oil lamps in it, and the open window with the long tune coming up through it, and the young summer night outside on the mountains. This loneliness was so much more intense than his familiar loneliness that it made him feel very young. Memories like this had come up again and again during these three days. It was like beginning life over again. It had tricked him into thinking, more than once, 'Next summer I'll make the strike, and this time I'll put it into something safe for the rest of my life, and stop this fool wandering around while I've still got some time left'—a way of thinking which he had really stopped a long time before.

It was getting darker rapidly in the pass. When a gust of wind brought the snow against Mike's face so hard that he noticed the flakes felt larger, he looked up. The light was still there, although the fire was dying out of it, and the snow swarmed across it more thickly. Mike remembered God. He did not think anything exact. He did not think about his own relationship to God. He merely felt the idea as a comforting presence. He'd always had a feeling about God whenever he looked at a sunset, especially a sunset which came through under a stormy sky. It had been the strongest feeling left in him until these memories like the one about Armandy had begun. Even in this last pass, his strange fear of the storm had come on him again a couple of times, but now that he had looked at the light and thought of God, it was gone. In a few minutes he would come to the summit and look down into his lighted city. He felt happily hurried by this anticipation.

He would take the burro down and stable her in John Hammersmith's shed, where he always kept her. He would spread fresh straw for her, and see that the shed was tight against the wind and snow, and get a measure of grain for her from John. Then he would go up to Mrs. Wright's house at the top of Fourth Street, and leave his things in the same room he always had, the one in front, which looked down over the roofs and chimneys of his city, and across at the east wall of the canyon, from which the sun rose late. He would trim his beard with Mrs. Wright's shears, and shave the upper part of his cheeks. He would bathe out of the blue bowl and pitcher, and wipe himself with the towel with yellow flowers on it, and dress in the good dark suit and the good black shoes with the gleaming box toes, and the good black hat which he had left in the chest in his room. In this way he would perform the ceremony which ended the life of the desert and began the life of Gold Rock. Then he would go down to the International House, and greet Arthur Morris in the gleaming bar, and go into the dining room and eat the best supper they had, with fresh meat and vegetables, and new-made pie, and two cups of hot clear coffee. He would be served by the plump blonde waitress who always joked with him, and gave him many little extra things with his first supper, including the drink which Arthur Morris always sent in from the bar.

At this point Mike Braneen stumbled in his mind, and his anticipation wavered. He could not be sure that the plump blonde waitress would serve him. For a moment he saw her in a long skirt, and the dining room of the International House, behind her, had potted palms standing in the corners, and was full of the laughter and loud, manly talk of many customers who wore high vests and mustaches and beards. These men leaned back from tables covered with empty dishes. They patted their tight vests and lighted expensive cigars. He knew all their faces. If he were to walk down the aisle between the tables on his side, they would all speak to him. But he also seemed to remember the dining room with only a few tables, with oil cloth on them instead of linen, and with moody young men sitting at them in their work clothes—strangers who worked for the highway department, or were just passing through, or talked mining in terms which he did not understand or which made him angry.

No, it would not be the plump blonde waitress. He did not know who it would be. It didn't matter. After supper he would go up Canyon Street under the arcade to the Lucky Boy Saloon, and there it would be the same as ever. There would be the laurel wreaths on the frosted glass panels of the doors, and the old sign upon the window, the sign that was older than Tom Connover, almost as old as Mike Braneen himself. He would open the door and see the bottles and the white women in the paintings, and the card table in the back corner and the big stove and the chairs along the wall. Tom would look around from his place behind the bar.

'Well, now,' he would roar, 'look who's here, boys.'

'Now will you believe it's winter?' he would roar at them.

Some of them would be the younger men, of course, and there might even be a few strangers, but this would only add to the dignity of his reception, and there would also be his friends. There would be Henry Bray with the gray walrus mustache, and Mark Wilton and Pat Gallagher. They would all welcome him loudly.

'Mike, how are you, anyway?' Tom would roar, leaning across the bar to shake hands with his big, heavy, soft hand with the diamond ring on it.

'And what'll it be, Mike? The same?' he'd ask, as if Mike had been in there no longer ago than the night before.

Mike would play that game too. 'The same,' he would say.

Then he would really be back in Gold Rock; never mind the plump blonde waitress.

Mike came to the summit of the old road and stopped and looked down. For a moment he felt lost again, as he had when he'd thought about the plump blonde waitress. He had expected Canyon Street to look much brighter. He had expected a lot of orange windows close together on the other side of the canyon. Instead there were only a few scattered lights across the darkness, and they were white. They made no communal glow upon the steep slope, but gave out only single, white needles of light, which pierced in darkness secretly and lonesomely, as if nothing could ever pass from one house to another over there. Canyon Street was very dark, too. There it went, the street he loved, steeply down into the bottom of the canyon, and down its length there were only the few street lights, more than a block apart, swinging in the wind and darting about that cold, small light. The snow whirled and swooped under the nearest street light below.

'You are getting to be an old fool,' Mike Braneen said out loud to himself, and felt better. This was the way Gold Rock was now, of course, and he loved it all the better. It was a place that grew old with a man, that was going to die sometime, too. There could be an understanding with it.

He worked his way slowly down into Canyon Street, with Annie slipping and checking behind him. Slowly, with the blown snow behind them, they came to the first built-up block, and passed the first dim light showing through a smudged window under the arcade. They passed the dark places after it, and the second light. Then Mike Braneen stopped in the middle of the street, and Annie stopped beside him, pulling her rump in and turning her head away from the snow. A highway truck, coming down from the head of the canyon, had to get way over onto the wrong side of the street to pass them. The driver leaned out as he went by, and yelled, 'Pull over, Pop. You're in town now.'

Mike Braneen didn't hear him. He was staring at the Lucky Boy. The Lucky Boy was dark, and there were boards nailed across the big window that had shown the sign. At last Mike went over onto the board walk to look more closely. Annie followed him, but stopped at the edge of the walk and scratched her neck against a post of the arcade. There was the other sign, hanging crossways under the arcade, and even in that gloom Mike could see that it said Lucky Boy and had a Jack of Diamonds painted on it. There was no mistake. The Lucky Boy sign, and others like it under the arcade, creaked and rattled in the wind.

There were footsteps coming along the boards. The boards sounded hollow, and sometimes one of them rattled. Mike Braneen looked down slowly from the sign and peered at the approaching figure. It was a man wearing a sheepskin coat with the collar turned up around his head. He was walking quickly, like a man who knew where he was going, and why, and where he had been. Mike almost let him pass. Then he spoke.

'Say, fella—'

He even reached out a hand as if to catch hold of the man's sleeve, though he didn't touch it. The man stopped, and asked, impatiently, 'Yeah?' and Mike let the hand down again slowly.

'Well, what is it?' the man asked.

'I don't want anything,' Mike said. 'I got plenty.'

'O.K., O.K.,' the man said. 'What's the matter?'

Mike moved his hand towards the Lucky Boy. 'It's closed,' he said.

'I see it is, Dad,' the man said. He laughed a little. He didn't seem to be in quite so much of a hurry now.

'How long has it been closed?' Mike asked.

'Since about June, I guess,' the man said. 'Old Tom Connover, the guy that ran it, died last June.'

Mike waited for a moment. 'Tom died?' he asked.

'Yup. I guess he'd just kept it open out of love of the place anyway. There hasn't been any real business for years. Nobody cared to keep it open after him.'

The man started to move on, but then he waited, peering, trying to see Mike better.

'This June?' Mike asked finally.

'Yup. This last June.'

'Oh,' Mike said. Then he just stood there. He wasn't thinking anything. There didn't seem to be anything to think.

'You knew him?' the man asked.

'Thirty years,' Mike said. 'No, more'n that,' he said, and started to figure out how long he had known Tom Connover, but lost it, and said, as if it would do just as well, 'He was a lot younger than I am, though.'

'Hey,' said the man, coming closer, and peering again. 'You're Mike Braneen, aren't you?'

'Yes,' Mike said.

'Gee, I didn't recognize you at first. I'm sorry.'

'That's all right,' Mike said. He didn't know who the man was, or what he was sorry about.

He turned his head slowly, and looked out into the street. The snow was coming down heavily now. The street was all white. He saw Annie with her head and shoulders in under the arcade, but the snow settling on her rump.

'Well, I guess I'd better get Molly under cover,' he said. He moved towards the burro a step, but then halted.

'Say, fella—'

The man had started on, but he turned back. He had to wait for Mike to speak.

'I guess this about Tom's mixed me up.'

'Sure,' the man said. 'It's tough, an old friend like that.'

'Where do I turn up to get to Mrs. Wright's place?'

'Mrs. Wright?'

'Mrs. William Wright,' Mike said. 'Her husband used to be a foreman in the Aztec. Got killed in the fire.'

'Oh,' the man said. He didn't say anything more, but just stood there, looking at the shadowy bulk of old Mike.

'She's not dead, too, is she?' Mike asked slowly.

'Yeah, I'm afraid she is, Mr. Braneen,' the man said.

'Look,' he said more cheerfully. 'It's Mrs. Branley's house you want right now, isn't it? Place where you stayed last winter?'

Finally Mike said, 'Yeah. Yeah, I guess it is.'

'I'm going up that way. I'll walk up with you,' the man said.

After they had started, Mike thought that he ought to take the burro down to John Hammersmith's first, but he was afraid to ask about it. They walked on down Canyon Street, with Annie walking along beside them in the gutter. At the first side street they turned right and began to climb the steep hill towards another of the little street lights dancing over a crossing. There was no sidewalk here, and Annie followed right at their heels. That one street light was the only light showing up ahead.

When they were half way up to the light, Mike asked, 'She die this summer, too?'

The man turned his body half around, so that he could hear inside his collar.

'What?'

'Did she die this summer, too?'

'Who?'

'Mrs. Wright,' Mike said.

The man looked at him, trying to see his face as they came up towards the light. Then he turned back again, and his voice was muffled by the collar.

'No, she died quite a while ago, Mr. Braneen.'

'Oh,' Mike said finally.

They came up onto the crossing under the light, and the snow-laden wind whirled around them again. They passed under the light, and their three lengthening shadows before them were obscured by the innumerable tiny shadows of the flakes.

NEBRASKA

A Jeeter Wedding

DOROTHY THOMAS

There was nothing about the dilapidated Jeeter farmstead to recommend it as a lodging place except its nearness to the schoolhouse and the fact that the Clay Creek teachers had always stayed there. The house was unpainted and eaveless, with a narrow front door that opened on to nothingness above a high stone foundation. There were hair-lined holes in the foundation where sleepy dogs crawled out of hiding to bark a time or two and wag their tails for visitors. A clay and cinder path led around to the littered back stoop and the one usable door.

Inside, the place was more cheerful, with checkered tablecloths, rag rugs, and the choicest farm calendars of the last decade.

There was a large family of Jeeters, but at the time I came to stay with them there were only five at home: the old mother, the two sons, a daughter, and a baby granddaughter. The other daughters, excepting the youngest, who was "working out" in a railway town "down the line a way," were married and lived on near-by farms. Before the first month was gone I met them all, big, blue-eyed, loud-voiced women, with the smell of the kitchen and the stable about them, and liked them well enough.

Ma Jeeter was a large woman with an enormous bosom that oozed down over the belt of her gray print dress and lay flat on her broad stomach. One of her eyes was gone. After I had been with her awhile she told me how she came to lose it.

"It was the spring I was carrying my third girl," she said. "I went out to holler the men-folks up for dinner and fell off the stoop and broke it on some bush stubs. I was scared it would mark the baby but it didn't.

I don't miss it much. Pa always said I should have a glass one but we just never got around to send off for it."

One of her knees was stiff so that she could not bend her leg at all.

"I don't know that it was really broke," she told me. "I was milkin' a heifer and she kicked me, and by night my leg was black to the hip and poulticin' didn't seem to help it none, and when I could get up and bear my weight on it again, that leg wouldn't bend. It's eleven years since I been upstairs. It's hard to piece the quilts I've pieced and never see 'em on the beds."

Some days her leg hurt her and she used a crutch her older son had made for her of a piece of gas pipe, bent at one end, and made comfortable for her arm with a piece of carpet wound about it. She had two chins. The upper one was bearded, and lay darkly upon the doughish whiteness of the lower one. She was a good cook and a good talker, and I liked to sit on the edge of the cob box and watch and listen while she lurched about the room getting supper.

The elder son was a broad-shouldered man of thirty with an entirely bald head. He had an impediment in his speech. When strangers spoke to him he fixed his blue eyes on them, and puckered his mouth and waited for the words he hoped to speak. While he waited a deep blush crept up over his baldness, and his Adam's apple rose and fell yearningly until the words came. In spite of his shyness and his speech difficulty, neighbors were always stopping their wagons to talk with him awhile.

The younger son was beginning his third year in the eighth grade of the school where I taught. He had the family good nature and was always willing to carry in the cobs for the stove.

Lena, the one girl at home, was the most quiet of the Jeeter women. She liked to get out of doors, and would spread up the beds, and do what sweeping she considered necessary, and be out about the stables, or in the cornfield with her brothers, early in the morning, leaving the cooking and the care of her two-year-old daughter to her mother. Cold winter mornings she plodded about the barnyard in an old green coat of her brother's, her red petticoat whipping about her legs.

Ma told me about Lena one Saturday morning when I was helping her tie a comforter.

"Lena's been awful unlucky," she said. "The neighbors will tell you if I don't, and I'd sooner you'd git the straight of it. This child here ain't her first. The other was a boy; he's in a home in Omaha if he ain't been adopted out. I guess she'd sooner have kept him than this little one if she'd knowed what was comin'. She was workin' out in town then. The father was a married man but he liked her a lot, and he done what he could for her. He sent her to a hospital in Omaha to have it, which is more than any of the other girls can boast. It was a fine boy; weighed twelve pounds. "This other fellow was our own hired man and a nicer man we never had on the place. He always shook his shoes out on a paper after he'd been in the fields, and he'd go out on the stoop to smoke his pipe after supper even when it was cold, and he could play the organ too. He didn't seem put out, much, when Lena told him, and said he'd marry her, all right. The afternoon of the day she told him he took a load of grain to town and about nine o'clock the elevator man calls up and asks if that was our team tied up by the mill, and we never heard of him again.

"Some families has one weakness, and some has another. The Marshall boys is drunk half the time, and those Peaveys have six or seven kids that has been caught stealin'. I say a weakness is just a weakness and there's worse than the weakness this family's got. I don't say our girls didn't have their babies sooner than they should of, but they was awful good girls, and they's awful good mothers. All their husbands seem satisfied with 'em, even if some of 'em did rear up a little about marryin' 'em. You'll hear it said round here, maybe, 'There'll be a Jeeter weddin' if you don't watch out,' when they're guyin' a fellow, instead of sayin', 'there'll be a sheriff weddin'.' That ain't just. There was some dispute all right over some of the weddin's, but we had to call the sheriff for only one, and we got four girls married, and then, there's Evie—"

Ma was almost certain to turn any conversation toward Evie, her best, smartest, and fairest daughter. I had not met Evie, but the school records, which showed that she had passed the county eighth-grade examinations the first try, and the fact that she had "worked out" three years without the breath of scandal coming near her, and the prettiness of her photograph on the living-room organ, upheld Ma's judgment.

There was a story Ma liked to tell about this favorite child. "The Kellys that Evie worked for before she went to town to work is awful good workers, and awful good Catholics. That family will get up in the middle of the night to get their chores done so as to get to the early church meetin' in town on time, but they've had their share of bad luck the same as anybody. Three different times they've had their barn buildings struck by lightnin' and their house struck once. They got so scared of thunderstorms that they kept a candle burnin' in front of a saint picture in the hall upstairs, all fixed so it couldn't set the house afire.

"That was to keep the house from bein' hit, and burnin' that candle wasn't all they done. They went to a church in Omaha, or Sioux City, or some place, and had a special mass-meetin' put on against thunder and lightnin', and come home with a jarful of holy water they'd had blessed to keep the kids from bein' struck. One night Mrs. Kelly woke Evie up yellin', 'Evie! Evie! Go down and get the holy water,' and Evie got up, and started downstairs, and she said it was enough to make your blood harden to see that candle puffin' up, and almost goin' out, and puttin' long shadders on the wall, and the lightnin' comin' about twice a minute, and the wind and the rain just terrible. She said it made her sick to her stummick. "She went into the pantry and climbed up and reached for the jar of holy water and just as she shut her hands on the jar, there comes a flash of lightnin' like to blind, and a terrible clap of thunder right on it, and she lost her footin' and down she come and busted the jar to shivers and spilled all the holy water. That stuff musta cost more than good whisky, and Mrs. Kelly was standin' at the top of the stairs jumpin' up and down, I guess, and yellin', 'Evie! Evie! Bring that holy water!' and Evie, quick as a trigger, fills another jar, and screws the cap on it, that had been on the holy water jar, because it had a red streak on it to mark it, and wiped the water off the side of it with her gown, and goes runnin' upstairs and Mrs. Kelly grabs it and sprinkles all the kids, and Evie gets back in bed and lays awake all the rest of the night so she'd be the first one down in the mornin' to sweep up the glass."

Lena sometimes seemed a little jealous of her mother's pride in Evie, but one Saturday morning when she was dusting the living room she took Evie's photograph from its place on the organ and squatted down and held the picture where her little girl could look at it. "See!" she said. "That's your Aunt Evie. Ain't she purty? Say 'Aunt Evie!'" and there was honest family pride in her voice.

If Lena's child had a real name I never heard it. Her mother seldom spoke to her, but her uncles and her grandmother talked to her a great deal, and called her Babe. When anyone spoke to her she put her thin hands up over her face, palms outward, and whimpered shyly. I think Ma was secretly ashamed of this unJeeter-like bad nature and tried to make it look like playfulness by saying, when the child put her hands over her eyes, "Babe want to play peek? Come play peek with Grandma!"

That fall I knitted the child a little red sweater. She was very proud of it and went about patting her stomach and saying "Pretty."

One evening shortly after the Christmas holidays I worked until dusk at the schoolhouse. When I came in through the kitchen, Lena met my hello with a sad sniff and a sullen stare. Babe was sitting in her high chair by the cupboard making the weary sounds she made when she had cried a long time and was about to give it up. I took a match from the box on the warming-oven and went into the living room to light the lamp. As I was feeling for the chimney I smelled the faint sour-dough smell that was Ma's and saw that she was huddled in her chair beside the base burner, crying. I knew that she wanted to talk to me.

"I am glad Pa died when he did," she began. "I'm glad he never lived till now. I was settin' here in this room the day he died, with the front door open to get a draft through, it was so hot. I was settin' right where the stove is now, shellin' a mess of peas, and all at once I heard Pa callin' me. I jumped up from where I was, and let the pan fall on the floor, and ran out the door, and there was Pa staggerin' up to the stoop, and Evie and the baby was standin' lookin' at him with their eyes big, and awful scared for their Pa. And he looked up at me breathin' hard and says, 'Ma, I'm took,' and sure 'nuf he was took, took with a stroke from workin' in the awful heat, and he sinked down with his back against the house and his legs stuck out stiff in front of him, and then little Evie, she come and stood up close, lookin' at him, and he opens his eyes, and sees her, and holds out his arms and says, 'Evie!' and then he give a shiver, and death comes on him, and he rolls up his eyes and flops over dead. But I'm glad he died when he did."

I waited with the chimney in my hand, knowing that some catastrophe more recent than Pa's death had fallen on the house.

"Light the lamp," she said at last, "and I'll show you the letter. I guess I don't need to make such a fuss about a thing that's happened so many times in this house. I guess I didn't have no reason to think she was so much better than the rest of 'em, but I did think it, and after this long time she's been workin' out and got along so well, and everyone sayin' how nice she is. Some days I've set here and think how she'd maybe go awhile with some awful nice man, and get engaged, and then be married with the preacher out from town, and all the neighbors in, and a cake and everything, but I guess it's like I said, a weakness is a weakness and there's no use hopin' against it."

Evie's letter was brief:

> "Dear Mama—I guess you will be surprised. I am coming home in a couple of weeks to get married. I can't wait. Bill says he is willing we should get married right away and at home. He is a brakeman and has a good run.
>
> Love,
> Evie."

Even the brothers seemed downcast about Evie's coming marriage. The bald one shook his head sadly when I got out the checkerboard that night, and the younger one sniffled over his arithmetic. Lena slapped Babe when the child got between the lamp and her mending and Ma sat by the stove and sighed.

The gloom did not lift. Summoned by Ma, the daughters came over one at a time to mourn with her. When I came in at night I would find one of them sitting with her in the living room, red-eyed with family sympathy. No one said, "I told you so," or "She's no better than the rest of us, and I always expected this to happen." Like Ma, they had loved her best, and believed that she would escape the shame they had each weathered so bravely, and come home some day to give them a fine Christian wedding, and save them from their sins.

Then one night, a week before they expected her, Evie came home. We were all in the living room, and none of us had noticed the car driving into the yard. We all started up when the door opened and Evie came in, laughing, and stamping the snow from her shoes. "Made the mailman bring me out," she said, and her voice was not loud like the other girls' voices.

Her brothers got to their feet and stood looking at her. Ma made an indefinite gesture toward her crutch and dropped her hands back on to her lap. She was crying. Evie went to her and laid a pink cheek against her hair. "Aren't you glad to see me?" she asked. Ma nodded toward me, and mumbled an introduction, and Evie said, "Pleased to know you," and smiled brightly. Evie kissed them all and then the boys went out to the kitchen and I rose too, but Ma said, "No, you stay," and, turning to Evie, "it's all right. I told her. She knows how it is."

Evie smiled at me again. "Sure, don't everybody run away. Lena, have you made me some gowns, or underthings, or anything?"

"No," said Lena, "and you don't need to be so smart about it."

Ma put her arm about Evie's little waist. "You still look real nice; that's something," she said. "If you'd have wrote that your patterns was still all right we'd have made you some clothes. We did talk about it, but the girls said likely you couldn't get into them, so we give it up. You won't need much. You wasn't plannin' on havin' anybody outside, was you?"

"Say," said Evie, "I'm going to have everybody, and a dress, and a veil, and a cake. Why, Ma, you didn't think I had to *make* Bill marry me, did you, that I was going to have a baby or anything?"

I thought Ma was fainting. She slipped down from her chair, her stiff leg thrust out in front of her like a gray log, and closed her arms about her girl. "Evie, Evie," she sobbed. "My good baby!"

Into Evie's wedding preparations the Jeeter women put all the dreams they ever had had of weddings. The sisters came by twos and threes now, and Babe had other children to play with. The boys brought a paperhanger out from town, and had the living room re-papered. I offered my room for a sewing room, and after school hours I sewed too. The sisters never tired of admiring the engagement ring. Evie explained the letter over and over again.

"I said he was willing to marry me at home because I went to so much bother to coax him into letting us be married here, instead of in town where all his friends is. I said I couldn't wait because I was afraid he would change his mind, if we waited, and hold out for being married in town, and besides he's going to get a leave and he's getting passes on his railroad for us to take a trip. The lady where I worked would have give me a wedding but I wanted to come home."

Ma could not go up to my room to sew because of her leg, so she sat at the bottom of the stairway and basted the pieces the girls tossed down to her, and kept her many grandchildren from getting in the paperhanger's paste. She and the girls called back and forth, and when a garment reached the trying-on stage Evie would be pinned into it and they would all go down to have Ma look it over.

Lena seemed no less happy than the rest. One day Evie found a picture in one of my magazines of a bridal party with a little tot in a Kate Greenaway costume carrying the ring in a lily, and called all the girls to come and look at it.

"We'll have it like that," she decided. "Babe can carry the lily. Won't she look cute in a pink dress?"

"Aw, she's too little," Lena protested. "You'd better have one of the other girls' kids."

But Evie had decided. "Babe is the one I want," she said, and Lena blushed, laughed, and bent her head over her sewing, and the married sisters looked at Evie with all their love in their faces.

The wedding day was perfect. Snow had fallen in the night and much of the ugliness of the farmyard was hidden. The sisters and their families came for breakfast. The groom was there by ten and the guests began to arrive before eleven. Ma's bed in the downstairs bedroom could not hold all the gifts. Each guest put down his present with a gesture which said, "We've brought something pretty nice. We like the Jeeters and we like this wedding. In fact, this gift is as nice as it is to make up for all the gifts we should have brought the Jeeter girls at all the weddings there should have been."

The groom was a big, good-looking fellow. The men who had married Jeeter girls at very quiet Jeeter weddings shook hands with him and told him he was getting the pick of the lot.

A neighbor played a march on the organ and Evie came down from my room, very pretty in white satin and tulle. Lena's Babe went before her in bright pink taffeta, her slightly dingy underwear showing a little at the neck, the stem of the lily clasped in her thin fists. No lily in bloom had been found in the greenhouses of the two nearest towns, but the lily idea was not to be given up, so Lena, who was handiest with scissors, had cut one from crepe paper, and fashioned it wondrously, bright green leaves and all, and one of the older girls had added the final touch by sprinkling it with sachet.

Though I stood across the room from Ma during the ceremony, I heard her breathing and saw her soft chins trembling. The daughter who had curled and arranged her hair had snipped off her beards, and dusted her well with pink powder so that she did not look like herself, but her teary blue eye was natural, and lively enough. Lena stood beside me, tall and proud, and kept her eyes on her little daughter. It was the happiest wedding I ever saw.

The dinner was Ma's particular triumph. Before they got past chicken and mashed potatoes the men of the party came out of the awed silence that had fallen on them when Evie first came down in her finery, and began to make good Clay Creek wedding jokes, and asked for second helpings. Babe set up a screech when they tried to take the lily away from her, so they let her keep it and she sat in her high chair and held the flower above her head with one hand while she stuffed food into her mouth with the other.

After dinner the bridal couple and most of the guests went out into the yard to take pictures. The groom carried the bride in his arms so that she would not soil her satin slippers that had cost her family half the price of a pig, and her youngest brother ran back to the stoop to get a box for her to stand on.

I went up to my room but I was not alone long before the bride came up with all her sisters in tow. They had come to help her change into her traveling suit. One of the sisters had brought her baby with her. She sat down on the edge of my bed and began to nurse him. "You sure are hungry," she said, spanking him playfully. "Had to wait a long time, didn't you?"

The other girls stood about handing Evie pieces of clothing, laughing and talking in loud happy voices. Babe whined at the door and I let her in. She put the lily behind her and looked sullenly about her, fearing she would be sent away.

"You don't realize how lucky you are," the one with the baby said, "to start in housekeeping with nothing to worry about but keeping house."

They all laughed at this, remembering.

"Never you mind," one of them said, "she'll have something to worry about, like as not, before the year is done."

Evie's head came up through the opening of a brown twill skirt. Her hair was mussed and I noticed that her eyes were not quite the Jeeter blue, but darker and steely.

"I will not," she said without smiling. "I won't have one this year, or the next, or the next."

One of the girls laughed rather uneasily. "You just think you won't," boomed the one with the baby. Evie slipped her arms into the blouse one of them held for her and put out a hand on either side waiting for the cuffs to be buttoned.

"No, I don't just *think* I won't," she said slowly. "I know good and well that I won't."

The room went silent, and the baby noticed, and let go his mother's breast with a loud smack, and lolled his head back on the thick arm that held him, and looked at Evie with wide-open blue eyes. Babe too felt that something was wrong. She raised her cake-sticky face from my wrist where she had been listening to my watch, went to her mother, and thrust the paper lily up into her face. "Smell," she whined. "Pretty."

Lena took the lily in her red hands and tore it into pieces.

COLORADO

Neither Jew Nor Greek

WILLIAM JOHN

Uncle Asy Mulberry threw back his head and expressed his skepticism with a laugh that was a cross between a chuckle and a whinny.

No, no—he said—you don't believe what you're sayin'. You may think you do, but you don't know your own mind. I ain't doubtin' the truth of your statement; it's as true as gospel. But when a man, and more particularly a woman, says to me, "We're all alike. Everybody's one under the skin," I know right off they haven't stopped to consider what they are talkin' about.

I've heard folks make that remark, in one form or another, off and on, for over seventy years; ever since I was old enough to be interested in what the other fellow was sayin'. Long before the institution you're leanin' against graduated out of the Feed and Livery class into a first-rate Automobile and Accessory business, neighbors and customers would drift in for a snack of small talk, and many's the time I've had 'em say to me, "Asy, you can't get away from it, we're all human, and bein' all human, we're all heir to the same faults and the same virtues."

Well, them are sentiments that would do credit to anybody, but here's the hitch: when you come to find out who the man or woman's referrin' to in such a brotherly or sisterly fashion, it's pretty sure to be somebody they don't know much about, or that they think is a mite better than they are.

Don't I recollect the stirrin' sermon Brother Millsap preached the one and only time Big Annie attended divine services here in the Hopeville Baptist Church? Don't I recollect the amount of brotherly and sisterly feelin' displayed at the close of that service? If I'd never seen it worked out before or since, that was enough to prove to me how much

---

Originally published in *The Century* magazine. Used by permission of the author.

store most folks put in the "We're all alike" idea. About all the education you ever need in this life is to learn to watch the average man and woman when they're just bein' themselves.

At the time Ike Bowan married Big Annie and brought her down here in Tumbleweed Valley to live, she was one of Miss May's steady girls. Miss May run the biggest and best house on Santa Fe Avenue, up in Dawson. A house of ill-repute it would be called now, I reckon, since the general wave of reform has swept over the country. But in them days our leadin' bankers and lawyers and cattlemen used to rub shoulders in Miss May's parlor, and nobody seemed to think much about it. I don't suppose there was a farmer or ranchman in the valley, that amounted to anything, who Big Annie couldn't call by his first name and not feel she was bein' overly intimate in doin' it.

There was some that said they couldn't understand why Ike married Big Annie, but that was never a mystery to me. Ike had run away from home, down in Texas, when he was nine years old and followed a trail herd north as far as Colorado. He'd been battered and knocked 'round, never knowin' a woman's lovin' care, for more than forty years, so when he found one that would have him, he was smart enough not to let the opportunity slip. He was short and weazened, had a cast in one eye, and if he ever got all the tobacco juice out of his beard at one time, I never happened to be 'round on that occasion.

What I couldn't understand was, why did Big Annie ever marry Ike? It may have been she had made up her mind to retire from active business and Ike was the first gate that opened on her lane, or it may have been that she was suddenly seized with a desire to become an honest woman in the eyes of the world. I ain't sayin' which, but I do know that no woman ever tried harder than Big Annie did to make her husband comfortable and happy, durin' the two years that Ike lived, after they was married.

Annie was big. Six feet tall, I reckon, and broad. Her hair was a light sorrel, and her profession hadn't hardened her blue eyes the way it does some women's. She was different, in one way at least, from most of the women in her trade—she was thrifty, kept most everything she got her hands on. Some said Big Annie owned a half interest in Miss May's house when she married Ike. Anyway, Ike added a hundred good white-faced cows to his herd the month after he brought Annie home. And I recollect, some years before that, hearin' Butch Gooch say,

"George Stevens was blowin' himself up at Miss May's last night. Big Annie had her rope on him. I'll bet he comes home without his shirt."

But Big Annie must of made up her mind to bury her past, and thought that other folks would be willin' to help her shovel the dirt in on it, for the second Sunday, after she landed in our midst, she walked into the Baptist Church and set down up front beside Lize Sharp, just as Brother Millsap was windin' up the announcements for the mornin'.

The men twisted their necks most off, tryin' to get a better view from their side of the church, and the women on Big Annie's side developed an epidemic of weak lungs, quicker than I ever seen it done before.

Brother Millsap stared at Big Annie as if he was witnessin' one of them miracles bein' performed he'd preached so much about. Then he coughed a couple of times himself and added a special exhortation to the women.

"Dip your hands deep into your lard pails," he roared. "Spare not your spices, cook liberally and your best, for when you cook for our big sociable to be held next Friday evening, you are preparin' for the Lord. Our organ is in bad shape. We have all prayed earnestly, but prayer without works availeth nothin'. Come early, bring plenty of food, ask all your friends. Let us make it a feast of good-fellowship. The cost of this glorious meal will be twenty-five cents for adults and fifteen cents for children."

Then, with a hitch at his white necktie, he opened the big Bible on the pulpit and begun the cheerin' message he'd prepared.

"Sisters and Brethern," he said, "I've chosen for my text this mornin' the twenty-eighth verse of the third chapter of Galatians."

I ain't up on the Bible, the way Ma is, but I can remember every word of that verse as plain as if Brother Millsap was standin' right here in front of us now, readin' it in that low, sanctimonious voice he used when he was in the pulpit. "There is neither Jew nor Greek, there is neither bond nor free, there is neither male nor female for ye are all one in Christ Jesus."

I reckon he'd of switched to some other subject if he'd had time, but Big Annie sort of took him by surprise, so to speak. He'd worked hard on that sermon, you could see that as he went along. He didn't stop with the one verse, but quoted more than half the Scriptures in his effort to prove how near we all come to bein' cut off the same pattern, in the eyes of God. He mentioned Mary Magdalene and several other right prominent folks who happened along at the time the Bible was set down. Before he finished, you was about convinced that Jesus was the first Democrat.

Big Annie never took her eyes off of Brother Millsap once while he was speakin'. She leaned forward and grasped the back of the bench in front of her with her big white cotton gloves, as if she was afraid she wouldn't catch every word he said. I 'low Big Annie had never been in any church before. It sort of surprised her, maybe, to find how helpful a sermon can be, if you happen to hit the kind suited to your needs.

Brother Millsap brought his talk to a close, with, "Carry this lesson through the week, next to your hearts, Sisters and Brethern. Treat your fellow-man as Jesus would have treated him. For remember, we are all one in Christ Jesus."

Big Annie stepped out into the aisle, after the benediction, flushed and beamin' like a child. Brother Millsap brushed past her to take his stand at the door for the handshakin'. But not another soul looked her way. Them of the men who had handkerchiefs was payin' strict attention to their noses. The women nearest the aisle turned their backs, plumb preoccupied in pickin' up their belongin's or chattin' with the women nearest them. Big Annie, head high, eyes bright, marched to the door alone. As I said, she could of called 'most any man in the gatherin' by his first name, but she didn't even nod to one of 'em.

She stopped at the door and held her hand out to the parson. "If that's what preachin's like, I'm for it," she boomed.

Brother Millsap turned an apple-red and stuttered, "We're—we're glad to have you with us this mornin', Mrs. Bowan, I hope you'll come again."

"I will," she says. "And I'm comin' to your sociable and bring my share of the grub." Then she stalked on out, untied her horse and drove away.

The tables was set outside, the night of the sociable. Some of the boys had cleared off a patch of sagebrush in front of the church and leveled up the ground. Most of the women were gathered 'round a small table where the food was bein' heaped as it arrived.

Big Annie was a little late in gettin' there. I seen her drive in, jump out of the buggy and tie her horse. Then she took what looked like a bread-board covered with a white cloth out of the back of her rig and walked to where the women was gathered.

It was a late May evenin' and the sun was just settin' in the crotch between the Spanish Peaks, yonder. Big Annie looked like a pink giant splotched with gold paint, she was that much bigger than most of the others. She laid the board on the table and uncovered three of the brownest, crispest pies it's ever been my pleasure to clap an eye on to. They may have smelt a bit too strong of the cup that cheers to be exactly suitable for a Baptist sociable, but my mouth waters to this day when I think of 'em.

"They're mince," she says.

The women melted away from Big Annie like sin before the wrath of the righteous; all but old lady Parsons, who was president and actin' manager of the Ladies' Aid at that time. Old lady Parsons took one good squint at them pies, then, with the back of her left hand, she shoved 'em off the table into a box of trash that was settin' beside it. "They ain't fit for hog food," she says, loud enough to be heard all over the lot.

Big Annie backed away a step or two, and her face got redder than the natural rays of the sun was paintin' it. Brother Millsap dodged into the church, no doubt to get somethin' he'd forgot to bring out, and the rest of us present just held our breath and waited for developments.

Big Annie picked up the board the pies had been on—she was still holdin' the white rag in her hand—and turned toward where her horse was tied. She stopped for a minute on her way to the buggy, looked us all over well and smiled. I've wondered many a time since whether Big Annie had seen enough of life to know that she might have done what old lady Parsons did if she had been in her place, or whether she had a sort of presentiment of what was goin' to happen a couple of years later and was takin' a bit of her pleasure in advance.

I don't have to tell you that that ended the Hopeville Baptist Church as far as Big Annie was concerned. Ike's health started failin' along in the summer and she spent most of her time with him, ridin' out lookin' after the cattle or decidin' what they'd have the Mexican help do. She was a heap of satisfaction to Ike, he told me so himself, a few months before he died.

Big Annie didn't have but one woman friend in the valley, and that woman was Clarence Shy's wife. Mrs. Shy was the helpless kind, that a smile or a friend meant a lot to. Ike Bowan's place laid on the other side of the river, on top of that bluff you see yonder, the south bank of the stream; but Shy's land was on this side, just across the creek from Ike's.

Clarence had inherited better than fifteen hundred acres from his pa, one of the first men to settle in the valley, a hard-drinkin', hard-fightin', money-gettin' old-timer. But by the time Big Annie was thrust upon us, as you might say, folks had worked Shy out of all but about a hundred acres. He wasn't any more like his pa than a rabbit's like a coyote. The Bible says the meek shall inherit the earth, but if you've ever noticed, you can't catch the Book up on one of its own statements. It don't say a word about how long the meek will keep the earth after they get it. Clarence was one of the meek, and he and his wife made a perfect matched team. They had four children who were like their parents both in body and spirit.

Big Annie took the Shy family under wing; sewed for the kids, put up preserves for Mrs. Shy, and told Clarence when to plant and when to harvest his crops. His land, what he had left of it, was good, and he had plenty of water. His pa built the first ditch on the river. The old man was far-sighted. He knew the land would never be worth much without the water.

With Big Annie to manage for him, Clarence begun to get ahead; paid off some of his debts and had a little money left over to live on. But prosperity is a right dangerous thing, at times. George Stevens looked over Shy's crops in the fall, and said, "Huh, we could all grow crops like them, if we had the water."

That was the beginnin' of the Tumbleweed Valley irrigation ditch. George persuaded a dozen or so of the other ranchers on this side of the river to throw in with him. They built a dam up above Shy's and took out a big ditch. That left Clarence high and dry, except at flood time. And if you know anything about irrigation, you know flood time ain't when you need the water the most.

If Ike hadn't died that fall, Big Annie would of probably figured out some way for Clarence to stop Stevens and his gang from stealin' the water. But after Ike took to his bed for the last time, Big Annie never left his room only to bring him things to make him easier.

I recollect the day Ike died. I was helpin' the Mexican lay adobes in this very wall you're leanin' against, when Big Annie drove up and motioned for me to come out. Me and Ma was livin' in that one room adobe on the back of the lot, at the time, and I had the rigs and horses I was fixin' to start my livery stable with, housed in a frame shed.

"Asy," Big Annie said, "Ike died this mornin'."

"I'm sorry to hear it, Annie," I says. "Is there anything I can do?"

"Well," she says, "maybe there is and maybe there ain't. Ike never was in a church in his life, but he was as good a man as ever wore boots. I've a hankerin' to give him a church burial. What do you think them buzzards would say if I asked for the loan of their church to bury Ike out of?"

"Annie," I says, "if I'd been born with the power to foretell the future, instead of bein' the ornery, no-account cuss I am, even then I'd hesitate to say; I'd rather bet on the weather than most folks I know. Let's drive over and have a talk with Brother Millsap."

I could tell, right away Brother Millsap wasn't hopeful. He said, "Mrs. Bowan, I'll be glad to preach the service and do everything I can, but—but as to usin' the church, that's a matter for the elders to decide." He glanced out of the window and I seen his face brighten. "There comes Amos Thompson this way. He's one of the elders. I'll go ask him," he says, jumpin' for the door.

His face had lost its cheerful look when he got back from talkin' to Amos. "Mrs. Bowan," he says, "Mr. Thompson don't like to decide a question of that nature without callin' a meetin' of the elders. Can I let you know later?"

Big Annie's shoulders squared. "I see how it is, parson," she says. "They've got to find out for sure that Ike wasn't neither a Jew nor a Greek. I don't believe we'd better put off havin' the funeral till they get through decidin'. If you'll let Mr. Mulberry drive you over to the ranch, day after tomorrow, we'll do the thing in a quiet way."

If it hadn't been for Mrs. Shy havin' to let her baby nurse every five minutes to keep it quiet, Ike's funeral would of been one of the nicest I ever attended. There was no outsider present, except Brother Millsap and myself and the Shy family. We buried Ike on the bluff overlookin' the river. As we was throwin' on the last of the dirt, Big Annie glanced across the stream and seen George Stevens and the rest of 'em, workin' like prairie-dogs on the new ditch.

"What's that gang doin' over there?" she asked, catchin' hold of Clarence's arm.

"I heard somebody say they was buildin' a ditch," Clarence said, pattin' the earth with his shovel.

"That's a funny idea," Big Annie says, and we all started for the house.

Irrigatin' time was here, before Big Annie realized what the new ditch had done to Clarence. When he went to turn the water into his ditch the stream was dry, but the big ditch above him was runnin' bank-full.

I reckon Big Annie did it, or stood by and told Clarence how to do it, for the next mornin' there was a hole cut in the new ditch and all the water was runnin' back into the river.

Amos Thompson and George Stevens rode up to see Clarence. He was out in the alfalfa, spreadin' the water.

"Shy," Thompson roared, "you cut our ditch last night, and if you ever set foot on the bank again, we'll throw you in jail for life."

Clarence wiped the mud off his shovel handle. "I've always had the water to use," he says.

"We've filed on this water accordin' to the laws of Colorado," Stevens put in. "It ain't our funeral if you've been asleep all these years, and if you can't farm without water, you'd better move off and find you another place."

I 'low that's exactly what Shy would of done, too, if it hadn't been for Big Annie. 'Course, he really owned what water he'd used, accordin' to law. But as I say, he was one of the meek. Big Annie's education had been limited to dealin' direct with mankind, so she wasn't up on legal matters. The only way she knew to fight was to cut the ditch, which she did or had Clarence do, the very next night.

The other side knew they was stealin' Shy's water, so they wasn't over anxious to drag him into court, for fear some smart lawyer would get hold of him and tie a knot in their scheme. Thompson and Stevens threatened some more but they didn't have Clarence arrested. Instead, they hired José Marufo, a burly, pock-marked Mexican, to guard the ditch nights.

Marufo hadn't been on the job more than a week till he turned up missin' one sunshiny mornin', and there was no water in the new ditch. When George Stevens rode up to the headgate to see what was the matter, he found the bank cut again, and Marufo's body, all sieved with buckshot, lyin' in a clump of willows, not fifty feet further on.

Well, I reckon there wasn't a person of thinkin' age in the valley who believed Clarence Shy killed Marufo. Clarence wasn't the kind of a man to kill anything. He even hired somebody to come do the butcherin' for him when he happened to have a hog or a heifer fat enough to slaughter. But every last man interested in the new ditch swore he knew for a fact that Shy done the shootin'.

There's nothin' much more annoyin' than to have somebody standin' in your way when you're tryin' to steal somethin', and that was the fix the Tumbleweed Valley Ditch Company was in. The quicker they got rid of Clarence, the quicker they could go about their thievin' unmolested. They had the sheriff down from Dawson to arrest Shy before the sun set that evenin', and persuaded Judge Beck to lay all other matters aside in order to try the nefarious murderer at once.

The trial was short and to the point, as you might say. The court-room was packed; 'most all of Tumbleweed Valley had come into Dawson to see justice meted out.

Clarence made as poor a witness in his own behalf as the opposin' side could of asked for. He confessed to cuttin' the ditch twice before, but denied killin' Marufo and breakin' the bank the night the Mexican was shot.

Mrs. Shy got on the stand and said, "It—it couldn't of been Clarence. He—he went to bed at the same time I did the night of—the—the night it happened." And when the prosecutin' attorney asked her how she knew he didn't get up later to go out and shoot Marufo, she turned an alkali-white, and stuttered, "I—I couldn't be sure. But I'm a light sleeper, on account of havin' to be up with the children so much, and I'm—I'm almost positive I'd of felt him get out of bed."

Big Annie set in the court-room every minute the trial was goin' on. She wore the black dress she'd bought when Ike died, and all the curl was combed out of her yellow hair. She'd look at Clarence and shake her head when he'd say somethin' on the stand that was hurtin' his case. He'd glance at her, then turn away quick, as if he was afraid.

The prosecutin' attorney made what come pretty near bein' a fatal mistake; he called Big Annie as his last witness. "Mrs. Bowan," he says, "you've been a close neighbor of the defendant for some time. Have you ever heard him say anything which would lead you to believe he was not on friendly terms with the deceased, José Marufo?"

Big Annie slapped her hands down on the arms of the witness-chair, and her eyes blazed. "If you mean," she shouted, "do I think Clarence Shy shot that worthless Mexican? No! And what's more, there ain't a man in this room who knows Shy, that believes it either, if they'd tell the truth."

"That'll do," says the attorney, and Big Annie stomped down off the stand.

Judge Beck made quite a speech on the evils of lettin' greed force you into acts you would afterwards repent of, when he sentenced Clarence. He finished by sayin', "Clarence Shy, you have been found guilty of murder in the first degree by a jury of twelve men. The court has the power to sentence you to life imprisonment at hard labor. But because this is your first offence, and when you enter the prison gates you are leavin' a wife and four children, the court is goin' to show the maximum leniency. I sentence you to hard labor in the penitentiary for twenty years."

When Judge Beck said, "twenty years," Big Annie rose up from the bench where she was settin', her mouth opened and closed, then she sank back without makin' a sound.

Her face was drawn and haggard when she shook Shy's hand, before they led him back into jail. "I'll look after the Missus and kids the best I can, Clarence, while you're away," I heard her say.

And I says to myself, "Well, Annie, you've got a family on your hands for the rest of your life, for they'd better hang a man like Clarence Shy and be done with it, than to send him up for twenty years. He won't last five."

The trial was about the middle of May, and I reckon Big Annie put in one of the busiest summers of her life from then on until fall, runnin' her own place and lookin' after the Shys. She come over to Billy Debusk's store on an average of twice a week to buy provisions, shoes for the kids and cloth to make 'em clothes.

I was busy roofin' this buildin', buildin' stalls for the horses and one thing and another. Sometimes when Big Annie would be passin', I'd yell and ask how things was movin' along; that is, if Ma wasn't anywheres 'round.

"We're makin' it," she'd call back, happy as a hen that's found herself a brood of chicks.

By September, I'd almost quit wonderin' about Clarence's family. Other folks' troubles have a way of slippin' out of your mind, easy-like. But one mornin' Big Annie pulled her horse to a stop right in front of the barn.

"Asy," she says, "we're havin' a hell of a time at Shy's. Three of the children are down with scarlet fever, and Mrs. Shy's in bed, expectin' another baby any day."

"That's tough, Annie," I says. "What do you suggest?"

"Money and somebody to help nurse," she snapped. "Somethin's got to be done."

"Well," I says, "they're havin' a harvest sociable at the church to-night. Crops have been good under the new ditch. I'll try takin' up a collection and you can count on me for twenty-five dollars."

"That's a grand idea, Asy. I'll count on your help," she says, chuckin' her horse into a trot.

That afternoon I told Ma I was ridin' out to look for a matched team, bein' about ready to open the livery-stable full force. But instead, I rode up the river to Shy's place. If I was goin' to make a plea for aid that evenin', I figured as how I ought to be an eyewitness to the misery.

The fences on the Shy place was down and Amos Thompson's cattle was trompin' the fields into dust. The adobes was showin' through the plasterin' on the house, as if it had just come through a hard case of smallpox.

Big Annie answered the door when I knocked. She was carryin' the youngest child in her arms, a baby less than two years old. The tears was streamin' down Big Annie's face like April rain. She stood there, shakin' her head without sayin' a word. Then she leaned over and kissed the baby. "It's dead!" she sobbed. "That gang killed it."

After a minute or two she straightened up and said, "You've got to go in and tell her, Asy, I can't."

Well, sir, by the time I landed at the sociable that night, I was so het up over the way the Shys had been treated, I was ready to go through the crowd with a gun and take their money away from them.

Brother Millsap suggested that we'd all go into the church and open the festivities with a prayer of thanks.

"When he gets through prayin'," I says to myself, "will be a good time for me to begin on 'em about the Shys."

He prayed at length, as most preachers do. He asked divine guidance for all the known races, singly and united. As I recollect, the Eskimo was the only one he overlooked. He advised the Lord as to their needs and how best to handle them. He mentioned the weather and suggested the kind most acceptable at that time. He thanked the Lord for bein' so generous with the farmers in the valley; told the Lord how we all appreciated the smile of His approval, and how hard we'd struggled to make ourselves worthy of His kindness and mercy and bountiful blessin's. He went on till I reckon there wasn't a person in the church, except myself, who didn't feel like their harp and halo was hangin' on the bench right in front of 'em.

As he breathed a fervent "Amen," I got to my feet and was in the act of clearin' my throat, when I heard somebody stridin' down the aisle. I glanced out the corner of my eye and seen Big Annie. Big Annie in a flamin' red dress, wearin' a whole garden of red poppies on her head, and carryin' a white sack under her arm. She couldn't of been redder, if she'd been the original pillar of fire.

She marched straight on to the platform, elbowed Brother Millsap to one side, and slapped down her sack, square on the big Bible.

"Christians," she says, without takin' time to catch her breath, "I've come here this evenin' to raise some money for the Shy family. They're in desperate need, and it'll take about five hundred dollars to see 'em through."

"I'll swan, you could almost see the walls of the church sway out and in, the folks settin' there was breathin' that hard.

"I've always made my own way," Big Annie went on, "ever since I can remember, and I ain't never asked anybody for a cent I didn't earn. So I ain't come here to beg off of you this evenin'. As most of the men in the audience know, I've been a savin' woman, and it's part of my savin's I've brought along with me." She touched the bag layin' on the Bible and stopped long enough to look us all over good.

"I've got what I call my keepsakes in that bag," she said. "Hat bands, silk shirts, a scatterin' of playin' cards, a letter or two, odds and ends too numerous to mention. But some place on every one of 'em is the name of the party who donated the gift, and in many instances there's a brief sentiment scratched above the name. These keepsakes are dear to me, for they remind me of the days when I had so many friends who were anxious to help me get along in the world. But I'm goin' to offer every one of 'em for sale tonight, auction 'em off to the highest bidders, in order to raise money for Mrs. Shy and her children."

George Stevens shuffled to his feet in the back of the church and took a step toward the door, lookin' as straight down his nose, as a man with a broken nose can.

"Set down, George," Big Annie yelled and George set down. "I wouldn't like to have you miss this sale. It'll be interestin'. But before we begin the auction, I think it's only fair to call on, say twelve of the most influential men here this evenin'. Some, or all of 'em, might be hankerin' to give as much as fifty dollars apiece, and me not know it. If that was the case, I might not have to part with all my keepsakes. Understand, though, I ain't askin' for the money to be donated. I'm here and ready to sell the last thing in that bag, if it's necessary."

She unfolded a piece of paper she had in her hand and held it off from her, as if she was tryin' to make out what was on it.

"Amos Thompson," Big Annie read.

"I give fifty dollars for the good of the cause," Amos shouted.

"Well done, brother," she said, imitatin' Brother Millsap to a T. "The next name appears to be George Stevens."

"Fifty for me, too," George groaned.

Big Annie went on down the list; Butch Gooch, Lipe Standard, Bruce East, Eli Jefferson, twelve of 'em, and every one of 'em donated the same amount. The walls of that church actually sprung three inches from the sigh of relief that was exhaled when she got through with her list.

The men started shufflin' their feet, gettin' ready to make a break for air, but Big Annie held up her hand and said, "Just a minute. I've got a couple of other little matters I want to call to your attention, before the meetin' adjourns. I know there's not a person in this church who believes that Clarence Shy shot José Marufo. That bein' the case, it won't strain your sense of justice or hurt your standin' as good Christians to do what I'm goin' to ask you."

She reached down into her bosom and pulled out a couple of papers. Her dress was cut low in front, and she brought 'em forth with a flourish.

"I got a lawyer in Dawson to write these papers for me," she said, holdin' 'em out in front of her, careful-like, "when I seen how bad off Mrs. Shy and her babies was gettin', so they're legal. One of 'em is a request for a pardon for Clarence Shy, and the lawyer says he'll have Clarence out of the pen inside of thirty days, if everybody who testified against him will sign it. The other paper is a deed to Shy for a fifth interest in that fine new ditch you've built. The deed's legal too. Step up, gentlemen. I know you'll all want to sign. The drinks are on the house."

A silence louder than a whole army of brass bands hung over that huddled bunch of church members for a minute. Then Big Annie reached out and touched the sack which was layin' on the Bible. If a bolt of lightnin' had struck the buildin', them men couldn't of been on their feet quicker, or struggled harder to reach the pulpit.

After everybody had signed up in full, and Big Annie was makin' her way out, she motioned to me to come too. I followed her 'round to the side of the church.

"Asy," she says, "there's somethin' on my mind that's troublin' me a lot. I want your advice."

"I don't own nothin' that I give as cheerful, Annie," I says.

"Well," she says, "I know who killed José Marufo. It was a Mexican girl by the name of Rafelita Montoya. She's livin' in an adobe shack on my place, now, and José's the father of her baby. She confessed to me because I've been helpin' her to get enough to eat. Do you think it's my duty to turn her over to the law?"

"Annie," I says, "it's always been my plan to let sleepin' dogs take their rest; if they didn't need it, they wouldn't be sleepin'."

"Thanks a lot, Asy, for them comfortin' words. That's the way I feel about it, too," she says, and started for her rig. Then she stopped, come back and chuckled in my ear, "And, Asy, I want to tell you that that there Bible book has got things down pretty pat. We're all alike, neither Jew nor Greek, free or tied up, when we get in a tight place. I ain't got a thing in this bag but some old rags and a strap or two." And she patted the sack under her arm.

SOUTH DAKOTA

Turkey Red

FRANCES GILCHRIST WOOD

The old mail-sled running between Haney and Le Beau, in the days when Dakota was still a Territory, was nearing the end of its hundred-mile route.

It was a desolate country in those days: geographers still described it as The Great American Desert, and in looks it certainly deserved the title. Never was there anything as lonesome as that endless stretch of snow reaching across the world until it cut into a cold gray sky, excepting the same desert burned to a brown tinder by the hot wind of summer.

Nothing but sky and plain and its voice, the wind, unless you might count a lonely sod shack blocked against the horizon, miles away from a neighbor, miles from anywhere, its red-curtained square of window glowing through the early twilight.

There were three men in the sled: Dan, the mail-carrier, crusty, belligerently Western, the self-elected guardian of everyone on his route; Hillas, a younger man, hardly more than a boy, living on his preemption claim near the upper reaches of the stage line; the third a stranger from that part of the country vaguely defined as 'the East.' He was traveling, had given his name as Smith, and was as inquisitive about the country as he was reticent about his business there. Dan plainly disapproved of him.

They had driven the last cold miles in silence when the stage-driver turned to his neighbor. 'Letter didn't say anything about coming out in the spring to look over the country, did it?'

Hillas shook his head. 'It was like all the rest, Dan. Don't want to build a railroad at all until the country's settled.'

'God! Can't they see the other side of it? What it means to the folks already here to wait for it?'

The stranger thrust a suddenly interested profile above the handsome collar of his fur coat. He looked out over the waste of snow.

'You say there's no timber here?'

Dan maintained unfriendly silence and Hillas answered. 'Nothing but scrub on the banks of the creeks. Years of prairie fires have burned out the trees, we think.'

'Any ores—mines?'

The boy shook his head as he slid farther down in his worn buffalo coat of the plains.

'We're too busy rustling for something to eat first. And you can't develop mines without tools.'

'Tools?'

'Yes, a railroad first of all.'

Dan shifted the lines from one fur-mittened hand to the other, swinging the freed numbed arm in rhythmic beating against his body as he looked along the horizon a bit anxiously. The stranger shivered visibly.

'It's a God-forsaken country. Why don't you get out?'

Hillas, following Dan's glance around the blurred sky-line, answered absently. 'Usual answer is, "Leave? It's all I can do to stay here!"'

Smith regarded him irritably. 'Why should any sane man ever have chosen this frozen wilderness?'

Hillas closed his eyes wearily. 'We came in the spring.'

'I see!' The edged voice snapped, 'Visionaries!'

Hillas's eyes opened again, wide, and then the boy was looking beyond the man with the far-seeing eyes of the plainsman. He spoke under his breath as if he were alone.

'Visionary, pioneer, American. That was the evolution in the beginning. Perhaps that is what we are.' Suddenly the endurance in his voice went down before a wave of bitterness. 'The first pioneers had to wait, too. How could they stand it so long!'

The young shoulders drooped as he thrust stiff fingers deep within the shapeless coat pockets. He slowly withdrew his right hand holding a parcel wrapped in brown paper. He tore a three-cornered flap in the cover, looked at the brightly colored contents, replaced the flap, and returned the parcel, his chin a little higher.

Dan watched the northern sky-line restlessly. 'It won't be snow. Look like a blizzard to you, Hillas?'

The traveler sat up. 'Blizzard?'

'Yes,' Dan drawled in willing contribution to his uneasiness, 'the real Dakota article where blizzards are made. None of your Eastern imitations, but a ninety-mile wind that whets slivers of ice off the frozen drifts all the way down from the North Pole. Only one good thing about a blizzard—it's over in a hurry. You get to shelter or you freeze to death.'

A gust of wind flung a powder of snow stingingly against their faces. The traveler withdrew his head turtlewise within the handsome collar in final condemnation. 'No man in his senses would ever have deliberately come here to live.'

Dan turned. 'Wouldn't, eh?'

'No.'

'You're American?'

'Yes.'

'Why?'

'I was born here. It's my country.'

'Ever read about your Pilgrim Fathers?'

'Why, of course.'

'Frontiersmen, same as us. You're living on what they did. We're getting this frontier ready for those who come after. Want our children to have a better chance than we had. Our reason's same as theirs. Hillas told you the truth. Country's all right if we had a railroad.'

'Humph!' With a contemptuous look across the desert. 'Where's your freight, your grain, cattle——'

'*West*-bound freight, coal, feed, seed-grain, work, and more neighbors.'

'One-sided bargain. Road that hauls empties one way doesn't pay. No Company would risk a line through here.'

The angles of Dan's jaw showed white. 'Maybe. Ever get a chance to pay your debt to those Pilgrim pioneers? Ever take it? Think the stock was worth saving?'

He lifted his whip-handle toward a pin-point of light across the stretch of snow. 'Donovan lives over there and Mis' Donovan. We call them "old folk" now; their hair has turned white as these drifts in two years. All they've got is here. He's a real farmer and a lot of help to the country, but they won't last long like this.'

Dan swung his arm toward a glimmer nor' by nor'east. 'Mis' Clark lives there, a mile back from the stage road. Clark's down in Yankton earning money to keep them going. She's alone with her baby holding down the claim.' Dan's arm sagged. 'We've had women go crazy out here.'

The whip-stock followed the empty horizon half round the compass to a lighted red square not more than two miles away.

'Mis' Carson died in the spring. Carson stayed until he was too poor to get away. There's three children—oldest's Katy, just eleven.' Dan's words failed, but his eyes told. 'Somebody will brag of them as ancestors some day. They'll deserve it if they live through this.'

Dan's jaw squared as he leveled his whip-handle straight at the traveler. 'I've answered your questions, now you answer mine! We know your opinion of the country—you're not traveling for pleasure or for your health. What are you here for?'

'Business. My own!'

'There's two kinds of business out here this time of year. 'Tain't healthy for either of them.' Dan's words were measured and clipped. 'You've damned the West and all that's in it good and plenty. Now I say, damn the people anywhere in the whole country that won't pay their debts from pioneer to pioneer; that lets us fight the wilderness barehanded and die fighting; that won't risk——'

A gray film dropped down over the world, a leaden shroud that was not the coming of twilight. Dan jerked about, his whip cracked out over the heads of the leaders, and they broke into a quick trot. The shriek of the runners along the frozen snow cut through the ominous darkness.

'Hillas,' Dan's voice came sharply, 'stand up and look for the light on Clark's guide-pole about a mile to the right. God help us if it ain't burning.'

Hillas struggled up, one clumsy mitten thatching his eyes from the blinding needles. 'I don't see it, Dan. We can't be more than a mile away. Hadn't you better break toward it?'

'Got to keep the track 'til we—see—light!'

The wind tore the words from his mouth as it struck them in lashing fury. The leaders had disappeared in a wall of snow, but Dan's lash whistled forward in reminding authority. There was a moment's lull.

'See it, Hillas?'

'No, Dan.'

Tiger-like the storm leaped again, bandying them about in its paws like captive mice. The horses swerved before the punishing blows, bunched, backed, tangled. Dan stood up, shouting his orders of menacing appeal above the storm.

Again a breathing space before the next deadly impact. As it came Hillas shouted: 'I see it—there, Dan! It's a red light. She's in trouble.'

Through the whirling smother and chaos of Dan's cries and the struggling horses the sled lunged out of the road into unbroken drifts. Again the leaders swung sidewise before the lashing of a thousand lariats of ice and bunched against the wheel-horses. Dan swore, prayed, mastered them with far-reaching lash, then the off leader went down. Dan felt behind him for Hillas and shoved the reins against his arm.

'I'll get him up—or cut leaders—loose! If I don't—come back—drive to light. *Don't—get—out!*'

Dan disappeared in the white fury. There were sounds of a struggle; the sled jerked sharply and stood still. Slowly it strained forward.

Hillas was standing, one foot outside on the runner, as they traveled a team's length ahead. He gave a cry—'Dan! Dan!' and gripped a furry bulk that lumbered up out of the drift.

'All—right—son.' Dan reached for the reins.

Frantically they fought their slow way toward the blurred light, staggering on in a fight with the odds too savage to last. They stopped abruptly as the winded leaders leaned against a wall interposed between themselves and insatiable fury.

Dan stepped over the dashboard, groped his way along the tongue between the wheel-horses, and reached the leeway of a shadowy square. 'It's the shed, Hillas. Help get the team in.' The exhausted animals crowded into the narrow space without protest.

'Find the guide-rope to the house, Dan.'

'On the other side, toward the shack. Where's—Smith?'

'Here, by the shed.'

Dan turned toward the stranger's voice.

'We're going 'round to the blizzard-line tied from shed to shack. Take hold of it and don't let go. If you do you'll freeze before we can find you. When the wind comes, turn your back and wait. Go on when it dies down and never let go the rope. Ready? The wind's dropped. Here, Hillas, next to me.'

Three blurs hugged the sod walls around to the northeast corner. The forward shadow reached upward to a swaying rope, lifted the hand of the second who guided the third.

'Hang on to my belt, too, Hillas. Ready—Smith? Got the rope?'

They crawled forward, three barely visible figures, six, eight, ten steps. With a shriek the wind tore at them, beat the breath from their bodies, cut them with stinging needle-points, and threw them aside. Dan reached back to make sure of Hillas who fumbled through the darkness for the stranger.

Slowly they struggled ahead, the cold growing more intense; two steps, four, and the mounting fury of the blizzard reached its zenith. The blurs swayed like battered leaves on a vine that the wind tore in two at last and flung the living beings wide. Dan, clinging to the broken rope, rolled over and found Hillas with the frayed end of the line in his hand, reaching about through the black drifts for the stranger. Dan crept closer, his mouth at Hillas's ear, shouting, 'Quick! Right behind me if we're to live through it!'

The next moment Hillas let go the rope. Dan reached madly. 'Boy, you can't find him—it'll only be two instead of one! Hillas! Hillas!'

The storm screamed louder than the plainsman and began heaping the snow over three obstructions in its path, two that groped slowly and one that lay still. Dan fumbled at his belt, unfastened it, slipped the rope through the buckle, knotted it, and crept its full length back toward the boy. A snow-covered something moved forward guiding another, one arm groping in blind search, reached and touched the man clinging to the belt.

Beaten and buffeted by the ceaseless fury that no longer gave quarter, they slowly fought their way hand-over-hand along the rope, Dan now crawling last. After a frozen eternity they reached the end of the line fastened man-high against a second haven of wall. Hillas pushed open the unlocked door, the three men staggered in and fell panting against the side of the room.

The stage-driver recovered first, pulled off his mittens, examined his fingers, and felt quickly of nose, ears, and chin. He looked sharply at Hillas and nodded. Unceremoniously they stripped off the stranger's gloves; reached for a pan, opened the door, dipped it into the drift, and plunged Smith's fingers down in the snow.

'Your nose is white, too. Thaw it out.'

Abruptly Dan indicated a bench against the wall where the two men seated would take up less space.

'I'm——' The stranger's voice was unsteady. 'I——' But Dan had turned his back and his attention to the homesteader.

The eight-by-ten room constituted the entire home. A shed roof slanted from eight feet high on the door and window side to a bit more than five on the other. A bed in one corner took up most of the space, and the remaining necessities were bestowed with the compactness of a ship's cabin. The rough boards of the roof and walls had been hidden by a covering of newspapers, with a row of illustrations pasted picture height. Cushions and curtains of turkey-red calico brightened the homely shack.

The driver had slipped off his buffalo coat and was bending over a baby exhaustedly fighting for breath that whistled shrilly through a closing throat. The mother, scarcely more than a girl, held her in tensely extended arms.

'How long's she been this way?'

'She began to choke up day before yesterday, just after you passed on the down trip.'

The driver laid big finger-tips on the restless wrist.

'She always has the croup when she cuts a tooth, Dan, but this is different. I've used all the medicines I have—nothing relieves the choking.'

The girl lifted heavy eyelids above blue semicircles of fatigue, and the compelling terror back of her eyes forced a question through dry lips.

'Dan, do you know what membranous croup is like? Is this it?'

The stage-driver picked up the lamp and held it close to the child's face, bringing out with distressing clearness the blue-veined pallor, sunken eyes, and effort of impeded breathing. He frowned, putting the lamp back quickly.

'Mebbe it is, Mis' Clark, but don't you be scared. We'll help you a spell.'

Dan lifted the red curtain from the cupboard, found an emptied lard-pail, half filled it with water, and placed it on an oil-stove that stood in the center of the room. He looked questioningly about the four walls, discovered a cleverly contrived tool-box beneath the cupboard shelves, sorted out a pair of pincers and bits of iron, laying the latter in a row over the oil blaze. He took down a can of condensed milk, poured a spoonful of the thick stuff into a cup of water, and made room for it near the bits of heating iron.

He turned to the girl, opened his lips as if to speak with a face full of pity.

Along the four-foot space between the end of the bed and the opposite wall the girl walked, crooning to the sick child she carried. As they watched, the low song died away, her shoulder rubbed heavily against the boarding, her eyelids dropped, and she stood sound asleep. The next hard-drawn breath of the baby roused her and she stumbled on, crooning a lullaby.

Smith clutched the younger man's shoulder. 'God, Hillas, look where she's marked the wall rubbing against it! Do you suppose she's been walking that way for three days and nights? Why, she's only a child—no older than my own daughter.'

Hillas nodded.

'Where are her people? Where's her husband?'

'Down in Yankton, Dan told you, working for the winter. Got to have the money to live.'

'Where's the doctor?'

'Nearest one's in Haney—four days' trip away by stage.'

The traveler stared, frowningly.

Dan was looking about the room again and after prodding the gay seat in the corner, lifted the cover and picked up a folded blanket, shaking out the erstwhile padded cushion. He hung the blanket over the back of a chair.

'Mis' Clark, there's nothing but steam will touch membreenous croup. We saved my baby that way last year. Set here and I'll fix things.'

He put the steaming lard-pail on the floor beside the mother and lifted the blanket over the baby's head. She put up her hand.

'She's so little, Dan, and weak. How am I going to know if she—if she——'

Dan rearranged the blanket tent. 'Jest get under with her yourself, Mis' Clark, then you'll know all that's happening.'

With the pincers he picked up a bit of hot iron and dropped it hissing into the pail, which he pushed beneath the tent. The room was oppressively quiet, walled in by the thick sod from the storm. The blanket muffled the sound of the child's breathing and the girl no longer stumbled against the wall.

Dan lifted the corner of the blanket and another bit of iron hissed as it struck the water. The older man leaned toward the younger.

'Stove—fire?' with a gesture of protest against the inadequate oil blaze.

Hillas whispered, 'Can't afford it. Coal is nine dollars in Haney, eighteen dollars here.'

They sat with heads thrust forward, listening in the intolerable silence. Dan lifted the blanket, hearkened a moment, then—'pst!' another bit of iron fell into the pail. Dan stooped to the tool chest for a reserve supply when a strangling cough made him spring to his feet and hurriedly lift the blanket.

The child was beating the air with tiny fists, fighting for breath. The mother stood rigid, arms out.

'Turn her this way!' Dan shifted the struggling child, face out. 'Now watch for the——'

The strangling cough broke and a horrible something—'It's the membrane! She's too weak—let me have her!'

Dan snatched the child and turned it face downward. The blue-faced baby fought in a supreme effort—again the horrible something—then Dan laid the child, white and motionless, in her mother's arms. She held the limp body close, her eyes wide with fear.

'Dan, is—is she—?'

A faint sobbing breath of relief fluttered the pale lips that moved in the merest ghost of a smile. The heavy eyelids half-lifted and the child nestled against its mother's breast. The girl swayed, shaking with sobs, 'Baby—baby!'

She struggled for self-control and stood up straight and pale. 'Dan, I ought to tell you. When it began to get dark with the storm and time to put up the lantern, I was afraid to leave the baby. If she strangled when I was gone—with no one to help her—she would die!'

Her lips quivered as she drew the child closer. 'I didn't go right away but—I did—at last. I propped her up in bed and ran. If I hadn't'—her eyes were wide with the shadowy edge of horror—'if I hadn't—you'd have been lost in the blizzard and—my baby would have died!'

She stood before the men as if for judgment, her face wet with unchecked tears. Dan patted her shoulder dumbly and touched a fresh, livid bruise that ran from the curling hair on her temple down across cheek and chin.

'Did you get this then?'

She nodded. 'The storm threw me against the pole when I hoisted the lantern. I thought I'd—never—get back!'

It was Smith who translated Dan's look of appeal for the cup of warm milk and held it to the girl's lips.

She made heroic attempts to swallow, her head drooped lower over the cup and fell against the driver's rough sleeve. 'Poor kid, dead asleep!'

Dan guided her stumbling feet toward the bed that the traveler sprang to open. She guarded the baby in the protecting angle of her arm into safety upon the pillow, then fell like a log beside her. Dan slipped off the felt boots, lifted her feet to the bed, and softly drew covers over mother and child.

'Poor kid; but she's grit, clear through!'

Dan walked to the window, looked out at the lessening storm, then at the tiny alarm-clock on the cupboard. 'Be over pretty soon now!' He seated himself by the table, dropped his head wearily forward on folded arms, and was asleep.

The traveler's face had lost some of its shrewdness. It was as if the white frontier had seized and shaken him into a new conception of life. He moved restlessly along the bench, then stepped softly to the side of the bed and straightened the coverlet into greater nicety while his lips twitched.

With consuming care he folded the blanket and restored the corner seat to its accustomed appearance of luxury. He looked about the room, picked up the gray kitten sleeping contentedly on the floor, and settled it on the red cushion with anxious attention to comfort.

He examined with curiosity the few books carefully covered in a corner shelf, took down an old hand-tooled volume and lifted his eyebrows at the ancient coat of arms on the book plate. He tiptoed across to the bench and pointed to the script beneath the plate. 'Edward Winslow (7) to his dear daughter, Alice (8).'

He motioned toward the bed. 'Her name?'

Hillas nodded. Smith grinned. 'Dan's right. Blood will tell, even to damning the rest of us.'

He sat down on the bench. 'I understand more than I did, Hillas, since—you crawled back after me—out there. But how can you stand it here? I know you and the Clarks are people of education and, oh, all the rest; you could make your way anywhere.'

Hillas spoke slowly. 'I think you have to live here to know. It means something to be a pioneer. You can't be one if you've got it in you to be a quitter. The country will be all right some day.' He reached for his greatcoat, bringing out a brown-paper parcel. He smiled at it oddly and went on as if talking to himself.

'When the drought and the hot winds come in the summer and burn the buffalo grass to a tinder and the monotony of the plains weighs on you as it does now, there's a common, low-growing cactus scattered over the prairie that blooms into the gayest red flower you ever saw.

'It wouldn't count for much anywhere else, but the pluck of it, without rain for months, dew even. It's the "colors of courage." '

He turned the torn parcel, showing the bright red within, and looked at the cupboard and window with shining, tired eyes.

'Up and down the frontier in these shacks, homes, you'll find things made of turkey-red calico, cheap, common elsewhere'—he fingered the three-cornered flap—'It's our "colors." ' He put the parcel back in his pocket. 'I bought two yards yesterday after—I got a letter at Haney.'

Smith sat looking at the gay curtains before him. The fury of the storm was dying down into fitful gusts. Dan stirred, looked quickly toward the bed, then the window, and got up quietly.

'I'll hitch up. We'll stop at Peterson's and tell her to come over.' He closed the door noiselessly.

The traveler was frowning intently. Finally he turned toward the boy who sat with his head leaning back against the wall, eyes closed.

'Hillas'—his very tones were awkward—'they call me a shrewd business man. I am; it's a selfish job and I'm not reforming now. But twice tonight you—children have risked your lives, without thought, for a stranger. I've been thinking about that railroad. Haven't you raised any grain or cattle that could be used for freight?'

The low answer was toneless. 'Drought killed the crops, prairie fires burned the hay, of course the cattle starved.'

'There's no timber, ore, nothing that could be used for east-bound shipment?'

The plainsman looked searchingly into the face of the older man. 'There's no timber this side the Missouri. Across the river, it's reservation—Sioux. We——' He frowned and stopped.

Smith stood up, his hands thrust deep in his pockets. 'I admitted I was shrewd, Hillas, but I'm not yellow clear through, not enough to betray this part of the frontier, anyhow. I had a man along here last fall spying for minerals. That's why I'm out here now. If you know the location, and we both think you do, I'll put capital in your way to develop the mines and use what pull I have to get the road in.'

He looked down at the boy and thrust out a masterful jaw. There was a ring of sincerity no one could mistake when he spoke again.

'This country's a desert now, but I'd back the Sahara peopled with your kind. This is on the square, Hillas; don't tell me you won't believe I'm American enough to trust?'

The boy tried to speak. With stiffened body and clenched hands he struggled for self-control. Finally in a ragged whisper: 'If I try to tell you what—it means—I can't talk! Dan and I know of outcropping coal over in the Buttes'—he nodded in the direction of the Missouri—'but we haven't had enough money to file mining claims.'

'Know where to dig for samples under this snow?'

The boy nodded. 'Some in my shack too. I——' His head went down upon the crossed arms. Smith laid an awkward hand on the heaving shoulders, then rose and crossed the room to where the girl had stumbled in her vigil. Gently he touched the darkened streak where her shoulders had rubbed and blurred the newspaper print. He looked from the relentless white desert outside to the gay bravery within and bent his head. 'Turkey-red—calico!'

There was a sound of jingling harness and the crunch of runners. The men bundled into fur coats.

'Hillas, the draw right by the house here.' Smith stopped and looked sharply at the plainsman, then went on with firm carelessness: 'This draw ought to strike a low grade that would come out near the river level. Does Dan know Clark's address?' Hillas nodded.

They tiptoed out and closed the door behind them softly. The wind had swept every cloud from the sky and the light of the Northern stars etched a dazzling world. Dan was checking up the leaders as Hillas caught him by the shoulder and shook him like a clumsy bear.

'Dan, you blind old mole, can you see the headlight of the Overland Freight blazing and thundering down that draw over the Great Missouri and Eastern?'

Dan stared.

'I knew you couldn't!' Hillas thumped him with furry fist. 'Dan'—the wind might easily have drowned the unsteady voice—'I've told Mr.

Smith about the coal—for freight. He's going to help us get capital for mining, and after that the road.'

'Smith! Smith! Well I'll be—aren't you a claim-spotter?'

He turned abruptly and crunched toward the stage. His passengers followed. Dan paused with his foot on the runner and looked steadily at the traveler from under lowered, shaggy brows.

'You're going to get a road out here?'

'I've told Hillas I'll put money in your way to mine the coal. Then the railroad will come.'

Dan's voice rasped with tension. 'We'll get out the coal. Are you going to see that the road's built?'

Unconsciously the traveler held up his right hand. 'I am!'

Dan searched his face sharply. Smith nodded. 'I'm making my bet on the people—friend!'

It was a new Dan who lifted his bronzed face to a white world. His voice was low and very gentle. 'To bring a road here'—he swung his whip-handle from Donovan's light around to Carson's square, sweeping in all that lay behind—'out here to them'—the pioneer faced the wide desert that reached into a misty space ablaze with stars—'would be like—playing God!'

The whip thudded softly into the socket and Dan rolled up on the driver's seat. Two men climbed in behind him. The long lash swung out over the leaders as Dan headed the old mail-sled across the drifted right-of-way of the Great Missouri and Eastern.

NORTH DAKOTA

A Coffin for Anna

ELISE RUSHFELDT

Thirty days lost in jail because of women's vanity.

Because Anna whined that she wanted a hat. He'd see to her. Didn't the Bible say that a man should be master of his own household? Just wait until he got home.

It had happened this way.

"Yes, we need money," she had agreed tonelessly the morning he had hitched up to drive away for harvest wages.

Her once pretty face was drawn. Her skirt sagged in back. She twisted her dirty blue check apron nervously in thin long hands, red and damp from dishwater, the blue veins standing out like cords with knots.

She had been one of the Servaas girls on the big farm on the crossroads before she married him. The Servaas girls were spoiled; always getting things.

Dully she had added, "But 'twill be hard to be left alone with the work. My back aches, and I ain't feeling so well. I don't know as I can care for the stock so very long. The baby might come."

The early breakfast was finished by the light of the kerosene lamp. The heavy white dishes stood in a group on one side of the brown-checked oilcloth-covered table, a group about his plate. She had not eaten. She had been frying cakes for him. She was standing now by the old kitchen stove doing things to pots and kettles. He pushed back his chair and took his overcoat from a nail by the kitchen door. Meanwhile he assuaged her worry with an easy carelessness.

"Won't come for a long time yet. You'll be durn lazy with only the stock to look after. It'll be bringing me in real money soon—that stock. Wouldn't take five hundred for it as it stands. And the calves will be

---

From *Frontier* magazine, March, 1929.

worth more later on." He stopped, and his large thoughts began to build air castles about that stock. "Phoo! Sure you can care for the stock."

He eyed her slyly. What did she mean to do with her time when he was gone? "And hev' all the rest of your time for visiting around, I s'pose?" If there was one thing he couldn't stand, it was this women's gadding. He had told her so, too.

"I ain't been visitin' for months and you know it. Not even to Mother's, since you quarreled with my only kin." The thin fingers had twisted the apron into a tighter knot. She leaned back against the door frame watching him as he checked and untied the horses that he had hitched, waiting, by the unpainted gray board fence. A clammy gray dawn was over all the unkempt little farm.

"Uppity kin," he growled. "Whoa there, Jumbo, back up a little! Back, I say! Yes, uppity. Trying to give you notions. I s'pose Selma Servaas says I ain't good enough for you, eh?"

She said nothing. Her sagging outline against the door gave him more visible evidence of the coming of the baby.

"Ain't a wife's place home with her husband, eh? But I ain't stopping you from runnin'. Go 'head."

This was irony.

"I can't leave the house, and you know it, without decent clothes. I ain't even got a hat left that I could go to a dog fight in. I'd be ashamed to be seen." She flared with resentment and defiance, her eyes challenging his.

He strode back to her, grabbed her bony arm, and swung her around. "That ain't the way to taunt yer pervider. But I ain't got time to 'tend to you now. The horses are waitin'."

But the memory of her sullen defiant eyes as she stood in the door of the unpainted sod-roofed shack, watching him drive away, stayed with him.

After a long day of slow jogging across a limitless prairie stretch broken by checkerboard fields he reached Fargo. But he did not delay there. He drove at once across the river to Moorhead, on the Minnesota side, to have a drink. Fargo, on the Dakota side of the river, had been voted dry by paternally minded city fathers. Moorhead was superlatively wet.

His thirst satisfied, he recrossed and once more rattled down Front Street, then found a hitching rail and tied his team to it.

Broadway was becoming so crowded with these danged automobiles. He preferred to walk down it. He walked rollingly over the city pavement as if the wavy sod of the prairie were billowing under his feet. It was nearly six o'clock on a Saturday night. The streets and pavements were crowded with out-of-town shoppers. The stores would be open on Saturday until late.

It was then that he saw the hat in the window. It was the only one there. A background of gray. Some posies in a narrow vase had spilled red petals on the soft gray. And the hat itself was a simple little thing of black and red. A feeling of lordly generosity came over him. Anna should see that he was a good provider. He would buy the hat for her.

"Want that bunnit in the window for my wife," he huskily told the girl in the shop. He sized her up as an awful stylish girl if she hadn't been dressed so plain.

As he stood awkwardly by the door, waiting, he glanced around him. Kinda like a sitting room. Not many hats around either. Selling out, maybe. Or like as not they hadn't the money to stock up the place. Just one little hat in the window. Gosh! That was no way to sell. Likely as not he could get the hat dirt cheap.

The saleswoman also appraised him. But no one can judge a man in Fargo by his outer apparel—especially if that apparel be the accouterments of a farmer.

Tipping the hat over in her hands she named the price. "It's an importation from Paris," she murmured. "It was a special order." Her tone bespoke that some sacred thing was near.

The Parisian trademark in the soft silk lining meant nothing to him, but the price staggered him. Fifty dollars for a hat. That little black and red thing no bigger than your fists. He'd be jiggered! He had never known that a hat cost more than four dollars and ninety-eight cents. Anna had pointed to some in the village shop that were marked that much, and her eyes were longing. But he had thought five dollars too much for a hat. Anna's had cost—but it was so long since he had bought a hat for Anna that he had forgotten how much it cost. Fifty dollars! His eyes were dismayed.

"Is it this hat you wish?" inquired the salesgirl, turning it reverently about. She didn't expect to sell it to him. He could see that. Maybe she was laffin' at him—inside. She'd say, "A big hick come in. . . ." He gulped and nodded. "Sure—I'll take it."

He carefully went through all his pockets twice for a mislaid check book. "Must hev' forgot it to home." She guided him to a counter checkbook. Some preliminary flourishes, a big scrawl and a blot, and then the hat, stowed in a neat round box with colored pictures on it, was his to carry away.

He carried it down the street, but not very far. He'd been crazy.

Fifty dollars for a hat for a female. It was a crime. It fostered women's vanity. It made them think themselves costly. Now, which of these places would he get the most for it?

He stopped farther up Broadway and Front Street before a brilliantly lighted department store all of four stories high. There was a window full of hats. Directed up an elevator. Almost a floor full of hats. Here he resold the Parisian hat and bought Anna a black sailor with a cabbage rose on it for three dollars.

It had meant thirty days.

And the hat, stowed under the seat of his wagon, was now all that he possessed for his strategy. He had lingered on the streets of Fargo the next two days. The young saleswoman, who had looked up his check immediately, had identified him and had him arrested.

Sentenced to thirty days in the county jail. He had checked off the days on the walls of his cell. All that time lost.

Anna's fault: whining and complaining about nothing to wear. Weren't women always saying that, anyway? And he, the generous, henpecked husband, had believed her. When he got home he would reason with her. 'Twas a man's duty toward weak woman.

He joggled over the rutty roads on the outskirts of Fargo with flat little buildings growing up from flat muddy places.

Thirty days. She had been big with a child. A son, of course. Although he had heard her say that she would like a daughter since she had lost their first, a little girl. But a little shaver, a boy, would be more useful when it came to doing the chores and running errands for his papa.

Thirty days. He wondered about the stock. Something might have happened to the stock without proper care. If Anna got to gadding, for instance. He'd better go home and see to the stock.

Natural for women to have babies, though. She needn't have looked so worrited. She wasn't the first woman in creation with a child. Nothing would happen. He wasn't worrit.

But before going home he must have money. It was necessary to keep Anna's respect for him. Life would not be the same—so full of thrills and power—if it were not for her. He dramatized himself before her in a variety of rôles. Her part to reflect wonder and amaze and sometimes fear of him. That was why her scornful look had stayed with him. Was he losing his grip on her? Yes, he had to have money. She ought to have come seen him, anyway. The livery man promised he'd tell her. Too stuck up because she was one of the Servaas girls. Only with money in his pocket could he make an effective home-coming and regain his ascendancy over her.

Before starting home he'd go to Moorhead and get a drink or two. The road home would be long and dusty. Hot fall sunshine spilled from the overflowing bowl of the sky. And a drink or two might start his brains working. "Giddap, Jumbo! Giddap, Stanley!" How the wooden bridge rumbled under their feet!

In Moorhead there were rows on rows of enticing saloons with damp penetrating aromas coming from behind closed doors. At Big Joe's Saloon they served a whopper of a lunch with the drinks. More terrible ruts that shook him into a greater thirst. Then the hitching rail before Big Joe's Saloon.

He slid into the place and took a seat at one of the tables in the rear near some men playing Norwegian whist. He was still afraid that someone might recognize him as the man who had been in jail for buying a hat for his wife without a bank account. Not that he had given his own name. He was too smart for that. You bet!

Leaning against the bar were a score of thirsty harvesters in old overalls and dusty shirts. But their pocketbooks were full. As he watched the glasses of cool liquor slip down their throats a poignant sorrow gripped him. Tears stood in his blue eyes.

Presently Red Nels, of freckled features and lurid hair, turned and saw him sitting pensively there. He greeted him loudly: "Why, Kettlesrud, old feller. Why weren't you threshing this year? We missed you on our outfit. Good eats and big wages this year. Yessir. What's the matter, ole man. Sure, yo're lookin' down in the mouth."

Kettlesrud gulped and murmured. It might have been that way. He turned his head away and brushed his sleeve across his eyes.

"Not passed away! Pshaw now, fellers. Will you listen to that! Don't it beat hell? His wife just passed away and left him with a little baby, he sez. He and me threshed on the same outfit last fall. Come and hev a drink, old feller. Best trouble chaser invented. Don't it beat hell how things happen!"

He walked up to the bar and with his flowing black hair and mild beneficent regard stood looking like a prophet out of the Old Testament. As the hot liquid flowed down his throat he felt comforted and alight with ideas. Such sympathetic fellers as one found in the old saloons. He amplified the story of Anna's death, added pathetic details, and wiped his eyes surreptitiously. They showed their sympathy by treating. But he told himself not to get soused. There was brain work to be done. All was not yet accomplished.

So he waved back more glasses with a regretful sad gesture. "No more, fellers. I gotta go and buy her a coffin. Best coffin money can buy. Nothin's too good fer Anna. 'Talways was that way with me. Thanks. No more."

They wrung his hand with fellow feeling, murmuring as he strode out, "Pore old feller. Dod blasted shame."

He told the rotund, red-faced undertaker on the Moorhead side of the banks of the Red River. "God be merciful unto me. It is the Lord that gives. And He has taken away. Blessed be His Holy Name. So I try to be submissive to His Will." As he spoke he felt a keen pang of resigned sorrow at poor Anna's fate, a heart-broken regret mitigated only by religious balm.

He explained the need of a coffin for Anna immediately, blinking hard the while, and biting his under lip to keep it in control. "Don't hev' to hev' any certificates or anything, do I? Ain't got 'em with me."

Since Kettlesrud had just allied himself to the big family of Olsens—Valmar-Olsen; and since Old Man Valmar-Olsen owned one of the largest farms in the state, as well as one of the biggest broods of children, the undertaker waived the matter of certificates for the present. He was quite moved by the quiet distress and religious resignation of the man. He showed it in customary fashion. "Come up and have a—" Then he remembered the religious fervor and changed his original plan. "Come up and have a cup of coffee. We live upstairs over the shop, my wife and me. She's always got the coffee pot on. Ya, we're Norske, that way. Come on up. You'll have a long drive across the prairie. No, well good luck." Then he coughed. He did not know whether it sounded sympathetic to offer good luck to a recently bereaved husband.

The coffin was loaded on the wagon, and Kettlesrud drove across the bridge into North Dakota. Undertakers, he told himself, were harpies preying on the sorrowful. Here he drew out a blue bandana, rather the worse for wear, and wiped his eyes. He was quite justified in getting the better of them. A coffin the better of them. He would sell it and have money to show to Anna.

Another undertaker's shop in Fargo on a side street. The lank Swede owner sprawled across the counter, picked his teeth, and listened sympathetically while the long-haired, good-looking but simple farmer huskily explained why he was trying to sell a coffin.

"It's been hell. The doctor said that Anna wouldn't live from one day to the next. I had to stop all farm work and care for her. The fields all rotted, but Anna was wuth more——"

He paused. He saw himself tenderly caring for a white-faced Anna who lay helpless, dependent upon him. He saw great overripe wheat fields spoiling for lack of a harvester. He gained control of himself and continued, quoting a Biblical verse concerning the things that come first.

"I had 'ter mortgage the farm to buy this coffin for her. Sent for it to mail-order house. Couldn't tend the fields, couldn't go to town. Only stayed there besides Anna. But she was getting well now. Gaining every day." He didn't s'pose the mail-order house would take the coffin back. He had kept it too long. He had to sell the coffin, however, to get delicacies for Anna. His name? Olsen. One of the Valmar-Olsens.

Richer by a hundred and fifty dollars he started at sunset across the prairies for home. Peace within and without. One hundred and fifty dollars in a fat wad in his leather wallet.

There was a time for everything. Even for sentiment about posies and sunsets. Anna always stared at both as if they were so much. Well, it was nice, this sunset. Gold spilled over the wide stubble fields, over the red foxtail and prairie grass, over the yellowing leaves of the fringe of trees on his right, where the Red River ran. If only it could be harvested, this wash of gold. And if all the fields whereon it lay were his.

But soon all the gold faded to a monotone of gray except that there flowed on the horizon a great afterglow: like the lights of a palace seen through smoked glasses. Something beyond? Anna had said so. All women were religious-like.

God and the Bible were worth knowing, though. They had helped him out of many a fix. Hadn't they helped him to-day—in Moorhead, to get the coffin?

Night came on. The wagon jolted monotonously along in deep sandy ruts. A continuous hummock of grass in the center of the road.

At least he wouldn't meet any of these dang automobiles on this road. If he did he wouldn't turn out for 'em. Let 'em honk and holler.

But say, with money in his pocket. Garn! Some day he might drive up before Anna in one of them contraptions. Then he'd get out and say, "That's the kind of man you married. The man that Selma Servaas says ain't good enough for you."

Jolted deeper into the ruts; blanketed deeper in a chilly grayness. What was beyond the grayness? He had seen headlines in the newspapers about bandits. He began intoning a hymn:

"Shall we, whose souls are lighted
With wisdom from on high . . ."

Ah, that willow hedge showed that he was nearing the crossroads. Nearing home. How he would flourish the money before Anna! And tell tales of the discomforts of threshing. Sleeping in the hay in barns. Getting up at clammy dawn to the shrieks of the discordant threshing engines. It had been dang cold and uncomfortable. Meanwhile she had been snug at home doing nothing except care for the stock.

Or perhaps she had been gadding again. Running over to the Servaas Place and listening to whose women's tongues clacking against him. He had never been an unreasonable husband in his demands; never beat her up unless he was drunk. Yet she would not respect a simple little request of not to gad.

His muscles grew more cramped and the chill more penetrating. The horse blankets that he had wrapped about his legs weren't enough to keep him warm. He had to descend from the wagon and walk along beside it, beating his arms over his chest.

All the more vividly he painted his meeting with Anna. She'd have to get up. He'd see that she got out of her warm bed to welcome her lawful husband. He'd see that she listened to him while he talked and that her eyes stopped defying him. Yes, there it was finally. The Servaas Farm and the crossroads. Anna's old home; a big, square white farmhouse with all modern improvements; great barns in the background, and a thriving grove about all. Anna's people; a stiff-necked generation of vipers. Said he wasn't good enough for her, eh?

There was already light in the Servaas kitchen, although it was only half-past three.

He jogged on the few separating miles between the Servaas Place and his eighty. Father Servaas had given it to him as a wedding present. Enoch had expected at least a quarter section.

By the bleak light of the late moon his unpainted sod-roofed shack looked tenantless and starved. The gates to the grass-grown driveway swung open on sagging hinges. The pasture bars were down. The little trees that Anna had induced him to plant the first year after marriage, stripped of their leaves, looked like a grotesque row of broomsticks. Beyond was the barn—and the barn doors yawned wide.

There came a hunch that Anna had been careless about closing up the stock. He retrieved a lantern hanging from the kitchen porch and strode with stiff legs toward the swinging barn door. He stumbled against a rusty scythe hidden among the tall brown rustling weeds. Hell! Anna ought to pick up a thing or two.

In the barn he looked about him with growing anger, the hot waves mounting to his brain. Anna had not taken in the cattle. And the bars to the pasture had been down, so of course they had wandered afar. Wandered, and were now bloating up through overeating in some wheat field. It was time he came home and tended to things.

He made his way to the house and stamped into the kitchen with ominous loudness. He lighted the pressed-glass oil lamp that swung from a bracket over the kitchen table. By its flickering yellow light he noted that the kitchen was dirty and uninviting.

"Anna. Anna. I want that you should get up," he ordered. He'd settle with her. "What you done to the stock?"

There was no reply. He tramped to the little bedroom, the lamp held high in his hand. "Anna," he ordered roughly again. "You get up."

An empty bed. No Anna.

She had gone to her mother's, of course. Gadding again, just as he had supposed. Listening to Selma Servaas say things against him. A heavy anger settled down upon him. He wasn't an unreasonable husband, as he had often told her. But a woman's place was in the house to welcome her husband instead of gadding about the neighborhood listening to gossip about him. He strode out into the yard and picked up the reins with hands that trembled.

"Giddap, you Jumbo. Giddap, Stanley." He jerked at the reins until the horses reared backward, settled down on four feet, and began a startled gallop.

Without knocking he tramped into the Servaas kitchen. "Selma

Servaas, I want to know what you done to my wife. I won't have her gadding about here."

Selma was at the table gathering up the breakfast dishes. At his question she dropped the pile of plates that she had in her hands. They crashed to the floor and were broken into slivers. She stood staring at the plates with such a woebegone expression that Enoch laughed at her. She was so careful of her things. A thrifty housewife. Garn, but her look was funny! He rocked with mirth.

She turned on him. "Laugh, will you! You—you—prairie actor. Ha, ha! Funny, ain't it? Funny life for all us North Dakota farm women. Ha, ha!" Then she turned her back to him.

"I want to know where my wife is," he shouted, his teeth clicking tight on his laughter. "Here I come home after working hard all fall and find her gadding about. Where is she, I say? She's my wife."

Selma Servaas took her time stacking the remainder of the dishes in the big granite-iron dishpan. Then, wiping her hands on the roller towel by the sink, she wheeled about and faced him, replying deliberately slow: "Anna is dead—in childbirth. Both her and the child are dead. She was alone. No one to take care of her. Your stock? They took it to pay for the coffin."

Enoch didn't speak. He just looked at her, tears welling out of his eyes. Then he said stupidly, "I—I had a coffin."

MONTANA

Chip Off the Old Block

WALLACE STEGNER

Sitting alone looking at the red eyes of the parlor heater, Chet thought how fast things happened. One day the flu hit. Two days after that his father left for Montana to get a load of whisky to sell for medicine. The next night he got back in the midst of a blizzard with his hands and feet frozen, bringing a sick homesteader he had picked up on the road; and now this morning all of them, the homesteader, his father, his mother, his brother Bruce, were loaded in a sled and hauled to the schoolhouse-hospital. It was scary how fast they all got it, even his father, who seldom got anything and was tougher than boiled owl. Everybody, he thought with some pride, but him. His mother's words as she left were a solemn burden on his mind. 'You'll have to hold the fort, Chet. You'll have to be the man of the house.' And his father, sweat on his face even in the cold, his frozen hands held tenderly in his lap, saying, 'Better let the whisky alone. Put it away somewhere till we get back.'

So he was holding the fort. He accepted the duty soberly. In the two hours since his family had left he had swept the floors, milked old Red and thrown down hay for her, brought in scuttles of lignite. And sitting now in the parlor he knew he was scared. He heard the walls tick and the floors creak. Every thirty seconds he looked up from his book, and finally he yawned, stretched, laid the book down, and took a stroll through the whole house, cellar to upstairs, as if for exercise. But his eyes were sharp, and he stepped back a little as he threw open the doors of bedrooms and closets. He whistled a little between his teeth and

From *The Virginia Quarterly Review,* copyright 1942 by Wallace Stegner. Used by permission of the author.

looked at the calendar in the hall to see what day it was. November 4, 1918.

A knock on the back door sent him running. It was the young man named Vickers who had taken his family away. He was after beds and blankets for the schoolhouse. Chet helped him knock the beds down and load them on the sled. He would sleep on the couch in the parlor; it was warmer there, anyway; no cold floors to worry about.

In the kitchen, making a list of things he had taken, Vickers saw the keg, the sacked cases of bottles, the pile of whisky-soaked straw sheaths from the bottles that had been broken on the trip. 'Your dad doesn't want to sell any of that, does he?' he said.

Chet thought briefly of his father's injunction to put the stuff away. But gee, the old man had frozen his hands and feet and caught the flu getting it, and now when people came around asking. . . . 'Sure,' he said. 'That's what he bought it for, flu medicine.'

'What've you got?'

'Rye and bourbon,' Chet said. 'There's some Irish, but I think he brought that special for somebody.' He rummaged among the sacks. 'Four dollars a bottle, I think it is,' he said, and looked at Vickers to see if that was too much. Vickers didn't blink. 'Or is it four-fifty?' Chet said.

Vickers' face was expressionless. 'Sure it isn't five? I wouldn't want to cheat you.' He took out his wallet, and under his eyes Chet retreated. 'I'll go look,' he said. 'I think there's a list.'

He stood in the front hall for a minute or two before he came back. 'Four-fifty,' he said casually. 'I thought probably it was.'

Vickers counted out twenty-seven dollars. 'Give me six rye,' he said. With the sack in his hand he stood in the back door and looked at Chet and laughed. 'What are you going to do with that extra three dollars?'

Chet felt his heart stop while he might have counted ten. His face began to burn. 'What three dollars?'

'Never mind,' Vickers said. 'I was just ragging you. Got all you need to eat here?'

'I got crocks of milk,' Chet said. He grinned at Vickers in relief, and Vickers grinned back. 'There's bread Ma baked the other day, and spuds. If I need any meat I can go shoot a rabbit.'

'Oh.' Vickers's eyebrows went up. 'You're a hunter, eh?'

'I shot rabbits all last fall for Mrs. Rieger,' Chet said. 'She's 'nemic and has to eat rabbits and prairie chickens and stuff. She lent me the shotgun and bought the shells.'

'Mmm,' Vickers said. 'I guess you can take care of yourself. How old are you?'

'Twelve.'

'That's old enough,' said Vickers. 'That's pretty old, in fact. Well, Mervin, if you need anything you call the school and I'll see that you get it.'

'My name isn't Mervin,' Chet said. 'It's Chet.'

'Okay,' Vickers said. 'Don't get careless with the fires.'

'What do you think I am?' Chet said in scorn. He raised his hand stiffly as Vickers went out. A little tongue of triumph licked up in him. That three bucks would look all right, all right. Next time he'd know better than to change the price, too. He took the bills out of his pocket and counted them. Twenty-seven dollars was a lot of dough. He'd show Ma and Pa whether he could hold the fort or not.

But holding the fort was tiresome. By two o'clock he was bored stiff, and the floors were creaking again in the silence. Then he remembered suddenly that he was the boss of the place. He could go or come as he pleased, as long as the cow was milked and the house kept warm. He thought of the two traps he had set in muskrat holes under the river bank. The blizzard and the flu had made him forget to see to them. And he might take Pa's gun and do a little hunting.

'Well,' he said in the middle of the parlor rug, 'I guess I will.'

For an hour and a half he prowled the river brush. Over on the path toward Heathcliff's he shot a snowshoe rabbit, and the second of his traps yielded a stiffly frozen muskrat. The weight of his game was a solid satisfaction as he came up the dugway swinging the rabbit by its feet, the muskrat by its plated tail.

Coming up past the barn, he looked over towards Van Dam's, then the other way, toward Chapman's, half hoping that someone might be out, and see him. He whistled loudly, sang a little into the cold afternoon air, but the desertion of the whole street, the unbroken fields of snow where ordinarily there would have been dozens of sled tracks and fox-and-goose paths, let a chill in upon his pride. He came up the back steps soberly and opened the door.

The muskrat's slippery tail slid out of his mitten and the frozen body thumped on the floor. Chet opened his mouth, shut it again, speechless with surprise and shock. Two men were in the kitchen. His eyes jumped from the one by the whisky keg to the other, sitting at the table drinking whisky from a cup. The one drinking he didn't know. The other was Louis Treat, a halfbreed who hung out down at the stable and sometimes worked a little for the Half-Diamond Bar. All Chet knew about him was that he could braid horsehair ropes and sing a lot of dirty songs.

'Aha!' said Louis Treat. He smiled at Chet and made a rubbing motion with his hands. 'We 'ave stop to get warm. You 'ave been hunting?'

'Yuh,' Chet said automatically. He stood where he was, his eyes swinging between the two men. The man at the table raised his eyebrows at Louis Treat.

'Ees nice rabbit there,' Louis said. His bright black button eyes went over the boy. Chet lifted the rabbit and looked at the frozen beads of blood on the white fur. 'Yuh,' he said. He was thinking about what his father always said. You could trust an Indian, if he was your friend, and you could trust a white man sometimes, if money wasn't involved, and you could trust a Chink more than either, but you couldn't trust a halfbreed.

Louis' voice went on, caressingly. 'You 'ave mushrat too, eh? You lak me to 'elp you peel thees mushrat?' His hand, dipping under the sheepskin and into his pants pocket, produced a long-bladed knife that jumped open with the pressure of his thumb on a button.

Chet dropped the rabbit and took off his mitts. 'No thanks,' he said. 'I can peel him.'

Shrugging, Louis put the knife away. He turned to thump the bung hard into the keg, and nodded at the other man, who rose. 'Ees tam we go,' Louis said. 'We 'ave been told to breeng thees wisky to the 'ospital.'

'Who told you?' Chet's insides grew tight, and his mind was setting like plaster of Paris. If Pa was here he'd scatter these thieves all the way to Chapman's. But Pa wasn't here. He watched Louis Treat. You could never trust a halfbreed.

'The doctor, O'Malley,' Louis said. Keeping his eye on Chet, he jerked his head at the other man. ' 'Ere, you tak' the other end.'

His companion, pulling up his sheepskin collar, stooped and took hold of the keg. Chet, with no blood in his face and no breath in his lungs, hesitated a split second and then jumped. Around the table, in the dining room door, he was out of their reach, and the shotgun was pointed straight at their chests. With his thumb he cocked both barrels, click, click.

Louis Treat swore. 'Put down that gun!'

'No, sir!' Chet said. 'I won't put it down till you drop that keg and get out of here!'

The two men looked at each other. Louis set his end gently back on the chair, and the other did the same. 'We 'ave been sent,' Louis said. 'You do not understan' w'at I mean.'

'I understand all right,' Chet said. 'If Doctor O'Malley had wanted that, he'd've sent Mr. Vickers for it this morning.'

The second man ran his tongue over his teeth and spat on the floor. 'Think he knows how to shoot that thing?'

Chet's chest expanded. The gun trembled so that he braced it against the frame of the door. 'I shot that rabbit, didn't I?' he said.

The halfbreed's teeth were bared in a bitter grin. 'You are a fool,' he said.

'And you're a thief!' Chet said. He covered the two carefully as they backed out, and when they were down the steps he slammed and bolted the door. Then he raced for the front hall, made sure that door was locked, and peeked out the front window. The two were walking side by side up the irrigation ditch toward town, pulling an empty box sled. Louis was talking furiously with his hand.

Slowly and carefully Chet uncocked the gun. Ordinarily he would have unloaded, but not now, not with thieves like those around. He put the gun above the mantel, looked in the door of the stove, threw in a half-scuttle of lignite, went to the window again to see if he could still see the two men. Then he looked at his hands. They were shaking. So were his knees. He sat down suddenly on the couch, unable to stand.

For days the only people he saw were those who came to buy whisky. They generally sat a while in the kitchen and talked about the flu and the war, but they weren't much company. Once Miss Landis, his schoolteacher, came apologetically and furtively with a two-quart fruit jar under her coat, and he charged her four dollars a quart for bulk rye out of the keg. His secret hoard of money mounted to eighty-five dollars, to a hundred and eight.

When there was none of that business (he had even forgotten by now that his father had told him not to meddle with it), he moped around the house, milked the cow, telephoned to the hospital to see how his folks were. One day his dad was pretty sick. Two days later he was better, but his mother had had a relapse because they were so short of beds they had had to put Brucie in with her. The milk crocks piled up in the cellarway, staying miraculously sweet, until he told the schoolhouse nurse over the phone about all the milk he had, and then Doctor O'Malley sent down old Gundar Moe to pick it up for the sick people.

Sometimes he stood on the porch on sunny, cold mornings and watched Lars Poulsen's sled go out along the road on the way to the graveyard, and the thought that maybe Mom or Bruce or Pa might die and be buried out there on the knoll by the sandhills made him swallow and go back inside where he couldn't see how deserted the street looked, and where he couldn't see the sled and the steaming gray horses move out toward the south bend of the river. He resolved to be a son his parents could be proud of, and sat down at the piano determined to learn a piece letter-perfect. But the dry silence of the house weighed on him; before long he would be lying with his forehead on the keyboard, his finger picking on one monotonous note. That way he could concentrate on how different it sounded with his head down, and forget to be afraid.

And at night, when he lay on the couch and stared into the sleepy red eyes of the heater, he heard noises that walked the house, and there were crosses in the lamp chimneys when he lighted them, and he knew that someone would die.

On the fifth day he sat down at the dining room table determined to write a book. In an old atlas he hunted up a promising locale. He found a tributary of the Amazon called the Tapajos, and firmly, his lips together in concentration, he wrote his title across the top of a school tablet: 'The Curse of the Tapajos.' All that afternoon he wrote enthusiastically. He created a tall, handsome young explorer and a halfbreed guide obscurely like Louis Treat. He plowed through steaming jungles, he wrestled pythons and other giant serpents which he spelled 'boy constructors.' All this time he was looking for the Lost City of Gold. And when the snakes got too thick even for his taste, and when he was beginning to wonder himself why the explorer didn't shoot the guide, who was constantly trying to poison the flour or stab his employer in his tent at midnight, he let the party come out on a broad pampa and see in the distance, crowning a golden hill, the lost city for which they searched. And then suddenly the explorer reeled and fell, mysteriously stricken, and the halfbreed guide, smiling with sinister satisfaction, disappeared quietly into the jungle. The curse of the Tapajos, which struck everyone who found that lost city, had struck again. But the young hero was not dead. . . .

Chet gnawed his pencil and stared across the room. It was going to be hard to figure out how his hero escaped. Maybe he was just stunned, not killed. Maybe a girl could find him there, and nurse him back to health. . . .

He rose, thinking, and wandered over to the window. A sled came across the irrigation ditch and pulled on over to Chance's house. Out of it got Mr. Chance and Mrs. Chance and Ed and Harvey Chance. They were well, then. People were starting to come home cured. He rushed to the telephone and called the hospital. No, the nurse said, his family weren't well yet; they wouldn't be home for three or four days at least. But they were all better. How was he doing? Did he need anything?

But at least he wasn't the only person on the street any more. That night after milking he took a syrup pail of milk to the Chances. They were all weak, all smiling. Mrs. Chance cried every time she spoke, and they were awfully grateful for the milk. He promised them, over their protests, that he would bring them some every day, and chop wood and haul water for them until they got really strong. Mr. Chance, who had the nickname of Dictionary because he strung off such jaw-breaking words, told him he was a benefactor and a Samaritan, and called upon his own sons to witness this neighborly kindness and be edified and enlarged. Chet went home in the dark, wondering if it might not be a good idea, later in his book somewhere, to have his explorer find a bunch of people, or maybe just a beautiful and ragged girl, kept in durance vile by some tribe of pigmies or spider men or something, and have him rescue them and confound their captors.

On the afternoon of the eighth day Chet sat in the kitchen at Chance's. His own house had got heavier and heavier to bear, and there wasn't much to eat there but milk and potatoes, and both stores were closed because of the flu. So he went a good deal to Chance's, doing their chores and talking about the hospital, and listening to Mr. Chance tell about the Death Ward where they put people who weren't going to get well. The Death Ward was the eighth-grade room, his own room, and he and Ed Chance speculated on what it would be like to go back to that room where so many people had died—Mrs. Rieger, and old Gypsy Davy from Poverty Flat, and John Chapman, and a lot of people.

Mrs. Chance sat by the stove and when anyone looked at her or spoke to her she shook her head and smiled and the tears ran down. She didn't seem unhappy about anything; she just couldn't help crying.

Mr. Chance said over and over that there was certainly going to be a multitude of familiar faces missing after this thing was over. The town would never be the same. He wouldn't be surprised if the destitute and friendless were found in every home in town, adopted and cared for by friends. They might have to build an institution to house the derelict and the bereaved.

He pulled his sagging cheeks and said to Chet, 'Mark my words, son, you are one of the fortunate. In that hospital I said to myself a dozen times, "Those poor Mason boys are going to lose their father." I lay there—myself in pain, mind you—and the first thing I'd hear some old and valued friend would be moved into the Death Ward. I thought your father was a goner when they moved him in.'

Chet's throat was suddenly dry as dust. 'Pa isn't in there!'

'Ira,' said Mrs. Chance, and shook her head and smiled and wiped the tears away. 'Now you've got the child all worked up.'

'He isn't in there now,' said Mr. Chance. 'By the grace of the Almighty—' he bent his head and his lips moved, 'he came out again. He's a hard man to kill. Hands and feet frozen, double pneumonia, and still he came out.'

'Is he all right now?' Chet said.

'Convalescing,' Mr. Chance said. 'Convalescing beautifully.' He raised a finger under Chet's nose. 'Some people are just hard to kill. But on the other hand, you take a person like that George Valet. I hesitate to say before the young what went on in that ward. Shameful, even though the man was sick.' His tongue ticked against his teeth, and his eyebrows raised at Chet. 'They cleaned his bed six times a day,' he said, and pressed his lips together. 'It makes a man wonder about God's wisdom,' he said. 'A man like that, his morals are as loose as his bowels.'

'Ira!' Mrs. Chance said.

'I would offer you a wager,' Mr. Chance said. 'I wager that a man as loose and discombobulated as that doesn't live through this epidemic.'

'I wouldn't bet on a person's life that way,' she said.

'Ma,' Harvey called from the next room, where he was lying down. 'What's all the noise about?'

They stopped talking and listened. The church bell was ringing madly. In a minute the bell in the firehouse joined it. The heavy bellow of a shotgun, both barrels, rolled over the snowflats between their street and the main part of town. A six-shooter went off, bang-bang-bang-bang-bang-bang, and there was the sound of distant yelling.

'Fire?' Mr. Chance said, stooping to the window.

'Here comes somebody,' Ed said. The figure of a boy was streaking across the flat. Mr. Chance opened the door and shouted at him. The boy ran closer, yelling something unintelligible. It was Spot Orullian.

'What?' Mr. Chance yelled.

Spot cupped his hands to his mouth, standing in the road in front of Chet's as if unwilling to waste a moment's time. 'War's over!' he shouted, and wheeled and was gone up the street toward Van Dam's.

Mr. Chance closed the door slowly. Mrs. Chance looked at him, and her lips jutted and trembled, her weak eyes ran over with tears, and she fell into his arms. The three boys, not quite sure how one acted when a war ended, but knowing it called for celebration, stood around uneasily. They shot furtive grins at one another, looked with furrowed brows at Mrs. Chance's shaking back.

'Now Uncle Joe can come home,' Ed said. 'That's what she's bawling about.'

Chet bolted out the door, raced over to his own house, pulled the loaded shotgun from the mantel, and burst out into the yard again. He blew the lid off the silence in their end of town, and followed the shooting with a wild yell. Ed and Harvey, leaning out their windows, answered him, and the heavy boom-boom of a shotgun came from the downtown district.

Carrying the gun, Chet went back to Chance's. He felt grown up, a householder. The end of the war had to be celebrated; neighbors had to get together and raise cain. He watched Mrs. Chance, still incoherent, rush to the calendar and put a circle around the date, November 11. 'I don't ever want to forget what day it happened on,' she said.

'Everyone in the world will remember this day,' said Mr. Chance, solemnly, like a preacher. Chet looked at him, his mind clicking.

'Mr. Chance,' he said, 'would you like a drink, to celebrate?'

Mr. Chance looked startled. 'What?'

'Pa's got some whisky. He'd throw a big party if he was home.

'I don't think we should,' said Mrs. Chance dubiously. 'Your father might . . . '

'Oh, Mama,' Mr. Chance said, and laid his arm across her back like a log. 'One bumper to honor the day. One leetle stirrup-cup to those boys of the Allies. Chester here is carrying on his father's tradition like a man.' He bowed and shook Chet's hand formally. 'We'd be delighted, sir,' he said, and they all laughed.

Somehow, nobody knew just how, the party achieved proportions. Mr. Chance suggested, after one drink, that it would be pleasant to have a neighbor or two, snatched from the terrors of the plague, come and join in the thanksgiving; and Chet, full of hospitality, said sure, that would be a keen idea. So Mr. Chance called Jewel King, and when Jewel came he brought Chubby Klein with him, and a few minutes later three more came, knocked, looked in to see the gathering with cups in their hands, and came in with alacrity when Chet held the door wide. Within an hour there were eight men, three women, and the two Chance boys, besides Chet. Mr. Chance wouldn't let the boys have any whisky, but Chet, playing bartender, sneaked a cup into the dining room and all sipped it and smacked their lips.

'Hey, look, I'm drunk,' Harvey said. He staggered, hiccoughed, caught himself, bowed low and apologized, staggered again. 'Hic,' he said. 'I had a drop too much.' The three laughed together secretly while loud voices went up in the kitchen.

'Gentlemen,' Mr. Chance was saying, 'I give you those heroic laddies in khaki who looked undaunted into the eyes of death and saved this ga-lorious empire from the rapacious Huns.'

'Yay!' the others said, banging cups on the table. 'Give her the other barrel, Dictionary.'

'I crave your indulgence for a moment,' Mr. Chance said. 'For one leetle moment, while I imbibe a few swallows of this delectable amber fluid.'

The noise went up and up. Chet went among them stiff with pride at having done all this, at being accepted here as host, at having men pat him on the back and shake his hand and tell him, 'You're all right, kid, you're a chip off the old block. What's the word from the folks?' He guggled liquor out of the sloshing cask into a milk crock, and the men dipped largely and frequently. About four o'clock, two more families arrived and were welcomed with roars. People bulged the big kitchen; their laughter rattled the window frames. Occasionally Dictionary Chance rose to propose a toast to 'those gems of purest ray serene, those unfailing companions on life's bitter pilgrimage, the ladies,

God bless 'em!' Every so often he suggested that it might be an idea worth serious consideration that some liquid refreshments be decanted from the aperture in the receptacle.

The more liquid refreshments Chet decanted from the aperture in the receptacle, the louder and more eloquent Mr. Chance became. He dominated the kitchen like an evangelist. He swung and swayed and stamped, he led a rendition of 'God Save the King,' he thundered denunciations on the Beast of Berlin, he thrust a large fist into the lapels of new arrivals and demanded detailed news of the war's end. Nobody knew more than that it was over.

But Dictionary didn't forget to be grateful, either. At least five times during the afternoon he caught Chet up in a long arm and publicly blessed him. Once he rose and cleared his throat for silence. Chubby Klein and Jewel King booed and hissed, but he bore their insults with dignity. 'Siddown!' they said. 'Speech!' said others. Mr. Chance waved his hands abroad, begging for quiet. Finally they gave it to him, snickering.

'Ladies and gen'lemen,' he said, 'we have come together on this auspicious occasion . . .'

'What's suspicious about it?' Jewel King said.

' . . . on this auspicious occasion, to do honor to our boys in Flanders' fields, to celebrate the passing of the dread incubus of Spanish influenza . . .'

'Siddown!' said Chubby Klein.

. . . and last, but not least, we are gathered here to honor our friendship with the owners of this good and hospitable house, Bo Mason and Sis, may their lives be long and strewn with flowers, and this noble scion of a noble stock, this tender youth who kept the home fires burning through shock and shell and who opened his house and his keg to us as his father would have done. Ladies and gen'lemen, the Right Honorable Chester Mason, may he live to bung many a barrel.'

Embarrassed and squirming and unsure of what to do with so many faces laughing at him, so many mouths cheering him, Chet crowded into the dining room door and tried to act casual, tried to pretend he didn't feel proud and excited and a man among men. And while he stood there with the noise beating at him in raucous approbation, the back door opened and the utterly flabbergasted face of his father looked in.

There was a moment of complete silence. Voices dropped away to nothing, cups hung at lips. Then in a concerted rush they were helping Bo Mason in. He limped heavily on bandaged and slippered feet, his hands wrapped in gauze, his face drawn and hollow-eyed and noticeably thinner than it had been ten days ago. After him came Chet's mother, half-carrying Bruce, and staggering under his weight. Hands took Bruce away from her, sat him on the open oven door, and led her to a chair. All three of them, hospital-pale, rested and looked around the room. And Chet's father did not look pleased.

'What the devil is this?' he said.

From his station in the doorway Chet squeaked, 'The war's over!'

'I know the war's over, but what's this?' He jerked a bandaged hand at the uncomfortable ring of people. Chet swallowed and looked at Dictionary Chance.

Dictionary's suspended talents came back to him. He strode to lay a friendly hand on his host's back; he swung and shook his hostess' hand; he twinkled at the white-faced, big-eyed Bruce on the oven door.

'This, sir,' he boomed, 'is a welcoming committee of your friends and neighbors, met here to rejoice over your escape from the dread sickness which has swept to untimely death so many of our good friends, God rest their souls! On the invitation of your manly young son here we have been celebrating not only that emancipation, but the emancipation of the entire world from the dread plague of war.' With the cup in his hand he bent and twinkled at Bo Mason. 'How's it feel to get back, old hoss?'

Bo grunted. He looked across at his wife and laughed a short, choppy laugh. The way his eyes came around and rested on Chet made Chet stop breathing. But his father's voice was hearty enough when it came. 'You got a snootful,' he said. 'Looks like you've all got a snootful.'

'Sir,' said Dictionary Chance, 'I haven't had such a delightful snootful since the misguided government of this province suspended the God-given right of its free people to purchase and imbibe and ingest intoxicating beverages.'

He drained his cup and set it on the table. 'And now,' he said, 'it is clear that our hosts are not completely recovered in their strength. I suggest that we do whatever small jobs our ingenuity and gratitude can suggest, and silently steal away.'

'Yeah,' the others said. 'Sure. Sure thing.' They brought in the one bed from the sled and set it up, swooped together blankets and mattresses and turned over to the women. Before the beds were made people began to leave. Dictionary Chance, voluble to the last, stopped to praise the excellent medicinal waters he had imbibed, and to say a word for Chet, before Mrs. Chance, with a quick pleading smile, led him away. The door had not even closed before Chet felt his father's cold eye on him.

'All right,' his father said. 'Will you please tell me why in the name of Christ you invited that God damned windbag and all the rest of those sponges over here to drink up my whisky?'

Chet stood sullenly in the door, boiling with sulky resentment. He had held the fort, milked the cow, kept the house, sold all that whisky for all it was worth, run Louis Treat and the other man out with a gun. Everybody else praised him, but you could depend on Pa to think more of that whisky the neighbors had drunk than of anything else. He wasn't going to explain or defend himself. If the old man was going to be that stingy, he could take a flying leap in the river.

'The war was over,' he said. 'I asked them over to celebrate.'

His father's head wagged. He looked incredulous and at his wits' end. 'You asked them over!' he said. 'You said, "Come right on over and drink up all the whisky my dad almost killed himself bringing in."' He stuck his bandaged hands out. 'Do you think I got these and damned near died in that hospital just to let a bunch of blotters . . . why, God damn you,' he said. 'Leave the house for ten days, tell you exactly what to do, and by Jesus everything goes wrong. How long have they been here?'

'Since about two.'

'How much did they drink?'

'I don't know. Three crocks full, I guess.'

His father's head weaved back and forth, he looked at his wife and then at the ceiling. 'Three crocks. At least a gallon, twelve dollars' worth. Oh Jesus Christ, if you had the sense of a piss-ant . . . '

Laboriously swearing with the pain, he hobbled to the keg. When he put his hand down to shake it, his whole body stiffened.

'It's half empty!' he said. He swung on Chet, and Chet met his furious look. Now! his mind said. Now let him say I didn't hold the fort.

'I sold some,' he said, and held his father's eyes for a minute before he marched out stiff-backed into the living room, dug the wad of bills from the vase on the mantel, and came back. He laid the money in his father's hand. 'I sold a hundred and twenty-four dollars' worth,' he said.

The muscles in his father's jaw moved. He glanced at Chet's mother, let the breath out hard through his nose. 'So you've been selling whisky,' he said. 'I thought I told you to leave that alone?'

'People wanted it for medicine,' Chet said. 'Should I've let them die with the flu? They came here wanting to buy it and I sold it. I thought that was what it was for.'

The triumph that had been growing in him ever since he went for the money was hot in his blood now. He saw the uncertainty in his father's face, and he almost beat down his father's eyes.

'I suppose,' his father said finally, 'you sold it for a dollar a bottle, or something.'

'I sold it for plenty,' Chet said. 'Four-fifty for bottles and four for quarts out of the keg. That's more than you were going to get, because I heard you tell Ma.'

His father sat down on the chair and fingered the bills, looking at him. 'You didn't have any business selling anything,' he said. 'And then you overcharge people.'

'Yeah!' Chet said, defying him now. 'If it hadn't been for me there wouldn't 'ave been any to sell. Louis Treat and another man came and tried to steal that whole keg, and I run 'em out with a shotgun.'

'What?' his mother said.

'I did!' Chet said. 'I made 'em put it down and get out.'

Standing in the doorway still facing his father, he felt the tears hot in his eyes and was furious at himself for crying. He hoped his father would try thrashing him. He just hoped he would. He wouldn't make a sound; he'd grit his teeth and show him whether he was man enough to stand it.... He looked at his father's gray expressionless face and shouted, 'I wish I'd let them take it! I just wish I had!'

And suddenly his father was laughing. He reared back in the chair and threw back his head and roared, his bandaged hands held tenderly before him like helpless paws. He stopped, caught his breath, looked at Chet again, and shook with a deep internal rumbling. 'Okay,' he said. 'Okay, kid. You're a man. I wouldn't take it away from you.'

'Well, there's no need to laugh,' Chet said. 'I don't see anything to laugh about.'

He watched his father twist in the chair and look at his mother. 'Look at him,' his father said. 'By God, he'd eat me if I made a pass at him.'

'Well, don't laugh!' Chet said. He turned and went into the living room, where he sat on the couch and looked at his hands the way he had when Louis Treat and the other man were walking up the ditch. His hands were trembling, the same way. But there was no need to laugh, any more than there was need to get sore over a little whisky given to the neighbors.

His mother came in and sat down beside him, laid a hand on his head. 'Don't be mad at Pa,' she said. 'He didn't understand. He's proud of you. We all are.'

'Yeah?' said Chet. 'Why doesn't *he* come and tell me that?'

His mother's smile was gentle and a little amused. 'Because he's ashamed of himself for losing his temper, I suppose,' she said. 'He never did know how to admit he was wrong.'

Chet set his jaw and looked at the shotgun above the mantel. He guessed he had looked pretty tough himself when he had the drop on Louis Treat and his thieving friend. He stiffened his shoulders under his mother's arm. 'Just let him start anything,' he said. 'Just let him try to get hard.'

His mother's smile broadened, but he glowered at her. 'And there's no need to laugh!' he said.

WASHINGTON

Happiness

MICHAEL FOSTER

While the sun's flame passed from the western sky, and the high waters of the flood tide faded from apricot to violet-ash, old man McCluskey sat in the window of his house on Alki Beach and smoked his pipe. A tug coming upsound with an immense tow of log rafts was just perceptibly rounding the buoy: he had been hearing the laboring throb of its engines for an hour or more. In the next room, his wife was moving methodically about, setting the table and humming somewhat uncertainly a popular song which, he supposed, she had heard at a movie that afternoon on her weekly shopping trip downtown.

Across the darkening bay the lights of the city glimmered against the smoky purple wall of night looming in the east. In the valley beyond Harbor Island a tongue of orange fire licked skyward from the stack of a steel mill and subsided to a pulsing red glow. Old man McCluskey arose finally and went into the kitchen. Pausing in the lighted doorway, he saw his wife, a heavy, pleasant woman whose hair was still quite dark, peering anxiously into the oven.

"The cake has fallen," she said, glancing at him absent-mindedly, "And I did want to have a real nice supper for the children."

Old man McCluskey pulled out his massive silver watch and blinked gravely at it.

"It's seven-nine," he stated with the scrupulous exactitude of a man who has nothing but leisure. "They'd ought to be here pretty soon, now."

"It's a long drive down from Vancouver." His wife closed the oven door and stood up. "It's mighty nice they could come down to spend

---

Sunday with us, I think. Since Emma got married we haven't seen much of her."

"Eddie is a good boy." Old man McCluskey fumbled with the buttons of his shabby brown sweater. "I wonder, now. . . . Do you suppose he'll bring me some more of that English tobacco, this time? That's a fine smoke, I'll tell you."

"Maybe. He's a good enough boy, all right, I guess. Emma is real fond of him, and she says he treats her elegantly. But he'll never get ahead in that job of his. I wish they'd move down here to Seattle. I'm sure Eddie could get work here. Then we could have Emma right near to us."

Old man McCluskey grunted non-committally and went out on the back porch, where he knocked the ashes from his pipe against the railing. A little wind had come with the change of the tide, and a moored rowboat, somewhere down there in the darkness, was bumping irregularly against a pile. The wind smelled of salt and tide-flats, tinged faintly with smoke; it was freshening from the southwest, he noted carefully.

Returning to the kitchen, he took off his sweater and hung it behind the door. After washing his hands and smoothing his straggling gray mustache, he put on his well-brushed blue coat and looked at his watch again with a touch of impatience.

He was on his way to the back room to refill his pipe when he heard three loud honks on an automobile horn in front of the house. As he turned toward the door he had a glimpse of his wife in the kitchen, hanging up her apron and hastily smoothing her hair. Before he could reach the door it flew open and Emma came in laughing.

"Hello, Pa," she said, giving him a perfunctory kiss. "Oh, there's Ma—well, we got here, all right." She was a large, robust girl, much like her mother. He looked past her to the doorway, where Eddie, a tall, studious-appearing young man, was waiting bashfully. The two men shook hands stiffly and stood vaguely smiling while Emma and her mother moved off, toward the bedroom, chattering volubly.

"Well, Eddie," old man McCluskey said as the bedroom door was closed firmly, "let me help you off with your coat, now. Make yourself at home." He noted with elaborate unconcern, as he took the coat and hung it on the hall-tree, that a round package, done up in pink wrapping paper, was in one of the side pockets.

"Come on in the parlor, Eddie," he added heartily, "supper is all ready, and as soon as the womenfolks come out, I guess we'll be eating."

They sat in the parlor, beginning a tentative dialogue concerning business and politics. Suddenly Eddie stood up with an exclamation.

"I came pretty near forgetting something," he muttered, and went out into the hall. He came back a moment later, carrying the pink package.

"Here," he handed it to his father-in-law, "I just happened to remember you liked this. So I thought I'd bring it along."

Old man McCluskey unwrapped the paper with fingers which trembled slightly, and held up to the light a can of the English tobacco.

"Now, that's mighty fine," he said. "You didn't need to do that, Eddie. You shouldn't have done it. You'd better let me pay you for it."

"I should say not." Eddie leaned back and lit a cigarette. "No, sir. I just brought that along in the hopes that you'd like it. They say it's pretty fair tobacco. I don't smoke a pipe, myself."

"Best I ever smoked," the old man told him earnestly, "and I'm much obliged to you, Eddie. I'll just take this along, now, and put it away where I can get at it first thing in the morning." He stopped in the doorway and looked back over the top of his spectacles. "I've got a little of my regular mixture left, about enough so's I can finish it up tonight. Then I can start smoking this tomorrow."

When he returned, his wife and Emma had come out of the bedroom, and they all went in to supper. He ate silently, enwrapped in tranquillity, while Emma and her mother carried on an animated conversation. Emma did most of the talking, recounting details of her new life in Vancouver, and occasionally appealing to Eddie for corroboration or approval.

As he finished his cake, he became aware that Emma was speaking to him.

"What did you say?" he asked, looking up.

"I wanted to know if you liked your tobacco that Eddie brought you," his daugher demanded. Before he could answer, his wife spoke brightly.

"Well, now, that was real nice of Eddie, I think," she said. "But isn't it awful expensive? I know from the way Father talks about it, it must—"

He gazed at his wife in alarm. But Eddie made a modest gesture.

"Oh, it didn't cost much," he assured her, "I was glad to do it."

After supper he went back to his favorite chair by the window, pleasantly conscious of the voices of his family from the kitchen, where his wife and Emma, with Eddie to help, were doing the dishes. Far to the northward, beyond the measured flicker of the West Point lighthouse, he could make out the blurred lights of a big steamer emerging from Admiralty Inlet—probably a Jap liner, he thought. A level bank of cloud, blowing in from sea, was slowly blotting out the stars in the west, and the wind was lacing the black waters of the bay with ghostly white crests.

He heard the doorbell ring, but he paid no attention to the subsequent murmurings in the front part of the house until his wife came into the room and switched on the light.

"There's a young man here to see you," she spoke urgently; "he says he's a newspaper reporter—from the *Post*. He says he wants to see you personally."

He stared at her in profound perturbation.

"What does he want with me? Maybe it's some other McCluskey he wants."

His wife shook her head.

"No, he wants to see you," she repeated. "He says he'd like to interview you. You'd better go in. Here, let me—"

She approached him and began fussing with his tie and brushing a few crumbs of tobacco off his vest with her hand. He saw that she was enormously impressed, and at once he assumed an air of calm sufficiency. With deliberate steps he preceded her down the hall. In the parlor he found a florid young man sitting on the sofa, smoking a cigarette with indifference. Emma had just finished saying something pleasant about the weather. Eddie leaned silently in the dining-room doorway, with the dish-towel still in his hand.

"Ah—Mr. McCluskey?" the reporter asked, arising and shaking hands, "I'm Smythe of the *Post*. Won't you sit down?"

Old man McCluskey took his seat in the large wooden rocking chair by the table and placed both hands upon his knees.

"What can I do for you?" he enquired firmly.

"Well, Mr. McCluskey, I am the Inquiring Reporter," the visitor said. "Every day I go out and ask people questions—important questions, such as everybody is interested in—and then we run their answers in a column called the Inquiring Reporter. You probably read it every morning. Now, Mr. McCluskey, I want to ask you for your definition of happiness."

He took pencil and paper from his pocket and prepared to write. Mrs.

McCluskey crossed the room, flurried and beaming, and stood behind her husband's chair.

"Mr. Smythe wants you to tell him what happiness is, Father," she prompted. "I guess you mean true happiness, don't you, Mr. Smythe?"

"Well, I'd like to have Mr. McCluskey tell me his idea of happiness," the reporter answered. "Almost everybody has a different idea of it. Some people say 'money to do good with'—that's what Mrs. E. A. Perkins on Phinney Ridge said; I just finished interviewing her—and others would like a good time, like Miss Krafft—she's a stenographer in the Marine—"

"Oh, but Mr. Smythe," Emma interrupted, "don't you think that true happiness, that is, I mean real, true happiness, comes from—"

Old man McCluskey cleared his throat.

"Where did you get my name?" he demanded. "What made you come out here to see me about that?"

"Well, what we do, Mr. McCluskey, is to pick out some names out of the City Directory at random, and then we call up the circulation department to make sure they are subscribers to the *Post*. Then I go out and ask them questions, like this one. So now, if you'll just tell me, I'll write your answer down. What would you say is your idea of happiness? Whatever you say is O. K. with me."

"Happiness? Well, I don't know. I hadn't thought about it, exactly," old man McCluskey said uncomfortably.

Sitting here, surrounded by his expectant family and watched by the stranger, he stared at his veined hands upon his knees and made a determined effort to think. Since he was under the impression that it was the proper thing to do in this connection, he thought of his wedding day: and the swift, blurred recollection of a rainy day in Autumn came to him. A day when the sea was gray, and the raw buildings of the new town clustered on the hill wore an air of desolate nostalgia against the forests and mountains. They walked alone, he and a slender, dark woman, from her house to the white church above the harbor. She was an orphan, and she had sewn her wedding gown herself, copying it carefully from a picture in a magazine. Because she wanted a fine wedding, they had worked together the night before, decorating the church with late flowers from her garden and evergreen boughs from the forest. There were people waiting in the church, when she left him at the door. The ceremony was as she had planned it, as fine a wedding as could be wished. Afterward, they walked back to her house, which she had scrubbed and swept and set in order, and where then, with the help of a neighbor woman, she cooked a wedding supper. . . . But he remembered most clearly coming into her room that night, after he had smoked a pipe alone on the porch, to find her awaiting him. . . .

He realized suddenly that the reporter was talking to him confidentially as he wrote on the paper he was holding in his hand. But as old man McCluskey strove to fix his attention upon what the young man was saying, another picture intruded itself, for the space of a heartbeat upon his mind. It was of a day in Summer, and the sea was glittering under a northern sun. As he leaned out the pilot-house window he could see a line of peaks, blue and silver, above a long, dark smudge of wooded shore away to the east. His fishing boat was rolling on a slow groundswell; on the scrubbed foredeck Bill Soames, his mate, was coiling a line, and he looked up with a seamed grin as McCluskey shouted something. . . . But that, of course, had nothing to do with the question he was supposed to answer for the paper .

"So I'll write that down," the reporter was saying quickly. "There. That ought to be enough. Now, Mr. McCluskey, I'll just read you what we've said, and you see if it's O. K.

"Happiness is found in unselfishness, and we are always the most contented when we are doing all we can for other people—let's change that to *others.* Now—*In my own case, my happiest moments have come from having kindly thoughts and from helping people, both loved ones and friends. True happiness cannot be bought with money. I have always believed in following the Golden Rule*—there's no need to quote that, everybody knows it, don't you think, Mr. McCluskey?—*and that should be enough to make anyone happy throughout life. My definition of happiness would be to do one's duty, lead an unselfish life and be kind to one's fellowmen."*

"How's that?"

Old man McCluskey blinked and fumbled for his pipe.

"Well, I guess that's about the size of it, all right," he said.

Mr. Smythe stood up and shook his hand.

"All right, Mr. McCluskey," he smiled cordially. "That's fine. Now, if I can borrow that photograph of you there on the piano, that will be all. We'll mail it back to you tomorrow. I've got a photographer outside in the car, but if I can have this picture we won't need to call him in. Ah, that's fine. Good night, everybody."

After the reporter had gone, old man McCluskey went back to his window and finished his pipe in silence. Lying in bed beside his wife that night, he listened for a while to the drowsy murmur from the other bedroom where Emma and Eddie were staying, and to the regular, heavy breathing of his wife. He thought with pleasure of the can of English tobacco Eddie had brought him, and as he fell asleep he could almost feel the pleasant bite of it upon his tongue. He would smoke the first pipeful of it, he decided, while he took his morning walk along the sea-wall after breakfast.

IDAHO

The Scarecrow

VARDIS FISHER

We were threshing on the ranch of Jon Weeg and when we went to the machine one morning we discovered that a stray animal had been to the piled sacks of grain and had ripped several of them wide open. Around the pile were the hoof-prints of a horse. We searched the yard and the outlying land, expecting to find the beast foundered; but there was no trace of it. In the evening of this day we built around the stacks of wheat a fence of barbed wire. "That'll hold him," we said.

But on the next morning we found another half-dozen sacks torn open; for the prowler had returned during the night, had leapt our three-wire fence, and had gone. In this evening we added two wires to the fence. It was now chin-high and we didn't think that even an elk could jump it. Our astonishment on the third morning left us speechless. The beast had come again, had vaulted our five-wire fence, and had plundered another half-dozen sacks. On the top wire was a little hair but that was all. And it was at this point that the matter began to be a little unreal for all of us. For Joe Burt, a huge and feeble-witted youth, it was nothing less than a miracle. Because ordinarily, as in turn we declared to one another, an animal does not gorge itself upon grain without foundering; does not come slyly under cover of darkness and vanish before daylight; and does not leap a five-wire fence.

"Mebbe it's a mule," said Curt Obbing. We searched and found tracks but they were not the tracks of a mule.

"I'm going to sleep out here," I said. "I'll find out."

And on the third night I laid my bed in the grain-yard and waited for the thief. I fell asleep; and later I was awakened by a terrific screeching of wire; and upon looking up, I saw a very tall gaunt horse caught on the fence. In the moonlight it seemed to be nothing but hide and bones and eyes. It had jumped and now stood with its front legs over the wire and with the taut wire under its belly; and a more forlorn and helpless creature I had never seen. I rose and went over to it, intending to flog the ungainly beast off the place, but something in its eyes made me pause. It was a kind of sad resignation, a hopeless surrender, mixed with shame for having got into such a predicament. And instead of flogging the thief I patted its gaunt and ancient head and looked at its eyes. "You old fool," I said. "Don't you know enough to keep off a wire fence?" I went over and stirred the torn sacks of wheat and watched the beast's eyes, but it gave no sign. It did not even lift an ear or turn its eyes to watch me. Then I put a halter on it and cut the wires to get it off the fence and tied it to a post.

On the next morning the men walked around the drooping skeleton and wondered what should be done. There was no agreement among us. Joe Burt wanted to tie tin cans to its tail and set the dogs on it; Curt wanted to turpentine it; and Jack Brody wanted to put a girth around it, with sharp nails set to the flesh and turn it loose. And as they spoke, the men smote the beast or cuffed its ears, but it did not flinch. It seemed to be a dead horse, tied to a post. I persuaded the men to let me take it down the road and point its nose valleyward. "It's a good Christian practice," I said, "to give all pests to your neighbors."

And I took the creature a mile down the road and threw clubs at it and as far as I could see that horse, it was going patiently westward and out of sight. But on the next morning, there that beast was, stuffed and contented, before those bags of grain. Even my patience was gone now.

"I suppose," Curt said, "you wanta play with it some more."

"Let me fix him," said Jack Brody. "Put a spiked cinch around him and then give him all the water he'n drink. He'll move plenty fast."

"No, if we're going to do anything we'll kill it."

We talked of the matter and decided it would be best to kill it; and in this night, which was very dark, we got Jon Weeg's double-barreled shotgun and led the horse into a patch of timber. And now all of us, I observed, were very quiet and mysterious, as if we plotted some crime. Joe Burt laughed queerly a time or two but none of us said a word. Curt took the horse and we followed in single file. The old beast led easily, never drawing back or turning aside, as if he had spent all his years on the end of a rope. I think it was his dumb surrender to our wish, the almost eager way in which he went with us, that explains what happened later.

Because after Curt stopped in a dark recess of the woods none of us wanted to be the executioner. This in itself was rather unusual; for we had all slain animals before and none of us thought anything of twisting the head off a rooster or putting pups into a sack with stones and throwing them into water. This execution was different somehow, and I am still at a loss to explain the difference. I don't know why we hesitated as if there would be guilt on our souls. We seemed to share a common friendliness for this old vagabond that had outraged our fence and another's property. Or perhaps it was because Joe began to whimper and put his hands to his ears.

No matter: I am convinced now that none of us would have slain this animal if there had been a protest. If Curt had led him back to the yard, I imagine we would have set food and drink to the thief. But we had brought this horse out to murder and none of us would confess any weakness or any change of mind. We were men and we were doing a man's job. And when Curt said, "Who's got the gun?" we all stepped forward, as though eager to slay the beast; but we did not look at one another.

One of the men stepped forward with the gun and there was another pause. We were waiting for a volunteer.

"Well," said Curt, "who's to blow his head off?"

"It don't make any difference," Jack Brody said.

But Joe Burt, shaking from head to feet, put his hands to his ears and chattered:

"It's—it's a cinch I don't want to!"

This declaration made us hesitate again. Then Curt swore a mighty oath and said we were a fine bunch of men.

"What's the matter you guys? Give me that gun!"

We all stepped back and Curt loaded both barrels. He took the halter off and threw it at our feet and then dug into a pocket for his tobacco and bit off a huge quid. He tongued the tobacco for a moment and looked at us and then raised the gun to his shoulder. We all stepped farther back and Joe, with fingers thrust into his ears, began to babble.

"I can't see the sights!" Curt shouted. "Someone light a match."

"You don't have to see," said Jack. "Just put it against his head."

"Light a match!"

I struck a match and in its feeble light we saw the horse like a gaunt shadow, waiting patiently with his head drooping. The match sputtered and went out. I struck another. We could all see the gleaming barrel of the gun and Curt squinting along the sights. Then there was a thundering roar, the match went out, and we stood in overwhelming darkness. I struck another match and we saw the beast, standing there as if propped, with blood running down its face. I stepped forward quickly with the light and Curt fired the other barrel. The horse squealed and dropped to earth.

On our way back we said nothing. Curt went ahead, with gun smoking on his shoulder; and as before, we followed him in single file. After we had gone fifty yards I stopped and listened but could hear no sound. We took our several ways to bed and I lay sleepless for a long while, thinking of that dead beast out in the woods.

What happened later is very strange and a little incredible and I am not sure that I can make it clear. On the next morning we went to the yard and found that horse again within our fence, standing forlornly before the bags of wheat. Still, this is not exactly the way it happened. As a matter of fact, Joe Burt went out first and made the discovery. He came running to the house, pale and gibbering; and like a frenzied fellow he tried to tell us what he had seen. "He's been dreaming," we said; and we jested with him and did not believe his story at all.

"You're cracked," Curt said. "You big simple lubber, stop that shakun around!" And Joe babbled at us and his teeth chattered.

And when we did go out, still unconvinced, we saw that creature before the grain. We all stopped and looked at him and looked at one another. He had not torn any sacks or eaten any wheat. Blood from his skull had run down to the bags, suggesting that he had been here most of the night: and the upper part of his head seemed to be a mass of clotted blood. One eye had been shot out and one ear had been blown off.

It is of what happened next that I cannot be certain, because it all seemed strange to me then and it seems very strange to me now. None of us ate much breakfast and none of us said anything after our first amazement. I went to the timber to be sure that this was the horse we had shot. I found signs of a terrific struggle, as if it had taken the beast a long while to recover its legs; and I found the bloody trail back to the yard. I also found the halter which in our excitement we had forgotten.

On this day we did not work and for hours we did not talk. We sat in the yard, smoking cigarettes one after another; or looking with fresh astonishment at the horse; or with shame at the world around us. For it seemed to be a new world and we did not understand it. And all the while the animal stood there without moving, and apparently without pain, like a horrible apparition from the dead. More than his return, I think, was the way he stood that filled us with strange emotion. He had possessed the yard and the pile of grain in spite of all our opposition. He seemed to have a serene, an almost unearthly, unconcern about his victory; and he looked as if he would stand there forever, having by some privilege unknown to us claimed his heritage and his rights.

Harold Dow sat on the doorstep with his chin in his hands. It occurred to me, time and again while walking around, that the whole situation was more comic than tragic; but Dow would not look at me, nor would Curt or Jack, when I passed them. Curt, in fact, pretended to be very busy tinkering with machinery in the yard. Jack lay in the sun with his hands under his head. But it was Joe Burt who acted most queerly and who made us all feel queer. During the whole forenoon he hid behind the bags of wheat and peered at that horse, his big round face like a moon against the sky. The big lubber with his stricken eyes and gibbering tongue made us all feel disembodied and lost. I have wondered since if what took place later would have happened if Joe had not been with us. I don't know. I do know that something persistent and inexplicable was busy in our minds and hearts; a notion which slowly took hold of us; the same thought. And when at last I said, "Fellows, let's get busy," they all knew what I meant. They all rose and followed me as if we had talked of the matter and planned what to do; and we went to the horse and looked at it. For a long moment we did not speak, but I knew that every one of us was thinking the same thing. And it is this part of the experience that most baffles me. I've no idea why we wanted to save that creature's life; for it was worthless and homeless and a nuisance to everybody. But here we were, who had suggested one torture and another, who had tried to blow its head off, now resolved to save its life. It may be that our experience—the attempt to kill the beast and then fetch it back to health—became in some strange way symbolic: a struggle between ourselves and all the blind forces of life which we did not understand. Death was our enemy, too, and against it we matched all our cunning and all our skill. And the fight we made here was more than a fight on the Antelope Hills. It was infinitely more than that to every one of us.

For three days and three nights we labored to save that horse's life. Not one of us suggested that we should call a veterinarian: this was our fight, our small epic of cunning and devotion, and we did not want professional skill. If a doctor had come the matter would not have been the same at all. There would not have been those tremendous implications that made silent men of us and chastened our hearts and hands. And so we devoted ourselves to this struggle and everything else in our lives stood aside and waited. With a pile of empty sacks we made a bed and forced the horse to lie; and we put liniments and salves on the wound and bandaged it; and hunted in coves for tender grass. We took turns sitting up with the creature, as if it were a human being, as if our whole life and happiness depended on it. And in everything that we did we moved and felt in common and were driven by the same overwhelming desire. In these three days we achieved the deepest kinship that I have ever known to exist among men.

On my night with the horse I did not sleep at all. I sat by it and looked at the sick eye and wondered what else I could do to relieve the pain and bring healing blood to the wound. Early in the morning Jack called to me from the bunkhouse where the men slept.

"How is he?"

"Better, I think."

"Does he—seem to be in much pain?"

"No, he's resting easily."

And then Curt appeared. "You say he's all right?"

"Yes, I think so."

At break of day they all left the bunkhouse and came to the yard. They looked at the horse and patted his lean hide or studied the sick eye. Jack went away and returned with an armful of grass, though the beast had not in forty-eight hours eaten a mouthful; and Curt warmed a pail of water. The horse drank on this morning and we were sure it was better. We smiled at one another and said the horse would be well soon, and when we sat to breakfast we ate with a little of our former appetites.

But in spite of all our efforts the animal died on the fourth day. Joe Burt wept; and the eyes of the other men, I observed, were as misty as my own. We ate no breakfast on this morning. Upon all of us there fell a depressing sadness; a great loneliness that ached in our throats, as if everything good and beautiful had been taken from life. Out in the woods we searched for a spot to dig a grave; and Curt said, "Here," and upon the ground where we had shot the horse we dug a grave. We did not drag it to the grave, as is the custom, with a log-chain around its neck. We rolled it to some planks and hauled it to the grave; and over the unsightly skull we placed a box, so that nothing would strike the wound; and upon the carcass we let the earth fall gently. . . .

And then as one man we returned to the yard and tore the fence down.

WYOMING

★

Wine of Wyoming

ERNEST HEMINGWAY

It was a hot afternoon in Wyoming; the mountains were a long way away and you could see snow on their tops, but they made no shadow, and in the valley the grain-fields were yellow, the road was dusty with cars passing, and all the small wooden houses at the edge of town were baking in the sun. There was a tree made shade over Fontan's back porch and I sat there at a table and Madame Fontan brought up cold beer from the cellar. A motor-car turned off the main road and came up the side road, and stopped beside the house. Two men got out and came in through the gate. I put the bottles under the table. Madame Fontan stood up.

"Where's Sam?" one of the men asked at the screen door.

"He ain't here. He's at the mines."

"You got some beer?"

"No. Ain't got any beer. That's a last bottle. All gone."

"What's he drinking?"

"That's a last bottle. All gone."

"Go on, give us some beer. You know me."

"Ain't got any beer. That's a last bottle. All gone."

"Come on, let's go some place where we can get some real beer," one of them said, and they went out to the car. One of them walked unsteadily. The motor-car jerked in starting, whirled on the road, and went on and away.

"Put the beer on the table," Madame Fontan said. "What's the matter, yes, all right. What's the matter? Don't drink off the floor."

"I didn't know who they were," I said.

"They're drunk," she said. "That's what makes the trouble. Then they go somewhere else and say they got it here. Maybe they don't even remember." She spoke French, but it was only French occasionally, and there were many English words and some English constructions.

"Where's Fontan?"

"Il fait de la vendange. Oh, my God, il est crazy pour le vin."

"But you like the beer?"

"Oui, j'aime la bière, mais Fontan, il est crazy pour le vin."

She was a plump old woman with a lovely ruddy complexion and white hair. She was very clean and the house was very clean and neat. She came from Lens.

"Where did you eat?"

"At the hotel."

"Mangez ici. Il ne faut pas manger à l'hôtel ou au restaurant. Mangez ici!"

"I don't want to make you trouble. And besides they eat all right at the hotel."

"I never eat at the hotel. Maybe they eat all right there. Only once in my life I ate at a restaurant in America. You know what they gave me? They gave me pork that was raw!"

"Really?"

"I don't lie to you. It was pork that wasn't cooked! Et mon fils il est marié avec une américaine, et tout le temps il a mangé les *beans* en *can*."

"How long has he been married?"

"Oh, my God, I don't know. His wife weighs two hundred twenty-five pounds. She don't work. She don't cook. She gives him beans en can."

"What does she do?"

"All the time she reads. Rien que des books. Tout le temps elle stay in the bed and read books. Already she can't have another baby. She's too fat. There ain't any room."

"What's the matter with her?"

"She reads books all the time. He's a good boy. He works hard. He worked in the mines; now he works on a ranch. He never worked on a ranch before, and the man that owns the ranch said to Fontan that he never saw anybody work better on that ranch than that boy. Then he comes home and she feeds him nothing."

"Why doesn't he get a divorce?"

"He ain't got no money to get a divorce. Besides, il est *crazy* pour elle."

"Is she beautiful?"

"He thinks *so*. When he brought her home I thought I would die. He's such a good boy and works hard all the time and never run around or make any trouble. Then he goes away to work in the oil-fields and brings home this Indienne that weighs right then one hundred eighty-five pounds."

"Elle est Indienne?"

"She's Indian all right. My God, yes. All the time she says sonofabitsh goddam. She don't work."

"Where is she now?"

"Au show."

"Where's that?"

"Au show. Moving pictures. All she does is read and go to the show."

"Have you got any more beer?"

"My God, yes. Sure. You come and eat with us tonight."

"All right. What should I bring?"

"Don't bring anything. Nothing at all. Maybe Fontan will have some of the wine."

That night I had dinner at Fontan's. We ate in the dining-room and there was a clean tablecloth. We tried the new wine. It was very light and clear and good, and still tasted of the grapes. At the table there were Fontan and Madame and the little boy, André.

"What did you do today?" Fontan asked. He was an old man with small mine-tired body, a drooping gray mustache, and bright eyes, and was from the Centre near Saint-Etienne.

"I worked on my book."

"Were your books all right?" asked Madame.

"He means he writes a book like a writer. Un roman," Fontan explained.

"Pa, can I go to the show?" André asked.

"Sure," said Fontan. André turned to me.

"How old do you think I am? Do you think I look fourteen years old?" He was a thin little boy, but his face looked sixteen.

"Yes. You look fourteen."

"When I go to the show I crouch down like this and try to look small." His voice was very high and breaking. "If I give them a quarter they keep it all but if I give them only fifteen cents they let me in all right."

"I only give you fifteen cents, then," said Fontan.

"No. Give me the whole quarter. I'll get it changed on the way."

"Il faut revenir tout de suite après le show," Madame Fontan said.

"I come right back." André went out the door. The night was cooling outside. He left the door open and a cool breeze came in.

"Mangez!" said Madame Fontan. "You haven't eaten anything." I had eaten two helpings of chicken and French fried potatoes, three ears of sweet corn, some sliced cucumbers, and two helpings of salad.

"Perhaps he wants some kek," Fontan said.

"I should have gotten some kek for him," Madame Fontan said. "Mangez du fromage. Mangez du crimcheez. Vous n'avez rien mangé. I ought have gotten kek. Americans always eat kek."

"Mais j'ai rudement bien mangé."

"Mangez! Vous n'avez rien mangé. Eat it all. We don't save anything. Eat it all up."

"Eat some more salad," Fontan said.

"I'll get some more beer," Madame Fontan said. "If you work all day in a book-factory you get hungry."

"Elle ne comprend pas que vous êtes écrivain," Fontan said. He was a delicate old man who used the slang and knew the popular songs of his period of military service in the end of the 1890's. "He writes the books himself," he explained to Madame.

"You write the books yourself?" Madame asked.

"Sometimes."

"Oh!" she said. "Oh! You write them yourself. Oh! Well, you get hungry if you do that too. Mangez! Je vais chercher de la bière."

We heard her walking on the stairs to the cellar. Fontan smiled at me. He was very tolerant of people who had not his experience and worldly knowledge.

When André came home from the show we were still sitting in the kitchen and were talking about hunting.

"Labor *day* we all went to Clear Creek," Madame said. "Oh, my God, you ought to have been there all right. We all went in the truck. Tout le monde est allé dans le truck. Nous sommes partis le dimanche. C'est le truck de Charley."

"On a mangé, on a bu du vin, de la bière, et il y avait aussi un français qui a apporté de l'absinthe," Fontan said. "Un français de la Californie!"

"My God, nous avons chanté. There's a farmer comes to see what's the matter, and we give him something to drink, and he stayed with us awhile. There was some Italians come too, and they want to stay with us too. We sung a song about the Italians and they don't understand it. They didn't know we didn't want them, but we didn't have nothing to do with them, and after a while they went away."

"How many fish did you catch?"

"Très peu. We went to fish a little while, but then we came back to sing again. Nous avons chanté, vous savez."

"In the night," said Madame, "toutes les femmes dort dans le truck. Les hommes à côté du feu. In the night I hear Fontan come to get some more wine, and I tell him, Fontan, my God, leave some for tomorrow. Tomorrow they won' have anything to drink, and then they'll be sorry."

"Mais nous avons tout bu," Fontan said. "Et le lendemain il ne reste rien."

"What did you do?"

"Nous avons pêché sérieusement."

"Good trout, all right, too. My God, yes. All the same; half-pound one ounce."

"How big?"

"Half-pound one ounce. Just right to eat. All the same size; half-pound one ounce."

"How do you like America?" Fontan asked me.

"It's my country, you see. So I like it, because it's my country. Mais on ne mange pas très bien. D'antan, oui. Mais maintenant, no."

"No," said Madame. "On ne mange pas bien." She shook her head. "Et aussi, il y a trop de Polack. Quand j'étais petite ma mère m'a dit, 'vous mangez comme les Polacks.' Je n'ai jamais compris ce que c'est qu'un Polack. Mais maintenant en Amérique je comprends. Il y a trop de Polack. Et, my God, ils sont sales, les Polacks."

"It is fine for hunting and fishing," I said.

"Oui. Ça, c'est le meilleur. La chasse et la pêche," Fontan said. "Qu'est-ce que vous avez comme fusil?"

"A twelve-gauge pump."

"Il est bon, le pump," Fontan nodded his head.

"Je veux aller à la chasse moi-même," André said in his high, little boy's voice.

"Tu ne peux pas," Fontan said. He turned to me.

"Ils sont des sauvages, les boys, vous savez. Ils sont des sauvages. Ils veulent shooter les uns les autres."

"Je veux aller tout seul," André said, very shrill and excited.

"You can't go," Madame Fontan said. "You are too young."

"Je veux aller tout seul," André said shrilly. "Je veux shooter les rats d'eau."

"What are rats d'eau?" I asked.

"You don't know them? Sure you know them. What they call the muskrats."

André had brought the twenty-two-calibre rifle out from the cupboard and was holding it in his hands under the light.

"Ils sont des sauvages," Fontan explained. "Ils veulent shooter les uns les autres."

"Je veux aller tout seul," André shrilled. He looked desperately along the barrel of the gun. "Je veux shooter les rats d'eau. Je connais beaucoup de rats d'eau."

"Give me the gun," Fontan said. He explained again to me. "They're savages. They would shoot one another."

André held tight on to the gun.

"On peut looker. On ne fait pas de mal. On peut looker."

"Il est crazy pour le shooting," Madame Fontan said. "Mais il est trop jeune."

André put the twenty-two-calibre rifle back in the cupboard.

"When I'm bigger I'll shoot the muskrats and the jack-rabbits too," he said in English. "One time I went out with papa and he shot a jack-rabbit just a little bit and I shot it and hit it."

"C'est vrai," Fontan nodded. "Il a tué un jack."

"But he hit it first," André said. "I want to go all by myself and shoot all by myself. Next year I can do it." He went over in a corner and sat down to read a book. I had picked it up when we came into the kitchen to sit after supper. It was a library book—*Frank on a Gunboat.*

"Il aime les books," Madame Fontan said. "But it's better than to run around at night with the other boys and steal things."

"Books are all right," Fontan said. "Monsieur il fait les books."

"Yes, that's so, all right. But too many books are bad," Madame Fontan said. "Ici, c'est une maladie, les books. C'est comme les churches.

Ici il y a trop de churches. En France il y a seulement les catholiques et les protestants—et très peu de protestants. Mais ici rien que de churches. Quand j'étais venu ici je disais, oh, my God, what are all the churches?"

"C'est vrai," Fontan said. "Il y a trop de churches."

"The other day," Madame Fontan said, "there was a little French girl here with her mother, the cousin of Fontan, and she said to me, 'En Amérique il ne faut pas être catholique. It's not good to be catholique. The Americans don't like you to be catholique. It's like the dry law.' I said to her, 'What you going to be? Heh? It's better to be catholique if you're catholique.' But she said, 'No, it isn't any good to be catholique in America.' But I think it's better to be catholique if you are. Ce n'est pas bon de changer sa religion. My God, no."

"You go to the mass here?"

"No. I don't go in America, only sometimes in a long while. Mais je reste catholique. It's no good to change the religion."

"On dit que Schmidt est catholique," Fontan said.

"On dit, mais on ne sait jamais," Madame Fontan said. "I don't think Schmidt is catholique. There's not many catholique in America."

"We are catholique," I said.

"Sure, but you live in France," Madame Fontan said. "Je ne crois pas que Schmidt est catholique. Did he ever live in France?"

"Les Polacks sont catholiques," Fontan said.

"That's true," Madame Fontan said. "They go to church, then they fight with knives all the way home and kill each other all day Sunday. But they're not real catholiques. They're Polack catholiques."

"All catholiques are the same," Fontan said. "One catholique is like another."

"I don't believe Schmidt is catholique," Madame Fontan said, "That's awful funny if he's catholique. Moi, je ne crois pas."

"Il est catholique," I said.

"Schmidt is catholique," Madame Fontan mused. "I wouldn't have believed it. My God, il est catholique."

"Marie va chercher de la bière," Fontan said. "Monsieur a soif—moi aussi."

"Yes, all right," Madame Fontan said from the next room. She went downstairs and we heard the stairs creaking. André sat reading in the corner. Fontan and I sat at the table, and he poured the beer from the last bottle into our two glasses, leaving a little in the bottom.

"C'est un bon pays pour la chasse," Fontan said. "J'aime beaucoup shooter les canards."

"Mais il y a très bonne chasse aussi en France," I said.

"C'est vrai," Fontan said. "Nous avons beaucoup de gibier là-bas."

Madame Fontan came up the stairs with the beer bottles in her hands. "Il est catholique," she said. "My God, Schmidt est catholique."

"You think he'll be the President?" Fontan asked.

"No," I said.

The next afternoon I drove out to Fontan's, through the shade of the town, then along the dusty road, turning up the side road and leaving the car beside the fence. It was another hot day. Madame Fontan came to the back door. She looked like Mrs. Santa Claus, clean and rosy-faced and white-haired, and waddling when she walked.

"My God, hello," she said. "It's hot, my God." She went back into the house to get some beer. I sat on the back porch and looked through the screen and the leaves of the tree at the heat and, away off, the mountains. There were furrowed brown mountains, and above them three peaks and a glacier with snow that you could see through the trees. The snow looked very white and pure and unreal. Madame Fontan came out and put down the bottles on the table.

"What you see out there?"

"The snow."

"C'est joli, la neige."

"Have a glass, too."

"All right."

She sat down on a chair beside me. "Schmidt," she said. "If he's the President, you think we get the wine and beer all right?"

"Sure," I said. "Trust Schmidt."

"Already we paid seven hundred fifty-five dollars in fines when they arrested Fontan. Twice the police arrested us and once the governments. All the money we made all the time Fontan worked in the mines and I did washing. We paid it all. They put Fontan in jail. Il n'a jamais fait de mal à personne."

"He's a good man," I said. "It's a crime."

"We don't charge too much money. The wine one dollar a litre. The beer ten cents a bottle. We never sell the beer before it's good. Lots of places they sell the beer right away when they make it, and then it gives everybody a headache. What's the matter with that? They put Fontan in jail and they take seven hundred fifty-five dollars."

"It's wicked," I said. "Where is Fontan?"

"He stays with the wine. He has to watch it now to catch it just right," she smiled. She did not think about the money any more. "Vous savez, il est crazy pour le vin. Last night he brought a little bit home with him, what you drank, and a little bit of the new. The last new. It ain't ready yet, but he drank a little bit, and this morning he put a little bit in his coffee. Dans son café, vous savez! Il est crazy pour le vin! Il est comme ça. Son pays est comme ça. Where I live in the north they don't drink any wine. Everybody drinks beer. By where we lived there was a big brewery right near us. When I was a little girl I didn't like the smell of the hops in the carts. Nor in the fields. Je n'aime pas les houblons. No, my God, not a bit. The man that owns the brewery said to me and my sister to go to the brewery and drink the beer, and then we'd like the hops. That's true. Then we liked them all right. He had them give us the beer. We liked them all right then. But Fontan, il est crazy pour le vin. One time he killed a jack-rabbit and he wanted me to cook it with a sauce with wine, make a black sauce with wine and butter and mushrooms and onion and everything in it, for the jack. My God, I make the sauce all right, and he eat it all and said, 'La sauce est meilleure que le jack.' Dans son pays c'est comme ça. Il y a beaucoup de gibier et de vin. Moi, j'aime les pommes de terre, le saucisson, et la bière. C'est bon, la bière. C'est très bon pour la santé."

"It's good," I said. "It and wine too."

"You're like Fontan. But there was a thing here that I never saw. I don't think you've ever seen it either. There were Americans came here and they put whiskey in the beer."

"No," I said.

"Oui. My God, yes, that's true. Et aussi une femme qui a vomis sur la table!"

"Comment?"

"C'est vrai. Elle a vomis sur la table. Et après elle a vomis dans ses shoes. And afterward they come back and say they want to come again and have another party the next Saturday, and I say no, my God, no! When they came I locked the door."

"They're bad when they're drunk."

"In the winter-time when the boys go to the dance they come in the cars and wait outside and say to Fontan, 'Hey, Sam, sell us a bottle wine,' or they buy the beer, and then they take the moonshine out of their pockets in a bottle and pour it in the beer and drink it. My God, that's the first time I ever saw that in my life. They put whiskey in the beer. My God, I don't understand *that!*"

"They want to get sick, so they'll know they're drunk."

"One time a fellow comes here came to me and said he wanted me to cook them a big supper and they drink one two bottles of wine, and their girls come too, and then they go to the dance. All right, I said. So I made a big supper, and when they come already they drank a lot. Then they put whiskey in the wine. My God, yes. I said to Fontan, 'On va être malade!' 'Oui,' il dit. Then these girls were sick, nice girls too, all-right girls. They were sick right at the table. Fontan tried to take them by the arm and show them where they could be sick all right in the cabinet, but the fellows said no, they were all right right there at the table."

Fontan had come in. "When they come again I locked the door. 'No,' I said. 'Not for hundred fifty dollars.' My God, no."

"There is a word for such people when they do like that, in French," Fontan said. He stood looking very old and tired from the heat.

"What?"

"Cochon," he said delicately, hesitating to use such a strong word. "They were like the cochon. C'est un mot très fort," he apologized, "mais vomir sur la table—" he shook his head sadly.

"Cochons," I said. "That's what they are—cochons. Salauds."

The grossness of the words was distasteful to Fontan. He was glad to speak of something else.

"Il y a des gens très gentils, très sensibles, qui viennent aussi," he said. "There are officers from the fort. Very nice men. Good fellas. Everybody that was ever in France they want to come and drink wine. They like wine all right."

"There was one man," Madame Fontan said, "and his wife never lets him get out. So he tells her he's tired, and goes to bed, and when she goes to the show he comes straight down here, sometimes in his pyjamas just with a coat over them. 'Maria, some beer,' he says, 'for God's sake.' He sits in his pyjamas and drinks the beer, and then he goes up to the fort and gets back in bed before his wife comes home from the show."

"C'est un original," Fontan said, "mais vraiment gentil. He's a nice fella."

"My God, yes, nice fella all right," Madame Fontan said. "He's always in bed when his wife gets back from the show."

"I have to go away tomorrow," I said. "To the Crow Reservation. We go there for the opening of the prairie-chicken season."

"Yes? You come back here before you go away. You come back here all right?"

"Absolutely."

"Then the wine will be done," Fontan said. "We'll drink a bottle together."

"Three bottles," Madame Fontan said.

"I'll be back," I said.

"We count on you," Fontan said.

"Good night," I said.

We got in early in the afternoon from the shooting-trip. We had been up that morning since five o'clock. The day before we had had good shooting, but that morning we had not seen a prairie-chicken. Riding in the open car, we were very hot and we stopped to eat our lunch out of the sun, under a tree beside the road. The sun was high and the patch of shade was very small. We ate sandwiches and crackers with sandwich filling on them, and were thirsty and tired, and glad when we finally were out and on the main road back to town. We came up behind a prairie-dog town and stopped the car to shoot at the prairie-dogs with the pistol. We shot two, but then stopped, because the bullets that missed glanced off the rocks and the dirt, and sung off across the fields, and beyond the fields there were some trees along a watercourse, with a house, and we did not want to get in trouble from stray bullets going toward the house. So we drove on, and finally were on the road coming down-hill toward the outlying houses of the town. Across the plain we could see the mountains. They were blue that day, and the snow on the high mountains shone like glass. The summer was ending, but the new snow had not yet come to stay on the high mountains; there was only the old sun-melted snow and the ice, and from a long way away it shone very brightly.

We wanted something cool and some shade. We were sunburned and our lips blistered from the sun and alkali dust. We turned up the side road to Fontan's, stopped the car outside the house, and went in. It was cool inside the dining-room. Madame Fontan was alone.

"Only two bottles beer," she said. "It's all gone. The new is no good yet."

I gave her some birds. "That's good," she said. "All right. Thanks. That's good." She went out to put the birds away where it was cooler. When we finished the beer I stood up. "We have to go," I said.

"You come back tonight all right? Fontan he's going to have the wine."

"We'll come back before we go away."

"You go away?"

"Yes. We have to leave in the morning."

"That's too bad you go away. You come tonight. Fontan will have the wine. We'll make a fête before you go."

"We'll come before we go."

But that afternoon there were telegrams to send, the car to be gone over—a tire had been cut by a stone and needed vulcanizing—and, without the car, I walked into the town, doing things that had to be done before we could go. When it was supper-time I was too tired to go out. We did not want a foreign language. All we wanted was to go early to bed.

As I lay in bed before I went to sleep, with all the things of the summer piled around ready to be packed, the windows open and the air coming in cool from the mountains, I thought it was a shame not to have gone to Fontan's—but in a little while I was asleep. The next day we were busy all morning packing and ending the summer. We had lunch and were ready to start by two o'clock.

"We must go and say good-by to the Fontans," I said.

"Yes, we must."

"I'm afraid they expected us last night."

"I suppose we could have gone."

"I wish we'd gone."

We said good-by to the man at the desk at the hotel, and to Larry and our other friends in the town, and then drove out to Fontan's. Both Monsieur and Madame were there. They were glad to see us. Fontan looked old and tired.

"We thought you would come last night," Madame Fontan said. "Fontan had three bottles of wine. When you did not come he drank it all up."

"We can only stay a minute," I said. "We just came to say good-by.

We wanted to come last night. We intended to come, but we were too tired after the trip."

"Go get some wine," Fontan said.

"There is no wine. You drank it all up."

Fontan looked very upset.

"I'll go get some," he said. "I'll just be gone a few minutes. I drank it up last night. We had it for you."

"I knew you were tired. 'My God,' I said, 'they're too tired all right to come,'" Madame Fontan said. "Go get some wine, Fontan."

"I'll take you in the car," I said.

"All right," Fontan said. "That way we'll go faster."

We drove down the road in the motor-car and turned up a side road about a mile away.

"You'll like that wine," Fontan said. "It's come out well. You can drink it for supper tonight."

We stopped in front of a frame house. Fontan knocked on the door. There was no answer. We went around to the back. The back door was locked too. There were empty tin cans around the back door. We looked in the window. There was nobody inside. The kitchen was dirty and sloppy, but all the doors and windows were tight shut."

"That son of a bitch. Where is she gone out?" Fontan said. He was desperate.

"I know where I can get a key," he said. "You stay here." I watched him go down to the next house down the road, knock on the door, talk to the woman who came out, and finally come back. He had a key. We tried it on the front door and the back, but it wouldn't work.

"That son of a bitch," Fontan said. "She's gone away somewhere."

Looking through the window I could see where the wine was stored. Close to the window you could smell the inside of the house. It smelled sweet and sickish like an Indian house. Suddenly Fontan took a loose board and commenced digging at the earth beside the back door.

"I can get in," he said. "Son of a bitch, I can get in."

There was a man in the back yard of the next house doing something to one of the front wheels of an old Ford.

"You better not," I said. "That man will see you. He's watching."

Fontan straightened up. "We'll try the key once more," he said. We tried the key and it did not work. It turned half-way in either direction.

"We can't get in," I said. "We better go back."

"I'll dig up the back," Fontan offered.

"No, I wouldn't let you take the chance."

"I'll do it."

"No," I said. "That man would see. Then they would seize it."

We went out to the car and drove back to Fontan's, stopping on the way to leave the key. Fontan did not say anything but swear in English. He was incoherent and crushed. We went in the house.

"That son of a bitch!" he said. "We couldn't get the wine. My own wine that I made."

All the happiness went from Madame Fontan's face. Fontan sat down in a corner with his head in his hands.

"We must go," I said. "It doesn't make any difference about the wine. You drink to us when we're gone."

"Where did that crazy go?" Madame Fontan asked.

"I don't know," Fontan said. "I don't know where she go. Now you go away without any wine."

"That's all right," I said.

"That's no good," Madame Fontan said. She shook her head.

"We have to go," I said. "Good-by and good luck. Thank you for the fine times."

Fontan shook his head. He was disgraced. Madame Fontan looked sad.

"Don't feel bad about the wine," I said.

"He wanted you to drink his wine," Madame Fontan said. "You can come back next year?"

"No. Maybe the year after."

"You see?" Fontan said to her.

"Good-by," I said. "Don't think about the wine. Drink some for us when we're gone." Fontan shook his head. He did not smile. He knew when he was ruined.

"That son of a bitch," Fontan said to himself.

"Last night he had three bottles," Madame Fontan said to comfort him. He shook his head.

"Good-by," he said.

Madame Fontan had tears in her eyes.

"Good-by," she said. She felt badly for Fontan.

"Good-by," we said. We all felt very badly. They stood in the doorway and we got in, and I started the motor. We waved. They stood together sadly on the porch. Fontan looked very old, and Madame Fontan looked sad. She waved to us and Fontan went in the house. We turned up the road.

"They felt so badly. Fontan felt terribly."

"We ought to have gone last night."

"Yes, we ought to have."

We were through the town and out on the smooth road beyond, with the stubble of grain-fields on each side and the mountains off to the right. It looked like Spain, but it was Wyoming.

"I hope they have a lot of good luck."

"They won't," I said, "and Schmidt won't be President either."

The cement road stopped. The road was gravelled now and we left the plain and started up between two foot-hills; the road in a curve and commencing to climb. The soil of the hills was red, the sage grew in gray clumps, and as the road rose we could see across the hills and away across the plain of the valley to the mountains. They were farther away now and they looked more like Spain than ever. The road curved and climbed again, and ahead there were some grouse dusting in the road. They flew as we came toward them, their wings beating fast, then sailing in long slants, and lit on the hillside below.

"They are so big and lovely. They're bigger than European partridges."

"It's a fine country for la chasse, Fontan says."

"And when the chasse is gone?"

"They'll be dead then."

"The boy won't."

"There's nothing to prove he won't be," I said.

"We ought to have gone last night."

"Oh, yes," I said. "We ought to have gone."

UTAH

Ike and Us Moons

NAOMI SHUMWAY

Sometime away back in Seventeen and Seventy, on the trek outa Virginia into Kentucky, one of Ike's ancestors saved one of our'ns life at the cost of his own, and ever since then our kin and his'n has sorta stuck together. Only our kin was the kind what prospered and become a power in the community, while Ike's was a fiddling fishing lot what always squatted on a piece of our land and expected us to feed them. I never heared tell of any of us Moons minding either. Reckon they liked having a nest of losels on their homeplace, same as My Dad did. But the Great Rebellion blowed everything to hell. Them of both families what wasn't kilt during the war died fighting the niggers afterwards, till long about Eighteen and Seventy they wasn't anybuddy left sept Ike and My Dad. They woulda stuck it out, even then, but Ike was only eight and My Dad twenty-two, and everything was mortgaged for more than it was worth, so one night they struck a match to their homeplace and climbed in a covered wagon and headed west.

But near the first I can recollect is Ike telling me of Us Moons. His memory seemed to stretch clean back to creation. He talked of Jonathan Moon, my first known kin, whats name and farm was all writ up in the Doomsday book like as if they had gone fishing together. 'The Moons always took their living rough handed from the earth,' Ike said. 'No Moon ever lived in any godforsaken city, or any else place but where all the land they could see from their doorsteps belonged to them. They was never a trapsing lot. They clung to their homeplaces as long as they could in honor. None of them was ever knighted, on

From *A Story Anthology: 1931-1933,* edited by Whit Burnett and Martha Foley, copyright, 1933, by Whit Burnett and Martha Foley. The Vanguard Press, 1933. Used by permission of the author.

accounta they never went fighting of any wars. They knowed how it was between a man and his homeplace and they was never the ones to drive any man off'n his. Only Moons what ever took up arms was your grandpa and uncles during the Great Rebellion, and they had to on accounta the Yanks was marching agin their land.'

This would be of a night, and I'd be sitting on Ike's lap, if it was winter, afore the kitchen fireplace, but happen it was summer, we'd sit out on the front porch steps. When I'd get sleepy, Ike would shake my chin and wake me up, for it was fitting I heared what he'd say. The Kids would have snuck away to their beds long afore and Em would be redding up for the night and My Dad would be in his study reading outa a book, it not mattering, for the future of the Moons was in nobuddy's hands but mine.

'No Moons ever worked for other men.' Ike would give my chin an extra hard shake when he'd say this, so's there'd be no danger of my missing it. 'If they planted a tree, or drove a fence post into the ground, it was for themselves and their children's children and not for some other man and his'n. When your Dad and me first come to the Yellowstone over thirty years gone, we slept in a dugout and et nothing but jackrabbits and dough-gods, on accounta we wouldn't join no outfit what wasn't our'n. But look at Moon Manor now! Two thousand acres of the best alfalfa pasturage in the state and racing men from coast to coast coming up to buy our hosses. And here's you, Jonathan Moon, living in a house exactly like what your great-great grandpa built back in Kentucky. Plenty of folks what come to this country same time as your Dad and me are still living in the same soddies they built then, on accounta they was always willing to be working of the railroad, or of somebody better off'n themselves.'

'Leave that baby go to bed,' Em would come with my night things and command. 'Ten o'clock and him wide awake as an owl.'

'Go away, woman!' Ike would start undressing of me then, whether it was on the porch or in the kitchen. It always took him about an hour, so I jest sit still and let him work at me as he talked.

'Everybuddy heared tell of the Sussex Moons. Old Queen Bess herself sent men to learn of them. 'Twas Jeremy Moon what growed the first potatoes in all England and 'twas none less than Sir Francis Drake give him the seed. The Moons ever showed other people the way. 'Twas your great-great grandpa Godfrey Moon what first saw that the Blue Grass was made for hosses. While up here in the Yellowstone where every man turned his hand to cows, your Dad was smart enough to round up the mustangs off'n the range. That's how we got our start, trading ten wild hosses for one thoroughbred.'

Happening we were out on the porch, My Dad woulda been listening at his study window and he'd poke out his head and ask extra serious of Ike, 'Wasn't it Thomas Watt Moon what discovered steam and Eli Whitney Moon what invented the cotton gin?'

Soon as I growed a little more bigger I got on to My Dad's joshing and would try it on Ike myself. I'd tell him stories out of Arabian Nights, and Gulliver's Travels and ask if the Moons had ever heared tell or done such. They wasn't no tale I could tell but what he could tell a taller one about Us Moons. This would generally be at the supper table on accounta I liked an audience.

'Give over, Jonathan,' My Dad would say when he'd see Ike's imagination was near to split from stretching. 'What you mean doubting the abilities of your ancestors?' His voice would be stern like, but there'd be a great twinkle in his eyes. 'Jest you go on Ike and tell this young heathen about Christopher Columbus Moon what discovered America.'

Ike's woman, Em, was so awed by his tales of Us Moons, that she always treated me like as if I was a crown prince or some such. Afore Ike took her she had been the Linden's hired girl. Karl Linden had sent back to the old country for her on accounta he couldn't get enough work outa American girls. She was big and sleepy-eyed, with braids like well ropes wrapped around her head, and she was that strong that when I hid my face agin her big soft breast, I felt that nothing could touch me. Not even death.

Em come to live on Moon Manor after Ike and My Dad built the big white house, and afore she had been there a year the kids come. Folks about were that aggravated, on accounta they couldn't decide who the father was. But Ike didn't keep them long worrit. Soon as ever Doc Sessions said 'Twins,' he got drunk as a lord and jumped on a hoss and rode so far and so fast to tell everybuddy that his mare dropped dead beneath him. When he come home he brought Em a pair of pink satin slippers what was too little for her, but he didn't bring no parson. Even My Dad failed of making him marry her. 'I done made my promises to Em,' Ike said. 'Ain't no skyrider going to hear them. Some things is private.'

The twins was named Jonathan and David, same as My Dad and me. But it was too mixing to call them that, so on accounta one being born a half a head taller than the other and they always staying that way, they was called the Big Kid and the Little Kid. The Big Kid was exactly like Ike, full of reasons and that skinny that My Dad said he ate so much it made him thin to carry it around. While the Little Kid was more Em's kind, squat and sturdy and slow thinking. They was always clinging to some part of each other's anatomy like as if they was Siamese and couldn't come apart nohow.

After Ike took up with Em, he kept at My Dad's heels like a barking dog to get him to take a woman. 'If you don't get yourself a son what's to become of the Moons?' He worrit My Dad with asking: 'Who's my kids going to work for? You want Moon Manor to fall into strange hands after all we sweat and dug?'

My Dad would agree with him, but would never do no more about it than to sit of nights studying the picture in the back of his watch of the girl he'd left behind him back in the Blue Grass. So if Big Melody hadn't sent him to Congress I probably would never of been born, on accounta Washington was where my mother lived. My Dad wanted a mother for his son and she wanted a lover. They was never no peace between them and when My Dad's term of office expired, she was plumb glad to take the money what he give her and to let him take me off to my homeplace.

Nobuddy ever tolt me anything about her, but once I overheared My Dad say to Ike, 'I've had another letter from Kathy; she wants me to let her have the boy for the summer.'

'Tell her you'll see her in hell first,' Ike said awful mad. 'Don't she know Jonathan is the only Moon left 'cept you?'

'You can't have a child by a woman and then jest pick up and leave,' My Dad said. 'And that's pretty much what I did. Kathy's a fine girl, it makes me feel like a skunk to say no, but the life she would give Jonathan would be death to a Moon.'

It didn't bother Ike none that My Dad fetched me home without my mother. He was plumb glad not to have a woman person interfering with how he should bring me up. Us Kids' education was a great concern of Ike's. He taught us to read outa Huntly's 'History of the World,' the same outa what My Dad had taught him. We never got very far in books though, on accounta Ike never agreeing with them and spending most of the time showing us they was all wrong. My Dad was always threatening to send back east for a tutor, but Us Kids would beg him not, for how could any strange person know so well as Ike what we'd a need to know? 'More men what's lived been fools than's not,' Ike would say, when we come to an extra disagreeable page. 'So a man's got to be careful, or he'll be believing their nonsense. The Moons never set much store by books anyway, they being mostly writ for folks not smart enough to figure things out for themselves.'

Both Ike and Em put me afore their own kids, but there was one thing Ike wouldn't learn me no matter how I begged. 'Us Wheelers have always fiddled for you Moons,' he said, and would go on learning the Big Kid to fiddle while I sulked in the corner. They was nobody in our parts what could play the fiddle like Ike. Nights when he took a fiddling fit the tall sage brush along the river bank back of our house was all filled up with our Outfit what had snuck up from the Bunkhouse to listen, and happen a stranger passed on the road he said, 'Whoa!' to his team for a spell. His music was awful sad; even when it was happy it was sad, on accounta it made you feel that the happiness had been dearly paid for and might be soon going.

I could never properly decide what I liked best, Ike's fiddling or his singing. He was plumb chuck full of songs. Mostly sad, too. All about homesick cowboys and separated sweethearts and wronged women and such. But the sorrowfullest of all was about a boy what starved to death in the great Irish famine. I recollect that night My Dad had got in late from Sundance and was having a plate of beans at the kitchen table while Ike was singing this'n. When he got to the part, 'Give me three grains of corn, mother, only three grains of corn, 'twill keep the little life I have till the coming of the morn,' Em and Us Kids was all weeping like as if it was a hoss-selling day. 'Will these beans put you outa your misery?' My Dad said, and then threw a spoonful what landed plunk against Ike's bald head.

'You want your son to grow up a hard-hearted losel like yourself?' Ike asked, mad as a wet hen. 'Cause you got no feelings, you got no call to discourage them in your son.'

Them two was always argufying. My Dad wanted Moon Manor to be modern, but Ike hated machinery. He took a ax and chopped up the first mow what My Dad bought on accounta it cut off a jackrabbit's leg and I recollect well the first time he saw a car.

Him and Us Kids had all been berrying and when we come up outa the river bottom we saw that our hitching posts was all filled up with teams and ponies, and that our big corral fence was lined with neighbors. This often happened; folks heard of something and then come to hear what Ike thought about it. As we come up, Big Melody what was sitting long side of My Dad on the corral gate called out, 'Well, Parson, what's the sermon tonight?'

Big Melody always said this and it always made Ike mad, but this night he didn't answer back on accounta we all had saw the thing. We knowed what it was from the papers, but we was all comfluttered to see one standing right there by our corral like as if it had a right. A city man was sitting on the front seat. Ike walked up to him looking so mad that the City Man put up his fists. Ike turned to My Dad. 'You sit there on your goddamned monkey tail and laugh, with a thing like that on your homeplace,' Ike said. 'David, you're a disgrace to the Moons.'

'Drive it around the corral a couple of times, Mr. Kalkins,' My Dad said, laughing so he had to put his hands over his heart where the pain always come. 'Let Ike see how it goes.'

It made a noise like thunder in the Firehole Divide when it moved. Ike dropped the berry pails and lifted Us Kids up to My Dad outa harm's way. The hosses began to scream and kick and one team broke loose and ran with the buggy right out in our potato patch afore the thing stopped.

'It's a magic wonder the earth don't open right up and swallow such a blasphemous thing,' Ike marveled. 'It's worse than a train, 'cause it ain't got no tracks so's you can figure out where it'll go.'

''Twould save a hoss a lot of work,' My Dad said, winking at Big Melody.

'You could go sparking the Merry Widow in Greacewood and be back before Em missed you,' Big Melody said, knowing well that Ike never looked at any woman save Em and was always argufying with men what went outa their own homes for such.

Ike paid them no heed. 'I'd be mortal shamed to be seen in one riding cross-country with all the animals and birds fleeing for their lives.'

'They're a thousand times better than a hoss,' the City Man said, thinking that on accounta all the men was laughing at Ike they was not for him. 'They can do anything.'

'Can they rope a steer?' Ike said quick-like, and reached out and yanked the City Man outa the thing.

My Dad and Big Melody was laughing so they could scarce pull Ike off'n the City Man. 'Best take that thing and get,' Big Melody tolt the City Man, looking kind of sheepish on accounta he didn't want Ike to know he had asked the stranger out.

Folks always laughed at Ike, but they didn't often go against what he said. He sized up new comers and tolt what to expect of them and he'd only to look at a piece of land to know what best would grow there. So our country was pretty slow at buying cars. Long after the happening at the corral, car dealers would meet up with the question, 'Can they rope steers?'

Every Sunday during the summer, Ike would take Us Kids on a walk over the Moon Manor what would last the whole day through. 'You can't know your homeplace too well,' Ike would say as we cut off through the fields. 'For the land can't really be your'n till you've walked over every inch of it.'

'Twas at the end of one of these hikes that our first trouble come, so I recollect it well. We started out afore sunup, the dew wetting us to our knees and Ike bending beneath the grub poke and chewing on a stalk of alfalfa. Ike always chewed alfalfa. He said folks missed a lot by not having a hoss's appetite of it.

We left the fields at Saddle Ridge and from there we could see way off, beyond Big Melody's Ten Sleep, the far purple mountains of the Park. Ike pointed out the divide in the highlands, where he and My Dad first saw Moon Manor. 'We was glad to get outa the mountains,' he said. 'They be no ways fitting for a homeplace, for their canyons yawn like open graves and their heights is a torment to the pride of man.'

The sun was breath warm on the ridge and Ike stretched out on a sandbar to dry his shoes. The Kids gathered sand lilies and got their noses all yellow from the deep smells they took. I walked a spell higher. Below the purple alfalfa moved in the breeze and half choked me with its sweet stinging smell. The big white house and the corrals seemed as growed to the earth as the cottonwoods what shaded them. Frail colored mists hung over the river what was overfull with June meltings. Across it in the pale green stretches of pasture, the young hosses had set themselves agin the mornglome and from the earth I felt the heavy thud of their feet. The ridge showed me my homeplace, and a meadow lark put a tune to what I saw.

'Look good to you, Jonathan?' Ike come up and put his hand on my shoulder. 'Men worshipped the earth afore they growed blasphemous and invented God.' Ike pointed to the highway beyond the Manor what was dotted here and there with buggies. 'Whole Yellowstone is turning out to church, and in strange parts other men are doing the same. They will shut themselves up in a house with windows made of glass what they can't see outa, and they'll read outa a book what's all about some god what was always hurting poor folks just to show them how strong he was. Ain't no need trying to make sense of it.'

The Kids had got so far ahead in their lily hunt that we had to run to catch up with them. At the foot of the ridge we come on a thicket a buffalo berries, and we all broke off branches an' et from them as we walked. Afore noon we was come to Bitter Creek and the old soddy what Ike and My Dad had put up their first year in the Yellowstone. Ike lifted us each up to read the faint printing of 'Moon Manor' above the door, what My Dad had scratched on so long ago with a piece of red sandstone. 'Folks laughed,' Ike said. 'They said as how Moon Manor was a mighty high sounding name for such diggings, but they be laughing outa the other sides of their mouths now.'

There wasn't any windows and only one door, and inside the air was damp like a cave. Hundreds of little lives lived in the walls, and the spiders were that many that between one week and the next we had to break their webs between the table and the chairs. Ike built a smudge in the fireplace to scare out everything, and then we all went down to the creek and stript and went in.

The creek was too shallow for Ike to do much swimming, so he found himself in a clay bed, where the water was only a few inches deep, and laid down. After a spell I left the Kids yelling at magpies what was sitting in the cottonwoods mocking us and waded over and joined him. The clay was as soft and smooth as Em's bosom when she had on her black satin dress. I stretched myself as far as I could in it. The warm live water ebbing up between my armpits and legs and the little threads of moss what drifted agin my skin and clung made me conscious of my body. I was all flesh like a pig in a pasture ditch. I liked it.

Rinsing ourselves off, but not bothering with clothes yet, we went back to the soddy and made us a snack. We had roast apples and potatoes and broiled beef strips, and we et so much Ike said he could see our bellies swelling up like bloated cows. Food always set Ike to recollecting. He tolt us happenings of the Yellowstone what made us mad with jealousy at being born so late.

Our shadows was long like as if we had stilts when we started out. The Kids ran ahead and filled their pockets with isinglass until they come to the collie where the tall sage growed, and then they waited for us. I knowed why they waited. They was scairt.

'I was only a little tad no bigger than you, Jonathan,' Ike said, shouldering the tall sage brush aside so we could pass. 'I was down here hunting our milk cow when I runs on their camp. They was after the corral full of mustangs what your Dad had spent all summer wrangling, and knowing we was all alone felt safe to camp right on our land..In the morning while one of them woulda shot your Dad and me, the others woulda made off with the hosses.

'I knowed they was the famous Rabbit Rustlers as soon as I saw them. Folks called them that on accounta they never give a man they robbed a rabbit's chance afore they kilt him. I ran back and tolt your Dad, but all he could do was to clean his guns and wait for dark, help being so far it was outa the question. So soon as it was good and black we snuck out, leaving the lantern still burning as though we was all unknowing in the soddy. We made a wide circle of their camp and come up on them from behind. All four a them was sitting round their campfire swapping yarns. We was in ten yards of them afore your Dad started to shoot. He shot so fast that only one a them had time to draw his gun afore they was all dead.

'It took us all night to dig their grave, but as soon as we could we took their hosses and outfit into Sundance and turned them over to Big Melody who was sheriff then. Your Dad said he found the rustler's outfit running loose in the hills. Big Melody knowed he was lying and tried to get him to own up, on accounta he thought your Dad should have the five thousand dollar reward what the government offered for them dead or alive, but your Dad went right on saying he didn't know nothing about nothing and he'd jest found the hosses loose in the hills.'

We was all standing around the bare sunken spot where the tall sage wouldn't grow, while Ike talked. He fished in his jumper for his handkerchief and wiped the wet from his eyes, and his voice was all choky when he went on. 'Your Dad was never properly proud of this piece of work. Years after I'd heard him talking in his sleep about it, but he'd no call to let it hurt his happiness. Without the money what the mustangs fetched, he'd not been able to fence Moon Manor, and the squatters woulda took it away from him. A man's got a right to fight for his homeplace, and land what is held at the price of blood grows dearer to the heart. Any Moon woulda done what he done.'

Ike had always a hard time to leave that place and this day Us Kids had to pull him along. He was glum all the way over the hills and cross the river on the highway bridge till we come to the pastures and the hosses started whinnying to him. They come running from all parts, and crowded round him like as if he was one of them. Us Kids couldn't see him at all, but we heared the denim of his pockets rip as they nosed for sugar. Ike tolt us each to get on while they was crowded up agin the fence, and when we did he swung up on Hannibal, the best bid of the year, and we all started off barebacked across the pastures with the unmounted hosses tagging like dogs behind.

The hard pressure of the young mare's back between my legs and the wind whipping down my shirt front and cross my bare body made me feel more than a man. The sky seemed only a step from the earth, and I thought any moment I would rise to it, and I thought that the feel of the red-gold clouds must be even grander than the wind, and I thought that the sun teetering on the tip of Troll Peak was a ripe apple for me to pick as I passed.

The scairt howl of a dog what smelt death come to us 'cross the river from the house. Ike was off'n Hannibal as soon as it reached his ears and running for the bridge and shouting back for Us Kids to follow. We saw Doc Sessions' hoss in the corral and knowed that it meant My Dad. For years the Doc had been telling him to mind his heart, but My Dad always answered, 'To hell with it. If it can't beat strong enough for a man, then the sooner it stops the better.'

Em was at the door to hurry us up the stairs to My Dad's room. Doc Sessions was bending over the bed. 'There's life in him,' he said to Ike, 'but it won't be there long.'

'He was pitching hoss shoes with the Outfit down behind the bunkhouse,' Em said, rolling her apron into a ball. 'And all at onct he jest toppled over and they had to fetch him in.'

I pushed past the grownups so I could see My Dad. His eyes was shut, but his forehead and cheeks peering outa his heavy white hair and beard showed dark red and the quilt scarce moved with his breath.

'Come here, Jonathan.' Ike knelt by the bed and pulled me down with him, Em and the Kids stood behind us. There wasn't any place for the Doc, so he went to the door and turned his back. Snige started howling agin. 'That goddamned dog,' Ike said.

My Dad's eyes opened at Ike's voice and moved back and forth between us till they understood. Then a great twinkle come in them, like as always when he talked to Ike. 'Don't forget to look after the Moons,' he said, his body sort of straightening out.

We looked at My Dad for a long time. Then Ike got up and pulled the sheet over My Dad's face, and it seemed like as if he ought to have pulled something over the purple gray of the sky and over the hills and fields, what was growing more beautiful in the glome. None of us was like I had ever knowed us, but outside the watery roar of the Shoshone hadn't so much as quivered, and the hosses went right on playing in the pastures. It made me mad. Em come up and put her hand on my hair. 'Don't you feel bad, Jonathan,' she said. 'You'll see your Dad some day in a much better world than this'n.'

'Don't lie to him!' Ike grabbed me fiercely from Em. 'He shan't be comforted by lies! Jonathan, your Dad is dead. What's happened to all the people in other years has happened to him, and it will one day happen to you. He's dead and he'll stay that way, and them that says different ain't got the guts to say the truth. But he had a grand life and he'd no kick coming. Don' let me hear none outa you.'

'I ain't kicking,' I said. 'Only I don't want the sky to be so fine, I don't——'

'The earth can't change on accounta one man has died,' Ike said. 'Not even him,' and he held me close.

That night after they had dressed My Dad up in his Sunday suit, and carried him down to the parlor lounge to wait for the coffin what Big Melody and the Outfit was making out in the back yard, Ike took me in where My Dad was and closed the door. He lifted down the great scythe what hung above the fireplace, what had belonged to Roland Moon the Strong, and handed it to me. Then he went into My Dad's study and fetched the iron chestful of earth, what Peter Moon had brought outa Sussex two hundred and fifty years before. 'A scythe and a bit of earth,' Ike said. 'These be your inheritance from the Moons. They had gold and jewels like other men, but 'twas these they saw fit to hand down to their sons and their sons' sons. They be yours now, Jonathan. Mind you keep faith with them as honorably as your Dad.'

We buried My Dad up on Saddle Ridge, where he'd often said all the Moon Manor was to lie. There was no parson, no nothing, jest us and Big Melody. Ike took a pinch of earth from the iron chest and flung it into the open grave. 'You and me wouldn't be worth that,' he said, as he lifted me up in the buggy for going home.

Them two had always quarreled, My Dad laughing and Ike in tears, but now that My Dad was up on the Ridge, he belonged to the Moons; the very best best of the lot and Ike almost forgot the others in remembering him. Moon Manor ran on, jest like as if My Dad was still with us. No problem ever come up but what Ike couldn't recollect something My Dad had said what would solve it. We was almost getting happy again, the autumn earth not letting us be sad, and then she come.

Ike was fiddling for us in the kitchen so we never heared her car on the road, or her knock at the door. We jest looked up and saw her peering through the screen door at us. She wore a yellow dress and hat and with the night behind her, she looked like as if she had jest stepped outa the moon. 'I'm David's wife,' she said as Ike bid her come in.

She came and stood on our kitchen hearth and shook the dust from her clothes. Her big black eyes searched me outa behind Em's chair. 'So you are Jonathan,' she said, and come and pushed my hair outa my eyes. I felt her studying every inch of me. 'Thank God, you're a Coniston,' she said, meaning her own people.

'He ain't, he's a Moon!' Ike fair snatched me from her.

His madness didn't scare her a bit, she jest looked at him cool like and said, 'You are Ike, aren't you? I remember David talking about you. Why wasn't I notified of his death? I learned of it quite by chance. A friend of mine summered in the Park and wrote me of it, so I came at once for my son.'

'You ain't got no son what I know of,' Ike said holding me behind him. 'You sold him to David for money! I know, 'cause he tolt me so.'

'I was a very young girl then,' she said, and the angry red in her cheeks made her look like the lady on the Bank of Cheyenne calendar. 'I had made an unhappy marriage, I wanted to forget it, and I thought that by giving up my son I could live again as though nothing had ever happened. But I couldn't. David knew I couldn't. I wrote him time after time and begged him for my son.'

'What you aim to do now?' Ike said.

'Why, take my son,' she said. 'And give him the life that belongs to him.'

'Jonathan belongs to Moon Manor,' Ike said.

'I've had enough of ranchmen,' she said. 'I shan't have one for my son. Jonathan's education will be expensive. My lawyer will dispose of the ranch for me.'

'I'm pretty much alive,' Ike said, 'and afore you could do that I'd have to be dead. Moon Manor belongs to Jonathan and Jonathan belongs to it. Ain't nothing going to separate them! Never!'

'Now don't be foolish,' she said. 'You have no lawful right to him.

David never left a will. I found that out at the bank in Sundance: and we were never divorced. I'm the child's mother and no law court in the world would take him from me.'

'Damn the law,' Ike said. 'A man's got a right to fight for his home-place. Jonathan ain't big enough, but he's got me.'

'If you were capable of reason,' she said, 'I could talk to you.'

'An' if you was a man I could talk to you.' Ike let go of me and reached for his gun what hanged on the door, handy for hawks and coyotes. He didn't point it at her, but held it down at his side. 'You'd better go,' he said.

She looked at him and laughed and then turned to me like as if she never cared what he had in his hand. She took a handkerchief outa her bag what was softer than anything I ever felt, and wiped my face with it. 'I'm your mother,' she said, 'and God only knows what they've told you about me.' Then she tipped my chin up to kiss me, but I drawed back and went and sat on the milk bench with the Kids. I didn't like nobuddy what Ike didn't.

'You understand who she is, Jonathan? You understand what she wants?' Ike waited for me to nod my head afore he went on. 'Then tell her how it strikes you.'

'I shan't give him a chance to say something to his mother that he will be sorry for afterwards.' She took hold of my hand tight and drew me off'n the bench. 'You're coming with me now. I should never feel safe to leave you here with this man another night.'

'You got the law on your side. I ain't fool enough not to know that. And if I was a man what was feared of it, you could do all you say and I'd stand by and let you. Only I ain't!' Ike pointed the gun square at her now. 'But you ain't got no law with you here tonight. Take your hands off'n that boy and get!'

'You'd never dare,' she said and kept holt my hand. 'You'd hang for it.'

'Not if I turned it on myself afterwards,' Ike said.

'You'd never dare,' she said again, and took a step towards the door pulling me with her. 'If I didn't know how faithfully you'd worked for David all these years, I'd have you arrested as soon as I get to Sundance,' she said, getting braver on accounta he didn't answer her.

She had me almost to the door when the shot come, and when she fell she pulled me down with her. The blood spouted like a little spring from the bosom of her yellow dress. I snatched my hand away and stood up. I looked at Ike and was afraid to go to him, so I ran to where Em and the Kids crouched in the dining room doorway screaming. Ike turned to us and waved the gun like as if it was a whip. 'Go upstairs, you all! Go!' he said.

'Maybe she ain't dead,' Em said. 'Maybe Big Melody can help us.'

'I took you off'n Karl Linden because you was smart,' Ike said. 'Now take the Kids outa here. Quick!'

We was half way up the stairs when the second shot come, and we turned and ran back to the kitchen. Ike lay on the hearth rug, its bright colors growing brighter with his blood. Em sit on the floor and took his head in her lap, and the Kids tugged at his boots.

I walked to the screen door, past her body, and stood studying my homeplace. The northern lights was playing green and red across the pale stubbles of the alfalfa fields, and for half a minute I saw the mound of My Dad's grave up on Saddle Ridge. Then the lights moved on to the river, coloring it like the spreading red on the floor. 'Land what is held at the price of blood grows dearer to the heart,' Ike had once said, and I looked, and knowed he was right.

OKLAHOMA

The Happiest Man on Earth

ALBERT MALTZ

Jesse felt ready to weep. He had been sitting in the shanty waiting for Tom to appear, grateful for the chance to rest his injured foot, quietly, joyously anticipating the moment when Tom would say, "Why of course, Jesse, you can start whenever you're ready!"

For two weeks he had been pushing himself, from Kansas City, Missouri, to Tulsa, Oklahoma, through nights of rain and a week of scorching sun, without sleep or a decent meal, sustained by the vision of that one moment. And then Tom had come into the office. He had come in quickly, holding a sheaf of papers in his hand; he had glanced at Jesse only casually, it was true—but long enough. He had not known him. He had turned away. . . . And Tom Brackett was his brother-in-law.

Was it his clothes? Jesse knew he looked terrible. He had tried to spruce up at a drinking fountain in the park, but even that had gone badly; in his excitement he had cut himself shaving, an ugly gash down the side of his cheek. And nothing could get the red gumbo dust out of his suit even though he had slapped himself till both arms were worn out. . . . Or was it just that he *had* changed so much?

True, they hadn't seen each other for five years; but Tom looked five years older, that was all. He was still Tom. God! was *he* so different?

Brackett finished his telephone call. He leaned back in his swivel chair and glanced over at Jesse with small, clear blue eyes that were suspicious and unfriendly. He was a heavy, paunchy man of forty-five, auburn-haired, rather dour looking; his face was meaty, his features pronounced and forceful, his nose somewhat bulbous and reddish-hued

---

From *Harper's Magazine,* June, 1938. Used by permission of Maxim Lieber.

at the tip. He looked like a solid, decent, capable business man who was commander of his local branch of the American Legion—which he was. He surveyed Jesse with cold indifference, manifestly unwilling to spend time on him. Even the way he chewed his toothpick seemed contemptuous to Jesse.

"Yes?" Brackett said suddenly. "What do you want?" His voice was decent enough, Jesse admitted. He had expected it to be worse. He moved up to the wooden counter that partitioned the shanty. He thrust a hand nervously through his tangled hair.

"I guess you don't recognize me, Tom," he said falteringly, "I'm Jesse Fulton."

"Huh?" Brackett said. That was all.

"Yes, I am, and Ella sends you her love."

Brackett rose and walked over to the counter until they were face to face. He surveyed Fulton incredulously, trying to measure the resemblance to his brother-in-law as he remembered him. This man was tall, about thirty. That fitted! He had straight good features and a lank erect body. That was right too. But the face was too gaunt, the body too spiny under the baggy clothes for him to be sure. His brother-in-law had been a solid, strong young man with muscle and beef to him. It was like looking at a faded, badly taken photograph and trying to recognize the subject: the resemblance was there but the difference was tremendous. He searched the eyes. They at least seemed definitely familiar, gray, with a curiously shy but decent look in them. He had liked that about Fulton.

Jesse stood quiet. Inside he was seething. Brackett was like a man examining a piece of broken-down horse flesh; there was a look of pure pity in his eyes. It made Jesse furious. He knew he wasn't as far gone as all that.

"Yes, I believe you are," Brackett said finally, "but you sure have changed."

"By God, it's five years, ain't it?" Jesse said resentfully. "You only saw me a couple of times anyway." Then, to himself, with his lips locked together, in mingled vehemence and shame, What if I have changed? Don't everybody? I ain't no corpse.

"You was solid looking," Brackett continued softly, in the same tone of incredulous wonder. "You lost weight, I guess?"

Jesse kept silent. He needed Brackett too much to risk antagonizing him. But it was only by deliberate effort that he could keep from boiling over. The pause lengthened, became painful. Brackett flushed. "Jiminy Christmas, excuse me," he burst out in apology. He jerked the counter up. "Come in. Take a seat. Good God, boy"—he grasped Jesse's hand and shook it—"I *am* glad to see you; don't think anything else! You just looked so peaked."

"It's all right," Jesse murmured. He sat down, thrusting his hand through his curly, tangled hair.

"Why are you limping?"

"I stepped on a stone; it jagged a hole through my shoe." Jesse pulled his feet back under the chair. He was ashamed of his shoes. They had come from the Relief originally, and two weeks on the road had about finished them. All morning, with a kind of delicious, foolish solemnity, he had been vowing to himself that before anything else, before even a suit of clothes, he was going to buy himself a brand new strong pair of shoes.

Brackett kept his eyes off Jesse's feet. He knew what was bothering the boy and it filled his heart with pity. The whole thing was appalling. He had never seen anyone who looked more down and out. His sister had been writing to him every week, but she hadn't told him they were as badly off as this.

"Well now, listen," Brackett began, "tell me things. How's Ella?"

"Oh, she's pretty good," Jesse replied absently. He had a soft, pleasing, rather shy voice that went with his soft gray eyes. He was worrying over how to get started.

"And the kids?"

"Oh, they're fine. . . . Well, you know," Jesse added, becoming more attentive, "the young one has to wear a brace. He can't run around, you know. But he's smart. He draws pictures and he does things, you know."

"Yes," Brackett said. "That's good." He hesitated. There was a moment's silence. Jesse fidgeted in his chair. Now that the time had arrived, he felt awkward. Brackett leaned forward and put his hand on Jesse's knee. "Ella didn't tell me things were so bad for you, Jesse. I might have helped."

"Well, goodness," Jesse returned softly, "you been having your own troubles, ain't you?"

"Yes." Brackett leaned back. His ruddy face became mournful and darkly bitter. "You know I lost my hardware shop?"

"Well sure, of course," Jesse answered, surprised. "You wrote us. That's what I mean."

"I forgot," Brackett said. "I keep on being surprised over it myself. Not that it was worth much," he added bitterly. "It was running down hill for three years. I guess I just wanted it because it was mine." He laughed pointlessly, without mirth. "Well tell me about yourself," he asked. "What happened to the job you had?"

Jesse burst out abruptly, with agitation, "Let it wait, Tom, I got something on my mind."

"It ain't you and Ella?" Brackett interrupted anxiously.

"Why no!" Jesse sat back. "Why however did you come to think that? Why Ella and me—" he stopped, laughing. "Why, Tom, I'm just crazy about Ella. Why she's just wonderful. She's just my whole life, Tom."

"Excuse me. Forget it." Brackett chuckled uncomfortably, turned away. The naked intensity of the youth's burst of love had upset him. It made him wish savagely that he could do something for them. They were both too decent to have had it so hard. Ella was like this boy too, shy and a little soft.

"Tom, listen," Jesse said, "I come here on purpose." He thrust his hand through his hair. "I want you to help me."

"Damn it, boy," Brackett groaned. He had been expecting this. "I can't much. I only get thirty-five a week and I'm damn grateful for it."

"Sure, I know," Jesse emphasized excitedly. He was feeling once again the wild, delicious agitation that had possessed him in the early hours of the morning. "I know you can't help us with money! But we met a man who works for you! He was in our city! He said you could give me a job!"

"Who said?"

"Oh, why didn't you tell me?" Jesse burst out reproachfully. "Why as soon as I heard it I started out. For two weeks now I been pushing ahead like crazy."

Brackett groaned aloud. "You come walking from Kansas City in two weeks so I could give you a job?"

"Sure, Tom, of course. What else could I do?"

"God Almighty, there ain't no jobs, Jesse! It's a slack season. And you don't know this oil business. It's special. I got my Legion friends here but they couldn't do nothing now. Don't you think I'd ask for you as soon as there was a chance?"

Jesse felt stunned. The hope of the last two weeks seemed rolling up into a ball of agony in his stomach. Then, frantically, he cried, "But listen, this man said *you* could hire! He *told* me! He drives trucks for you! He said you *always* need men!"

"Oh! . . . You mean *my* department?" Brackett said in a low voice.

"*Yes,* Tom. That's it!"

"Oh, no, you don't want to work in my department," Brackett told him in the same low voice. "You don't know what it is."

"Yes, I do," Jesse insisted. "He told me all about it, Tom. You're a dispatcher, ain't you? You send the dynamite trucks out?"

"Who was the man, Jesse?"

"Everett, Everett, I think."

"Egbert? Man about my size?" Brackett asked slowly.

"Yes, Egbert. He wasn't a phony, was he?"

Brackett laughed. For the second time his laughter was curiously without mirth. "No, he wasn't a phony." Then, in a changed voice: "Jiminy, boy, you should have asked me before you trekked all the way down here."

"Oh, I didn't want to," Jesse explained with naïve cunning. "I knew you'd say 'no.' He told me it was risky work, Tom. But I don't care."

Brackett locked his fingers together. His solid, meaty face became very hard. "I'm going to say 'no' anyway, Jesse."

Jesse cried out. It had not occurred to him that Brackett would not agree. It had seemed as though reaching Tulsa were the only problem he had to face. "Oh, no," he begged, "you can't. Ain't there any jobs, Tom?"

"Sure, there's jobs. There's even Egbert's job if you want it."

"He's quit?"

"He's dead!"

"Oh!"

"On the job, Jesse. Last night if you want to know."

"Oh!" . . . Then, "I don't care!"

"Now you listen to me," Brackett said. "I'll tell you a few things that you should have asked before you started out. It ain't dynamite you drive. They don't use anything as safe as dynamite in drilling oil wells. They wish they could, but they can't. It's nitroglycerin! Soup!"

"But I know," Jesse told him reassuringly. "He advised me, Tom. You don't have to think I don't know."

"Shut up a minute," Brackett ordered angrily. "Listen! You just have to *look* at this soup, see? You just *cough* loud and it blows! You know how they transport it? In a can that's shaped like this, see, like a fan? That's to give room for compartments, because each compartment has to be lined with rubber. That's the only way you can even *think* of handling it."

"Listen, Tom—"

"Now wait a minute, Jesse. For God's sake just put your mind to this. I know you had your heart set on a job, but you've got to understand. This stuff goes only in special trucks! At night! They got to follow a special route! They can't go through any city! If they lay over, it's got to be in a special garage! Don't you see what that means? Don't that tell you how dangerous it is?"

"I'll drive careful," Jesse said. "I know how to handle a truck. I'll drive slow."

Brackett groaned. "Do you think Egbert didn't drive careful or know how to handle a truck?"

"Tom," Jesse said earnestly, "you can't scare me. I got my mind fixed on only one thing: Egbert said he was getting a dollar a mile. He was making five to six hundred dollars a month for half a month's work, he said. Can I get the same?"

"Sure, you can get the same," Brackett told him savagely. "A dollar a mile. It's easy. But why do you think the company has to pay so much? It's easy—until you run over a stone that your headlights didn't pick out, like Egbert did. Or get a blowout! Or get something in your eye, so the wheel twists and you jar the truck! Or any other God damn thing that nobody ever knows! We can't ask Egbert what happened to him. There's no truck to give any evidence. There's no corpse. There's nothing! Maybe tomorrow somebody'll find a piece of twisted steel way off in a cornfield. But we never find the driver. Not even a finger nail. All we know is that he don't come in on schedule. Then we wait for the police to call us. You know what happened last night? Something went wrong on the bridge. Maybe Egbert was nervous. Maybe he brushed the side with his fender. Only there's no bridge any more. No truck. No Egbert. Do you understand now? That's what you get for your God damn dollar a mile!"

There was a moment of silence. Jesse sat twisting his long thin hands. His mouth was sagging open, his face was agonized. Then he shut his eyes and spoke softly. "I don't care about that, Tom. You told me. Now you got to be good to me and give me the job."

Brackett slapped the palm of his hand down on his desk. "No!"

"Listen, Tom," Jesse said softly, "you just don't understand." He opened his eyes. They were filled with tears. They made Brackett turn away. "Just look at me, Tom. Don't that tell you enough? What did you think of me when you first saw me? You thought: 'Why don't that bum go away and stop panhandling?' Didn't you, Tom? Tom, I just can't live like this any more. I got to be able to walk down the street with my head up."

"You're crazy," Brackett muttered. "Every year there's one out of five drivers gets killed. That's the average. What's worth that?"

"Is my life worth anything now? We're just starving at home, Tom. They ain't put us back on relief yet."

"Then you should have told me," Brackett exclaimed harshly. "It's your own damn fault. A man has no right to have false pride when his family ain't eating. I'll borrow some money and we'll telegraph it to Ella. Then you go home and get back on relief."

"And then what?"

"And then wait, God damn it! You're no old man. You got no right to throw your life away. Sometime you'll get a job."

"No!" Jesse jumped up. "No. I believed that too. But I don't now," he cried passionately. "I ain't getting a job no more than you're getting your hardware store back. I lost my skill, Tom. Linotyping is skilled work. I'm rusty now. I've been six years on relief. The only work I've had is pick and shovel. When I got that job this spring I was supposed to be an A-1 man. But I wasn't. And they got new machines now. As soon as the slack started they let me out."

"So what?" Brackett said harshly. "Ain't there other jobs?"

"How do I know?" Jesse replied. "There ain't been one for six years. I'd even be afraid to take one now. It's been too hard waiting so many weeks to get back on relief."

"Well you got to have some courage," Brackett shouted. "You've got to keep up hope."

"I got all the courage you want," Jesse retorted vehemently, "but no, I ain't got no hope. The hope has dried up in me in six years' waiting. You're the only hope I got."

"You're crazy," Brackett muttered. "I won't do it. For God's sake think of Ella for a minute."

"Don't you *know* I'm thinking about her?" Jesse asked softly. He plucked at Brackett's sleeve. "That's what decided me, Tom." His voice became muted into a hushed, pained whisper. "The night Egbert was at our house I looked at Ella like I'd seen her for the first time. *She ain't pretty any more, Tom!"* Brackett jerked his head and moved away. Jesse followed him, taking a deep, sobbing breath. "Don't that tell you, Tom? Ella was like a little doll or something, you remember. I couldn't walk down the street without somebody turning to look at her. She ain't twenty-nine yet, Tom, and she ain't pretty no more."

Brackett sat down with his shoulders hunched up wearily. He gripped his hands together and sat leaning forward, staring at the floor.

Jesse stood over him, his gaunt face flushed with emotion, almost unpleasant in its look of pleading and bitter humility. "I ain't done right for Ella, Tom. Ella deserved better. This is the only chance I see in my whole life to do something for her. I've just been a failure."

"Don't talk nonsense," Brackett commented, without rancor. "You ain't a failure. No more than me. There's millions of men in the identical situation. It's just the depression, or the recession, or the God damn New Deal, or . . . !" He swore and lapsed into silence.

"Oh, no," Jesse corrected him, in a knowing, sorrowful tone, "those things maybe excuse other men. But not me. It was up to me to do better. This is my own fault!"

"Oh, beans!" Brackett said. "It's more sun spots than it's you!"

Jesse's face turned an unhealthy mottled red. It looked swollen. "Well, I don't care," he cried wildly. "I don't care! You got to give me this! I got to lift my head up. I went through one stretch of hell but I can't go through another. You want me to keep looking at my little boy's legs and tell myself if I had a job he wouldn't be like that? Every time he walks he says to me, 'I got soft bones from the rickets and you give it to me because you didn't feed me right.' Jesus Christ, Tom, you think I'm going to sit there and watch him like that another six years?"

Brackett leaped to his feet. "So what if you do?" he shouted. "You say you're thinking about Ella. How's she going to like it when you get killed?"

"Maybe I won't," Jesse pleaded. "I've got to have some luck sometime."

"That's what they all think," Brackett replied scornfully. "When you take this job your luck is a question mark. The only thing certain is that sooner or later you get killed."

"Okay then," Jesse shouted back. "Then I do! But meanwhile I got something, don't I? I can buy a pair of shoes. Look at me! I can buy a suit that don't say 'Relief' by the way it fits. I can smoke cigarettes. I can buy some candy for the kids. I can eat some myself. Yes, by God, I want to eat some candy. I want a glass of beer once a day. I want Ella dressed up. I want her to eat meat three times a week, four times maybe. I want to take my family to the movies."

Brackett sat down. "Oh, shut up," he said wearily.

"No," Jesse told him softly, passionately, "you can't get rid of me. Listen, Tom," he pleaded, "I got it all figured out. On six hundred a month look how much I can save! If I last only three months, look how much it is—a thousand dollars—more! And maybe I'll last longer. Maybe a couple years. I can fix Ella up for life!"

"You said it," Brackett interposed. "I suppose you think she'll enjoy living when you're on a job like that?"

"I got it all figured out," Jesse answered excitedly. "She don't know, see? I tell her I make only forty. You put the rest in a bank account for her, Tom."

"Oh, shut up," Brackett said. "You think you'll be happy? Every minute, waking and sleeping, you'll be wondering if to-morrow you'll be dead. And the worst days will be your days off, when you're not driving. They have to give you every other day free to get your nerve back. And you lay around the house eating your heart out. That's how happy you'll be."

Jesse laughed. "I'll be happy! Don't you worry, I'll be so happy, I'll be singing. Lord God, Tom, I'm going to feel *proud* of myself for the first time in seven years!"

"Oh, shut up, shut up," Brackett said.

The little shanty became silent. After a moment Jesse whispered: "You got to, Tom. You got to. You got to."

Again there was silence. Brackett raised both hands to his head, pressing the palms against his temples.

"Tom, Tom—" Jesse said.

Brackett sighed. "Oh God damn it," he said finally, "all right, I'll take you on, God help me." His voice was low, hoarse, infinitely weary. "If you're ready to drive to-night, you can drive to-night."

Jesse didn't answer. He couldn't. Brackett looked up. The tears were running down Jesse's face. He was swallowing and trying to speak, but only making an absurd, gasping noise.

"I'll send a wire to Ella," Brackett said in the same hoarse, weary voice. "I'll tell her you got a job, and you'll send her fare in a couple of days. You'll have some money then—that is, if you last the week out, you jackass!"

Jesse only nodded. His heart felt so close to bursting that he pressed both hands against it, as though to hold it locked within his breast.

"Come back here at six o'clock," Brackett said. "Here's some money. Eat a good meal."

"Thanks," Jesse whispered.

"Wait a minute," Brackett said. "Here's my address." He wrote it on a piece of paper. "Take any car going that way. Ask the conductor where to get off. Take a bath and get some sleep."

"Thanks," Jesse said. "Thanks, Tom."

"Oh, get out of here," Brackett said.

"Tom."

"What?"

"I just—" Jesse stopped. Brackett saw his face. The eyes were still glistening with tears, but the gaunt face was shining now, with a kind of fierce radiance.

Brackett turned away. "I'm busy," he said.

Jesse went out. The wet film blinded him but the whole world seemed to have turned golden. He limped slowly, with the blood pounding his temples and a wild, incommunicable joy in his heart. "I'm the happiest man in the world," he whispered to himself. "I'm the happiest man on the whole earth."

Brackett sat watching till finally Jesse turned the corner of the alley and disappeared. Then he hunched himself over, with his head in his hands. His heart was beating painfully, like something old and clogged. He listened to it as it beat. He sat in desperate tranquillity, gripping his head in his hands.

NEW MEXICO

Love Charm

OLIVER LAFARGE

In those days Governor Jaramillo at Santa Fe was trying to maintain friendship with the Jicarilla Apaches, because they were a bulwark against the Comanches in the east and the Navajo Apaches in the west, a counterbalance to the always restive Taos, and even the Mescalero Apaches down to the southward hesitated to raid in territory the Jicarillas defended. The Governor employed many of them as scouts and paid them well, besides subsidizing their chiefs, so Strong Walker's Son, as his name was then, took service with the troops. He acquired a mild fondness for liquor and a determination to earn enough to get a rifle if he couldn't steal one. His people called him Mexican Scout and then Buffalo Grass; the whites named him Jose Agapito. He was twenty years old, a big, lean, powerful man and a seasoned fighter when he went to work for Don Miguel Palacios, on the Palacios grant west of Jemez.

The Navajos had stolen ten of Don Miguel's best horses and Buffalo Grass was hired to bring them back. The money was good, but he was interested even more in the reputation to be acquired among his own people, for this was different from raiding white men or even fighting Comanches. Navajos are a kind of Apache; they know how to think, how to master themselves and war and the enemy in their minds. That makes them dangerous, whereas with even the best fighters who are not Apache, one has to do with men of weak thought.

He had to follow a hidden trail into enemy country after a man who was awake and watching, reaching out behind him after whomever might follow. Buffalo Grass traveled afoot, cautiously, thinking about not being seen and about the almost unreadable signs his enemy had left in windblown sand, the bent twigs of bushes, the quality on the surfaces of bald rock which warned him that his adversary and the unshod horses had passed that way. Far within his own country the Navajo relaxed his thought, and Buffalo Grass felt safe to overtake him. He lay in wait in a good place, having drawn himself in, the way a quail draws in its scent, so that it was almost impossible that he should be seen. The Navajo came by loping and singing. Buffalo Grass put an arrow in him neatly, his enemy never knew who did it, at his end was only defeat and astonishment. It was the perfection of warfare.

Then he had to get himself and his horses out of there. By the time he reached his own country, he was half starved and his brain was tired. He gave five horses to his brother to take care of for him and took five to Don Miguel, explaining that those were all he could recover. Don Miguel was satisfied and paid the full reward, with which at last he bought his rifle. Back at home, he remarked that he had been generous with the Mexican, so his name became Generous Man from that time on.

A year or so later he went to work for Juan Funes who had a ranch northeast of Abiquiu, not far from the Jicarilla country. Funes had a daughter Conchita, who seemed as immodest, fidgety and infantile as most other attractive white women, although Generous Man noticed some vague quality in her from the outset. He discovered shortly that she had a lover, which caused him no surprise; she looked as if she would and he paid little attention to her until the day of San Ysidro, patron of the ranch. That evening many people danced, there was singing and plenty of drinking. About halfway through the celebration Conchita and a young man danced alone.

Generous Man sat in the corner, where he could see and not be noticed and there allowed himself to relax. He had chosen a place pointedly far from a group of Pueblo Indians, fluent in Spanish, who were visiting the party. He enjoyed the music, but thought most of it too mournful, the dancing was amusing though indecent. Like any other Indian, he responded to those arts and was keenly aware of what they had to say. Now he was watching one of the finest dancers in New Mexico performing her best dance with a mediocre partner. Slowly he began to feel her power, it came out from her and filled the room, it was strong with a strength that was grotesquely sexual. Whatever might be the white men's foolishness, they also had their strength and in Conchita one part of it was summarized and carried to perfection. He had seen Mexicans in battle show a blind ability to upset reasonable fate and he appreciated that; now he saw something else which disturbed him profoundly, and at the same time heated his blood until with startling clarity he imagined possessing this woman and knew that his face was naked among strangers. He pulled his blanket up over his head and left the room quietly.

He sat in his hut by the corral feeling the night coldness, listening to the faint music; he must master this quality, he must conquer it in his mind or be unsure of himself. One could not be carried away by desire like that, that was the white man's way.

The next day when she passed him as she went to get water, he felt the same disturbance. He saddled up and went home without speaking to anyone, or collecting his money due him. It offended his pride to turn up empty-handed with no story, but he needed the shelter of his people.

There for a month he battled with Conchita until one day when he was stalking sheep, with his whole being concentrated on silence and invisibility, out of nothing he thought of her, the fire ran through him, he snapped a twig and lost his quarry. He made camp where he was and for four days struggled to drive this thing out of his system. He succeeded only in driving it in so deep that it was fundamental to all his thoughts and upon that basis he could again master himself. He went home, reflected long and faced the issue. There was only one thing to do, distasteful though it might be.

He returned to Juan Funes, said he had been called away by family matters and asked for work. Funes had mounted guard for a week after the Apache left, fearing a raid, but none had materialized and as this man was a good worker, he took him back. Indians are queer and Apaches queerest of all.

The whole family was astounded when he came in to supper that night. Instead of dirty shirt and old leggings, he wore the whitest and finest buckskin with gleaming quill decoration. His hair was freshly combed and braided, wrapped in otter fur, and with feathers at the top of each braid; his face was carefully painted. He was a splendid figure and even handsome.

Funes looked at his wife, she looked at Conchita who made a little face. One of the younger children giggled. Generous Man remained silent and grave throughout the meal. Afterward the parents talked it over. The idea of an Apache falling in love with one's daughter was so grotesque that the mind kept rejecting it, but it was inescapable. Conchita was indiscreet, they knew, but in this matter they felt full trust in her, the whole thing was so ridiculous. The Indian was a good worker; Funes, after a period of anger, became amused and decided to keep him on.

For four successive evenings Generous Man continued this manner of courtship, although each evening he found it more difficult. On the fourth after supper, he sat in front of the corral and began to play on the flute, then he heard laughter from the house door. He finished the tune, rose slowly and walked over to his hut. In the morning he told Funes that he would be gone for about eight days and rode back to his people.

With greatest reluctance, because he felt it to be shameful, he explained the situation to Stone Medicine Bead, his great-uncle. He was dominated, he no longer belonged to himself. He had tried everything; only by making the woman his could he regain mastery. Stone Medicine Bead listened gravely, smoking his pipe, and then questioned the young man closely about his thoughts and his efforts to free himself. Generous Man's sincerity was great, his need almost desperate. His great-uncle began to make medicine. It took four days during which Generous Man neither ate nor slept; at the end of it he was equipped within himself with the most powerful love charm a man could have, and he carried in a pouch the most powerful charm that could be given to a woman. He turned to the Funes ranch without fine raiment, but this time he brought his precious gun.

He arrived fairly late in the afternoon and turned to work that needed doing, just as though he had never been away. When he came in to supper in his ragged clothes, there was a faint stir among the family. He paid no attention to any of them; they disturbed him no longer, his thought was out over them, out over Conchita as it had covered the Navajo and his weapons. While food was being brought in, before they were all seated, his hand passed once across Conchita's coffee-cup. No one noticed that. Through supper he kept his eyes on vacancy; when they rose his passing glance took in the empty cup. Then he allowed himself to look at her briefly. She caught a puzzling expression of satisfaction in the moment their eyes met. After he had returned, her parents commented with amusement on the Indian's return to sanity. Conchita wondered.

Generous Man seemed to take no more notice of her; going and coming about the ranch he passed her by as though she were anyone—and yet it was not like that. Increasingly she felt that his attitude arose, not from having given her up, but from some strange assurance. Then one day she caught his eyes again looking her over with calm possessiveness. He did not look down or turn away, but went on considering her. Feeling angry and alarmed, she turned and hurried to the house and sat down inside to recover herself. What had come over the Indian? Now she was painfully aware of him whenever they were together; even just in passing, she felt that incomprehensible confidence and possession. Much as when she danced her personality had come home to him, so now she felt his force, something almost as though she would have had to obey, had he given her an order, and she could not get him out of her mind. She half hated him, avoided his presence and spoke to him only when necessary. Then she saw, or thought she saw, that he knew what she was doing and was pleased by it. She began to fear the man.

She was out in front of the house one afternoon when Generous Man came in with a string of horses. Since it was a very hot day, he had stripped to breechclout and moccasins when he went out on foot to find them. Now he rode bareback, a big sinewy man, his thighs hard as iron and corded with long lines of strength, ripples of lean muscle in his arms, sweaty and dusty, at ease on the lively pony, concentrated, strong in his face. He passed at a slight distance heading for the corral, then when the loose horses were in, he rode back to the house to speak to her father. She stepped inside and watched through the crack in the door.

As soon as he drew his rein, he looked right in at her, half smiled and turned his head to speak to Funes. She fled back to the small inner room, where she slept, and sat down on the bed. Of course he had seen her outside and seen her run in, Indians always do. It pleased him—worse, it was just what he expected. And she knew how every sinew on him looked, the color of his skin, the way he smelled of dry sweat and the dust caked on his face and chest. She knew frightfully just how very much he was a man. She hated him and she would kill him.

She went out for a walk as soon as the coast was clear, down through the cottonwoods, by the arroyo. When the trees hid the house, she became terrified lest he might be following her and ran back. But he was working with her father in the corral. She returned to the shade of the trees and sat down. That was the worst of all. He wasn't even doubtful enough to try. The dirty Apache, she'd kill him. She fingered her knife. She'd call him to her, in the dusk of an evening, stab and then scream. As she thought of it, she saw him clearly, smelt him, felt his strength and could not imagine his death.

Her lovers courted her with passion, humbly. Those to whom she surrendered were destroyed by victory. She owned them and abused them. This man frightened her, she wanted to see him crawl. He would be absurd then, she could—she must—laugh at him. Then she would see. She thought of him abject, and herself sure and scornful, her nostrils dilating as she imagined it, and her instinct depicted with a vivid flash his very feel and smell.

She came in late for supper and stormy, in a turmoil, hating the Indian. She paid no attention to him, but after they were done with the business of eating, she talked gaily and flashed her teeth. Then when she let her eyes pass over him, she felt a chill perhaps because he was just as ever; she seemed to make no dent in him, and yet he caught at her nerves and there was something in her which he made to bend and acknowledge his certainty.

She could not stand this, the savage must be taught and cured. Thus she explained and went on explaining, partly to herself and partly to the little shrine over her bed, while all the time there burned inside of her the knowledge of what this man's embrace would be like. She would not give in to him, of course, not for a moment, but she craved to feel him subject to her, she said. He would be a little bit like a mountain lion.

During the next day she observed him frankly. He did not seem surprised or embarrassed when she watched him. Neither that day nor the next could she bring herself to speak to him, but on the third she manages a *buenos dias,* and then found occasion to talk idly with him on nothing. He was so calm that she went back to the house in a fury, wondering if he were interested in her at all. But Indians were queer that way, she had heard. Behind the quietness of his face she half perceived a fire, but a fire that acted and controlled itself, an inhuman mastery; he would not stay so. The flame would leap out and consume him, and bow to her. She was frightened, as she imagined him broken loose and the little thrills again ran up and down her body. That night she hardly slept.

In the morning as she took clothes down to the arroyo to wash, she passed him. He answered her greeting and stood still, she stopped and faced him.

"I shall be under the cottonwoods tonight," he said. "By the gray rock."

Then he passed on. He appointed no hour, did not question her wish or convenience, he made himself inevitable. She was afraid, while she beat out the clothes at the water's edge, by the familiar, intimate stream and the home trees and rocks and sand. It was strange and she was afraid. All day she imagined him there, she saw his big shoulders and his head in darkness. Of course he picked that place. It was the only one, but he was so much bigger than the others, like a mountain. Fear and desire fluctuated.

He made no sign at supper. She caught his eye, but drew no help from it, only a terrific disturbance from the sense of his presence, a repetition of the certainty that he would be there.

The evening with her family dragged heavily; she was afraid of her parents and at the same time wanted to cling to them. She was not able to join in their talk. They all turned in early, but when they actually started to go to bed Conchita began to chatter, trying to delay them. At last she was in bed herself, in the darkness of her room, listening to her sister's snores, seeing the starlit, small square of the window, and the irregular, dark patch of the shrine on the opposite wall. Everything was quiet, her family as ever slept deep, and down under the cottonwoods that Apache was waiting.

It would be so simple not to go—would he then come here, would he kill her tomorrow, would this business just continue? So easy not to go —she could not imagine what might happen. She thought of herself going; she was dressed save for shoes and shawl, she would crawl through the window, follow the dark path to where there was no starlight under the cottonwoods. And then there would be that big man among the echoes of those other, lesser men's whispers. A thrill of passion rose under her fear; she told herself and the shrine that she would not give in to him, that she went only to teach him.

She slipped out of bed carefully. If only her sister would have stirred, if some member of her family might have waked, she could have stopped, but nothing prevented her. She put on her shoes, knife and shawl, then did each thing as she had foreseen it, save that the time was endless, her heart shook her and she could hardly catch her breath. In the first darkness of the cottonwoods she stopped, appalled. Why did he not come to meet her? Was he so certain? She turned back, stopped again, hesitated and went in under the trees. Now she could see.

He stood by the rock, seeming enormous, and silent. Now she would touch him and this control would end. He said something in Apache, then,

"Good. Come along."

He took her hand and led her a few steps to the edge of the trees; she stopped short as she saw two horses standing. Catching the rope of one, he drew it near and said,

"Mount. It is your horse. I have a blanket on the saddle."

She recognized her own pony, and in the other, one of her father's best horses. That was so utterly and typically Apache that it brought her partially to herself. She drew back with a little snort of revulsion. His hand took her elbow, the big fingers closed along her arm and pressing upward.

"Mount," he said. I am lost, she thought, I am lost. Fumblingly and with his hands urging her she obeyed him; unhelped she could never have lifted herself to the saddle. He wrapped the blanket around her carefully, picked up his rifle and swung to the back of the other horse. Then he took the lead rope—her pony had no bridle and started off.

The pony had other ideas. It laid back its ears and pulled, it even half reared. Conchita had a sudden spasm of wild hope, even as she knew it to be hopeless. Generous Man pulled the noose tight with a wrench and spoke softly. Wise in lariats and slip-knots, the animal gave in, quietly following the lead horse's fast walk. Conchita sat as though paralyzed, having no coherent thought, nothing that could be shaped in words, while they moved slowly into the gully, out the other end, past the clay butte and so onto the flats—achingly familiar places, turned hostile on this night.

Once well away from the ranch he jerked the ponies into a trot. Conchita had been sitting so limp that the new motion almost threw her, then she readjusted herself. The jerky gait and changed position restored her blood; now she began to think confusedly, with single words like ejaculations in her mind, and to comprehend the state and cause of her own terror. The big savage, erect and easy on his barebacked horse, rode silently ahead of her. She was his prisoner, she was an Apache slave. She did not need to tell herself what the phrase meant, it went back in earliest childhood's tales of fear, it was a knowledge of every frontier woman. You would hear it in the course of a narrative, by firelight, "The Apaches took her and made her a slave," and there would be a pause, women would say *pobrecita,* and *Maria Santisima,* pityingly. The Apaches, the Apaches—Apache slave. How could she ever have come near this man? But she never dreamed he would do this. Her life ran reasonably, up to that fatal moment of indecision on the edge of the cottonwoods; all that was she, and true. This could not be, but it was.

Far off to the right, perhaps a mile away, she saw a tiny point of light framed in a square. There must be a house there and people stirring. It was late, perhaps they were having a celebration or sickness or childbirth. She saw the bearded men and kindly women and the big fire, knew the homely voices and bustle and warmth and smell in that house, the guns on the wall and the hands hardy to use them. If she could call and be heard, if she could call. It was useless and she dared not try, though she drew in a half breath at the thought, and let it out again in a quavering sigh.

The Apache heard that small noise, and turned to look at her, saying, "A little more. Rest your hands on the pommel."

She had hardly been audible to herself but they can hear everything. With his back to her, riding, he was watching minutely.

A rise of ground hid the light and shortly they began to descend a wide canada. Generous Man stirred the horses to a lope. His voice had been kind. That was curious, they have no kindness. Then she remembered, as something long ago, that this man desired her and she had wanted him. Shortly, in his own good time, he was going to take her. The concept froze her vitals. As though Gallinas Peak in all its winter ruggedness of ice and snow and cliff leant down to seize her in abominable, frigid rape. How had she ever wanted this man, by what charm? This was no love such as human beings knew, but a ruthless inscrutable lust in which she would be crushed, as by slow, heavy rocks.

Inch by inch, like a mouse sneaking along a threshold, her right hand slid down along the pommel, under the blanket, and touched her knee. Her fingers felt along the outside of her leg at the edge of her skirt until they touched her knife, the little bone handle and the narrow sharp blade, scarcely a hand's breadth long. From it a faint warmth and courage stole up into her fingers, her hand, her arm, her heart. She drew it and with the same minute care brought hand and knife back to the high pommel. He was not altogether master. Herself or him—it did not matter.

Generous Man was thinking that white women are easily tired, and so he must stop soon and let her rest. Now that she no longer threatened him he did not wish to be hard on her. He postponed halting, because he was excited. Love-making must wait till later; a woman should be accustomed to a man, they said, no matter how powerful was the charm. He was thinking about this trail, still in enemy country, and also that he did not care if none of his people understood how precious his prize was. Later he could give his mind to that, not now, for it dissolved him inside. They were reaching a place where one could hide all day and she could sleep on good sand under some pinon trees. By midnight tomorrow they would be home.

He is going to do it now, she thought, *ay Maria Santisima, Madre de Dios,* strength. The Indian was on her left side. She put that hand on his shoulder and turned toward him. Her touch almost made him quake, although her hand was cold. She must be tired and perhaps frightened, needing his support. When he put his arm across her shoulders to steady her, he was surprised by the convulsive start she gave, and a sudden intensity of motion. Her right arm swung in a wide arc, desperately, while she drew in a quick, gasping breath. By a fighter's quick reflex he struck up her hand so that the sharp pain shot into his left shoulder. Astonished and bewildered, he released his instinctive reaction to an enemy, swinging to earth in one smooth, wide leap to stand with feet braced and ready rifle. Fear was war.

Her second thrust met only air, both horses shied, and she fell, landing on all fours. She began to rise, facing him with terrified courage, still clutching the knife. The white bone foresight was invisible against her white blouse, but above the muzzle of his rifle he saw her face, the lips drawn back almost into a square around her teeth.

The vivid splash of fire and deep boom were shocking, they seemed to rend the whole night. He had forgotten guns were so loud. He stood rigid, still staring along the barrel, while she sank down until she was flat and small and huddled on the sand. After some seconds he lowered the gun and stepped over to her, looking down.

Even now, as she lay dead, you could see her beauty. The mould of the flame of her life still shaped her. How was he ever to understand? He squatted there for a long time while high winds tore to and fro inside him, until the immediate crisis passed and he could act with the outward appearance of reason. His shoulder ached and blood was running freely down his chest. He put dust on the wound to cake it. Then he rose slowly and began to walk away. After he had gone a few yards, he looked at his rifle, lifted it, hesitated, and then threw it away with a sudden, violent gesture.

He went carefully, masking his tracks from enemies and from the dead, until he was a mile or more to the westward. Then he continued more rapidly. There was a place which he could reach before noon, known to very few, where there was water. A man could stay there many days without seeing anyone, and perhaps in long solitude, a lost man might find himself.

ARIZONA

Papago Kid

MARY AUSTIN

The first time I met him, said the engineer of Socorro Float, who told me this story, was on the trail called Jornada del Muerte, Journey of Death, which sure is well named. And that's an odd sort of coincidence when you come to think of it. Jornada del Muerte is the only passable trail from Sonora to the California Gulf, and in the whole two hundred miles there are only two certain places where a man can find water. I was about all in myself when I reached the Tinajas Altas, and found this Papago Kid, as we afterward called him, camping alongside of it.

He'd had a bad fall making the first stage of the journey, and all the water his cracked canteen would hold wouldn't have kept a gopher's tongue from going black between there and Yuma. But there he was with his grub-sack nearer empty than even yet I like to remember, but quite comfortable in his mind because he had begun to feel me come about the time I must have been sagging over Two Angels Dip twelve hours earlier. He said he had felt me there, and again at Cabeza de Torro, which is a way of talking I have noticed in men whose work keeps them loose in the open, as if they spread themselves with an odd kind of certainty over a great deal more territory than a man can actually cover with his five senses. But the Papago Kid . . .

No, he wasn't a Papago. Irish. Black Irish from New Jersey. I've no doubt he was descended from kings and his people at home had a banshee, but all that was left of his Irish inheritance was the touch of mysticism and the incurable youth that started everybody calling him 'Kid' as soon as they knew him. He told me his name once, but it

From *One-Smoke Stories* by Mary Austin. Published by Houghton, Mifflin. Used by permission.

is as 'the Kid' we always spoke of him. 'Papago' was added because of a kind of jealous infatuation he had for the country that is as lovely as a woman and has all a woman's trick of looking soft as a summer and being utterly ruthless. Also there was a girl over toward Comobabi—but that came afterward.

Naturally I took the Kid into Yuma with me and paid myself for it by lecturing him in a fatherly kind of way for roaming around reckless in a country that even buzzards abandon.

'One of these days, Kid,' I told him, 'you'll be lying down between water-holes and you won't get up again, and then what?'

'Oh, then, my soul will go marchin' on,' he flipped. 'I was on my way,' he said, 'to see the *palo verde* bloom around Tumummoc. I don't doubt I'd have made it.'

Somehow the country is like that; gets a grip on you that's stronger than anything living, stronger than death maybe . . .

Well . . . I left the Kid at Yuma waiting for a train to take him back to Tucson in time for the *palo verde*. He had a little money, he told me, that came to him regularly, but I never found that he used it for any purpose but taking him from place to place in a country too big for any man to get around in satisfactorily on his own feet. For the little that he needed to live on—and it was little enough—he would tie up for a job of work for a few weeks or months at some of the mines. That was how I ran into him again at Quijotoa where I was cleaning up a lot of old tailings. He stayed with me the whole of one fall and winter, and I'd have given him anything in reason to keep him on, for the Kid was the sort of company a man grows to hanker for when he is set down beside a hole in the ground years on end, a day and a half from anywhere in particular. He was better educated than the common run of mining men, and had read extensively the oddest, most unrelated things. He told me that he was quite alone, had been brought up by a maiden aunt who had died when he was about seventeen—it was from what she had left him that his remittance came—and that a year or two after her death a weakness of the lungs had developed. This had brought him to the West and the open, to Ashfork to be exact, and from there he had worked across between the Rio Grande and the Colorado, as far north as the Cañon de Chelly and south pretty much all over Sonora.

If you think that *you* have seen the West—I tell you it was the Kid's peep-show! For a matter of ten years nothing worth seeing went on in it, but waited until he had arrived from Mesa Verde or Indio or Chilchilicalli, for the curtain to go up.

I am a practical man, and an engineer. I deal with material things, and materials the most stubborn and irreducible, ores and raw metals and the solid matrix of the earth. But I ended by believing that the Kid had a special faculty for knowing what was, at any given moment, going on in any one of the places he loved.

'I'm feelin' the day at Oraibi,' he would say. 'The peach orchards at the foot of the third mesa will be bustin' out to bloom.' Or, 'You'll overlook my bein' late with the balance sheets, Mr. Strangworth, but there's a wind turnin' up the undersides of the sage beyond Tumummoc, white like the feet of a girl under green water.' It didn't in the least matter that it was three or five days to the place he'd been mooning about. And when the spell was on him to take the road, there was nothing would keep him. I know because I tried once, when I was fearfully shorthanded, holding back his wages on one excuse or another. He filled up his grub-sack from my stores one night, and the next morning all I found was a note saying where I could send his pay-check.

He visited me several times at Quijotoa, staying from three to five months at a time, and when I was managing the Silver Lead in the Santa Catalinas, he turned up again. It was there that he fell in with Red Morgan.

Red was plain hobo. Drink and a general distrust of all forms of industry had reduced him to a state in which he had lost control of his life to the chance of the hour. He would hire himself out to get money for drink—atrocious *aguardiente* the Greasers smuggled in to him—and drink until he was fired. Then he would drift on to the next mine or the next camp as the case might be, and begin all over. He was strong as an ox, and for that sort of man, sympathetic; and he had the remnants of an inherited refinement. I shouldn't wonder, indeed, if he had come from social strata a little above that of the Kid's, and had taken to bumming through being naturally deficient in the capacity for self-direction. At any rate, they struck up the sort of relationship that one finds occasionally between a boy and an ownerless pup. The Kid did about as he pleased with Morgan, and Morgan groveled and came back for more.

The Kid, who just naturally hated drunkenness the way the Irish do hate it when they don't take to it like ducks to water, used regularly to banish Red from his society when the drinking bouts would begin.

Then Morgan would weep in his cups and insist that between friends there should be complete personal autonomy. Finally he would discover that the Kid had taken the road without him and he would set out, half sober, his tongue literally hanging out with anxiety to find him and be taken on again.

I suspect that Morgan's abounding health and physical energy was one of the bonds between them. Probably he knew more of his friend's own weakness in that direction than the rest of us, for with all his bitter tirades against the Kid's misuse of him, I never heard Red complain of what we all knew to be the case, that he carried not only the primitive camp outfit, but often, in addition to his own, the Kid's blanket. Except to tell me that the infection which had driven him West in the first place, had been completely healed, the Kid never talked of his ailment. But it had left him practically with only one lung, and more than ordinarily sensitive to altitude sickness. Anyway, for one reason or another, this oddly assorted pair kept together for the better part of six years, dropping in on us when they were hard up, or occasionally, I like to believe, because the Kid really enjoyed a chin with me.

He had worked out quite a philosophy of life in his travels, but he grew more and more silent concerning the things he saw in them, so that it was really from Red Morgan that we heard about the girl at Comobabi. I don't know if the girl comes into this story. I don't really know. However, it's to find out the rights of the story that I'm telling it at all. Maybe when I am through you'll know.

Papagueria is a wonderful country . . . white bean country! It begins about the Gila River and the Rio Santa Cruz, and goes indefinitely south into Sonora. From San Xavier del Bac to Quitovaquita it is about a hundred and twenty miles in an air line. Up one side and down the other of the great edgewise ranges, it's farther than a well man can travel in a week. In between there are lovely valleys where the ground is yielding under foot, the foliage of the *palo verde* is delicate as a woman's hair, and the air is soft against the skin like veils. It is a blue country, blue and white, white cloud and white sand, with all the ranges melting into blueness, and the pale greens turning to blue in the shadows. There's bisnaga, that's barrel cactus, and great marching sahuaros and feathery mesquite with hundred-year-old twisted trunks. By the time you get past Robles Pass into one of those little villages where time goes by as still as the drift of foam on a wave, you don't wonder they called themselves the People of the Bean. I give you my word that the bean, with its broad quiet leaves, its white, scented blossoms above them, and its delicately inquiring tip, is a beautiful, a magical plant. There's corn there and melons, quail calling in the mesquite, and rest.

The girl was the daughter of the head man in one of their villages. He'd squatted on one of those little water-sinks like some old sheik on an oasis, and between his beans and a few head of stock he'd picked up, he was pretty well fixed for that country. The Kid used to drop in on him ever so often, and once they nursed him through one of his bad spells, so that it came perfectly natural, when the girl fell in love with him, for the old *capitán* to make an offer of her and her affection to the Papago Kid, at one of their big eats in the presence of all the company. By all accounts the Kid must have been horribly embarrassed, trying to get out of it and at the same time save the girl's feelings. I had Red Morgan's word for it that she was both pretty and good. Red was indignant with the Kid for not falling in with what he considered a particularly soft snap. As I said, Red knew more of his *compadre's* weakness than any of us, and I think he was tormented by the fear that the time would come, and that soon, when the Kid would need a good deal more than his income or than Red could earn, to make him comfortable. These lungers sometimes take a long time dying. But get out of marrying her the Kid did, with some kind of credit, owing to his being Irish and to the girl's not understanding white custom. He established himself as a kind of perpetual, official fiancé, who turned up regularly with presents and no end of ceremony.

I took the liberty of speaking to him about it once after Red had been indulging in one of his tirades. It seemed somehow a pity, seeing the lad wasn't long for this world, that he shouldn't have something of the common destiny—a home, you know, and kids . . . even brown ones. Those Papagos aren't a bad sort, and the little he could have left the girl when he went out would have made up to her. So I spoke to him one evening when the world had turned all holy, as it does sometimes about sundown, and we were sitting together with a pipe on the dump outside the Silver Lead.

The Kid sort of flushed up. 'It isn't because she's Papago,' he broke out; 'she's as white inside as anybody!'

'And it isn't because you're too good for her,' I put in; 'I'll lay my hat you were brought up a Catholic, and you could make it all right with Father Saladra.'

'Oh, I'd marry her, if I did anything,' he admitted. 'You see that streak of road out there?' he said, pointing where it went winding away between the hills as if it were in a hurry to get somewhere it never reached. 'Well, I'd naturally up and die if ever there came a time when I couldn't just take the road when it calls me. It's Death maybe that's been chasin' me all these years, but I know that I just got to keep goin'. And how would that do for a wife and kids?'

'You'd come back,' I told him.

'Not if I thought I had to. It's knowin' that I don't have to that keeps me goin' there regular. Gee!' he said, 'but I can't bear the thought of lyin' still, even in my grave.'

That was the last talk I ever had with him.

Along in the early winter Red slouched in looking for a job, soberer than I'd ever known him to be. He wouldn't tell me anything at first about the Kid except that he was in the lunger's hospital at Tucson, and by degrees he let out that it wouldn't have happened if the Kid hadn't been such a Quixotic fool about the girl. It seemed that the Kid, who had felt a bad spell coming on, had turned in at the oasis for a rest and a few weeks of regular meals. He'd a more than ordinarily handsome present for the girl in his pack, and according to Red he was more than ordinarily in the mood to settle down with her and behave in a fashion that Red never characterized by any word but 'regular.' They were pretty well spent by the time they got in, for the nights had suddenly turned cold and they had traveled all the last day in one of those blinding storms of dust that rise about the beginning of the rains. The Kid was coughing steadily in the dust, and saying more than Red had known him to say before, of how good it would be to get between the clean dark walls of a *jacal* to rest. All the time, as if he had a kind of sense of its being necessary to get there somehow in spite of everything, he kept on beating his way through the wall of dust when he ought to have been lying under a mesquite asleep. They dropped the wind behind them in the night, and about mid-morning, as they sighted the smoke of the *jacal* between the little oaks, they heard the *tombes* going, and one of those four-stringed Yaqui harps.

You see the girl's old man had got tired of this ceremonious engagement that never came to anything. He wanted a regular son-in-law, and what Red and the Kid had stumbled on was the infare of the girl's marriage to a regular husband which had taken place the night before.

The present came in handily, but I take it the groom was none too well pleased or the girl too much so. Red and the Kid slept under a

folded handkerchief, or, if he preferred to take the month he had been given in which to make his decision, all he had to do was write to the unpronounceable address on the same page of the same notebook, and he was a dean, not at Harvard, true, but at twice the salary Harvard had been and would be paying him. That was all there was to it, but, as he got out of the car and closed the door without slamming it because the hinge was loose, Crossett knew he was kidding himself. There was a hell of a lot more to it. There was what Crossett called his trouble.

He crossed the square and went into the Pershing Building through the back entrance. The guard in the swivel chair near the revolving door looked up from his copy of the *Times-Herald,* recognized Crossett, and nodded. Crossett nodded back, and walked down the black and gray marble hallway to the elevator, and punched the gold button. The elevator came and the handsome, stout Negro woman, in the neat blue uniform with PB embroidered in silver over her left pocket, smiled and pressed the number five button without waiting for Crossett to call his floor. She smiled again when he got out on the fifth floor, and Crossett knew there wouldn't be anything like this in Ohio, dean or no dean.

"You're late," Miss Gough said as he walked into his office. "They started at two-thirty sharp, when Captain Iverson arrived."

"They'll wait," Crossett said, crossing to the door of his own room. "I got stuck."

Miss Gough shook her head at him with a half smile, as though he were a little boy, and it occurred to Crossett that one of the advantages of Ohio would be that there would be no Miss Gough. He closed the door behind him and went into his private washroom. There were only three offices with private washrooms on the fifth floor of the Pershing Building and, as he dried his hands on the small towel with the initials PB stamped in blue in one corner, it seemed to Crossett that here was his trouble in a nutshell: Miss Gough and the private washroom.

If he had not insisted on a room with an outside window before he came down from Harvard in 1941, he would not have drawn one of the three private washrooms, they would have thought of him as just another professor and, after the shooting war was over, they would have let him go quietly, the way they were letting other professors go. Instead, they had looked around, noticed the private washroom, decided anyone who rated one of them was obviously too important to be let go, and he had been saddled with reconversion. Anybody who knew the score knew that the shooting war had been a picnic by comparison with the mess of reconversion, and Crossett knew the score.

If he had not insisted on a secretary who didn't chew gum, he might have drawn any one of the hundreds of nice little girls, from Arkansas or New Hampshire or Kentucky, who wagged their jaws while they typed and pasted picture postcards from vacationing friends on the wall over their desks and let their bosses alone. But Crossett had insisted on a non-gum chewer and he had drawn Miss Gough, who had gone to Smith and spelled beautifully and wore tailored suits and was so damned efficient and devoted to her job that she would cut her own lunch hour, and hang on to a phone for ten minutes, while he was paged at the Hay-Adams, to remind him that he was due at a two-thirty meeting of the Planning Committee. A man with a desk in one of the crowded offices down the hall and a girl with nothing more on her mind than tomorrow's blind date could pack up when the shooting war was over and go back to whatever he had been doing before Pearl Harbor or take an attractive, better offer. A man with a private washroom and Miss Gough had a conscience. Crossett rinsed his mouth and he was drinking a glass of water when Miss Gough came in.

"They just called from the Conference Room to ask if you were back," she said. "I's two-forty, Mr. Crossett. Is that cold enough? I could get you a glass from the cooler?"

"No, this is all right," Crossett said. It wasn't cold enough but all at once, with the alcohol dying inside him, he was so sick of Washington and the war effort and reconversion and Miss Gough's bright devotion, that he could scarcely swallow. Why couldn't they let him alone? He had done his job. Four years were enough. Why couldn't they get along with the bright young men, with this Captain Iverson and his prize-winning plans and the scores of others like him? Crossett put the glass down on the edge of the black marble basin, came out into the office, and kicked the washroom door shut. "What's on the agenda?" he said.

"Final approval of the master memorandum for the President," Miss Gough said. "And the preamble you wrote. That's all."

"All right, I'll go in now," Crossett said. "Oh, say, look. The left front door of my car is going to fall off any minute unless I do something about that hinge. Do you think you could?"

"Why didn't you tell me?" Miss Gough said. "Of course I can. I know the man at the filling station on Wisconsin and Q. He'll do anything for me. You go on ahead to the meeting, Mr. Crossett. I'll call him right away."

"Thanks," Crossett said and went out, wishing he hadn't asked her, yet knowing it was the only way the car would ever be fixed. He went down the hall to the conference room and turned the knob quietly, but not quietly enough. The Director was at the head of the long table, reading from the thick memorandum, and he stopped to look across his glasses at the door. He smiled at Crossett and nodded and waited while Crossett came into the room and closed the door. Crossett started for his usual chair, halfway down the table, facing the window, and then he saw that it was occupied by a man in uniform. Crossett went around the table, to the other side, and he slipped into the vacant chair facing his regular seat, his back to the window. The Director resumed reading and Crossett looked around.

All the deputies were there, as well as the liaison boys from FEA and WPB and WMC, and Crossett remembered, now that he was here, how important the meeting was and how much he had wanted to be on time. His head ached slightly and his mouth felt furry, the way it always did in the afternoon if he drank at lunch, and now he really regretted that second martini. His glance came down the long table and stopped on the man in uniform, the man in Crossett's chair, and Crossett sat up straighter.

The man had two silver bars on his shoulder, and his face was dark and thin, and there was a narrow, black, very new mustache, so narrow and so new that it looked as though it had been drawn on with an eyebrow pencil, running in a straight line across the middle of the wide space between his nose and his upper lip. Crossett knew very little about medicine but he was willing to bet, from the shape of the young man's head, that Captain Iverson had suffered from rickets or some other disease of malnutrition when he was a boy. Crossett turned and looked out the window, down the long double line of cars parked along the grassy island, to the public parking lot at the end, and there it was, the shiny pale blue Oldsmobile, the 1941 or 1942 model. It was parked arrogantly, facing Seventh Street, taking up more room than one car was entitled to, but ready for getting away without turning. Crossett swung back and looked at Captain Iverson with interest.

A month before, Iverson had won the fifteen-thousand-dollar first prize in a national contest, sponsored by a breakfast food company, for the best manuscript plan on the problems of the postwar world. The newspapers, in which his picture had appeared in the news columns as well as in full-page advertisements paid for by the breakfast food company, had said he was twenty-seven years old. He looked older, though, with his gaunt face and his thick black hair falling forward over his eyes. Crossett wondered how he had found the time, while on active duty, to prepare a book-length manuscript on such a subject. Crossett examined Captain Iverson's uniform. There were no campaign or area ribbons over his left pocket and, on the shoulder of his left sleeve, he wore the red, white, and blue patch of the Service Forces. That, Crossett said to himself, explained that. After four years in the nation's capital, much of that time spent at meetings in the Pentagon and Navy buildings, it was Crossett's belief that, if Tolstoy had served at a desk in the Service Forces in Washington, he could have written *War and Peace* without turning down a single cocktail invitation.

Crossett had not read the prize-winning plan, nobody but the contest judges had read it yet because the rumor around town in agency circles was that no trade publisher was interested, but the Director of Crossett's outfit had been impressed by the newspaper accounts, and he had asked the army to allow Captain Iverson to sit in on the meetings of the agency's Planning Committee. This was Captain Iverson's first visit, and it looked as though he was not impressed, but Crossett had seen too many men look like that at too many meetings to feel that his appearance was conclusive. The young captain sat slouched down in Crossett's chair, his thin little body hunched over, his lips twisted in what might not have been a contemptuous sneer, his eyes half closed, and his nervous fingers played with a beautiful gold fountain pen, obviously purchased quite recently, like the pale blue 1941 or 1942 Oldsmobile, out of the prize money.

"We've all read copies of the memorandum itself prior to this meeting," the Director said. "And before you arrived, we found that we're all in substantial agreement on the main points, so there's not much to be gained by rehashing the document itself here." Crossett realized with a start that the Director was talking to him, and he swung his glance down the table. "The plan itself, then, with all our main recommendations, goes to the President's desk as is. Is that correct, gentlemen?" Everybody nodded and Crossett noticed that the Director's glance remained on Captain Iverson. Everybody, including Crossett, turned and looked at the young man. He pursed his lips and, after a pause that seemed to Crossett just a little too long even for a much older man, Captain Iverson nodded grudgingly, without straightening in the chair. "Very well," the Director said. "The only thing about which there seems to be some disagreement, then, is the preamble you wrote, Crossett."

"The preamble?" Crossett said. "Why?"

"The point has been raised that it is, well—" The Director hesitated. "That it is needlessly belligerent, shall we say," the Director said. "I don't say that I agree with the objection, Crossett, but it has been raised, and I think we ought to get it settled at this meeting. The memorandum must go to the printer tomorrow."

"Would you read it aloud, sir?" Crossett said.

"I just did," the Director said. "Weren't you listening?"

"It didn't sound belligerent when I wrote it," Crossett said, evading the question. "I didn't intend it to be belligerent. I don't know what that word means in this connection. I'd like to hear it read again and see where there's anything in it that anybody can object to."

The Director cleared his throat and started to read again. He didn't read particularly well, but it seemed to Crossett that you couldn't read that sort of thing badly. Half of it was direct quotation from Roosevelt's speeches. The rest was practically a restatement of President Truman's affirmation, in his first address to Congress, of his administration's objectives. The artless words and phrases, about education, work for all, a decent standard of living, came through the Director's bad reading voice with all the old simplicity and power. The Director finished and looked up. Crossett looked around the table. Nobody met his glance. He turned back to the Director. Their eyes met and then the Director looked away quickly. He cleared his throat.

"Captain Iverson?" the Director said.

"It's pointless," Captain Iverson said, talking to his gold fountain pen. "I think it will do more harm than good."

"Why?" Crossett said, leaning forward slightly, talking directly across the table at the younger man. "How can it do harm?"

"The President presents it to Congress," Captain Iverson said, still addressing the gorgeous fountain pen. "They're fed up with that Utopia stuff. It'll get their backs up."

"I don't think it's our job to worry about the backs of Congress," Crossett said. "Those few paragraphs, that's what this agency was created for. That's the whole point of the document itself. Let's do our job, and let's let the President worry about getting it through Congress."

"It's not practical," Captain Iverson said. "It's like looking for a neat Mexican. There ain't no such animal." Half the people around the table laughed, and Captain Iverson's eyelids lifted for a moment as his lips and his mustache twisted a little more to the left in what was apparently a modest smile. "I say nuts to the high-flown words and the fancy preambles," he said, his attention fixed once more on the gold fountain pen. "There's too much of that around. Let's show the President and Congress that we're not a bunch of long-haired dreamers," Captain Iverson said. "Let's show them we're as good businessmen as they are," he said. "That way we don't get their backs up, and we've got a chance to really sell a program."

Crossett opened his mouth, but the words wouldn't come, and he closed his lips without speaking. It was just as well. They would have been the wrong words. He leaned back in the chair, which was exactly like the chair in which he always sat at these meetings, but this one didn't feel comfortable or right because his back was to the window and he couldn't see the Potomac, and he realized that it wasn't the martinis at all. It was the accumulation, the four years, that was all. He had been at it too long. Crossett remembered a phrase the sportswriters used about a pitcher who began to walk too many men and allowed too many hits: he has lost the zip on his fast one.

"I'll tell you what," the Director said, gathering the loose pages and jogging them into an even pile on the glass table top. "I'll think this over and make the decision myself before I send the memorandum to the printer. Thank you, gentlemen."

The chairs scraped and the men broke up into small groups as they moved toward the door. The WPB man, who was on loan from Yale, fell in beside Crossett and said something humorous about the reconversion job the universities would have to do on themselves but, before Crossett could reply, one of the deputies pulled the WPB man aside and, as he went through the door, Crossett found himself next to Captain Iverson. Crossett was surprised by how short the younger man was. He had seemed taller behind the wheel of the Oldsmobile.

"Quite seriously," Crossett said. "What was your real objection to the preamble?"

Captain Iverson looked up and, as his lips twisted, he glanced quickly to his right and then to his left, as though to see if anybody was listening. Half a dozen men were.

"All that stuff about milk for babies, hell," Captain Iverson said through his thin smile. "I don't want everybody to be the same size."

Crossett was off balance when he hit him, so he recoiled with the impact and his own shoulder hit the marble wall, spoiling his view. But he must have connected in a good place because, when he turned around, all he could see, sticking out from the group of excited executives bending over the younger man, was a pair of brown strap shoes and six or seven inches of cuffless pinks. Captain Iverson was out cold. Cold enough, anyway. Crossett stepped on something, saw it was the gold fountain pen, and he paused just long enough to kick the damned thing back toward the jabbering group. Then he walked on down the hall to his own office and went in.

"I talked to my man at the filling station on Wisconsin and Q," Miss Gough said. "He said if you drive by there tonight on your way home he thinks he'll be able to fix that door for you, but you'd better not work late tonight because he closes at seven. What's all that excitement out in the hall?"

"A top executive just resigned," Crossett said. He crossed the room and opened the door of his private office. "Get me the Raleigh, will you, Miss Gough?" he said across his shoulder.

Crossett closed the door and sat down at his desk, still breathing irregularly, and he pulled the small looseleaf leather notebook from behind the folded handkerchief in his outer breast pocket. He flipped it to the page with the room number on it, and he set the open book flat in the middle of the green blotter, and he waited for his breathing to become regular again. When the phone rang Crossett was sucking his knuckles. They burned slightly.

"I've got the Raleigh," Miss Gough said. "Who did you want there, Mr. Crossett?"

"Just put me on," Crossett said and she did and then, as he read off the room number to the girl at the Raleigh switchboard, he remembered another phone call. Crossett had made that one almost four years ago, from the faculty lounge, between classes, to the man at the Copley-Plaza who had come up to Boston from Washington for a few days and had taken Crossett out and fed him two martinis before lunch.

"Five oh nine is busy," the girl at the Raleigh switchboard said. "Will you wait, sir?"

"Yes, I'll wait," Crossett said and he waited, for the man from Ohio who two hours before had pointed the way out that Crossett had just taken with his bruised knuckles, and he waited also for the suddenly remembered feeling that was four years old but still as fresh and hard and exciting as it had been then, that day in the faculty lounge, when martinis before lunch did not die until late afternoon, when he was forty-six.

"Here's five oh nine now, sir," the girl at the Raleigh switchboard said. "Thanks for waiting."

There was a click at the other end and Crossett looked around the room quickly, in a sudden panic of regret, not for the private washroom, or the guard in the swivel chair at the back door, or the stout woman in the gilded elevator who knew his floor without asking, or even for parking place number 168, but for something else, for the endless foolish meetings, and for the few quiet minutes every morning while the car pools from Chevy Chase and Alexandria were unloading, and even for Miss Gough's relentless efficiency, for something he had been part of for four years. He would never have that again. Not in Ohio.

"Hello," Crossett said in a tired voice, and he turned with the phone to look out the window. It was a clear day and you could see the Potomac.

BIOGRAPHICAL NOTES

Nelson Algren was born in Detroit in 1909, of Scandinavian descent. After attending the Chicago public schools and the University of Illinois, he began writing in 1933 while working as a migratory laborer in the Southwest. A short story written in an abandoned filling station in the Rio Grande Valley sold and gained him a half interest in the station. It was followed by other short stories which appeared in both *The Best American Short Stories* and the O. Henry Memorial Award volume, and by a first novel *Somebody in Boots.* He is at present living in the Chicago area. Ernest Hemingway recently spoke of him as the best of the young writers in America.

Sherwood Anderson was born in Camden, Ohio, in 1876. His family moved aimlessly about Ohio, and each of the seven Anderson children was born in a different town. Most of his boyhood was spent in Clyde, Ohio. His schooling was spotty although he attended Wittenberg College for a short time. He became a manager of a paint factory on his return from Cuba after the Spanish-American War, and it was out of this factory that he walked suddenly one day. He did not immediately begin to write but went to Chicago to live with his brother Karl, a well-known painter, and here Anderson became an advertising copy writer. Dreiser, Floyd Dell and Sandburg helped secure a publisher for *Winesburg, Ohio* and though this brought him public notice, his only book to approach "best-seller" class was one of the poorest of them, *Dark Laughter.* Anderson's best work is found in the short stories of *Winesburg, Ohio* and *The Triumph of the Egg.* His simplicity, sensitivity and psychological acuity made him a great influence in the development of the American short story.

Mary Austin, whose unique mental equipment earned her the epithet, "the most intelligent woman in America," died in 1934 at her Casa Querida in Santa Fe at the age of 65. In 1903, when the doctors gave her nine months at the risk of a major operation, "she counted her money and decided that she had enough to die on; she went abroad because she understood that there were places in Italy where one in great pain could die quietly." Born of pioneer ancestry in Illinois, Mary Austin was self-educated. Susan B. Anthony and Frances Willard directed her attention to the Suffrage and Prohibition Movements before she moved West to witness the end of the cowboy period and the decline of the Spanish culture of California. Her marriage took her to the Mojave Desert where she developed a lasting interest in the art and lore of the American Indian. Henry Smith has written of her in the *New Mexico Quarterly Review*: ". . . she is impelled toward the integration of the human personality as it actually exists, everywhere in some specific environment, and particularly in America in the environment which has seemed to her . . . most fundamentally American . . . the Southwest."

Sanora Babb was born in Arizona but spent much of her life in the plains of the Oklahoma Panhandle and its Indian country farther east, Colorado, New Mexico and in Kansas. Of the latter country she says, "Kansas is almost as much two separate states as is California because of the difference in its eastern and western sections. I have lived in both, but mostly in western Kansas, the wheat section." Miss Babb taught school on the plains, living on a sheep ranch, and later moved to California where she now lives. Many of her short stories have appeared in various magazines, including *The New Mexico Quarterly Review, Antioch Review, New Masses* and *Mainstream* and in the anthology, *Cross Section*. A forthcoming novel by her will be published by Random House.

John Peale Bishop was a native of Charleston, West Virginia, although he spent most of his life outside the South. Educated at Princeton with Edmund Wilson and F. Scott Fitzgerald, he published a book of poems and sketches called *The Undertaker's Garland* in 1922 in collaboration with Edmund Wilson. He served in World War I and subsequently was an editor on *Vanity Fair*. For a number of years he lived in Europe. In 1930 he received the Scribner's award of $5000 for a short novel called *Many Thousands Gone*. He published two volumes of poems, *Now with His Love,* and *Minute Particulars,* and a novel, *Act of Darkness.*

ROARK BRADFORD was born in Lauderdale County, Tennessee, in 1896. Although he was a direct descendant of Governor William Bradford of Massachusetts, his family has been resident in the South since colonial days. Aside from country schools in Tennessee and Arkansas, his only education was in the Artillery Schools of the Army. He worked as a newspaperman in Atlanta and then in New Orleans where he was night editor of the *Times-Picayune*. His first published fiction was about Negroes—a series of stories for the New York *World*—and that has been his main subject ever since. His second story won the O. Henry Prize for the best short story of 1927. The *World* stories eventually became the book *Ol' Man Adam an' His Chillun,* which was made into an immensely successful play, *Green Pastures,* by Marc Connelly, and won the Pulitzer Prize in 1930. Mr. Bradford's *John Henry,* published in 1931, was a Literary Guild selection. Until his death recently, he lived in New Orleans with his wife and son in the French Quarter, and frequently went to his plantation near Shreveport to replenish his source material.

ERSKINE CALDWELL, born in 1903 in White Oak, Coweta County, Georgia, was the son of a Presbyterian minister and the first years of his life were spent in various parts of the South. He had almost no schooling until he entered the University of Virginia where he spent three years studying, but he came to know the poor white of Georgia intimately. Deeply interested in social problems, he gave at the New School for Social Research a series of lectures on "Southern Tenant Farmers" and he has written much on the subject of economic conditions in the South. Both his novels, *Tobacco Road* and *God's Little Acre* treat this topic, as do a large number of his short stories. In 1933 he was awarded the thousand-dollar prize of the *Yale Review* for his short story "Country Full of Swedes." His work has appeared widely.

DOROTHY CANFIELD, equally well known as Dorothy Canfield Fisher, was born in Lawrence, Kansas, in 1879. Her father was an educator and president of several state universities. She was graduated from Ohio State University and received her Ph.D. degree in Romance Languages from Columbia University after studying both there and in France. In 1907 she married John R. Fisher and had a son and a daughter. In 1912 she published her first novel, *The Squirrel Cage*. Since then she has written about twenty-five books, including novels, juveniles, non-fiction, translations of foreign works, collections of short stories, and one play. Her books have had great popularity in England and have been translated into several foreign languages. Always interested in education, she holds eight degrees from American universities, and has written and lectured widely on education. She has studied both the New England and Middle Western milieus with an acute psychological touch and a literary sureness. Her stories have been reprinted in numerous anthologies and have appeared in various magazines. She has been one of the judges of the Book-of-the-Month Club since its inception.

GLADYS HASTY CARROLL, though born in Rochester, New Hampshire, in 1904 insists that where seems "less important, in view both of my personal devotions and my literary material, than the fact that my home from earliest memory has been in South Berwick, Maine." She was educated at Bates College and "scarcely spent a night outside the State of Maine" until she was married. She believes that New England is not a ghost region living only in the glory of its literary and cultural past, but that it is still a living and growing community, full of material for the writer with the seeing eye. "Life," she says, "is and always has been more interesting and precious to me than literature; I read and write only out of eagerness for further clarification of what I see and hear and feel." Her best-known work includes *As the Earth Turns, Neighbor of the Sky* and a collection of short stories, *Head of the Line,* from which "So Clyde Was Born" is taken.

WALTER VAN TILBURG CLARK was born in Maine in 1909, moved to Nevada at the age of eight, and attended school and college there. His father was president of the state university in Reno, Nevada, where he did his undergraduate work. He also had a year of graduate study at Stanford and studied philosophy and literature at the University of Vermont afterwards. He is married, has three children, and recently has moved to Taos, New Mexico, to devote himself completely to writing. He made a strong impression with his first novel, *The Ox-Bow Incident,* the scene of which was also in Nevada, and a second novel *The City of Trembling Leaves* has also received a good deal of critical attention. The story included here, "The Wind and the Snow of Winter" received the first prize in the O. Henry Memorial Award volume of 1945. Mr. Clark has also been awarded a Guggenheim Fellowship.

PIETRO DI DONATO was born in West Hoboken, New Jersey, in 1911, the son of Italian immigrants. His father was a bricklayer. In fact, anyone who has read his only novel, *Christ in Concrete,* knows his life-story for the book is autobiographical in almost every detail. He left grammar school to take up his father's trowel when his father died. In spite of everything he managed to attend night classes and read voluminously. In 1937, *Esquire* published his first work, the story "Christ in Concrete," which later became the first chapter of the novel of the same name. He finally was able to take a year off from work to do the novel and then returned to bricklaying, working on the New York World's Fair.

WILLIAM FAULKNER grew up in Oxford, Mississippi, a descendant of a once wealthy family. His schooling was intermittent and he spent most of his youth loafing around his father's livery stable. He wrote poetry, strongly influenced by Omar Khayyam and Swinburne, but, he says, it was no good except as an aid to love-making. Jolted out of his lazy life by the first World War, he joined the Canadian Air Force. After the war he turned to earning a living at odd jobs such as house-painting. He started writing fiction and suddenly, he explains, "I discovered that writing was a mighty fine thing. It enables you to make men stand on their hind legs and cast a shadow." Faulkner, at loose ends, drifted down to New Orleans, where he became a friend of Sherwood Anderson, through whom he came to the notice of the *Double Dealer,* one of the pioneer small literary magazines, and it was here that his first published work, a poem, appeared in 1922. After being unable to sell *The Sound and the Fury,* generally considered his finest novel, he deliberately set out to write a commercial horror story to make money. This novel, *Sanctuary,* made his fortune and Faulkner has since not had to worry about money. Not only has he come to be one of the most controversial figures in the American novel, but he is unquestionably one of the finest short story writers in America, a fact not generally recognized. "That Evening Sun Go Down" is one of his best short stories and comes from a collection called *These Thirteen.*

VARDIS FISHER was born in 1895 in a one-room cottonwood-log shack in Annis, Idaho, where his Mormon pioneer parents had settled. His mother was his only teacher until he first entered school at the age of fifteen in Rigby, Idaho. In the first World War, he enlisted as a flying cadet and later transferred to the heavy artillery. He studied at the University of Utah and the University of Chicago. He taught nine years in various universities and left teaching in 1931. He was director of the Federal Writers' Project in Idaho. He says, "My career began, I suppose, early in high school; for before I was halfway through a wild-eyed and sentimental adolescence, I wrote what I called a novel as well as a ton of horrible verse. Inasmuch as by that time I had an incurable feeling of inferiority, I decided to be a writer." His novel *Children of God* on the history of Mormonism won the Harper Novel Prize in 1939. He lives in Thousand Springs Valley, Idaho, where he describes himself as "an enthusiastic and wholly incompetent horticulturist; but I stick to those plants which will grow no matter which end you thrust into the earth."

MICHAEL FOSTER was born in Hardy, Arkansas, in 1904. He has worked as a press agent, cartoonist, designer, and reporter. His work deals with the Northwest and in an area where there has been very little good writing, his work stands out in sharp contrast to what has been done. He makes his home at Orcas Island, Washington, in the Pacific Northwest which he knows and loves. His books include *Forgive Adam,* and *The American Dream.* His short stories have been published both in *Story* and *Colliers.*

MARY WILKINS FREEMAN traced her descent on both sides of the family back to old New England stock. Her ancestors were Puritan colonists from whom she inherited in large measure her taste for simple things and from whom she received her dislike for ostentation. She was born in Randolph, Massachusetts, in 1852 and died in 1930. Probably no author whose writings have so definite a literary value has worked and achieved distinction more quietly than Mary Wilkins Freeman. Indeed, she was always averse to self-advertisements of any kind so that even now the general public knows but little of her personality and life. Yet her stories and novels are read not only in the English-speaking world but have been translated into many other languages. As John Macy said, "her genius was original, not of a school. . . . Her material was close at hand, plain and simple; she had the genius to see it and render it objectively." Her field is the New England village and she is credited with 238 short stories, twelve novels, a play and a volume of verse.

ZONA GALE was born in 1874 at Portage, Wisconsin, once a pioneer fur-trading center. She was graduated from the University of Wisconsin in 1895 and took her M.A. there in 1899. Subsequently her alma mater awarded her an honorary Litt.D. She wrote from her early childhood and her first "book" was printed and bound by herself at the age of seven. She worked for various newspapers in Milwaukee from 1899 to 1901, and then came to New York and became a reporter on the *World*. She wrote short stories indefatigably but it was not until 1904 that her first story was published. She was awarded the Pulitzer Prize for her dramatization of *Miss Lulu Bett* in 1920. Her work began as a regional writer, with sharp observation and fidelity to reality, and she matured into a fellow-realist with Sinclair Lewis and Dreiser.

SUSAN GLASPELL was born in Iowa in 1882 and spent most of her early life in the Middle West and most of her later life in New England. She worked her way through college by writing for Des Moines newspapers and, after graduating from Drake University there, joined the staff of the Des Moines *News*. She kept running into material which appealed to her as short story material and finally gave up newspaper work, went back to Davenport, and decided to earn her living writing. She sold stories to *Harper's* and the *American* and then decided to do a novel. It was *The Glory of the Conquered*. In 1915 her husband organized the Provincetown Players and she became interested in writing for the theater. She wrote a number of plays and one of them, *Alison's House,* was awarded the Pulitzer Prize for 1931. After a long silence, she published in 1939 a new novel, *The Morning Is Near Us*. She wrote a number of short stories, the best of which is probably "A Jury of Her Peers."

Paul Green was born on a farm near the town of Lillington, North Carolina, in 1894. The life that Green grew up to know was much the same as that of his ancestors. On his father's farm he and his brothers worked the cotton and corn and cut timber, shoulder to shoulder with the Negro laborers. His imagination was fed on the beauty and the loneliness of the wide fields and the sky, the ever changing life of the wooded swamps and hills, and the pathos and humor of the Negroes and fervid poor whites. Finally he saved enough money to attend the state university at Chapel Hill, where he won a prize for a one-act play. He spent some time in Belgium and Northern France in the American Expeditionary Force during World War I. He returned to Chapel Hill and then to Cornell to continue studying philosophy. In 1927 he won the Pulitzer Prize for *In Abraham's Bosom* and in 1928 received a Guggenheim Fellowship. Although famous as a dramatist, he has done a good many fine short stories, of which "A Tempered Fellow" is one of the best.

Sara Haardt was born in Montgomery, Alabama, in 1898. She has written and published forty stories which, according to her husband, H. L. Mencken, ". . . picture also the conflict of a new generation with the lingering traditions of an old and decaying culture, the dramatic contrast between the old dying and the young struggling to live and thrive. . . ." In 1919, barely twenty-one years old, she served as chairwoman of the Alabama branch of the National Woman's Party. She was educated at Goucher College in Baltimore and won the college magazine short story contest there at the beginning of her writing career. In November, 1919, she became editor-in-chief of that magazine, Goucher College's *Kalends*. Subsequently she taught both at the Margaret Booth School in Montgomery, and later at Goucher. She took advanced work at Johns Hopkins. She wrote articles, short stories and editorials for the Baltimore *Evening Sun,* as well as scenarios for Hollywood. In 1930, she married H. L. Mencken. Her work includes a novel, *The Making of a Lady,* and a collection of her short stories published posthumously and called *Southern Album*. She died in Baltimore in 1935.

Nancy Hale was born in Boston in 1908, the daughter of parents who both were painters. She herself was educated to be an artist but turned to writing. She has been a magazine editor in New York and a reporter for the New York *Times*. She is best known for her novel *Prodigal Women* and a collection of short stories *Between the Dark and the Daylight*. She is married to Fredson Bowers, Associate Professor of English Literature at the University of Virginia, where her son attends college, and she resides. Her stories have appeared in many magazines and have been widely reprinted.

Ernest Hemingway was born in 1898 in Oak Park, Illinois. He worked for the Kansas City *Star* after graduating from high school in 1917 but in a few months left for Italy to serve in the first World War. He continued his newspaper career after the war but in Paris, he met a man who had a profound effect on his career—Sherwood Anderson. After his first successful novel, *The Sun Also Rises,* he awoke to find himself famous; automatically he became the voice of the "lost generation." He is a master of the short story and his work in this form shows his mastery of dialogue at its best, short, clipped and bare, the very essence of speech. As John Peale Bishop has said: ". . . [he has made] Midwestern speech into a prose living and alert, capable of saying at all times exactly what he wanted it to say." Among his most important works are *The Sun Also Rises, A Farewell to Arms, For Whom the Bell Tolls, Men Without Women,* and *Winner Take Nothing*. An enthusiastic sportsman, he is an expert fisherman, skiier, hunter, and a good drinker as well. He has had an abiding interest in Spain and in bullfighting and most of his best work, both in the novel and short story, has been done against a foreign setting, unlike most of the other writing of his contemporaries.

DuBose Heyward was born in Charleston, South Carolina, in 1885. The family, though of the innermost circle of South Carolina aristocracy, was impoverished by the Civil War and the boy had to sell newspapers at nine, left school at fourteen to clerk in a hardware store. His first writing was poetry in collaboration with his friend Hervey Allen. After his marriage in 1923, to Dorothy Hartzell Kuhns, with whom he collaborated on *Porgy* and *Mamba's Daughters,* he was persuaded by her to quit his job in the insurance business and devote himself to writing. His first novel, *Porgy,* was an immense success as a serial, novel, and later on as a play and an opera (*Porgy and Bess,* with music by George Gershwin). From then he was established as a novelist and playwright, his subject nearly always being the primitive Gullah Negroes of South Carolina and the Sea Islands.

William M. John was born in Trinidad, Colorado, in 1888 and has been occupied with his ranches in Colorado and the Farms in the Tumbleweed Valley, places about which he writes. It is only recently that he has begun to translate the characters he has known in his corner of the West into fiction. He was educated at Princeton and subsequently worked as a cattleman, a reporter for the Denver *Times,* and later in private investments. "Neither Jew Nor Greek" was awarded first prize in the O. Henry Memorial Award volume in 1930, and since then, Mr. John has been published widely in both fiction and articles. At present, he makes his home in Alamo Verde, Golden, Colorado.

Josephine Winslow Johnson was born in Kirkwood, Missouri, in 1910. She attended Washington University and has been an art student, volunteer social worker and writer. She says: "I have lived on a farm in St. Louis County since 1922. I am irritated by the creeping-in of roads, houses and estates. My uncle is a dairy farmer in Boone County. The land around his is farmed by tenants or share-croppers. Their condition is almost hopeless under the present system. Farming appears to be tolerated as an evil necessity. The country is beautiful but its people are wretched. I hate standardization, ugliness, narrowness of life—its unrest and quicksand quality. It makes me feel as though I were on the margin of a whirlpool. I love poetry and cooking and all the little things. Salamanders and fungus seem more exciting to me than war or politics but it is cowardly and impossible to ignore them or try to escape. I love sincerity and simplicity and am always being disillusioned by people . . . the only complete peace and happiness seems to be in the fields or woods when one is alone, and even that isn't sufficient for always." Her novel, *Now in November,* was a Pulitzer Prize winner. She is married to Grant G. Cannon and has two children.

Oliver La Farge was born in New York City in 1901, the grandson of the famous painter John La Farge, and brother of writer Christopher La Farge. His interest in and sympathy with the American Indian dates almost from his infancy, when he dubbed himself "Indian Man," the name he was always known by as a child. At Harvard, this interest became specialized into a B.A. in anthropology in 1924 and an M.A. in 1929. He has lived off and on in Arizona and New Mexico since 1921 and settled in New Mexico to live there permanently in 1941, but was dislodged by the war. Separated from the Army in 1946, he returned immediately to New Mexico and intends to stay there. His novel, *Laughing Boy,* won the Pulitzer Prize for Fiction in 1929. "Love Charm" was conceived, he says, "in the course of listening disgustedly to an Italian Opera called (approximately) *Il Filtre de Amore.*"

Meridel le Sueur was born in Murray, Iowa, and was raised, not reared, so she says, in Oklahoma, Texas, Kansas, Illinois, the Dakotas and Minnesota. She had little formal education. The *Dial* printed her first short story and she has been published and reprinted widely since. A book of her short stories, *Salute to Spring,* was published in 1940 and *North Country,* another collection of short stories has recently been put out. *Autumnal Village,* one of the books in the American Folkways Series edited by Erskine Caldwell, has also been recently printed. At present she is working on a Guggenheim grant doing historical research. Her special interests are her two daughters Rachel and Deborah, aged fourteen and fifteen. She is the sister of Hollywood actress Joan Crawford, who was born Le Sueur.

Victoria Lincoln was born in Fall River, Massachusetts, in 1904. She was educated at Radcliffe College, spent some time abroad and in various parts of the United States especially New England. She is the wife of Victor Lowe, Professor of Philosophy at Ohio State University and the mother of three children. She has been writing for quite a number of years and is the author of the very successful novel, *February Hill,* published in 1934 and dramatized later as *The Primrose Path.* In 1944, *Grandmother and the Comet,* a collection of her short stories, from which "Embarkation Point" was taken, was published by Farrar and Rinehart. Her latest book, *The Wind at My Back,* appeared in 1946. She is now living in a suburb of Columbus, Ohio, running her household and working on a new novel.

Vernon Loggins is a native Texan and a graduate of the University of Texas. He is a lecturer on literature and teaches creative writing at Columbia University. He has published fiction, verse, literary criticism and biography. His latest book, *Two Romantics,* is a life of two of the most illustrious of Texans, the sculptress Elizabeth Ney and her husband Edmund Montgomery, the philosopher. An earlier book, *The Negro Author,* is generally recognized as the standard history of American Negro literature. Mr. Loggins is at present at work on a new biography of Nathaniel Hawthorne.

Albert Maltz is short story writer, novelist and dramatist. He was born in Brooklyn in 1908, educated at Columbia University and the Yale

School of Drama. He began his writing as a dramatist with *Merry Go Round, Peace on Earth,* and *Black Pit* all emphasizing Mr. Maltz's conviction that "all my work is and will be based (on the conclusion) that individuals live not in a vacuum but in a society, and that a writer cannot write truly of people or characters unless the world in which they live is equally illumined." Next he turned to short story writing and one of his stories, "Man on the Road," almost was a forecast of the Congressional investigation of silicosis among West Virginia miners. "The Happiest Man on Earth" won first prize in the 1938 O. Henry Memorial Award volume. Since then he has written two novels. *The Cross and the Arrow* and *The Underground Stream* and has had his short stories reprinted in some thirty-odd other anthologies.

ALAN MARSHALL was born in Rutherglen, Scotland, in 1905. In 1912, his parents brought him to America, where he was educated at the Carnegie Institute of Technology and at Columbia University. He has taught at the College of the City of New York. He has published few short stories. "Death and Transfiguration" is generally considered his most important piece of work. In this story, Edward J. O'Brien says, "He has succeeded in cloaking simple realism with a poetic treatment that is not unlike the best of Hawthorne."

JOHN O'HARA, the eldest of eight children, was born in Pottsville, Pennsylvania in 1905. His father was a physician of more than local fame and it is probable that "The Doctor's Son" comes out of experience that Mr. O'Hara knew first hand. He has worked at many occupations from laborer in a steel mill to secretary to Heywood Broun. Subsequently he became a newspaper reporter and feature editor for various papers and magazines. He has written many stories for the *New Yorker* and since 1934 has been a screen writer. He has been called "the voice of the hang-over generation" since 1929 and the Boswell of the "post-Scott Fitzgerald era." "The Doctor's Son" however is not in that stream of Mr. O'Hara's work, and is perhaps a better and richer vein. He is best known for his *Appointment in Samarra, Butterfield 8* and *Pal Joey.*

Marjorie Kinnan Rawlings was born in Washington, D. C., in 1896. She studied at the University of Wisconsin under William Ellery Leonard and went from college to the National Headquarters of the Y.M.C.A. as publicity writer. From 1925 to 1927 she was a syndicated verse writer for United Features. Finally, in 1928, she gave up newspaper work and bought a seventy-two-acre orange grove, with four thousand trees, at Cross Creek, Hawthorn, Florida. Here she settled down to devote her time to fiction. Her first book, *South Moon Under,* was a Book-of-the-Month Club choice and *The Yearling* also was a Book-of-the-Month Club choice and won the Pulitzer Prize for Fiction in 1939 as well. Her stories have been widely printed, and one, "Gal Young Un," won the O. Henry Memorial Award in 1933. "Writing," she says, "is agony. I stay at my typewriter for eight hours every day when I'm working and keep as free as possible from all distractions for the rest of the day. I aim to do six pages a day, but I'm satisfied with three. Often there are only a few lines to show. . . ." She works carefully with Florida material, where she is more at home than in her father's farm in Maryland, and she knows the Florida Crackers, their conversation, and their rapidly disappearing backwoods life thoroughly.

Elise M. Rushfeldt is the child of Norse pioneers on the Minnesota frontier. She was born in a prairie town and has lived most of her life there with brief intermissions for travel abroad. Some years ago she relinquished teaching to devote herself to free-lance journalism. Since then she has written a number of short stories which have been published and have attracted some attention.

Allan Seager was born in Adrian, Michigan, in 1906. He moved to Memphis, Tennessee, when he was eleven years old and lived there until he went to college at the University of Michigan. Following that he was one of the editors of *Vanity Fair* for a year and a half. He is married and has two daughters. At present he is a teacher at the University of Michigan and was recently the winner of a contest for the best short story from a college faculty member given by *Good Housekeeping* magazine. He is the author of two novels, and the author of a number of short stories which have received considerable critical attention. He has traveled in Europe and South America and was a Rhodes Scholar at Oxford after his graduation from the University of Michigan.

Irwin Shaw is a native New Yorker, having been born in Brooklyn. His writing career began in high school and at Brooklyn College he was simultaneously involved in playwrighting and football. Upon graduation, he began to write serial dramatizations of comic strips for radio, the success of which gave him the leisure necessary to write two plays. One of them, *Bury the Dead,* was produced on Broadway in 1936 when the author was only twenty-three years old. Since then, in addition to writing occasional motion pictures, he has written several plays, among them *The Gentle People, The Assassin, Sons and Soldiers,* and *Siege.* His short stories have appeared in many magazines but most frequently in the *New Yorker.* Three collections of his short stories have been published by Random House—*Sailor Off the Bremen, Welcome to the City,* and most recently, *Act of Faith.* During the war, Mr. Shaw served on the staff of *Stars and Stripes.* Random House has published his first novel *The Young Lions.*

Naomi Shumway was born on a ranch in northwestern Wyoming about 1909. She had a public school education which she abandoned at seventeen to go on a mission for the Mormon Church. She lost her faith and came to New York to do housework. She is now a librarian in New York. She has only written occasional short stories of which "Ike and Us Moons" is the best. Probably this is one of the finest stories written in America.

Wallace Stegner, although born in Lake Mills, Iowa, in 1909, received his high-school and college education in Salt Lake City, Utah, and did graduate work at the University of California and later received his Ph.D. at the University of Iowa. He has lived in various parts of the United States as well as in Saskatchewan. At present, Mr. Stegner is at

Stanford University in charge of the creative writing program there. His first novel, *Remembering Laughter,* won the Little, Brown novelette contest in 1937. His best-known work since then is *On a Darkling Plain, Fire and Ice, The Big Rock Candy Mountain,* and *One Nation,* a Life in America prize book which won an Anisfield-Wolf Award in 1946. He has had stories in many magazines and has been reprinted in both *The Best American Short Stories* and the O. Henry Memorial Award volume.

John Steinbeck was born in Salinas, California, in 1902, peculiarly the product of the California interior valleys. Much of his work is a reflection of his native district, and of the Monterey coast where he lived after his marriage. He studied Marine Biology at Stanford and led a private expedition to the Galapagos Islands to escape the hullabaloo occasioned by his novel of the migrant workers, *The Grapes of Wrath,* which won the Pulitzer Prize. His work has a remarkable versatility ranging from romantic history in his novel of Henry Morgan the Pirate called *Cup of Gold* through the sociological awareness of *In Dubious Battle* and *The Grapes of Wrath.* His other work includes the now famous *Tortilla Flat,* a play *Of Mice and Men,* and a number of other novels. His book of short stories, *The Long Valley,* shows Steinbeck at his sensitive best, and it is from this that this section of "The Red Pony" was chosen.

James Stevens has been writing about Pacific Northwest for a long time. Born in Iowa in 1892, he moved to Idaho at an early age and then, at fifteen, he was driving four mule trucks; later he worked in logging camps and sawmills in Oregon and Washington and it is from his intimate knowledge of the lumber country of Oregon that his story "Bulldogger" comes. In 1924, when he sold his first story, he gave up his sedan and wardrobe and resigned himself to the frugal life of a writer. He says he still envies the enormous—as they appear to him—wages earned by sawmill hands but you'd never get that idea from reading "Bulldogger." He is best known for his book *Paul Bunyan* published in 1925.

Jesse Stuart was born in 1907 in W-Hollow near Riverton, Kentucky. After desperate struggles to get through Lincoln Memorial University, he went to Vanderbilt, still working his way through school, this time living on a meal a day, and having all his clothing, poems and his master's thesis burned to ashes. He decided to farm and leave school, to write only for his own amusement and then was asked to take over the county school system which resulted in thirty-two lawsuits which he had to fight. Finally he finished his first book of poetry called *Man with a Bull-Tongue Plow*. In 1937 he was given a Guggenheim Fellowship and visited twenty-seven European countries. He returned, began a newspaper, wrote his first editorials on a Congressman, was trailed, beaten up, shot at twice and cut once with a knife but, he says, "I'm very much alive, and if I continue to be alive—so help me God—I'll portray the section of America that gave me birth." About "Dawn of Remembered Spring," he writes, "Strange about this story. Here is one for you. I sent the story out to magazines 37 times. It was rejected by all editors, yet the majority of them always sent a little note saying it was a good story but they couldn't use a snake story for fear of losing their women readers. . . . I sent six stories to *Harper's Bazaar,* accidentally dropping in the snake story, for I knew that the editors of *Harper's Bazaar* were all women, and perhaps, according to other reports, haters of snakes or snake stories. All stories were returned but "Dawn of Remembered Spring." It was accepted. And how I needed money! Thirty-eight trips for a story, one about snakes, and a woman editor, Lady Editor, bought it . . . Then the surprise came! Another woman editor, Martha Foley, picked it up and used it in *The Best American Short Stories.*"

Ruby Pickens Tartt was born in Livingston, Alabama, in the house her great-grandparents built, and has lived there all her life. Mrs. Tartt studied art at Newcomb in New Orleans and at the Chase School in New York. She became a photographer and some of her work attracted the attention of Arnold Genthe. She worked on the Alabama Writers' Project and was particularly interested in Negro lore. A specialist in portrait painting until three years ago, when she was badly hurt in a tornado, Mrs. Tartt has since been unable to use her right hand for painting. Her work has appeared in the *Southwest Review* and all of it has since been reprinted.

David Thibault died in 1934, when he stood at the brink of literary success. He was a native of Arkansas and the manager of a cotton plantation in the Arkansas delta where he became acquainted with the Negro life that he made the basis for a number of his stories. He was interested in agricultural experiments and published a book *Modern Farming* on his own. In 1933 he collaborated with Carl Liddle on a head-hunter's romance entitled *Tunchi.* Afterwards he began writing a series of stories which were to fit logically into a novel of Negro life called *Salt Mule.* He received a telegram from Richard J. Walsh of John Day Company expressing enthusiasm for what he had seen of Thibault's stories, saying that they would make a great book, and that Walsh would take all of his writings to come. That day Thibault was taken ill and within a week he died of tubercular meningitis. His death has been mourned as a loss to American writing.

Dorothy Thomas was born in Kansas, descended from generations of Welsh clergymen on her father's side. She was the sixth child and the second daughter in a family of ten. When she was seven years old, the family moved to Alberta, Canada, and homesteaded in the brush country forty-four miles from a railroad. Her father taught her to read. Her playthings were homemade. After her father's death, her brothers, mere boys, brought in a sawmill and worked what timber forest fires had left them. After six years in Canada, they returned to the States, lived two years in Kansas and then moved to Lincoln, Nebraska. There she attended Bethany High School and had three years of college at Cotner College and the University of Nebraska, with years of teaching in between. During the summers, she clerked in stores. She traveled and sold books and then went back to Lincoln to live with her mother, a sister and a brother.

James Thurber was born in Columbus, Ohio, in 1894. He went to Ohio State University from which he was not graduated because of failure in botany and military drill. He served two years as a code clerk in the diplomatic service and afterward was a newspaperman for seven years. His cartoons in the *New Yorker* have aroused nation-wide mirth. His short stories and sketches have been published in book form. He has settled permanently in Cornwall, Connecticut. He was managing editor of *New Yorker* magazine until 1933 when he resigned, but he is still a regular contributor. In 1940, in collaboration with Elliott Nugent, he wrote his first play, *The Male Animal.* Robert Coates says of him, ". . . [Thurber] regards himself primarily as a writer, and is at once a little jealous of the Artist-Thurber and suspicious of anyone who admires the one in preference to the other. . . ." Some of his best-known works include, *Is Sex Necessary?, My Life and Hard Times* and *My World—and Welcome to It!*

Ella Middleton Tybout was born in the country about five miles from the small town of New Castle, in Delaware. Here, on her grandfather's land, she spent most of her childhood. She was the only child and she played with the little Negro children on the place, went with them into their homes, heard them talk and knew how they lived. The first story of *Poketown People* was written when Miss Tybout was sixteen, and not published for several years later, when a friend sent it to *Lippincott's* Magazine. She later moved to Washington and worked for the Navy Department there. Out of her stay there came her book *The Wife of the Secretary of State.* She has traveled a good deal, crossed both the Equator and the Arctic Circle, and traveled extensively in the United States as well. She was educated at home, in a "sporadic manner; in fact, I am much like Topsy, for I jest growed." She now makes her home in a little town situated in the foothills of the Allegheny Mountains.

Jerome Weidman was born, raised and educated in New York. He attended public schools and evening sessions at both the College of the City of New York and New York University, where he studied accountancy and law. Before turning to writing, Mr. Weidman, in his own words, "was a newsboy, a soda jerker, a mail clerk, a delivery boy for a firm that rented tuxedos made—I'll take my oath—of pure lead, a printer, a stenographer, a window cleaner, a switchboard operator, and an operator in a necktie factory." Except for the war years, when he served with the Office of War Information both in the United States and in England, he has been writing ever since. He has published a number of books among them, *I Can Get It For You Wholesale, I'll Never Go There Any More* and *The Captain's Tiger,* a book of short stories from which "The Neat Mexicans" was taken.

JESSAMYN WEST was born in Indiana of Quaker parents. Miss West has spent part of her life in California where she was graduated from Whittier College and did postgraduate work at the University of California. Her first book, *The Friendly Persuasion,* was published by Harcourt, Brace in 1945. It has had a large success and is soon to be made into a motion picture by Frank Capra. She has written innumerable stories for many magazines and has just completed the book and lyrics for a musical stage production on the life of Audubon, probably to be produced in New York this fall. She is married, lives in Napa, California, intends to write a novel soon and also to continue with her short story writing.

FRANCES GILCHRIST WOOD was born in 1859 in Hillsgrove, near the small prairie town of Carthage, Illinois. She was educated at Carthage College and later received her M.A. and Ph.D. at Columbia University. She has had experience both in business and as a newspaper woman in the Dakotas and other Western states. She began to write short stories in later life and her first short story was "The White Battalion" which appeared in the *Bookman* in 1918. Edward J. O'Brien said, "'Turkey Red' is one of the best pioneer stories ever written by an American. As a feat of construction, it has seldom been surpassed. There was a danger in the very elaborateness of the construction, but the vitality of the characterization and the sheer human interest of the story itself overcame the structural difficulty." Her stories have appeared in many magazines and in several of The Best American Short Story collections.

RICHARD WRIGHT was born on a plantation near Natchez, Mississippi, in 1908, the son of a Negro farm- and mill-worker and a country schoolteacher. When he was five, the father deserted the family and the mother supported her children as best she could in Memphis, Tennessee, and later in Arkansas. After reading H. L. Mencken's *Book of Prefaces,* he determined to become a writer. He "bummed all over the country" and, later, on the strength of a few free-verse poems gained a place on the Federal Writers' Project in 1935. Two years later he went to New York where again he wrote on the Writers' Project and wrote the *Guide to Harlem* which it brought out. In 1938 he won the $500 prize offered by *Story* for the best story written by a worker on the Writers' Project, with the novella *Uncle Tom's Children,* which gave the title to a book of four long tales. The following year he was awarded a Guggenheim Fellowship. Then, he wrote *Native Son,* a best-selling novel, which was a Book-of-the-Month Club choice. In 1940, he won the Spingarn medal, highest award for achievement in the field of Negro interests, for his "powerful description . . . of the effect of proscription, segregation and the denial of opportunity to the American Negro."